PENGUIN CLASSICS

COMPLETE SHORT STORIES

GRAHAM GREENE, whose long life (1904–1991) nearly spanned the twentieth century, was one of its greatest novelists. Educated at Berkhamsted School and Balliol College, Oxford, he started his career as a sub-editor of the London *Times*. He began to attract notice as a novelist with his fourth book, *Orient Express,* in 1932. In 1935, he trekked across northern Liberia, his first experience in Africa, told in *A Journey Without Maps.* He converted to Catholicism in 1926 and reported on religious persecution in Mexico in 1938 in *The Lawless Roads,* which served as a background for his famous *The Power and the Glory,* one of several "Catholic" novels (*Brighton Rock, The Heart of the Matter, The End of the Affair*). During the war he worked for the British secret service in Sierra Leone; afterward, he began wide-ranging travels as a journalist, reflected in novels such as *The Quiet American, Our Man in Havana, The Comedians, Travels with My Aunt, The Honorary Consul, The Human Factor, Monsignor Quixote,* and *The Captain and the Enemy.* As well as his many novels, Graham Greene wrote several collections of short stories, four travel books, six plays, two books of autobiography, *A Sort of Life* and *Ways of Escape,* two of biography, and four books for children. He also contributed hundreds of essays and film and book reviews to *The Spectator* and other journals, many of which appear in the late collection *Reflections.* Most of his novels have been filmed, including *The Third Man,* which was first written as a film treatment. Graham Greene was named Companion of Honour and received the Order of Merit and many other awards.

PICO IYER, born in Oxford, England, and partly raised in California, is the author of several books about cultures mixing, including *Video Night in Kathmandu, The Lady and the Monk, Cuba and the Night, The Global Soul,* and *Abandon.* He now lives in suburban Japan.

GRAHAM GREENE

Complete Short Stories

Introduction by PICO IYER

PENGUIN BOOKS

PENGUIN BOOKS

Published by the Penguin Group

Penguin Group (USA) Inc., 375 Hudson Street, New York, New York 10014, U.S.A.
Penguin Group (Canada), 90 Eglinton Avenue East, Suite 700, Toronto,
Ontario, Canada M4P 2Y3 (a division of Pearson Penguin Canada Inc.)
Penguin Books Ltd, 80 Strand, London WC2R 0RL, England
Penguin Ireland, 25 St Stephen's Green, Dublin 2, Ireland
(a division of Penguin Books Ltd)
Penguin Group (Australia), 250 Camberwell Road, Camberwell, Victoria 3124, Australia
(a division of Pearson Australia Group Pty Ltd)
Penguin Books India Pvt Ltd, 11 Community Centre, Panchsheel Park,
New Delhi – 110 017, India
Penguin Group (NZ), 67 Apollo Drive, Rosedale, North Shore 0632, New Zealand
(a division of Pearson New Zealand Ltd)
Penguin Books (South Africa) (Pty) Ltd, 24 Sturdee Avenue, Rosebank,
Johannesburg 2196, South Africa

Penguin Books Ltd, Registered Offices: 80 Strand, London WC2R 0RL, England

Complete Short Stories first published in Penguin books 2005

9 10 8

Copyright © Graham Greene, 1923, 1929, 1935, 1940, 1941, 1942, 1946, 1947, 1949,
1954, 1955, 1956, 1957, 1962, 1963, 1964, 1965, 1966, 1982, 1988, 1989, 1990
Introduction copyright © Pico Iyer, 2005
All rights reserved

An extension of this copyright appears on p. 595.

PUBLISHER'S NOTE
This is a work of fiction. Names, characters, places, and incidents are either the
product of the author's imagination or are used fictitiously, and any resemblance to
actual persons, living or dead, business establishments, events, or locales is entirely
coincidental.

LIBRARY OF CONGRESS CATALOGING IN PUBLICATION DATA
Greene, Graham, 1904–1991
[Short stories]
Complete short stories / Graham Greene ; introduction by Pico Iyer.
p.   cm.(Penguin classics)
Includes bibliographical references.
Contents: Twenty-one stories—A sense of reality—May we borrow your husband?—
The last word and other stories.
ISBN 978-0-14-303910-5
I. Title.   II. Series.
PR6013.R44A6   2005
823'.912—dc22   2004057255

Printed in the United States of America
Set in Sabon

Contents

Introduction by Pico Iyer   vii
Suggestions for Further Reading by Michael Gorra   xix

TWENTY-ONE STORIES

THE DESTRUCTORS	3
SPECIAL DUTIES	19
THE BLUE FILM	25
THE HINT OF AN EXPLANATION	30
WHEN GREEK MEETS GREEK	42
MEN AT WORK	56
ALAS, POOR MALING	63
THE CASE FOR THE DEFENCE	67
A LITTLE PLACE OFF THE EDGWARE ROAD	71
ACROSS THE BRIDGE	77
A DRIVE IN THE COUNTRY	87
THE INNOCENT	101
THE BASEMENT ROOM	106
A CHANCE FOR MR LEVER	132
BROTHER	148
JUBILEE	156
A DAY SAVED	162
I SPY	167
PROOF POSITIVE	170
THE SECOND DEATH	175
THE END OF THE PARTY	181

A SENSE OF REALITY

UNDER THE GARDEN	193
A VISIT TO MORIN	249

DREAM OF A STRANGE LAND   264
A DISCOVERY IN THE WOODS   278

MAY WE BORROW YOUR HUSBAND?

MAY WE BORROW YOUR HUSBAND?   301
BEAUTY   333
CHAGRIN IN THREE PARTS   337
THE OVER-NIGHT BAG   344
MORTMAIN   350
CHEAP IN AUGUST   361
A SHOCKING ACCIDENT   385
THE INVISIBLE JAPANESE GENTLEMEN   391
AWFUL WHEN YOU THINK OF IT   396
DOCTOR CROMBIE   400
THE ROOT OF ALL EVIL   407
TWO GENTLE PEOPLE   420

THE LAST WORD AND OTHER STORIES

THE LAST WORD   431
THE NEWS IN ENGLISH   443
THE MOMENT OF TRUTH   453
THE MAN WHO STOLE THE EIFFEL TOWER   460
THE LIEUTENANT DIED LAST   464
A BRANCH OF THE SERVICE   474
AN OLD MAN'S MEMORY   487
THE LOTTERY TICKET   490
THE NEW HOUSE   502
WORK NOT IN PROGRESS   506
MURDER FOR THE WRONG REASON   513
AN APPOINTMENT WITH THE GENERAL   534

NEWLY COLLECTED

THE BLESSING   547
CHURCH MILITANT   554
DEAR DR FALKENHEIM   560
THE OTHER SIDE OF THE BORDER   566

Introduction

A foreigner sits in a square in a border town, looking at the bright lights, the big hotels of the land across the bridge. He has been watching, as everyone in town has, a famous con man, in flight from his creditors, walking around the square with his dog. The foreigner feels a kind of kinship with the fugitive—he, too, we sense, is in flight from something—and savors the fact that (this being Mexico) everyone in town knows the man is a criminal, except for the two foreign detectives sent to find him. When finally they do catch up with the stranger, the detectives quickly become his friends and the crook's safety seems guaranteed. Then, going across the bridge, in search of his dog, the fugitive gets hit, by chance, by a passing car. The dog bays pitifully beside his master.

"It was comic and it was pitiable," the narrator says, "but it wasn't less comic because the man was dead." Nor, one might add, less pitiable. "It all seemed to me a little too touching to be true," he confesses, "as the old crook lay there with his arm around the dog's neck, dead with his million between the money-changers' huts, but it's as well to be humble in the face of human nature." Art, he might be saying, is seldom so neat (or cynical) as one might wish.

To some, perhaps, such a scene might sound almost like a parody of Graham Greene: when an English paper ran a competition, asking its readers to send in a parody of Greene, the author himself sent in an entry, and, by some accounts, came in second. Yet all that is strong and touching about Greene is caught in the short vignette, written before any of the major novels came out: the love of paradox; the surrender to a sense of human frailty that makes all paradox redundant; the position on the wrong side of the border, among the fallen; and the sense of companionship being often no more than a fellowship of thieves, but no less real for that. "The man who believes that the secrets of this world are forever hidden," writes Cormac McCarthy in *Blood Meridian,* "lives in mystery and fear." So, too, Greene might suggest, does the man who knows that the secrets of the world are forever known.

Greene's ability to weave wistfulness and comedy together, his skill at constructing emotional and political spiderwebs so intricate that the lightest touch leaves them shaking, has often meant that his short fiction has been overlooked. The classic masters of short stories (Chekhov, say, or Greene's friend and contemporary V. S. Pritchett) are masters of a single mood, or character, or air of ironic humanity; Greene's characteristic domain, by comparison, was doubleness. Divided loyalties were his thing, conflicted feelings. To play out the full logic of a man reaching out for a man he distrusts, or a swindler doing good things for bad reasons, he seemed to need the measured space of a tightly plotted novel.

Yet the stories collected at four points in his career, written over a course of sixty years, catch their elusive maker in silhouette, in a way, and sometimes, less distracted by protagonist and plot, show us more of him than do any of the novels. With perhaps typical perverseness, Greene structured his first collection of stories backward, beginning with the last and ending with the earliest (as if to chronicle a passage toward innocence); but even the smallest of them, like that story on the frontier, have titles ("Across the Bridge") that suggest they were aiming at something more. Sometimes amusements, sometimes parables, sometimes ways for him to try out a mood or idea, sometimes just "escapes," Greene's stories show us the writer in his off hours, less guarded.

You can draw certain conclusions about his development when you read them together: noting, perhaps, that he made a more attractive older man than a young one, because his sense of human folly and confinement was mixed with a sense of fun and youth—

seen from a distance—or realizing how the youthful stories are often preoccupied with disenchantment, where the later ones rejoice in their freedom from illusion. The earliest pieces here, frank in their restlessness and anger, end often in murder, where the final ones are haunted by death, the damage no longer done to others but oneself. Yet what haunts one most of all, reading the stories all at once, is how much his concerns were steady from the beginning, even as they took in more tolerance and irony. Nearly all the stories, it seems to me, are about innocence, and turn upon the fact that the innocent, those still inside the garden, long for adventure, danger, flight; while those on the far side of the fence wish that they could go back again.

Not surprisingly, perhaps, Greene was least able to take on this theme, or to approach it, when he was young. His earliest exercises are largely set in England, which is to say the familiar and the gray; when wartime comes, with its austerities and precautionary rites, its long bureaucratic corridors and paper shuffling, it seems only to intensify a sense of privation that was there from the beginning. In the first set of stories Greene wrote, initially entitled *Nineteen Stories,* and then *Twenty-One Stories,* the mood is sullen, often violent. The stories with the most everyday titles—"A Drive in the Country" or "A Little Place off the Edgware Road"—are taken up with darkness, a sense of oppression. The mere recitation of English place names—"Maidenhead" is a recurring favorite—carries a kind of salacious charge, and the overall mood can best be caught by the sound of "Fetter Lane" and "Leadenhall Street."

Indeed, those who know that a Catholic writer is behind the pieces may be surprised at how little solace is to be found in them—or will have to adjust, at least, to a provisional believer's sense that redemption is a never-ending if. Greene was as singular a Catholic as he was everything else, and the faith he took on at the age of twenty-two seems never to have left him with a sense of happy endings. His interest, in fact, is almost never in what is above us, and almost always in what lies beneath, often quite literally. Everything that lies below the conscious mind, or the bland surface of our formal lives: the underground and the basement. When writing of the king's jubilee, Greene concentrates, quite typically, on a gigolo (dressed like a "retired Governor from the Colonies") and a madam, each taking the other for something else, but bound together in a kind of companionship. As the two of them carry on their conversation in a hotel lounge, the most commonplace phrases—"trips to the London underworld," "I cleaned up the streets"—acquire a happily shaded second meaning. Greene was always interested in the (sometimes better) parts of us we don't acknowledge.

The archetypal early story, in that regard, may well be "When Greek Meets Greek," in which all four of the characters, as in classic Greene, are con men, who are somehow innocent enough to believe that their deceits are cunning—and, more than that, innocent enough to fall for another con man's devices. As a fraudulent schemer pretending to be the head of an Oxford college hands over a diploma to a would-be lord, in some borrowed rooms in London (while the young accomplices of each go off, linked together, just as the older men hoped), one comes upon the perfect Greenian tableau in which lack of virtue is rewarded and errant trust becomes a kind of faith. From here it is not a very long step to the whiskey priests of his first great novel, *The Power and the Glory*, who, for all their shabbiness and impiety, can perform a mass, or administer simple human compassion, as well as any cardinal.

Insofar as Greene was drawn to the shabby or the secret—a charge he always denied—it was because he was always unable to turn away from the human, or to give up on the prospects of even the most moth-eaten. Many of these early stories are inchoate, or mere scenes almost, but in the richest of them you can see the smiling skeptic of *Our Man in Havana* or *Travels with My Aunt*. Greene never had an entirely innocent reading of the world—he seems to have been something of an ironist from birth—and yet he never lost respect for childhood and for all the things we do when we don't know better. And it is the stubborn, recidivist innocence of even the con men in his stories that makes them so endearing; we laugh at them from a distance, and then realize that we're somehow within them, and on their side.

There is a story in that first collection actually called "The Innocent" and in it Greene reveals another factor that complicated his abiding sense of loss. A character not dissimilar to his creator goes back to his drab boyhood hometown—Bishop's Hendron—to rummage through the past. On his arm, though, is a woman he's just picked up, one Lola, who, of course, contradicts with her every movement the search for innocence he's undertaking. One part of Greene, it seems, was always eager to poke away at what he'd left behind, the root of him, while another was hungry for the worldly and the new. In his finest stories the language of both moods comes together in the sound of a well-bred diffidence trying to tamp down something stronger. "She wasn't anything in particular," says the narrator of "Across the Bridge," of another Lola, "but she looked beautiful at a distance."

Greene's next set of stories, titled (mischievously, of course) *A Sense of Reality* and brought out sixteen years after the first, shows him going back to that boyhood town without a Lola beside him. The pieces are among the most inward and private things he ever wrote, haunted by a mysterious sense of having been written more for himself than for any reader. Greene was the rare writer of his time and class who went to a psychoanalyst (at sixteen); some years later, going to Liberia, he was, more or less explicitly, going to explore his subconscious, undertaking a journey to the interior.

In these stories that same impetus is evident, to peel back the official story of our lives we tell ourselves and find its truth. One of the pieces in the first collection actually draws upon that trip to Africa (noting, with typical mordancy, that the man who flees London to get away from boredom may only find a different kind of boredom in the jungle). But the heart of the second collection—and, really, of much of Greene—seems to me to lie in that long excursion called "Under the Garden." As its title suggests, it is about everything that hides out from the daylight world, all that the child (and then the dying man, returning to his boyhood home) longs to find hidden beneath the bourgeois surface. Always a lover of the renegade—in perpetual flight from the wisdom of headmasters (one of whom was his father)—Greene here offers up a counter-example, in the form of a literally under-ground savant. "Be disloyal," the ragged sage tells a suggestible boy, "be a double agent."

This is, of course, what Greene himself chose to do all his life; the story has the feel of a psychic autobiography, whose sequel, perhaps, is the last major book Greene ever published, a record of dreams that came out after his death. When tossing off two books of official memoir, he characteristically chose to raise more questions than he answered; here, however, rooting about at the dark edges of the garden, and enshrining everything that would draw him on (the sexual and the forbidden), he shows himself uncensored. Much more than most writers he always kept up a keen sense of how the child's intimations and fears lie at the core of us—Robert Louis Stevenson, he seldom forgot, was his mother's first cousin—and there is an echo here of William Golding, even of Stephen King, in the sudden shock of a child coming upon a dead body for the first time. The names them-selves enforce the air of allegory—characters are called "Miss Ramsgate" or "Mr. Strangeways"—and the boy who descends under the garden has all his creator's restlessness and longing for rebellion in his name, "Wilditch." The story's setting is its theme, really: "The Dark Walk."

These pieces do not always work as stories, or as works of fic-tion; but they do show that Greene, at some level, was always writing fairy tales for grown-ups (or for children who know more than they should); the form appealed to him as less reduc-tive, more open to mystery, than any theory. "A fairy story in such an event would be a more valuable asset than a Fabian graph," says Wilditch, going mournfully over his dead mother's things. Yet for all this sense of impendingness, the stories never lose their hold on comedy. Greene habitually called upon poignancy as a way to save his farces from becoming cartoonish, and on satire to rescue his sense of poignancy from the maudlin. At times, in this surreal world that feels more dreamed than plot-ted, it's almost as if P. G. Wodehouse is bumping into Gregor Samsa.

"The tenth is difficult for the clinic, but the fifteenth—Sir Nigel doesn't think we should delay longer than the fifteenth."

"Is he a great fisherman?"

"Fisherman? Sir Nigel? I have no idea."

The humor, the pathos, and much of the terror of Greene, we recall, come from his simple ability to set down a typical specimen of the English middle class in a setting of real urgency and suffering. So, too, does the aching sense of vulnerability that makes one long, at times, for anything to believe in, if it can make the pain go away. As he moved toward the rounded stories of his final collection—I am excepting for the moment the almost posthumous *The Last Word and Other Stories,* which I leave readers to discover for themselves—he moved toward a blend of shrewdness and forgiveness that, at its best, has some of the ripened mellowness of Shakespeare's final plays: realism and hope in balance.

"Absolute reality belongs to dreams and not to life." That, I think, is the central line of the middle collection. And it begins to explain to us that the title of the collection, which first might have seemed just a prank is, in fact, a way to nudge us toward the mystic's (or the believer's) sense that what we call real is only a charade, and what is truly real is everything we can't see or even guess at. In that sense, it serves to show us how this most guarded and contrarian of souls would hold himself to a faith, so long as he could find no reason for it.

This element of dream, leavened and made more interesting by a light serving of the human comedy, comes to its intricate climax in the last real set of stories Greene ever wrote, which might have taken their cue from his beloved master, James (who wrote that short stories are situated "at that exquisite point where poetry ends and reality begins"). The beauty of his best work is that it was located on precisely that cusp, as if on the wall of Eden, as the door begins to open to let its subjects out (or to let its former inhabitants look in). "What is cowardice in the young is wisdom in the old," he writes, "but all the same one can be ashamed of wisdom."

In his recent book *How to Read and Why,* the critic Harold Bloom declares, with an authority as unqualified as his title, that "Short stories are not parables or wise sayings, and so cannot be fragments; we ask them for the pleasures of closure." Yet Greene's work, it seems to me, asks for precisely the opposite: open-endedness, a humbled sense that life is always wiser than our notions of it, a refusal to settle down into one category or the other. Asked, near the end of his life, what he traveled for, he said, simply, "Ambiguity."

The very title of *May We Borrow Your Husband?* catches this mingledness, the sense that we're hovering somewhere between comedy and something much more sinister, but can no longer tell which is which. When first I saw this book on my parents' bookshelf, as a teenager, it seemed to me as everyday and banal a description of adultery as could be imagined (and, in fact, sat on the shelf next to Updike's *Couples*); with each passing year, though, the title troubles me more, and in the context of the eponymous story, stands in fact for a quite manipulative cunning hidden behind the polite enquiry. Greene's stories are tales of guile and innocence, except that Iago is helplessly in love with Desdemona; and the awful import of that is itself made more unsettling by the fact the drollery is handled so lightly.

On the surface, the stories Greene wrote in his later years are all urbane amusements, worldly fables of corruption and death graced with such a light touch and such wise humanity that they might almost have come from his neighbor on the Riviera (whose work he claimed to dislike), Somerset Maugham: *Up at the Neighboring Villa* perhaps. They are written in the first person, mostly, and Greene goes out of his way to suggest, unusually, that the observing narrator is himself. He mentions restaurants he was known to haunt—Felix au Port in Antibes, Bentley's in London—and tells his little parables as if they were just scenes he chanced to overhear while sitting in a corner.

The settings and ostensible concerns are nearly all domestic; such politics as exist here are mostly sexual. The pieces turn often around a man and a woman whose relations are strained; and many of the characters, all of whom sound alike (Greene was never a master of voices), are in mourning at some level for an innocence lost. The central moments of his novels, often, come with two men talking in the dark; here, more unsettlingly, they center around a male and a female more divided than they know (those who complain about the treatment of women in Greene's novels tend to glide over the fact that friendship, however qualified or temporary, is his thing; between the sexes there is always a rueful consciousness of distance). These are, you could say, love stories about people who shouldn't be in love.

Their theme, always, is innocence, but it is innocence observed from afar, innocence threatened or already spoiled. Like the worldly Frenchmen that he loved, Greene was a connoisseur of those grown-up truths that make honesty, often, the worst policy, and kindness a form of cruelty wearing a smiling face. In a particular favorite of mine, "Mortmain" (the name becomes more unnerving because it never actually appears in the story), a small chapter of marital bliss becomes a wry story of the Fall. The moments of greatest innocence or hope, these stories suggest, are precisely the ones that portend the greatest doom. Innocence is a liability because it can't see beyond its rosy expectations.

Greene always wrote of innocence with the knowing poignancy of one who knew better, but sometimes wished he didn't; with the earnestness, even, of one who longs for a kind of justice, while knowing that infallible justice seldom comes to mortals. He pledged himself to a faith that would always leave him disappointed: in a careworn hope somewhere between the complacency of the solid believer and the nonchalance of the skeptic. In the title story, a biographer of Rochester, like our author, encounters a near-virgin on her honeymoon, and, of course, her innocence begins to corrupt his experience; a part of him wishes to protect her, while another part longs to take advantage of what she has. "The more you love," a schoolboy paraphrases his doctor, in another story, "the greater the danger." And the perspective of the story is that of a man close to the end who sees "that at the end of what is called 'the sexual life' the only love which has lasted is the love that has accepted everything, every disappointment, every failure and every betrayal, which has accepted even the sad fact that in the end there is no desire so deep as the simple desire for companionship." When "Je ne regrette rien" sounds in his head, it elicits more sadness than relief in one approaching death who feels he has almost everything to regret.

All the compression of the novels is alive and rich in these pages (Henry Hickslaughter trudges toward "the shallow end" of the pool), and even the smallest sentences, sometimes, can set off an almost silent detonation. "Suddenly," Greene writes of another couple returning from their honeymoon, "it was autumn when they arrived back in London." Autumn haunts everything in these final sunlit tales, whether the boarded-up striptease parlor on the beach or a nickname ("Poopy") so funny that it becomes quite sad. The sense of amusement is everywhere, too—you can hear the private hell and horses' confinement hiding out in the name "Josephine Heckstall-Jones"—but the humor is always spiked and deepened by the sadness. The stiff man carrying an overnight case on a plane claims it contains not embezzled money or illicit drugs, but a dead baby. The name of the "little grey man" is Henry Cooper (in life, that name belonged to England's most prized heavyweight boxer).

" 'That's wonderful,' he said sadly, 'wonderful,'" we read in another story, and are reminded of how Greene could violate the writer's rule never to use adverbs, simply by putting such English on them.

Comedy and human frailty together: that is the particular blend of Greene at his strongest, sitting in the shadows with his "splinter of ice" and quietly mocking the character who suddenly becomes too vulnerable for the author's liking, or for ours. In perhaps the strongest of all the tales in this volume, "Cheap in August," Greene introduces us to a scene that seems to offer all the easy satire and simple delight of a jeu d'esprit. A woman is on holiday in Jamaica, and, like many a Greene character, she's longing for danger and adventure during her rare freedom from a good, clean, all-American husband. "After ten years of being happily married, she thought, one undervalues security and tranquility."

A Jamesian story in reverse, one thinks: an Englishwoman longing to be educated in some form in the New World. Stories about women alone on holiday in the tropics, and not getting any younger, tend to follow a familiar itinerary. Her search for romance or "ambiguity" will meet with a sticky end, we assume, and our expectations of gentle irony are met when the one redeemer she encounters is an overweight aging American who might be a compound of what Greene, and even his characters, regard as laughable. Even his shoes are of the kind "known as co-respondent."

We read along, toward the expected comic, perhaps comforting, climax—maybe they'll find a surprising kind of love together—when the door swings open, and there is exactly what we didn't expect: a figure of fun seen on his bed in tears, lonely, fragile, and terrified of the dark. Coming from a writer who is writing more and more of death as he nears his seventies, it takes on an extra poignancy and strength. There's no great concentration on the exotic setting, there's no particular complication of plot. There is simply a sudden lurch into human frailty and the longing to be held and loved. The reader, embarking on the story with the wish to be amused, suddenly finds that she's involved. And the person who commands our sympathy is precisely the one we knew was there only as a comic prop. We're on the border again, we see, but this time we know that it separates something much more universal than just Mexico and America.

Suggestions for Further Reading

Norman Sherry's *Life of Graham Greene* is now available complete in three volumes: the first, which appeared in 1989, covers Greene's life from 1904 to 1939; the second (1995) covers the period from 1939 to 1955; and the third (2004) takes the story from 1955 until the writer's death in 1991. There is a competing, and prosecutorial, one-volume life by Michael Shelden, *Graham Greene: The Enemy Within* (London: Heinemann, 1994). Two of Greene's own books provide a useful context for his fiction. His comments on other novelists invariably supply a commentary on his practice, and he was also an acute critic of his own work. See the *Collected Essays* (New York: Viking, 1969) and *Ways of Escape* (New York: Simon and Schuster, 1980). The essential critical volume remains the collection edited by Samuel Hynes, *Graham Greene: A Collection of Critical Essays* (Englewood Cliffs, NJ: Prentice-Hall, 1973). It reprints seminal essays by Morton Dauwen Zabel, R.W.B. Lewis, and Richard Hoggart; reviews by Evelyn Waugh and George Orwell; a fine essay on the theology of *The End of the Affair* by Ian Gregor; and an overview of Greene's career by Frank Kermode. Interested readers may also find the following of use:

Adamson, Judith. *Graham Greene and Cinema*. Norman, OK: Pilgrim Books, 1984.
———. *Graham Greene: The Dangerous Edge*. New York: St. Martin's, 1990.
Baldridge, Cates. *Graham Greene's Fictions: The Virtues of Extremity*. Columbia and London: University of Missouri Press, 2000.

Lodge, David. *Graham Greene*. New York and London: Columbia University Press, 1966.

Mudford, Peter. *Graham Greene*. Plymouth, England: Northcote House in association with the British Council, 1996.

Sharrock, Roger. *Saints, Sinners and Comedians: The Novels of Graham Greene*. Notre Dame, IN: University of Notre Dame Press, 1984.

Smith, Grahame. *The Achievement of Graham Greene*. Sussex: The Harvester Press, 1986.

Spurling, John. *Graham Greene*. London and New York: Methuen, 1983.

Complete Short Stories

TWENTY-ONE STORIES

THE DESTRUCTORS

It was on the eve of August Bank Holiday that the latest recruit became the leader of the Wormsley Common Gang. No one was surprised except Mike, but Mike at the age of nine was surprised by everything. 'If you don't shut your mouth,' somebody once said to him, 'you'll get a frog down it.' After that Mike kept his teeth tightly clamped except when the surprise was too great.

The new recruit had been with the gang since the beginning of the summer holidays, and there were possibilities about his brooding silence that all recognized. He never wasted a word even to tell his name until that was required of him by the rules. When he said 'Trevor' it was a statement of fact, not as it would have been with the others a statement of shame or defiance. Nor did anyone laugh except Mike, who finding himself without support and meeting the dark gaze of the newcomer opened his mouth and was quiet again. There was every reason why T, as he was afterwards referred to, should have been an object of mockery—there was his name (and they substituted the initial because otherwise they had no excuse not to laugh at it), the fact that his father, a former architect and present clerk, had 'come down in the world' and that his mother considered herself better than the neighbours. What but an odd quality of danger, of the unpredictable, established him in the gang without any ignoble ceremony of initiation?

The gang met every morning in an impromptu car-park, the site of the last bomb of the first blitz. The leader, who was known as Blackie, claimed to have heard it fall, and no one was precise enough in his dates to point out that he would have been one year old and fast asleep on the down platform of Wormsley Common Underground Station. On one side of the car-park leant the first occupied house, No. 3, of the shattered Northwood Terrace—literally leant, for it had suffered from the blast of the bomb and the side walls were supported on wooden struts. A smaller bomb and incendiaries had fallen beyond, so that the house stuck up like a jagged tooth and carried on the further wall relics of its neighbour, a dado, the remains of a fireplace. T, whose words were almost confined to voting 'Yes' or 'No' to the plan of operations proposed each day by Blackie, once startled the whole gang by saying broodingly, 'Wren built that house, father says.'

'Who's Wren?'

'The man who built St Paul's.'

'Who cares?' Blackie said. 'It's only Old Misery's.'

Old Misery—whose real name was Thomas—had once been a builder and decorator. He lived alone in the crippled house, doing for himself: once a week you could see him coming back across the common with bread and vegetables, and once as the boys played in the car-park he put his head over the smashed wall of his garden and looked at them.

'Been to the lav,' one of the boys said, for it was common knowledge that since the bombs fell something had gone wrong with the pipes of the house and Old Misery was too mean to spend money on the property. He could do the redecorating himself at cost price, but he had never learnt plumbing. The lav was a wooden shed at the bottom of the narrow garden with a star-shaped hole in the door: it had escaped the blast which had smashed the house next door and sucked out the window-frames of No. 3.

The next time the gang became aware of Mr Thomas was more surprising. Blackie, Mike and a thin yellow boy, who for some reason was called by his surname Summers, met him on the common coming back from the market. Mr Thomas stopped them. He said glumly, 'You belong to the lot that play in the car-park?'

Mike was about to answer when Blackie stopped him. As the leader he had responsibilities. 'Suppose we are?' he said ambiguously.

'I got some chocolates,' Mr Thomas said. 'Don't like 'em myself. Here you are. Not enough to go round, I don't suppose. There never is,' he added with sombre conviction. He handed over three packets of Smarties.

The gang was puzzled and perturbed by this action and tried to explain it away. 'Bet someone dropped them and he picked 'em up,' somebody suggested.

'Pinched 'em and then got in a bleeding funk,' another thought aloud.

'It's a bribe,' Summers said. 'He wants us to stop bouncing balls on his wall.'

'We'll show him we don't take bribes,' Blackie said, and they sacrificed the whole morning to the game of bouncing that only Mike was young enough to enjoy. There was no sign from Mr Thomas.

Next day T astonished them all. He was late at the rendezvous, and the voting for that day's exploit took place without him. At Blackie's suggestion the gang was to disperse in pairs, take buses at random and see how many free rides could be snatched from unwary conductors (the operation was to be carried out in pairs to avoid cheating). They were drawing lots for their companions when T arrived.

'Where you been, T?' Blackie asked. 'You can't vote now. You know the rules.'

'I've been *there*,' T said. He looked at the ground, as though he had thoughts to hide.

'Where?'

'At Old Misery's.' Mike's mouth opened and then hurriedly closed again with a click. He had remembered the frog.

'At Old Misery's?' Blackie said. There was nothing in the rules against it, but he had a sensation that T was treading on dangerous ground. He asked hopefully, 'Did you break in?'

'No. I rang the bell.'

'And what did you say?'

'I said I wanted to see his house.'

'What did he do?'

'He showed it me.'

'Pinch anything?'

'No.'

'What did you do it for then?'

The gang had gathered round: it was as though an impromptu court were about to form and try some case of deviation. T said, 'It's a beautiful house,' and still watching the ground, meeting no one's eyes, he licked his lips first one way, then the other.

'What do you mean, a beautiful house?' Blackie asked with scorn.

'It's got a staircase two hundred years old like a corkscrew. Nothing holds it up.'

'What do you mean, nothing holds it up. Does it float?'

'It's to do with opposite forces, Old Misery said.'

'What else?'

'There's panelling.'

'Like in the Blue Boar?'

'Two hundred years old.'

'Is Old Misery two hundred years old?'

Mike laughed suddenly and then was quiet again. The meeting was in a serious mood. For the first time since T had strolled into the car-park on the first day of the holidays his position was in danger. It only needed a single use of his real name and the gang would be at his heels.

'What did you do it for?' Blackie asked. He was just, he had no jealousy, he was anxious to retain T in the gang if he could. It was the word 'beautiful' that worried him—that belonged to a class world that you could still see parodied at the Wormsley Common Empire by a man wearing a top hat and a monocle, with a haw-haw accent. He was tempted to say, 'My dear Trevor, old chap,' and unleash his hell hounds. 'If you'd broken in,' he said sadly—that indeed would have been an exploit worthy of the gang.

'This was better,' T said. 'I found out things.' He continued to stare at his feet, not meeting anybody's eye, as though he were absorbed in some dream he was unwilling—or ashamed—to share.

'What things?'

'Old Misery's going to be away all tomorrow and Bank Holiday.'

Blackie said with relief, 'You mean we could break in?'

'And pinch things?' somebody asked.

Blackie said, 'Nobody's going to pinch things. Breaking in—that's good enough, isn't it? We don't want any court stuff.'

'I don't want to pinch anything,' T said. 'I've got a better idea.'

'What is it?'

T raised eyes, as grey and disturbed as the drab August day. 'We'll pull it down,' he said. 'We'll destroy it.'

Blackie gave a single hoot of laughter and then, like Mike, fell quiet, daunted by the serious implacable gaze. 'What'd the police be doing all the time?' he said.

'They'd never know. We'd do it from inside. I've found a way in.' He said with a sort of intensity, 'We'd be like worms, don't you see, in an apple. When we came out again there'd be nothing there, no staircase, no panels, nothing but just walls, and then we'd make the walls fall down—somehow.'

'We'd go to jug,' Blackie said.

'Who's to prove? and anyway we wouldn't have pinched anything.' He added without the smallest flicker of glee, 'There wouldn't be anything to pinch after we'd finished.'

'I've never heard of going to prison for breaking things,' Summers said.

'There wouldn't be time,' Blackie said. 'I've seen housebreakers at work.'

'There are twelve of us,' T said. 'We'd organize.'

'None of us know how . . .'

'I know,' T said. He looked across at Blackie. 'Have you got a better plan?'

'Today,' Mike said tactlessly, 'we're pinching free rides . . .'

'Free rides,' T said. 'Kid stuff. You can stand down, Blackie, if you'd rather . . .'

'The gang's got to vote.'

'Put it up then.'

Blackie said uneasily, 'It's proposed that tomorrow and Monday we destroy Old Misery's house.'

'Here, here,' said a fat boy called Joe.

'Who's in favour?'

T said, 'It's carried.'

'How do we start?' Summers asked.

'He'll tell you,' Blackie said. It was the end of his leadership.

He went away to the back of the car-park and began to kick a stone, dribbling it this way and that. There was only one old Morris in the park, for few cars were left there except lorries: without an attendant there was no safety. He took a flying kick at the car and scraped a little paint off the rear mudguard. Beyond, paying no more attention to him than to a stranger, the gang had gathered round T; Blackie was dimly aware of the fickleness of favour. He thought of going home, of never returning, of letting them all discover the hollowness of T's leadership, but suppose after all what T proposed was possible—nothing like it had ever been done before. The fame of the Wormsley Common car-park gang would surely reach around London. There would be headlines in the papers. Even the grown-up gangs who ran the betting at the all-in wrestling and the barrow-boys would hear with respect of how Old Misery's house had been destroyed. Driven by the pure, simple and altruistic ambition of fame for the gang, Blackie came back to where T stood in the shadow of Old Misery's wall.

T was giving his orders with decision: it was as though this plan had been with him all his life, pondered through the seasons, now in his fifteenth year crystallized with the pain of puberty. 'You,' he said to Mike, 'bring some big nails, the biggest you can find, and a hammer. Anybody who can, better bring a hammer and a screwdriver. We'll need plenty of them. Chisels too. We can't have too many chisels. Can anybody bring a saw?'

'I can,' Mike said.

'Not a child's saw,' T said. 'A real saw.'

Blackie realized he had raised his hand like any ordinary member of the gang.

'Right, you bring one, Blackie. But now there's a difficulty. We want a hacksaw.'

'What's a hacksaw?' someone asked.

'You can get 'em at Woolworth's,' Summers said.

The fat boy called Joe said gloomily, 'I knew it would end in a collection.'

'I'll get one myself,' T said. 'I don't want your money. But I can't buy a sledge-hammer.'

Blackie said, 'They are working on No. 15. I know where they'll leave their stuff for Bank Holiday.'

'Then that's all,' T said. 'We meet here at nine sharp.'

'I've got to go to church,' Mike said.

'Come over the wall and whistle. We'll let you in.'

2

On Sunday morning all were punctual except Blackie, even Mike. Mike had a stroke of luck. His mother felt ill, his father was tired after Saturday night, and he was told to go to church alone with many warnings of what would happen if he strayed. Blackie had difficulty in smuggling out the saw, and then in finding the sledge-hammer at the back of No. 15. He approached the house from a lane at the rear of the garden, for fear of the policeman's beat along the main road. The tired evergreens kept off a stormy sun: another wet Bank Holiday was being prepared over the Atlantic, beginning in swirls of dust under the trees. Blackie climbed the wall into Misery's garden.

There was no sign of anybody anywhere. The lav stood like a tomb in a neglected graveyard. The curtains were drawn. The house slept. Blackie lumbered nearer with the saw and the sledge-hammer. Perhaps after all nobody had turned up: the plan had been a wild invention: they had woken wiser. But when he came close to the back door he could hear a confusion of sound hardly louder than a hive in swarm: a clickety-clack, a bang bang, a scraping, a creaking, a sudden painful crack. He thought: it's true, and whistled.

They opened the back door to him and he came in. He had at once the impression of organization, very different from the old happy-go-lucky ways under his leadership. For a while he wandered up and down stairs looking for T. Nobody addressed him: he had a sense of great urgency, and already he could begin to see the plan. The interior of the house was being carefully demolished without touching the walls. Summers with hammer and chisel was ripping out the skirting-boards in the ground-floor dining-room: he had already smashed the panels of the door. In the same room Joe was heaving up the parquet blocks, exposing the soft wood floorboards over the cellar. Coils of wire came out

of the damaged skirting and Mike sat happily on the floor clip-
ping the wires.

On the curved stairs two of the gang were working hard with
an inadequate child's saw on the banisters—when they saw
Blackie's big saw they signalled for it wordlessly. When he next
saw them a quarter of the banisters had been dropped into the
hall. He found T at last in the bathroom—he sat moodily in the
least cared-for room in the house, listening to the sounds coming
up from below.

'You've really done it,' Blackie said with awe. 'What's going to
happen?'

'We've only just begun,' T said. He looked at the sledge-
hammer and gave his instructions. 'You stay here and break the
bath and the wash-basin. Don't bother about the pipes. They
come later.'

Mike appeared at the door. 'I've finished the wires, T,' he said.

'Good. You've just got to go wandering round now. The
kitchen's in the basement. Smash all the china and glass and bottles you can lay hold of. Don't turn on the taps—we don't want a
flood—yet. Then go into all the rooms and turn out the drawers.
If they are locked get one of the others to break them open. Tear
up any papers you find and smash all the ornaments. Better take
a carving knife with you from the kitchen. The bedroom's opposite here. Open the pillows and tear up the sheets. That's enough
for the moment. And you, Blackie, when you've finished in here
crack the plaster in the passage up with your sledge-hammer.'

'What are you going to do?' Blackie asked.

'I'm looking for something special,' T said.

It was nearly lunch-time before Blackie had finished and went
in search of T. Chaos had advanced. The kitchen was a sham-
bles of broken glass and china. The dining-room was stripped of
parquet, the skirting was up, the door had been taken off its
hinges, and the destroyers had moved up a floor. Streaks of light
came in through the closed shutters where they worked with the
seriousness of creators—and destruction after all is a form of
creation. A kind of imagination had seen this house as it had
now become.

Mike said, 'I've got to go home for dinner.'

'Who else?' T asked, but all the others on one excuse or another had brought provisions with them.

They squatted in the ruins of the room and swapped unwanted sandwiches. Half an hour for lunch and they were at work again. By the time Mike returned they were on the top floor, and by six the superficial damage was completed. The doors were all off, all the skirtings raised, the furniture pillaged and ripped and smashed—no one could have slept in the house except on a bed of broken plaster. T gave his orders—eight o'clock next morning, and to escape notice they climbed singly over the garden wall, into the car-park. Only Blackie and T were left: the light had nearly gone, and when they touched a switch, nothing worked—Mike had done his job thoroughly.

'Did you find anything special?' Blackie asked.

T nodded. 'Come over here,' he said, 'and look.' Out of both pockets he drew bundles of pound notes. 'Old Misery's savings,' he said. 'Mike ripped out the mattress, but he missed them.'

'What are you going to do? Share them?'

'We aren't thieves,' T said. 'Nobody's going to steal anything from this house. I kept these for you and me—a celebration.' He knelt down on the floor and counted them out—there were seventy in all. 'We'll burn them,' he said, 'one by one,' and taking it in turns they held a note upwards and lit the top corner, so that the flame burnt slowly towards their fingers. The grey ash floated above them and fell on their heads like age. 'I'd like to see Old Misery's face when we are through,' T said.

'You hate him a lot?' Blackie asked.

'Of course I don't hate him,' T said. 'There'd be no fun if I hated him.' The last burning note illuminated his brooding face. 'All this hate and love,' he said, 'it's soft, it's hooey. There's only things, Blackie,' and he looked round the room crowded with the unfamiliar shadows of half things, broken things, former things. 'I'll race you home, Blackie,' he said.

3

Next morning the serious destruction started. Two were missing—Mike and another boy whose parents were off to Southend and Brighton in spite of the slow warm drops that had begun to fall and the rumble of thunder in the estuary like the first guns of the old blitz. 'We've got to hurry,' T said.

Summers was restive. 'Haven't we done enough?' he asked. 'I've been given a bob for slot machines. This is like work.'

'We've hardly started,' T said. 'Why, there's all the floors left, and the stairs. We haven't taken out a single window. You voted like the others. We are going to *destroy* this house. There won't be anything left when we've finished.'

They began again on the first floor picking up the top floor-boards next the outer wall, leaving the joists exposed. Then they sawed through the joists and retreated into the hall, as what was left of the floor heeled and sank. They had learnt with practice, and the second floor collapsed more easily. By the evening an odd exhilaration seized them as they looked down the great hollow of the house. They ran risks and made mistakes: when they thought of the windows it was too late to reach them. 'Cor,' Joe said, and dropped a penny down into the dry rubble-filled well. It cracked and span amongst the broken glass.

'Why did we start this?' Summers asked with astonishment; T was already on the ground, digging at the rubble, clearing a space along the outer wall. 'Turn on the taps,' he said. 'It's too dark for anyone to see now, and in the morning it won't matter.' The water overtook them on the stairs and fell through the floorless rooms.

It was then they heard Mike's whistle at the back. 'Something's wrong,' Blackie said. They could hear his urgent breathing as they unlocked the door.

'The bogies?' Summers asked.

'Old Misery,' Mike said. 'He's on his way,' he said with pride.

'But why?' T said. 'He told me . . .' He protested with the fury of the child he had never been, 'It isn't fair.'

'He was down at Southend,' Mike said, 'and he was on the train coming back. Said it was too cold and wet.' He paused and gazed at the water. 'My, you've had a storm here. Is the roof leaking?'

'How long will he be?'

'Five minutes. I gave Ma the slip and ran.'

'We better clear,' Summers said. 'We've done enough, anyway.'

'Oh no, we haven't. Anybody could do this—' 'this' was the shattered hollowed house with nothing left but the walls. Yet walls could be preserved. Façades were valuable. They could build inside again more beautifully than before. This could again be a home. He said angrily, 'We've got to finish. Don't move. Let me think.'

'There's no time,' a boy said.

'There's got to be a way,' T said. 'We couldn't have got this far . . .'

'We've done a lot,' Blackie said.

'No. No, we haven't. Somebody watch the front.'

'We can't do any more.'

'He may come in at the back.'

'Watch the back too.' T began to plead. 'Just give me a minute and I'll fix it. I swear I'll fix it.' But his authority had gone with his ambiguity. He was only one of the gang. 'Please,' he said.

'Please,' Summers mimicked him, and then suddenly struck home with the fatal name. 'Run along home, Trevor.'

T stood with his back to the rubble like a boxer knocked groggy against the ropes. He had no words as his dreams shook and slid. Then Blackie acted before the gang had time to laugh, pushing Summers backward. 'I'll watch the front, T,' he said, and cautiously he opened the shutters of the hall. The grey wet common stretched ahead, and the lamps gleamed in the puddles. 'Someone's coming, T. No, it's not him. What's your plan, T?'

'Tell Mike to go out to the lav and hide close beside it. When he hears me whistle he's got to count ten and start to shout.'

'Shout what?'

'Oh, "Help", anything.'

'You hear, Mike,' Blackie said. He was the leader again. He took a quick look between the shutters. 'He's coming, T.'

'Quick, Mike. The lav. Stay here, Blackie, all of you, till I yell.'

'Where are you going, T?'

'Don't worry. I'll see to this. I said I would, didn't I?'

Old Misery came limping off the common. He had mud on his shoes and he stopped to scrape them on the pavement's edge. He didn't want to soil his house, which stood jagged and dark between the bomb-sites, saved so narrowly, as he believed, from destruction. Even the fan-light had been left unbroken by the bomb's blast. Somewhere somebody whistled. Old Misery looked sharply round. He didn't trust whistles. A child was shouting: it seemed to come from his own garden. Then a boy ran into the road from the car-park. 'Mr Thomas,' he called, 'Mr Thomas.'

'What is it?'

'I'm terribly sorry, Mr Thomas. One of us got taken short, and we thought you wouldn't mind, and now he can't get out.'

'What do you mean, boy?'

'He's got stuck in your lav.'

'He'd no business . . . Haven't I seen you before?'

'You showed me your house.'

'So I did. So I did. That doesn't give you the right to . . .'

'Do hurry, Mr Thomas. He'll suffocate.'

'Nonsense. He can't suffocate. Wait till I put my bag in.'

'I'll carry your bag.'

'Oh no, you don't. I carry my own.'

'This way, Mr Thomas.'

'I can't get in the garden that way. I've got to go through the house.'

'But you *can* get in the garden this way, Mr Thomas. We often do.'

'You often do?' He followed the boy with a scandalized fascination. 'When? What right . . . ?'

'Do you see . . . ? the wall's low.'

'I'm not going to climb walls into my own garden. It's absurd.'

'This is how we do it. One foot here, one foot there, and over.' The boy's face peered down, an arm shot out, and Mr Thomas found his bag taken and deposited on the other side of the wall.

'Give me back my bag,' Mr Thomas said. From the loo a boy yelled and yelled. 'I'll call the police.'

'Your bag's all right, Mr Thomas. Look. One foot there. On

your right. Now just above. To your left.' Mr Thomas climbed over his own garden wall. 'Here's your bag, Mr Thomas.'

'I'll have the wall built up,' Mr Thomas said, 'I'll not have you boys coming over here, using my loo.' He stumbled on the path, but the boy caught his elbow and supported him. 'Thank you, thank you, my boy,' he murmured automatically. Somebody shouted again through the dark. 'I'm coming, I'm coming,' Mr Thomas called. He said to the boy beside him, 'I'm not unreasonable. Been a boy myself. As long as things are done regular. I don't mind you playing round the place Saturday mornings. Sometimes I like company. Only it's got to be regular. One of you asks leave and I say Yes. Sometimes I'll say No. Won't feel like it. And you come in at the front door and out at the back. No garden walls.'

'Do get him out, Mr Thomas.'

'He won't come to any harm in my loo,' Mr Thomas said, stumbling slowly down the garden. 'Oh, my rheumatics,' he said. 'Always get 'em on Bank Holiday. I've got to be careful. There's loose stones here. Give me your hand. Do you know what my horoscope said yesterday? "Abstain from any dealings in first half of week. Danger of serious crash." That might be on this path,' Mr Thomas said. 'They speak in parables and double meanings.' He paused at the door of the loo. 'What's the matter in there?' he called. There was no reply.

'Perhaps he's fainted,' the boy said.

'Not in my loo. Here, you, come out,' Mr Thomas said, and giving a great jerk at the door he nearly fell on his back when it swung easily open. A hand first supported him and then pushed him hard. His head hit the opposite wall and he sat heavily down. His bag hit his feet. A hand whipped the key out of the lock and the door slammed. 'Let me out,' he called, and heard the key turn in the lock. 'A serious crash,' he thought, and felt dithery and confused and old.

A voice spoke to him softly through the star-shaped hole in the door. 'Don't worry, Mr Thomas,' it said, 'we won't hurt you, not if you stay quiet.'

Mr Thomas put his head between his hands and pondered. He had noticed that there was only one lorry in the car-park, and he felt certain that the driver would not come for it before the morning. Nobody could hear him from the road in front, and the lane at the back was seldom used. Anyone who passed there would be hurrying home and would not pause for what they would certainly take to be drunken cries. And if he did call 'Help,' who, on a lonely Bank Holiday evening, would have the courage to investigate? Mr Thomas sat on the loo and pondered with the wisdom of age.

After a while it seemed to him that there were sounds in the silence—they were faint and came from the direction of his house. He stood up and peered through the ventilation-hole—between the cracks in one of the shutters he saw a light, not the light of a lamp, but the wavering light that a candle might give. Then he thought he heard the sound of hammering and scraping and chipping. He thought of burglars—perhaps they had employed the boy as a scout, but why should burglars engage in what sounded more and more like a stealthy form of carpentry? Mr Thomas let out an experimental yell, but nobody answered. The noise could not even have reached his enemies.

4

Mike had gone home to bed, but the rest stayed. The question of leadership no longer concerned the gang. With nails, chisels, screwdrivers, anything that was sharp and penetrating, they moved around the inner walls worrying at the mortar between the bricks. They started too high, and it was Blackie who hit on the damp course and realized the work could be halved if they weakened the joints immediately above. It was a long, tiring, un-amusing job, but at last it was finished. The gutted house stood there balanced on a few inches of mortar between the damp course and the bricks.

There remained the most dangerous task of all, out in the open at the edge of the bomb-site. Summers was sent to watch the road for passers-by, and Mr Thomas, sitting on the loo, heard clearly now the sound of sawing. It no longer came from the house, and that a little reassured him. He felt less concerned. Perhaps the other noises too had no significance.

A voice spoke to him through the hole. 'Mr Thomas.'

'Let me out,' Mr Thomas said sternly.

'Here's a blanket,' the voice said, and a long grey sausage was worked through the hole and fell in swathes over Mr Thomas's head.

'There's nothing personal,' the voice said. 'We want you to be comfortable tonight.'

'Tonight,' Mr Thomas repeated incredulously.

'Catch,' the voice said. 'Penny buns—we've buttered them, and sausage-rolls. We don't want you to starve, Mr Thomas.'

Mr Thomas pleaded desperately. 'A joke's a joke, boy. Let me out and I won't say a thing. I've got rheumatics. I got to sleep comfortable.'

'You wouldn't be comfortable, not in your house, you wouldn't. Not now.'

'What do you mean, boy?' But the footsteps receded. There was only the silence of night: no sound of sawing. Mr Thomas tried one more yell, but he was daunted and rebuked by the silence—a long way off an owl hooted and made away again on its muffled flight through the soundless world.

At seven next morning the driver came to fetch his lorry. He climbed into the seat and tried to start the engine. He was vaguely aware of a voice shouting, but it didn't concern him. At last the engine responded and he backed the lorry until it touched the great wooden shore that supported Mr Thomas's house. That way he could drive right out and down the street without reversing. The lorry moved forward, was momentarily checked as though something were pulling it from behind, and then went on to the sound of a long rumbling crash. The driver was astonished to see bricks bouncing ahead of him, while stones hit the roof of his cab. He put on his brakes. When he climbed out the whole landscape had suddenly altered. There was no house beside the car-park, only a hill of rubble. He went round and examined the back of his lorry for damage, and found a rope tied there that was still twisted at the other end round part of a wooden strut.

The driver again became aware of somebody shouting. It came from the wooden erection which was the nearest thing to a house in that desolation of broken brick. The driver climbed the smashed wall and unlocked the door. Mr Thomas came out of the loo. He was wearing a grey blanket to which flakes of pastry adhered. He gave a sobbing cry. 'My house,' he said. 'Where's my house?'

'Search me,' the driver said. His eye lit on the remains of a bath and what had once been a dresser and he began to laugh. There wasn't anything left anywhere.

'How dare you laugh,' Mr Thomas said. 'It was my house. My house.'

'I'm sorry,' the driver said, making heroic efforts, but when he remembered the sudden check of his lorry, the crash of bricks falling, he became convulsed again. One moment the house had stood there with such dignity between the bomb-sites like a man in a top hat, and then, bang, crash, there wasn't anything left— not anything. He said, 'I'm sorry. I can't help it, Mr Thomas. There's nothing personal, but you got to admit it's funny.'

1954

SPECIAL DUTIES

William Ferraro of Ferraro & Smith lived in a great house in Montagu Square. One wing was occupied by his wife who believed herself to be an invalid and obeyed strictly the dictate that one should live every day as if it were one's last. For this reason her wing for the last ten years had invariably housed some Jesuit or Dominican priest with a taste for good wine and whisky and an emergency bell in his bedroom. Mr Ferraro looked after his salvation in more independent fashion. He retained the firm grasp on practical affairs that had enabled his grandfather, who had been a fellow exile with Mazzini, to found the great business of Ferraro & Smith in a foreign land. God has made man in his image, and it was not unreasonable for Mr Ferraro to return the compliment and to regard God as the director of some supreme business which yet depended for certain of its operations on Ferraro & Smith. The strength of a chain is in its weakest link, and Mr Ferraro did not forget his responsibility.

Before leaving for his office at 9.30 Mr Ferraro as a matter of courtesy would telephone to his wife in the other wing. 'Father Dewes speaking,' a voice would say.

'How is my wife?'

'She passed a good night.'

The conversation seldom varied. There had been a time when Father Dewes' predecessor made an attempt to bring Mr and Mrs Ferraro into a closer relationship, but he had desisted when he realized how hopeless his aim was, and how on the few occasions when Mr Ferraro dined with them in the other wing an inferior claret was served at table and no whisky was drunk before dinner.

Mr Ferraro, having telephoned from his bedroom where he took his breakfast, would walk, rather as God walked in the Garden, through his library lined with the correct classics and his drawing-room, on the walls of which hung one of the most expensive art collections in private hands. Where one man would treasure a single Degas, Renoir, Cézanne, Mr Ferraro bought wholesale—he had six Renoirs, four Degas, five Cézannes. He never tired of their presence, they represented a substantial saving in death-duties.

On this particular Monday morning it was also May the first. The sense of spring had come punctually to London and the sparrows were noisy in the dust. Mr Ferraro too was punctual, but unlike the seasons he was as reliable as Greenwich time. With his confidential secretary—a man called Hopkinson—he went through the schedule for the day. It was not very onerous, for Mr Ferraro had the rare quality of being able to delegate responsibility. He did this the more readily because he was accustomed to make unexpected checks, and woe betide the employee who failed him. Even his doctor had to submit to a sudden counter-check from a rival consultant. 'I think,' he said to Hopkinson, 'this afternoon I will drop in to Christie's and see how Maverick is getting on.' (Maverick was employed as his agent in the purchase of pictures.) What better could be done on a fine May afternoon than check on Maverick? He added, 'Send in Miss Saunders,' and drew forward a personal file which even Hopkinson was not allowed to handle.

Miss Saunders moused in. She gave the impression of moving close to the ground. She was about thirty years old with indeterminate hair and eyes of a startling clear blue which gave her otherwise anonymous face a resemblance to a holy statue. She was described in the firm's books as 'assistant confidential secretary' and her duties were 'special' ones. Even her qualifications were special: she had been head girl at the Convent of Saint Latitudinaria, Woking, where she had won in three successive years the special prize for piety—a little triptych of Our Lady with a background of blue silk, bound in Florentine leather and supplied by Burns Oates & Washbourne. She also had a long record of unpaid service as a Child of Mary.

'Miss Saunders,' Mr Ferraro said, 'I find no account here of the indulgences to be gained in June.'

'I have it here, sir. I was late home last night as the plenary indulgence at St Etheldreda's entailed the Stations of the Cross.'

She laid a typed list on Mr Ferraro's desk: in the first column the date, in the second the church or place of pilgrimage where the indulgence was to be gained, and in the third column in red ink the number of days saved from the temporal punishments of Purgatory. Mr Ferraro read it carefully.

'I get the impression, Miss Saunders,' he said, 'that you are spending too much time on the lower brackets. Sixty days here, fifty days there. Are you sure you are not wasting your time on these? One indulgence of 300 days will compensate for many such. I noticed just now that your estimate for May is lower than your April figures, and your estimate for June is nearly down to the March level. Five plenary indulgences and 1,565 days—a very good April work. I don't want you to slacken off.'

'April is a very good month for indulgences, sir. There is Easter. In May we can depend only on the fact that it is Our Lady's month. June is not very fruitful, except at Corpus Christi. You will notice a little Polish church in Cambridgeshire . . .'

'As long as you remember, Miss Saunders, that none of us is getting younger. I put a great deal of trust in you, Miss Saunders. If I were less occupied here, I could attend to some of these indulgences myself. You pay great attention, I hope, to the conditions.'

'Of course I do, Mr Ferraro.'

'You are always careful to be in a State of Grace?'

Miss Saunders lowered her eyes. 'That is not very difficult in my case, Mr Ferraro.'

'What is your programme today?'

'You have it there, Mr Ferraro.'

'Of course. St Praxted's, Canon Wood. That is rather a long way to go. You have to spend the whole afternoon on a mere sixty days' indulgence?'

'It was all I could find for today. Of course there are always the plenary indulgences at the Cathedral. But I know how you feel about not repeating during the same month.'

'My only point of superstition,' Mr Ferraro said. 'It has no basis, of course, in the teaching of the Church.'

'You wouldn't like an occasional repetition for a member of your family, Mr Ferraro, your wife . . . ?'

'We are taught, Miss Saunders, to pay first attention to our own souls. My wife should be looking after her own indulgences—she has an excellent Jesuit adviser—I employ you to look after mine.'

'You have no objection to Canon Wood?'

'If it is really the best you can do. So long as it does not involve overtime.'

'Oh no, Mr Ferraro. A decade of the Rosary, that's all.'

After an early lunch—a simple one in a City chop-house which concluded with some Stilton and a glass of excellent port—Mr Ferraro visited Christie's. Maverick was satisfactorily on the spot and Mr Ferraro did not bother to wait for the Bonnard and the Monet which his agent had advised him to buy. The day remained warm and sunny, but there were confused sounds from the direction of Trafalgar Square which reminded Mr Ferraro that it was Labour Day. There was something inappropriate to the sun and the early flowers under the park trees in these processions of men without ties carrying dreary banners covered with bad lettering. A desire came to Mr Ferraro to take a real holiday, and he nearly told his chauffeur to drive to Richmond Park. But he always preferred, if it were possible, to combine business with pleasure, and it occurred to him that if he drove out now to Canon Wood, Miss Saunders should be arriving about the same time, after her lunch interval, to start the afternoon's work.

Canon Wood was one of those new suburbs built around an old estate. The estate was a public park, the house, formerly famous as the home of a minor Minister who served under Lord North at the time of the American rebellion, was now a local museum, and a street had been built on the little windy hill-top once a hundred-acre field: a Charrington coal agency, the window dressed with one large nugget in a metal basket, a Home & Colonial Stores, an Odeon cinema, a large Anglican church.

Mr Ferraro told his driver to ask the way to the Roman Catholic church.

'There isn't one here,' the policeman said.

'St Praxted's?'

'There's no such place,' the policeman said.

Mr Ferraro, like a Biblical character, felt a loosening of the bowels.

'St Praxted's, Canon Wood.'

'Doesn't exist, sir,' the policeman said. Mr Ferraro drove slowly back towards the City. This was the first time he had checked on Miss Saunders—three prizes for piety had won his trust. Now on his homeward way he remembered that Hitler had been educated by the Jesuits, and yet hopelessly he hoped.

In his office he unlocked the drawer and took out the special file. Could he have mistaken Canonbury for Canon Wood? But he had not been mistaken, and suddenly a terrible doubt came to him how often in the last three years Miss Saunders had betrayed her trust. (It was after a severe attack of pneumonia three years ago that he had engaged her—the idea had come to him during the long insomnias of convalescence.) Was it possible that not one of these indulgences had been gained? He couldn't believe that. Surely a few of that vast total of 36,892 days must still be valid. But only Miss Saunders could tell him how many. And what had she been doing with her office time—those long hours of pilgrimage? She had once taken a whole week-end at Walsingham.

He rang for Mr Hopkinson, who could not help remarking on the whiteness of his employer's face. 'Are you feeling quite well, Mr Ferraro?'

'I have had a severe shock. Can you tell me where Miss Saunders lives?'

'She lives with an invalid mother near Westbourne Grove.'

'The exact address, please.'

Mr Ferraro drove into the dreary wastes of Bayswater: great family houses had been converted into private hotels or fortunately bombed into car parks. In the terraces behind, dubious girls leant against the railings, and a street band blew harshly round a corner. Mr Ferraro found the house, but he could not bring himself to ring the bell. He sat crouched in his Daimler waiting for something to happen. Was it the intensity of his gaze that brought Miss Saunders to an upper window, a coincidence, or retribution? Mr Ferraro thought at first that it was the warmth of the day that had caused her to be so inefficiently clothed, as she slid the window a little wider open. But then an arm circled her waist, a young man's face looked down into the street, a hand pulled a curtain across with the familiarity of habit. It became obvious to Mr Ferraro that not even the conditions for an indulgence had been properly fulfilled.

If a friend could have seen Mr Ferraro that evening mounting the steps of Montagu Square, he would have been surprised at the way he had aged. It was almost as though he had assumed during the long afternoon those 36,892 days he had thought to have saved during the last three years from Purgatory. The curtains were drawn, the lights were on, and no doubt Father Dewes was pouring out the first of his evening whiskies in the other wing. Mr Ferraro did not ring the bell, but let himself quietly in. The thick carpet swallowed his footsteps like quicksand. He switched on no lights: only a red-shaded lamp in each room had been lit ready for his use and now guided his steps. The pictures in the drawing-room reminded him of death-duties: a great Degas bottom like an atomic explosion mushroomed above a bath: Mr Ferraro passed on into the library: the leather-bound classics reminded him of dead authors. He sat down in a chair and a slight pain in his chest reminded him of his double pneumonia. He was three years nearer death than when Miss Saunders was appointed first. After a long while Mr Ferraro knotted his fingers together in the shape some people use for prayer. With Mr Ferraro it was an indication of decision. The worst was over: time lengthened again ahead of him. He thought: 'Tomorrow I will set about getting a really reliable secretary.'

1954

THE BLUE FILM

'Other people enjoy themselves,' Mrs Carter said.

'Well,' her husband replied, 'we've seen . . .'

'The reclining Buddha, the emerald Buddha, the floating markets,' Mrs Carter said. 'We have dinner and then go home to bed.'

'Last night we went to Chez Eve . . .'

'If you weren't with *me*,' Mrs Carter said, 'you'd find . . . you know what I mean, Spots.'

It was true, Carter thought, eyeing his wife over the coffee-cups: her slave bangles chinked in time with her coffee-spoon: she had reached an age when the satisfied woman is at her most beautiful, but the lines of discontent had formed. When he looked at her neck he was reminded of how difficult it was to un-string a turkey. Is it my fault, he wondered, or hers—or was it the fault of her birth, some glandular deficiency, some inherited characteristic? It was sad how when one was young, one so often mistook the signs of frigidity for a kind of distinction.

'You promised we'd smoke opium,' Mrs Carter said.

'Not here, darling. In Saigon. Here it's "not done" to smoke.'

'How conventional you are.'

'There'd be only the dirtiest of coolie places. You'd be con-spicuous. They'd stare at you.' He played his winning card. 'There'd be cockroaches.'

'I should be taken to plenty of Spots if I wasn't with a hus-band.'

He tried hopefully, 'The Japanese strip-teasers . . .' but she had heard all about them. 'Ugly women in bras,' she said. His irritation rose. He thought of the money he had spent to take his wife with him and to ease his conscience—he had been away too often without her, but there is no company more cheerless than that of a woman who is not desired. He tried to drink his coffee calmly: he wanted to bite the edge of the cup.

'You've spilt your coffee,' Mrs Carter said.

'I'm sorry.' He got up abruptly and said, 'All right. I'll fix something. Stay here.' He leant across the table. 'You'd better not be shocked,' he said. 'You've asked for it.'

'I don't think I'm usually the one who is shocked,' Mrs Carter said with a thin smile.

Carter left the hotel and walked up towards the New Road. A boy hung at his side and said, 'Young girl?'

'I've got a woman of my own,' Carter said gloomily.

'Boy?'

'No thanks.'

'French films?'

Carter paused. 'How much?'

They stood and haggled a while at the corner of the drab street. What with the taxi, the guide, the films, it was going to cost the best part of eight pounds, but it was worth it, Carter thought, if it closed her mouth for ever from demanding 'Spots'. He went back to fetch Mrs Carter.

They drove a long way and came to a halt by a bridge over a canal, a dingy lane overcast with indeterminate smells. The guide said, 'Follow me.'

Mrs Carter put a hand on Carter's arm. 'Is it safe?' she asked.

'How would I know?' he replied, stiffening under her hand.

They walked about fifty unlighted yards and halted by a bamboo fence. The guide knocked several times. When they were admitted it was to a tiny earth-floored yard and a wooden hut. Something—presumably human—was humped in the dark under a mosquito-net. The owner showed them into a tiny stuffy room with two chairs and a portrait of the King. The screen was about the size of a folio volume.

The first film was peculiarly unattractive and showed the rejuvenation of an elderly man at the hands of two blonde masseuses. From the style of the women's hairdressing the film must have been made in the late twenties. Carter and his wife sat in mutual embarrassment as the film whirled and clicked to a stop.

'Not a very good one,' Carter said, as though he were a connoisseur.

'So that's what they call a blue film,' Mrs Carter said. 'Ugly and not exciting.'

A second film started.

There was very little story in this. A young man—one couldn't see his face because of the period soft hat—picked up a girl in the street (her cloche hat extinguished her like a meat-cover) and accompanied her to her room. The actors were young: there was some charm and excitement in the picture. Carter thought, when the girl took off her hat, I know that face, and a memory which had been buried for more than a quarter of a century moved. A doll over a telephone, a pin-up girl of the period over the double bed. The girl undressed, folding her clothes very neatly: she leant over to adjust the bed, exposing herself to the camera's eye and to the young man: he kept his head turned from the camera. Afterwards, she helped him in turn to take off his clothes. It was only then he remembered—that particular playfulness confirmed by the birthmark on the man's shoulder.

Mrs Carter shifted on her chair. 'I wonder how they find the actors,' she said hoarsely.

'A prostitute,' he said. 'It's a bit raw, isn't it? Wouldn't you like to leave?' he urged her, waiting for the man to turn his head. The girl knelt on the bed and held the youth around the waist— she couldn't have been more than twenty. No, he made a calculation, twenty-one.

'We'll stay,' Mrs Carter said, 'we've paid.' She laid a dry hot hand on his knee.

'I'm sure we could find a better place than this.'

'No.'

The young man lay on his back and the girl for a moment left him. Briefly, as though by accident, he looked at the camera. Mrs Carter's hand shook on his knee. 'Good God,' she said, 'it's you.'

'It *was* me,' Carter said, 'thirty years ago.' The girl was climbing back on to the bed.

'It's revolting,' Mrs Carter replied.

'I don't remember it as revolting,' Carter replied.

'I suppose you went and gloated, both of you.'

'No, I never saw it.'

'Why did you do it? I can't look at you. It's shameful.'

'I asked you to come away.'

'Did they pay you?'

'They paid her. Fifty pounds. She needed the money badly.'

'And you had your fun for nothing?'

'Yes.'

'I'd never have married you if I'd known. Never.'

'That was a long time afterwards.'

'You still haven't said why. Haven't you any excuse?' She stopped. He knew she was watching, leaning forward, caught up herself in the heat of that climax more than a quarter of a century old.

Carter said, 'It was the only way I could help her. She'd never acted in one before. She wanted a friend.'

'A friend,' Mrs Carter said.

'I loved her.'

'You couldn't love a tart.'

'Oh yes, you can. Make no mistake about that.'

'You queued for her, I suppose.'

'You put it too crudely,' Carter said.

'What happened to her?'

'She disappeared. They always disappear.'

The girl leant over the young man's body and put out the light. It was the end of the film. 'I have new ones coming next week,' the Siamese said, bowing deeply. They followed their guide back down the dark lane to the taxi.

In the taxi Mrs Carter said, 'What was her name?'

'I don't remember.' A lie was easiest.

As they turned into the New Road she broke her bitter silence again. 'How could you have brought yourself . . . ? It's so degrading. Suppose someone you knew—in business—recognized you.'

'People don't talk about seeing things like that. Anyway, I wasn't in business in those days.'

'Did it never worry you?'

'I don't believe I have thought of it once in thirty years.'

'How long did you know her?'

'Twelve months perhaps.'

'She must look pretty awful by now if she's alive. After all she was common even then.'

'I thought she looked lovely,' Carter said.

They went upstairs in silence. He went straight to the bathroom and locked the door. The mosquitoes gathered around the lamp and the great jar of water. As he undressed he caught glimpses of himself in the small mirror: thirty years had not been kind: he felt his thickness and his middle age. He thought: I hope to God she's dead. Please, God, he said, let her be dead. When I go back in there, the insults will start again.

But when he returned Mrs Carter was standing by the mirror. She had partly undressed. Her thin bare legs reminded him of a heron waiting for fish. She came and put her arms round him: a slave bangle joggled against his shoulder. She said, 'I'd forgotten how nice you looked.'

'I'm sorry. One changes.'

'I didn't mean that. I like you as you are.'

She was dry and hot and implacable in her desire. 'Go on,' she said, 'go on,' and then she screamed like an angry and hurt bird. Afterwards she said, 'It's years since that happened,' and continued to talk for what seemed a long half hour excitedly at his side. Carter lay in the dark silent, with a feeling of loneliness and guilt. It seemed to him that he had betrayed that night the only woman he loved.

1954

THE HINT OF AN
EXPLANATION

A long train journey on a late December evening, in this new version of peace, is a dreary experience. I suppose that my fellow traveller and I could consider ourselves lucky to have a compartment to ourselves, even though the heating apparatus was not working, even though the lights went out entirely in the frequent Pennine tunnels and were too dim anyway for us to read our books without straining the eyes, and though there was no restaurant car to give at least a change of scene. It was when we were trying simultaneously to chew the same kind of dry bun bought at the same station buffet that my companion and I came together. Before that we had sat at opposite ends of the carriage, both muffled to the chin in overcoats, both bent low over type we could barely make out, but as I threw the remains of my cake under the seat our eyes met, and he laid his book down.

By the time we were half-way to Bedwell Junction we had found an enormous range of subjects for discussion; starting with buns and the weather, we had gone on to politics, the Government, foreign affairs, the atom bomb, and by an inevitable progression, God. We had not, however, become either shrill or acid. My companion, who now sat opposite me, leaning a little forward, so that our knees nearly touched, gave such an impression of serenity that it would have been impossible to quarrel with him, however much our views differed, and differ they did profoundly.

I had soon realized I was speaking to a Roman Catholic—to someone who believed—how do they put it?—in an omnipotent and omniscient Deity, while I am what is loosely called an agnostic. I have a certain intuition (which I do not trust, founded as it may well be on childish experiences and needs) that a God exists, and I am surprised occasionally into belief by the extraordinary coincidences that beset our path like the traps set for leopards in the jungle, but intellectually I am revolted at the whole notion of such a God who can so abandon his creatures to the enormities of Free Will. I found myself expressing this view to my companion who listened quietly and with respect. He made no attempt to interrupt—he showed none of the impatience or the intellectual arrogance I have grown to expect from Catholics; when the lights of a wayside station flashed across his face which had escaped hitherto the rays of the one globe working in the compartment, I caught a glimpse suddenly of—what? I stopped speaking, so strong was the impression. I was carried back ten years, to the other side of the great useless conflict, to a small town, Gisors in Normandy. I was again, for a moment, walking on the ancient battlements and looking down across the grey roofs, until my eyes for some reason lit on one stony 'back' out of the many, where the face of a middle-aged man was pressed against a window pane (I suppose that face has ceased to exist now, just as perhaps the whole town with its medieval memories has been reduced to rubble). I remembered saying to myself with astonishment, 'That man is happy—completely happy.' I looked across the compartment at my fellow traveller, but his face was already again in shadow. I said weakly, 'When you think what God—if there is a God—allows. It's not merely the physical agonies, but think of the corruption, even of children . . .'

He said, 'Our view is so limited,' and I was disappointed at the conventionality of his reply. He must have been aware of my disappointment (it was as though our thoughts were huddled as closely as ourselves for warmth), for he went on, 'Of course there is no answer here. We catch hints . . .' and then the train roared into another tunnel and the lights again went out. It was the longest tunnel yet; we went rocking down it and the cold seemed to become more intense with the darkness, like an icy fog (when one sense—of sight—is robbed, the others grow more acute).

When we emerged into the mere grey of night and the globe lit up once more, I could see that my companion was leaning back on his seat.

I repeated his last word as a question, 'Hints?'

'Oh, they mean very little in cold print—or cold speech,' he said, shivering in his overcoat. 'And they mean nothing at all to another human being than the man who catches them. They are not scientific evidence—or evidence at all for that matter. Events that don't, somehow, turn out as they were intended—by the human actors, I mean, or by the thing behind the human actors.'

'The thing?'

'The word Satan is so anthropomorphic.' I had to lean forward now: I wanted to hear what he had to say. I am—I really am, God knows—open to conviction. He said, 'One's words are so crude, but I sometimes feel pity for that thing. It is so continually finding the right weapon to use against its Enemy and the weapon breaks in its own breast. It sometimes seems to me so— powerless. You said something just now about the corruption of children. It reminded me of something in my own childhood. You are the first person—except for one—that I have thought of telling it to, perhaps because you are anonymous. It's not a very long story, and in a way it's relevant.'

I said, 'I'd like to hear it.'

'You mustn't expect too much meaning. But to me there seems to be a hint. That's all. A hint.'

He went slowly on turning his face to the pane, though he could have seen nothing in the whirling world outside except an occasional signal lamp, a light in a window, a small country station torn backwards by our rush, picking his words with precision. He said, 'When I was a child they taught me to serve at Mass. The church was a small one, for there were very few Catholics where I lived. It was a market town in East Anglia, surrounded by flat chalky fields and ditches—so many ditches. I don't suppose there were fifty Catholics all told, and for some reason there was a tradition of hostility to us. Perhaps it went back to the burning of a Protestant martyr in the sixteenth century—there was a stone marking the place near where the meat stalls stood on Wednesdays. I was only half aware of the enmity, though I knew that my school nickname of Popey Martin had something to do with my religion and I had heard that my father was very nearly excluded from the Constitutional Club when he first came to the town.

'Every Sunday I had to dress up in my surplice and serve Mass. I hated it—I have always hated dressing up in any way (which is funny when you come to think of it), and I never ceased to be afraid of losing my place in the service and doing something which would put me to ridicule. Our services were at a different hour from the Anglican, and as our small, far-from-select band trudged out of the hideous chapel the whole of the townsfolk seemed to be on the way past to the proper church—I always thought of it as the proper church. We had to pass the parade of their eyes, indifferent, supercilious, mocking; you can't imagine how seriously religion can be taken in a small town—if only for social reasons.

'There was one man in particular; he was one of the two bakers in the town, the one my family did not patronize. I don't think any of the Catholics patronized him because he was called a freethinker—an odd title, for, poor man, no one's thoughts were less free than his. He was hemmed in by his hatred—his hatred of us. He was very ugly to look at, with one wall-eye and a head the shape of a turnip, with the hair gone on the crown, and he was unmarried. He had no interests, apparently, but his baking and his hatred, though now that I am older I begin to see other sides of his nature—it did contain, perhaps, a certain furtive love. One would come across him suddenly, sometimes, on a country walk, especially if one was alone and it was Sunday. It was as though he rose from the ditches and the chalk smear on his clothes reminded one of the flour on his working overalls. He would have a stick in his hand and stab at the hedges, and if his mood were very black he would call out after you strange, abrupt words that were like a foreign tongue—I know the meaning of those words, of course, now. Once the police went to his house because of what a boy said he had seen, but nothing came of it except that the hate shackled him closer. His name was Blacker, and he terrified me.

'I think he had a particular hatred of my father—I don't know why. My father was manager of the Midland Bank, and it's possible that at some time Blacker may have had unsatisfactory dealings with the bank—my father was a very cautious man who suffered all his life from anxiety about money—his own and other people's. If I try to picture Blacker now I see him walking along a narrowing path between high windowless walls, and at the end of the path stands a small boy of ten—me. I don't know whether it's a symbolic picture or the memory of one of our encounters—our encounters somehow got more and more frequent. You talked just now about the corruption of children. That poor man was preparing to revenge himself on everything he hated—my father, the Catholics, the God whom people persisted in crediting—by corrupting me. He had evolved a horrible and ingenious plan.

'I remember the first time I had a friendly word from him. I was passing his shop as rapidly as I could when I heard his voice call out with a kind of sly subservience as though he were an under-servant. "Master David," he called, "Master David," and I hurried on. But the next time I passed that way he was at his door (he must have seen me coming) with one of those curly cakes in his hand that we called Chelsea buns. I didn't want to take it, but he made me, and then I couldn't be other than polite when he asked me to come into his parlour behind the shop and see something very special.

'It was a small electric railway—a rare sight in those days, and he insisted on showing me how it worked. He made me turn the switches and stop and start it, and he told me that I could come in any morning and have a game with it. He used the word "game" as though it were something secret, and it's true that I never told my family of this invitation and of how, perhaps twice a week those holidays, the desire to control that little railway became overpowering, and looking up and down the street to see if I were observed, I would dive into the shop.'

Our larger, dirtier, adult train drove into a tunnel and the light went out. We sat in darkness and silence, with the noise of the train blocking our ears like wax. When we were through we didn't speak at once and I had to prick him into continuing.

'An elaborate seduction,' I said.

'Don't think his plans were as simple as that,' my companion said, 'or as crude. There was much more hate than love, poor man, in his make-up. Can you hate something you don't believe in? And yet he called himself a free-thinker. What an impossible paradox, to be free and to be so obsessed. Day by day all through those holidays his obsession must have grown, but he kept a grip; he bided his time. Perhaps that thing I spoke of gave him the strength and the wisdom. It was only a week from the end of the holidays that he spoke to me of what concerned him so deeply.

'I heard him behind me as I knelt on the floor, coupling two coaches. He said, "You won't be able to do this, Master David, when school starts." It wasn't a sentence that needed any comment from me any more than the one that followed, "You ought to have it for your own, you ought," but how skilfully and unemphatically he had sowed the longing, the idea of a possibility . . . I was coming to his parlour every day now; you see I had to cram every opportunity in before the hated term started again, and I suppose I was becoming accustomed to Blacker, to that wall-eye, that turnip head, that nauseating subservience. The Pope, you know, describes himself as "The servant of the servants of God", and Blacker—I sometimes think, that Blacker was "the servant of the servants of . . ." well, let it be.

'The very next day, standing in the doorway watching me play, he began to talk to me about religion. He said, with what untruth even I recognized, how much he admired the Catholics; he wished he could believe like that, but how could a baker believe? He accented "a baker" as one might say a biologist, and the tiny train spun round the gauge-O track. He said, "I can bake the things you eat just as well as any Catholic can," and disappeared into his shop. I hadn't the faintest idea what he meant. Presently he emerged again, holding in his hand a little wafer. "Here," he said, "eat that and tell me . . ." When I put it in my mouth I could tell that it was made in the same way as our wafers for communion—he had got the shape a little wrong, that was all, and I felt guilty and irrationally scared. "Tell me," he said, "what's the difference?"

' "Difference?" I asked.

' "Isn't that just the same as you eat in church?"

'I said smugly, "It hasn't been consecrated."

'He said, "Do you think if I put the two of them under a microscope, you could tell the difference?" But even at ten I had the answer to that question. "No," I said, "the—accidents don't change," stumbling a little on the word "accidents" which had suddenly conveyed to me the idea of death and wounds.

'Blacker said with sudden intensity, "How I'd like to get one of yours in my mouth—just to see . . ."

'It may seem odd to you, but this was the first time that the idea of transubstantiation really lodged in my mind. I had learnt it all by rote; I had grown up with the idea. The Mass was as lifeless to me as the sentences in *De Bello Gallico,* communion a routine like drill in the school-yard, but here suddenly I was in the presence of a man who took it seriously, as seriously as the priest whom naturally one didn't count—it was his job. I felt more scared than ever.

'He said, "It's all nonsense, but I'd just like to have it in my mouth."

' "You could if you were a Catholic," I said naïvely. He gazed at me with his one good eye like a Cyclops. He said, "You serve at Mass, don't you? It would be easy for you to get at one of those things. I tell you what I'd do—I'd swap this electric train set for one of your wafers—consecrated, mind. It's got to be consecrated."

' "I could get you one out of the box," I said. I think I still imagined that his interest was a baker's interest—to see how they were made.

' "Oh, no," he said. "I want to see what your God tastes like."

' "I couldn't do that."

' "Not for a whole electric train, just for yourself? You wouldn't have any trouble at home. I'd pack it up and put a label inside that your Dad could see—'For my bank manager's little boy from a grateful client.' He'd be pleased as Punch with that."

'Now that we are grown men it seems a trivial temptation, doesn't it? But try to think back to your own childhood. There was a whole circuit of rails on the floor at our feet, straight rails and curved rails, and a little station with porters and passengers, a tunnel, a foot-bridge, a level crossing, two signals, buffers, of course—and above all, a turntable. The tears of longing came into my eyes when I looked at the turntable. It was my favourite piece—it looked so ugly and practical and true. I said weakly, "I wouldn't know how."

'How carefully he had been studying the ground. He must have slipped several times into Mass at the back of the church. It would have been no good, you understand, in a little town like that, presenting himself for communion. Everybody there knew him for what he was. He said to me, "When you've been given communion you could just put it under your tongue a moment. He serves you and the other boy first, and I saw you once go out behind the curtain straight afterwards. You'd forgotten one of those little bottles."

' "The cruet," I said.

' "Pepper and salt." He grinned at me jovially, and I—well, I looked at the little railway which I could no longer come and play with when term started. I said, "You'd just swallow it, wouldn't you?"

' "Oh, yes," he said, "I'd just swallow it."

'Somehow I didn't want to play with the train any more that day. I got up and made for the door, but he detained me, gripping my lapel. He said, "This will be a secret between you and me. Tomorrow's Sunday. You come along here in the afternoon. Put it in an envelope and post it in. Monday morning the train will be delivered bright and early."

' "Not tomorrow," I implored him.

' "I'm not interested in any other Sunday," he said. "It's your only chance." He shook me gently backwards and forwards. "It will always have to be a secret between you and me," he said. "Why, if anyone knew they'd take away the train and there'd be me to reckon with. I'd bleed you something awful. You know how I'm always about on Sunday walks. You can't avoid a man like me. I crop up. You wouldn't even be safe in your own house. I know ways to get into houses when people are asleep." He pulled me into the shop after him and opened a drawer. In the drawer was an odd-looking key and a cut-throat razor. He said, "That's a master key that opens all locks and that—that's what I bleed people with." Then he patted my cheek with his plump floury fingers and said, "Forget it. You and me are friends."

'That Sunday Mass stays in my head, every detail of it, as though it had happened only a week ago. From the moment of the Confession to the moment of Consecration it had a terrible importance; only one other Mass has ever been so important to me—perhaps not even one, for this was a solitary Mass which could never happen again. It seemed as final as the last Sacrament, when the priest bent down and put the wafer in my mouth where I knelt before the altar with my fellow server.

'I suppose I had made up my mind to commit this awful act— for, you know, to us it must always seem an awful act—from the moment when I saw Blacker watching from the back of the church. He had put on his best Sunday clothes, and as though he could never quite escape the smear of his profession, he had a dab of dried talcum on his cheek, which he had presumably applied after using that cut-throat of his. He was watching me closely all the time, and I think it was fear—fear of that terrible undefined thing called bleeding—as much as covetousness that drove me to carry out my instructions.

'My fellow server got briskly up and taking the communion plate preceded Father Carey to the altar rail where the other Communicants knelt. I had the Host lodged under my tongue: it felt like a blister. I got up and made for the curtain to get the cruet that I had purposely left in the sacristy. When I was there I looked quickly round for a hiding-place and saw an old copy of the *Universe* lying on a chair. I took the Host from my mouth and inserted it between two sheets—a little damp mess of pulp. Then I thought: perhaps Father Carey has put the paper out for a particular purpose and he will find the Host before I have time to remove it, and the enormity of my act began to come home to me when I tried to imagine what punishment I should incur. Murder is sufficiently trivial to have its appropriate punishment, but for this act the mind boggled at the thought of any retribution at all. I tried to remove the Host, but it had stuck clammily between the pages and in desperation I tore out a piece of the newspaper and, screwing the whole thing up, stuck it in my trouser pocket. When I came back through the curtain carrying the cruet my

eyes met Blacker's. He gave me a grin of encouragement and unhappiness—yes, I am sure, unhappiness. Was it perhaps that the
poor man was all the time seeking something incorruptible?

'I can remember little more of that day. I think my mind was
shocked and stunned and I was caught up too in the family bus-
tle of Sunday. Sunday in a provincial town is the day for relations. All the family are at home and unfamiliar cousins and
uncles are apt to arrive packed in the back seats of other people's
cars. I remember that some crowd of that kind descended on us
and pushed Blacker temporarily out of the foreground of my
mind. There was somebody called Aunt Lucy with a loud hollow
laugh that filled the house with mechanical merriment like the
sound of recorded laughter from inside a hall of mirrors, and I
had no opportunity to go out alone even if I had wished to. When
six o'clock came and Aunt Lucy and the cousins departed and
peace returned, it was too late to go to Blacker's and at eight it
was my own bed-time.

'I think I had half forgotten what I had in my pocket. As I emptied my pocket the little screw of newspaper brought quickly back
the Mass, the priest bending over me, Blacker's grin. I laid the
packet on the chair by my bed and tried to go to sleep, but I was
haunted by the shadows on the wall where the curtains blew, the
squeak of furniture, the rustle in the chimney, haunted by the
presence of God there on the chair. The Host had always been to
me—well, the Host. I knew theoretically, as I have said, what I had
to believe, but suddenly, as someone whistled in the road outside,
whistled secretively, knowingly, to me, I knew that this which I
had beside my bed was something of infinite value—something a
man would pay for with his whole peace of mind, something that
was so hated one could love it as one loves an outcast or a bullied
child. These are adult words and it was a child of ten who lay
scared in bed, listening to the whistle from the road, Blacker's
whistle, but I think he felt fairly clearly what I am describing now.
That is what I meant when I said this Thing, whatever it is, that
seizes every possible weapon against God, is always, everywhere,
disappointed at the moment of success. It must have felt as certain
of me as Blacker did. It must have felt certain, too, of Blacker. But
I wonder, if one knew what happened later to that poor man,

whether one would not find again that the weapon had been turned against its own breast.

'At last I couldn't bear that whistle any more and got out of bed. I opened the curtains a little way, and there right under my window, the moonlight on his face, was Blacker. If I had stretched my hand down, his fingers reaching up could almost have touched mine. He looked up at me, flashing the one good eye, with hunger—I realize now that near-success must have developed his obsession almost to the point of madness. Desperation had driven him to the house. He whispered up at me, "David, where is it?"

'I jerked my head back at the room. "Give it me," he said, "quick. You shall have the train in the morning."

'I shook my head. He said, "I've got the bleeder here, and the key. You'd better toss it down."

'"Go away," I said, but I could hardly speak with fear.

'"I'll bleed you first and then I'll have it just the same."

'"Oh no, you won't," I said. I went to the chair and picked it—Him—up. There was only one place where He was safe. I couldn't separate the Host from the paper, so I swallowed both. The newsprint stuck like a prune to the back of my throat, but I rinsed it down with water from the ewer. Then I went back to the window and looked down at Blacker. He began to wheedle me. "What have you done with it, David? What's the fuss? It's only a bit of bread," looking so longingly and pleadingly up at me that even as a child I wondered whether he could really think that, and yet desire it so much.

'"I swallowed it," I said.

'"Swallowed it?"

'"Yes," I said. "Go away." Then something happened which seems to me now more terrible than his desire to corrupt or my thoughtless act: he began to weep—the tears ran lopsidedly out of the one good eye and his shoulders shook. I only saw his face for a moment before he bent his head and strode off, the bald turnip head shaking, into the dark. When I think of it now, it's almost as if I had seen that Thing weeping for its inevitable defeat. It had tried to use me as a weapon and now I had broken in its hands and it wept its hopeless tears through one of Blacker's eyes.'

The black furnaces of Bedwell Junction gathered around the line. The points switched and we were tossed from one set of rails to another. A spray of sparks, a signal light changed to red, tall chimneys jetting into the grey night sky, the fumes of steam from stationary engines—half the cold journey was over and now remained the long wait for the slow cross-country train. I said, 'It's an interesting story. I think I should have given Blacker what he wanted. I wonder what he would have done with it.'

'I really believe,' my companion said, 'that he would first of all have put it under his microscope—before he did all the other things I expect he had planned.'

'And the hint?' I said. 'I don't quite see what you mean by that.'

'Oh, well,' he said vaguely, 'you know for me it was an odd beginning, that affair, when you come to think of it,' but I should never have known what he meant had not his coat, when he rose to take his bag from the rack, come open and disclosed the collar of a priest.

I said, 'I suppose you think you owe a lot to Blacker.'

'Yes,' he said. 'You see, I am a very happy man.'

1948

WHEN GREEK
MEETS GREEK

When the chemist had shut his shop for the night he went through a door at the back of the hall that served both him and the flats above, and then up two flights and a half of stairs carrying an offering of a little box of pills. The box was stamped with his name and address: Priskett, 14 New End Street, Oxford. He was a middle-aged man with a thin moustache and scared evasive eyes: he wore his long white coat even when he was off duty as if it had the power of protecting him like a King's uniform from his enemies. So long as he wore it he was free from summary trial and execution.

On the top landing was a window: outside Oxford spread through the spring evening: the peevish noise of innumerable bicycles, the gasworks, the prison, and the grey spires, beyond the bakers and confectioners, like paper frills. A door was marked with a visiting-card Mr Nicholas Fennick, BA: the chemist rang three short times.

The man who opened the door was sixty years old at least with snow-white hair and a pink babyish skin. He wore a mulberry velvet dinner jacket, and his glasses swung on the end of a wide black ribbon. He said with a kind of boisterousness, 'Ah, Priskett, step in, Priskett. I had just sported my oak for a moment . . .'

'I brought you some more of my pills.'

'Invaluable, Priskett. If only you had taken a degree—the Society of Apothecaries would have been enough—I would have appointed you resident medical officer of St Ambrose's.'

'How's the college doing?'

'Give me your company for a moment in the common-room, and you shall know all.'

Mr Fennick led the way down a little dark passage cluttered with mackintoshes: Mr Priskett, feeling his way uneasily from mackintosh to mackintosh, kicked in front of him a pair of girl's shoes. 'One day,' Mr Fennick said, 'we must build . . .' and he made a broad confident gesture with his glasses that seemed to press back the walls of the common-room: a small round table covered with a landlady's cloth, three or four shiny chairs and a glass-fronted bookcase containing a copy of *Every Man His Own Lawyer*. 'My niece Elisabeth,' Mr Fennick said, 'my medical adviser.' A very young girl with a lean pretty face nodded perfunctorily from behind a typewriter. 'I am going to train Elisabeth,' Mr Fennick said, 'to act as bursar. The strain of being both bursar and president of the college is upsetting my stomach. The pills . . . thank you.'

Mr Priskett said humbly, 'And what do you think of the college, Miss Fennick?'

'My name's Cross,' the girl said. 'I think it's a good idea. I'm surprised my uncle thought of it.'

'In a way it was—partly—my idea.'

'I'm more surprised still,' the girl said firmly.

Mr Priskett, folding his hands in front of his white coat as though he were pleading before a tribunal, went on: 'You see, I said to your uncle that with all these colleges being taken over by the military and the tutors having nothing to do they ought to start teaching by correspondence.'

'A glass of audit ale, Priskett?' Mr Fennick suggested. He took a bottle of brown ale out of a cupboard and poured out two gaseous glasses.

'Of course,' Mr Priskett pleaded, 'I hadn't thought of all this—the common-room, I mean, and St Ambrose's.'

'My niece,' Mr Fennick said, 'knows very little of the set-up.' He began to move restlessly around the room touching things with his hand. He was rather like an aged bird of prey inspecting the grim components of its nest.

The girl said briskly, 'As I see it, Uncle is running a swindle called St Ambrose's College, Oxford.'

'Not a swindle, my dear. The advertisement was very carefully worded.' He knew it by heart: every phrase had been carefully checked with his copy of *Every Man His Own Lawyer* open on the table. He repeated it now in a voice full and husky with bottled brown ale. 'War conditions prevent you going to Oxford. St Ambrose's—Tom Brown's old college—has made an important break with tradition. For the period of the war only it will be possible to receive tuition by post wherever you may be, whether defending the Empire on the cold rocks of Iceland or on the burning sands of Libya, in the main street of an American town or a cottage in Devonshire . . .'

'You've overdone it,' the girl said. 'You always do. That hasn't got a cultured ring. It won't catch anybody but suckers.'

'There are plenty of suckers,' Mr Fennick said.

'Go on.'

'Well, I'll skip that bit. "Degree-diplomas will be granted at the end of three terms instead of the usual three years."' He explained, 'That gives a quick turnover. One can't wait for money these days. "Gain a real Oxford education at Tom Brown's old college. For full particulars of tuition fees, battels, etc., write to the Bursar."'

'And do you mean to say the University can't stop that?'

'Anybody,' Mr Fennick said with a kind of pride, 'can start a college anywhere. I've never said it was part of the University.'

'But battels—battels mean board and lodgings.'

'In this case,' Mr Fennick said, 'it's quite a nominal fee—to keep your name in perpetuity on the books of the old firm—I mean the college.'

'And the tuition . . .'

'Priskett here is the science tutor. I take history and classics. I thought that you, my dear, might tackle—economics?'

'I don't know anything about them.'

'The examinations, of course, have to be rather simple—within the capacity of the tutors. (There is an excellent public library here.) And another thing—the fees are returnable if the diploma-degree is not granted.'

'You mean . . .'

'Nobody will ever fail,' Mr Priskett brought breathlessly out with scared excitement.

'And you are really getting results?'

'I waited, my dear, until I could see the distinct possibility of at least six hundred a year for the three of us before I wired you. And today—beyond all my expectations—I have received a letter from Lord Driver. He is entering his son at St Ambrose's.'

'But how can he come here?'

'In his absence, my dear, on his country's service. The Drivers have always been a military family. I looked them up in Debrett.'

'What do you think of it?' Mr Priskett asked with anxiety and triumph.

'I think it's rich. Have you arranged a boat-race?'

'There, Priskett,' Mr Fennick said proudly, raising his glass of audit ale, 'I told you she was a girl of the old stock.'

2

Directly he heard his landlady's feet upon the stairs the elderly man with the grey shaven head began to lay his wet tea-leaves round the base of the aspidistra. When she opened the door he was dabbing the tea-leaves in tenderly with his fingers. 'A lovely plant, my dear.'

But she wasn't going to be softened at once: he could tell that: she waved a letter at him. 'Listen,' she said, 'what's this Lord Driver business?'

'My name, my dear: a good Christian name like Lord George Sanger had.'

'Then why don't they put Mr Lord Driver on the letter?'

'Ignorance, just ignorance.'

'I don't want any hanky-panky from my house. It's always been honest.'

'Perhaps they didn't know if I was an esquire or just a plain mister, so they left it blank.'

'It's sent from St Ambrose's College, Oxford: people like that ought to know.'

'It comes, my dear, of having such a good address. W1. And all the gentry live in Mewses.' He made a half-hearted snatch at the letter, but the landlady held it out of reach.

'What are the likes of you writing to Oxford College about?'

'My dear,' he said with strained dignity, 'I may have been a little unfortunate: it may even be that I have spent a few years in chokey, but I have the rights of a free man.'

'And a son in quod.'

'Not in quod, my dear. Borstal is quite another institution. It is—a kind of college.'

'Like St Ambrose's.'

'Perhaps not quite of the same rank.'

He was too much for her: he was usually in the end too much for her. Before his first stay at the Scrubs he had held a number of positions as manservant and even butler: the way he raised his eyebrows he had learned from Lord Charles Manville: he wore his clothes like an eccentric peer, and you might say that he had even learned the best way to pilfer from old Lord Bellen who had a penchant for silver spoons.

'And now, my dear, if you'd just let me have my letter?' He put his hand tentatively forward: he was as daunted by her as she was by him: they sparred endlessly and lost to each other; interminably the battle was never won—they were always afraid. This time it was his victory. She slammed the door. Suddenly, ferociously, when the door had closed, he made a little vulgar noise at the aspidistra. Then he put on his glasses and began to read.

His son had been accepted for St Ambrose's, Oxford. The great fact stared up at him above the sprawling decorative signature of the President. Never had he been more thankful for the coincidence of his name. 'It will be my great pleasure,' the President wrote, 'to pay personal attention to your son's career at St Ambrose's. In these days it is an honour to welcome a member of a great military family like yours.' Driver felt an odd mixture of amusement and of genuine pride. He'd put one over on them, but his breast swelled within his waistcoat at the idea that now he had a son at Oxford.

But there were two snags—minor snags when he considered how far he'd got already. It was apparently an old Oxford custom that fees should be paid in advance, and then there were the examinations. His son couldn't do them himself: Borstal would not allow it, and he wouldn't be out for another six months. Besides the whole beauty of the idea was that he should receive the gift of an Oxford degree as a kind of welcome home. Like a chess player who is always several moves ahead he was already seeing his way around these difficulties.

The fees he felt sure in his case were only a matter of bluff: a peer could always get credit, and if there was any trouble after the degree had been awarded, he could just tell them to sue and be damned. No Oxford college would like to admit that it had been imposed on by an old lag. But the examinations? A funny little knowing smile twitched the corners of his mouth: a memory of the Scrubs five years ago and the man they called Daddy, the Reverend Simon Milan. He was a short-time prisoner—they were all short-time prisoners at the Scrubs: no sentence of over three years was ever served there. He remembered the tall lean aristocratic parson with his iron-grey hair and his narrow face like a lawyer's which had gone somehow soft inside with too much love. A prison, when you came to think of it, contained as much knowledge as a University: there were doctors, financiers, clergy. He knew where he could find Mr Milan: he was employed in a boarding-house near Euston Square, and for a few drinks he would do most things—he would certainly make out some fine examination papers. 'I can just hear him now,' Driver reminded himself ecstatically, 'talking Latin to the warders.'

3

It was autumn in Oxford: people coughed in the long queues for sweets and cakes, and the mists from the river seeped into the cinemas past the commissionaires on the look-out for people without gas-masks. A few undergraduates picked their way through the evacuated swarm: they always looked in a hurry: so much had to be got through in so little time before the army claimed them. There were lots of pickings for racketeers, Elisabeth Cross thought, but not much of a chance for a girl to find a husband: the oldest Oxford racket had been elbowed out by the black markets in Woodbines, toffees, tomatoes.

There had been a few days last spring when she had treated St Ambrose's as a joke, but when she saw the money actually coming in, the whole thing seemed less amusing. Then for some weeks she was acutely unhappy—until she realized that of all the war-time rackets this was the most harmless. They were not reducing supplies like the Ministry of Food, or destroying confidence like the Ministry of Information: her uncle paid income tax, and they even to some extent educated people. The suckers, when they took their diploma-degrees, would know several things they hadn't known before.

But that didn't help a girl to find a husband.

She came moodily out of the matinée, carrying a bunch of papers she should have been correcting. There was only one 'student' who showed any intelligence at all, and that was Lord Driver's son. The papers were forwarded from 'somewhere in England' via London by his father; she had nearly found herself caught out several times on points of history, and her uncle she knew was straining his rusty Latin to the limit.

When she got home she knew that there was something in the air: Mr Priskett was sitting in his white coat on the edge of a chair and her uncle was finishing a stale bottle of beer. When something went wrong he never opened a new bottle: he believed in happy drinking. They watched her in silence. Mr Priskett's silence was gloomy, her uncle's preoccupied. Something had to be got round—it couldn't be the university authorities: they had stopped bothering him long ago—a lawyer's letter, an irascible interview, and their attempt to maintain 'a monopoly of local education'—as Mr Fennick put it—had ceased.

'Good evening,' Elisabeth said. Mr Priskett looked at Mr Fennick and Mr Fennick frowned.

'Has Mr Priskett run out of pills?'

Mr Priskett winced.

'I've been thinking,' Elisabeth said, 'that as we are now in the third term of the academic year, I should like a rise in salary.'

Mr Priskett drew in his breath sharply, keeping his eyes on Mr Fennick.

'I should like another three pounds a week.'

Mr Fennick rose from his table; he glared ferociously into the top of his dark ale, his frown beetled. The chemist scraped his chair a little backward. And then Mr Fennick spoke.

'We are such stuff as dreams are made on,' he said and hic-cupped slightly.

'Kidneys,' Elisabeth said.

'Rounded by a sleep. And these our cloud-capped towers . . .'

'You are misquoting.'

'Vanished into air, into thin air.'

'You've been correcting the English papers.'

'Unless you allow me to think, to think rapidly and deeply, there won't be any more examination papers,' Mr Fennick said.

'Trouble?'

'I've always been a Republican at heart. I don't see why we want a hereditary peerage.'

'*À la lanterne,*' Elisabeth said.

'This man Lord Driver: why should a mere accident of birth . . . ?'

'He refuses to pay?'

'It isn't that. A man like that expects credit: it's right that he should have credit. But he's written to say that he's coming down tomorrow to see his boy's college. The old fat-headed sentimental fool,' Mr Fennick said.

'I knew you'd be in trouble sooner or later.'

'That's the sort of damn fool comfortless thing a girl would say.'

'It just needs brain.'

Mr Fennick picked up a brass ash-tray—and then put it down again carefully.

'It's quite simple as soon as you begin to think.'

'Think?'

Mr Priskett scraped a chair-leg.

'I'll meet him at the station with a taxi, and take him to—say Balliol. Lead him straight through into the inner quad, and there you'll be, just looking as if you'd come out of the Master's lodging.'

'He'll know it's Balliol.'

'He won't. Anybody who knew Oxford couldn't be stupid enough to send his son to St Ambrose's.'

'Of course it's true. These military families are a bit crass.'

'You'll be in an enormous hurry. Convocation or something. Whip him round the Hall, the Chapel, the Library, and hand him back to me outside the Master's. I'll take him out to lunch and see him into his train. It's simple.'

Mr Fennick said broodingly, 'Sometimes I think you're a terrible girl, terrible. Is there nothing you wouldn't think up?'

'I believe,' Elisabeth said, 'that if you're going to play your own game in a world like this, you've got to play it properly. Of course,' she said, 'if you are going to play a different game, you go to a nunnery or to the wall and like it. But I've only got one game to play.'

4

It really went off very smoothly. Driver found Elisabeth at the barrier: she didn't find him because she was expecting something different. Something about him worried her; it wasn't his clothes or the monocle he never seemed to use—it was something subtler than that. It was almost as though he were afraid of her, he was so ready to fall in with her plans. 'I don't want to be any trouble, my dear, any trouble at all. I know how busy the President must be.' When she explained that they would be lunching together in town, he even seemed relieved. 'It's just the bricks of the dear old place,' he said. 'You mustn't mind my being a sentimentalist, my dear.'

'Were you at Oxford?'

'No, no. The Drivers, I'm afraid, have neglected the things of the mind.'

'Well, I suppose a soldier needs brains?'

He took a sharp look at her, and then answered in quite a different sort of voice, 'We believed so in the Lancers.' Then he strolled beside her to the taxi, twirling his monocle, and all the way up from the station he was silent, taking little quiet sideways peeks at her, appraising, approving.

'So this is St Ambrose's,' he said in a hearty voice just before the porter's lodge and she pushed him quickly by, through the first quad, towards the Master's house, where on the doorstep with a BA gown over his arm stood Mr Fennick permanently posed like a piece of garden statuary. 'My uncle, the President,' Elisabeth said.

'A charming girl, your niece,' Driver said as soon as they were alone together. He had really only meant to make conversation, but as soon as he had spoken the old two crooked minds began to move in harmony.

'She's very home-loving,' Mr Fennick said. 'Our famous elms,' he went on, waving his hand skywards. 'St Ambrose's rooks.'

'Crooks?' Driver exclaimed.

'Rooks. In the elms. One of our great modern poets wrote about them. "St Ambrose elms, oh St Ambrose elms", and about "St Ambrose rooks calling in wind and rain".'

'Pretty. Very pretty.'

'Nicely turned, I think.'

'I meant your niece.'

'Ah, yes. This way to the Hall. Up these steps. So often trodden, you know, by Tom Brown.'

'Who was Tom Brown?'

'The great Tom Brown—one of Rugby's famous sons.' He added thoughtfully, 'She'll make a fine wife—and mother.'

'Young men are beginning to realize that the flighty ones are not what they want for a lifetime.'

They stopped by mutual consent on the top step: they nosed towards each other like two old blind sharks who each believes that what stirs the water close to him is tasty meat.

'Whoever wins her,' Mr Fennick said, 'can feel proud. She'll make a fine hostess . . .'

'I and my son,' Driver said, 'have talked seriously about marriage. He takes rather an old-fashioned view. He'll make a good husband . . .'

They walked into the hall, and Mr Fennick led the way round the portraits. 'Our founder,' he said, pointing at a full-bottomed wig. He chose it deliberately: he felt it smacked a little of himself. Before Swinburne's portrait he hesitated: then pride in St Ambrose's conquered caution. 'The great poet Swinburne,' he said. 'We sent him down.'

'Expelled him?'

'Yes. Bad morals.'

'I'm glad you are strict about those.'

'Ah, your son is in safe hands at St Amb's.'

'It makes me very happy,' Driver said. He began to scrutinize the portrait of a nineteenth-century divine. 'Fine brushwork,' he said. 'Now religion—I believe in religion. Basis of the family.' He said with a burst of confidence. 'You know our young people ought to meet.'

Mr Fennick gleamed happily. 'I agree.'

'If he passes . . .'

'Oh, he'll certainly pass,' Mr Fennick said.

'He'll be on leave in a week or two. Why shouldn't he take his degree in person?'

'Well, there'd be difficulties.'

'Isn't it the custom?'

'Not for postal graduates. The Vice-Chancellor likes to make a small distinction . . . but Lord Driver, in the case of so distinguished an alumnus, I suggest that I should be deputed to present the degree to your son in London.'

'I'd like him to see his college.'

'And so he shall in happier days. So much of the college is shut now. I would like him to visit it for the first time when its glory is restored. Allow me and my niece to call on you.'

'We are living very quietly.'

'Not serious financial trouble, I hope?'

'Oh, no, no.'

'I'm so glad. And now let us rejoin the dear girl.'

5

It always seemed to be more convenient to meet at railway stations. The coincidence didn't strike Mr Fennick who had fortified himself for the journey with a good deal of audit ale, but it struck Elisabeth. The college lately had not been fulfilling expectations, and that was partly due to the laziness of Mr Fennick: from his conversation lately it almost seemed as though he had

begun to regard the college as only a step to something else—
what she couldn't quite make out. He was always talking about
Lord Driver and his son Frederick and the responsibilities of the
peerage. His Republican tendencies had quite lapsed. 'That dear
boy,' was the way he referred to Frederick, and he marked him
100% for Classics. 'It's not often Latin and Greek go with military genius,' he said. 'A remarkable boy.'

'He's not so hot on economics,' Elisabeth said.

'We mustn't demand too much book-learning from a soldier.'

At Paddington Lord Driver waved anxiously to them through
the crowd; he wore a very new suit—one shudders to think how
many coupons had been gambled away for the occasion. A little
behind him was a very young man with a sullen mouth and a scar
on his cheek. Mr Fennick bustled forward; he wore a black raincoat over his shoulder like a cape and carrying his hat in his hand
he disclosed his white hair venerably among the porters.

'My son—Frederick,' Lord Driver said. The boy sullenly took
off his hat and put it on again quickly: they wore their hair in the
army very short.

'St Ambrose's welcomes her new graduate,' Mr Fennick said.
Frederick grunted.

The presentation of the degree was made in a private room at
Mount Royal. Lord Driver explained that his house had been
bombed—a time bomb, he added, a rather necessary explanation
since there had been no raids recently. Mr Fennick was satisfied if
Lord Driver was. He had brought up a BA gown, a mortar-board
and a Bible in his suitcase, and he made quite an imposing little
ceremony between the book-table, the sofa and the radiator,
reading out a Latin oration and tapping Frederick lightly on the
head with the Bible. The degree-diploma had been expensively
printed in two colours by an Anglo-Catholic firm. Elisabeth was
the only uneasy person there. Could the world, she wondered, really contain two such suckers? What was this painful feeling
growing up in her that perhaps it contained four?

After a little light lunch with bottled brown beer—'almost as
good, if I may say so, as our audit ale,' Mr Fennick beamed—the
President and Lord Driver made elaborate moves to drive the two
young people together. 'We've got to talk a little business,' Mr

Fennick said, and Lord Driver hinted, 'You've not been to the movies for a year, Frederick.' They were driven out together into bombed shabby Oxford Street while the old men rang cheerfully down for whisky.

'What's the idea?' Elisabeth said.

He was good-looking; she liked his scar and his sullenness; there was almost too much intelligence and purpose in his eyes. Once he took off his hat and scratched his head: Elisabeth again noticed his short hair. He certainly didn't look a military type. And his suit, like his father's, looked new and ready-made. Hadn't he had any clothes to wear when he came on leave?

'I suppose,' she said, 'they are planning a wedding.'

His eyes lit gleefully up. 'I wouldn't mind,' he said.

'You'd have to get leave from your CO, wouldn't you?'

'CO?' he asked in astonishment, flinching a little like a boy who has been caught out, who hasn't been prepared beforehand with that question. She watched him carefully, remembering all the things that had seemed to her odd since the beginning.

'So you haven't been to the movies for a year,' she said.

'I've been on service.'

'Not even an Ensa show?'

'Oh, I don't count those.'

'It must be awfully like being in prison.'

He grinned weakly, walking faster all the time, so that she might easily have been pursuing him through the Hyde Park gates.

'Come clean,' she said. 'Your father's not Lord Driver.'

'Oh yes, he is.'

'Any more than my uncle's President of a College.'

'What?' He began to laugh—it was an agreeable laugh, a laugh you couldn't trust but a laugh which made you laugh back and agree that in a crazy world like this all sorts of things didn't matter a hang. 'I'm just out of Borstal,' he said. 'What's yours?'

'Oh, I haven't been in prison yet.'

He said, 'You'll never believe me, but all that ceremony—it looked phoney to me. Of course Dad swallowed it.'

'And my uncle swallowed you . . . I couldn't quite.'

'Well, the wedding's off. In a way I'm sorry.'

'I'm still free.'

'Well,' he said, 'we might discuss it,' and there in the pale Autumn sunlight of the Park they did discuss it—from all sorts of angles. There were bigger frauds all round them: officials of the Ministries passed carrying little portfolios; controllers of this and that purred by in motor-cars, and men with the big blank faces of advertisement hoardings strode purposefully in khaki with scarlet tabs down Park Lane from the Dorchester. Their fraud was a small one by the world's standard, and a harmless one: the boy from Borstal and the girl from nowhere at all—from the draper's counter and the semi-detached villa. 'He's got a few hundred stowed away, I'm sure of that,' said Fred. 'He'd make a settlement if he thought he could get the President's niece.'

'I wouldn't be surprised if Uncle had five hundred. He'd put it all down for Lord Driver's son.'

'We'd take over this college business. With a bit of capital we could really make it go. It's just chicken-feed now.'

They fell in love for no reason at all, in the park, on a bench to save twopences, planning their fraud on the old frauds they knew they could outdo. Then they went back and Elisabeth declared herself before she'd got properly inside the door. 'Frederick and I want to get married.' She almost felt sorry for the old fools as their faces lit up, suddenly, simultaneously, because everything had been so easy, and then darkened with caution as they squinted at each other. 'This is very surprising,' Lord Driver said, and the President said, 'My goodness, young people work fast.'

All night the two old men planned their settlements, and the two young ones sat happily back in a corner, watching them fence, with the secret knowledge that the world is always open to the young.

1941

MEN AT WORK

Richard Skate had taken a couple of hours away from the Ministry to see whether his house was still standing after the previous night's raid. He was a thin, pale, hungry-looking man of early middle age. All his life had been spent in keeping his nose above water, lecturing at night-schools and acting as temporary English master at some of the smaller public schools and in the process he had acquired a small house, a wife and one child—a rather precocious girl with a talent for painting who despised him. They lived in the country, his house was cut off from him by the immeasurable distance of bombed London—he visited it hurriedly twice a week, and his whole world was now the Ministry, the high heartless building with complicated lifts and long passages like those of a liner and lavatories where the water never ran hot and the nail-brushes were chained like Bibles. Central heating gave it a stuffy smell of mid-Atlantic except in the passages where the windows were always open for fear of blast and the cold winds whistled in. One expected to see people wrapped in rugs lying in deckchairs and the messengers carried round minutes like soup. Skate slept downstairs in the basement on a camp-bed, emerging at about ten o'clock for breakfast, and these imprisoned weeks were beginning to give him the appearance of a pit-pony— a purblind air as of something that lived underground. The Establishments branch of the Ministry of Information thought it wise to send a minute to the staff advising them to spend an hour or two a day in the open air, and some members did indeed reach the King's Arms at the corner. But Skate didn't drink.

And yet in spite of everything he was happy. Showing his pass at the outer gate, nodding to the Home Guard who was a specialist in early Icelandic customs, he was happy. For his nose was now well above water: he had a permanent job, he was a Civil Servant. His ambition had been to be a playwright (one Sunday performance in St John's Wood had enabled him to register as a dramatist in the Central Register), and now that the London theatres were most of them closed, he was no longer taunted by the sight of other men's success.

He opened the door of his dark room. It had been built of plywood in a passage, for as the huge staff of the Ministry accumulated like a kind of fungoid life—old divisions sprouting daily new sections which then broke away and became divisions and spawned in turn—the five hundred rooms of the great university block became inadequate: corners of passages were turned into rooms, and corridors disappeared overnight.

'All well?' his assistant asked: the large-breasted young woman who mothered him, bringing him cups of coffee when he looked peaky and guarding the telephone.

'Oh, yes, thanks. It's still there. A pane of glass gone, that's all.'

'A Mr Savage rang up.'

'Oh, did he? What did he want?'

'He said he'd joined the Air Force and wanted to show you his uniform.'

'Old Savage,' Skate said. 'He always was a bit wild.'

The telephone rang, and Miss Manners grasped it like an enemy.

'Yes,' she said, 'yes, RS is back. It's HG,' she explained to Skate. All the junior staff called people by initials: it was a sort of social compromise, between a Christian name and a Mr. It made telephone conversations as obscure as a cable in code.

'Hello, Graves. Yes, it's still standing. Will you be at the Book Committee? I simply haven't got any agenda. Can't you invent something?' He said to Miss Manners, 'Graves wants to know who'll be at the Committee.'

Miss Manners recited quickly down the phone, 'RK, DH, FL, and BL says he'll be late. All right, I'll tell RS. Goodbye.' She said to Skate, 'HG asks why you don't just put Report on Progress down on the agenda.'

'He will have his little joke,' Skate said miserably. 'As if there could be any progress.'

'You want your tea,' Miss Manners said. She unlocked a drawer and took out Skate's teaspoon. No teaspoons had been supplied in the Ministry after the initial loss of 6,000 in the opening months of the war, and indeed it was becoming more and more necessary to lock everything portable up. Even the blankets disappeared from the ARP shelters. Like the wreck of a German plane the place seemed to be the prey of the relic-hunters, so that one could foresee the day when only the heavy Portland stone would remain, stripped bare, scorched by incendiaries and pitted with bullet-holes where the Home Guard unloaded their rifles.

'Oh dear, oh dear,' Skate said, 'I must get this agenda done.' His worry was only skin deep: it was all a game played in a corner under the gigantic shadow. Propaganda was a means of passing the time: work was not done for its usefulness but for its own sake—simply as an occupation. He wrote wearily down 'The Problem of India' on the agenda.

Leaving his room Skate stood aside for an odd little procession of old men in robes, led by a mace-bearer. They passed—one of them sneezing—towards the Chancellor's Hall, like humble ghosts still carrying out the ritual of another age. They had once been kings in this palace, the gigantic building had been built to house them, and now the civil servants passed up and down through their procession as though it had no more consistency than smoke. Long before he reached the room where the Book Committee sat he heard a familiar voice saying, 'What we want is a really colossal campaign . . .' It was King, of course, putting his shoulder to the war-effort: these outbreaks occurred periodically like desire. King had been an advertising man, and the need to sell something would regularly overcome him. Memories of Ovaltine and Halitosis and the Mustard Club sought an outlet all the time, until suddenly, overwhelmingly, he would begin to sell the war. The Treasury and the Stationery Office always saw to it that his great schemes came to nothing: only once, because somebody was on holiday, a King campaign really got under way. It was when the meat ration went down to a shilling; the hoardings all over London carried a curt King message. 'DON'T GROUSE ABOUT MUTTON. WHAT'S WRONG WITH YOUR GREENS?' A ribald Labour member asked a question in Parliament, the posters were withdrawn at a cost of twenty thousand pounds, the Permanent Secretary resigned, the Prime Minister stood by the Minister who stood by his staff ('I consider we are one of the fighting services'), and King, after being asked to resign, was instead put in charge of the Books Division of the Ministry at a higher salary. Here it was felt he could do no harm.

Skate slid in and handed round copies of the agenda unobtrusively like a maid laying napkins. He didn't bother to listen to King: something about a series of pamphlets to be distributed free to six million people really explaining what we were fighting for. 'Tell 'em what freedom means,' King said. 'Democracy. Don't use long words.'

Hill said, 'I don't think the Stationery Office . . .' Hill's thin voice was always the voice of reason. He was said to be the author of the official explanation and defence of the Ministry's existence: 'A negative action may have positive results.'

On Skate's agenda was written:

1. Arising from the Minutes.
2. Pamphlet in Welsh on German labour conditions.
3. Facilities for Wilkinson to visit the ATS.
4. Objections to proposed Bone pamphlet.
5. Suggestion for a leaflet from Meat Marketing Board.
6. The Problem of India.

The list, Skate thought, looked quite impressive.

'Of course,' King went on, 'the details need working out. We've got to get the right authors. Priestley and people like him. I feel there won't be any difficulty about money if we can present a really clear case. Would you look into it, Skate, and report back?'

Skate agreed. He didn't know what it was all about, but that didn't matter. A few minutes would be passed to and fro, and

King's blood would cool in the process. To send a minute to any-body else in the great building and to receive a reply took at least twenty-four hours; on an urgent matter an exchange of three minutes might be got through in a week. Time outside the Min-istry went at quite a different pace. Skate remembered how the minutes on who should write a 'suggested' pamphlet about the French war-effort were still circulating indecisively while Ger-many broke the line, passed the Somme, occupied Paris and re-ceived the delegates at Compiègne.

The committee as usual lasted an hour—it was always, to Skate, an agreeable meeting with men from other divisions, the Religions Division, the Empire Division and so on. Sometimes they co-opted another man they thought was nice. It gave an op-portunity for all sorts of interesting discussions—on books and authors and artists and plays and films. The agenda didn't really matter: it was quite easy to invent one at the last moment.

Today everybody was in a good temper; there hadn't been any bad news for a week, and as the policy of the latest Permanent Secretary was that the Ministry should not do anything to attract attention, there was no reason to fear a purge in the immediate future. The decision, too, eased everybody's work. And there was quite a breath of the larger life in the matter of Wilkinson. Wilkinson was a very popular novelist who wanted to sound a clarion-note to women, and he had asked permission to make a special study of the ATS. Now the military authorities refused permission—nobody knew why. Speculation continued for ten minutes. Skate said he thought Wilkinson was a bad writer and King disagreed—that led to a general literary discussion. Lewis from the Empire Division, who had fought in Gallipoli during the last war, dozed uneasily.

He woke up when they got on to the Bone pamphlet. Bone had been asked to write a pamphlet about the British Empire: it was to be distributed, fifty thousand copies of it, free at public meetings. But now that it was in type, all sorts of tactless phrases were dis-covered by the experts. India objected to a reference to Canadian dairy herds, and Australia objected to a phrase about Botany Bay. The Canadian authority was certain that mention of Wolfe would antagonize the French-Canadians, and the New Zealand authority felt that undue emphasis had been laid on the Australian fruit-farms. Meanwhile the public meetings had all been held, so that there was no means of distributing the pamphlet. Somebody suggested that it might be sent to America for the New York World Fair, but the American Division then demanded certain cuts in the references to the War of Independence, and by the time those had been made the World Fair had closed. Now Bone had written objecting to his own pamphlet which he said was unrecognizable.

'We could get somebody else to sign it,' Skate suggested—but that meant paying another fee, and the Treasury, Hill said, would never sanction that.

'Look here, Skate,' King said, 'you're a literary man. You write to Bone and sort of smooth things over.'

Lowndes came in hurriedly, smelling a little of wine. He said, 'Sorry to be late. Had to lunch a man on business. Seen the news?'

'No.'

'Daylight raids again. Fifty Nazi planes shot down. They are turning on the heat. Fifteen of ours lost.'

'We must really get Bone's pamphlet out,' Hill said.

Skate suddenly, to his surprise, said savagely, 'That'll show them,' and then sat down in humble collapse as though he had been caught out in treachery.

'Well,' Hill said, 'we mustn't get rattled, Skate. Remember what the Minister said: It's our duty just to carry on our work whatever happens.'

'Yes, I didn't mean anything.'

Without reaching a decision on the Bone pamphlet they passed on to the Meat Marketing Leaflet. Nobody was interested in this, so the matter was left in Skate's hands to report back. 'You talk to 'em, Skate,' King said. 'Good idea. You know about these things. Might ask Priestley,' he vaguely added, and then frowned thoughtfully at that old-timer on the minutes, 'The Problem of India'. 'Need we really discuss it this week?' he said. 'There's nobody here who knows about India. Let's get in Lawrence next week.'

'Good chap, Lawrence,' Lowndes said. 'Wrote a naughty novel once called *Parson's Pleasure*.'

'We'll co-opt him,' King said.

The Book Committee was over for another week, and since the room would be empty now until morning, Skate opened the big windows against the night's blast. Far up in the pale enormous sky little white lines, like the phosphorescent spoor of snails, showed where men were going home after work.

1940

ALAS, POOR MALING

Poor inoffensive ineffectual Maling! I don't want you to smile at Maling and his borborygmi, as the doctors always smiled when he consulted them, as they must have smiled even after the sad climax of September 3rd, 1940, when his borborygmi held up for twenty-four fatal hours the amalgamation of the Simcox and Hythe Newsprint Companies. Simcox's interests had always been dearer to Maling than life: hard-driven, conscientious, happy in his work, he wanted no position higher than their secretary, and those twenty-four hours happened—for reasons it is unwise to go into here, for they involve intricacies in British income-tax law—to be fatal to the company's existence. After that day he dropped altogether out of sight, and I shall always believe he crept away to die of a broken heart in some provincial printing works. Alas, poor Maling!

It was the doctors who called his complaint borborygmi: in England we usually call it just 'tummy rumbles'. I believe it's quite a harmless kind of indigestion, but in Maling's case it took a rather odd form. His stomach, he used to complain, blinking sadly downwards through his semi-circular reading glasses, had 'an ear'. It used to pick up notes in an extraordinary way and give them out again after meals. I shall never forget one embarrassing tea at the Piccadilly Hotel in honour of a party of provincial printers: it was the year before the war, and Maling had been attending the Symphony Concerts at Queen's Hall (he never went again). In the distance a dance orchestra had been playing 'The Lambeth Walk' (how tired one got of that tune in 1938 with its waggery and false bonhomie and its 'ois'). Suddenly in the happy silence between dances, as the printers sat back from a ruin of toasted tea-cakes, there emerged—faint as though from a distant part of the hotel, sad and plangent—the opening bars of a Brahms Concerto. A Scottish printer, who had an ear for good music, exclaimed with dour relish, 'My goodness, how that mon can play.' Then the music stopped abruptly, and an odd suspicion made me look at Maling. He was red as beetroot. Nobody noticed because the dance orchestra began again to the Scotsman's disgust with 'Boomps-a-Daisy', and I think I was the only one who detected a curious faint undertone of 'The Lambeth Walk' apparently coming from the chair where Maling sat.

It was after ten, when the printers had piled into taxis and driven away to Euston, that Maling told me about his stomach. 'It's quite unaccountable,' he said, 'like a parrot. It seems to pick up things at random.' He added with tears in his voice, 'I can't enjoy food any more. I never know what's going to happen afterwards. This afternoon wasn't the worst. Sometimes it's quite loud.' He brooded forlornly. 'When I was a boy I liked listening to German bands . . .'

'Haven't you seen a doctor?'

'They don't understand. They say it's just indigestion and nothing to worry about. Nothing to worry about! But then when I've been seeing a doctor it's always lain quiet.' I noticed that he spoke of his stomach as if it were a detested animal. He gazed bleakly at his knuckles and said, 'Now I've become afraid of any new noise. I never know. It doesn't take any notice of some, but others seem . . . well, to fascinate it. At a first hearing. Last year when they took up Piccadilly it was the road drills. I used to get them all over again after dinner.'

I said rather stupidly, 'I suppose you've tried the usual salts,' and I remember—it was my last sight of him—his expression of despair as though he had ceased to expect comprehension from any living soul.

It was my last sight of him because the war pitched me out of the printing trade into all sorts of odd occupations, and it was only at second-hand that I heard the account of the strange board meeting which broke poor Maling's heart.

What the papers called the blitz-and-pieces krieg against

Britain had been going on for about a week: in London we were just settling down to air-raid alarms at the rate of five or six a day, but the 3rd of September, the anniversary of the war, had so far been relatively peaceful. There was a general feeling, however, that Hitler might celebrate the anniversary with a big attack. It was therefore in an atmosphere of some tension that Simcox and Hythe had their joint meeting.

It took place in the traditional grubby little room above the Simcox offices in Fetter Lane: the round table dating from the original Joshua Simcox, the steel engraving of a printing works dated 1875, and an irrelevant copy of a Bible which had always been the only book in the big glass bookcase except for a volume of type faces. Old Sir Joshua Simcox was in the chair: you can picture his snow-white hair and the pale pork-like Nonconformist features. Wesby Hythe was there, and half a dozen other directors with narrow canny faces and neat black coats: they all looked a little strained. If the new income-tax regulations were to be evaded, they had to work quickly. As for Maling he crouched over his pad, nervously ready to advise anybody on anything.

There was one interruption during the reading of the minutes. Wesby Hythe, who was an invalid, complained that a typewriter in the next room was getting on his nerves. Maling blushed and went out: I think he must have swallowed a tablet because the typewriter stopped. Hythe was impatient. 'Hurry up,' he said, 'hurry up. We haven't all night.' But that was exactly what they had.

After the minutes had been read Sir Joshua began explaining elaborately in a Yorkshire accent that their motives were entirely patriotic: they hadn't any intention of evading tax: they just wanted to contribute to the war effort, drive, economy . . . He said, 'The proof of the pudden' . . .' and at that moment the air-raid sirens started. As I have said a mass attack was expected: it wasn't the time for delay: a dead man couldn't evade income tax. The directors gathered up their papers and bolted for the basement.

All except Maling. You see, he knew the truth. I think it had been the reference to pudding which had roused the sleeping animal. Of course he should have confessed, but think for a moment: would you have had the courage, after watching those elderly men with white slips to their waistcoats pelt with a horrifying lack of dignity to safety? I know I should have done exactly what Maling did, have followed Sir Joshua down to the basement in the desperate hope that for once the stomach would do the right thing and make amends. But it didn't. The joint boards of Simcox and Hythe stayed in the basement for twelve hours, and Maling stayed with them, saying nothing. You see, for some unaccountable reason of taste, poor Maling's stomach had picked up the note of the Warning only too effectively, but it had somehow never taken to the All Clear.

1940

THE CASE FOR
THE DEFENCE

It was the strangest murder trial I ever attended. They named it the Peckham murder in the headlines, though Northwood Street, where the old woman was found battered to death, was not strictly speaking in Peckham. This was not one of those cases of circumstantial evidence in which you feel the jurymen's anxiety—because mistakes *have* been made—like domes of silence muting the court. No, this murderer was all but found with the body; no one present when the Crown counsel outlined his case believed that the man in the dock stood any chance at all.

He was a heavy stout man with bulging bloodshot eyes. All his muscles seemed to be in his thighs. Yes, an ugly customer, one you wouldn't forget in a hurry—and that was an important point because the Crown proposed to call four witnesses who hadn't forgotten him, who had seen him hurrying away from the little red villa in Northwood Street. The clock had just struck two in the morning.

Mrs Salmon in 15 Northwood Street had been unable to sleep; she heard a door click shut and thought it was her own gate. So she went to the window and saw Adams (that was his name) on the steps of Mrs Parker's house. He had just come out and he was wearing gloves. He had a hammer in his hand and she saw him drop it into the laurel bushes by the front gate. But before he moved away, he had looked up—at her window. The fatal instinct that tells a man when he is watched exposed him in the light of a street-lamp to her gaze—his eyes suffused with horrifying and brutal fear, like an animal's when you raise a whip. I talked afterwards to Mrs Salmon, who naturally after the astonishing verdict went in fear herself. As I imagine did all the witnesses—Henry MacDougall, who had been driving home from Benfleet late and nearly ran Adams down at the corner of Northwood Street. Adams was walking in the middle of the road looking dazed. And old Mr Wheeler, who lived next door to Mrs Parker, at No. 12, and was wakened by a noise—like a chair falling—through the thin-as-paper villa wall, and got up and looked out of the window, just as Mrs Salmon had done, saw Adams's back and, as he turned, those bulging eyes. In Laurel Avenue he had been seen by yet another witness—his luck was badly out; he might as well have committed the crime in broad daylight.

'I understand,' counsel said, 'that the defence proposes to plead mistaken identity. Adams's wife will tell you that he was with her at two in the morning on February 14, but after you have heard the witnesses for the Crown and examined carefully the features of the prisoner, I do not think you will be prepared to admit the possibility of a mistake.'

It was all over, you would have said, but the hanging.

After the formal evidence had been given by the policeman who had found the body and the surgeon who examined it, Mrs Salmon was called. She was the ideal witness, with her slight Scotch accent and her expression of honesty, care and kindness.

The counsel for the Crown brought the story gently out. She spoke very firmly. There was no malice in her, and no sense of importance at standing there in the Central Criminal Court with a judge in scarlet hanging on her words and the reporters writing them down. Yes, she said, and then she had gone downstairs and rung up the police station.

'And do you see the man here in court?'

She looked straight at the big man in the dock, who stared hard at her with his pekingese eyes without emotion.

'Yes,' she said, 'there he is.'

'You are quite certain?'

She said simply, 'I couldn't be mistaken, sir.'

It was all as easy as that.

'Thank you, Mrs Salmon.'

Counsel for the defence rose to cross-examine. If you had reported as many murder trials as I have, you would have known beforehand what line he would take. And I was right, up to a point.

'Now, Mrs Salmon, you must remember that a man's life may depend on your evidence.'

'I do remember it, sir.'

'Is your eyesight good?'

'I have never had to wear spectacles, sir.'

'You are a woman of fifty-five?'

'Fifty-six, sir.'

'And the man you saw was on the other side of the road?'

'Yes, sir.'

'And it was two o'clock in the morning. You must have re-markable eyes, Mrs Salmon?'

'No, sir. There was moonlight, and when the man looked up, he had the lamplight on his face.'

'And you have no doubt whatever that the man you saw is the prisoner?'

I couldn't make out what he was at. He couldn't have ex-pected any other answer than the one he got.

'None whatever, sir. It isn't a face one forgets.'

Counsel took a look round the court for a moment. Then he said, 'Do you mind, Mrs Salmon, examining again the people in court? No, not the prisoner. Stand up, please, Mr Adams,' and there at the back of the court with thick stout body and muscular legs and a pair of bulging eyes, was the exact image of the man in the dock. He was even dressed the same—tight blue suit and striped tie.

'Now think very carefully, Mrs Salmon. Can you still swear that the man you saw drop the hammer in Mrs Parker's garden was the prisoner—and not this man, who is his twin brother?'

Of course she couldn't. She looked from one to the other and didn't say a word.

There the big brute sat in the dock with his legs crossed, and there he stood too at the back of the court and they both stared at Mrs Salmon. She shook her head.

What we saw then was the end of the case. There wasn't a wit-ness prepared to swear that it was the prisoner he'd seen. And the brother? He had his alibi, too; he was with his wife.

And so the man was acquitted for lack of evidence. But whether—if he did the murder and not his brother—he was punished or not, I don't know. That extraordinary day had an extraordinary end. I followed Mrs Salmon out of court and we got wedged in the crowd who were waiting, of course, for the twins. The police tried to drive the crowd away, but all they could do was keep the road-way clear for traffic. I learned later that they tried to get the twins to leave by a back way, but they wouldn't. One of them—no one knew which—said, 'I've been acquitted, haven't I?' and they walked bang out of the front entrance. Then it happened. I don't know how, though I was only six feet away. The crowd moved and somehow one of the twins got pushed on to the road right in front of a bus.

He gave a squeal like a rabbit and that was all; he was dead, his skull smashed just as Mrs Parker's had been. Divine vengeance? I wish I knew. There was the other Adams getting on his feet from beside the body and looking straight over at Mrs Salmon. He was crying, but whether he was the murderer or the innocent man nobody will ever be able to tell. But if you were Mrs Salmon, could you sleep at night?

1939

A LITTLE PLACE OFF
THE EDGWARE ROAD

Craven came up past the Achilles statue in the thin summer rain. It was only just after lighting-up time, but already the cars were lined up all the way to the Marble Arch, and the sharp acquisitive faces peered out ready for a good time with anything possible which came along. Craven went bitterly by with the collar of his mackintosh tight round his throat: it was one of his bad days.

All the way up the park he was reminded of passion, but you needed money for love. All that a poor man could get was lust. Love needed a good suit, a car, a flat somewhere, or a good hotel. It needed to be wrapped in cellophane. He was aware all the time of the stringy tie beneath the mackintosh, and the frayed sleeves: he carried his body about with him like something he hated. (There were moments of happiness in the British Museum reading-room, but the body called him back.) He bore, as his only sentiment, the memory of ugly deeds committed on park chairs. People talked as if the body died too soon—that wasn't the trouble, to Craven, at all. The body kept alive—and through the glittering tinselly rain, on his way to a rostrum, he passed a little man in a black suit carrying a banner, 'The Body shall rise again.' He remembered a dream from which three times he had woken trembling: he had been alone in the huge dark cavernous burying ground of all the world. Every grave was connected to another under the ground: the globe was honeycombed for the sake of the dead, and on each occasion of dreaming he had discovered anew the horrifying fact that the body doesn't decay. There are no worms and dissolution. Under the ground the world was littered with masses of dead flesh ready to rise again with their warts and boils and eruptions. He had lain in bed and remembered—as 'tidings of great joy'—that the body after all was corrupt.

He came up into the Edgware Road walking fast—the Guardsmen were out in couples, great languid elongated beasts—the bodies like worms in their tight trousers. He hated them, and hated his hatred because he knew what it was, envy. He was aware that every one of them had a better body than himself: indigestion creased his stomach: he felt sure that his breath was foul—but who could he ask? Sometimes he secretly touched himself here and there with scent: it was one of his ugliest secrets. Why should he be asked to believe in the resurrection of this body he wanted to forget? Sometimes he prayed at night (a hint of religious belief was lodged in his breast like a worm in a nut) that *his* body at any rate should never rise again.

He knew all the side streets round the Edgware Road only too well: when a mood was on, he simply walked until he tired, squinting at his own image in the windows of Salmon & Gluckstein and the ABCs. So he noticed at once the posters outside the disused theatre in Culpar Road. They were not unusual, for sometimes Barclays Bank Dramatic Society would hire the place for an evening—or an obscure film would be trade-shown there. The theatre had been built in 1920 by an optimist who thought the cheapness of the site would more than counter-balance its disadvantage of lying a mile outside the conventional theatre zone. But no play had ever succeeded, and it was soon left to gather rat-holes and spider-webs. The covering of the seats was never renewed, and all that ever happened to the place was the temporary false life of an amateur play or a trade show.

Craven stopped and read—there were still optimists it appeared, even in 1939, for nobody but the blindest optimist could hope to make money out of the place as 'The Home of the Silent Film'. The first season of 'primitives' was announced (a highbrow phrase): there would never be a second. Well, the seats were cheap, and it was perhaps worth a shilling to him, now that he was tired, to get in somewhere out of the rain. Craven bought a ticket and went in to the darkness of the stalls.

In the dead darkness a piano tinkled something monotonous recalling Mendelssohn: he sat down in a gangway seat, and could immediately feel the emptiness all round him. No, there would never be another season. On the screen a large woman in a kind of toga wrung her hands, then wobbled with curious jerky movements towards a couch. There she sat and stared out like a sheepdog distractedly through her loose and black and stringy hair. Sometimes she seemed to dissolve altogether into dots and flashes and wiggly lines. A sub-title said, 'Pompilia betrayed by her beloved Augustus seeks an end to her troubles.'

Craven began at last to see—a dim waste of stalls. There were not twenty people in the place—a few couples whispering with their heads touching, and a number of lonely men like himself, wearing the same uniform of the cheap mackintosh. They lay about at intervals like corpses—and again Craven's obsession returned: the tooth-ache of horror. He thought miserably—I am going mad: other people don't feel like this. Even a disused theatre reminded him of those interminable caverns where the bodies were waiting for resurrection.

'*A slave to his passion Augustus calls for yet more wine.*'

A gross middle-aged Teutonic actor lay on an elbow with his arm round a large woman in a shift. The Spring Song tinkled ineptly on, and the screen flickered like indigestion. Somebody felt his way through the darkness, scrabbling past Craven's knees—a small man: Craven experienced the unpleasant feeling of a large beard brushing his mouth. Then there was a long sigh as the newcomer found the next chair, and on the screen events had moved with such rapidity that Pompilia had already stabbed herself—or so Craven supposed—and lay still and buxom among her weeping slaves.

A low breathless voice sighed out close to Craven's ear, 'What's happened? Is she asleep?'

'No. Dead.'

'Murdered?' the voice asked with a keen interest.

'I don't think so. Stabbed herself.'

Nobody said 'Hush': nobody was enough interested to object to a voice. They drooped among the empty chairs in attitudes of weary inattention.

The film wasn't nearly over yet: there were children somehow to be considered: was it all going on to a second generation? But

the small bearded man in the next seat seemed to be interested
only in Pompilia's death. The fact that he had come in at that
moment apparently fascinated him. Craven heard the word 'coincidence' twice, and he went on talking to himself about it in
low out-of-breath tones. 'Absurd when you come to think of it,'
and then 'no blood at all'. Craven didn't listen: he sat with his
hands clasped between his knees, facing the fact as he had faced
it so often before, that he was in danger of going mad. He had to
pull himself up, take a holiday, see a doctor (God knew what infection moved in his veins). He became aware that his bearded
neighbour had addressed him directly. 'What?' he asked impatiently, 'what did you say?'

'There would be more blood than you can imagine.'

'What are you talking about?'

When the man spoke to him, he sprayed him with damp
breath. There was a little bubble in his speech like an impedi-
ment. He said, 'When you murder a man . . .'

'This was a woman,' Craven said impatiently.

'That wouldn't make any difference.'

'And it's got nothing to do with murder anyway.'

'That doesn't signify.' They seemed to have got into an absurd
and meaningless wrangle in the dark.

'I know, you see,' the little bearded man said in a tone of
enormous conceit.

'Know what?'

'About such things,' he said with guarded ambiguity.

Craven turned and tried to see him clearly. Was he mad? Was
this a warning of what he might become—babbling incompre-
hensibly to strangers in cinemas? He thought, By God, no, trying
to see: I'll be sane yet. I *will* be sane. He could make out nothing
but a small black hump of body. The man was talking to himself
again. He said, 'Talk. Such talk. They'll say it was all for fifty
pounds. But that's a lie. Reasons and reasons. They always take
the first reason. Never look behind. Thirty years of reasons. Such
simpletons,' he added again in that tone of breathlessness and
unbounded conceit. So this was madness. So long as he could realize that, he must be sane himself—relatively speaking. Not so

sane perhaps as the seekers in the park or the Guardsmen in the Edgware Road, but saner than this. It was like a message of encouragement as the piano tinkled on.

Then again the little man turned and sprayed him. 'Killed herself, you say? But who's to know that? It's not a mere question of what hand holds the knife.' He laid a hand suddenly and confidingly on Craven's: it was damp and sticky: Craven said with horror as a possible meaning came to him, 'What are you talking about?'

'I know,' the little man said. 'A man in my position gets to know almost everything.'

'What is your position?' Craven asked, feeling the sticky hand on his, trying to make up his mind whether he was being hysterical or not—after all, there were a dozen explanations—it might be treacle.

'A pretty desperate one *you'd* say.' Sometimes the voice almost died in the throat altogether. Something incomprehensible had happened on the screen—take your eyes from these early pictures for a moment and the plot had proceeded on at such a pace . . . Only the actors moved slowly and jerkily. A young woman in a night-dress seemed to be weeping in the arms of a Roman centurion: Craven hadn't seen either of them before. '*I am not afraid of death, Lucius—in your arms.*'

The little man began to titter—knowingly. He was talking to himself again. It would have been easy to ignore him altogether if it had not been for those sticky hands which he now removed: he seemed to be fumbling at the seat in front of him. His head had a habit of lolling sideways—like an idiot child's. He said distinctly and irrelevantly: 'Bayswater Tragedy.'

'What was that?' Craven said. He had seen those words on a poster before he entered the park.

'What?'

'About the tragedy.'

'To think they call Cullen Mews Bayswater.' Suddenly the little man began to cough—turning his face towards Craven and coughing right at him: it was like vindictiveness. The voice said, 'Let me see. My umbrella.' He was getting up.

'You didn't have an umbrella.'

'My umbrella,' he repeated. 'My—' and seemed to lose the word altogether. He went scrabbling out past Craven's knees.

Craven let him go, but before he had reached the billowy dusty curtains of the Exit the screen went blank and bright—the film had broken, and somebody immediately turned up one dirt-choked chandelier above the circle. It shone down just enough for Craven to see the smear on his hands. This wasn't hysteria: this was a fact. He wasn't mad: he had sat next to a madman who in some mews—what was the name, Colon, Collin . . . Craven jumped up and made his own way out: the black curtain flapped in his mouth. But he was too late: the man had gone and there were three turnings to choose from. He chose instead a telephone-box and dialled with a sense odd for him of sanity and decision 999.

It didn't take two minutes to get the right department. They were interested and very kind. Yes, there had been a murder in a mews—Cullen Mews. A man's neck had been cut from ear to ear with a bread knife—a horrid crime. He began to tell them how he had sat next the murderer in a cinema: it couldn't be anyone else: there was blood on his hands—and he remembered with re-pulsion as he spoke the damp beard. There must have been a ter-rible lot of blood. But the voice from the Yard interrupted him. 'Oh no,' it was saying, 'we have the murderer—no doubt of it at all. It's the body that's disappeared.'

Craven put down the receiver. He said to himself aloud, 'Why should this happen to *me*? Why to *me*?' He was back in the hor-ror of his dream—the squalid darkening street outside was only one of the innumerable tunnels connecting grave to grave where the imperishable bodies lay. He said, 'It was a dream, a dream,' and leaning forward he saw in the mirror above the telephone his own face sprinkled by tiny drops of blood like dew from a scent-spray. He began to scream, 'I won't go mad. I won't go mad. I'm sane. I won't go mad.' Presently a little crowd began to collect, and soon a policeman came.

1939

ACROSS THE BRIDGE

'They say he's worth a million,' Lucia said. He sat there in the little hot damp Mexican square, a dog at his feet, with an air of immense and forlorn patience. The dog attracted your attention at
once; for it was very nearly an English setter, only something had
gone wrong with the tail and the feathering. Palms wilted over
his head, it was all shade and stuffiness round the bandstand, ra-
dios talked loudly in Spanish from the little wooden sheds where
they changed your pesos into dollars at a loss. I could tell he
didn't understand a word from the way he read his newspaper—
as I did myself picking out the words which were like English
ones. 'He's been here a month,' Lucia said, 'they turned him out
of Guatemala and Honduras.'

You couldn't keep any secrets for five hours in this border
town. Lucia had only been twenty-four hours in the place, but
she knew all about Mr Joseph Calloway. The only reason I didn't
know about him (and I'd been in the place two weeks) was because I couldn't talk the language any more than Mr Calloway
could. There wasn't another soul in the place who didn't know
the story—the whole story of Halling Investment Trust and the
proceedings for extradition. Any man doing dusty business in
any of the wooden booths in the town is better fitted by long observation to tell Mr Calloway's tale than I am, except that I was
in—literally—at the finish. They all watched the drama proceed
with immense interest, sympathy and respect. For, after all, he
had a million.

Every once in a while through the long steamy day, a boy
came and cleaned Mr Calloway's shoes: he hadn't the right

words to resist them—they pretended not to know his English. He must have had his shoes cleaned the day Lucia and I watched him at least half a dozen times. At midday he took a stroll across the square to the Antonio Bar and had a bottle of beer, the setter sticking to heel as if they were out for a country walk in England (he had, you may remember, one of the biggest estates in Norfolk). After his bottle of beer, he would walk down between the money-changers' huts to the Rio Grande and look across the bridge into the United States: people came and went constantly in cars. Then back to the square till lunch-time. He was staying in the best hotel, but you don't get good hotels in this border town: nobody stays in them more than a night. The good hotels were on the other side of the bridge: you could see their electric signs twenty storeys high from the little square at night, like lighthouses marking the United States.

You may ask what I'd been doing in so drab a spot for a fortnight. There was no interest in the place for anyone; it was just damp and dust and poverty, a kind of shabby replica of the town across the river. Both had squares in the same spots; both had the same number of cinemas. One was cleaner than the other, that was all, and more expensive, much more expensive. I'd stayed across there a couple of nights waiting for a man a tourist bureau said was driving down from Detroit to Yucatan and would sell a place in his car for some fantastically small figure—twenty dollars, I think it was. I don't know if he existed or was invented by the optimistic half-caste in the agency; anyway, he never turned up and so I waited, not much caring, on the cheap side of the river. It didn't much matter; I was living. One day I meant to give up the man from Detroit and go home or go south, but it was easier not to decide anything in a hurry. Lucia was just waiting for a car the other way, but she didn't have to wait so long. We waited together and watched Mr Calloway waiting—for God knows what.

I don't know how to treat this story—it was a tragedy for Mr Calloway, it was poetic retribution, I suppose, in the eyes of the shareholders whom he'd ruined with his bogus transactions, and to Lucia and me, at this stage, it was comedy—except when he kicked the dog. I'm not a sentimentalist about dogs, I prefer people to be cruel to animals rather than to human beings, but I couldn't help being revolted at the way he'd kick that animal—with a hint of cold-blooded venom, not in anger but as if he were getting even for some trick it had played him a long while ago. That generally happened when he returned from the bridge: it was the only sign of anything resembling emotion he showed. Otherwise he looked a small, set, gentle creature with silver hair and a silver moustache and gold-rimmed glasses, and one gold tooth like a flaw in character.

Lucia hadn't been accurate when she said he'd been turned out of Guatemala and Honduras; he'd left voluntarily when the extradition proceedings seemed likely to go through and moved north. Mexico is still not a very centralized state, and it is possible to get round governors as you can't get round cabinet ministers or judges. And so he waited there on the border for the next move. That earlier part of the story was, I suppose, dramatic, but I didn't watch it and I can't invent what I haven't seen—the long waiting in ante-rooms, the bribes taken and refused, and growing fear of arrest, and then the flight—in gold-rimmed glasses—covering his tracks as well as he could, but this wasn't finance and he was an amateur at escape. And so he'd washed up here, under my eyes and Lucia's eyes, sitting all day under the bandstand, nothing to read but a Mexican paper, nothing to do but look across the river at the United States, quite unaware, I suppose, that everyone knew everything about him, once a day kicking his dog. Perhaps in its semi-setter way it reminded him too much of the Norfolk estate—though that, too, I suppose, was the reason he kept it.

And the next act again was pure comedy. I hesitate to think what this man worth a million was costing his country as they edged him out from this land and that. Perhaps somebody was getting tired of the business, and careless; anyway, they sent across two detectives with an old photograph. He'd grown his silvery moustache since that had been taken, and he'd aged a lot, and they couldn't catch sight of him. They hadn't been across the bridge two hours when everybody knew that there were two foreign detectives in town looking for Mr Calloway—everybody knew, that is to say, except Mr Calloway, who couldn't talk

Spanish. There were plenty of people who could have told him in English, but they didn't. It wasn't cruelty, it was a sort of awe and respect: like a bull, he was on show, sitting there mournfully in the plaza with his dog, a magnificent spectacle for which we all had ring-side seats.

I ran into one of the policemen in the Bar Antonio. He was disgusted; he had had some idea that when he crossed the bridge life was going to be different, so much more colour and sun, and—I suspect—love, and all he found were wide mud streets where the nocturnal rain lay in pools, and mangy dogs, smells and cockroaches in his bedroom, and the nearest to love, the open door of the Academia Comercial, where pretty mestizo girls sat all morning learning to typewrite. Tip-tap-tip-tap-tip—perhaps they had a dream too—jobs on the other side of the bridge, where life was going to be so much more luxurious, refined and amusing.

We got into conversation; he seemed surprised that I knew who they both were and what they wanted. He said, 'We've got information this man Calloway's in town.'

'He's knocking around somewhere,' I said.

'Could you point him out?'

'Oh, I don't know him by sight,' I said.

He drank his beer and thought a while. 'I'll go out and sit in the plaza. He's sure to pass sometime.'

I finished my beer and went quickly off and found Lucia. I said, 'Hurry, we're going to see an arrest.' We didn't care a thing about Mr Calloway, he was just an elderly man who kicked his dog and swindled the poor, and deserved anything he got. So we made for the plaza; we knew Calloway would be there, but it had never occurred to either of us that the detectives wouldn't recognize him. There was quite a surge of people round the place; all the fruit-sellers and boot-blacks in town seemed to have arrived together; we had to force our way through, and there in the little green stuffy centre of the place, sitting on adjoining seats, were the two plain-clothes men and Mr Calloway. I've never known the place so silent; everybody was on tiptoe, and the plain-clothes men were staring at the crowd for Mr Calloway, and Mr Calloway sat on his usual seat staring out over the money-changing booths at the United States.

'It can't go on. It just can't,' Lucia said. But it did. It got more fantastic still. Somebody ought to write a play about it. We sat as close as we dared. We were afraid all the time we were going to laugh. The semi-setter scratched for fleas and Mr Calloway watched the USA. The two detectives watched the crowd, and the crowd watched the show with solemn satisfaction. Then one of the detectives got up and went over to Mr Calloway. That's the end, I thought. But it wasn't, it was the beginning. For some reason they had eliminated him from their list of suspects. I shall never know why. The man said:

'You speak English?'

'I *am* English,' Mr Calloway said.

Even that didn't tear it, and the strangest thing of all was the way Mr Calloway came alive. I don't think anybody had spoken to him like that for weeks. The Mexicans were too respectful—he was a man with a million—and it had never occurred to Lucia and me to treat him casually like a human being; even in our eyes he had been magnified by the colossal theft and the world-wide pursuit.

He said, 'This is rather a dreadful place, don't you think?'

'It is,' the policeman said.

'I can't think what brings anybody across the bridge.'

'Duty,' the policeman said gloomily. 'I suppose you are passing through.'

'Yes,' Mr Calloway said.

'I'd have expected over here there'd have been—you know what I mean—life. You read things about Mexico.'

'Oh, life,' Mr Calloway said. He spoke firmly and precisely, as if to a committee of shareholders. 'That begins on the other side.'

'You don't appreciate your own country until you leave it.'

'That's very true,' Mr Calloway said. 'Very true.'

At first it was difficult not to laugh, and then after a while there didn't seem to be much to laugh at: an old man imagining all the fine things going on beyond the international bridge. I think he thought of the town opposite as a combination of London and Norfolk—theatres and cocktail bars, a little shooting and a walk round the field at evening with the dog—that miserable imitation of a setter—poking the ditches. He'd never been across, he couldn't know it was just the same thing over again—even the same layout; only the streets were paved and the hotels had ten more storeys, and life was more expensive, and everything was a little bit cleaner. There wasn't anything Mr Calloway would have called living—no galleries, no bookshops, just *Film Fun* and the local paper, and *Click* and *Focus* and the tabloids.

'Well,' said Mr Calloway, 'I think I'll take a stroll before lunch. You need an appetite to swallow the food here. I generally go down and look at the bridge about now. Care to come, too?'

The detective shook his head. 'No,' he said, 'I'm on duty. I'm looking for a fellow.' And that, of course, gave *him* away. As far as Mr Calloway could understand, there was only one 'fellow' in the world anyone was looking for—his brain had eliminated friends who were seeking their friends, husbands who might be waiting for their wives, all objectives of any search but just the one. The power of elimination was what had made him a financier—he could forget the people behind the shares.

That was the last we saw of him for a while. We didn't see him going into the Botica Paris to get his aspirin, or walking back from the bridge with his dog. He simply disappeared, and when he disappeared, people began to talk and the detectives heard the talk. They looked silly enough, and they got busy after the very man they'd been sitting next to in the garden. Then they, too, disappeared. They, as well as Mr Calloway, had gone to the state capital to see the Governor and the Chief of Police, and it must have been an amusing sight there, too, as they bumped into Mr Calloway and sat with him in the waiting-rooms. I suspect Mr Calloway was generally shown in first, for everyone knew he was worth a million. Only in Europe is it possible for a man to be a criminal as well as a rich man.

Anyway, after about a week the whole pack of them returned by the same train. Mr Calloway travelled Pullman, and the two policemen travelled in the day coach. It was evident that they hadn't got their extradition order.

Lucia had left by that time. The car came and went across the bridge. I stood in Mexico and watched her get out at the United States Customs. She wasn't anything in particular, but she looked beautiful at a distance as she gave me a wave out of the United

States and got back into the car. And I suddenly felt sympathy for Mr Calloway, as if there were something over there which you couldn't find here, and turning round I saw him back on his old beat, with the dog at his heels.

I said, 'Good afternoon,' as if it had been all along our habit to greet each other. He looked tired and ill and dusty, and I felt sorry for him—to think of the kind of victory he'd been winning, with so much expenditure of cash and care—the prize this dirty and dreary town, the booths of the money-changers, the awful little beauty parlours with their wicker chairs and sofas looking like the reception rooms of brothels, that hot and stuffy garden by the bandstand.

He replied gloomily, 'Good afternoon,' and the dog started to sniff at some ordure and he turned and kicked it with fury, with depression, with despair.

And at that moment a taxi with the two policemen in it passed us on its way to the bridge. They must have seen that kick; perhaps they were cleverer than I had given them credit for, perhaps they were just sentimental about animals, and thought they'd do a good deed, and the rest happened by accident. But the fact remains— those two pillars of the law set about the stealing of Mr Calloway's dog.

He watched them go by. Then he said, 'Why don't you go across?'

'It's cheaper here,' I said.

'I mean just for an evening. Have a meal at that place we can see at night in the sky. Go to the theatre.'

'There isn't one.'

He said angrily, sucking his gold tooth, 'Well, anyway, get away from here.' He stared down the hill and up the other side. He couldn't see that the street climbing up from the bridge contained only the same money-changers' booths as this one.

I said, 'Why don't *you* go?'

He said evasively, 'Oh—business.'

I said, 'It's only a question of money. You don't *have* to pass by the bridge.'

He said with faint interest, 'I don't talk Spanish.'

'There isn't a soul here,' I said, 'who doesn't talk English.'

He looked at me with surprise. 'Is that so?' he said. 'Is that so?'

It's as I have said; he'd never tried to talk to anyone, and they respected him too much to talk to him—he was worth a million. I don't know whether I'm glad or sorry that I told him that. If I hadn't, he might be there now, sitting by the bandstand having his shoes cleaned—alive and suffering.

Three days later his dog disappeared. I found him looking for it calling softly and shamefacedly between the palms of the garden. He looked embarrassed. He said in a low angry voice, 'I *hate* that dog. The beastly mongrel,' and called 'Rover, Rover' in a voice which didn't carry five yards. He said, 'I bred setters once. I'd have shot a dog like that.' It reminded him, I *was* right, of Norfolk, and he lived in the memory, and he hated it for its imperfection. He was a man without a family and without friends, and his only enemy was that dog. You couldn't call the law an enemy; you have to be intimate with an enemy.

Late that afternoon someone told him they'd seen the dog walking across the bridge. It wasn't true, of course, but we didn't know that then—they paid a Mexican five pesos to smuggle it across. So all that afternoon and the next Mr Calloway sat in the garden having his shoes cleaned over and over again, and thinking how a dog could just walk across like that, and a human being, an immortal soul, was bound here in the awful routine of the little walk and the unspeakable meals and the aspirin at the botica. That dog was seeing things he couldn't see—that hateful dog. It made him mad—I think literally mad. You must remember the man had been going on for months. He had a million and he was living on two pounds a week, with nothing to spend his money on. He sat there and brooded on the hideous injustice of it. I think he'd have crossed over one day in any case, but the dog was the last straw.

Next day when he wasn't to be seen, I guessed he'd gone across and I went too. The American town is as small as the Mexican. I knew I couldn't miss him if he was there, and I was still curious. A little sorry for him, but not too much.

I caught sight of him first in the only drug-store, having a Coca-Cola, and then once outside a cinema looking at the posters; he had dressed with extreme neatness, as if for a party, but there was no party. On my third time round, I came on the detectives—they were having Coca-Colas in the drug-store, and they must have missed Mr Calloway by inches. I went in and sat down at the bar.

'Hello,' I said, 'you still about.' I suddenly felt anxious for Mr Calloway. I didn't want them to meet.

One of them said, 'Where's Calloway?'

'Oh,' I said, 'he's hanging on.'

'But not his dog,' he said and laughed. The other looked a little shocked, he didn't like anyone to *talk* cynically about a dog. Then they got up—they had a car outside.

'Have another?' I said.

'No thanks. We've got to keep going.'

The men bent close and confided to me, 'Calloway's on this side.'

'No!' I said.

'And his dog.'

'He's looking for it,' the other said.

'I'm damned if he is,' I said, and again one of them looked a little shocked, as if I'd insulted the dog.

I don't think Mr Calloway was looking for his dog, but his dog certainly found him. There was a sudden hilarious yapping from the car and out plunged the semi-setter and gambolled furiously down the street. One of the detectives—the sentimental one—was into the car before we got to the door and was off after the dog. Near the bottom of the long road to the bridge was Mr Calloway—I do believe he'd come down to look at the Mexican side when he found there was nothing but the drug-store and the cinemas and the paper shops on the American. He saw the dog coming and yelled at it to go home—'home, home, home,' as if they were in Norfolk—it took no notice at all, pelting towards him. Then he saw the police car coming, and ran. After that, everything happened too quickly, but I think the order of events was this—the dog started across the road right in front of the car, and Mr Calloway yelled, at the dog or the car, I don't know which. Anyway, the detective swerved—he said later, weakly, at the inquiry, that he couldn't run over a dog, and down went Mr Calloway, in a mess of broken glass and gold rims and silver hair, and blood. The dog was on to him before any of us could reach him, licking and whimpering and licking. I saw Mr Calloway put up his hand, and down it went across the dog's neck and the whimper rose to a stupid bark of triumph, but Mr Calloway was dead—shock and a weak heart.

'Poor old geezer,' the detective said, 'I bet he really loved that dog,' and it's true that the attitude in which he lay looked more like a caress than a blow. I thought it was meant to be a blow, but the detective may have been right. It all seemed to me a little too touching to be true as the old crook lay there with his arm over the dog's neck, dead with his million between the money-changers' huts, but it's as well to be humble in the face of human nature. He had come across the river for something, and it may, after all, have been the dog he was looking for. It sat there, baying its stupid and mongrel triumph across his body, like a piece of sentimental statuary: the nearest he could get to the fields, the ditches, the horizon of his home. It was comic and it was pitiable, but it wasn't less comic because the man was dead. Death doesn't change comedy to tragedy, and if that last gesture was one of affection, I suppose it was only one more indication of a human being's capacity for self-deception, our baseless optimism that is so much more appalling than our despair.

1938

A DRIVE IN THE COUNTRY

As every other night she listened to her father going round the house, locking the doors and windows. He was head clerk at Bergson's Export Agency, and lying in bed she would think with dislike that his home was like his office, run on the same lines, its safety preserved with the same meticulous care, so that he could present a faithful steward's account to the managing-director. Regularly every Sunday he presented the account, accompanied by his wife and two daughters, in the little neo-Gothic church in Park Road. They always had the same pew, they were always five minutes early, and her father sang loudly with no sense of tune, holding an outsize prayer book on the level of his eyes. 'Singing songs of exultation'—he was presenting the week's account (one household duly safeguarded)—'marching to the Promised Land.' When they came out of church, she looked carefully away from the corner by the 'Bricklayers' Arms' where Fred always stood, a little lit because the Arms had been open for half an hour, with his air of unbalanced exultation.

She listened: the back door closed, she could hear the catch of the kitchen window click, and the restless pad of his feet going back to try the front door. It wasn't only the outside doors he locked: he locked the empty rooms, the bathroom, the lavatory. He was locking something out, but obviously it was something capable of penetrating his first defences. He raised his second line all the way up to bed.

She laid her ear against the thin wall of the jerry-built villa and could hear the faint voices from the neighbouring room; as she listened they came clearer as though she were turning the knob of a wireless set. Her mother said '. . . margarine in the cooking . . .' and her father said '. . . much easier in fifteen years.' Then the bed creaked and there were dim sounds of tenderness and comfort between the two middle-aged strangers in the next room. In fifteen years, she thought unhappily, the house will be his; he had paid twenty-five pounds down and the rest he was paying month by month as rent. 'Of course,' he was in the habit of saying after a good meal, 'I've improved the property,' and he expected at least one of them to follow him into his study. 'I've wired this room for power,' he padded back past the little downstairs lavatory, 'this radiator', the final stroke of satisfaction, 'the garden', and if it was a fine evening he would fling the french window of the dining-room open on the little carpet of grass as carefully kept as a college lawn. 'A pile of bricks,' he'd say, 'that's all it was.' Five years of Saturday afternoons and fine Sundays had gone into the patch of turf, the surrounding flower-bed, the one apple-tree which regularly produced one crimson tasteless apple more each year.

'Yes,' he said, 'I've improved the property,' looking round for a nail to drive in, a weed to be uprooted. 'If we had to sell now, we should get back more than I've paid from the society.' It was more than a sense of property, it was a sense of honesty. Some people who bought their houses through the society let them go to rack and ruin and then cleared out.

She stood with her ear against the wall, a small, furious, immature figure. There was no more to be heard from the other room, but in her inner ear she still heard the chorus of a property owner, the tap-tap of a hammer, the scrape of a spade, the whistle of radiator steam, a key turning, a bolt pushed home, the little trivial sounds of men building barricades. She stood planning her treachery.

It was a quarter past ten; she had an hour in which to leave the house, but it did not take so long. There was really nothing to fear. They had played their usual rubber of three-handed bridge while her sister altered a dress for the local 'hop' next night; after the rubber she had boiled a kettle and brought in a pot of tea; then she had filled the hot-water bottles and put them in the beds while her father locked up. He had no idea whatever that she was an enemy.

She put on a scarf and a heavy coat because it was still cold at night; the spring was late that year, as her father commented, watching for the buds on the apple-tree. She didn't pack a suitcase; that would have reminded her too much of week-ends at the sea, a family expedition to Ostend from all of which one returned; she wanted to match the odd reckless quality of Fred's mind. This time she wasn't going to return. She went softly downstairs into the little crowded hall, unlocked the door. All was quiet upstairs, and she closed the door behind her.

She was touched by a faint feeling of guilt because she couldn't lock it from the outside. But her guilt vanished by the time she reached the end of the crazy-paved path and turned to the left down the road which after five years was still half made, past the gaps between the villas where the wounded fields remained grimly alive in the form of thin grass and heaps of clay and dandelions.

She walked fast, passing a long line of little garages like the graves in a Latin cemetery where the coffin lies below the fading photograph of its occupant. The cold night air touched her with exhilaration. She was ready for anything, as she turned by the Belisha beacon into the shuttered shopping street; she was like a recruit in the first months of a war. The choice made she could surrender her will to the strange, the exhilarating, the gigantic event.

Fred, as he had promised, was at the corner where the road turned down towards the church; she could taste the spirit on his lips as they kissed, and she was satisfied that no one else could have so adequately matched the occasion; his face was bright and reckless in the lamp-light, he was as exciting and strange to her as the adventure. He took her arm and ran her into a blind unlighted alley, then left her for a moment until two headlamps beamed softly at her out of the cavern. She cried with astonishment, 'You've got a car?' and felt the jerk of his nervous hand urging her towards it. 'Yes,' he said, 'do you like it?' grinding into second gear, changing clumsily into top as they came out between the shuttered windows.

She said, 'It's lovely. Let's drive a long way.'

'We will,' he said, watching the speedometer needle go quivering to fifty-five.

'Does it mean you've got a job?'

'There are no jobs,' he said, 'they don't exist any more than the Dodo. Did you see that bird?' he asked sharply, turning his headlights full on as they passed the turning to the housing estate and quite suddenly came out into the country between a café ('Draw in here'), a boot-shop ('Buy the shoes worn by your favourite film star'), and an undertaker's with a large white angel lit by a neon light.

'I didn't see any bird.'

'Not flying at the windscreen?'

'No.'

'I nearly hit it,' he said. 'It would have made a mess. Bad as those fellows who run someone down and don't stop. Should *we* stop?' he asked, turning out his switchboard light so that they couldn't see the needle vibrate to sixty.

'Whatever you say,' she said, sitting deep in a reckless dream.

'You going to love me tonight?'

'Of course I am.'

'Never going back there?'

'No,' she said, abjuring the tap of hammer, the click of latch, the pad of slippered feet making the rounds.

'Want to know where we are going?'

'No.' A little flat cardboard copse ran forward into the green light and darkly by. A rabbit turned its scut and vanished into a hedge. He said, 'Have you any money?'

'Half a crown.'

'Do you love me?' For a long time she expended on his lips all she had patiently had to keep in reserve, looking the other way on Sunday mornings, saying nothing when his name came up at meals with disapproval. She expended herself against dry unresponsive lips as the car leapt ahead and his foot trod down on the accelerator. He said, 'It's the hell of a life.'

She echoed him, 'The hell of a life.'

He said, 'There's a bottle in my pocket. Have a drink.'

'I don't want one.'

'Give me one then. It has a screw top,' and with one hand on her and one on the wheel he tipped his head, so that she could pour a little whisky into his mouth out of the quarter bottle. 'Do you mind?' he said.

'Of course I don't mind.'

'You can't save,' he said, 'on ten shillings a week pocket-money. I lay it out the best I can. It needs a hell of a lot of thought. To give variety. Half a crown on Weights. Three and six on whisky. A shilling on the pictures. That leaves three shillings for beer. I take my fun once a week and get it over.'

The whisky had dribbled on to his tie and the smell filled the small coupé. It pleased her. It was *his* smell. He said, 'They grudge it me. They think I ought to get a job. When you're that age you don't realize there aren't any jobs for some of us—any more for ever.'

'I know,' she said. 'They are old.'

'How's your sister?' he asked abruptly; the bright glare swept the road ahead of them clean of small scurrying birds and animals.

'She's going to the hop tomorrow. I wonder where we shall be.'

He wouldn't be drawn; he had his own idea and kept it to himself.

'I'm loving this.'

He said, 'There's a club out this way. At a road-house. Mick made me a member. Do you know Mick?'

'No.'

'Mick's all right. If they know you, they'll serve you drinks till midnight. We'll look in there. Say hullo to Mick. And then in the morning—we'll decide that later when we've had a few drinks.'

'Have you the money?' A small village, a village fast asleep already behind closed doors and windows, sailed down the hill towards them as if it was being carried smoothly by a landslide into the scarred plain from which they'd come. A low grey Norman church, an inn without a sign, a clock striking eleven. He said, 'Look in the back. There's a suitcase there.'

'It's locked.'

'I forgot the key,' he said.

'What's in it?'

'A few things,' he said vaguely. 'We could pop them for drinks.'

'What about a bed?'

'There's the car. You are not scared, are you?'

'No,' she said. 'I'm not scared. This is—' but she hadn't words for the damp cold wind, the darkness, the strangeness, the smell of whisky and the rushing car. 'It moves,' she said. 'We must have gone a long way already. This is real country,' seeing an owl sweep low on furry wings over a ploughed field.

'You've got to go farther than this for real country,' he said. 'You won't find it yet on *this* road. We'll be at the road-house soon.'

She discovered in herself a nostalgia for their dark windy solitary progress. She said, 'Need we go to the club? Can't we go farther into the country?'

He looked sideways at her; he had always been open to *any* suggestion: like some meteorological instrument, he was made for the winds to blow through. 'Of course,' he said, 'anything you like.' He didn't give the club a second thought; they swept past it a moment later, a long lit Tudor bungalow, a crash of voices, a bathing-pool filled for some reason with hay. It was immediately behind them, a patch of light whipping round a corner out of sight.

He said, 'I suppose this is country now. They none of them get farther than the club. We're quite alone now. We could lie in these fields till doomsday as far as *they* are concerned, though I suppose a ploughman . . . if they do plough here.' He raised his foot from the accelerator and let the car's speed gradually diminish. Somebody had left a wooden gate open into a field and he turned the car in; they jolted a long way down the field beside the hedge and came to a standstill. He turned out the headlamps and they sat in the tiny glow of the switchboard light. 'Peaceful,' he said uneasily; and they heard a screech owl hunting overhead and a small rustle in the hedge where something went into hiding. They belonged to the city; they hadn't a name for anything round them; the tiny buds breaking in the bushes were nameless. He nodded at a group of dark trees at the hedge ends. 'Oaks?'

'Elms?' she asked, and their mouths went together in a mutual ignorance. The touch excited her; she was ready for the most reckless act; but from his mouth, the dry spiritous lips, she gained a sense that he was less excited than he had hoped to be.

She said, to reassure herself, 'It's good to be here—miles away from anyone we know.'

'I dare say Mick's there. Down the road.'

'Does he know?'

'Nobody knows.'

She said, 'That's how I wanted it. How did you get this car?'

He grinned at her with unbalanced amusement. 'I saved from the ten shillings.'

'No but how? Did someone lend it you?'

'Yes,' he said. He suddenly pushed the door open and said, 'Let's take a walk.'

'We've never walked in the country before.' She took his arm, and she could feel the tense nerves responding to her touch. It was what she liked; she couldn't tell what he would do next. She said, 'My father calls you crazy. I like you crazy. What's all this stuff?' kicking at the ground.

'Clover,' he said, 'isn't it? I don't know.' It was like being in a foreign city where you can't understand the names on shops, the traffic signs: nothing to catch hold of, to hold you down to this and that, adrift together in a dark vacuum. 'Shouldn't you turn on the headlamps?' she said. 'It won't be so easy finding our way back. There's not much moon.' Already they seemed to have gone a long way from the car; she couldn't see it clearly any longer.

'We'll find our way,' he said. 'Somehow. Don't worry.' At the hedge end they came to the trees. He pulled a twig down and felt the sticky buds. 'What is it? Beech?'

'I don't know.'

He said, 'If it had been warmer, we could have slept out here. You'd think we might have had that much luck, tonight of all nights. But it's cold and it's going to rain.'

'Let's come in the summer,' but he didn't answer. Some other wind had blown, she could tell it, and already he had lost interest in her. There was something hard in his pocket; it hurt her side; she put her hand in. The metal chamber had absorbed all the cold there had been in the windy ride. She whispered fearfully,

'Why are you carrying that?' She had always before drawn a line round his recklessness. When her father had said he was crazy she had secretly and possessively smiled because she thought she knew the extent of his craziness. Now, while she waited for him to answer her, she could feel his craziness go on and on, out of her reach, out of her sight; she couldn't see where it ended; it had no end, she couldn't possess it any more than she could possess a darkness or a desert.

'Don't be scared,' he said. 'I didn't mean you to find that tonight.' He suddenly became more tender than he had ever been; he put his hand on her breast; it came from his fingers, a great soft meaningless flood of tenderness. He said, 'Don't you see? Life's hell. There's nothing we can do.' He spoke very gently, but she had never been more aware of his recklessness: he was open to every wind, but the wind now seemed to have set from the east: it blew like sleet through his words. 'I haven't a penny,' he said. 'We can't live on nothing. It's no good hoping that I'll get a job.' He repeated, 'There aren't any more jobs any more. And every year, you know, there's less chance, because there are more people younger than I am.'

'But why,' she said, 'have we come—?'

He became softly and tenderly lucid. 'We do love each other, don't we? We can't live without each other. It's no good hanging around, is it, waiting for our luck to change. We don't even get a fine night,' he said, feeling for rain with his hand. 'We can have a good time tonight—in the car—and then in the morning—'

'No, no,' she said. She tried to get away from him. 'I couldn't. It's horrible. I never said—'

'You wouldn't know anything,' he said gently and inexorably. Her words, she could realize now, had never made any real impression; he was swayed by them but no more than he was swayed by anything: now that the wind had set, it was like throwing scraps of paper towards the sky to speak at all, or to argue. He said, 'Of course we neither of us believe in God, but there may be a chance, and it's company, going together like that.' He added with pleasure, 'It's a gamble,' and she remembered more occasions than she could count when their last coppers had gone ringing down in fruit machines.

He pulled her closer and said with complete assurance, 'We love each other. It's the only way, you know. You can trust me.' He was like a skilled logician; he knew all the stages of the argument. She despaired of catching him out on any point but the premise: we love each other. *That* she doubted for the first time, faced by the mercilessness of his egotism. He repeated, 'It will be company.'

She said, 'There must be some way . . .'

'Why *must*?'

'Otherwise, people would be doing it all the time—everywhere!'

'They are,' he said triumphantly, as if it were more important for him to find his argument flawless than to find—well, a way, a way to go on living. 'You've only got to read the papers,' he said. He whispered gently, endearingly, as if he thought the very sound of the words tender enough to dispel all fear. 'They call it a suicide pact. It's happening all the time.'

'I couldn't. I haven't the nerve.'

'You needn't do anything,' he said. 'I'll do it all.'

His calmness horrified her. 'You mean—you'd kill me?'

He said, 'I love you enough for that, I promise it won't hurt you.' He might have been persuading her to play some trivial and uncongenial game. 'We shall be together always.' He added rationally, 'Of course, if there *is* an always,' and suddenly she saw his love as a mere flicker of gas flame playing on the marshy depth of his irresponsibility, but now she realized that it was without any limit at all; it closed over the head. She pleaded, 'There are things we can sell. That suitcase.'

She knew that he was watching her with amusement, that he had rehearsed all her arguments and had an answer; he was only pretending to take her seriously. 'We might get fifteen shillings,' he said. 'We could live a day on that—but we shouldn't have much fun.'

'The things inside it?'

'Ah, that's another gamble. They might be worth thirty shillings. Three days, that would give us—with economy.'

'We might get a job.'

'I've been trying for a good many years now.'

'Isn't there the dole?'

'I'm not an insured worker. I'm one of the ruling class.'

'Your people, they'd give us something.'

'But we've got our pride, haven't we?' he said with remorse-less conceit.

'The man who lent you the car?'

He said, 'You remember Cortez, the fellow who burnt his boats? I've burned mine. I've *got* to kill myself. You see, I stole that car. We'd be stopped in the next town. It's too late even to go back.' He laughed; he had reached the climax of his argument and there was nothing more to dispute about. She could tell that he was perfectly satisfied and perfectly happy. It infuriated her. '*You've* got to, maybe. But I haven't. Why should I kill myself? What right have you—?' She dragged herself away from him and felt against her back the rough massive trunk of the living tree.

'Oh,' he said in an irritated tone, 'of course if you like to go on without me.' She had admired his conceit; he had always carried his unemployment with a manner. Now you could no longer call it conceit: it was a complete lack of any values. 'You can go home,' he said, 'though I don't quite know how—I can't drive you back because I'm staying here. You'll be able to go to the hop tomorrow night. And there's a whist-drive, isn't there, in the church hall? My dear, I wish you joy of home.'

There was a savagery in his manner. He took security, peace, order in his teeth and worried them so that she couldn't help feeling a little pity for what they had joined in despising: a hammer tapped at her heart, driving in a nail here and a nail there. She tried to think of a bitter retort, for after all there was something to be said for the negative virtues of doing no injury, of simply going on, as her father was going on for another fifteen years. But the next moment she felt no anger. They had trapped each other. He had always wanted this: the dark field, the weapon in his pocket, the escape and the gamble; but she less honestly had wanted a little of both worlds: irresponsibility and a safe love, danger and a secure heart.

He said, 'I'm going now. Are you coming?'

'No,' she said. He hesitated; the recklessness for a moment wavered; a sense of something lost and bewildered came to her through the dark. She wanted to say: Don't be a fool. Leave the car where it is. Walk back with me, and we'll get a lift home, but she knew any thought of hers had occurred to him and been answered already: ten shillings a week, no job, getting older. Endurance was a virtue of one's fathers.

He suddenly began to walk fast down the hedge; he couldn't see where he was going; he stumbled on a root and she heard him swear. 'Damnation'—the little commonplace sound in the darkness overwhelmed her with pain and horror. She cried out, 'Fred. Fred. Don't do it,' and began to run in the opposite direction. She couldn't stop him and she wanted to be out of hearing. A twig broke under her foot like a shot, and the owl screamed across the ploughed field beyond the hedge. It was like a rehearsal with sound effects. But when the real shot came, it was quite different: a thud like a gloved hand striking a door and no cry at all. She didn't notice it at first and afterwards she thought that she had never been conscious of the exact moment when her lover ceased to exist.

She bruised herself against the car, running blindly; a blue-spotted Woolworth handkerchief lay on the seat in the light of the switchboard bulb. She nearly took it, but no, she thought, no one must know that I have been here. She turned out the light and picked her way as quietly as she could across the clover. She could begin to be sorry when she was safe. She wanted to close a door behind her, thrust a bolt down, hear the catch grip.

It wasn't ten minutes walk down the deserted lane to the roadhouse. Tipsy voices spoke a foreign language, though it was the language Fred had spoken. She could hear the clink of coins in fruit machines, the hiss of soda; she listened to these sounds like an enemy, planning her escape. They frightened her like something mindless: there was no appeal one could make to that egotism. It was simply a Want to be satisfied; it gaped at her like a mouth. A man was trying to wind up his car; the self-starter wouldn't work. He said, 'I'm a Bolshie. Of course I'm a Bolshie. I believe—'

A thin girl with red hair sat on the step and watched him. 'You're all wrong,' she said.

'I'm a Liberal Conservative.'

'You *can't* be a liberal Conservative.'

'Do you love me?'

'I love Joe.'

'You *can't* love Joe.'

'Let's go home, Mike.'

The man tried to wind up the car again, and she came up to them as if she'd come out of the club and said, 'Give me a lift?'

'Course. Delighted. Get in.'

'Won't the car go?'

'No.'

'Have you flooded—?'

'That's an idea.' He lifted the bonnet and she pressed the self-starter. It began to rain slowly and heavily and drenchingly, the kind of rain you always expect to fall on graves, and her thoughts went down the lane towards the field, the hedge, the trees—oak, beech, elm? She imagined the rain on his face, the pool collecting in each eye-socket and streaming down on either side the nose. But she could feel nothing but gladness because she had escaped from him.

'Where are you going?' she said.

'Devizes.'

'I thought you might be going to London.'

'Where do you want to go to?'

'Golding's Park.'

'Let's go to Golding's Park.'

The red-haired girl said, 'I am going in, Mike. It's raining.'

'Aren't you coming?'

'I'm going to find Joe.'

'All right.' He smashed his way out of the little car-park, bending his mudguard on a wooden post, scraping the paint of another car.

'That's the wrong way,' she said.

'We'll turn.' He backed the car into a ditch and out again. 'Was a good party,' he said. The rain came down harder; it blinded the windscreen and the electric wiper wouldn't work, but her companion didn't care. He drove straight on at forty miles an hour; it was an old car, it wouldn't do any more; the rain leaked through the hood. He said, 'Twis' that knob. Have a tune,' and when she turned it and the dance music came through, he said, 'That's Harry Roy. Know him anywhere,' driving into the thick wet night carrying the hot music with them. Presently he said, 'A friend of mine, one of the best, you'd know him, Peter Weatherall. You know him.'

'No.'

'You must know Peter. Haven't seen him about lately. Goes off on the drink for weeks. They sent out an SOS for Peter once in the middle of the dance music. "Missing from Home". We were in the car. We had a laugh about that.'

She said, 'Is that what people do—when people are missing?'

'Know this tune,' he said. 'This isn't Harry Roy. This is Alf Cohen.'

She said suddenly, 'You're Mike, aren't you? Wouldn't *you* lend—'

He sobered up. 'Stony broke,' he said. 'Comrades in misfortune. Try Peter. Why do you want to go to Golding's Park?'

'My home.'

'You mean you live there?'

'Yes.' She said, 'Be careful. There's a speed limit here.' He was perfectly obedient. He raised his foot and let the car crawl at fifteen miles an hour. The lamp standards marched unsteadily to meet them and lit his face: he was quite old, forty if a day, ten years older than Fred. He wore a striped tie and she could see his sleeve was frayed. He had more than ten shillings a week, but perhaps not so very much more. His hair was going thin.

'You can drop me here,' she said. He stopped the car and she got out and the rain went on. He followed her on to the road. 'Let me come in?' he asked. She shook her head; the rain wetted them through; behind her was the pillar-box, the Belisha beacon, the road through the housing estate. 'Hell of a life,' he said politely, holding her hand, while the rain drummed on the hood of the cheap car and ran down his face, across his collar and the school tie. But she felt no pity, no attraction, only a faint horror and repulsion. A kind of dim recklessness gleamed in his wet eye, as the hot music of Alf Cohen's band streamed from the car, a faded irresponsibility. 'Le's go back,' he said, 'le's go somewhere. Le's go for a ride in the country. Le's go to Maidenhead,' holding her hand limply.

She pulled it away, he didn't resist, and walked down the half-made road to No. 64. The crazy paving in the front garden seemed to hold her feet firmly up. She opened the door and heard through the dark and the rain a car grind into second gear and drone away—certainly not towards Maidenhead or Devizes or the country. Another wind must have blown.

Her father called down from the first landing: 'Who's there?'

'It's me,' she said. She explained, 'I had a feeling you'd left the door unbolted.'

'And had I?'

'No,' she said gently, 'it's bolted all right,' driving the bolt softly and firmly home. She waited till his door closed. She touched the radiator to warm her fingers—he had put it in himself, he had improved the property; in fifteen years, she thought, it will be ours. She was quite free from pain, listening to the rain on the roof; he had been over the whole roof that winter inch by inch, there was nowhere for the rain to enter. It was kept outside, drumming on the shabby hood, pitting the clover field. She stood by the door, feeling only the faint repulsion she always had for things weak and crippled, thinking, 'It isn't tragic at all,' and looking down with an emotion like tenderness at the flimsy bolt from a sixpenny store any man could have broken, but which a Man had put in, the head clerk of Bergson's.

1937

THE INNOCENT

It was a mistake to take Lola there. I knew it the moment we alighted from the train at the small country station. On an autumn evening one remembers more of childhood than at any other time of year, and her bright veneered face, the small bag which hardly pretended to contain our things for the night, simply didn't go with the old grain warehouses across the small canal, the few lights up the hill, the posters of an ancient film. But she said, 'Let's go into the country,' and Bishop's Hendron was, of course, the first name which came into my head. Nobody would know me there now, and it hadn't occurred to me that it would be I who remembered.

Even the old porter touched a chord. I said, 'There'll be a four-wheeler at the entrance,' and there was, though at first I didn't notice it, seeing the two taxis and thinking; 'The old place is coming on.' It was very dark, and the thin autumn mist, the smell of wet leaves and canal water were deeply familiar.

Lola said, 'But why did you choose this place? It's grim.' It was no use explaining to her why it wasn't grim to me, that that sand heap by the canal had always been there (when I was three I remember thinking it was what other people meant by the sea-side). I took the bag (I've said it was light; it was simply a forged passport of respectability) and said we'd walk. We came up over the little humpbacked bridge and passed the alms-houses. When I was five I saw a middle-aged man run into one to commit suicide; he carried a knife and all the neighbours pursued him up the stairs. She said, 'I never thought the country was like *this*.' They were ugly alms-houses, little grey stone boxes, but I knew them as I knew nothing else. It was like listening to music, all that walk.

But I had to say something to Lola. It wasn't her fault that she didn't belong here. We passed the school, the church, and came round into the old wide High Street and the sense of the first twelve years of life. If I hadn't come, I shouldn't have known that sense would be so strong, because those years hadn't been particularly happy or particularly miserable; they had been ordinary years, but now with the smell of wood fires, of the cold striking up from the dark damp paving stones, I thought I knew what it was that held me. It was the smell of innocence.

I said to Lola, 'It's a good inn, and there'll be nothing here, you'll see, to keep us up. We'll have dinner and drinks and go to bed.' But the worst of it was that I couldn't help wishing that I were alone. I hadn't been back all these years; I hadn't realized how well I remembered the place. Things I'd quite forgotten, like that sand heap, were coming back with an effect of pathos and nostalgia. I could have been very happy that night in a melancholy autumnal way, wandering about the little town, picking up clues to that time of life when, however miserable we are, we have expectations. It wouldn't be the same if I came back again, for then there would be the memories of Lola, and Lola meant just nothing at all. We had happened to pick each other up at a bar the day before and liked each other. Lola was all right, there was no one I would rather spend the night with, but she didn't fit in with *these* memories. We ought to have gone to Maidenhead. That's country too.

The inn was not quite where I remembered it. There was the Town Hall, but they had built a new cinema with a Moorish dome and a café, and there was a garage which hadn't existed in my time. I had forgotten too the turning to the left up a steep villaed hill.

'I don't believe that road was there in my day,' I said.

'Your day?' Lola asked.

'Didn't I tell you? I was born here.'

'You must get a kick out of bringing me here,' Lola said. 'I suppose you used to think of nights like this when you were a boy.'

'Yes,' I said, because it wasn't her fault. She was all right. I liked her scent. She used a good shade of lipstick. It was costing me a lot, a fiver for Lola and then all the bills and fares and drinks, but I'd have thought it money well spent anywhere else in the world.

I lingered at the bottom of that road. Something was stirring in the mind, but I don't think I should have remembered what, if a crowd of children hadn't come down the hill at that moment into the frosty lamplight, their voices sharp and shrill, their breath fuming as they passed under the lamps. They all carried linen bags, and some of the bags were embroidered with initials. They were in their best clothes and a little self-conscious. The small girls kept to themselves in a kind of compact beleaguered group, and one thought of hair ribbons and shining shoes and the sedate tinkle of a piano. It all came back to me: they had been to a dancing lesson, just as I used to go, to a small square house with a drive of rhododendrons half-way up the hill. More than ever I wished that Lola were not with me, less than ever did she fit, as I thought 'something's missing from the picture,' and a sense of pain glowed dully at the bottom of my brain.

We had several drinks at the bar, but there was half an hour before they would agree to serve dinner. I said to Lola, 'You don't want to drag round this town. If you don't mind, I'll just slip out for ten minutes and look at a place I used to know.' She didn't mind. There was a local man, perhaps a schoolmaster, at the bar simply longing to stand her a drink. I could see how he envied me, coming down with her like this from town just for a night.

I walked up the hill. The first houses were all new. I resented them. They hid such things as fields and gates I might have remembered. It was like a map which had got wet in the pocket and pieces had stuck together; when you opened it there were whole patches hidden. But half-way up, there the house really was, the drive; perhaps the same old lady was giving lessons. Children exaggerate age. She may not in those days have been more than thirty-five. I could hear the piano. She was following the same routine. Children under eight, 6–7 p.m. Children eight to thirteen, 7–8. I opened the gate and went in a little way. I was trying to remember.

I don't know what brought it back. I think it was simply the autumn, the cold, the wet frosting leaves, rather than the piano, which had played different tunes in those days. I remembered the small girl as well as one remembers anyone without a photograph to refer to. She was a year older than I was: she must have been just on the point of eight. I loved her with an intensity I have never felt since, I believe, for anyone. At least I have never made the mistake of laughing at children's love. It has a terrible inevitability of separation because there *can* be no satisfaction. Of course one invents tales of houses on fire, of war and forlorn charges which prove one's courage in her eyes, but never of marriage. One knows without being told that that can't happen, but the knowledge doesn't mean that one suffers less. I remembered all the games of blind-man's buff at birthday parties when I vainly hoped to catch her, so that I might have the excuse to touch and hold her, but I never caught her; she always kept out of my way.

But once a week for two winters I had my chance: I danced with her. That made it worse (it was cutting off our only contact) when she told me during one of the last lessons of the winter that next year she would join the older class. She liked me too, I knew it, but we had no way of expressing it. I used to go to her birthday parties and she would come to mine, but we never even ran home together after the dancing class. It would have seemed odd; I don't think it occurred to us. I had to join my own boisterous teasing male companions, and she the besieged, the hustled, the shrilly indignant sex on the way down the hill.

I shivered there in the mist and turned my coat collar up. The piano was playing a dance from an old C. B. Cochran revue. It seemed a long journey to have taken to find only Lola at the end of it. There *is* something about innocence one is never quite resigned to lose. Now when I am unhappy about a girl, I can simply go and buy another one. Then the best I could think of was to write some passionate message and slip it into a hole (it was extraordinary how I began to remember everything) in the woodwork of the gate. I had once told her about the hole, and sooner or later I was sure she would put in her fingers and find the message. I wondered what the message could have been. One wasn't able to express much, I thought, in those days; but because the expression was inadequate, it didn't mean that the pain was shallower than what one sometimes suffered now. I remembered how for days I had felt in the hole and always found the message there. Then the dancing lessons stopped. Probably by the next winter I had forgotten.

As I went out of the gate I looked to see if the hole existed. It was there. I put in my finger, and, in its safe shelter from the seasons and the years, the scrap of paper rested yet. I pulled it out and opened it. Then I struck a match, a tiny glow of heat in the mist and dark. It was a shock to see by its diminutive flame a picture of crude obscenity. There could be no mistake; there were my initials below the childish inaccurate sketch of a man and woman. But it woke fewer memories than the fume of breath, the linen bags, a damp leaf, or the pile of sand. I didn't recognize it; it might have been drawn by a dirty-minded stranger on a lavatory wall. All I could remember was the purity, the intensity, the pain of that passion.

I felt at first as if I had been betrayed. 'After all,' I told myself, 'Lola's not so much out of place here.' But later that night, when Lola turned away from me and fell asleep, I began to realize the deep innocence of that drawing. I had believed I was drawing something with a meaning and beautiful; it was only now after thirty years of life that the picture seemed obscene.

1937

THE BASEMENT ROOM

I

When the front door had shut the two of them out and the butler Baines had turned back into the dark and heavy hall, Philip began to live. He stood in front of the nursery door, listening until he heard the engine of the taxi die out along the street. His parents were safely gone for a fortnight's holiday; he was 'between nurses', one dismissed and the other not arrived; he was alone in the great Belgravia house with Baines and Mrs Baines.

He could go anywhere, even through the green baize door to the pantry or down the stairs to the basement living-room. He felt a happy stranger in his home because he could go into any room and all the rooms were empty.

You could only guess who had once occupied them: the rack of pipes in the smoking-room beside the elephant tusks, the carved wood tobacco jar; in the bedroom the pink hangings and the pale perfumes and three-quarter finished jars of cream which Mrs Baines had not yet cleared away for her own use; the high glaze on the never-opened piano in the drawing-room, the china clock, the silly little tables and the silver. But here Mrs Baines was already busy, pulling down the curtains, covering the chairs in dust-sheets.

'Be off out of here, Master Philip,' and she looked at him with her peevish eyes, while she moved round, getting everything in order, meticulous and loveless and doing her duty.

Philip Lane went downstairs and pushed at the baize door; he looked into the pantry, but Baines was not there, then he set foot for the first time on the stairs to the basement. Again he had the sense: this is life. All his seven nursery years vibrated with the strange, the new experience. His crowded brain was like a city which feels the earth tremble at a distant earthquake shock. He was apprehensive, but he was happier than he had ever been. Everything was more important than before.

Baines was reading a newspaper in his shirt-sleeves. He said, 'Come in, Phil, and make yourself at home. Wait a moment and I'll do the honours,' and going to a white cleaned cupboard he brought out a bottle of ginger-beer and half a Dundee cake. 'Half past eleven in the morning,' Baines said. 'It's opening time, my boy,' and he cut the cake and poured out the ginger-beer. He was more genial than Philip had ever known him, more at his ease, a man in his own home.

'Shall I call Mrs Baines?' Philip asked, and he was glad when Baines said no. She was busy. She liked to be busy, so why interfere with her pleasure?

'A spot of drink at half past eleven,' Baines said, pouring himself out a glass of ginger-beer, 'gives an appetite for chop and does no man any harm.'

'A chop?' Philip asked.

'Old Coasters,' Baines said, 'they call all food chop.'

'But it's not a chop?'

'Well, it might be, you know, if cooked with palm oil. And then some paw-paw to follow.'

Philip looked out of the basement window at the dry stone yard, the ash-can and the legs going up and down beyond the railings.

'Was it hot there?'

'Ah, you never felt such heat. Not a nice heat, mind, like you get in the park on a day like this. Wet,' Baines said, 'corruption.' He cut himself a slice of cake. 'Smelling of rot,' Baines said, rolling his eyes round the small basement room, from clean cupboard to clean cupboard, the sense of bareness, of nowhere to hide a man's secrets. With an air of regret for something lost he took a long draught of ginger-beer.

'Why did father live out there?'

'It was his job,' Baines said, 'same as this is mine now. And it was mine then too. It was a man's job. You wouldn't believe it now, but I've had forty niggers under me, doing what I told them to.'

'Why did you leave?'

'I married Mrs Baines.'

Philip took the slice of Dundee cake in his hand and munched it round the room. He felt very old, independent and judicial; he was aware that Baines was talking to him as man to man. He never called him Master Philip as Mrs Baines did, who was servile when she was not authoritative.

Baines had seen the world; he had seen beyond the railings. He sat there over his ginger pop with the resigned dignity of an exile; Baines didn't complain; he had chosen his fate, and if his fate was Mrs Baines he had only himself to blame.

But today—the house was almost empty and Mrs Baines was upstairs and there was nothing to do—he allowed himself a little acidity.

'I'd go back tomorrow if I had the chance.'

'Did you ever shoot a nigger?'

'I never had any call to shoot,' Baines said. 'Of course I carried a gun. But you didn't need to treat them bad. That just made them stupid. Why,' Baines said, bowing his thin grey hair with embarrassment over the ginger pop, 'I loved some of those damned niggers. I couldn't help loving them. There they'd be laughing, holding hands; they liked to touch each other; it made them feel fine to know the other fellow was around. It didn't mean anything we could understand; two of them would go about all day without loosing hold, grown men; but it wasn't love; it didn't mean anything we could understand.'

'Eating between meals,' Mrs Baines said. 'What would your mother say, Master Philip?'

She came down the steep stairs to the basement, her hands full of pots of cream and salve, tubes of grease and paste. 'You oughtn't to encourage him, Baines,' she said, sitting down in a wicker armchair and screwing up her small ill-humoured eyes at the Coty lipstick, Pond's cream, the Leichner rouge and Cyclax powder and Elizabeth Arden astringent.

She threw them one by one into the wastepaper basket. She

saved only the cold cream. 'Tell the boy stories,' she said. 'Go along to the nursery, Master Philip, while I get lunch.'

Philip climbed the stairs to the baize door. He heard Mrs Baines's voice like the voice in a nightmare when the small Price light has guttered in the saucer and the curtains move; it was sharp and shrill and full of malice, louder than people ought to speak, exposed.

'Sick to death of your ways, Baines, spoiling the boy. Time you did some work about the house,' but he couldn't hear what Baines said in reply. He pushed open the baize door, came up like a small earth animal in his grey flannel shorts into a wash of sunlight on a parquet floor, the gleam of mirrors dusted and polished and beautified by Mrs Baines.

Something broke downstairs, and Philip sadly mounted the stairs to the nursery. He pitied Baines; it occurred to him how happily they could live together in the empty house if Mrs Baines were called away. He didn't want to play with his Meccano sets; he wouldn't take out his train or his soldiers; he sat at the table with his chin on his hands: this is life; and suddenly he felt responsible for Baines, as if he were the master of the house and Baines an ageing servant who deserved to be cared for. There was not much one could do; he decided at least to be good.

He was not surprised when Mrs Baines was agreeable at lunch; he was used to her changes. Now it was 'another helping of meat, Master Philip', or 'Master Philip, a little more of this nice pudding'. It was a pudding he liked, Queen's pudding with a perfect meringue, but he wouldn't eat a second helping lest she might count that a victory. She was the kind of woman who thought that any injustice could be counterbalanced by something good to eat.

She was sour, but she liked making sweet things; one never had to complain of a lack of jam or plums; she ate well herself and added soft sugar to the meringue and the strawberry jam. The half-light through the basement window set the motes moving above her pale hair like dust as she sifted the sugar, and Baines crouched over his plate saying nothing.

Again Philip felt responsibility. Baines had looked forward to this, and Baines was disappointed: everything was being spoilt.

The sensation of disappointment was one which Philip could share; he could understand better than anyone this grief, something hoped for not happening, something promised not fulfilled, something exciting which turned dull. 'Baines,' he said, 'will you take me for a walk this afternoon?'

'No,' Mrs Baines said, 'no. That he won't. Not with all the silver to clean.'

'There's a fortnight to do it in,' Baines said.

'Work first, pleasure afterwards.'

Mrs Baines helped herself to some more meringue.

Baines put down his spoon and fork and pushed his plate away. 'Blast,' he said.

'Temper,' Mrs Baines said, 'temper. Don't you go breaking any more things, Baines, and I won't have you swearing in front of the boy. Master Philip, if you've finished you can get down.'

She skinned the rest of the meringue off the pudding.

'I want to go for a walk,' Philip said.

'You'll go and have a rest.'

'I want to go for a walk.'

'Master Philip,' Mrs Baines said. She got up from the table, leaving her meringue unfinished, and came towards him, thin, menacing, dusty in the basement room. 'Master Philip, you just do as you're told.' She took him by the arm and squeezed it; she watched him with a joyless passionate glitter and above her head the feet of typists trudged back to the Victoria offices after the lunch interval.

'Why shouldn't I go for a walk?'

But he weakened; he was scared and ashamed of being scared. This was life; a strange passion he couldn't understand moving in the basement room. He saw a small pile of broken glass swept into a corner by the wastepaper basket. He looked at Baines for help and only intercepted hate; the sad hopeless hate of something behind bars.

'Why shouldn't I?' he repeated.

'Master Philip,' Mrs Baines said, 'you've got to do as you're told. You mustn't think just because your father's away there's nobody here to—'

'You wouldn't dare,' Philip cried, and was startled by Baines's low interjection:

'There's nothing she wouldn't dare.'

'I hate you,' Philip said to Mrs Baines. He pulled away from her and ran to the door, but she was there before him; she was old, but she was quick.

'Master Philip,' she said, 'you'll say you're sorry.' She stood in front of the door quivering with excitement. 'What would your father do if he heard you say that?'

She put a hand out to seize him, dry and white with constant soda, the nails cut to the quick, but he backed away and put the table between them, and suddenly to his surprise she smiled; she became again as servile as she had been arrogant. 'Get along with you, Master Philip,' she said with glee, 'I see I'm going to have my hands full till your father and mother come back.'

She left the door unguarded and when he passed her she slapped him playfully. 'I've got too much to do today to trouble about you. I haven't covered half the chairs,' and suddenly even the upper part of the house became unbearable to him as he thought of Mrs Baines moving around shrouding the sofas, laying out the dust-sheets.

So he wouldn't go upstairs to get his cap but walked straight out across the shining hall into the street, and again, as he looked this way and looked that way, it was life he was in the middle of.

2

The pink sugar cakes in the window on a paper doily, the ham, the slab of mauve sausage, the wasps driving like small torpedoes across the pane caught Philip's attention. His feet were tired by pavements; he had been afraid to cross the road, had simply walked first in one direction, then in the other. He was nearly home now; the square was at the end of the street; this was a shabby outpost of Pimlico, and he smudged the pane with his nose looking for sweets, and saw between the cake and ham a different Baines. He hardly recognized the bulbous eyes, the bald forehead. This was a happy, bold and buccaneering Baines, even though it was, when you looked closer, a desperate Baines.

Philip had never seen the girl, but he remembered Baines had a niece. She was thin and drawn, and she wore a white mackintosh; she meant nothing to Philip; she belonged to a world about which he knew nothing at all. He couldn't make up stories about her, as he could make them up about withered Sir Hubert Reed, the Permanent Secretary, about Mrs Wince-Dudley who came up once a year from Penstanley in Suffolk with a green umbrella and an enormous black handbag, as he could make them up about the upper servants in all the houses where he went to tea and games. She just didn't belong. He thought of mermaids and Undine, but she didn't belong there either, nor to the adventures of Emil, nor to the Bastables. She sat there looking at an iced pink cake in the detachment and mystery of the completely disinherited, looking at the half-used pots of powder which Baines had set out on the marble-topped table between them.

Baines was urging, hoping, entreating, commanding, and the girl looked at the tea and the china pots and cried. Baines passed his handkerchief across the table, but she wouldn't wipe her eyes; she screwed it in her palm and let the tears run down, wouldn't do anything, wouldn't speak, would only put up a silent resistance to what she dreaded and wanted and refused to listen to at any price. The two brains battled over the tea-cups loving each other, and there came to Philip outside, beyond the ham and wasps and dusty Pimlico pane, a confused indication of the struggle.

He was inquisitive and he didn't understand and he wanted to know. He went and stood in the doorway to see better, he was less sheltered than he had ever been; other people's lives for the first time touched and pressed and moulded. He would never escape that scene. In a week he had forgotten it, but it conditioned his career, the long austerity of his life; when he was dying, rich and alone, it was said that he asked: 'Who is she?'

Baines had won; he was cocky and the girl was happy. She wiped her face, she opened a pot of powder, and their fingers touched across the table. It occurred to Philip that it might be amusing to imitate Mrs Baines's voice and to call 'Baines' to him from the door.

His voice shrivelled them; you couldn't describe it in any other way, it made them smaller, they weren't together any more. Baines was the first to recover and trace the voice, but that didn't make things as they were. The sawdust was spilled out of the afternoon; nothing you did could mend it, and Philip was scared. 'I didn't mean . . .' He wanted to say that he loved Baines, that he had only wanted to laugh at Mrs Baines. But he had discovered you couldn't laugh at Mrs Baines. She wasn't Sir Hubert Reed, who used steel nibs and carried a pen-wiper in his pocket; she wasn't Mrs Wince-Dudley; she was darkness when the night-light went out in a draught; she was the frozen blocks of earth he had seen one winter in a graveyard when someone said, 'They need an electric drill'; she was the flowers gone bad and smelling in the little closet room at Penstanley. There was nothing to laugh about. You had to endure her when she was there and forget about her quickly when she was away, suppress the thought of her, ram it down deep.

Baines said, 'It's only Phil,' beckoned him in and gave him the pink iced cake the girl hadn't eaten, but the afternoon was broken, the cake was like dry bread in the throat. The girl left them at once: she even forgot to take the powder. Like a blunt icicle in her white mackintosh she stood in the doorway with her back to them, then melted into the afternoon.

'Who is she?' Philip asked. 'Is she your niece?'

'Oh, yes,' Baines said, 'that's who she is; she's my niece,' and poured the last drops of water on to the coarse black leaves in the teapot.

'May as well have another cup,' Baines said.

'The cup that cheers,' he said hopelessly, watching the bitter black fluid drain out of the spout.

'Have a glass of ginger pop, Phil?'

'I'm sorry. I'm sorry, Baines.'

'It's not your fault, Phil. Why, I could really believe it wasn't you at all, but her. She creeps in everywhere.' He fished two leaves out of his cup and laid them on the back of his hand, a thin soft flake and a hard stalk. He beat them with his hand: 'Today,' and the stalk detached itself, 'tomorrow, Wednesday, Thursday, Friday, Saturday, Sunday,' but the flake wouldn't come, stayed where it was, drying under his blows, with a resistance you wouldn't believe it to possess. 'The tough one wins,' Baines said.

He got up and paid the bill and out they went into the street. Baines said, 'I don't ask you to say what isn't true. But you needn't actually *tell* Mrs Baines you met us here.'

'Of course not,' Philip said, and catching something of Sir Hubert Reed's manner, 'I understand, Baines.' But he didn't understand a thing; he was caught up in other people's darkness.

'It was stupid,' Baines said. 'So near home, but I hadn't time to think, you see. I'd got to see her.'

'I haven't time to spare,' Baines said. 'I'm not young. I've got to see that she's all right.'

'Of course you have, Baines.'

'Mrs Baines will get it out of you if she can.'

'You can trust me, Baines,' Philip said in a dry important Reed voice; and then, 'Look out. She's at the window watching.' And there indeed she was, looking up at them, between the lace curtains, from the basement room, speculating. 'Need we go in, Baines?' Philip asked, cold lying heavy on his stomach like too much pudding; he clutched Baines's arm.

'Careful,' Baines said softly, 'careful.'

'But need we go in, Baines? It's early. Take me for a walk in the park.'

'Better not.'

'But I'm frightened, Baines.'

'You haven't any cause,' Baines said. 'Nothing's going to hurt you. You just run along upstairs to the nursery. I'll go down by the area and talk to Mrs Baines.' But he stood hesitating at the top of the stone steps pretending not to see her, where she watched between the curtains. 'In at the front door, Phil, and up the stairs.'

Philip didn't linger in the hall; he ran, slithering on the parquet Mrs Baines had polished, to the stairs. Through the drawing-room doorway on the first floor he saw the draped chairs; even the china clock on the mantel was covered like a canary's cage. As he passed, it chimed the hour, muffled and secret under the duster. On the nursery table he found his supper laid out: a glass of milk and a piece of bread and butter, a sweet biscuit, and a little cold Queen's pudding without the meringue. He had no appetite; he strained his ears for Mrs Baines's coming, for the sound of voices, but the basement held its secrets; the green baize door shut off that world. He drank the milk and ate the biscuit, but he didn't touch the rest, and presently he could hear the soft precise footfalls of Mrs Baines on the stairs: she was a good servant, she walked softly; she was a determined woman, she walked precisely.

But she wasn't angry when she came in; she was ingratiating as she opened the night nursery door—'Did you have a good walk, Master Philip?'—pulled down the blinds, laid out his pyjamas, came back to clear his supper. 'I'm glad Baines found you. Your mother wouldn't have liked your being out alone.' She examined the tray. 'Not much appetite, have you, Master Philip? Why don't you try a little of this nice pudding? I'll bring you up some more jam for it.'

'No, no, thank you, Mrs Baines,' Philip said.

'You ought to eat more,' Mrs Baines said. She sniffed round the room like a dog. 'You didn't take any pots out of the wastepaper basket in the kitchen, did you, Master Philip?'

'No,' Philip said.

'Of course you wouldn't. I just wanted to make sure.' She patted his shoulder and her fingers flashed to his lapel; she picked off a tiny crumb of pink sugar. 'Oh, Master Philip,' she said, 'that's why you haven't any appetite. You've been buying sweet cakes. That's not what your pocket money's for.'

'But I didn't,' Philip said, 'I didn't.'

She tasted the sugar with the tip of her tongue.

'Don't tell lies to me, Master Philip. I won't stand for it any more than your father would.'

'I didn't, I didn't,' Philip said. 'They gave it me. I mean Baines,' but she had pounced on the word 'they'. She had got what she wanted; there was no doubt about that, even when you didn't know what it was she wanted. Philip was angry and miserable and disappointed because he hadn't kept Baines's secret. Baines oughtn't to have trusted him; grown-up people should keep their own secrets, and yet here was Mrs Baines immediately entrusting him with another.

'Let me tickle your palm and see if you can keep a secret.' But he put his hand behind him; he wouldn't be touched. 'It's a secret between us, Master Philip, that I know all about them. I suppose she was having tea with him,' she speculated.

'Why shouldn't she?' he asked, the responsibility for Baines weighing on his spirit, the idea that he had got to keep her secret when he hadn't kept Baines's making him miserable with the unfairness of life. 'She was nice.'

'She was nice, was she?' Mrs Baines said in a bitter voice he wasn't used to.

'And she's his niece.'

'So that's what he said,' Mrs Baines struck softly back at him like the clock under the duster. She tried to be jocular. 'The old scoundrel. Don't you tell him I know, Master Philip.' She stood very still between the table and the door, thinking very hard, planning something. 'Promise you won't tell. I'll give you that Meccano set, Master Philip . . .'

He turned his back on her; he wouldn't promise, but he wouldn't tell. He would have nothing to do with their secrets, the responsibilities they were determined to lay on him. He was only anxious to forget. He had received already a larger dose of life than he had bargained for, and he was scared. 'A 2A Meccano set, Master Philip.' He never opened his Meccano set again, never built anything, never created anything, died the old dilettante, sixty years later with nothing to show rather than preserve the memory of Mrs Baines's malicious voice saying good night, her soft determined footfalls on the stairs to the basement, going down, going down.

3

The sun poured in between the curtains and Baines was beating a tattoo on the water-can. 'Glory, glory,' Baines said. He sat down on the end of the bed and said, 'I beg to announce that Mrs Baines has been called away. Her mother's dying. She won't be back till tomorrow.'

'Why did you wake me up so early?' Philip complained. He watched Baines with uneasiness; he wasn't going to be drawn in; he'd learnt his lesson. It wasn't right for a man of Baines's age to be so merry. It made a grown person human in the same way that you were human. For if a grown-up could behave so childishly, you were liable to find yourself in their world. It was enough that it came at you in dreams: the witch at the corner, the man with a knife. So 'It's very early,' he whined, even though he loved Baines, even though he couldn't help being glad that Baines was happy. He was divided by the fear and the attraction of life.

'I want to make this a long day,' Baines said. 'This is the best time.' He pulled the curtains back. 'It's a bit misty. The cat's been out all night. There she is, sniffing round the area. They haven't taken in any milk at 59. Emma's shaking out the mats at 63.' He said, 'This was what I used to think about on the Coast: somebody shaking mats and the cat coming home. I can see it today,' Baines said, 'just as if I was still in Africa. Most days you don't notice what you've got. It's a good life if you don't weaken.' He put a penny on the washstand. 'When you've dressed, Phil, run and get a *Mail* from the barrow at the corner. I'll be cooking the sausages.'

'Sausages?'

'Sausages,' Baines said. 'We're going to celebrate today.' He celebrated at breakfast, restless, cracking jokes, unaccountably merry and nervous. It was going to be a long, long day, he kept on coming back to that: for years he had waited for a long day, he had sweated in the damp Coast heat, changed shirts, gone down with fever, lain between the blankets and sweated, all in the hope of this long day, that cat sniffing round the area, a bit of mist, the mats beaten at 63. He propped the *Mail* in front of the coffee-pot and read pieces aloud. He said, 'Cora Down's been married for the fourth time.' He was amused, but it wasn't his idea of a long day. His long day was the Park, watching the riders in the Row, seeing Sir Arthur Stillwater pass beyond the rails ('He dined with us once in Bo; up from Freetown; he was governor there'), lunch at the Corner House for Philip's sake (he'd have preferred himself a glass of stout and some oysters at the York bar), the Zoo, the long bus ride home in the last summer light: the leaves in the Green Park were beginning to turn and the motors nuzzled out of Berkeley Street with the low sun gently glowing on their windscreens. Baines envied no one, not Cora Down, or Sir Arthur Stillwater, or Lord Sandale, who came out on to the steps of the Army and Navy and then went back again—he hadn't anything to do and might as well look at another paper. 'I said don't let me see you touch that black again.' Baines had led a man's life; everyone on top of the bus pricked his ears when he told Philip all about it.

'Would you have shot him?' Philip asked, and Baines put his head back and tilted his dark respectable manservant's hat to a better angle as the bus swerved round the Artillery Memorial.

'I wouldn't have thought twice about it. I'd have shot to kill,' he boasted, and the bowed figure went by, the steel helmet, the heavy cloak, the down-turned rifle and the folded hands.

'Have you got the revolver?'

'Of course I've got it,' Baines said. 'Don't I need it with all the burglaries there've been?' This was the Baines whom Philip loved: not Baines singing and carefree, but Baines responsible, Baines behind barriers, living his man's life.

All the buses streamed out from Victoria like a convoy of aeroplanes to bring Baines home with honour. 'Forty blacks under me,' and there waiting near the area steps was the proper reward, love at lighting-up time.

'It's your niece,' Philip said, recognizing the white mackintosh, but not the happy sleepy face. She frightened him like an unlucky number; he nearly told Baines what Mrs Baines had said; but he didn't want to bother, he wanted to leave things alone.

'Why, so it is,' Baines said. 'I shouldn't wonder if she was going to have a bit of supper with us.' But he said, they'd play a game, pretend they didn't know her, slip down the area steps, 'and here,' Baines said, 'we are,' lay the table, put out the cold sausages, a bottle of beer, a bottle of ginger pop, a flagon of harvest burgundy. 'Everyone his own drink,' Baines said. 'Run upstairs, Phil, and see if there's been a post.'

Philip didn't like the empty house at dusk before the lights went on. He hurried. He wanted to be back with Baines. The hall lay there in quiet and shadow prepared to show him something he didn't want to see. Some letters rustled down and someone knocked. 'Open in the name of the Republic.' The tumbrils rolled, the head bobbed in the bloody basket. Knock, knock, and the postman's footsteps going away. Philip gathered the letters. The slit in the door was like the grating in a jeweller's window. He remembered the policeman he had seen peer through. He had said to his nurse, 'What's he doing?' and when she said, 'He's seeing if everything's all right,' his brain immediately filled with images of all that might be wrong. He ran to the baize door and the stairs. The girl was already there and Baines was kissing her. She leant breathless against the dresser.

'Here's Emmy, Phil.'

'There's a letter for you, Baines.'

'Emmy,' Baines said, 'it's from her.' But he wouldn't open it. 'You bet she's coming back.'

'We'll have supper, anyway,' Emmy said. 'She can't harm that.'

'You don't know her,' Baines said. 'Nothing's safe. Damn it,' he said, 'I was a man once,' and he opened the letter.

'Can I start?' Philip asked, but Baines didn't hear; he presented in his stillness an example of the importance grown-up people attached to the written word: you had to write your thanks, not wait and speak them, as if letters couldn't lie. But Philip knew better than that, sprawling his thanks across a page to Aunt Alice who had given him a teddy bear he was too old for. Letters could lie all right, but they made the lie permanent. They lay as evidence against you: they made you meaner than the spoken word.

'She's not coming back till tomorrow night,' Baines said. He opened the bottles, he pulled up the chairs, he kissed Emmy again against the dresser.

'You oughtn't to,' Emmy said, 'with the boy here.'

'He's got to learn,' Baines said, 'like the rest of us,' and he helped Philip to three sausages. He only took one himself; he said he wasn't hungry, but when Emmy said she wasn't hungry either he stood over her and made her eat. He was timid and rough with her and made her drink the harvest burgundy because he said she needed building up; he wouldn't take no for an answer, but when he touched her his hands were light and clumsy too, as if he was afraid to damage something delicate and didn't know how to handle anything so light.

'This is better than milk and biscuits, eh?'

'Yes,' Philip said, but he was scared, scared for Baines as much as for himself. He couldn't help wondering at every bite, at every draught of the ginger pop, what Mrs Baines would say if she ever learnt of this meal; he couldn't imagine it, there was a depth of bitterness and rage in Mrs Baines you couldn't sound. He said, 'She won't be coming back tonight?' but you could tell by the way they immediately understood him that she wasn't really away at all; she was there in the basement with them, driving them to longer drinks and louder talk, biding her time for the right cutting word. Baines wasn't really happy; he was only watching happiness from close to instead of from far away.

'No,' he said, 'she'll not be back till late tomorrow.' He couldn't keep his eyes off happiness. He'd played around as much as other men; he kept on reverting to the Coast as if to excuse himself for his innocence. He wouldn't have been so innocent if he'd lived his life in London, so innocent when it came to tenderness. 'If it was you, Emmy,' he said, looking at the white dresser, the scrubbed chairs, 'this'd be like a home.' Already the room was not quite so harsh; there was a little dust in corners, the silver needed a final polish, the morning's paper lay untidily on a chair. 'You'd better go to bed, Phil; it's been a long day.'

They didn't leave him to find his own way up through the dark shrouded house; they went with him, turning on lights, touching each other's fingers on the switches. Floor after floor they drove the night back. They spoke softly among the covered chairs. They watched him undress, they didn't make him wash or clean his teeth, they saw him into bed and lit his night-light and left his door ajar. He could hear their voices on the stairs, friendly like the guests he heard at dinner-parties when they moved down the hall, saying good night. They belonged; wherever they were they made a home. He heard a door open and a clock strike, he heard their voices for a long while, so that he felt they were not far away and he was safe. The voices didn't dwindle, they simply went out, and he could be sure that they were still somewhere not far from him, silent together in one of the many empty rooms, growing sleepy together as he grew sleepy after the long day.

He just had time to sigh faintly with satisfaction, because this too perhaps had been life, before he slept and the inevitable terrors of sleep came round him: a man with a tricolour hat beat at the door on His Majesty's service, a bleeding head lay on the kitchen table in a basket, and the Siberian wolves crept closer. He was bound hand and foot and couldn't move; they leapt round him breathing heavily; he opened his eyes and Mrs Baines was there, her grey untidy hair in threads over his face, her black hat askew. A loose hairpin fell on the pillow and one musty thread brushed his mouth. 'Where are they?' she whispered. 'Where are they?'

4

Philip watched her in terror. Mrs Baines was out of breath as if she had been searching all the empty rooms, looking under loose covers.

With her untidy grey hair and her black dress buttoned to her throat, her gloves of black cotton, she was so like the witches of his dreams that he didn't dare to speak. There was a stale smell in her breath.

'She's here,' Mrs Baines said, 'you can't deny she's here.' Her face was simultaneously marked with cruelty and misery; she wanted to 'do things' to people, but she suffered all the time. It would have done her good to scream, but she daren't do that: it would warn them. She came ingratiatingly back to the bed where Philip lay rigid on his back and whispered, 'I haven't forgotten the Meccano set. You shall have it tomorrow, Master Philip. We've got secrets together, haven't we? Just tell me where they are.'

He couldn't speak. Fear held him as firmly as any nightmare. She said, 'Tell Mrs Baines, Master Philip. You love your Mrs

Baines, don't you?' That was too much; he couldn't speak, but he could move his mouth in terrified denial, wince away from her dusty image.

She whispered, coming closer to him, 'Such deceit. I'll tell your father. I'll settle with you myself when I've found them. You'll smart; I'll see you smart.' Then immediately she was still, listening. A board had creaked on the floor below, and a moment later, while she stooped listening above his bed, there came the whispers of two people who were happy and sleepy together after a long day. The night-light stood beside the mirror and Mrs Baines could see there her own reflection, misery and cruelty wavering in the glass, age and dust and nothing to hope for. She sobbed without tears, a dry, breathless sound, but her cruelty was a kind of pride which kept her going; it was her best quality, she would have been merely pitiable without it. She went out of the door on tiptoe, feeling her way across the landing, going so softly down the stairs that no one behind a shut door could hear her. Then there was complete silence again; Philip could move; he raised his knees; he sat up in bed; he wanted to die. It wasn't fair, the walls were down again between his world and theirs, but this time it was something worse than merriment that the grown people made him share; a passion moved in the house he recognized but could not understand.

It wasn't fair, but he owed Baines everything: the Zoo, the ginger pop, the bus ride home. Even the supper called to his loyalty. But he was frightened; he was touching something he touched in dreams; the bleeding head, the wolves, the knock, knock, knock. Life fell on him with savagery, and you couldn't blame him if he never faced it again in sixty years. He got out of bed. Carefully from habit he put on his bedroom slippers and tiptoed to the door: it wasn't quite dark on the landing below because the curtains had been taken down for the cleaners and the light from the street washed in through the tall windows. Mrs Baines had her hand on the glass door-knob; she was very carefully turning it; he screamed: 'Baines, Baines.'

Mrs Baines turned and saw him cowering in his pyjamas by the banisters; he was helpless, more helpless even than Baines, and cruelty grew at the sight of him and drove her up the stairs.

The nightmare was on him again and he couldn't move; he hadn't any more courage left, he couldn't even scream.

But the first cry brought Baines out of the best spare bedroom and he moved quicker than Mrs Baines. She hadn't reached the top of the stairs before he'd caught her round the waist. She drove her black cotton gloves at his face and he bit her hand. He hadn't time to think, he fought her like a stranger, but she fought back with knowledgeable hate. She was going to teach them all and it didn't really matter whom she began with; they had all deceived her; but the old image in the glass was by her side, telling her she must be dignified, she wasn't young enough to yield her dignity; she could beat his face, but she mustn't bite; she could push, but she mustn't kick.

Age and dust and nothing to hope for were her handicaps. She went over the banisters in a flurry of black clothes and fell into the hall; she lay before the front door like a sack of coals which should have gone down the area into the basement. Philip saw; Emmy saw; she sat down suddenly in the doorway of the best spare bedroom with her eyes open as if she were too tired to stand any longer. Baines went slowly down into the hall.

It wasn't hard for Philip to escape; they'd forgotten him completely. He went down the back, the servants' stairs, because Mrs Baines was in the hall. He didn't understand what she was doing lying there; like the pictures in a book no one had read to him, the things he didn't understand terrified him. The whole house had been turned over to the grown-up world; he wasn't safe in the night nursery; their passions had flooded in. The only thing he could do was to get away, by the back stairs, and up through the area, and never come back. He didn't think of the cold, of the need for food and sleep; for an hour it would seem quite possible to escape from people for ever.

He was wearing pyjamas and bedroom slippers when he came up into the square, but there was no one to see him. It was that hour of the evening in a residential district when everyone is at the theatre or at home. He climbed over the iron railings into the little garden: the plane-trees spread their large pale palms between him and the sky. It might have been an illimitable forest into which he had escaped. He crouched behind a trunk and the wolves retreated; it seemed to him between the little iron seat and the tree-trunk that no one would ever find him again. A kind of embittered happiness and self-pity made him cry; he was lost; there wouldn't be any more secrets to keep; he surrendered responsibility once and for all. Let grown-up people keep to their world and he would keep to his, safe in the small garden between the plane-trees.

Presently the door of 48 opened and Baines looked this way and that; then he signalled with his hand and Emmy came; it was as if they were only just in time for a train, they hadn't a chance of saying good-bye. She went quickly by like a face at a window swept past the platform, pale and unhappy and not wanting to go. Baines went in again and shut the door; the light was lit in the basement, and a policeman walked round the square, looking into the areas. You could tell how many families were at home by the lights behind the first-floor curtains.

Philip explored the garden: it didn't take long: a twenty-yard square of bushes and plane-trees, two iron seats and a gravel path, a padlocked gate at either end, a scuffle of old leaves. But he couldn't stay: something stirred in the bushes and two illuminated eyes peered out at him like a Serbian wolf, and he thought how terrible it would be if Mrs Baines found him there. He'd have no time to climb the railings; she'd seize him from behind.

He left the square at the unfashionable end and was immediately among the fish-and-chip shops, the little stationers selling *Bagatelle*, among the accommodation addresses and the dingy hotels with open doors. There were few people about because the pubs were open, but a blowsy woman carrying a parcel called out to him across the street and the commissionaire outside a cinema would have stopped him if he hadn't crossed the road. He went deeper: you could go farther and lose yourself more completely here than among the plane-trees. On the fringe of the square he was in danger of being stopped and taken back: it was obvious where he belonged; but as he went deeper he lost the marks of his origin. It was a warm night: any child in those free-living parts might be expected to play truant from bed. He found a kind of camaraderie even among grown-up people; he might have been a neighbour's child as he went quickly by, but they weren't going to tell on him, they'd been young once themselves. He picked up a protective coating of dust from the pavements, of smuts from the trains which passed along the backs in a spray of fire. Once he was caught in a knot of children running away from something or somebody, laughing as they ran; he was whirled with them round a turning and abandoned, with a sticky fruit-drop in his hand.

He couldn't have been more lost, but he hadn't the stamina to keep on. At first he feared that someone would stop him; after an hour he hoped that someone would. He couldn't find his way back, and in any case he was afraid of arriving home alone; he was afraid of Mrs Baines, more afraid than he had ever been. Baines was his friend, but something had happened which gave Mrs Baines all the power. He began to loiter on purpose to be noticed, but no one noticed him. Families were having a last breather on the doorsteps, the refuse bins had been put out and bits of cabbage stalks soiled his slippers. The air was full of voices, but he was cut off; these people were strangers and would always now be strangers; they were marked by Mrs Baines and he shied away from them into a deep class-consciousness. He had been afraid of policemen, but now he wanted one to take him home; even Mrs Baines could do nothing against a policeman. He sidled past a constable who was directing traffic, but he was too busy to pay him any attention. Philip sat down against a wall and cried.

It hadn't occurred to him that that was the easiest way, that all you had to do was to surrender, to show you were beaten and accept kindness . . . It was lavished on him at once by two women and a pawnbroker. Another policeman appeared, a young man with a sharp incredulous face. He looked as if he noted everything he saw in pocket-books and drew conclusions. A woman offered to see Philip home, but he didn't trust her: she wasn't a match for Mrs Baines immobile in the hall. He wouldn't give his address; he said he was afraid to go home. He had his way; he got his protection. 'I'll take him to the station,' the policeman said, and holding him awkwardly by the hand (he wasn't married; he had his career to make) he led him round the corner, up the stone stairs into the little bare over-heated room where Justice lived.

5

Justice waited behind a wooden counter on a high stool; it wore a heavy moustache; it was kindly and had six children ('three of them nippers like yourself'); it wasn't really interested in Philip, but it pretended to be, it wrote the address down and sent a constable to fetch a glass of milk. But the young constable was interested; he had a nose for things.

'Your home's on the telephone, I suppose,' Justice said. 'We'll ring them up and say you are safe. They'll fetch you very soon. What's your name, sonny?'

'Philip.'

'Your other name?'

'I haven't got another name.' He didn't want to be fetched; he wanted to be taken home by someone who would impress even Mrs Baines. The constable watched him, watched the way he drank the milk, watched him when he winced away from questions.

'What made you run away? Playing truant, eh?'

'I don't know.'

'You oughtn't to do it, young fellow. Think how anxious your father and mother will be.'

'They are away.'

'Well, your nurse.'

'I haven't got one.'

'Who looks after you, then?' The question went home. Philip saw Mrs Baines coming up the stairs at him, the heap of black cotton in the hall. He began to cry.

'Now, now, now,' the sergeant said. He didn't know what to do; he wished his wife were with him; even a policewoman might have been useful.

'Don't you think it's funny,' the constable said, 'that there hasn't been an inquiry?'

'They think he's tucked up in bed.'

'You are scared, aren't you?' the constable said. 'What scared you?'

'I don't know.'

'Somebody hurt you?'

'No.'

'He's had bad dreams,' the sergeant said. 'Thought the house was on fire, I expect. I've brought up six of them. Rose is due back. She'll take him home.'

'I want to go home with you,' Philip said; he tried to smile at the constable, but the deceit was immature and unsuccessful.

'I'd better go,' the constable said. 'There may be something wrong.'

'Nonsense,' the sergeant said. 'It's a woman's job. Tact is what you need. Here's Rose. Pull up your stockings, Rose. You're a disgrace to the Force. I've got a job of work for you.' Rose shambled in: black cotton stockings drooping over her boots, a gawky Girl Guide manner, a hoarse hostile voice. 'More tarts, I suppose.'

'No, you've got to see this young man home.' She looked at him owlishly.

'I won't go with her,' Philip said. He began to cry again. 'I don't like her.'

'More of that womanly charm, Rose,' the sergeant said. The telephone rang on his desk. He lifted the receiver. 'What? What's that?' he said. 'Number 48? You've got a doctor?' He put his hand over the telephone mouth. 'No wonder this nipper wasn't reported,' he said. 'They've been too busy. An accident. Woman slipped on the stairs.'

'Serious?' the constable asked. The sergeant mouthed at him; you didn't mention the word death before a child (didn't he know? he had six of them), you made noises in the throat, you grimaced, a complicated shorthand for a word of only five letters anyway.

'You'd better go, after all,' he said, 'and make a report. The doctor's there.'

Rose shambled from the stove; pink apply-dapply cheeks, loose stockings. She stuck her hands behind her. Her large morgue-like mouth was full of blackened teeth. 'You told me to take him and now just because something interesting . . . I don't expect justice from a man . . .'

'Who's at the house?' the constable asked.

'The butler.'

'You don't think,' the constable said, 'he saw . . .'

'Trust me,' the sergeant said. 'I've brought up six. I know 'em through and through. You can't teach me anything about children.'

'He seemed scared about something.'

'Dreams,' the sergeant said.

'What name?'

'Baines.'

'This Mr Baines,' the constable said to Philip, 'you like him, eh? He's good to you?' They were trying to get something out of him; he was suspicious of the whole roomful of them; he said 'yes' without conviction because he was afraid at any moment of more responsibilities, more secrets.

'And Mrs Baines?'

'Yes.'

They consulted together by the desk. Rose was hoarsely aggrieved; she was like a female impersonator, she bore her womanhood with an unnatural emphasis even while she scorned it in her creased stockings and her weather-exposed face. The charcoal shifted in the stove; the room was over-heated in the mild late summer evening. A notice on the wall described a body found in the Thames, or rather the body's clothes: wool vest, wool pants, wool shirt with blue stripes, size ten boots, blue serge suit worn at the elbows, fifteen and a half celluloid collar. They couldn't find anything to say about the body, except its measurements, it was just an ordinary body.

'Come along,' the constable said. He was interested, he was glad to be going, but he couldn't help being embarrassed by his company, a small boy in pyjamas. His nose smelt something, he didn't know what, but he smarted at the sight of the amusement they caused: the pubs had closed and the streets were full again of men making as long a day of it as they could. He hurried through the less frequented streets, chose the darker pavements, wouldn't loiter, and Philip wanted more and more to loiter, pulling at his hand, dragging with his feet. He dreaded the sight of Mrs Baines waiting in the hall: he knew now that she was dead. The sergeant's mouthing had conveyed that; but she wasn't buried, she wasn't out of sight: he was going to see a dead person in the hall when the door opened.

The light was on in the basement, and to his relief the constable made for the area steps. Perhaps he wouldn't have to see Mrs Baines at all. The constable knocked on the door because it was too dark to see the bell, and Baines answered. He stood there in the doorway of the neat bright basement room and you could see the sad complacent plausible sentence he had prepared wither at the sight of Philip; he hadn't expected Philip to return like that in the policeman's company. He had to begin thinking all over again; he wasn't a deceptive man. If it hadn't been for Emmy he would have been quite ready to let the truth lead him where it would.

'Mr Baines?' the constable asked.

He nodded; he hadn't found the right words; he was daunted by the shrewd knowing face, the sudden appearance of Philip there.

'This little boy from here?'

'Yes,' Baines said. Philip could tell that there was a message he was trying to convey, but he shut his mind to it. He loved Baines, but Baines had involved him in secrets, in fears he didn't understand. That was what happened when you loved—you got involved; and Philip extricated himself from life, from love, from Baines.

'The doctor's here,' Baines said. He nodded at the door, moistened his mouth, kept his eyes on Philip, begging for something like a dog you can't understand, 'There's nothing to be done. She slipped on these stone basement stairs. I was in here. I heard her fall.' He wouldn't look at the notebook, at the constable's spidery writing which got a terrible lot on one page.

'Did the boy see anything?'

'He can't have done. I thought he was in bed. Hadn't he better go up? It's a shocking thing. O,' Baines said, losing control, 'it's a shocking thing for a child.'

'She's through there?' the constable asked.

'I haven't moved her an inch,' Baines said.

'He'd better then—'

'Go up the area and through the hall,' Baines said, and again he begged dumbly like a dog: one more secret, keep this secret, do this for old Baines, he won't ask another.

'Come along,' the constable said. 'I'll see you up to bed.
You're a gentleman. You must come in the proper way through
the front door like the master should. Or will you go along with
him, Mr Baines, while I see the doctor?'

'Yes,' Baines said, 'I'll go.' He came across the room to Philip,
begging, begging, all the way with his old soft stupid expression:
this is Baines, the old Coaster; what about a palm-oil chop, eh?; a
man's life; forty niggers; never used a gun; I tell you I couldn't help
loving them; it wasn't what we call love, nothing we could understand. The messages flickered out from the last posts at the border,
imploring, beseeching, reminding: this is your old friend Baines;
what about an elevenses; a glass of ginger pop won't do you any
harm; sausages; a long day. But the wires were cut, the messages
just faded out into the vacancy of the scrubbed room in which
there had never been a place where a man could hide his secrets.

'Come along, Phil, it's bedtime. We'll just go up the steps . . .'
Tap, tap, tap, at the telegraph; you may get through, you can't tell,
somebody may mend the right wire. 'And in at the front door.'

'No,' Philip said, 'no. I won't go. You can't make me go. I'll
fight. I won't see her.'

The constable turned on them quickly. 'What's that? Why
won't you go?'

'She's in the hall,' Philip said. 'I know she's in the hall. And
she's dead. I won't see her.'

'You moved her then?' the constable said to Baines. 'All the
way down here? You've been lying, eh? That means you had to
tidy up . . . Were you alone?'

'Emmy,' Philip said, 'Emmy.' He wasn't going to keep any
more secrets: he was going to finish once and for all with everything, with Baines and Mrs Baines and the grown-up life beyond
him. 'It was all Emmy's fault,' he protested with a quaver which
reminded Baines that after all he was only a child; it had been
hopeless to expect help there; he was a child; he didn't understand what it all meant; he couldn't read this shorthand of terror;
he'd had a long day and he was tired out. You could see him
dropping asleep where he stood against the dresser, dropping
back into the comfortable nursery peace. You couldn't blame

him. When he woke in the morning, he'd hardly remember a thing.

'Out with it,' the constable said, addressing Baines with professional ferocity, 'who is she?' just as the old man sixty years later startled his secretary, his only watcher, asking, 'Who is she? Who is she?' dropping lower and lower to death, passing on the way perhaps the image of Baines: Baines hopeless, Baines letting his head drop, Baines 'coming clean'.

1936

A CHANCE FOR MR LEVER

Mr Lever knocked his head against the ceiling and swore. Rice was stored above, and in the dark the rats began to move. Grains of rice fell between the slats on to his Revelation suitcase, his bald head, his cases of tinned food, the little square box in which he kept his medicines. His boy had already set up the camp-bed and mosquito-net, and outside in the warm damp dark his folding table and chair. The thatched pointed huts streamed away towards the forest and a woman went from hut to hut carrying fire. The glow lit her old face, her sagging breasts, her tattooed diseased body.

It was incredible to Mr Lever that five weeks ago he had been in London.

He couldn't stand upright; he went down on hands and knees in the dust and opened his suitcase. He took out his wife's photograph and stood it on the chop-box; he took out a writing-pad and an indelible pencil: the pencil had softened in the heat and left mauve stains on his pyjamas. Then, because the light of the hurricane lamp disclosed cockroaches the size of black-beetles flattened against the mud wall, he carefully closed the suitcase. Already in ten days he had learnt that they'd eat anything—socks, shirts, the laces out of your shoes.

Mr Lever went outside; moths beat against his lamp, but there were no mosquitoes; he hadn't seen or heard one since he landed. He sat in a circle of light carefully observed. The blacks squatted outside their huts and watched him; they were friendly, interested, amused, but their strict attention irritated Mr Lever. He could feel the small waves of interest washing round him, when he began to write, when he stopped writing, when he wiped his damp hands with a handkerchief. He couldn't touch his pocket without a craning of necks.

Dearest Emily, he wrote, *I've really started now. I'll send this letter back with a carrier when I've located Davidson. I'm very well. Of course everything's a bit strange. Look after yourself, my dear, and don't worry.*

'Massa buy chicken,' his cook said, appearing suddenly between the huts. A small stringy fowl struggled in his hands.

'Well,' Mr Lever said, 'I gave you a shilling, didn't I?'

'They no like,' the cook said. 'These low bush people.'

'Why don't they like? It's good money.'

'They want king's money,' the cook said, handing back the Victorian shilling. Mr Lever had to get up, go back into his hut, grope for his money-box, search through twenty pounds of small change: there was no peace.

He had learnt that very quickly. He had to economize (the whole trip was a gamble which scared him); he couldn't afford hammock carriers. He would arrive tired out after seven hours of walking at a village of which he didn't know the name and not for a minute could he sit quietly and rest. He must shake hands with the chief, he must see about a hut, accept presents of palm wine he was afraid to drink, buy rice and palm oil for the carriers, give them salts and aspirin, paint their sores with iodine. They never left him alone for five minutes on end until he went to bed. And then the rats began, rushing down the walls like water when he put out the light, gambolling among his cases.

I'm too old, Mr Lever told himself, I'm too old, writing damply, indelibly, *I hope to find Davidson tomorrow. If I do, I may be back almost as soon as this letter. Don't economize on the stout and milk, dear, and call in the doctor if you feel bad. I've got a premonition this trip's going to turn out well. We'll take a holiday, you need a holiday,* and staring ahead past the huts and the black faces and the banana trees towards the forest from which he had come, into which he would sink again next day, he thought, Eastbourne, Eastbourne would do her a world of good; and he continued to write the only kind of lies he had ever told Emily, the lies which comforted. *I ought to draw at least three hundred in commission and expenses.* But it wasn't the sort of place where he'd been accustomed to sell heavy machinery; thirty years of it, up and down Europe and in the States, but never anything like this. He could hear his filter dripping in the hut, and somewhere somebody was playing something (he was so lost he hadn't got the simplest terms to his hands), something monotonous, melancholy, superficial, a twanging of palm fibres which seemed to convey that you weren't happy, but it didn't matter, everything would always be the same.

Look after yourself, Emily, he repeated. It was almost the only thing he found himself capable of writing to her; he couldn't describe the narrow, steep, lost paths, the snakes sizzling away like flames, the rats, the dust, the naked diseased bodies. He was unbearably tired of nakedness. *Don't forget*—It was like living with a lot of cows.

'The chief,' his boy whispered, and between the huts under a waving torch came an old stout man wearing a robe of native cloth and a battered bowler hat. Behind him his men carried six bowls of rice, a bowl of palm oil, two bowls of broken meat. 'Chop for the labourers,' the boy explained, and Mr Lever had to get up and smile and nod and try to convey without words that he was pleased, that the chop was excellent, that the chief would get a good dash in the morning. At first the smell had been almost too much for Mr Lever.

'Ask him,' he said to his boy, 'if he's seen a white man come through here lately. Ask him if a white man's been digging around here. Damn it,' Mr Lever burst out, the sweat breaking on the backs of his hands and on his bald head, 'ask him if he's seen Davidson?'

'Davidson?'

'Oh, hell,' Mr Lever said, 'you know what I mean. The white man I'm looking for.'

'White man?'

'What do you imagine I'm here for, eh? White man? Of course white man. I'm not here for my health.' A cow coughed, rubbed its horns against the hut and two goats broke through between the chief and him, upsetting the bowls of meat scraps; nobody cared, they picked the meat out of the dust and dung.

Mr Lever sat down and put his hands over his face, fat white well-cared-for hands with wrinkles of flesh over the rings. He felt too old for this.

'Chief say no white man been here long time.'

'How long?'

'Chief say not since he pay hut tax.'

'How long's that?'

'Long long time.'

'Ask him how far is it to Greh, tomorrow.'

'Chief say too far.'

'Nonsense,' Mr Lever said.

'Chief say too far. Better stay here. Fine town. No humbug.'

Mr Lever groaned. Every evening there was the same trouble. The next town was always too far. They would invent any excuse to delay him, to give themselves a rest.

'Ask the chief how many hours—?'

'Plenty, plenty.' They had no idea of time.

'This fine chief. Fine chop. Labourers tired. No humbug.'

'We are going on,' Mr Lever said.

'This fine town. Chief say—'

He thought: if this wasn't the last chance, I'd give up. They nagged him so, and suddenly he longed for another white man (not Davidson, he daren't say anything to Davidson) to whom he could explain the desperation of his lot. It wasn't fair that a man, after thirty years' commercial travelling, should need to go from door to door asking for a job. He had been a good traveller, he had made money for many people, his references were excellent, but the world had moved on since his day. He wasn't stream-lined; he certainly wasn't streamlined. He had been ten years re-tired when he lost his money in the depression.

Mr Lever walked up and down Victoria Street showing his references. Many of the men knew him, gave him cigars, laughed at him in a friendly way for wanting to take on a job at his age ('I can't somehow settle at home. The old warhorse you know . . .'), cracked a joke or two in the passage, went back that night to Maidenhead silent in the first-class carriage, shut in with age and ruin and how bad things were and poor devil his wife's probably sick.

It was in the rather shabby little office off Leadenhall Street that Mr Lever met his chance. It called itself an engineering firm, but there were only two rooms, a typewriter, a girl with gold teeth and Mr Lucas, a thin narrow man with a tic in one eyelid. All through the interview the eyelid flickered at Mr Lever. Mr Lever had never before fallen so low as this.

But Mr Lucas struck him as reasonably honest. He put 'all his cards on the table'. He hadn't got any money, but he had expectations; he had the handling of a patent. It was a new crusher. There was money in it. But you couldn't expect the big trusts to change over their machinery now. Things were too bad. You'd got to get in at the start, and that was where—why, that was where this chief, the bowls of chop, the nagging and the rats and the heat came in. They called themselves a republic, Mr Lucas said, he didn't know anything about that, they were not as black as they were painted, he supposed (ha, ha, nervously, ha, ha); anyway, this company had slipped agents over the border and grabbed a concession: gold and diamonds. He could tell Mr Lever in confidence that the trust was frightened of what they'd found. Now an enterprising man could just slip across (Mr Lucas liked the word slip, it made everything sound easy and secret) and introduce this new crusher to them: it would save them thousands when they started work, there'd be a fat commission, and afterwards, with that start . . . There was a fortune for them all.

'But can't you fix it up in Europe?'

Tic, tic, went Mr Lucas's eyelid. 'A lot of Belgians; they are leaving all decisions to the man on the spot. An Englishman called Davidson.'

'How about expenses?'

'That's the trouble,' Mr Lucas said. 'We are only beginning. What we want is a partner. We can't afford to send a man. But if you like a gamble . . . Twenty per cent commission.'

'Chief say excuse him.' The carriers squatted round the basins and scooped up the rice in their left hands. 'Of course. Of course,' Mr Lever said absent-mindedly. 'Very kind, I'm sure.'

He was back out of the dust and dark, away from the stink of goats and palm oil and whelping bitches, back among the rotarians and lunch at Stone's, 'the pint of old', and the trade papers; he was a good fellow again, finding his way back to Golders Green just a bit lit; his masonic emblem rattled on his watch-chain, and he bore with him from the tube station to his house in Finchley Road a sense of companionship, of broad stories and belches, a sense of bravery.

He needed all his bravery now; the last of his savings had gone into the trip. After thirty years he knew a good thing when he saw it, and he had no doubts about the new crusher. What he doubted was his ability to find Davidson. For one thing there weren't any maps; the way you travelled in the Republic was to write down a list of names and trust that someone in the villages you passed would understand and know the route. But they always said 'Too far'. Good fellowship wilted before the phrase.

'Quinine,' Mr Lever said. 'Where's my quinine?' His boy never remembered a thing; they just didn't care what happened to you; their smiles meant nothing, and Mr Lever, who knew better than anyone the value of a meaningless smile in business, resented their heartlessness, and turned towards the dilatory boy an expression of disappointment and dislike.

'Chief say white man in bush five hours away.'

'That's better,' Mr Lever said. 'It must be Davidson. He's digging for gold?'

'Ya. White man dig for gold in bush.'

'We'll be off early tomorrow,' Mr Lever said.

'Chief say better stop this town. Fever humbug white man.'

'Too bad,' Mr Lever said, and he thought with pleasure: my luck's changed. He'll want help. He won't refuse me a thing. A friend in need is a friend indeed, and his heart warmed towards Davidson, seeing himself arrive like an answer to prayer out of the forest, feeling quite biblical and vox humana. He thought: Prayer. I'll pray tonight, that's the kind of thing a fellow gives up, but it pays, there's something in it, remembering the long agonizing prayer on his knees, by the sideboard, under the decanters, when Emily went to hospital.

'Chief say white man dead.'

Mr Lever turned his back on them and went into his hut. His

sleeve nearly overturned the hurricane lamp. He undressed
quickly, stuffing his clothes into a suitcase away from the cockroaches. He wouldn't believe what he had been told; it wouldn't
pay him to believe. If Davidson were dead, there was nothing he
could do but return; he had spent more than he could afford; he
would be a ruined man. He supposed that Emily might find a
home with her brother, but he could hardly expect her brother—
he began to cry, but you couldn't have told in the shadowy hut
the difference between sweat and tears. He knelt down beside his
camp-bed and mosquito-net and prayed on the dust of the earth
floor. Up till now he had always been careful never to touch
ground with his naked feet for fear of jiggers; there were jiggers
everywhere, they only waited an opportunity to dig themselves in
under the toe-nails, lay their eggs and multiply.

'O God,' Mr Lever prayed, 'don't let Davidson be dead; let
him be just sick and glad to see me.' He couldn't bear the idea
that he might not any longer be able to support Emily. 'O God,
there's nothing I wouldn't do.' But that was an empty phrase; he
had no real notion as yet of what he would do for Emily. They
had been happy together for thirty-five years; he had never been
more than momentarily unfaithful to her when he was lit after a
rotarian dinner and egged on by the boys; whatever skirt he'd
been with in his time, he had never for a moment imagined that
he could be happy married to anyone else. It wasn't fair if, just
when you were old and needed each other most, you lost your
money and couldn't keep together.

But of course Davidson wasn't dead. What would he have
died of? The blacks were friendly. People said the country was
unhealthy, but he hadn't so much as heard a mosquito. Besides,
you didn't die of malaria; you just lay between the blankets and
took quinine and felt like death and sweated it out of you. There
was dysentery, but Davidson was an old campaigner; you were
safe if you boiled and filtered the water. The water was poison
even to touch; it was unsafe to wet your feet because of guinea
worm, but you didn't die of guinea worm.

Mr Lever lay in bed and his thoughts went round and round
and he couldn't sleep. He thought: you don't die of a thing like
guinea worm. It makes a sore on your foot, and if you put your

foot in water you can see the eggs dropping out. You have to find the end of the worm, like a thread of cotton, and wind it round a match and wind it out of your leg without breaking; it stretches as high as the knee. I'm too old for this country, Mr Lever thought.

Then his boy was beside him again. He whispered urgently to Mr Lever through the mosquito-net. 'Massa, the labourers say they go home.'

'Go home?' Mr Lever asked wearily; he had heard it so often before. 'Why do they want to go home? What is it now?' but he didn't really want to hear the latest squabble: that the Bande men were never sent to carry water because the headman was a Bande, that someone had stolen an empty treacle tin and sold it in the village for a penny, that someone wasn't made to carry a proper load, that the next day's journey was 'too far'. He said, 'Tell 'em they can go home. I'll pay them off in the morning. But they won't get any dash. They'd have got a good dash if they'd stayed.' He was certain it was just another try-on; he wasn't as green as all that.

'Yes, massa. They no want dash.'

'What's that?'

'They frightened fever humbug them like white man.'

'I'll get carriers in the village. They can go home.'

'Me too, massa.'

'Get out,' Mr Lever said; it was the last straw; 'get out and let me sleep.' The boy went at once, obedient even though a deserter, and Mr Lever thought: sleep, what a hope. He lifted the net and got out of bed (bare-footed again: he didn't care a damn about the jiggers) and searched for his medicine box. It was locked, of course, and he had to open his suitcase and find the key in a trouser pocket. His nerves were more on edge than ever by the time he found the sleeping tablets and he took three of them. That made him sleep, heavily and dreamlessly, though when he woke he found that something had made him fling out his arms and open the net. If there had been a single mosquito in the place, he'd have been bitten, but of course there wasn't one.

He could tell at once that the trouble hadn't blown over. The village—he didn't know its name—was perched on a hill-top;

east and west the forest flowed out beneath the little plateau; to the west it was a dark unfeatured mass like water, but in the east you could already discern the unevenness, the great grey cotton trees lifted above the palms. Mr Lever was always called before dawn, but no one had called him. A few of his carriers sat outside a hut sullenly talking; his boy was with them. Mr Lever went back inside and dressed; he thought all the time, I must be firm, but he was scared, scared of being deserted, scared of being made to return.

When he came outside again the village was awake: the women were going down the hill to fetch water, winding silently past the carriers, past the flat stones where the chiefs were buried, the little grove of trees where the rice birds, like green and yellow canaries, nested. Mr Lever sat down on his folding chair among the chickens and whelping bitches and cow dung and called his boy. He took 'a strong line'; but he didn't know what was going to happen. 'Tell the chief I want to speak to him,' he said.

There was some delay; the chief wasn't up yet, but presently he appeared in his blue and white robe, setting his bowler hat straight. 'Tell him,' Mr Lever said, 'I want carriers to take me to the white man and back. Two days.'

'Chief no agree,' the boy said.

Mr Lever said furiously, 'Damn it, if he doesn't agree, he won't get any dash from me, not a penny.' It occurred to him immediately afterwards how hopelessly dependent he was on these people's honesty. There in the hut for all to see was his money-box; they had only to take it. This wasn't a British or French colony; the blacks on the coast wouldn't bother, could do nothing if they did bother, because a stray Englishman had been robbed in the interior.

'Chief say how many?'

'It's only for two days,' Mr Lever said. 'I can do with six.'

'Chief say how much?'

'Sixpence a day and chop.'

'Chief no agree.'

'Ninepence a day then.'

'Chief say too far. A shilling.'

'All right, all right,' Mr Lever said. 'A shilling then. You others can go home if you want to. I'll pay you off now, but you won't get any dash, not a penny.'

He had never really expected to be left, and it gave him a sad feeling of loneliness to watch them move sullenly away (they were ashamed of themselves) down the hill to the west. They hadn't any loads, but they weren't singing; they drooped silently out of sight, his boy with them, and he was alone with his pile of boxes and the chief who couldn't talk a word of English. Mr Lever smiled tremulously.

It was ten o'clock before his new carriers were chosen; he could tell that none of them wanted to go, and they would have to walk through the heat of the middle day if they were to find Davidson before it was dark. He hoped the chief had explained properly where they were going; he couldn't tell; he was completely shut off from them, and when they started down the eastward slope, he might just as well have been alone.

They were immediately caught up in the forest. Forest conveys a sense of wildness and beauty, of an active natural force, but this Liberian forest was simply a dull green wilderness. You passed, on the path a foot or so wide, through an endless back garden of tangled weeds; it didn't seem to be growing round you, so much as dying. There was no life at all, except for a few large birds whose wings creaked overhead through the invisible sky like an unoiled door. There was no view, no way out for the eyes, no change of scene. It wasn't the heat that tired, so much as the boredom; you had to think of things to think about; but even Emily failed to fill the mind for more than three minutes at a time. It was a relief, a distraction, when the path was flooded and Mr Lever had to be carried on a man's back. At first he had disliked the strong bitter smell (it reminded him of a breakfast food he was made to eat as a child), but he soon got over that. Now he was unaware that they smelt at all; any more than he was aware that the great swallow-tailed butterflies, which clustered at the water's edge and rose in green clouds round his waist, were beautiful. His senses were dulled and registered very little except his boredom.

But they did register a distinct feeling of relief when his leading carrier pointed to a rectangular hole dug just off the path. Mr Lever understood. Davidson had come this way. He stopped and looked at it. It was like a grave dug for a small man, but it went down deeper than graves usually do. About twelve feet below there was black water, and a few wooden props which held the sides from slipping were beginning to rot; the hole must have been dug since the rains. It didn't seem enough, that hole, to have brought out Mr Lever with his plans and estimates for a new crusher. He was used to big industrial concerns, the sight of pitheads, the smoke of chimneys, the dingy rows of cottages back to back, the leather armchair in the office, the good cigar, the masonic hand-grips, and again it seemed to him, as it had seemed in Mr Lucas's office, that he had fallen very low. It was as if he was expected to do business beside a hole a child had dug in an overgrown and abandoned back garden; percentages wilted in the hot damp air. He shook his head; he mustn't be discouraged; this was an old hole. Davidson had probably done better since. It was only common sense to suppose that the gold rift which was mined at one end in Nigeria, at the other in Sierra Leone, would pass through the republic. Even the biggest mines had to begin with a hole in the ground. The company (he had talked to the directors in Brussels) were quite confident: all they wanted was the approval of the man on the spot that the crusher was suitable for local conditions. A signature, that was all he had to get, he told himself, staring down into the puddle of black water.

Five hours, the chief had said, but after six hours they were still walking. Mr Lever had eaten nothing; he wanted to get to Davidson first. All through the heat of the day he walked. The forest protected him from the direct sun, but it shut out the air, and the occasional clearings, shrivelled though they were in the vertical glare, seemed cooler than the shade because there was a little more air to breathe. At four o'clock the heat diminished, but he began to fear they wouldn't reach Davidson before dark. His foot pained him; he had caught a jigger the night before; it was as if someone were holding a lighted match to his toe. Then at five they came on a dead black.

Another rectangular hole in a small cleared space among the dusty greenery had caught Mr Lever's eye. He peered down and was shocked to see a face return his stare, white eyeballs like phosphorus in the black water. The black had been bent almost double to fit him in; the hole was really too small to be a grave, and he had swollen. His flesh was like a blister you could prick with a needle. Mr Lever felt sick and tired; he might have been tempted to return if he could have reached the village before dark, but now there was nothing to do but go on; the carriers luckily hadn't seen the body. He waved them forward and stumbled after them among the roots, fighting his nausea. He fanned himself with his sun helmet; his wide fat face was damp and pale. He had never seen an uncared-for body before; his parents he had seen carefully laid out with closed eyes and washed faces; they 'fell asleep' quite in accordance with their epitaphs, but you couldn't think of sleep in connection with the white eyeballs and the swollen face. Mr Lever would have liked very much to say a prayer, but prayers were out of place in the dead drab forest; they simply didn't 'come'.

With the dusk a little life did waken: something lived in the dry weeds and brittle trees, if only monkeys. They chattered and screamed all round you, but it was too dark to see them; you were like a blind man in the centre of a frightened crowd who wouldn't say what scared them. The carriers too were frightened. They ran under their fifty-pound loads behind the dipping light of the hurricane lamp, their huge flat carriers' feet flapping in the dust like empty gloves. Mr Lever listened nervously for mosquitoes; you would have expected them to be out by now, but he didn't hear one.

Then at the top of a rise above a small stream they came on Davidson. The ground had been cleared in a square of twelve feet and a small tent pitched; he had dug another hole; the scene came dimly into view as they climbed the path; the chop-boxes piled outside the tent, the syphon of soda water, the filter, an enamel basin. But there wasn't a light, there wasn't a sound, the flaps of the tent were not closed, and Mr Lever had to face the possibility that after all the chief might have told the truth.

Mr Lever took the lamp and stooped inside the tent. There was a body on the bed. At first Mr Lever thought Davidson was covered with blood, but then he realized it was a black vomit which stained his shirt and khaki shorts, the fair stubble on his chin. He put out a hand and touched Davidson's face, and if he hadn't felt a slight breath on his palm he would have taken him for dead; his skin was so cold. He moved the lamp closer, and now the lemon-yellow face told him all he wanted to know: he hadn't thought of that when his boy said fever. It was quite true that a man didn't die of malaria, but an odd piece of news read in New York in '98 came back to mind: there had been an outbreak of yellow jack in Rio and ninety-four per cent of the cases had been fatal. It hadn't meant anything to him then, but it did, now. While he watched, Davidson was sick, quite effortlessly; he was like a tap out of which something flowed.

It seemed at first to Mr Lever to be the end of everything, of his journey, his hopes, his life with Emily. There was nothing he could do for Davidson, the man was unconscious, there were times when his pulse was so low and irregular that Mr Lever thought that he was dead until another black stream spread from his mouth; it was no use even cleaning him. Mr Lever laid his own blankets over the bed on top of Davidson's because he was so cold to the touch, but he had no idea whether he was doing the right, or even the fatally wrong, thing. The chance of survival, if there were any chance at all, depended on neither of them. Outside his carriers had built a fire and were cooking the rice they had brought with them. Mr Lever opened his folding chair and sat by the bed. He wanted to keep awake: it seemed right to keep awake. He opened his case and found his unfinished letter to Emily. He sat by Davidson's side and tried to write, but he could think of nothing but what he had already written too often: *Look after yourself. Don't forget that stout and milk.*

He fell asleep over his pad and woke at two and thought that Davidson was dead. But he was wrong again. He was very thirsty and missed his boy. Always the first thing his boy did at the end of a march was to light a fire and put on a kettle; after that, by the time his table and chair were set up, there was water ready for the filter. Mr Lever found half a cup of soda water left in Davidson's syphon; if it had been only his health at stake he would have gone down to the stream, but he had Emily to remember. There was a typewriter by the bed, and it occurred to Mr Lever that he might just as well begin to write his report of failure now; it might keep him awake; it seemed disrespectful to the dying man to sleep. He found paper under some letters which had been typed and signed but not sealed. Davidson must have been taken ill very suddenly. Mr Lever wondered whether it was he who had crammed the black into the hole; his boy perhaps, for there was no sign of a servant. He balanced the typewriter on his knee and headed the letter 'In Camp near Greh'.

It seemed to him unfair that he should have come so far, spent so much money, worn out a rather old body to meet his inevitable ruin in a dark tent beside a dying man, when he could have met it just as well at home with Emily in the plush parlour. The thought of the prayers he had uselessly uttered on his knees by the camp-bed among the jiggers, the rats and the cockroaches made him re-bellious. A mosquito, the first he had heard, went humming round the tent. He slashed at it savagely; he wouldn't have recognized himself among the rotarians. He was lost and he was set free. Moralities were what enabled a man to live happily and success-fully with his fellows, but Mr Lever wasn't happy and he wasn't successful, and his only fellow in the little stuffy tent wouldn't be troubled by Untruth in Advertising or by Mr Lever coveting his neighbour's oxen. You couldn't keep your ideas intact when you discovered their geographical nature. The Solemnity of Death: death wasn't solemn; it was a lemon-yellow skin and a black vomit. Honesty is the Best Policy: he saw quite suddenly how false that was. It was an anarchist who sat happily over the typewriter, an anarchist who recognized nothing but one personal relation-ship, his affection for Emily. Mr Lever began to type: *I have ex-amined the plans and estimates of the new Lucas crusher . . .*

Mr Lever thought with savage happiness: I win. This letter would be the last the company would hear from Davidson. The junior partner would open it in the dapper Brussels office; he would tap his false teeth with a Waterman pen and go in to talk to M. Golz. *Taking all these factors into consideration I recom-mend acceptance . . .* They would telegraph to Lucas. As for Davidson, that trusted agent of the company would have died of yellow fever at some never accurately determined date. Another agent would come out, and the crusher . . . Mr Lever carefully copied Davidson's signature on a spare sheet of paper. He wasn't satisfied. He turned the original upside-down and copied it that way, so as not to be confused by his own idea of how a letter should be formed. That was better, but it didn't satisfy him. He searched until he found Davidson's own pen and began again to copy and copy the signature. He fell asleep copying it and woke again an hour later to find the lamp was out; it had burnt up all the oil. He sat there beside Davidson's bed till daylight; once he was bitten by a mosquito in the ankle and clapped his hand to the place too late: the brute went humming out. With the light Mr Lever saw that Davidson was dead. 'Dear, dear,' he said. 'Poor fellow.' He spat out with the words, quite delicately in a corner, the bad morning taste in his mouth. It was like a little sediment of his conventionality.

Mr Lever got two of his carriers to cram Davidson tidily into his hole. He was no longer afraid of them or of failure or of separation. He tore up his letter to Emily. It no longer represented his mood in its timidity, its secret fear, its gentle fussing phrases, *Don't forget the stout. Look after yourself.* He would be home as soon as the letter, and they were going to do things together now they'd never dreamt of doing. The money for the crusher was only the beginning. His ideas stretched farther now than Eastbourne, they stretched as far as Switzerland; he had a feeling that, if he really let himself go, they'd stretch as far as the Riviera. How happy he was on what he thought of as 'the trip home'. He was freed from what had held him back through a long pedantic career, the fear of a conscious fate that notes the dishonesty, notes the skirt in Piccadilly, notes the glass too many of Stone's special. Now he had said Boo to that goose . . .

But you who are reading this, who know so much more than Mr Lever, who can follow the mosquito's progress from the dead swollen black to Davidson's tent, to Mr Lever's ankle, you may possibly believe in God, a kindly god tender towards human frailty, ready to give Mr Lever three days of happiness, three days off the galling chain, as he carried back through the forest his amateurish forgeries and the infection of yellow fever in the blood. The story might very well have encouraged my faith in that loving omniscience if it had not been shaken by personal knowledge of the drab forest through which Mr Lever now went so merrily, where it is impossible to believe in any spiritual life, in anything outside the nature dying round you, the shrivelling of the weeds. But of course, there are two opinions about everything; it was Mr Lever's favourite expression, drinking beer in the Ruhr, Pernod in Lorraine, selling heavy machinery.

1936

BROTHER

The Communists were the first to appear. They walked quickly, a group of about a dozen, up the boulevard which runs from Combat to Ménilmontant; a young man and a girl lagged a little way behind because the man's leg was hurt and the girl was helping him along. They looked impatient, harassed, hopeless, as if they were trying to catch a train which they knew already in their hearts they were too late to catch.

The proprietor of the café saw them coming when they were still a long way off; the lamps at that time were still alight (it was later that the bullets broke the bulbs and dropped darkness over all that quarter of Paris), and the group showed up plainly in the wide barren boulevard. Since sunset only one customer had entered the café, and very soon after sunset firing could be heard from the direction of Combat; the Metro station had closed hours ago. And yet something obstinate and undefeatable in the proprietor's character prevented him from putting up the shutters; it might have been avarice; he could not himself have told what it was as he pressed his broad yellow forehead against the glass and stared this way and that, up the boulevard and down the boulevard.

But when he saw the group and their air of hurry he began immediately to close the café. First he went and warned his only customer who was practising billiard shots, walking round and round the table, frowning and stroking a thin moustache between shots, a little green in the face under the low diffused lights.

'The Reds are coming,' the proprietor said, 'you'd better be off. I'm putting up the shutters.'

'Don't interrupt. They won't harm me,' the customer said. 'This is a tricky shot. Red's in baulk. Off the cushion. Screw on spot.' He shot his ball straight into a pocket.

'I knew you couldn't do anything with that,' the proprietor said, nodding his bald head. 'You might just as well go home. Give me a hand with the shutters first. I've sent my wife away.' The customer turned on him maliciously, rattling the cue between his fingers. 'It was your talking that spoilt the shot. You've cause to be frightened, I dare say. But I'm a poor man. I'm safe. I'm not going to stir.' He went across to his coat and took out a dry cigar. 'Bring me a bock.' He walked round the table on his toes and the balls clicked and the proprietor padded back to the bar, elderly and irritated. He did not fetch the beer but began to close the shutters; every move he made was slow and clumsy. Long before he had finished the group of Communists was outside.

He stopped what he was doing and watched them with furtive dislike. He was afraid that the rattle of the shutters would attract their attention. If I am very quiet and still, he thought, they may go on, and he remembered with malicious pleasure the police barricade across the Place de la République. That will finish them. In the meanwhile I must be very quiet, very still, and he felt a kind of warm satisfaction at the idea that worldly wisdom dictated the very attitude most suited to his nature. So he stared through the edge of a shutter, yellow, plump, cautious, hearing the billiard balls crackle in the other room, seeing the young man come limping up the pavement on the girl's arm, watching them stand and stare with dubious faces up the boulevard towards Combat.

But when they came into the café he was already behind the bar, smiling and bowing and missing nothing, noticing how they had divided forces, how six of them had begun to run back the way they had come.

The young man sat down in a dark corner above the cellar stairs and the others stood round the door waiting for something to happen. It gave the proprietor an odd feeling that they should stand there in his café not asking for a drink, knowing what to expect, when he, the owner, knew nothing, understood nothing. At last the girl said 'Cognac,' leaving the others and coming to the bar, but when he poured it out for her, very careful to give a fair and not a generous measure, she simply took it to the man sitting in the dark and held it to his mouth.

'Three francs,' the proprietor said. She took the glass and sipped a little and turned it so that the man's lips might touch the same spot. Then she knelt down and rested her forehead against the man's forehead and so they stayed.

'Three francs,' the proprietor said, but he could not make his voice bold. The man was no longer visible in his corner, only the girl's back, thin and shabby in a black cotton frock, as she knelt, leaning forward to find the man's face. The proprietor was daunted by the four men at the door, by the knowledge that they were Reds who had no respect for private property, who would drink his wine and go away without paying, who would rape his women (but there was only his wife, and she was not there), who would rob his bank, who would murder him as soon as look at him. So with fear in his heart he gave up the three francs as lost rather than attract any more attention.

Then the worst that he contemplated happened.

One of the men at the door came up to the bar and told him to pour out four glasses of cognac. 'Yes, yes,' the proprietor said, fumbling with the cork, praying secretly to the Virgin to send an angel, to send the police, to send the Gardes Mobiles, now, immediately, before the cork came out, 'that will be twelve francs.'

'Oh, no,' the man said, 'we are all comrades here. Share and share alike. Listen,' he said, with earnest mockery, leaning across the bar, 'all we have is yours just as much as it's ours, comrade,' and stepping back a pace he presented himself to the proprietor, so that he might take his choice of stringy tie, of threadbare trousers, of starved features. 'And it follows from that, comrade, that all you have is ours. So four cognacs. Share and share alike.'

'Of course,' the proprietor said, 'I was only joking.' Then he stood with bottle poised, and the four glasses tinkled upon the counter. 'A machine-gun,' he said, 'up by Combat,' and smiled to see how for the moment the men forgot their brandy, as they fidgeted near the door. Very soon now, he thought, and I shall be quit of them.

'A machine-gun,' the Red said incredulously, 'they're using machine-guns?'

'Well,' the proprietor said, encouraged by this sign that the Gardes Mobiles were not very far away, 'you can't pretend that you aren't armed yourselves.' He leant across the bar in a way that was almost paternal. 'After all, you know, your ideas—they wouldn't do in France. Free love.'

'Who's talking of free love?' the Red said.

The proprietor shrugged and smiled and nodded at the corner. The girl knelt with her head on the man's shoulder, her back to the room. They were quite silent and the glass of brandy stood on the floor beside them. The girl's beret was pushed back on her head and one stocking was laddered and darned from knee to ankle.

'What, those two? They aren't lovers.'

'I,' the proprietor said, 'with my bourgeois notions would have thought . . .'

'He's her brother,' the Red said.

The men came clustering round the bar and laughed at him, but softly as if a sleeper or a sick person were in the house. All the time they were listening for something. Between their shoulders the proprietor could look out across the boulevard; he could see the corner of the Faubourg du Temple.

'What are you waiting for?'

'For friends,' the Red said. He made a gesture with open palm as if to say: You see, we share and share alike. We have no secrets.

Something moved at the corner of the Faubourg du Temple.

'Four more cognacs,' the Red said.

'What about those two?' the proprietor asked.

'Leave them alone. They'll look after themselves. They're tired.'

How tired they were. No walk up the boulevard from Ménilmontant could explain the tiredness. They seemed to have come farther and fared a great deal worse than their companions. They were more starved; they were infinitely more hopeless, sitting in their dark corner away from the friendly gossip, the amicable voices which now confused the proprietor's brain, until for a moment he believed himself to be a host entertaining friends.

He laughed and made a broad joke directed at the two of them, but they made no sign of understanding. Perhaps they were to be pitied, cut off from the camaraderie round the counter; perhaps they were to be envied for their deeper comradeship. The proprietor thought for no reason at all of the bare grey trees of the Tuileries like a series of exclamation marks drawn against the winter sky. Puzzled, disintegrated, with all his bearings lost, he stared out through the door towards the Faubourg.

It was as if they had not seen each other for a long while, and would soon again be saying good-bye. Hardly aware of what he was doing he filled four glasses with brandy. They stretched out worn blunted fingers for them.

'Wait,' he said. 'I've got something better than this'; then paused, conscious of what was happening across the boulevard. The lamplights splashed down on blue steel helmets; the Gardes Mobiles were lining out across the entrance to the Faubourg, and a machine-gun pointed directly at the café windows.

So, the proprietor thought, my prayers are answered. Now I must do my part, not look, not warn them, save myself. Have they covered the side door?

'I will get the other bottle. Real Napoleon brandy. Share and share alike.' He felt a curious lack of triumph as he opened the trap of the bar and came out. He tried not to walk quickly back towards the billiard room. Nothing that he did must warn these men; he tried to spur himself with the thought that every slow casual step he took was a blow for France, for his café, for his savings. He had to step over the girl's feet to pass her; she was asleep. He noted the sharp shoulder blades thrusting through the cotton, and raised his eyes and met her brother's, filled with pain and despair.

He stopped. He found he could not pass without a word. It was as if he needed to explain something, as if he belonged to the wrong party. With false bonhomie he waved the corkscrew he carried in the other's face. 'Another cognac, eh?'

'It's no good talking to them,' the Red said, 'they're German. They don't understand a word.'

'German?'

'That's what's wrong with his leg. A concentration camp.'

The proprietor told himself that he must be quick, that he must put a door between him and them, that the end was very close, but he was bewildered by the hopelessness in the man's gaze. 'What's he doing here?' Nobody answered him. It was as if his question were too foolish to need a reply. With his head sunk upon his breast the proprietor went past, and the girl slept on. He was like a stranger leaving a room where all the rest are friends. A German. They don't understand a word; and up, up through the heavy darkness of his mind, through the avarice and the dubious triumph, a few German words remembered from the very old days climbed like spies into the light: a line from the *Lorelei* learnt at school, *Kamerad* with its wartime suggestion of fear and surrender, and oddly from nowhere the phrase *mein Bruder*. He opened the door of the billiard room and closed it behind him and softly turned the key.

'Spot in baulk,' the customer explained and leant across the great green table, but while he took aim, wrinkling his narrow peevish eyes, the firing started. It came in two bursts with a rip of glass between. The girl cried out something, but it was not one of the words he knew. Then feet ran across the floor, the trap of the bar slammed. The proprietor sat back against the table and listened for any further sound; but silence came in under the door and silence through the keyhole.

'The cloth. My God, the cloth,' the customer said, and the proprietor looked down at his own hand which was working the corkscrew into the table.

'Will this absurdity never end?' the customer said. 'I shall go home.'

'Wait,' the proprietor said, 'wait.' He was listening to voices and footsteps in the other room. They were voices he did not recognize. Then a car drove up and presently drove away again. Somebody rattled the handle of the door.

'Who is it?' the proprietor called.

'Who are you? Open that door.'

'Ah,' the customer said with relief, 'the police. Where was I now? Spot in baulk.' He began to chalk his cue. The proprietor opened the door. Yes, the Gardes Mobiles had arrived; he was safe again, though his windows were smashed. The Reds had vanished as if they had never been. He looked at the raised trap, at the smashed electric bulbs, at the broken bottle which dripped behind the bar. The café was full of men, and he remembered with odd relief that he had not had time to lock the side door.

'Are you the owner?' the officer asked. 'A bock for each of these men and a cognac for myself. Be quick about it.'

The proprietor calculated, 'Nine francs fifty,' and watched closely with bent head the coins rattle upon the counter.

'You see,' the officer said with significance, 'we pay.' He nodded towards the side door. 'Those others: did they pay?'

No, the proprietor admitted, they had not paid, but as he counted the coins and slipped them into the till, he caught himself silently repeating the officer's order—'A bock for each of these men.' Those others, he thought, one's got to say that for them, they weren't mean about the drink. It was four cognacs with them. But, of course, they did not pay. 'And my windows,' he complained aloud with sudden asperity, 'what about my windows?'

'Never you mind,' the officer said, 'the government will pay. You have only to send in your bill. Hurry up now with my cognac. I have no time for gossip.'

'You can see for yourself,' the proprietor said, 'how the bottles have been broken. Who will pay for that?'

'Everything will be paid for,' the officer said.

'And now I must go to the cellar to fetch more.'

He was angry at the reiteration of the word pay. They enter my café, he thought, they smash my windows, they order me about and think that all is well if they pay, pay, pay. It occurred to him that these men were intruders.

'Step to it,' the officer said, and turned and rebuked one of the men who had leant his rifle against the bar.

At the top of the cellar stairs the proprietor stopped. They were in darkness, but by the light from the bar he could just make out a body half-way down. He began to tremble violently, and it was some seconds before he could strike a match. The young German lay head downwards, and the blood from his head had dropped on to the step below. His eyes were open and stared back at the proprietor with the old despairing expression of life. The proprietor would not believe that he was dead. 'Kamerad,' he said, bending down, while the match singed his fingers and went out, trying to recall some phrase in German, but he could only remember, as he bent lower still, 'mein Bruder'. Then suddenly he turned and ran up the steps, waved the match-box in the officer's face, and called out in a low hysterical voice to him and his men and to the customer stooping under the low green shade, 'Salauds! Salauds!'

'What was that? What was that?' the officer exclaimed. 'Did you say that he was your brother? It's impossible,' and he frowned incredulously at the proprietor and rattled the coins in his pocket.

1936

JUBILEE

Mr Chalfont ironed his trousers and his tie. Then he folded up his ironing-board and put it away. He was tall and he had preserved his figure; he looked distinguished even in his pants in the small furnished bed-sitting room he kept off Shepherd's Market. He was fifty, but he didn't look more than forty-five; he was stony broke, but he remained unquestionably Mayfair.

He examined his collar with anxiety; he hadn't been out of doors for more than a week, except to the public-house at the corner to eat his morning and evening ham roll, and then he always wore an overcoat and a soiled collar. He decided that it wouldn't damage the effect if he wore it once more; he didn't believe in economizing too rigidly over his laundry, you had to spend money in order to earn money, but there was no point in being extravagant. And somehow he didn't believe in his luck this cocktail time; he was going out for the good of his morale, because after a week away from the restaurants it would have been so easy to let everything slide, to confine himself to his room and his twice daily visit to the public-house.

The Jubilee decorations were still out in the cold windy May. Soiled by showers and soot the streamers blew up across Piccadilly, draughty with desolation. They were the reminder of a good time Mr Chalfont hadn't shared; he hadn't blown whistles or thrown paper ribbons; he certainly hadn't danced to any harmoniums. His neat figure was like a symbol of Good Taste as he waited with folded umbrella for the traffic lights to go green; he had learned to hold his hand so that one frayed patch on his sleeve didn't show, and the rather exclusive club tie, freshly ironed, might have been bought that morning. It wasn't lack of patriotism or loyalty which had kept Mr Chalfont indoors all through Jubilee week. Nobody drank the toast of the King more sincerely than Mr Chalfont so long as someone else was standing the drink, but an instinct deeper than good form had warned him not to be about. Too many people whom he had once known (so he explained it) were coming up from the country; they might want to look him up, and a fellow just couldn't ask them back to a room like this. That explained his discretion; it didn't explain his sense of oppression while he waited for the Jubilee to be over.

Now he was back at the old game.

He called it that himself, smoothing his neat grey military moustache. The old game. Somebody going rapidly round the corner into Berkeley Street nudged him playfully and said, 'Hullo, you old devil,' and was gone again, leaving the memory of many playful nudges in the old days, of Merdy and the Boob. For he couldn't disguise the fact that he was after the ladies. He didn't want to disguise it. It made his whole profession appear even to himself rather gallant and carefree. It disguised the fact that the ladies were not so young as they might be and that it was the ladies (God bless them!) who paid. It disguised the fact that Merdy and the Boob had long ago vanished from his knowledge. The list of his acquaintances included a great many women but hardly a single man; no one was more qualified by a long grimy experience to tell smoking-room stories, but the smoking-room in which Mr Chalfont was welcome did not nowadays exist.

Mr Chalfont crossed the road. It wasn't an easy life, it exhausted him nervously and physically, he needed a great many sherries to keep going. The first sherry he had always to pay for himself; that was the thirty pounds he marked as expenses on his income-tax return. He dived through the entrance, not looking either way, for it would never do for the porter to think that he was soliciting any of the women who moved heavily like seals through the dim aquarium light of the lounge. But his usual seat was occupied.

He turned away to look for another chair where he could exhibit himself discreetly: the select tie, the tan, the grey distinguished hair, the strong elegant figure, the air of a retired Governor from the Colonies. He studied the woman who sat in his chair covertly: he thought he'd seen her somewhere, the mink coat, the overblown figure, the expensive dress. Her face was familiar but unnoted, like that of someone you pass every day at the same place. She was vulgar, she was cheerful, she was undoubtedly rich. He couldn't think where he had met her.

She caught Mr Chalfont's eye and winked. He blushed, he was horrified, nothing of this sort had ever happened to him before; the porter was watching and Mr Chalfont felt scandal at his elbow, robbing him of his familiar restaurant, his last hunting ground, turning him perhaps out of Mayfair altogether into some bleak Paddington parlour where he couldn't keep up the least appearance of gallantry. Am I so obvious, he thought, so obvious? He went hastily across to her before she could wink again. 'Excuse me,' he said, 'you must remember me. What a long time . . . '

'Your face is familiar, dear,' she said. 'Have a cocktail.'

'Well,' Mr Chalfont said, 'I should certainly not mind a sherry, Mrs—Mrs—I've quite forgotten your surname.'

'You're a sport,' the woman said, 'but Amy will do.'

'Ah,' Mr Chalfont said, 'you are looking very well, Amy. It gives me much pleasure to see you sitting there again after all these—months—why, years it must be. The last time we met . . . '

'I don't remember you clearly, dear, though of course when I saw you looking at me . . . I suppose it was in Jermyn Street.'

'Jermyn Street,' Mr Chalfont said. 'Surely not Jermyn Street. I've never . . . Surely it must have been when I had my flat in Curzon Street. Delectable evenings one had there. I've moved since then to a rather humbler abode where I wouldn't dream of inviting you . . . But perhaps we could slip away to some little nest of your own. Your health, my dear. You look younger than ever.'

'Happy days,' Amy said. Mr Chalfont winced. She fingered her mink coat. 'But you know—I've retired.'

'Ah, lost money, eh,' Mr Chalfont said. 'Dear lady, I've suffered in that way too. We must console each other a little. I suppose business is bad. Your husband—I seem to recall a trying man who did his best to interfere with our idyll. It was quite an idyll, wasn't it, those evenings in Curzon Street?'

'You've got it wrong, dear. I never was in Curzon Street. But if you date back to the time I tried that husband racket, why that goes years back, to the mews off Bond Street. Fancy your remembering. It was wrong of me. I can see that now. And it never really worked. I don't think he looked like a husband. But now I've retired. Oh, no,' she said, leaning forward until he could smell the brandy on her plump little lips, 'I haven't lost money; I've made it.'

'You're lucky,' Mr Chalfont said.

'It was all the Jubilee,' Amy explained.

'I was confined to my bed during the Jubilee,' Mr Chalfont said. 'I understand it all went off very well.'

'It was lovely,' Amy said. 'Why, I said to myself, everyone ought to do something to make it a success. So I cleaned up the streets.'

'I don't quite understand,' Mr Chalfont said. 'You mean the decorations?'

'No, no,' Amy said, 'that wasn't it at all. But it didn't seem to me nice, when all these Colonials were in London, for them to see the girls in Bond Street and Wardour Street and all over the place. I'm proud of London, and it didn't seem right to me that we should get a reputation.'

'People must live.'

'Of course they must live. Wasn't I in the business myself, dear?'

'Oh,' Mr Chalfont said, 'you were in the business?' It was quite a shock to him; he looked quickly this way and that, fearing that he might have been observed.

'So you see I opened a House and split with the girls. I took all the risk, and then of course I had my other expenses. I had to advertise.'

'How did you—how did you get it known?' He couldn't help having a kind of professional interest.

'Easy, dear. I opened a tourist bureau. Trips to the London underworld. Limehouse and all that. But there was always an old fellow who wanted the guide to show him something privately afterwards.'

'Very ingenious,' Mr Chalfont said.

'And loyal too, dear. It cleaned up the streets properly. Though of course I only took the best. I was very select. Some of them jibbed, because they said they did all the work, but as I said to them, it was My Idea.'

'So now you're retired?'

'I made five thousand pounds, dear. It was really my jubilee as well, though you mightn't think it to look at me. I always had the makings of a business woman, and I saw, you see, how I could extend the business. I opened at Brighton too. I cleaned up England in a way of speaking. It was ever so much nicer for the Colonials. There's been a lot of money in the country these last weeks. Have another sherry, dear, you are looking poorly.'

'Really, really you know I ought to be going.'

'Oh, come on. It's Jubilee, isn't it? Celebrate. Be a sport.'

'I think I see a friend.'

He looked helplessly around: a friend: he couldn't even think of a friend's name. He wilted before a personality stronger than his own. She bloomed there like a great dressy autumn flower. He felt old: my jubilee. His frayed cuffs showed; he had forgotten to arrange his hand. He said, 'Perhaps. Just one. It ought really to be on me,' and as he watched her bang for the waiter in the dim genteel place and dominate his disapproval when he came, Mr Chalfont couldn't help wondering at the unfairness of her confidence and her health. He had a touch of neuritis, but she was carnival; she really seemed to belong to the banners and drinks and plumes and processions. He said quite humbly, 'I should like to have seen the procession, but I wasn't up to it. My rheumatism,' he excused himself. His little withered sense of good taste could not stand the bright plebeian spontaneity. He was a fine dancer, but they'd have outdanced him on the pavements; he made love attractively in his formal well-bred way, but they'd have outloved him, blind and drunk and crazy and happy in the park. He had known that he would be out of place, he'd kept away; but it was humiliating to realize that Amy had missed nothing.

'You look properly done, dear,' Amy said. 'Let me lend you a couple of quid.'

'No, no,' Mr Chalfont said. 'Really I couldn't.'

'I expect you've given me plenty in your time.'

But had he? He couldn't remember her; it was such a long time since he'd been with a woman except in the way of business. He said, 'I couldn't. I really couldn't.' He tried to explain his attitude while she fumbled in her bag.

'I never take money—except, you know, from friends.' He admitted desperately, 'or except in business.' But he couldn't take his eyes away. He was broke and it was cruel of her to show him a five-pound note. 'No. Really.' It was a long time since his market price had been as high as five pounds.

'I know how it is, dear,' Amy said, 'I've been in the business myself, and I know just how you feel. Sometimes a gentleman would come home with me, give me a quid and run away as if he was scared. It was insulting. I never did like taking money for nothing.'

'But you're quite wrong,' Mr Chalfont said. 'That's not it at all. Not it at all.'

'Why, I could tell almost as soon as you spoke to me. You don't need to keep up pretences with me, dear,' Amy went inexorably on, while Mayfair faded from his manner until there remained only the bed-sitting room, the ham rolls, the iron heating on the stove. 'You don't need to be proud. But if you'd rather (it's all the same to me, it doesn't mean a thing to me) we'll go home, and let you do your stuff. It's all the same to me, dear, but if you'd rather—I know how you feel,' and presently they went out together arm-in-arm into the decorated desolate street.

'Cheer up, dear,' Amy said, as the wind picked up the ribbons and tore them from the poles and lifted the dust and made the banners flap, 'a girl likes a cheerful face.' And suddenly she became raucous and merry, slapping Mr Chalfont on his back, pinching his arm, saying, 'Let's have a little Jubilee spirit, dear,' taking her revenge for a world of uncongenial partners on old Mr Chalfont. You couldn't call him anything else now but old Mr Chalfont.

1936

A DAY SAVED

I had stuck closely to him, as people say like a shadow. But that's absurd. I'm no shadow. You can feel me, touch me, hear me, smell me. I'm Robinson. But I had sat at the next table, followed twenty yards behind down every street, when he went upstairs I waited at the bottom, and when he came down I passed out before him and paused at the first corner. In that way I was really like a shadow, for sometimes I was in front of him and sometimes I was behind him.

Who was he? I never knew his name. He was short and ordinary in appearance and he carried an umbrella; his hat was a bowler, and he wore brown gloves. But this was his importance to me: he carried something I dearly, despairingly wanted. It was beneath his clothes, perhaps in a pouch, a purse, perhaps dangling next to his skin. Who knows how cunning the most ordinary man can be? Surgeons can make clever insertions. He may have carried it even closer to his heart than the outer skin.

What was it? I never knew. I can only guess, as I might guess at his name, calling him Jones or Douglas, Wales, Canby, Fotheringay. Once in a restaurant I said 'Fotheringay' softly to my soup and I thought he looked up and round about him. I don't know. This is the horror I cannot escape: knowing nothing, his name, what it was he carried, why I wanted it so, why I followed him.

Presently we came to a railway bridge and underneath it he met a friend. I am using words again very inexactly. Bear with me. I try to be exact. I pray to be exact. All I want in the world is to know. So when I say he met a friend, I do not know that it was a friend, I know only that it was someone he greeted with apparent affection. The friend said to him, 'When do you leave?' He said, 'At two from Dover.' You may be sure I felt my pocket to make sure the ticket was there.

Then his friend said, 'If you fly you will save a day.'

He nodded, he agreed, he would sacrifice his ticket, he would save a day.

I ask you, what does a day saved matter to him or to you? A day saved from what? for what? Instead of spending the day travelling, you will see your friend a day earlier, but you cannot stay indefinitely, you will travel home twenty-four hours sooner, that is all. But you will fly home and again save a day? Save it from what, for what? You will begin work a day earlier, but you cannot work on indefinitely. It only means that you will cease work a day earlier. And then, what? You cannot die a day earlier. So you will realize perhaps how rash it was of you to save a day, when you discover how you cannot escape those twenty-four hours you have so carefully preserved; you may push them forward and push them forward, but some time they must be spent, and then you may wish you had spent them as innocently as in the train from Ostend.

But this thought never occurred to him. He said, 'Yes, that's true. It would save a day. I'll fly.' I nearly spoke to him then. The selfishness of the man. For that day which he thought he was saving might be his despair years later, but it was my despair at the instant. For I had been looking forward to the long train journey in the same compartment. It was winter, and the train would be nearly empty, and with the least luck we should be alone together. I had planned everything. I was going to talk to him. Because I knew nothing about him, I should begin in the usual way by asking whether he minded the window being raised a little or a little lowered. That would show him that we spoke the same language and he would probably be only too ready to talk, feeling himself in a foreign country; he would be grateful for any help I might be able to give him, translating this or that word.

Of course I never believed that talk would be enough. I should learn a great deal about him, but I believed that I should have to kill him before I knew all. I should have killed him, I think, at night, between the two stations which are the farthest parted, after the customs had examined our luggage and our passports had been stamped at the frontier, and we had pulled down the blinds and turned out the light. I had even planned what to do with his body, with the bowler hat and the umbrella and the brown gloves, but only if it became necessary, only if in no other way he would yield what I wanted. I am a gentle creature, not easily roused.

But now he had chosen to go by aeroplane and there was nothing that I could do. I followed him, of course, sat in the seat behind, watched his tremulousness at his first flight, how he avoided for a long while the sight of the sea below, how he kept his bowler hat upon his knees, how he gasped a little when the grey wing tilted up like the arm of a windmill to the sky and the houses were set on edge. There were times, I believe, when he regretted having saved a day.

We got out of the aeroplane together and he had a small trouble with the customs. I translated for him. He looked at me curiously and said, 'Thank you.' He was—again I suggest that I know when all I mean is I assume by his manner and his conversation—stupid and good-natured, but I believe for a moment he suspected me, thought he had seen me somewhere, in a tube, in a bus, in a public baths, below the railway bridge, on how many stairways. I asked him the time. He said, 'We put our clocks back an hour here,' and beamed with an absurd pleasure because he had saved an hour as well as a day.

I had a drink with him, several drinks with him. He was absurdly grateful for my help. I had beer with him at one place, gin at another, and at a third he insisted on my sharing a bottle of wine. We became for the time being friends. I felt more warmly towards him than towards any other man I have known, for, like love between a man and a woman, my affection was partly curiosity. I told him that I was Robinson; he meant to give me a card, but while he was looking for one he drank another glass of wine and forgot about it. We were both a little drunk. Presently I began to call him Fotheringay. He never contradicted me and it may have been his name, but I seem to remember also calling him Douglas, Wales and Canby without correction. He was very generous and I found it easy to talk with him; the stupid are often companionable. I told him that I was desperate and he offered me money. He could not understand what I wanted.

I said, 'You've saved a day. You can afford to come with me tonight to a place I know.'

He said, 'I have to take a train tonight.' He told me the name of the town, and he was not surprised when I told him that I was coming too.

We drank together all that evening and went to the station together. I was planning, if it became necessary, to kill him. I thought in all friendliness that perhaps after all I might save him from having saved a day. But it was a small local train; it crept from station to station, and at every station people got out of the train and other people got into the train. He insisted on travelling third class and the carriage was never empty. He could not speak a word of the language and he simply curled up in his corner and slept; it was I who remained awake and had to listen to the weary painful gossip, a servant speaking of her mistress, a peasant woman of the day's market, a soldier of the Church, and a man who, I believe, was a tailor of adultery, wire-worms and the harvest of three years ago.

It was two o'clock in the morning when we reached the end of our journey. I walked with him to the house where his friends lived. It was quite close to the station and I had no time to plan or carry out any plan. The garden gate was open and he asked me in. I said no. I would go to the hotel. He said his friends would be pleased to put me up for the remainder of the night, but I said no. The lights were on in a downstairs room and the curtains were not drawn. A man was asleep in a chair by a great stove and there were glasses on a tray, a decanter of whisky, two bottles of beer and a long thin bottle of Rhine wine. I stepped back and he went in and almost immediately the room was full of people. I could see his welcome in their eyes and in their gestures. There was a woman in a dressing-gown and a girl who sat with thin knees drawn up to her chin and three men, two of them old. They did not draw the curtains, though he must surely have guessed that I was watching them. The garden was cold; the winter beds were furred with weeds. I laid my hand on some prickly bush. It was as if they gave a deliberate display of their unity and companionship. My friend—I call him my friend, but he was really no more than an acquaintance and was my friend only for so long as we both were drunk—sat in the middle of them all, and I could tell from the way his lips were moving that he was telling them many things which he had never told me. Once I thought I could detect from his lip movements, 'I have saved a day.' He looked stupid and good-natured and happy. I could not bear the sight for long. It was an impertinence to display himself like that to me. I have never ceased to pray from that moment that the day he saved may be retarded and retarded until eventually he suffers its eighty-six thousand four hundred seconds when he has the most desperate need, when he is following another as I followed him, closely as people say like a shadow, so that he has to stop, as I have had to stop, to reassure himself: you can smell me, you can touch me, you can hear me, I am not a shadow: I am Fotheringay, Wales, Canby, I am Robinson.

1935

I SPY

Charlie Stowe waited until he heard his mother snore before he got out of bed. Even then he moved with caution and tiptoed to the window. The front of the house was irregular, so that it was possible to see a light burning in his mother's room. But now all the windows were dark. A searchlight passed across the sky, lighting the banks of cloud and probing the dark deep spaces between, seeking enemy airships. The wind blew from the sea, and Charlie Stowe could hear behind his mother's snores the beating of the waves. A draught through the cracks in the window-frame stirred his night-shirt. Charlie Stowe was frightened.

But the thought of the tobacconist's shop which his father kept down a dozen wooden stairs drew him on. He was twelve years old, and already boys at the County School mocked him because he had never smoked a cigarette. The packets were piled twelve deep below, Gold Flake and Player's, De Reszke, Abdulla, Woodbines, and the little shop lay under a thin haze of stale smoke which would completely disguise his crime. That it was a crime to steal some of his father's stock Charlie Stowe had no doubt, but he did not love his father; his father was unreal to him, a wraith, pale, thin, indefinite, who noticed him only spasmodically and left even punishment to his mother. For his mother he felt a passionate demonstrative love; her large boisterous presence and her noisy charity filled the world for him; from her speech he judged her the friend of everyone, from the rector's wife to the 'dear Queen', except the 'Huns', the monsters who lurked in Zeppelins in the clouds. But his father's affection and dislike were as indefinite as his movements. Tonight he had said he would be in Norwich, and yet you never knew. Charlie Stowe had no sense of safety as he crept down the wooden stairs. When they creaked he clenched his fingers on the collar of his night-shirt.

At the bottom of the stairs he came out quite suddenly into the little shop. It was too dark to see his way, and he did not dare touch the switch. For half a minute he sat in despair on the bottom step with his chin cupped in his hands. Then the regular movement of the searchlight was reflected through an upper window and the boy had time to fix in memory the pile of cigarettes, the counter, and the small hole under it. The footsteps of a policeman on the pavement made him grab the first packet to his hand and dive for the hole. A light shone along the floor and a hand tried the door, then the footsteps passed on, and Charlie cowered in the darkness.

At last he got his courage back by telling himself in his curiously adult way that if he were caught now there was nothing to be done about it, and he might as well have his smoke. He put a cigarette in his mouth and then remembered that he had no matches. For a while he dared not move. Three times the searchlight lit the shop, as he muttered taunts and encouragements. 'May as well be hung for a sheep,' 'Cowardy, cowardy custard,' grown-up and childish exhortations oddly mixed.

But as he moved he heard footfalls in the street, the sound of several men walking rapidly. Charlie Stowe was old enough to feel surprise that anybody was about. The footsteps came nearer, stopped; a key was turned in the shop door, a voice said: 'Let him in,' and then he heard his father, 'If you wouldn't mind being quiet, gentlemen. I don't want to wake up the family.' There was a note unfamiliar to Charlie in the undecided voice. A torch flashed and the electric globe burst into blue light. The boy held his breath; he wondered whether his father would hear his heart beating, and he clutched his night-shirt tightly and prayed, 'O God, don't let me be caught.' Through a crack in the counter he could see his father where he stood, one hand held to his high stiff collar, between two men in bowler hats and belted mackintoshes. They were strangers.

'Have a cigarette,' his father said in a voice dry as a biscuit.

One of the men shook his head. 'It wouldn't do, not when we are on duty. Thank you all the same.' He spoke gently, but without kindness: Charlie Stowe thought his father must be ill.

'Mind if I put a few in my pocket?' Mr Stowe asked, and when the man nodded he lifted a pile of Gold Flake and Players from a shelf and caressed the packets with the tips of his fingers.

'Well,' he said, 'there's nothing to be done about it, and I may as well have my smokes.' For a moment Charlie Stowe feared discovery, his father stared round the shop so thoroughly; he might have been seeing it for the first time. 'It's a good little business,' he said, 'for those that like it. The wife will sell out, I suppose. Else the neighbours'll be wrecking it. Well, you want to be off. A stitch in time. I'll get my coat.'

'One of us'll come with you, if you don't mind,' said the stranger gently.

'You needn't trouble. It's on the peg here. There, I'm all ready.'

The other man said in an embarrassed way, 'Don't you want to speak to your wife?' The thin voice was decided, 'Not me. Never do today what you can put off till tomorrow. She'll have her chance later, won't she?'

'Yes, yes,' one of the strangers said and he became very cheerful and encouraging. 'Don't you worry too much. While there's life . . . ' and suddenly his father tried to laugh.

When the door had closed Charlie Stowe tiptoed upstairs and got into bed. He wondered why his father had left the house again so late at night and who the strangers were. Surprise and awe kept him for a little while awake. It was as if a familiar photograph had stepped from the frame to reproach him with neglect. He remembered how his father had held tight to his collar and fortified himself with proverbs, and he thought for the first time that, while his mother was boisterous and kindly, his father was very like himself, doing things in the dark which frightened him. It would have pleased him to go down to his father and tell him that he loved him, but he could hear through the window the quick steps going away. He was alone in the house with his mother, and he fell asleep.

1930

PROOF POSITIVE

The tired voice went on. It seemed to surmount enormous obstacles to speech. The man's sick, Colonel Crashaw thought, with pity and irritation. When a young man he had climbed in the Himalayas, and he remembered how at great heights several breaths had to be taken for every step advanced. The five-foot-high platform in the Music Rooms of The Spa seemed to entail for the speaker some of the same effort. He should never have come out on such a raw afternoon, thought Colonel Crashaw, pouring out a glass of water and pushing it across the lecturer's table. The rooms were badly heated, and yellow fingers of winter fog felt for cracks in the many windows. There was little doubt that the speaker had lost all touch with his audience. It was scattered in patches about the hall—elderly ladies who made no attempt to hide their cruel boredom, and a few men, with the appearance of retired officers, who put up a show of attention.

Colonel Crashaw, as president of the local Psychical Society, had received a note from the speaker a little more than a week before. Written by a hand which trembled with sickness, age or drunkenness, it asked urgently for a special meeting of the society. An extraordinary, a really impressive, experience was to be described while still fresh in the mind, though what the experience had been was left vague. Colonel Crashaw would have hesitated to comply if the note had not been signed by a Major Philip Weaver, Indian Army, retired. One had to do what one could for a brother officer; the trembling of the hand must be either age or sickness.

It proved principally to be the latter when the two men met for the first time on the platform. Major Weaver was not more than sixty, thin, and dark, with an ugly obstinate nose and satire in his eye, the most unlikely person to experience anything unexplainable. What antagonized Crashaw most was that Weaver used scent; a white handkerchief which drooped from his breast pocket exhaled as rich and sweet an odour as a whole altar of lilies. Several ladies prinked their noses, and General Leadbitter asked loudly whether he might smoke.

It was quite obvious that Weaver understood. He smiled provocatively and asked very slowly, 'Would you mind not smoking? My throat has been bad for some time.' Crashaw murmured that it was terrible weather; influenza throats were common. The satirical eye came round to him and considered him thoughtfully, while Weaver said in a voice which carried half-way across the hall, 'It's cancer in my case.'

In the shocked vexed silence that followed the unnecessary intimacy he began to speak without waiting for any introduction from Crashaw. He seemed at first to be in a hurry. It was only later that the terrible impediments were placed in the way of his speech. He had a high voice, which sometimes broke into a squeal, and must have been peculiarly disagreeable on the parade-ground. He paid a few compliments to the local society; his remarks were just sufficiently exaggerated to be irritating. He was glad, he said, to give them the chance of hearing him; what he had to say might alter their whole view of the relative values of matter and spirit.

Mystic stuff, thought Crashaw.

Weaver's high voice began to shoot out hurried platitudes. The spirit, he said, was stronger than anyone realized; the physiological action of heart and brain and nerves were subordinate to the spirit. The spirit was everything. He said again, his voice squeaking up like bats into the ceiling, 'The spirit is so much stronger than you think.' He put his hand across his throat and squinted sideways at the window-panes and the nuzzling fog, and upwards at the bare electric globe sizzling with heat and poor light in the dim afternoon. 'It's immortal,' he told them very seriously, and they shifted, restless, uncomfortable and weary, in their chairs.

It was then that his voice grew tired and his speech impeded. The knowledge that he had entirely lost touch with his audience may have been the cause. An elderly lady at the back had taken her knitting from a bag, and her needles flashed along the walls when the light caught them, like a bright ironic spirit. Satire for a moment deserted Weaver's eyes, and Crashaw saw the vacancy it left, as though the ball had turned to glass.

'This is important,' the lecturer cried to them. 'I can tell you a story—' His audience's attention was momentarily caught by his promise of something definite, but the stillness of the lady's needles did not soothe him. He sneered at them all: 'Signs and wonders,' he said.

Then he lost the thread of his speech altogether.

His hand passed to and fro across his throat and he quoted Shakespeare, and then St Paul's Epistle to the Galatians. His speech, as it grew slower, seemed to lose all logical order, though now and then Crashaw was surprised by the shrewdness in the juxtaposition of two irrelevant ideas. It was like the conversation of an old man which flits from subject to subject, the thread a subconscious one. 'When I was at Simla,' he said, bending his brows as though to avoid the sunflash on the barrack square, but perhaps the frost, the fog, the tarnished room broke his memories. He began to assure the wearied faces all over again that the spirit did not die when the body died, but that the body only moved at the spirit's will. One had to be obstinate, to grapple . . .

Pathetic, Crashaw thought, the sick man's clinging to his belief. It was as if life were an only son who was dying and with whom he wished to preserve some form of communication . . .

A note was passed to Crashaw from the audience. It came from a Dr Brown, a small alert man in the third row; the society cherished him as a kind of pet sceptic. The note read: 'Can't you make him stop? The man's obviously very ill. And what good is his talk, anyway?'

Crashaw turned his eyes sideways and upwards and felt his

pity vanish at sight of the roving satirical eyes that gave the lie to the tongue, and at the smell, overpoweringly sweet, of the scent in which Weaver had steeped his handkerchief. The man was an 'outsider'; he would look up his record in the old Army Lists when he got home.

'Proof positive,' Weaver was saying, sighing a shrill breath of exhaustion between the words. Crashaw laid his watch upon the table, but Weaver paid him no attention. He was supporting himself on the rim of the table with one hand. 'I'll give you,' he said, speaking with increasing difficulty, 'proof pos . . . ' His voice scraped into stillness, like a needle at a record's end, but the quiet did not last. From an expressionless face, a sound which was more like a high mew than anything else, jerked the audience into attention. He followed it up, still without a trace of any emotion or understanding, with a succession of incomprehensible sounds, a low labial whispering, an odd jangling note, while his fingers tapped on the table. The sounds brought to mind innumerable séances, the bound medium, the tambourine shaken in mid-air, the whispered trivialities of ghosts in the darkness, the dinginess, the airless rooms.

Weaver sat down slowly in his chair and let his head fall backwards. An old lady began to cry nervously, and Dr Brown scrambled on to the platform and bent over him. Colonel Crashaw saw the doctor's hand tremble as he picked the handkerchief from the pocket and flung it away from him. Crashaw, aware of another and more unpleasant smell, heard Dr Brown whisper, 'Send them all away. He's dead.'

He spoke with a distress unusual in a doctor accustomed to every kind of death. Crashaw, before he complied, glanced over Dr Brown's shoulder at the dead man. Major Weaver's appearance disquieted him. In a long life he had seen many forms of death, men shot by their own hand, and men killed in the field, but never such a suggestion of mortality. The body might have been one fished from the sea a long while after death; the flesh of the face seemed as ready to fall as an over-ripe fruit. So it was with no great shock of surprise that he heard Dr Brown's whispered statement: 'The man must have been dead a week.'

What the Colonel thought of most was Weaver's claim—
'Proof positive'—proof, he had probably meant, that the spirit
outlived the body, that it tasted eternity. But all he had certainly
revealed was how, without the body's aid, the spirit in seven days
decayed into whispered nonsense.

1930

THE SECOND DEATH

She found me in the evening under the trees that grew outside the village. I had never cared for her and would have hidden myself if I'd seen her coming. She was to blame, I'm certain, for her son's vices. If they were vices, but I'm very far from admitting that they were. At any rate he was generous, never mean, like others in the village I could mention if I chose.

I was staring hard at a leaf or she would never have found me. It was dangling from the twig, its stalk torn across by the wind or else by a stone one of the village children had flung. Only the green tough skin of the stalk held it there suspended. I was watching closely, because a caterpillar was crawling across the surface making the leaf sway to and fro. The caterpillar was aiming at the twig, and I wondered whether it would reach it in safety or whether the leaf would fall with it into the water. There was a pool underneath the trees, and the water always appeared red, because of the heavy clay in the soil.

I never knew whether the caterpillar reached the twig, for, as I've said, the wretched woman found me. The first I knew of her coming was her voice just behind my ear.

'I've been looking in all the pubs for you,' she said in her old shrill voice. It was typical of her to say 'all the pubs' when there were only two in the place. She always wanted credit for the trouble she hadn't really taken.

I was annoyed and I couldn't help speaking a little harshly. 'You might have saved yourself the trouble,' I said, 'you should have known I wouldn't be in a pub on a fine night like this.'

The old vixen became quite humble. She was always smooth

enough when she wanted anything. 'It's for my poor son,' she said. That meant that he was ill. When he was well I never heard her say anything better than 'that dratted boy'. She'd make him be in the house by midnight every day of the week, as if there were any serious mischief a man could get up to in a little village like ours. Of course we soon found a way to cheat her, but it was the principle of the thing I objected to—a grown man of over thirty ordered about by his mother, just because she hadn't a husband to control. But when he was ill, though it might be with only a small chill, it was 'my poor son'.

'He's dying,' she said, 'and God knows what I shall do without him.'

'Well, I don't see how I can help you,' I said. I was angry, because he'd been dying once before and she'd done everything but actually bury him. I imagined it was the same sort of dying this time, the sort a man gets over. I'd seen him about the week before on his way up the hill to see the big-breasted girl at the farm. I'd watched him till he was like a little black dot, which stayed suddenly by a square box in a field. That was the barn where they used to meet. I have very good eyes and it amuses me to try how far and how clearly they can see. I met him again some time after midnight and helped him get into the house without his mother knowing, and he was well enough then—only a little sleepy and tired.

The old vixen was at it again. 'He's been asking for you,' she shrilled at me.

'If he's as ill as you make out,' I said, 'it would be better for him to ask for a doctor.'

'Doctor's there, but he can't do anything.' That startled me for a moment, I'll admit it, until I thought, 'The old devil's malingering. He's got some plan or other.' He was quite clever enough to cheat a doctor. I had seen him throw a fit that would have deceived Moses.

'For God's sake come,' she said, 'he seems frightened.' Her voice broke quite genuinely, for I suppose in her way she was fond of him. I couldn't help pitying her a little, for I knew that he had never cared a mite for her and had never troubled to disguise the fact.

I left the trees and the red pool and the struggling caterpillar, for I knew that she would never leave me alone, now that her 'poor boy' was asking for me. Yet a week ago there was nothing she wouldn't have done to keep us apart. She thought me responsible for his ways, as though any mortal man could have kept him off a likely woman when his appetite was up.

I think it must have been the first time I had entered their cottage by the front door, since I came to the village ten years ago. I threw an amused glance at his window. I thought I could see the marks on the wall of the ladder we'd used the week before. We'd had a little difficulty in putting it straight, but his mother slept sound. He had brought the ladder down from the barn, and when he'd got safely in, I carried it up there again. But you could never trust his word. He'd lie to his best friend, and when I reached the barn I found the girl had gone. If he couldn't bribe you with his mother's money, he'd bribe you with other people's promises.

I began to feel uneasy directly I got inside the door. It was natural that the house should be quiet, for the pair of them never had any friends to stay, although the old woman had a sister-in-law living only a few miles away. But I didn't like the sound of the doctor's feet, as he came downstairs to meet us. He'd twisted his face into a pious solemnity for our benefit, as though there was something holy about death, even about the death of my friend.

'He's conscious,' he said, 'but he's going. There's nothing I can do. If you want him to die in peace, better let his friend go along up. He's frightened about something.'

The doctor was right. I could tell that as soon as I bent under the lintel and entered my friend's room. He was propped up on a pillow, and his eyes were on the door, waiting for me to come. They were very bright and frightened, and his hair lay across his forehead in sticky stripes. I'd never realized before what an ugly fellow he was. He had got sly eyes that looked at you too much out of the corners, but when he was in ordinary health, they held a twinkle that made you forget the slyness. There was something pleasant and brazen in the twinkle, as much as to say, 'I know I'm sly and ugly. But what does that matter? I've got guts.' It was that twinkle, I think, some women found attractive and stimulating. Now when the twinkle was gone, he looked a rogue and nothing else.

I thought it my duty to cheer him up, so I made a small joke out of the fact that he was alone in bed. He didn't seem to relish it, and I was beginning to fear that he, too, was taking a religious view of his death, when he told me to sit down, speaking quite sharply.

'I'm dying,' he said, talking very fast, 'and I want to ask you something. That doctor's no good—he'd think me delirious. I'm frightened, old man. I want to be reassured,' and then after a long pause, 'someone with common sense.' He slipped a little farther down in his bed.

'I've only once been badly ill before,' he said. 'That was before you settled here. I wasn't much more than a boy. People tell me that I was even supposed to be dead. They were carrying me out to burial, when a doctor stopped them just in time.'

I'd heard plenty of cases like that, and I saw no reason why he should want to tell me about it. And then I thought I saw his point. His mother had not been too anxious once before to see if he were properly dead, though I had little doubt that she made a great show of grief—'My poor boy. I don't know what I shall do without him.' And I'm certain that she believed herself then, as she believed herself now. She wasn't a murderess. She was only inclined to be premature.

'Look here, old man,' I said, and I propped him a little higher on his pillow, 'you needn't be frightened. You aren't going to die, and anyway I'd see that the doctor cut a vein or something before they moved you. But that's all morbid stuff. Why, I'd stake my shirt that you've got plenty more years in front of you. And plenty more girls too,' I added to make him smile.

'Can't you cut out all that?' he said, and I knew then that he had turned religious. 'Why,' he said, 'if I lived, I wouldn't touch another girl. I wouldn't, not one.'

I tried not to smile at that, but it wasn't easy to keep a straight face. There's always something a bit funny about a sick man's morals. 'Anyway,' I said, 'you needn't be frightened.'

'It's not that,' he said. 'Old man, when I came round that

other time, I thought that I'd been dead. It wasn't like sleep at all. Or rest in peace. There was someone there all round me, who knew everything. Every girl I'd ever had. Even that young one who hadn't understood. It was before your time. She lived a mile down the road, where Rachel lives now, but she and her family went away afterwards. Even the money I'd taken from mother. I don't call that stealing. It's in the family. I never had a chance to explain. Even the thoughts I'd had. A man can't help his thoughts.'

'A nightmare,' I said.

'Yes, it must have been a dream, mustn't it? The sort of dream people do get when they are ill. And I saw what was coming to me too. I can't bear being hurt. It wasn't fair. And I wanted to faint and I couldn't, because I was dead.'

'In the dream,' I said. His fear made me nervous. 'In the dream,' I said again.

'Yes, it must have been a dream—mustn't it?—because I woke up. The curious thing was I felt quite well and strong. I got up and stood in the road, and a little farther down, kicking up the dust, was a small crowd, going off with a man—the doctor who had stopped them burying me.'

'Well?' I said.

'Old man, he said, 'suppose it was true. Suppose I had been dead. I believed it then, you know, and so did my mother. But you can't trust her. I went straight for a couple of years. I thought it might be a sort of second chance. Then things got fogged and somehow . . . It didn't seem really possible. It's not possible. Of course it's not possible. You know it isn't, don't you?'

'Why, no,' I said. 'Miracles of that sort don't happen nowadays. And anyway, they aren't likely to happen to you, are they? And here of all places under the sun.'

'It would be so dreadful,' he said, 'if it had been true, and I'd got to go through all that again. You don't know what things were going to happen to me in that dream. And they'd be worse now.' He stopped and then, after a moment, he added as though he were stating a fact: 'When one's dead there's no unconsciousness any more for ever.'

'Of course it was a dream,' I said, and squeezed his hand. He was frightening me with his fancies. I wished that he'd die quickly, so that I could get away from his sly, bloodshot and terrified eyes and see something cheerful and amusing, like the Rachel he had mentioned, who lived a mile down the road.

'Why,' I said, 'if there had been a man about working miracles like that, we should have heard of others, you may be sure. Even poked away in this God-forsaken spot,' I said.

'There were some others,' he said. 'But the stories only went round among the poor, and they'll believe anything, won't they? There were lots of diseased and crippled they said he'd cured. And there was a man, who'd been born blind, and he came and just touched his eyelids and sight came to him. Those were all old wives' tales, weren't they?' he asked me, stammering with fear, and then lying suddenly still and bunched up at the side of the bed.

I began to say, 'Of course, they were all lies,' but I stopped, because there was no need. All I could do was to go downstairs and tell his mother to come up and close his eyes. I wouldn't have touched them for all the money in the world. It was a long time since I thought of that day, ages and ages ago, when I felt a cold touch like spittle on my lids and opening my eyes had seen a man like a tree surrounded by other trees walking away.

1929

THE END OF THE PARTY

Peter Morton woke with a start to face the first light. Rain tapped against the glass. It was January the fifth.

He looked across a table on which a night-light had guttered into a pool of water, at the other bed. Francis Morton was still asleep, and Peter lay down again with his eyes on his brother. It amused him to imagine it was himself whom he watched, the same hair, the same eyes, the same lips and line of cheek. But the thought palled, and the mind went back to the fact which lent the day importance. It was the fifth of January. He could hardly believe a year had passed since Mrs Henne-Falcon had given her last children's party.

Francis turned suddenly upon his back and threw an arm across his face, blocking his mouth. Peter's heart began to beat fast, not with pleasure now but with uneasiness. He sat up and called across the table, 'Wake up.' Francis's shoulders shook and he waved a clenched fist in the air, but his eyes remained closed. To Peter Morton the whole room seemed to darken, and he had the impression of a great bird swooping. He cried again, 'Wake up,' and once more there was silver light and the touch of rain on the windows. Francis rubbed his eyes. 'Did you call out?' he asked.

'You are having a bad dream,' Peter said. Already experience had taught him how far their minds reflected each other. But he was the elder, by a matter of minutes, and that brief extra interval of light, while his brother still struggled in pain and darkness, had given him self-reliance and an instinct of protection towards the other who was afraid of so many things.

'I dreamed that I was dead,' Francis said.

'What was it like?' Peter asked.

'I can't remember,' Francis said.

'You dreamed of a big bird.'

'Did I?'

The two lay silent in bed facing each other, the same green eyes, the same nose tilting at the tip, the same firm lips, and the same premature modelling of the chin. The fifth of January, Peter thought again, his mind drifting idly from the image of cakes to the prizes which might be won. Egg-and-spoon races, spearing apples in basins of water, blind man's buff.

'I don't want to go,' Francis said suddenly. 'I suppose Joyce will be there . . . Mabel Warren.' Hateful to him, the thought of a party shared with those two. They were older than he. Joyce was eleven and Mabel Warren thirteen. The long pigtails swung superciliously to a masculine stride. Their sex humiliated him, as they watched him fumble with his egg, from under lowered scornful lids. And last year . . . he turned his face away from Peter, his cheeks scarlet.

'What's the matter?' Peter asked.

'Oh, nothing. I don't think I'm well. I've got a cold. I oughtn't to go to the party.' Peter was puzzled. 'But Francis, is it a bad cold?'

'It will be a bad cold if I go to the party. Perhaps I shall die.'

'Then you mustn't go,' Peter said, prepared to solve all difficulties with one plain sentence, and Francis let his nerves relax, ready to leave everything to Peter. But though he was grateful he did not turn his face towards his brother. His cheeks still bore the badge of a shameful memory, of the game of hide and seek last year in the darkened house, and of how he had screamed when Mabel Warren put her hand suddenly upon his arm. He had not heard her coming. Girls were like that. Their shoes never squeaked. No boards whined under the tread. They slunk like cats on padded claws.

When the nurse came in with hot water Francis lay tranquil leaving everything to Peter. Peter said, 'Nurse, Francis has got a cold.'

The tall starched woman laid the towels across the cans and

said, without turning, 'The washing won't be back till tomorrow. You must lend him some of your handkerchiefs.'

'But, Nurse,' Peter asked, 'hadn't he better stay in bed?'

'We'll take him for a good walk this morning,' the nurse said. 'Wind'll blow away the germs. Get up now, both of you,' and she closed the door behind her.

'I'm sorry,' Peter said. 'Why don't you just stay in bed? I'll tell mother you felt too ill to get up.' But rebellion against destiny was not in Francis's power. If he stayed in bed they would come up and tap his chest and put a thermometer in his mouth and look at his tongue, and they would discover he was malingering. It was true he felt ill, a sick empty sensation in his stomach and a rapidly beating heart, but he knew the cause was only fear, fear of the party, fear of being made to hide by himself in the dark, uncompanioned by Peter and with no night-light to make a blessed breach.

'No, I'll get up,' he said, and then with sudden desperation, 'But I won't go to Mrs Henne-Falcon's party. I swear on the Bible I won't.' Now surely all would be well, he thought. God would not allow him to break so solemn an oath. He would show him a way. There was all the morning before him and all the afternoon until four o'clock. No need to worry when the grass was still crisp with the early frost. Anything might happen. He might cut himself or break his leg or really catch a bad cold. God would manage somehow.

He had such confidence in God that when at breakfast his mother said, 'I hear you have a cold, Francis,' he made light of it. 'We should have heard more about it,' his mother said with irony, 'if there was not a party this evening,' and Francis smiled, amazed and daunted by her ignorance of him. His happiness would have lasted longer if, out for a walk that morning, he had not met Joyce. He was alone with his nurse, for Peter had leave to finish a rabbit-hutch in the woodshed. If Peter had been there he would have cared less; the nurse was Peter's nurse also, but now it was as though she were employed only for his sake, because he could not be trusted to go for a walk alone. Joyce was only two years older and she was by herself.

She came striding towards them, pigtails flapping. She glanced scornfully at Francis and spoke with ostentation to the nurse. 'Hello, Nurse. Are you bringing Francis to the party this evening? Mabel and I are coming.' And she was off again down the street in the direction of Mabel Warren's home, consciously alone and self-sufficient in the long empty road. 'Such a nice girl,' the nurse said. But Francis was silent, feeling again the jump-jump of his heart, realizing how soon the hour of the party would arrive. God had done nothing for him, and the minutes flew.

They flew too quickly to plan any evasion, or even to prepare his heart for the coming ordeal. Panic nearly overcame him when, all unready, he found himself standing on the doorstep, with coat-collar turned up against a cold wind, and the nurse's electric torch making a short trail through the darkness. Behind him were the lights of the hall and the sound of a servant laying the table for dinner, which his mother and father would eat alone. He was nearly overcome by the desire to run back into the house and call out to his mother that he would not go to the party, that he dared not go. They could not make him go. He could almost hear himself saying those final words, breaking down for ever the barrier of ignorance which saved his mind from his parents' knowledge. 'I'm afraid of going. I won't go. I daren't go. They'll make me hide in the dark, and I'm afraid of the dark. I'll scream and scream and scream.' He could see the expression of amazement on his mother's face, and then the cold confidence of a grown-up's retort.

'Don't be silly. You must go. We've accepted Mrs Henne-Falcon's invitation.' But they couldn't make him go; hesitating on the doorstep while the nurse's feet crunched across the frost-covered grass to the gate, he knew that. He would answer: 'You can say I'm ill. I won't go. I'm afraid of the dark.' And his mother: 'Don't be silly. You know there's nothing to be afraid of in the dark.' But he knew the falsity of that reasoning; he knew how they taught also that there was nothing to fear in death, and how fearfully they avoided the idea of it. But they couldn't make him go to the party. 'I'll scream. I'll scream.'

'Francis, come along.' He heard the nurse's voice across the dimly phosphorescent lawn and saw the yellow circle of her torch wheel from tree to shrub. 'I'm coming,' he called with despair; he

couldn't bring himself to lay bare his last secrets and end reserve
between his mother and himself, for there was still in the last resort a further appeal possible to Mrs Henne-Falcon. He comforted himself with that, as he advanced steadily across the hall,
very small, towards her enormous bulk. His heart beat unevenly,
but he had control now over his voice, as he said with meticulous
accent, 'Good evening, Mrs Henne-Falcon. It was very good of
you to ask me to your party.' With his strained face lifted towards the curve of her breasts, and his polite set speech, he was
like an old withered man. As a twin he was in many ways an
only child. To address Peter was to speak to his own image in a
mirror, an image a little altered by a flaw in the glass, so as to
throw back less a likeness of what he was than of what he wished
to be, what he would be without his unreasoning fear of darkness, footsteps of strangers, the flight of bats in dusk-filled gardens.

'Sweet child,' said Mrs Henne-Falcon absent-mindedly, before, with a wave of her arms, as though the children were a
flock of chickens, she whirled them into her set programme of
entertainments: egg-and-spoon races, three-legged races, the
spearing of apples, games which held for Francis nothing worse
than humiliation. And in the frequent intervals when nothing
was required of him and he could stand alone in corners as far removed as possible from Mabel Warren's scornful gaze, he was
able to plan how he might avoid the approaching terror of the
dark. He knew there was nothing to fear until after tea, and not
until he was sitting down in a pool of yellow radiance cast by the
ten candles on Colin Henne-Falcon's birthday cake did he become fully conscious of the imminence of what he feared. He
heard Joyce's high voice down the table, 'After tea we are going
to play hide and seek in the dark.'

'Oh, no,' Peter said, watching Francis's troubled face, 'don't
let's. We play that every year.'

'But it's in the programme,' cried Mabel Warren. 'I saw it myself. I looked over Mrs Henne-Falcon's shoulder. Five o'clock tea.
A quarter to six to half past, hide and seek in the dark. It's all
written down in the programme.'

Peter did not argue, for if hide and seek had been inserted in

Mrs Henne-Falcon's programme, nothing which he could say would avert it. He asked for another piece of birthday cake and sipped his tea slowly. Perhaps it might be possible to delay the game for a quarter of an hour, allow Francis at least a few extra minutes to form a plan, but even in that Peter failed, for children were already leaving the table in twos and threes. It was his third failure, and again he saw a great bird darken his brother's face with its wings. But he upbraided himself silently for his folly, and finished his cake encouraged by the memory of that adult refrain, 'There's nothing to fear in the dark.' The last to leave the table, the brothers came together to the hall to meet the mustering and impatient eyes of Mrs Henne-Falcon.

'And now,' she said, 'we will play hide and seek in the dark.'

Peter watched his brother and saw the lips tighten. Francis, he knew, had feared this moment from the beginning of the party, had tried to meet it with courage and had abandoned the attempt. He must have prayed for cunning to evade the game, which was now welcomed with cries of excitement by all the other children. 'Oh, do let's.' 'We must pick sides.' 'Is any of the house out of bounds?' 'Where shall home be?'

'I think,' said Francis Morton, approaching Mrs Henne-Falcon, his eyes focused unwaveringly on her exuberant breasts, 'it will be no use my playing. My nurse will be calling for me very soon.'

'Oh, but your nurse can wait, Francis,' said Mrs Henne-Falcon, while she clapped her hands together to summon to her side a few children who were already straying up the wide staircase to upper floors. 'Your mother will never mind.'

That had been the limit of Francis's cunning. He had refused to believe that so well-prepared an excuse could fail. All that he could say now, still in the precise tone which other children hated, thinking it a symbol of conceit, was, 'I think I had better not play.' He stood motionless, retaining, though afraid, unmoved features. But the knowledge of his terror, or the reflection of the terror itself, reached his brother's brain. For the moment, Peter Morton could have cried aloud with the fear of bright lights going out, leaving him alone in an island of dark surrounded by the gentle lappings of strange footsteps. Then he remembered that the fear was not his own, but his brother's. He said impulsively to Mrs Henne-Falcon, 'Please, I don't think Francis should play. The dark makes him jump so.' They were the wrong words. Six children began to sing, 'Cowardy cowardy custard,' turning torturing faces with the vacancy of wide sunflowers towards Francis Morton.

Without looking at his brother, Francis said, 'Of course I'll play. I'm not afraid, I only thought . . .' But he was already forgotten by his human tormentors. The children scrambled round Mrs Henne-Falcon, their shrill voices pecking at her with questions and suggestions. 'Yes, anywhere in the house. We will turn out all the lights. Yes, you can hide in the cupboards. You must stay hidden as long as you can. There will be no home.'

Peter stood apart, ashamed of the clumsy manner in which he had tried to help his brother. Now he could feel, creeping in at the corners of his brain, all Francis's resentment of his championing. Several children ran upstairs, and the lights on the top floor went out. Darkness came down like the wings of a bat and settled on the landing. Others began to put out the lights at the edge of the hall, till the children were all gathered in the central radiance of the chandelier, while the bats squatted round on hooded wings and waited for that, too, to be extinguished.

'You and Francis are on the hiding side,' a tall girl said, and then the light was gone, and the carpet wavered under his feet with the sibilance of footfalls, like small cold draughts, creeping away into corners.

'Where's Francis?' he wondered. 'If I join him he'll be less frightened of all these sounds.' 'These sounds' were the casing of silence: the squeak of a loose board, the cautious closing of a cupboard door, the whine of a finger drawn along polished wood.

Peter stood in the centre of the dark deserted floor, not listening but waiting for the idea of his brother's whereabouts to enter his brain. But Francis crouched with fingers on his ears, eyes uselessly closed, mind numbed against impressions, and only a sense of strain could cross the gap of dark. Then a voice called 'Coming,' and as though his brother's self-possession had been shattered by the sudden cry, Peter Morton jumped with his fear. But it was not his own fear. What in his brother was a burning panic was in him an altruistic emotion that left the reason unimpaired. 'Where, if I were Francis, should I hide?' And because he was, if not Francis himself, at least a mirror to him, the answer was immediate. 'Between the oak book-case on the left of the study door, and the leather settee.' Between the twins there could be no jargon of telepathy. They had been together in the womb, and they could not be parted.

Peter Morton tiptoed towards Francis's hiding-place. Occasionally a board rattled, and because he feared to be caught by one of the soft questers through the dark, he bent and untied his laces. A tag struck the floor and the metallic sound set a host of cautious feet moving in his direction. But by that time he was in his stockings and would have laughed inwardly at the pursuit had not the noise of someone stumbling on his abandoned shoes made his heart trip. No more boards revealed Peter Morton's progress. On stockinged feet he moved silently and unerringly towards his object. Instinct told him he was near the wall, and, extending a hand, he laid the fingers across his brother's face.

Francis did not cry out, but the leap of his own heart revealed to Peter a proportion of Francis's terror. 'It's all right,' he whispered, feeling down the squatting figure until he captured a clenched hand. 'It's only me. I'll stay with you.' And grasping the other tightly, he listened to the cascade of whispers his utterance had caused to fall. A hand touched the book-case close to Peter's head and he was aware of how Francis's fear continued in spite of his presence. It was less intense, more bearable, he hoped, but it remained. He knew that it was his brother's fear and not his own that he experienced. The dark to him was only an absence of light; the groping hand that of a familiar child. Patiently he waited to be found.

He did not speak again, for between Francis and himself was the most intimate communion. By way of joined hands thought could flow more swiftly than lips could shape themselves round words. He could experience the whole progress of his brother's emotion, from the leap of panic at the unexpected contact to the steady pulse of fear, which now went on and on with the regularity of a heart-beat. Peter Morton thought with intensity, 'I am

here. You needn't be afraid. The lights will go on again soon.
That rustle, that movement is nothing to fear. Only Joyce, only
Mabel Warren.' He bombarded the drooping form with thoughts
of safety, but he was conscious that the fear continued. 'They are
beginning to whisper together. They are tired of looking for us.
The lights will go on soon. We shall have won. Don't be afraid.
That was someone on the stairs. I believe it's Mrs Henne-Falcon.
Listen. They are feeling for the lights.' Feet moving on a carpet,
hands brushing a wall, a curtain pulled apart, a clicking handle,
the opening of a cupboard door. In the case above their heads a
loose book shifted under a touch. 'Only Joyce, only Mabel Warren, only Mrs Henne-Falcon,' a crescendo of reassuring thought
before the chandelier burst, like a fruit-tree, into bloom.

The voices of the children rose shrilly into the radiance.
'Where's Peter?' 'Have you looked upstairs?' 'Where's Francis?'
but they were silenced again by Mrs Henne-Falcon's scream. But
she was not the first to notice Francis Morton's stillness, where he
had collapsed against the wall at the touch of his brother's hand.
Peter continued to hold the clenched fingers in an arid and puzzled
grief. It was not merely that his brother was dead. His brain, too
young to realize the full paradox, wondered with an obscure self-
pity why it was that the pulse of his brother's fear went on and on,
when Francis was now where he had always been told there was
no more terror and no more darkness.

1929

A SENSE OF REALITY

UNDER THE GARDEN

PART ONE

I

It was only when the doctor said to him, 'Of course the fact that you don't smoke is in your favour,' Wilditch realized what it was he had been trying to convey with such tact. Dr Cave had lined up along one wall a series of X-ray photographs, the whorls of which reminded the patient of those pictures of the earth's surface taken from a great height that he had pored over at one period during the war, trying to detect the tiny grey seed of a launching ramp.

Dr Cave had explained, 'I want you clearly to understand my problem.' It was very similar to an intelligence briefing of such 'top secret' importance that only one officer could be entrusted with the information. Wilditch felt gratified that the choice had fallen on him, and he tried to express his interest and enthusiasm, leaning forward and examining more closely than ever the photographs of his own interior.

'Beginning at this end,' Dr Cave said, 'let me see, April, May, June, three months ago, the scar left by the pneumonia is quite obvious. You can see it here.'

'Yes, sir,' Wilditch said absent-mindedly. Dr Cave gave him a puzzled look.

'Now if we leave out the intervening photographs for the moment and come straight to yesterday's, you will observe that this latest one is almost entirely clear, you can only just detect . . .'

'Good,' Wilditch said. The doctor's finger moved over what might have been tumuli or traces of prehistoric agriculture.

'But not entirely, I'm afraid. If you look now along the whole series you will notice how very slow the progress has been. Really by this stage the photographs should have shown no trace.'

'I'm sorry,' Wilditch said. A sense of guilt had taken the place of gratification.

'If we had looked at the last plate in isolation I would have said there was no cause for alarm.' The doctor tolled the last three words like a bell. Wilditch thought, is he suggesting tuberculosis?

'It's only in relation to the others, the slowness . . . it suggests the possibility of an obstruction.'

'Obstruction?'

'The chances are that it's nothing, nothing at all. Only I wouldn't be *quite* happy if I let you go without a deep examination. Not *quite* happy.' Dr Cave left the photographs and sat down behind his desk. The long pause seemed to Wilditch like an appeal to his friendship.

'Of course,' he said, 'if it would make you happy . . .'

It was then the doctor used those revealing words, 'Of course the fact that you don't smoke is in your favour.'

'Oh.'

'I think we'll ask Sir Nigel Sampson to make the examination. In case there is something there, we couldn't have a better surgeon . . . for the operation.'

Wilditch came down from Wimpole Street into Cavendish Square looking for a taxi. It was one of those summer days which he never remembered in childhood: grey and dripping. Taxis drew up outside the tall liver-coloured buildings partitioned by dentists and were immediately caught by the commissionaires for the victims released. Gusts of wind barely warmed by July drove the rain aslant across the blank eastern gaze of Epstein's virgin and dripped down the body of her fabulous son. 'But it hurt,' the child's voice said behind him. 'You make a fuss about nothing,' a mother—or a governess—replied.

2

This could not have been said of the examination Wilditch endured a week later, but he made no fuss at all, which perhaps aggravated his case in the eyes of the doctors who took his calm for lack of vitality. For the unprofessional to enter a hospital or to enter the services has very much the same effect; there is a sense of relief and indifference; one is placed quite helplessly on a conveyor-belt with no responsibility any more for anything. Wilditch felt himself protected by an organization, while the English summer dripped outside on the coupés of the parked cars. He had not felt such freedom since the war ended.

The examination was over—a bronchoscopy; and there remained a nightmare memory, which survived through the cloud of the anaesthetic, of a great truncheon forced down his throat into the chest and then slowly withdrawn; he woke next morning bruised and raw so that even the act of excretion was a pain. But that, the nurse told him, would pass in one day or two; now he could dress and go home. He was disappointed at the abruptness with which they were thrusting him off the belt into the world of choice again.

'Was everything satisfactory?' he asked, and saw from the nurse's expression that he had shown indecent curiosity.

'I couldn't say, I'm sure,' the nurse said. 'Sir Nigel will look in, in his own good time.'

Wilditch was sitting on the end of the bed tying his tie when Sir Nigel Sampson entered. It was the first time Wilditch had been conscious of seeing him: before he had been a voice addressing him politely out of sight as the anaesthetic took over. It was the beginning of the week-end and Sir Nigel was dressed for the country in an old tweed jacket. He had tousled white hair and he looked at Wilditch with a far-away attention as though he were a float bobbing in midstream.

'Ah, feeling better,' Sir Nigel said incontrovertibly.

'Perhaps.'

'Not very agreeable,' Sir Nigel said, 'but you know we couldn't let you go, could we, without taking a look?'

'Did you see anything?'

Sir Nigel gave the impression of abruptly moving downstream to a quieter reach and casting his line again.

'Don't let me stop you dressing, my dear fellow.' He looked vaguely around the room before choosing a strictly upright chair, then lowered himself on to it as though it were a tuffet which might 'give'. He began feeling in one of his large pockets—for a sandwich?

'Any news for me?'

'I expect Dr Cave will be along in a few minutes. He was caught by a rather garrulous patient.' He drew a large silver watch out of his pocket—for some reason it was tangled up in a piece of string. 'Have to meet my wife at Liverpool Street. Are *you* married?'

'No.'

'Oh well, one care the less. Children can be a great responsibility.'

'I have a child—but she lives a long way off.'

'A long way off? I see.'

'We haven't seen much of each other.'

'Doesn't care for England?'

'The colour-bar makes it difficult for her.' He realized how childish he sounded directly he had spoken, as though he had been trying to draw attention to himself by a bizarre confession, without even the satisfaction of success.

'Ah yes,' Sir Nigel said. 'Any brothers or sisters? You, I mean.'

'An elder brother. Why?'

'Oh well, I suppose it's all on the record,' Sir Nigel said, rolling in his line. He got up and made for the door. Wilditch sat on the bed with the tie over his knee. The door opened and Sir Nigel said, 'Ah, here's Dr Cave. Must run along now. I was just telling Mr Wilditch that I'll be seeing him again. You'll fix it, won't you?' and he was gone.

'Why should I see him again?' Wilditch asked and then, from Dr Cave's embarrassment, he saw the stupidity of the question. 'Oh yes, of course, you did find something?'

'It's really very lucky. If caught in time . . .'

'There's sometimes hope?'

'Oh, there's always hope.'

So, after all, Wilditch thought, I am—if I so choose—on the conveyor-belt again.

Dr Cave took an engagement-book out of his pocket and said briskly, 'Sir Nigel has given me a few dates. The tenth is difficult for the clinic, but the fifteenth—Sir Nigel doesn't think we should delay longer than the fifteenth.'

'Is he a great fisherman?'

'Fisherman? Sir Nigel? I have no idea.' Dr Cave looked aggrieved, as though he were being shown an incorrect chart. 'Shall we say the fifteenth?'

'Perhaps I could tell you after the week-end. You see, I have not made up my mind to stay as long as that in England.'

'I'm afraid I haven't properly conveyed to you that this is serious, really serious. Your only chance—I repeat your only chance,' he spoke like a telegram, 'is to have the obstruction removed in time.'

'And then, I suppose, life can go on for a few more years.'

'It's impossible to guarantee . . . but there have been complete cures.'

'I don't want to appear dialectical,' Wilditch said, 'but I do have to decide, don't I, whether I want my particular kind of life prolonged.'

'It's the only one we have,' Dr Cave said.

'I see you are not a religious man—oh, please don't misunderstand me, nor am I. I have no curiosity at all about the future.'

3

The past was another matter. Wilditch remembered a leader in the Civil War who rode from an undecided battle mortally wounded. He revisited the house where he was born, the house in which he was married, greeted a few retainers who did not recognize his condition, seeing him only as a tired man upon a horse, and finally—but Wilditch could not recollect how the biography had ended: he saw only a figure of exhaustion slumped over the saddle, as he also took, like Sir Nigel Sampson, a train from Liverpool Street. At Colchester he changed on to the branch line to Winton, and suddenly summer began, the kind of summer he always remembered as one of the conditions of life at Winton. Days had become so much shorter since then. They no longer began at six in the morning before the world was awake.

Winton Hall had belonged, when Wilditch was a child, to his uncle, who had never married, and every summer he lent the house to Wilditch's mother. Winton Hall had been virtually Wilditch's, until school cut the period short, from late June to early September. In memory his mother and brother were shadowy background figures. They were less established even than the machine upon the platform of 'the halt' from which he bought Fry's chocolates for a penny a bar: than the oak tree spreading over the green in front of the red-brick wall—under its shade as a child he had distributed apples to soldiers halted there in the hot August of 1914: the group of silver birches on the Winton lawn and the broken fountain, green with slime. In his memory he did not share the house with others: he owned it.

Nevertheless the house had been left to his brother not to him; he was far away when his uncle died and he had never returned since. His brother married, had children (for them the fountain had been mended), the paddock behind the vegetable garden and the orchard, where he used to ride the donkey, had been sold (so his brother had written to him) for building council-houses, but the hall and the garden which he had so scrupulously remembered nothing could change.

Why then go back now and see it in other hands? Was it that at the approach of death one must get rid of everything? If he had accumulated money he would now have been in the mood to distribute it. Perhaps the man who had ridden the horse around the countryside had not been saying goodbye, as his biographer imagined, to what he valued most: he had been ridding himself of illusions by seeing them again with clear and moribund eyes, so that he might be quite bankrupt when death came. He had the will to possess at that absolute moment nothing but his wound.

His brother, Wilditch knew, would be faintly surprised by this visit. He had become accustomed to the fact that Wilditch never came to Winton; they would meet at long intervals at his brother's club in London, for George was a widower by this time, living alone. He always talked to others of Wilditch as a man un-happy in the country, who needed a longer range and stranger people. It was lucky, he would indicate, that the house had been left to him, for Wilditch would probably have sold it in order to travel further. A restless man, never long in one place, no wife, no children, unless the rumours were true that in Africa . . . or it might have been in the East . . . Wilditch was well aware of how his brother spoke of him. His brother was the proud owner of the lawn, the goldfish-pond, the mended fountain, the laurel-path which they had known when they were children as the Dark Walk, the lake, the island . . . Wilditch looked out at the flat hard East Anglian countryside, the meagre hedges and the stubbly grass, which had always seemed to him barren from the salt of Danish blood. All these years his brother had been in occupation, and yet he had no idea of what might lie underneath the garden.

4

The chocolate-machine had gone from Winton Halt, and the halt had been promoted—during the years of nationalization—to a station; the chimneys of a cement-factory smoked along the hori-zon and council-houses now stood three deep along the line.

Wilditch's brother waited in a Humber at the exit. Some famil-iar smell of coal-dust and varnish had gone from the waiting-room and it was a mere boy who took his ticket instead of a stooped and greying porter. In childhood nearly all the world is older than oneself.

'Hullo, George,' he said in remote greeting to the stranger at the wheel.

'How are things, William?' George asked as they ground on their way—it was part of his character as a countryman that he had never learnt how to drive a car well.

The long chalky slope of a small hill—the highest point before the Ural mountains he had once been told—led down to the vil-lage between the bristly hedges. On the left was an abandoned chalk-pit—it had been just as abandoned forty years ago, when he had climbed all over it looking for treasure, in the form of brown nuggets of iron pyrites which when broken showed an interior of starred silver.

'Do you remember hunting for treasure?'

'Treasure?' George said. 'Oh, you mean that iron stuff.'

Was it the long summer afternoons in the chalk-pit which had made him dream—or so vividly imagine—the discovery of a real treasure? If it was a dream it was the only dream he remembered from those years, or, if it was a story which he had elaborated at night in bed, it must have been the final effort of a poetic imagination that afterwards had been rigidly controlled. In the various services which had over the years taken him from one part of the world to another, imagination was usually a quality to be suppressed. One's job was to provide facts, to a company (import and export), a newspaper, a government department. Speculation was discouraged. Now the dreaming child was dying of the same disease as the man. He was so different from the child that it was odd to think the child would not outlive him and go on to quite a different destiny.

George said, 'You'll notice some changes, William. When I had the bathroom added, I found I had to disconnect the pipes from the fountain. Something to do with pressure. After all there are no children now to enjoy it.'

'It never played in my time either.'

'I had the tennis-lawn dug up during the war, and it hardly seemed worth while to put it back.'

'I'd forgotten that there *was* a tennis-lawn.'

'Don't you remember it, between the pond and the goldfish tank?'

'The pond? Oh, you mean the lake and the island.'

'Not much of a lake. You could jump on to the island with a short run.'

'I had thought of it as much bigger.'

But all measurements had changed. Only for a dwarf does the world remain the same size. Even the red-brick wall which separated the garden from the village was lower than he remembered—a mere five feet, but in order to look over it in those days he had always to scramble to the top of some old stumps covered deep with ivy and dusty spiders' webs. There was no sign of these when they drove in: everything was very tidy everywhere, and a handsome piece of ironmongery had taken the place of the swing-gate which they had ruined as children.

'You keep the place up very well,' he said.

'I couldn't manage it without the market-garden. That enables me to put the gardener's wages down as a professional expense. I have a very good accountant.'

He was put into his mother's room with a view of the lawn and the silver birches; George slept in what had been his uncle's. The little bedroom next door which had once been his was now converted into a tiled bathroom—only the prospect was unchanged. He could see the laurel bushes where the Dark Walk began, but they were smaller too. Had the dying horseman found as many changes?

Sitting that night over coffee and brandy, during the long family pauses, Wilditch wondered whether as a child he could possibly have been so secretive as never to have spoken of his dream, his game, whatever it was. In his memory the adventure had lasted for several days. At the end of it he had found his way home in the early morning when everyone was asleep: there had been a dog called Joe who bounded towards him and sent him sprawling in the heavy dew of the lawn. Surely there must have been some basis of fact on which the legend had been built. Perhaps he had run away, perhaps he had been out all night—on the island in the lake or hidden in the Dark Walk—and during those hours he had invented the whole story.

Wilditch took a second glass of brandy and asked tentatively, 'Do you remember much of those summers when we were children here?' He was aware of something unconvincing in the question: the apparently harmless opening gambit of a wartime interrogation.

'I never cared for the place much in those days,' George said surprisingly. 'You were a secretive little bastard.'

'Secretive?'

'And uncooperative. I had a great sense of duty towards you, but you never realized that. In a year or two you were going to follow me to school. I tried to teach you the rudiments of cricket. You weren't interested. God knows what you were interested in.'

'Exploring?' Wilditch suggested, he thought with cunning.

'There wasn't much to explore in fourteen acres. You know, I had such plans for this place when it became mine. A swimming-pool where the tennis-lawn was—it's mainly potatoes now. I meant to drain the pond too—it breeds mosquitoes. Well, I've added two bathrooms and modernized the kitchen, and even that has cost me four acres of pasture. At the back of the house now you can hear the children caterwauling from the council-houses. It's all been a bit of a disappointment.'

'At least I'm glad you haven't drained the lake.'

'My dear chap, why go on calling it a lake? Have a look at it in the morning and you'll see the absurdity. The water's nowhere more than two feet deep.' He added, 'Oh well, the place won't outlive me. My children aren't interested, and the factories are beginning to come out this way. They'll get a reasonably good price for the land—I haven't much else to leave them.' He put some more sugar in his coffee. 'Unless, of course, you'd like to take it on when I am gone?'

'I haven't the money and anyway there's no cause to believe that I won't be dead first.'

'Mother was against my accepting the inheritance,' George said. 'She never liked the place.'

'I thought she loved her summers here.' The great gap between their memories astonished him. They seemed to be talking about different places and different people.

'It was terribly inconvenient, and she was always in trouble with the gardener. You remember Ernest? She said she had to wring every vegetable out of him. (By the way he's still alive, though retired of course—you ought to look him up in the morning. It would please him. He still feels he owns the place.) And then, you know, she always thought it would have been better for us if we could have gone to the seaside. She had an idea that she was robbing us of a heritage—buckets and spades and seawater-bathing. Poor mother, she couldn't afford to turn down Uncle Henry's hospitality. I think in her heart she blamed father for dying when he did without providing for holidays at the sea.'

'Did you talk it over with her in those days?'

'Oh no, not then. Naturally she had to keep a front before the children. But when I inherited the place—you were in Africa—she warned Mary and me about the difficulties. She had very decided views, you know, about any mysteries, and that turned her against the garden. Too much shrubbery, she said. She wanted everything to be very clear. Early Fabian training, I dare say.'

'It's odd. I don't seem to have known her very well.'

'You had a passion for hide-and-seek. She never liked that. Mystery again. She thought it a bit morbid. There was a time when we couldn't find you. You were away for hours.'

'Are you sure it was hours? Not a whole night?'

'I don't remember it at all myself. Mother told me.' They drank their brandy for a while in silence. Then George said, 'She asked Uncle Henry to have the Dark Walk cleared away. She thought it was unhealthy with all the spiders' webs, but he never did anything about it.'

'I'm surprised *you* didn't.'

'Oh, it was on my list, but other things had priority, and now it doesn't seem worth while to make more changes.' He yawned and stretched. 'I'm used to early bed. I hope you don't mind. Breakfast at 8.30?'

'Don't make any changes for me.'

'There's just one thing I forgot to show you. The flush is tricky in your bathroom.'

George led the way upstairs. He said, 'The local plumber didn't do a very good job. Now, when you've pulled this knob, you'll find the flush never quite finishes. You have to do it a second time—sharply like this.'

Wilditch stood at the window looking out. Beyond the Dark Walk and the space where the lake must be, he could see the splinters of light given off by the council-houses; through one gap in the laurels there was even a street-light visible, and he could hear the faint sound of television-sets joining together different programmes like the discordant murmur of a mob.

He said, 'That view would have pleased mother. A lot of the mystery gone.'

'I rather like it this way myself,' George said, 'on a winter's evening. It's a kind of companionship. As one gets older one doesn't want to feel quite alone on a sinking ship. Not being a churchgoer myself . . .' he added, leaving the sentence lying like a torso on its side.

'At least we haven't shocked mother in that way, either of us.'

'Sometimes I wish I'd pleased her, though, about the Dark Walk. And the pond—how she hated that pond too.'

'Why?'

'Perhaps because you liked to hide on the island. Secrecy and mystery again. Wasn't there something you wrote about it once? A story?'

'Me? A story? Surely not.'

'I don't remember the circumstances. I thought—in a school magazine? Yes, I'm sure of it now. She was very angry indeed and she wrote rude remarks in the margin with a blue pencil. I saw them somewhere once. Poor mother.'

George led the way into the bedroom. He said, 'I'm sorry there's no bedside light. It was smashed last week, and I haven't been into town since.'

'It's all right. I don't read in bed.'

'I've got some good detective-stories downstairs if you wanted one.'

'Mysteries?'

'Oh, mother never minded those. They came under the heading of puzzles. Because there was always an answer.'

Beside the bed was a small bookcase. He said, 'I brought some of mother's books here when she died and put them in her room. Just the ones that she had liked and no bookseller would take.' Wilditch made out a title, *My Apprenticeship* by Beatrice Webb. 'Sentimental, I suppose, but I didn't want actually to *throw away* her favourite books. Good night.' He repeated, 'I'm sorry about the light.'

'It really doesn't matter.'

George lingered at the door. He said, 'I'm glad to see you here, William. There were times when I thought you were avoiding the place.'

'Why should I?'

'Well, you know how it is. I never go to Harrod's now because I was there with Mary a few days before she died.'

'Nobody has died here. Except Uncle Henry, I suppose.'

'No, of course not. But why did you, suddenly, decide to come?'

'A whim,' Wilditch said.

'I suppose you'll be going abroad again soon?'

'I suppose so.'

'Well, good night.' He closed the door.

Wilditch undressed, and then, because he felt sleep too far away, he sat down on the bed under the poor centre-light and looked along the rows of shabby books. He opened Mrs Beatrice Webb at some account of a trade union congress and put it back. (The foundations of the future Welfare State were being truly and uninterestingly laid.) There were a number of Fabian pamphlets heavily scored with the blue pencil which George had remembered. In one place Mrs Wilditch had detected an error of one decimal point in some statistics dealing with agricultural imports. What passionate concentration must have gone to that discovery. Perhaps because his own life was coming to an end, he thought how little of this, in the almost impossible event of a future, she would have carried with her. A fairy-story in such an event would be a more valuable asset than a Fabian graph, but his mother had not approved of fairy-stories. The only children's book on these shelves was a history of England. Against an enthusiastic account of the battle of Agincourt she had pencilled furiously,

> And what good came of it at last?
> Said little Peterkin.

The fact that his mother had quoted a poem was in itself remarkable.

The storm which he had left behind in London had travelled east in his wake and now overtook him in short gusts of wind and wet that slapped at the pane. He thought, for no reason, It will be a rough night on the island. He had been disappointed to discover from George that the origin of the dream which had travelled with him round the world was probably no more than a story invented for a school magazine and forgotten again, and just as that thought occurred to him, he saw a bound volume called *The Warburian* on the shelf.

He took it out, wondering why his mother had preserved it, and found a page turned down. It was the account of a cricket-match against Lancing and Mrs Wilditch had scored the margin: 'Wilditch One did good work in deep field.' Another turned-down leaf produced a passage under the heading Debating Society: 'Wilditch One spoke succinctly to the motion.' The motion was 'That this House has no belief in the social policies of His Majesty's Government'. So George in those days had been a Fabian too.

He opened the book at random this time and a letter fell out. It had a printed heading, Dean's House, Warbury, and it read, 'Dear Mrs Wilditch, I was sorry to receive your letter of the 3rd and to learn that you were displeased with the little fantasy published by your younger son in *The Warburian*. I think you take a rather extreme view of the tale which strikes me as quite a good imaginative exercise for a boy of thirteen. Obviously he has been influenced by the term's reading of *The Golden Age*—which after all, fanciful though it may be, was written by a governor of the Bank of England.' (Mrs Wilditch had made several blue exclamation marks in the margin—perhaps representing her view of the Bank.) 'Last term's *Treasure Island* too may have contributed. It is always our intention at Warbury to foster the imagination—which I think you rather harshly denigrate when you write of "silly fancies". We have scrupulously kept our side of the bargain, knowing how strongly you feel, and the boy is not "subjected", as you put it, to any religious instruction at all. Quite frankly, Mrs Wilditch, I cannot see any trace of religious feeling in this little fancy—I have read it through a second time before writing to you—indeed the treasure, I'm afraid, is only too material, and quite at the mercy of those "who break in and steal".'

Wilditch tried to find the place from which the letter had fallen, working back from the date of the letter. Eventually he found it: 'The Treasure on the Island' by W.W.

Wilditch began to read.

5

'In the middle of the garden there was a great lake and in the middle of the lake an island with a wood. Not everybody knew about the lake, for to reach it you had to find your way down a long dark walk, and not many people's nerves were strong enough to reach the end. Tom knew that he was likely to be undisturbed in that frightening region, and so it was there that he constructed a raft out of old packing cases, and one drear wet day when he knew that everybody would be shut in the house, he dragged the raft to the lake and paddled it across to the island. As far as he knew he was the first to land there for centuries.

'It was all overgrown on the island, but from a map he had found in an ancient sea-chest in the attic he made his measurements, three paces north from the tall umbrella pine in the middle and then two paces to the right. There seemed to be nothing but scrub, but he had brought with him a pick and a spade and with the dint of almost superhuman exertions he uncovered an iron ring sunk in the grass. At first he thought it would be impossible to move, but by inserting the point of the pick and levering it he raised a kind of stone lid and there below, going into the darkness, was a long narrow passage.

'Tom had more than the usual share of courage, but even he would not have ventured further if it had not been for the parlous state of the family fortunes since his father had died. His elder brother wanted to go to Oxford but for lack of money he would probably have to sail before the mast, and the house itself, of which his mother was passionately fond, was mortgaged to the hilt to a man in the City called Sir Silas Dedham whose name did not belie his nature.'

Wilditch nearly gave up reading. He could not reconcile this childish story with the dream which he remembered. Only the 'drear wet night' seemed true as the bushes rustled and dripped and the birches swayed outside. A writer, so he had always understood, was supposed to order and enrich the experience which was the source of his story, but in that case it was plain that the young Wilditch's talents had not been for literature. He read with growing irritation, wanting to exclaim again and again to this thirteen-year-old ancestor of his, 'But why did you leave that out? Why did you alter this?'

'*The passage opened out into a great cave stacked from floor to ceiling with gold bars and chests overflowing with pieces of eight. There was a jewelled crucifix*'—Mrs Wilditch had underlined the word in blue—'*set with precious stones which had once graced the chapel of a Spanish galleon and on a marble table were goblets of precious metal.*'

But, as he remembered, it was an old kitchen-dresser, and there were no pieces of eight, no crucifix, and as for the Spanish galleon . . .

'*Tom thanked the kindly Providence which had led him first to the map in the attic*' (but there had been no map. Wilditch wanted to correct the story, page by page, much as his mother had done with her blue pencil) '*and then to this rich treasure trove*' (his mother had written in the margin, referring to the kindly Providence, 'No trace of religious feeling!!'). '*He filled his pockets with the pieces of eight and taking one bar under each arm, he made his way back along the passage. He intended to keep his discovery secret and slowly day by day to transfer the treasure to the cupboard in his room, thus surprising his mother at the end of the holidays with all this sudden wealth. He got safely home unseen by anyone and that night in bed he counted over his new riches while outside it rained and rained. Never had he heard such a storm. It was as though the wicked spirit of his old pirate ancestor raged against him*' (Mrs Wilditch had written, 'Eternal punishment I suppose!') '*and indeed the next day, when he returned to the island in the lake, whole trees had been uprooted and now lay across the entrance to the passage. Worse still there had been a landslide, and now the cavern must lie hidden forever below the waters of the lake. However,*' the young Wilditch had added briefly forty years ago, '*the treasure already recovered was sufficient to save the family home and send his brother to Oxford.*'

Wilditch undressed and got into bed, then lay on his back listening to the storm. What a trivial conventional day-dream W.W. had constructed—out of what? There had been no attic-room— probably no raft: these were preliminaries which did not matter, but why had W.W. so falsified the adventure itself? Where was the man with the beard? The old squawking woman? Of course it had all been a dream, it could have been nothing else but a dream, but a dream too was an experience, the images of a dream had their own integrity, and he felt professional anger at this false report just as his mother had felt at the mistake in the Fabian statistics.

All the same, while he lay there in his mother's bed and thought of her rigid interrogation of W.W.'s story, another theory of the falsifications came to him, perhaps a juster one. He remembered how agents parachuted into France during the bad years after 1940 had been made to memorize a cover-story which they could give, in case of torture, with enough truth in it to be checked. Perhaps forty years ago the pressure to tell had been almost as great on W.W., so that he had been forced to find relief in fantasy. Well, an agent dropped into occupied territory was always given a time-limit after capture. 'Keep the interrogators at bay with silence or lies for just so long, and then you may tell all.' The time-limit had surely been passed in his case a long time ago, his mother was beyond the possibility of hurt, and Wilditch for the first time deliberately indulged his passion to remember.

He got out of bed and, after finding some notepaper stamped, presumably for income-tax purposes, Winton Small Holdings Limited, in the drawer of the desk, he began to write an account of what he had found—or dreamed that he found—under the garden of Winton Hall. The summer night was nosing wetly around the window just as it had done fifty years ago, but, as he wrote, it began to turn grey and recede; the trees of the garden became visible, so that, when he looked up after some hours from his writing, he could see the shape of the broken fountain and what he supposed were the laurels in the Dark Walk, looking like old men humped against the weather.

PART TWO

I

Never mind how I came to the island in the lake, never mind whether in fact, as my brother says, it is a shallow pond with water only two feet deep (I suppose a raft can be launched on two feet of water, and certainly I must have always come to the lake by way of the Dark Walk, so that it is not at all unlikely that I built my raft there). Never mind what hour it was—I think it was evening, and I had hidden, as I remember it, in the Dark Walk because George had not got the courage to search for me there. The evening turned to rain, just as it's raining now, and George must have been summoned into the house for shelter. He would have told my mother that he couldn't find me and she must have called from the upstair windows, front and back—perhaps it was the occasion George spoke about tonight. I am not sure of these facts, they are plausible only, I can't yet *see* what I'm describing. But I know that I was not to find George and my mother again for many days . . . It cannot, whatever George says, have been less than three days and nights that I spent below the ground. Could he really have forgotten so inexplicable an experience?

And here I am already checking my story as though it were something which had really happened, for what possible relevance has George's memory to the events of a dream?

I dreamed that I crossed the lake, I dreamed . . . that is the only certain fact and I must cling to it, the fact that I dreamed. How my poor mother would grieve if she could know that, even for a moment, I had begun to think of these events as true . . . but, of course, if it were possible for her to know what I am thinking now, there would be no limit to the area of possibility. I dreamed then that I crossed the water (either by swimming—I could already swim at seven years old—or by wading if the lake is really as small as George makes out, or by paddling a raft) and scrambled up the slope of the island. I can remember grass, scrub, brushwood, and at last a wood. I would describe it as a forest if I had not already seen, in the height of the garden-wall, how age diminishes size. I don't remember the umbrella pine which W.W. described—I suspect he stole the sentinel-tree from *Treasure Island*, but I do know that when I got into the wood I was completely hidden from the house and the trees were close enough together to protect me from the rain. Quite soon I was lost, and yet how could I have been lost if the lake were no bigger than a pond, and the island therefore not much larger than the top of a kitchen-table?

Again I find myself checking my memories as though they were facts. A dream does not take account of size. A puddle can contain a continent, and a clump of trees stretch in sleep to the world's edge. I dreamed, I *dreamed* that I was lost and that night began to fall. I was not frightened. It was as though even at seven I was accustomed to travel. All the rough journeys of the future were already in me then, like a muscle which had only to develop. I curled up among the roots of the trees and slept. When I woke I could still hear the pit-pat of the rain in the upper branches and the steady zing of an insect near by. All these noises come as clearly back to me now as the sound of the rain on the parked cars outside the clinic in Wimpole Street, the music of yesterday.

The moon had risen and I could see more easily around me. I was determined to explore further before the morning came, for then an expedition would certainly be sent in search of me. I knew, from the many books of exploration George had read to me, of the danger to a person lost of walking in circles until eventually he dies of thirst or hunger, so I cut a cross in the bark of the tree (I had brought a knife with me that contained several blades, a small saw and an instrument for removing pebbles from horses' hooves). For the sake of future reference I named the place where I had slept Camp Hope. I had no fear of hunger, for I had apples in both pockets, and as for thirst I had only to continue in a straight line and I would come eventually to the lake again where the water was sweet, or at worst a little brackish. I go into all these details, which W.W. unaccountably omitted, to test my memory. I had forgotten until now how far or how deeply it extended. Had W.W. forgotten or was he afraid to remember?

I had gone a little more than three hundred yards—I paced the distances and marked every hundred paces or so on a tree—it was the best I could do, without proper surveying instruments, for the map I already planned to draw—when I reached a great oak of apparently enormous age with roots that coiled away above the surface of the ground. (I was reminded of those roots once in

Africa where they formed a kind of shrine for a fetish—a seated human figure made out of a gourd and palm fronds and unidentifiable vegetable matter gone rotten in the rains and a great penis of bamboo. Coming on it suddenly, I was frightened, or was it the memory that it brought back which scared me?) Under one of these roots the earth had been disturbed; somebody had shaken a mound of charred tobacco from a pipe and a sequin glistened like a snail in the moist moonlight. I struck a match to examine the ground closer and saw the imprint of a foot in a patch of loose earth—it was pointing at the tree from a few inches away and it was as solitary as the print Crusoe found on the sands of another island. It was as though a one-legged man had taken a leap out of the bushes straight at the tree.

Pirate ancestor! What nonsense W.W. had written, or had he converted the memory of that stark frightening footprint into some comforting thought of the kindly scoundrel, Long John Silver, and his wooden leg?

I stood astride the imprint and stared up the tree, half expecting to see a one-legged man perched like a vulture among the branches. I listened and there was no sound except last night's rain dripping from leaf to leaf. Then—I don't know why—I went down on my knees and peered among the roots. There was no iron ring, but one of the roots formed an arch more than two feet high like the entrance to a cave. I put my head inside and lit another match—I couldn't see the back of the cave.

It's difficult to remember that I was only seven years old. To the self we remain always the same age. I was afraid at first to venture further, but so would any grown man have been, any one of the explorers I thought of as my peers. My brother had been reading aloud to me a month before from a book called *The Romance of Australian Exploration*—my own powers of reading had not advanced quite as far as that, but my memory was green and retentive and I carried in my head all kinds of new images and evocative words—aboriginal, sextant, Murumbidgee, Stony Desert, and the points of the compass with their big capital letters ESE and NNW had an excitement they have never quite lost. They were like the figure on a watch which at last comes round to pointing the important hour. I was comforted by the thought that Sturt had been sometimes daunted and that Burke's bluster often hid his fear. Now, kneeling by the cave, I remembered a cavern which George Grey, another hero of mine, had entered and how suddenly he had come on the figure of a man ten feet high painted on the wall, clothed from the chin down to the ankles in a red garment. I don't know why, but I was more afraid of that painting than I was of the aborigines who killed Burke, and the fact that the feet and hands which protruded from the garment were said to be badly executed added to the terror. A foot which looked like a foot was only human, but my imagination could play endlessly with the faults of the painter—a club-foot, a claw-foot, the worm-like toes of a bird. Now I associated this strange footprint with the ill-executed painting, and I hesitated a long time before I got the courage to crawl into the cave under the root. Before doing so, in reference to the footprint, I gave the spot the name of Friday's Cave.

2

For some yards I could not even get upon my knees, the roof grated my hair, and it was impossible for me in that position to strike another match. I could only inch along like a worm, making an ideograph in the dust. I didn't notice for a while in the darkness that I was crawling down a long slope, but I could feel on either side of me roots rubbing my shoulders like the banisters of a staircase. I was creeping through the branches of an underground tree in a mole's world. Then the impediments were passed— I was out the other side; I banged my head again on the earth-wall and found that I could rise to my knees. But I nearly toppled down again, for I had not realized how steeply the ground sloped. I was more than a man's height below ground and, when I struck a match, I could see no finish to the long gradient going down. I cannot help feeling a little proud that I continued on my way, on my knees this time, though I suppose it is arguable whether one can really show courage in a dream.

I was halted again by a turn in the path, and this time I found I could rise to my feet after I had struck another match. The track had flattened out and ran horizontally. The air was stuffy with an odd disagreeable smell like cabbage cooking, and I wanted to go back. I remembered how miners carried canaries with them in cages to test the freshness of the air, and I wished I had thought of bringing our own canary with me which had accompanied us to Winton Hall—it would have been company too in that dark tunnel with its tiny song. There was something, I remembered, called coal-damp which caused explosions, and this passage was certainly damp enough. I must be nearly under the lake by this time, and I thought to myself that, if there was an explosion, the waters of the lake would pour in and drown me.

I blew out my match at the idea, but all the same I continued on my way in the hope that I might come on an exit a little easier than the long crawl back through the roots of the trees.

Suddenly ahead of me something whistled, only it was less like a whistle than a hiss: it was like the noise a kettle makes when it is on the boil. I thought of snakes and wondered whether some giant serpent had made its nest in the tunnel. There was something fatal to man called a Black Mamba . . . I stood stock-still and held my breath, while the whistling went on and on for a long while, before it whined out into nothing. I would have given anything then to have been safe back in bed in the room next to my mother's, with the electric-light switch close to my hand and the firm bed-end at my feet. There was a strange clanking sound and a duck-like quack. I couldn't bear the darkness any more and I lit another match, reckless of coal-damp. It shone on a pile of old newspapers and nothing else—it was strange to find I had not been the first person here. I called out 'Hullo!' and my voice went on in diminishing echoes down the long passage. Nobody answered, and when I picked up one of the papers I saw it was no proof of a human presence. It was the *East Anglian Observer* for April 5th 1885—'with which is incorporated the *Colchester Guardian*.' It's funny how even the date remains in my mind and the Victorian Gothic type of the titling. There was a faint fishy smell about it as though—oh, eons ago—it had been wrapped around a bit of pre-historic cod. The match burnt my fingers and went out. Perhaps I was the first to come here for all those years, but suppose whoever had brought those papers were lying somewhere dead in the tunnel . . .

Then I had an idea. I made a torch of the paper in my hand, tucked the others under my arm to serve me later, and with the stronger light advanced more boldly down the passage. After all wild beasts—so George had read to me—and serpents too in all likelihood—were afraid of fire, and my fear of an explosion had been driven out by the greater terror of what I might find in the dark. But it was not a snake or a leopard or a tiger or any other cavern-haunting animal that I saw when I turned the second corner. Scrawled with the simplicity of ancient man upon the left-hand wall of the passage—done with a sharp tool like a chisel—was the outline of a gigantic fish. I held up my paper-torch higher and saw the remains of lettering either half-obliterated or in a language I didn't know.

I was trying to make sense of the symbols when a hoarse voice out of sight called, 'Maria, Maria.'

I stood very still and the newspaper burned down in my hand. 'Is that you, Maria?' the voice said. It sounded to me very angry. 'What kind of a trick are you playing? What's the clock say? Surely it's time for my broth.' And then I heard again that strange quacking sound which I had heard before. There was a long whispering and after that silence.

$$\int^{\cdot} \! \mathit{cn} \quad \mathit{rc} \quad \mathit{ch_{\cdot)}} \mathit{r}$$

3

I suppose I was relieved that there were human beings and not wild beasts down the passage, but what kind of human beings could they be except criminals hiding from justice or gypsies who are notorious for stealing children? I was afraid to think what they might do to anyone who discovered their secret. It was also possible, of course, that I had come on the home of some aboriginal tribe . . . I stood there unable to make up my mind whether to go on or to turn back. It was not a problem which my Australian peers could help me to solve, for they had sometimes found the aboriginals friendly folk who gave them fish (I thought of the fish on the wall) and sometimes enemies who attacked with spears. In any case—whether these were criminals or gypsies or aboriginals—I had only a pocket-knife for my defence. I think it showed the true spirit of an explorer that in spite of my fears I thought of the map I must one day draw if I survived and so named this spot Camp Indecision.

My indecision was solved for me. An old woman appeared suddenly and noiselessly around the corner of the passage. She wore an old blue dress which came down to her ankles covered with sequins, and her hair was grey and straggly and she was going bald on top. She was every bit as surprised as I was. She stood there gaping at me and then she opened her mouth and squawked. I learned later that she had no roof to her mouth and was probably saying, 'Who are you?' but then I thought it was some foreign tongue she spoke—perhaps aboriginee—and I replied with an attempt at assurance, 'I'm English.'

The hoarse voice out of sight said, 'Bring him along here, Maria.'

The old woman took a step towards me, but I couldn't bear the thought of being touched by her hands, which were old and curved like a bird's and covered with the brown patches that Ernest, the gardener, had told me were 'grave-marks'; her nails were very long and filled with dirt. Her dress was dirty too and I thought of the sequin I'd seen outside and imagined her scrabbling home through the roots of the tree. I backed up against the side of the passage and somehow squeezed around her. She quacked after me, but I went on. Round a second—or perhaps a third—corner I found myself in a great cave some eight feet high. On what I thought was a throne, but I later realized was an old lavatory-seat, sat a big old man with a white beard yellowing round the mouth from what I suppose now to have been nicotine. He had one good leg, but the right trouser was sewn up and looked stuffed like a bolster. I could see him quite well because an oil-lamp stood on a kitchen-table, beside a carving-knife and two cabbages, and his face came vividly back to me

the other day when I was reading Darwin's description of a
carrier-pigeon: 'Greatly elongated eyelids, very large external
orifices to the nostrils, and a wide gape of mouth.'

He said, 'And who would you be and what are you doing here
and why are you burning my newspaper?'

The old woman came squawking around the corner and then
stood still behind me, barring my retreat.

I said, 'My name's William Wilditch, and I come from Winton
Hall.'

'And where's Winton Hall?' he asked, never stirring from his
lavatory-seat.

'Up there,' I said and pointed at the roof of the cave.

'That means precious little,' he said. 'Why, everything is up
there, China and all America too and the Sandwich Islands.'

'I suppose so,' I said. There was a kind of reason in most of
what he said, as I came to realize later.

'But down here there's only us. We are exclusive,' he said,
'Maria and me.'

I was less frightened of him now. He spoke English. He was a
fellow-countryman. I said, 'If you'll tell me the way out I'll be going on my way.'

'What's that you've got under your arm?' he asked me sharply.
'More newspapers?'

'I found them in the passage . . .'

'Finding's not keeping here,' he said, 'whatever it may be up
there in China. You'll soon discover that. Why, that's the last lot
of papers Maria brought in. What would we have for reading if
we let you go and pinch them?'

'I didn't mean . . .'

'Can you read?' he asked, not listening to my excuses.

'If the words aren't too long.'

'Maria can read, but she can't see very well any more than I
can, and she can't articulate much.'

Maria went kwahk, kwahk behind me, like a bull-frog it
seems to me now, and I jumped. If that was how she read I wondered how he could understand a single word. He said, 'Try a
piece.'

'What do you mean?'

'Can't you understand plain English? You'll have to work for your supper down here.'

'But it's not supper-time. It's still early in the morning,' I said.

'What o'clock is it, Maria?'

'Kwahk,' she said.

'Six. That's supper-time.'

'But it's six in the morning, not the evening.'

'How do you know? Where's the light? There aren't such things as mornings and evenings here.'

'Then how do you ever wake up?' I asked. His beard shook as he laughed. 'What a shrewd little shaver he is,' he exclaimed. 'Did you hear that, Maria? "How do you ever wake up?" he said. All the same you'll find that life here isn't all beer and skittles and who's your Uncle Joe. If you are clever, you'll learn and if you are not clever . . .' He brooded morosely. 'We are deeper here than any grave was ever dug to bury secrets in. Under the earth or over the earth, it's here you'll find all that matters.' He added angrily, 'Why aren't you reading a piece as I told you to? If you are to stay with us, you've got to jump to it.'

'I don't want to stay.'

'You think you can just take a peek, is that it? and go away. You are wrong—but take all the peek you want and then get on with it.'

I didn't like the way he spoke, but all the same I did as he suggested. There was an old chocolate-stained chest of drawers, a tall kitchen-cupboard, a screen covered with scraps and transfers; and a wooden crate which perhaps served Maria for a chair, and another larger one for a table. There was a cooking-stove with a kettle pushed to one side, steaming yet. That would have caused the whistle I had heard in the passage. I could see no sign of any bed, unless a heap of potato-sacks against the wall served that purpose. There were a lot of breadcrumbs on the earth-floor and a few bones had been swept into a corner as though awaiting interment.

'And now,' he said, 'show your young paces. I've yet to see whether you are worth your keep.'

'But I don't want to be kept,' I said. 'I really don't. It's time I went home.'

'Home's where a man lies down,' he said, 'and this is where you'll lie from now. Now take the first page that comes and read to me. I want to hear the news.'

'But the paper's nearly fifty years old,' I said. 'There's no news in it.'

'News is news however old it is.' I began to notice a way he had of talking in general statements like a lecturer or a prophet. He seemed to be less interested in conversation than in the recital of some articles of belief, odd crazy ones, perhaps, yet somehow I could never put my finger convincingly on an error. 'A cat's a cat even when it's a dead cat. We get rid of it when it's smelly, but news never smells, however long it's dead. News keeps. And it comes round again when you least expect. Like thunder.'

I opened the paper at random and read: 'Garden fête at the Grange. The fête at the Grange, Long Wilson, in aid of Distressed Gentlewomen was opened by Lady (Isobel) Montgomery.' I was a bit put out by the long words coming so quickly, but I acquitted myself with fair credit. He sat on the lavatory-seat with his head sunk a little, listening with attention. 'The Vicar presided at the White Elephant Stall.'

The old man said with satisfaction, 'They are royal beasts.'

'But these were not really elephants,' I said.

'A stall is part of a stable, isn't it? What do you want a stable for if they aren't real? Go on. Was it a good fate or an evil fate?'

'It's not that kind of fate either,' I said.

'There's no other kind,' he said. 'It's your fate to read to me. It's *her* fate to talk like a frog, and mine to listen because my eyesight's bad. This is an underground fate we suffer from here, and that was a garden fate—but it all comes to the same fate in the end.' It was useless to argue with him and I read on: 'Unfortunately the festivities were brought to an untimely close by a heavy rainstorm.'

Maria gave a kwahk that sounded like a malicious laugh, and 'You see,' the old man said, as though what I had read proved somehow he was right, 'that's fate for you.'

'The evening's events had to be transferred indoors, including the Morris Dancing and the Treasure Hunt.'

'Treasure Hunt?' the old man asked sharply.

'That's what it says here.'

'The impudence of it,' he said. 'The sheer impudence. Maria, did you hear that?'

She kwahked—this time, I thought, angrily.

'It's time for my broth,' he said with deep gloom, as though he were saying, 'It's time for my death.'

'It happened a long time ago,' I said, trying to soothe him.

'Time,' he exclaimed, 'you can —— time,' using a word quite unfamiliar to me which I guessed—I don't know how—was one that I could not with safety use myself when I returned home. Maria had gone behind the screen—there must have been other cupboards there, for I heard her opening and shutting doors and clanking pots and pans.

I whispered to him quickly, 'Is she your luba?'

'Sister, wife, mother, daughter,' he said, 'what difference does it make? Take your choice. She's a woman, isn't she?' He brooded there on the lavatory-seat like a king on a throne. 'There are two sexes,' he said. 'Don't try to make more than two with definitions.' The statement sank into my mind with the same heavy mathematical certainty with which later on at school I learned the rule of Euclid about the sides of an isosceles triangle. There was a long silence.

'I think I'd better be going,' I said, shifting up and down. Maria came in. She carried a dish marked Fido filled with hot broth. Her husband, her brother, whatever he was, nursed it on his lap a long while before he drank it. He seemed to be lost in thought again, and I hesitated to disturb him. All the same, after a while, I tried again.

'They'll be expecting me at home.'

'Home?'

'Yes.'

'You couldn't have a better home than this,' he said. 'You'll see. In a bit of time—a year or two—you'll settle down well enough.'

I tried my best to be polite. 'It's very nice here, I'm sure, but . . .'

'It's no use your being restless. I didn't ask you to come, did I, but now you are here, you'll stay. Maria's a great hand with cabbage. You won't suffer any hardship.'

'But I can't stay. My mother . . .'

'Forget your mother and your father too. If you need anything from up there Maria will fetch it down for you.'

'But I can't stay here.'

'Can't's not a word that you can use to the likes of me.'

'But you haven't any right to keep me . . .'

'And what right had you to come busting in like a thief, getting Maria all disturbed when she was boiling my broth?'

'I couldn't stay here with you. It's not—sanitary.' I don't know how I managed to get that word out. 'I'd die . . .'

'There's no need to talk of dying down here. No one's ever died here, and you've no reason to believe that anyone ever will. We aren't dead, are we, and we've lived a long long time, Maria and me. You don't know how lucky you are. There's treasure here beyond all the riches of Asia. One day, if you don't go disturbing Maria, I'll show you. You know what a millionaire is?' I nodded. 'They aren't one quarter as rich as Maria and me. And they die too, and where's their treasure then? Rockefeller's gone and Fred's gone and Columbus. I sit here and just read about dying—it's an entertainment that's all. You'll find in all those papers what they call an obituary—there's one about a Lady Caroline Winterbottom that made Maria laugh and me. It's summerbottoms we have here, I said, all the year round, sitting by the stove.'

Maria kwahked in the background, and I began to cry more as a way of interrupting him than because I was really frightened.

It's extraordinary how vividly after all these years I can remember that man and the words he spoke. If they were to dig down now on the island below the roots of the tree, I would half expect to find him sitting there still on the old lavatory-seat which seemed to be detached from any pipes or drainage and serve no useful purpose, and yet, if he had really existed, he must have passed his century a long time ago. There was something of a monarch about him and something, as I said, of a prophet and something of the gardener my mother disliked and of a police-man in the next village; his expressions were often countrylike and coarse, but his ideas seemed to move on a deeper level, like roots spreading below a layer of compost. I could sit here now in this room for hours remembering the things he said—I haven't made out the sense of them all yet: they are stored in my memory like a code uncracked which waits for a clue or an inspiration.

He said to me sharply, 'We don't need salt here. There's too much as it is. You taste any bit of earth and you'll find it salt. We live in salt. We are pickled, you might say, in it. Look at Maria's hands, and you'll see the salt in the cracks.'

I stopped crying at once and looked (my attention could al-ways be caught by bits of irrelevant information), and, true enough, there seemed to be grey-white seams running between her knuckles.

'You'll turn salty too in time,' he said encouragingly and drank his broth with a good deal of noise.

I said, 'But I really am going, Mr . . .'

'You can call me Javitt,' he said, 'but only because it's not my real name. You don't believe I'd give you that, do you? And Maria's not Maria—it's just a sound she answers to, you under-stand me, like Jupiter.'

'No.'

'If you had a dog called Jupiter, you wouldn't believe he was really Jupiter, would you?'

'I've got a dog called Joe.'

'The same applies,' he said and drank his soup. Sometimes I think that in no conversation since have I found the interest I dis-covered in those inconsequent sentences of his to which I listened during the days (I don't know how many) that I spent below the garden. Because, of course, I didn't leave that day. Javitt had his way.

He might be said to have talked me into staying, though if I had proved obstinate I have no doubt at all that Maria would have blocked my retreat, and certainly I would not have fancied struggling to escape through the musty folds of her clothes. That was the strange balance—to and fro—of those days; half the time I was frightened as though I were caged in a nightmare and half the time I only wanted to laugh freely and happily at the strangeness of his speech and the novelty of his ideas. It was as if, for those hours or days, the only important things in life were two, laughter and fear. (Perhaps the same ambivalence was there when I first began to know a woman.) There are people whose laughter has always a sense of superiority, but it was Javitt who taught me that laughter is more often a sign of equality, of pleasure and not of malice. He sat there on his lavatory-seat and he said, 'I shit dead stuff every day, do I? How wrong you are.' (I was already laughing because that was a word I knew to be obscene and I had never heard it spoken before.) 'Everything that comes out of me is alive, I tell you. It's squirming around there, germs and bacilli and the like, and it goes into the ground like a womb, and it comes out somewhere, I dare say, like my daughter did—I forgot I haven't told you about her.'

'Is she here?' I said with a look at the curtain, wondering what monstrous woman would next emerge.

'Oh, no, she went upstairs a long time ago.'

'Perhaps I could take her a message from you,' I said cunningly.

He looked at me with contempt. 'What kind of a message,' he asked, 'could the likes of you take to the likes of her?' He must have seen the motive behind my offer, for he reverted to the fact of my imprisonment. 'I'm not unreasonable,' he said, 'I'm not one to make hailstorms in harvest time, but if you went back up there you'd talk about me and Maria and the treasure we've got, and people would come digging.'

'I swear I'd say nothing' (and at least I have kept that promise, whatever others I have broken, through all the years until now).

'You talk in your sleep maybe. A boy's never alone. You've got a brother, I dare say, and soon you'll be going to school and hinting of things to make you seem important. There are plenty of ways of keeping an oath and breaking it in the same moment. Do you know what I'd do then? If they came searching? I'd go further in.'

Maria kwahk-kwahked her agreement where she listened from somewhere behind the curtains.

'What do you mean?'

'Give me a hand to get off this seat,' he said. He pressed his hand down on my shoulder and it was like a mountain heaving. I looked at the lavatory-seat and I could see that it had been placed exactly to cover a hole which went down down down out of sight. 'A moit of the treasure's down there already,' he said, 'but I wouldn't let the bastards enjoy what they could find here. There's a little matter of subsidence I've got fixed up so that they'd never see the light of day again.'

'But what would you do below there for food?'

'We've got tins enough for another century or two,' he said. 'You'd be surprised at what Maria's stored away there. We don't use tins up here because there's always broth and cabbage and that's more healthy and keeps the scurvy off, but we've no more teeth to lose and our gums are fallen as it is, so if we had to fall back on tins we would. Why, there's hams and chickens and red salmons' eggs and butter and steak-and-kidney pies and caviar, venison too and marrow-bones, I'm forgetting the fish—cods' roe and sole in white wine, langouste legs, sardines, bloaters, and herrings in tomato-sauce, and all the fruits that ever grew, apples, pears, strawberries, figs, raspberries, plums and greengages and passion fruit, mangoes, grapefruit, loganberries and cherries, mulberries too and sweet things from Japan, not to speak of vegetables, Indian corn and taties, salsify and spinach and that thing they call endive, asparagus, peas and the hearts of bamboo, and I've left out our old friend the tomato.' He lowered himself heavily back on to his seat above the great hole going down.

'You must have enough for two lifetimes,' I said.

'There's means of getting more,' he added darkly, so that I pictured other channels delved through the undersoil of the garden like the section of an ant's nest, and I remembered the sequin on the island and the single footprint.

Perhaps all this talk of food had reminded Maria of her duties because she came quacking out from behind her dusty curtain, carrying two bowls of broth, one medium size for me and one almost as small as an egg-cup for herself. I tried politely to take the small one, but she snatched it away from me.

'You don't have to bother about Maria,' the old man said.

'She's been eating food for more years than you've got weeks. She knows her appetite.'

'What do you cook with?' I asked.

'Calor,' he said.

That was an odd thing about this adventure or rather this dream: fantastic though it was, it kept coming back to ordinary life with simple facts like that. The man could never, if I really thought it out, have existed all those years below the earth, and yet the cooking, as I seem to remember it, was done on a cylinder of calor-gas.

The broth was quite tasty and I drank it to the end. When I had finished I fidgeted about on the wooden box they had given me for a seat—nature was demanding something for which I was too embarrassed to ask aid.

'What's the matter with you?' Javitt said. 'Chair not comfortable?'

'Oh, it's very comfortable,' I said.

'Perhaps you want to lie down and sleep?'

'No.'

'I'll show you something which will give you dreams,' he said. 'A picture of my daughter.'

'I want to do number one,' I blurted out.

'Oh, is that all?' Javitt said. He called to Maria, who was still clattering around behind the curtain, 'The boy wants to piss. Fetch him the golden po.' Perhaps my eyes showed interest, for he added to me diminishingly, with the wave of a hand, 'It's the least of my treasures.'

All the same it was remarkable enough in my eyes, and I can remember it still, a veritable chamber-pot of gold. Even the young dauphin of France on that long road back from Varennes with his father had only a silver cup at his service. I would have been more embarrassed, doing what I called number one in front of the old man Javitt, if I had not been so impressed by the pot. It lent the everyday affair the importance of a ceremony, almost of a sacrament. I can remember the tinkle in the pot like far-away chimes as though a gold surface resounded differently from china or base metal.

Javitt reached behind him to a shelf stacked with old papers and picked one out. He said, 'Now you look at that and tell me what you think.'

It was a kind of magazine I'd never seen before—full of pictures which are now called cheese-cake. I have no earlier memory of a woman's unclothed body, or as nearly unclothed as made no difference to me then, in the skin-tight black costume. One whole page was given up to a Miss Ramsgate, shot from all angles. She was the favourite contestant for something called Miss England and might later go on, if she were successful, to compete for the title of Miss Europe, Miss World and after that Miss Universe. I stared at her as though I wanted to memorize her for ever. And that is exactly what I did.

'That's our daughter,' Javitt said.

'And did she become . . .'

'She was launched,' he said with pride and mystery, as though he were speaking of some moon-rocket which had at last after many disappointments risen from the pad and soared to outer space. I looked at the photograph, at the wise eyes and the inexplicable body, and I thought, with all the ignorance children have of age and generations, I never want to marry anybody but her. Maria put her hand through the curtains and quacked, and I thought, she would be my mother then, but not a hoot did I care. With that girl for my wife I could take anything, even school and growing up and life. And perhaps I could have taken them, if I had ever succeeded in finding her.

Again my thoughts were interrupted. For if I am remembering a vivid dream—and dreams do stay in all their detail far longer than we realize—how would I have known at that age about such absurdities as beauty-contests? A dream can only contain what one has experienced, or, if you have sufficient faith in Jung, what our ancestors have experienced. But calor-gas and the Ramsgate Beauty Queen? . . . They are not ancestral memories, nor the memories of a child of seven. Certainly my mother did not allow us to buy with our meagre pocket-money—sixpence a week?—such papers as that. And yet the image is there, caught once and for all, not only the expression of the eyes, but the expression of the body too, the particular tilt of the breasts, the shallow scoop of the navel like something carved in sand, the little trim buttocks—the dividing line swung between them close and regular like the single sweep of a pencil. Can a child of seven fall in love for life with a body? And there is a further mystery which did not occur to me then: how could a couple as old as Javitt and Maria have had a daughter so young in the period when such contests were the vogue?

'She's a beauty,' Javitt said, 'you'll never see her like where your folks live. Things grow differently underground, like a mole's coat. I ask you where there's softness softer than that?' I'm not sure whether he was referring to the skin of his daughter or the coat of a mole.

I sat on the golden po and looked at the photograph and listened to Javitt as I would have listened to my own father if I had possessed one. His sayings are fixed in my memory like the photograph. Gross some of them seem now, but they did not appear gross to me then when even the graffiti on walls were innocent. Except when he called me 'boy' or 'snapper' or something of the kind he seemed unaware of my age: it was not that he talked to me as an equal but as someone from miles away, looking down from his old lavatory-seat to my golden po, from so far away that he couldn't distinguish my age, or perhaps he was so old that anyone under a century or so seemed much alike to him. All that I write here was not said at that moment. There must have been many days or nights of conversation—you couldn't down there tell the difference—and now I dredge the sentences up, in no particular order, just as they come to mind, sitting at my mother's desk so many years later.

4

'You laugh at Maria and me. You think we look ugly. I tell you she could have been painted if she had chosen by some of the greatest—there's one that painted women with three eyes—she'd have suited him. But she knew how to tunnel in the earth like me, when to appear and when not to appear. It's a long time now that we've been alone down here. It gets more dangerous all the

time—if you can speak of time—on the upper floor. But don't
think it hasn't happened before. But when I remember . . .' But
what he remembered has gone from my head, except only his
concluding phrase and a sense of desolation: 'Looking round at
all those palaces and towers, you'd have thought they'd been
made like a child's castle of the desert-sand.

'In the beginning you had a name only the man or woman
knew who pulled you out of your mother. Then there was a name
for the tribe to call you by. That was of little account, but of
more account all the same than the name you had with strangers;
and there was a name used in the family—by your pa and ma if
it's those terms you call them by nowadays. The only name without any power at all was the name you used to strangers. That's
why I call myself Javitt to you, but the name the man who pulled
me out knew—that was so secret I had to keep him as a friend
for life, so that he wouldn't even tell me because of the responsibility it would bring—I might let it slip before a stranger. Up
where you come from they've begun to forget the power of the
name. I wouldn't be surprised if you only had the one name and
what's the good of a name everyone knows? Do you suppose
even I feel secure here with my treasure and all—because, you
see, as it turned out, I got to know the first name of all. He told
it me before he died, before I could stop him, with a hand over
his mouth. I doubt if there's anyone in the world except me who
knows his first name. It's an awful temptation to speak it out
loud—introduce it casually into the conversation like you might
say by Jove, by George, for Christ's sake. Or whisper it when I
think no one's attentive.

'When I was born, time had a different pace to what it has now.
Now you walk from one wall to another, and it takes you twenty
steps—or twenty miles—who cares?—between the towns. But
when I was young we took a leisurely way. Don't bother me with
"I must be gone now" or "I've been away so long". I can't talk to
you in terms of time—your time and my time are different. Javitt
isn't my usual name either even with strangers. It's one I thought
up fresh for you, so that you'll have no power at all. I'll change it
right away if you escape. I warn you that.

'You get a sense of what I mean when you make love with a

girl. The time isn't measured by clocks. Time is fast or slow or it stops for a while altogether. One minute is different to every other minute. When you make love it's a pulse in a man's part which measures time and when you spill yourself there's no time at all. That's how time comes and goes, not by an alarm-clock made by a man with a magnifying glass in his eye. Haven't you ever heard them say, "It's —— time" up there?' and he used again the word which I guessed was forbidden like his name, perhaps because it had power too.

'I dare say you are wondering how Maria and me could make a beautiful girl like that one. That's an illusion people have about beauty. Beauty doesn't come from beauty. All that beauty can produce is prettiness. Have you never looked around upstairs and counted the beautiful women with their pretty daughters? Beauty diminishes all the time, it's the law of diminishing returns, and only when you get back to zero, to the real ugly base of things, there's a chance to start again free and independent. Painters who paint what they call ugly things know that. I can still see that little head with its cap of blonde hair coming out from between Maria's thighs and how she leapt out of Maria in a spasm (there wasn't any doctor down here or midwife to give her a name and rob her of power—and she's Miss Ramsgate to you and to the whole world upstairs). Ugliness and beauty; you see it in war too; when there's nothing left of a house but a couple of pillars against the sky, the beauty of it starts all over again like before the builder ruined it. Perhaps when Maria and I go up there next, there'll only be pillars left, sticking up around the flattened world like it was fucking time.' (The word had become a familiar to me by this time and no longer had the power to shock.)

'Do you know, boy, that when they make those maps of the universe you are looking at the map of something that looked like that six thousand million years ago? You can't be much more out of date than that, I'll swear. Why, if they've got pictures up there of us taken yesterday, they'll see the world all covered with ice—if their photos are a bit more up to date than ours, that is. Otherwise we won't be there at all, maybe, and it might just as well be a photo of the future. To catch a star while it's alive you have to be as nippy as if you were snatching at a racehorse as it goes by.

'You are a bit scared still of Maria and me because you've never seen anyone like us before. And you'd be scared to see our daughter too, there's no other like her in whatever country she's in now, and what good would a scared man be to her? Do you know what a rogue-plant is? And do you know that white cats with blue eyes are deaf? People who keep nursery-gardens look around all the time at the seedlings and they throw away any oddities like weeds. They call them rogues. You won't find many white cats with blue eyes and that's the reason. But sometimes you find someone who wants things different, who's tired of all the plus signs and wants to find zero, and he starts breeding away with the differences. Maria and I are both rogues and we are born of generations of rogues. Do you think I lost this leg in an accident? I was born that way just like Maria with her squawk. Generations of us uglier and uglier, and suddenly out of Maria comes our daughter, who's Miss Ramsgate to you. I don't speak her name even when I'm asleep. We're unique like the Red Grouse. You ask anybody if they can tell you where the Red Grouse came from.

'You are still wondering why we are unique. It's because for generations we haven't been thrown away. Man kills or throws away what he doesn't want. Somebody once in Greece kept the wrong child and exposed the right one, and then one rogue at least was safe and it only needed another. Why, in Tierra del Fuego in starvation years they kill and eat their old women because the dogs are of more value. It's the hardest thing in the world for a rogue to survive. For hundreds of years now we've been living underground and we'll have the laugh of you yet, coming up above for keeps in a dead world. Except I'll bet you your golden po that Miss Ramsgate will be there somewhere— her beauty's rogue too. We have long lives, we—Javitts to you. We've kept our ugliness all those years and why shouldn't she keep her beauty? Like a cat does. A cat is as beautiful the last day as the first. And it keeps its spittle. Not like a dog.

'I can see your eye light up whenever I say Miss Ramsgate, and you still wonder how it comes Maria and I have a child like that in spite of all I'm telling you. Elephants go on breeding till they are ninety years old, don't they, and do you suppose a rogue like Javitt (which isn't my real name) can't go on longer than a beast so stupid it lets itself be harnessed and draw logs? There's another thing we have in common with elephants. No one sees us dead.

'We know the sex-taste of female birds better than we know the sex-taste of women. Only the most beautiful in the hen's eyes survives, so when you admire a peacock you know you have the same taste as a pea-hen. But women are more mysterious than birds. You've heard of beauty and the beast, haven't you? They have rogue-tastes. Just look at me and my leg. You won't find Miss Ramsgate by going round the world preening yourself like a peacock to attract a beautiful woman—she's our daughter and she had rogue-tastes too. She isn't for someone who wants a beautiful wife at his dinner-table to satisfy his vanity, and an understanding wife in bed who'll treat him just the same number of times as he was accustomed to at school—so many times a day or week. She went away, our daughter did, with a want looking for a want—and not a want you can measure in inches either or calculate in numbers by the week. They say that in the northern countries people make love for their health, so it won't be any good looking for her in the north. You might have to go as far as Africa or China. And talking of China . . . '

5

Sometimes I think that I learned more from Javitt—this man who never existed—than from all my schoolmasters. He talked to me while I sat there on the po or lay upon the sacks as no one had ever done before or has ever done since. I could not have expected my mother to take time away from the Fabian pamphlets to say, 'Men are like monkeys—they don't have any season in love, and the monkeys aren't worried by this notion of dying. They tell us from pulpits we're immortal and then they try to frighten us with death. I'm more a monkey than a man. To the monkeys death's an accident. The gorillas don't bury their dead with hearses and crowns of flowers, thinking one day it's going to happen to them and they better put on a show if they want one for themselves too. If one of them dies, it's a special case, and so they can leave it in the ditch. I feel like them. But I'm not a special case yet. I keep clear of hackney-carriages and railway-trains, you won't find horses, wild dogs or machinery down here. I love life and I survive. Up there they talk about natural death, but it's natural death that's unnatural. If we lived for a thousand years—and there's no reason we shouldn't—there'd always be a smash, a bomb, tripping over your left foot—those are the natural deaths. All we need to live is a bit of effort, but nature sows booby-traps in our way.

'Do you believe those skulls monks have in their cells are set there for contemplation? Not on your life. They don't believe in death any more than I do. The skulls are there for the same reason you'll see a queen's portrait in an embassy—they're just part of the official furniture. Do you believe an ambassador ever looks at that face on the wall with a diamond tiara and an empty smile?

'Be disloyal. It's your duty to the human race. The human race needs to survive and it's the loyal man who dies first from anxiety or a bullet or overwork. If you have to earn a living, boy, and the price they make you pay is loyalty, be a double agent—and never let either of the two sides know your real name. The same applies to women and God. They both respect a man they don't own, and they'll go on raising the price they are willing to offer. Didn't Christ say that very thing? Was the prodigal son loyal or the lost shilling or the strayed sheep? The obedient flock didn't give the shepherd any satisfaction or the loyal son interest his father.

'People are afraid of bringing May blossom into the house. They say it's unlucky. The real reason is it smells strong of sex and they are afraid of sex. Why aren't they afraid of fish then, you may rightly ask? Because when they smell fish they smell a holiday ahead and they feel safe from breeding for a short while.'

I remember Javitt's words far more clearly than the passage of time; certainly I must have slept at least twice on the bed of sacks, but I cannot remember Javitt sleeping until the very end— perhaps he slept like a horse or a god, upright. And the broth— that came at regular intervals, so far as I could tell, though there was no sign anywhere of a clock, and once I think they opened for me a tin of sardines from their store (it had a very Victorian label on it of two bearded sailors and a seal, but the sardines tasted good).

I think Javitt was glad to have me there. Surely he could not have been talking quite so amply over the years to Maria who could only quack in response, and several times he made me read to him from one of the newspapers. The nearest to our time I ever found was a local account of the celebrations for the relief of Mafeking. ('Riots,' Javitt said, 'purge like a dose of salts.')

Once he told me to pick up the oil-lamp and we would go for a walk together, and I was able to see how agile he could be on his one leg. When he stood upright he looked like a rough carv-ing from a tree-trunk where the sculptor had not bothered to separate the legs, or perhaps, as with the image on the cave, they were 'badly executed'. He put one hand on each wall and hopped gigantically in front of me, and when he paused to speak (like many old people he seemed unable to speak and move at the same time) he seemed to be propping up the whole passage with his arms as thick as pit-beams. At one point he paused to tell me that we were now directly under the lake. 'How many tons of water lie up there?' he asked me—I had never thought of water in tons before that, only in gallons, but he had the exact figure ready, I can't remember it now. Further on, where the passage sloped upwards, he paused again and said, 'Listen,' and I heard a kind of rumbling that passed overhead and after that a rattling as little cakes of mud fell around us. 'That's a motor-car,' he said, as an explorer might have said, 'That's an elephant.'

I asked him whether perhaps there was a way out near there since we were so close to the surface, and he made his answer, even to that direct question, ambiguous and general like a proverb. 'A wise man has only one door to his house,' he said.

What a boring old man he would have been to an adult mind, but a child has a hunger to learn which makes him sometimes hang on the lips of the dullest schoolmaster. I thought I was learning about the world and the universe from Javitt, and still to this day I wonder how it was that a child could have invented these details, or have they accumulated year by year, like coral, in the sea of the unconscious around the original dream?

There were times when he was in a bad humour for no apparent reason, or at any rate for no adequate reason. An example: for all his freedom of speech and range of thought, I found there were tiny rules which had to be obeyed, else the thunder of his invective broke—the way I had to arrange the spoon in the empty broth-bowl, the method of folding a newspaper after it had been read, even the arrangement of my limbs on the bed of sacks.

'I'll cut you off,' he cried once and I pictured him lopping off one of my legs to resemble him. 'I'll starve you, I'll set you alight like a candle for a warning. Haven't I given you a kingdom here of all the treasures of the earth and all the fruits of it, tin by tin, where time can't get in to destroy you and there's no day or night, and you go and defy me with a spoon laid down longways in a saucer? You come of an ungrateful generation.' His arms waved about and cast shadows like wolves on the wall behind the oil-lamp, while Maria sat squatting behind a cylinder of calor-gas in an attitude of terror.

'I haven't even seen your wonderful treasure,' I said with feeble defiance.

'Nor you won't,' he said, 'nor any lawbreaker like you. You lay last night on your back grunting like a small swine, but did I curse you as you deserved? Javitt's patient. He forgives and he forgives seventy times seven, but then you go and lay your spoon longways . . .' He gave a great sigh like a wave withdrawing. He said, 'I forgive even that. There's no fool like an old fool and you will search a long way before you find anything as old as I am—even among the tortoises, the parrots and the elephants. One day I'll show you the treasure, but not now. I'm not in the right mood now. Let time pass. Let time heal.'

I had found the way, however, on an earlier occasion to set him in a good humour and that was to talk to him about his daughter. It came quite easily to me, for I found myself to be passionately in love, as perhaps one can only be at an age when all one wants is to give and the thought of taking is very far removed. I asked him whether he was sad when she left him to go 'upstairs' as he liked to put it.

'I knew it had to come,' he said. 'It was for that she was born. One day she'll be back and the three of us will be together for keeps.'

'Perhaps I'll see her then,' I said.

'You won't live to see that day,' he said, as though it was I who was the old man, not he.

'Do you think she's married?' I asked anxiously.

'She isn't the kind to marry,' he said. 'Didn't I tell you she's a rogue like Maria and me? She has her roots down here. No one marries who has his roots down here.'

'I thought Maria and you were married,' I said anxiously.

He gave a sharp crunching laugh like a nut-cracker closing. 'There's no marrying in the ground,' he said. 'Where would you find the witnesses? Marriage is public. Maria and me, we just grew into each other, that's all, and then she sprouted.'

I sat silent for a long while, brooding on that vegetable picture. Then I said with all the firmness I could muster, 'I'm going to find her when I get out of here.'

'If you get out of here,' he said, 'you'd have to live a very long time and travel a very long way to find her.'

'I'll do just that,' I replied.

He looked at me with a trace of humour. 'You'll have to take a look at Africa,' he said, 'and Asia—and then there's America, North and South, and Australia—you might leave out the Arctic and the other Pole—she was always a warm girl.' And it occurs to me now when I think of the life I have led since, that I have been in most of those regions—except Australia where I have only twice touched down between planes.

'I will go to them all,' I said, 'and I'll find her.' It was as though the purpose of life had suddenly come to me as it must have come often enough to some future explorer when he noticed on a map for the first time an empty space in the heart of a continent.

'You'll need a lot of money,' Javitt jeered at me.

'I'll work my passage,' I said, 'before the mast.' Perhaps it was
a reflection of that intention which made the young author W.W.
menace his elder brother with such a fate before preserving him
for Oxford of all places. The mast was to be a career sacred to
me—it was not for George.

'It'll take a long time,' Javitt warned me.

'I'm young,' I said.

I don't know why it is that when I think of this conversation
with Javitt the doctor's voice comes back to me saying hopelessly, 'There's always hope.' There's hope perhaps, but there
isn't so much time left now as there was then to fulfil a destiny.

That night, when I lay down on the sacks, I had the impression that Javitt had begun to take a favourable view of my case.
I woke once in the night and saw him sitting there on what is
popularly called a throne, watching me. He closed one eye in a
wink and it was like a star going out.

Next morning after my bowl of broth, he suddenly spoke up.
'Today,' he said, 'you are going to see my treasure.'

6

It was a day heavy with the sense of something fateful coming
nearer—I call it a day but for all I could have told down there it
might have been a night. And I can only compare it in my later
experience with those slow hours I have sometimes experienced
before I have gone to meet a woman with whom for the first time
the act of love is likely to come about. The fuse has been lit, and
who can tell the extent of the explosion? A few cups broken or a
house in ruins?

For hours Javitt made no further reference to the subject, but
after the second cup of broth (or was it perhaps, on that occasion, the tin of sardines?) Maria disappeared behind the screen
and when she reappeared she wore a hat. Once, years ago perhaps, it had been a grand hat, a hat for the races, a great black
straw affair; now it was full of holes like a colander decorated
with one drooping scarlet flower which had been stitched and re-
stitched and stitched again. I wondered when I saw her dressed

like that whether we were about to go 'upstairs'. But we made no move. Instead she put a kettle upon the stove, warmed a pot and dropped in two spoonfuls of tea. Then she and Javitt sat and watched the kettle like a couple of soothsayers bent over the steaming entrails of a kid, waiting for a revelation. The kettle gave a thin preliminary whine and Javitt nodded and the tea was made. He alone took a cup, sipping it slowly, with his eyes on me, as though he were considering and perhaps revising his decision.

On the edge of his cup, I remember, was a tea-leaf. He took it on his nail and placed it on the back of my hand. I knew very well what that meant. A hard stalk of tea indicated a man upon the way and the soft leaf a woman; this was a soft leaf. I began to strike it with the palm of my other hand counting as I did so, 'One, two, three.' It lay flat, adhering to my hand. 'Four, five.' It was on my fingers now and I said, triumphantly, 'In five days,' thinking of Javitt's daughter in the world above.

Javitt shook his head. 'You don't count time like that with us,' he said. 'That's five decades of years.' I accepted his correction— he must know his own country best, and it's only now that I find myself calculating, if every day down there were ten years long, what age in our reckoning could Javitt have claimed?

I have no idea what he had learned from the ceremony of the tea, but at least he seemed satisfied. He rose on his one leg, and now that he had his arms stretched out to either wall, he reminded me of a gigantic crucifix, and the crucifix moved in great hops down the way we had taken the day before. Maria gave me a little push from behind and I followed. The oil-lamp in Maria's hand cast long shadows ahead of us.

First we came under the lake and I remembered the tons of water hanging over us like a frozen falls, and after that we reached the spot where we had halted before, and again a car went rumbling past on the road above. But this time we continued our shuffling march. I calculated that now we had crossed the road which led to Winton Halt; we must be somewhere under the inn called The Three Keys, which was kept by our gardener's uncle, and after that we should have arrived below the Long Mead, a field with a small minnowy stream along its northern border owned by a farmer called Howell. I had not given up all idea of escape and I noted our route carefully and the distance we had gone. I had hoped for some side-passage which might indicate that there was another entrance to the tunnel, but there seemed to be none and I was disappointed to find that, before we travelled below the inn, we descended quite steeply, perhaps in order to avoid the cellars—indeed at one moment I heard a groaning and a turbulence as though the gardener's uncle were taking delivery of some new barrels of beer.

We must have gone nearly half a mile before the passage came to an end in a kind of egg-shaped hall. Facing us was a kitchen-dresser of unstained wood, very similar to the one in which my mother kept her stores of jam, sultanas, raisins and the like.

'Open up, Maria,' Javitt said, and Maria shuffled by me, clanking a bunch of keys and quacking with excitement, while the lamp swung to and fro like a censer.

'She's heated up,' Javitt said. 'It's many days since she saw the treasure last.' I do not know which kind of time he was referring to then, but judging from her excitement I think the days must really have represented decades—she had even forgotten which key fitted the lock and she tried them all and failed and tried again before the tumbler turned.

I was disappointed when I first saw the interior—I had expected gold bricks and a flow of Maria Theresa dollars spilling on the floor, and there were only a lot of shabby cardboard-boxes on the upper shelves and the lower shelves were empty. I think Javitt noted my disappointment and was stung by it. 'I told you,' he said, 'the moit's down below for safety.' But I wasn't to stay disappointed very long. He took down one of the biggest boxes off the top shelf and shook the contents on to the earth at my feet, as though defying me to belittle *that*.

And *that* was a sparkling mass of jewellery such as I had never seen before—I was going to say in all the colours of the rainbow, but the colours of stones have not that pale girlish simplicity. There were reds almost as deep as raw liver, stormy blues, greens like the underside of a wave, yellow sunset colours, greys like a shadow on snow, and stones without colour at all that sparkled brighter than all the rest. I say I'd seen nothing like it: it is the scepticism of middle age which leads me now to compare that treasure trove with the caskets overflowing with artificial jewellery which you sometimes see in the shop-windows of Italian tourist-resorts.

And there again I find myself adjusting a dream to the kind of criticism I ought to reserve for some agent's report on the import or export value of coloured glass. If this was a dream, these were real stones. Absolute reality belongs to dreams and not to life. The gold of dreams is not the diluted gold of even the best gold-smith, there are no diamonds in dreams made of paste—what seems is. 'Who seems most kingly is the king.'

I went down on my knees and bathed my hands in the trea-sure, and while I knelt there Javitt opened box after box and poured the contents upon the ground. There is no avarice in a child. I didn't concern myself with the value of this horde: it was simply a treasure, and a treasure is to be valued for its own sake and not for what it will buy. It was only years later, after a deal of literature and learning and knowledge at second hand, that W.W. wrote of the treasure as something with which he could save the family fortunes. I was nearer to the jackdaw in my dream, caring only for the glitter and the sparkle.

'It's nothing to what lies below out of sight,' Javitt remarked with pride.

There were necklaces and bracelets, lockets and bangles, pins and rings and pendants and buttons. There were quantities of those little gold objects which girls like to hang on their bracelets: the Vendôme column and the Eiffel Tower and a Lion of St Mark's, a champagne bottle and a tiny booklet with leaves of gold inscribed with the names of places important perhaps to a pair of lovers—Paris, Brighton, Rome, Assisi and Moreton-in-Marsh. There were gold coins too—some with the heads of Ro-man emperors and others of Victoria and George IV and Frederick Barbarossa. There were birds made out of precious stone with diamond-eyes, and buckles for shoes and belts, hairpins too with the rubies turned into roses, and vinaigrettes. There were tooth-picks of gold, and swizzlesticks, and little spoons to dig the wax out of your ears of gold too, and cigarette-holders studded with di-amonds, and small boxes of gold for pastilles and snuff, horse-shoes for the ties of hunting men, and emerald-hounds for the lapels of hunting women: fishes were there too and little carrots of ruby for luck, diamond-stars which had perhaps decorated generals or statesmen, golden key-rings with emerald-initials, and sea-shells picked out with pearls, and a portrait of a dancing-girl in gold and enamel, with Haidee inscribed in what I suppose were rubies.

'Enough's enough,' Javitt said, and I had to drag myself away, as it seemed to me, from all the riches in the world, its pursuits and enjoyments. Maria would have packed everything that lay there back into the cardboard-boxes, but Javitt said with his lordliest voice, 'Let them lie,' and back we went in silence the way we had come, in the same order, our shadows going ahead. It was as if the sight of the treasure had exhausted me. I lay down on the sacks without waiting for my broth and fell asleep at once. In my dream within a dream somebody laughed and wept.

7

I have said that I can't remember how many days and nights I spent below the garden. The number of times I slept is really no guide, for I slept simply when I had the inclination or when Javitt commanded me to lie down, there being no light or darkness save what the oil-lamp determined, but I am almost sure it was after this sleep of exhaustion that I woke with the full intention somehow to reach home again. Up till now I had acquiesced in my captivity with little complaint; perhaps the meals of broth were palling on me, though I doubt if that was the reason, for I have fed for longer, with as little variety and less appetite, in Africa; perhaps the sight of Javitt's treasure had been a climax which robbed my story of any further interest; perhaps, and I think this is the most likely reason, I wanted to begin my search for Miss Ramsgate.

Whatever the motive, I came awake determined from my deep sleep, as suddenly as I had fallen into it. The wick was burning low in the oil-lamp and I could hardly distinguish Javitt's features and Maria was out of sight somewhere behind the curtain. To my astonishment Javitt's eyes were closed—it had never occurred to me before that there were moments when these two might sleep. Very quietly, with my eyes on Javitt, I slipped off my shoes—it was now or never. When I had got them off with less sound than a mouse makes, an idea came to me and I withdrew the laces—I can still hear the sharp ting of the metal tag ringing on the gold po beside my sacks. I thought I had been too clever by half, for Javitt stirred—but then he was still again and I slipped off my makeshift bed and crawled over to him where he sat on the lavatory-seat. I knew that, unfamiliar as I was with the tunnel, I could never outpace Javitt, but I was taken aback when I realized that it was impossible to bind together the ankles of a one-legged man.

But neither could a one-legged man travel without the help of his hands—the hands which lay now conveniently folded like a statue's on his lap. One of the things my brother had taught me was to make a slip-knot. I made one now with the laces joined and very gently, millimetre by millimetre, passed it over Javitt's hands and wrists, then pulled it tight.

I had expected him to wake with a howl of rage and even in my fear felt some of the pride Jack must have experienced at outwitting the giant. I was ready to flee at once, taking the lamp with me, but his very silence detained me. He only opened one eye, so that again I had the impression that he was winking at me. He tried to move his hands, felt the knot, and then acquiesced in their imprisonment. I expected him to call for Maria, but he did nothing of the kind, just watching me with his one open eye.

Suddenly I felt ashamed of myself. 'I'm sorry,' I said.

'Ha, ha,' he said, 'my prodigal, the strayed sheep, you're learning fast.'

'I promise not to tell a soul.'

'They wouldn't believe you if you did,' he said.

'I'll be going now,' I whispered with regret, lingering there absurdly, as though with half of myself I would have been content to stay for always.

'You better,' he said. 'Maria might have different views from me.' He tried his hands again. 'You tie a good knot.'

'I'm going to find your daughter,' I said, 'whatever you may think.'

'Good luck to you then,' Javitt said. 'You'll have to travel a long way; you'll have to forget all your schoolmasters try to teach you; you must lie like a horse-trader and not be tied up with loyalties any more than you are here, and who knows? I doubt it, but you might, you just might.'

I turned away to take the lamp, and then he spoke again. 'Take your golden po as a souvenir,' he said. 'Tell them you found it in an old cupboard. You've got to have something when you start a search to give you substance.'

'Thank you,' I said, 'I will. You've been very kind.' I began—absurdly in view of his bound wrists—to hold out my hand like a departing guest; then I stooped to pick up the po just as Maria, woken perhaps by our voices, came through the curtain. She took the situation in as quick as a breath and squawked at me—what I don't know—and made a dive with her bird-like hand.

I had the start of her down the passage and the advantage of the light, and I was a few feet ahead when I reached Camp Indecision, but at that point, what with the wind of my passage and the failing wick, the lamp went out. I dropped it on the earth and groped on in the dark. I could hear the scratch and whimper of Maria's sequin dress, and my nerves leapt when her feet set the lamp rolling on my tracks. I don't remember much after that. Soon I was crawling upwards, making better speed on my knees than she could do in her skirt, and a little later I saw a grey light where the roots of the tree parted. When I came up into the open it was much the same early morning hour as the one when I had entered the cave. I could hear kwahk, kwahk, kwahk, come up from below the ground—I don't know if it was a curse or a menace or just a farewell, but for many nights afterwards I lay in bed afraid that the door would open and Maria would come in to fetch me, when the house was silent and asleep. Yet strangely enough I felt no fear of Javitt, then or later.

Perhaps—I can't remember—I dropped the gold po at the entrance of the tunnel as a propitiation to Maria; certainly I didn't have it with me when I rafted across the lake or when Joe, our dog, came leaping out of the house at me and sent me sprawling on my back in the dew of the lawn by the green broken fountain.

PART THREE

I

Wilditch stopped writing and looked up from the paper. The night had passed and with it the rain and the wet wind. Out of the window he could see thin rivers of blue sky winding between the banks of cloud, and the sun as it slanted in gleamed weakly on the cap of his pen. He read the last sentence which he had written and saw how again at the end of his account he had described his adventure as though it were one which had really happened and not something that he had dreamed during the course of a night's truancy or invented a few years later for the school-magazine. Somebody, early though it was, trundled a wheelbarrow down the gravel-path beyond the fountain. The sound, like the dream, belonged to childhood.

He went downstairs and unlocked the front door. There unchanged was the broken fountain and the path which led to the Dark Walk, and he was hardly surprised when he saw Ernest, his uncle's gardener, coming towards him behind the wheelbarrow. Ernest must have been a young man in the days of the dream and he was an old man now, but to a child a man in the twenties approaches middle-age and so he seemed much as Wilditch remembered him. There was something of Javitt about him, though he had a big moustache and not a beard—perhaps it was only a brooding and scrutinizing look and that air of authority and possession which had angered Mrs Wilditch when she approached him for vegetables.

'Why, Ernest,' Wilditch said, 'I thought you had retired?'

Ernest put down the handle of the wheelbarrow and regarded Wilditch with reserve. 'It's Master William, isn't it?'

'Yes. George said—'

'Master George was right in a way, but I have to lend a hand still. There's things in this garden others don't know about.' Perhaps he *had* been the model for Javitt, for there was something in his way of speech that suggested the same ambiguity.

'Such as . . . ?'

'It's not everyone can grow asparagus in chalky soil,' he said, making a general statement out of the particular in the same way Javitt had done. 'You've been away a long time, Master William.'

'I've travelled a lot.'

'We heard one time you was in Africa and another time in Chinese parts. Do you like a black skin, Master William?'

'I suppose at one time or another I've been fond of a black skin.'

'I wouldn't have thought they'd win a beauty prize,' Ernest said.

'Do you know Ramsgate, Ernest?'

'A gardener travels far enough in a day's work,' he said. The wheelbarrow was full of fallen leaves after the night's storm. 'Are the Chinese as yellow as people say?'

'No.'

There *was* a difference, Wilditch thought: Javitt never asked for information, he gave it: the weight of water, the age of the earth, the sexual habits of a monkey. 'Are there many changes in the garden,' he asked, 'since I was here?'

'You'll have heard the pasture was sold?'

'Yes. I was thinking of taking a walk before breakfast—down the Dark Walk perhaps to the lake and the island.'

'Ah.'

'Did you ever hear any story of a tunnel under the lake?'

'There's no tunnel there. For what would there be a tunnel?'

'No reason that I know. I suppose it was something I dreamed.'

'As a boy you was always fond of that island. Used to hide there from the missus.'

'Do you remember a time when I ran away?'

'You was always running away. The missus used to tell me to go and find you. I'd say to her right out, straight as I'm talking to you, I've got enough to do digging the potatoes you are always asking for. I've never known a woman get through potatoes like she did. You'd have thought she ate them. She could have been living on potatoes and not on the fat of the land.'

'Do you think I was treasure-hunting? Boys do.'

'You was hunting for something. That's what I said to the folk round here when you were away in those savage parts—not even coming back here for your uncle's funeral. "You take my word," I said to them, "he hasn't changed, he's off hunting for something, like he always did, though I doubt if he knows what he's after," I said to them. "The next we hear," I said, "he'll be standing on his head in Australia."'

Wilditch remarked with regret, 'Somehow I never looked there'; he was surprised that he had spoken aloud. 'And The Three Keys, is it still in existence?'

'Oh, it's there all right, but the brewers bought it when my uncle died and it's not a free house any more.'

'Did they alter it much?'

'You'd hardly know it was the same house with all the pipes and tubes. They put in what they call pressure, so you can't get an honest bit of beer without a bubble in it. My uncle was content to go down to the cellar for a barrel, but it's all machinery now.'

'When they made all those changes you didn't hear any talk of a tunnel under the cellar?'

'Tunnel again. What's got you thinking of tunnels? The only tunnel I know is the railway tunnel at Bugham and that's five miles off.'

'Well, I'll be walking on, Ernest, or it will be breakfast time before I've seen the garden.'

'And I suppose now you'll be off again to foreign parts. What's it to be this time? Australia?'

'It's too late for Australia now.'

Ernest shook his brindled head at Wilditch with an air of sober disapproval. 'When I was born,' he said, 'time had a different pace to what it seems to have now,' and, lifting the handle of the wheelbarrow, he was on his way towards the new iron gate before Wilditch had time to realize he had used almost the very words of Javitt. The world was the world he knew.

2

The Dark Walk was small and not very dark—perhaps the laurels had thinned with the passing of time, but the cobwebs were there as in his childhood to brush his face as he went by. At the end of the walk there was the wooden gate on to the green which had always in his day been locked—he had never known why that route out of the garden was forbidden him, but he had discovered a way of opening the gate with the rim of a halfpenny. Now he could find no halfpennies in his pocket.

When he saw the lake he realized how right George had been. It was only a small pond, and a few feet from the margin there was an island the size of the room in which last night they had dined. There *were* a few bushes growing there, and even a few trees, one taller and larger than the others, but certainly it was neither the sentinel-pine of W.W.'s story nor the great oak of his memory. He took a few steps back from the margin of the pond and jumped.

He hadn't quite made the island, but the water in which he landed was only a few inches deep. Was any of the water deep enough to float a raft? He doubted it. He sloshed ashore, the water not even penetrating his shoes. So this little spot of earth had contained Camp Hope and Friday's Cave. He wished that he had the cynicism to laugh at the half-expectation which had brought him to the island.

The bushes came only to his waist and he easily pushed through them towards the largest tree. It was difficult to believe that even a small child could have been lost here. He was in the world that George saw every day, making his round of a not very remarkable garden. For perhaps a minute, as he pushed his way through the bushes, it seemed to him that his whole life had been wasted, much as a man who has been betrayed by a woman wipes out of his mind even the happy years with her. If it had not been for his dream of the tunnel and the bearded man and the hidden treasure, couldn't he have made a less restless life for himself, as George in fact had done, with marriage, children, a home? He tried to persuade himself that he was exaggerating the importance of a dream. His lot had probably been decided months before that when George was reading him *The Romance of Australian Exploration*. If a child's experience does really form his future life, surely he had been formed, not by Javitt, but by Grey and Burke. It was his pride that at least he had never taken his various professions seriously: he had been loyal to no one—not even to the girl in Africa (Javitt would have approved his disloyalty). Now he stood beside the ignoble tree that had no roots above the ground which could possibly have formed the entrance to a cave and he looked back at the house: it was so close that he could see George at the window of the bathroom lathering his face. Soon the bell would be going for breakfast and they would be sitting opposite each other exchanging the morning small talk. There was a good train back to London at 10.25. He supposed that it was the effect of his disease that he was so tired—not sleepy but achingly tired as though at the end of a long journey.

After he had pushed his way a few feet through the bushes he came on the blackened remains of an oak; it had been split by lightning probably and then sawed close to the ground for logs. It could easily have been the source of his dream. He tripped on the old roots hidden in the grass, and squatting down on the ground he laid his ear close to the earth. He had an absurd desire to hear from somewhere far below the kwahk, kwahk from a roofless mouth and the deep rumbling of Javitt's voice saying, 'We are hairless, you and I,' shaking his beard at him, 'so's the hippopotamus and the elephant and the dugong—you wouldn't know, I suppose, what a dugong is. We survive the longest, the hairless ones.'

But, of course, he could hear nothing except the emptiness you hear when a telephone rings in an empty house. Something tickled his ear, and he almost hoped to find a sequin which had survived the years under the grass, but it was only an ant staggering with a load towards its tunnel.

Wilditch got to his feet. As he levered himself upright, his hand was scraped by the sharp rim of some metal object in the earth. He kicked the object free and found it was an old tin chamber-pot. It had lost all colour in the ground except that inside the handle there adhered a few flakes of yellow paint.

3

How long he had been sitting there with the pot between his knees he could not tell; the house was out of sight: he was as small now as he had been then—he couldn't see over the tops of the bushes, and he was back in Javitt's time. He turned the pot over and over; it was certainly not a golden po, but that proved nothing either way; a child might have mistaken it for one when it was newly painted. Had he then really dropped this in his flight—which meant that somewhere underneath him now Javitt sat on his lavatory-seat and Maria quacked beside the calor-gas . . . ? There was no certainty; perhaps years ago, when the paint was fresh, he had discovered the pot, just as he had done this day, and founded a whole afternoon-legend around it. Then why had W.W. omitted it from his story?

Wilditch shook the loose earth out of the po, and it rang on a pebble just as it had rung against the tag of his shoelace fifty years ago. He had a sense that there was a decision he had to make all over again. Curiosity was growing inside him like the cancer. Across the pond the bell rang for breakfast and he thought, 'Poor mother—she had reason to fear,' turning the tin chamber-pot on his lap.

A VISIT TO MORIN

Le Diable au Ciel—there it was on a shelf in the Colmar book-shop causing a memory to reach out to me from the past of twenty years ago. One didn't often, in the 1950s, see Pierre Morin's novels on display, and yet here were two copies of his once famous book, and looking along the rows of paper-bindings I discovered others, as though there existed in Alsace a secret *cave*, like those hidden cellars where wines were once pre-served from the enemy for the days when peace would return.

I had admired Pierre Morin when I was a boy, but I had al-most forgotten him. He was even then an older writer on the point of abandonment by his public, but the language-class in an English public school is always a long way behind the Paris fashions. We happened at Collingworth to have a Roman Cath-olic master who belonged to the generation which Morin had pleased or offended. He had offended the orthodox Catholics in his own country and pleased the liberal Catholics abroad; he had pleased, too, the French Protestants who believed in God with the same intensity he seemed to show, and he found enthusiastic readers among non-Christians who, when once they had ac-cepted imaginatively his premises, perhaps detected in his work the freedom of speculation which put his fellow Catholics on their guard. How fresh and exciting his work had appeared to my schoolmaster's generation; and to me, brought up in a lower form on *Les Misérables* and the poems of Lamartine, he was a revolutionary writer. But it is the fate of revolutionaries that the world accepts them. The excitement has gone from Morin's pages. Only the orthodox read him now, when the whole world seems prepared to believe in a god, except strangely enough—but I will not anticipate the point of my small anecdote which may yet provide a footnote to the literary history of Morin's day. When I publish it no harm can be done. Morin will be dead in the flesh as well as being dead as a writer, and he has left, so far as I am aware, no descendants and no disciples.

I yet recall with pleasure those French classes presided over by a Mr Strangeways from Chile; his swarthy complexion was said by his enemies to indicate Spanish blood (it was the period of the Spanish Civil War when anything Spanish and Roman was regarded as Fascist) and by his friends, of whom I was one, a dash of Indian. In dull fact his father was an engineer from Wolverhampton and his mother came from Louisiana and was only Latin after three removes. At these senior classes we no longer studied syntax—at which Mr Strangeways was in any case weak. Mr Strangeways read aloud to us and we read aloud to him, but after five minutes we would launch into literary criticism, pulling to pieces with youthful daring—Mr Strangeways like so many schoolmasters remained always youthful—the great established names and building up with exaggerated appreciation those who had not yet 'arrived'. Of course Morin had arrived years before, but of that we were unaware in our brick prison five hundred miles from the Seine—he hadn't reached the school text-books; he hadn't yet been mummified by Messrs Hachette et Cie. Where we didn't understand his meaning, there were no editor's notes to kill speculation.

'Can he really believe that?' I remember exclaiming to Mr Strangeways when a character in *Le Diable au Ciel* made some dark and horrifying statement on the Atonement or the Redemption, and I remember Mr Strangeways' blunt reply, flapping the sleeves of his short black gown, 'But I believe it too, Dunlop.' He did not leave it at that or allow himself to get involved in a theological debate, which might have imperilled his post in my Protestant school. He went on to indicate that we were unconcerned with what the author believed. The author had chosen as his viewpoint the character of an orthodox Catholic—all his thoughts therefore must be affected, as they would be in life, by his orthodoxy. Morin's technique forbade him to play a part in the story himself; even to show irony would be to cheat, though perhaps we might detect something of Morin's view from the fact that the orthodoxy of Durobier was extended to the furthest possible limits, so that at the close of the book we had the impression of a man stranded on a long strip of sand from which there was no possibility of advance, and to retreat towards the shore would be to surrender. 'Is this true or is it not true?' His whole creed was concerned in the answer.

'You mean,' I asked Mr Strangeways, 'that perhaps Morin does not believe?'

'I mean nothing of the kind. No one has seriously questioned his Catholicism, only his prudence. Anyway that's not true criticism. A novel is made up of words and characters. Are the words well chosen and do the characters live? All the rest belongs to literary gossip. You are not in this class to learn how to be gossip-writers.'

And yet in those days I would have liked to know. Sometimes Mr Strangeways, recognizing my interest in Morin, would lend me Roman Catholic literary periodicals which contained notices of the novelist's work that often offended his principle of leaving the author's views out of account. I found Morin was sometimes accused of Jansenism—whatever that might be: others called him an Augustinian—a name which meant as little to me—and in the better-printed and bulkier reviews I thought I detected a note of grievance. He believed all the right things, they could find no specific fault, and yet . . . it was as though some of his characters accepted a dogma so wholeheartedly that they drew out its implications to the verge of absurdity, while others examined a dogma as though they were constitutional lawyers determined on confining it to a kind of legal minimum. Durobier, I am sure, would have staked his life on a literal Assumption: at some point in history, somewhere in the latter years of the first century AD, the body of the Virgin had floated skywards, leaving an empty tomb. On the other hand there was a character called Sagrin, in one of the minor novels, perhaps *Le Bien Pensant,* who believed that the holy body had rotted in the grave like other bodies. The strange thing was that both views seemed to possess irritating qualities to Catholic reviewers, and yet both proved to be equally in accordance with the dogmatic pronouncement when it came. One could assert therefore that they were orthodox; yet the orthodox critics seemed to scent heresy like a rat dead somewhere under the boards, at a spot they could not locate.

These, of course, were ancient criticisms, fished out of Mr Strangeways' cupboard, full of old French magazines dating back to his long-lost sojourn in Paris some time during the late 'twenties, when he had attended lectures at the Sorbonne and drunk beer at the Dôme. The word 'paradox' was frequently used with an air of disapproval. Perhaps after all the orthodox were proved right, for I certainly was to discover just how far Morin carried in his own life the sense of paradox.

2

I am not one of those who revisit their old school, or what a disappointment I would have proved to Mr Strangeways, who must by now be on the point of retirement. I think he had pictured me in the future as a distinguished writer for the weeklies on the subject of French literature—perhaps even as the author of a scholarly biography of Corneille. In fact, after an undistinguished war-record, I obtained a post, with the help of influential connections, in a firm of wine-merchants. My French syntax, so neglected by Mr Strangeways, had been improved by the war and proved useful to the firm, and I suppose I had a certain literary flair which enabled me to improve on the rather old-fashioned style of the catalogues. The directors had been content for too long with the jargon of the Wine and Food Society—'An unimportant but highly sympathetic wine for light occasions among friends'. I introduced a more realistic note and substituted knowledge for knowingness. 'This wine comes from a small vineyard on the western slopes of the Mont Soleil range. The soil in this region has Jurassic elements, as the vineyard is on the edge of the great Jurassic fissure which extends across Europe from the Urals, and this encourages the cultivation of a small, strong, dark grape with a high sugar-content, less vulnerable than more famous wines to the chances of weather.' Of course it was the same 'unimportant' wine, but my description gave the host material for his vanity.

Business had brought me to Colmar—we had found it necessary to change our agent there, and as I am a single man and find the lonely Christmases of London sad and regretful, I had chosen to combine my visit with the Christmas holiday. One does not feel alone abroad; I imagined drinking my way through the festival itself in some *bierhaus* decorated with holly, myself invisible behind the fume of cigars. A German Christmas is Christmas *par excellence*: singing, sentiment, gluttony.

I said to the shop assistant, 'You seem to have a good supply of M. Morin's books.'

'He is very popular,' she said.

'I got the impression that in Paris he is no longer much read.'

'We are Catholics here,' she said with a note of reproof. 'Besides, he lives near Colmar, and we are very proud he chose to settle in our neighbourhood.'

'How long has he been here?'

'He came immediately after the war. We consider him almost one of us. We have all his books in German also—you will see them over there. Some of us feel he is even finer in German than in French. German,' she said, scrutinizing me with contempt as I picked up a French edition of *Le Diable au Ciel*, 'has a better vocabulary for the profundities.'

I told her I had admired M. Morin's novels since my schooldays. She softened towards me then, and I left the shop with M. Morin's address—a village fifteen miles from Colmar. I was uncertain all the same whether I would call on him. What really had I to say to him to excuse the vulgarity of my curiosity? Writing is the most private of all the arts, and yet few of us hesitate to invade the writer's home. We have all heard of that one caller from Porlock, but hundreds of callers every day are ringing doorbells, lifting receivers, thrusting themselves into the secret room where a writer works and lives.

I doubt whether I should have ventured to ring M. Morin's bell, but I caught sight of him two days later at the Midnight Mass in a village outside Colmar; it was not the village where I had been told he lived, and I wondered why he had come such a distance alone. Midnight Mass is a service which even a non-believer like myself finds inexplicably moving. Perhaps there is some memory of childhood which makes the journey through the darkness, the lighted windows and the frosty night, the slow gathering of silent strangers from the four quarters of the countryside moving and significant. There was a crib to the left of the door as I came in—the plaster-baby sprawled in the plaster-lap, and the cows, the sheep and the shepherd cast long shadows in the candlelight. Among the kneeling women was an old man whose face I seemed to remember: a round head like a peasant's, the skin wrinkled like a stale apple, with the hair gone from the crown. He knelt, bowed his head, and rose again. There had just been time, I suppose, for a formal prayer, but it must have been a short one. His chin was stubbled white like the field ouside, and there was so little about him to suggest a member of the French Academy that I might have taken him for the peasant he appeared to be, in his suit of respectable and shiny black and his black tie like a bootlace, if I had not been attracted by the eyes. The eyes gave him away: they seemed to know too much and to have seen further than the season and the fields. Of a very clear pale blue, they continually shifted focus, looking close and looking away, observant, sad and curious like those of a man caught in some great catastrophe which it is his duty to record, but which he cannot bear to contemplate for any length of time. It was not, of course, during his short prayer before the crib that I had time to watch Morin so closely; but when the congregation was shuffling up towards the altar for Communion, Morin and I found ourselves alone among the empty chairs. It was then I recognized him—perhaps from memories of old photographs in Mr Strangeways' reviews. I do not know, yet I was convinced of his identity, and I wondered what it was that kept this old distinguished Catholic from going up with the others, at this Mass of all Masses in the year, to receive the Sacrament. Had he perhaps inadvertently broken his fast, or was he a man who suffered from scruples and did he believe that he had been guilty of some act of uncharity or greed? There could not be many serious temptations, I thought, for a man who must be approaching his eightieth year. And yet I would not have believed him scrupulous; it was from his own novels I had learnt of the existence of this malady of the religious, and I would never have supposed the creator of Durobier to have suffered from the same disease as his character. However, a novelist may sometimes write most objectively of his own failings.

We sat there alone at the back of the church. The air was as cold and still as a frozen tree and the candles burned straight on the altar and God, so they believed, passed along the altar-rail. This was the birth of Christianity: outside in the dark was old savage Judea, but in here the world was only a few minutes old. It was the Year One again, and I felt the old sentimental longing to believe as those, I suppose, believed who came back one by one from the rail, with lips set like closed doors around the dissolving wafer and with crossed hands. If I had said to one of them, 'Teach me why you believe,' what would the answer have been? I thought perhaps I knew, for once in the war—driven by fear and disgust at the sight of the dead—I had spoken to a Catholic chaplain in just that way. He didn't belong to my unit, he was a busy man—it isn't the job of a chaplain in the line to instruct or convert and he was not to blame that he could convey nothing of his faith to an outsider like myself. He lent me two books—one a penny-catechism with its catalogue of preposterous questions and answers, smug and explanatory—mystery like a butterfly killed by cyanide, stiffened and laid out with pins and paper-strips; the other a sober enough study of gospel dates. I lost them both in a few days, with three bottles of whisky, my jeep and the corporal whose name I had not had time to learn before he was killed, while I was peeing in the green canal close by. I don't suppose I'd have kept the books much longer anyway. They were not the kind of help I needed, nor was the chaplain the man to give it me. I remember asking him if he had read Morin's novels. 'I haven't time to waste with him,' he said abruptly.

'They were the first books,' I said, 'to interest me in your faith.'

'You'd have done much better to read Chesterton,' he said.

So it was odd to find myself there at the back of the church with Morin himself. He was the first to leave and I followed him out. I was glad to go, for the sentimental attraction of a Midnight Mass was lost in the long *ennui* of the communions.

'M. Morin,' I said in that low voice we assume in a church or hospital.

He looked quickly, and I thought defensively, up.

I said, 'Forgive my speaking to you like this, M. Morin, but your books have given me such great pleasure.' Had the man from Porlock employed the same banal phrases?

'You are English?' he asked.

'Yes.'

He spoke to me then in English. 'You write yourself? Forgive my asking, but I do not know your name.'

'Dunlop. But I don't write. I buy and sell wine.'

'A profession more worthy of respect,' M. Morin said. 'If you would care to drive with me—I live only ten kilometres from here—I think I could show you a wine you may not have encountered.'

'Surely, it's rather late, M. Morin. And I have a driver . . .'

'Send him home. After Midnight Mass I find it difficult to sleep. You would be doing me a kindness.' When I hesitated he said, 'As for tomorrow, that is just any day of the year, and I don't like visitors.'

I tried to make a joke of it. 'You mean it's my only chance?' and he replied 'Yes' with seriousness. The doors of the church swung open and the congregation came slowly out into the frosty glitter, pecking at the holy water stoup with their forefingers, chatting cheerfully again as the mystery receded, greeting neighbours. A wailing child marked the lateness of the hour like a clock. M. Morin strode away and I followed him.

3

M. Morin drove with clumsy violence, wrenching at his gears, scraping the right-hand hedgerows as though the car were a new invention and he a courageous pioneer in its use. 'So you have read some of my books?' he asked.

'A great many, when I was a schoolboy . . .'

'You mean they are fit only for children?'

'I mean nothing of the sort.'

'What can a child find in them?'

'I was sixteen when I began to read them. That's not a child.'

'Oh well, now they are only read by the old—and the pious. Are you pious, Mr Dunlop?'

'I'm not a Catholic.'

'I'm glad to hear that. Then I shan't offend you.'

'Once I thought of becoming one.'

'Second thoughts are best.'

'I think it was your books that made me curious.'

'I will not take responsibility,' he said. 'I am not a theologian.' We bumped over a little branch railway-track without altering speed and swerved right through a gateway much in need of repair. A light hanging in a porch shone on an open door.

'Don't you lock up,' I asked him, 'in these parts?'

He said, 'Ten years ago—times were bad then—a hungry man was frozen to death near here on Christmas morning. He could find no one to open a door: there was a blizzard, but they were all at church. Come in,' he said angrily from the porch; 'are you looking round, making notes of how I live? Have you deceived me? Are you a journalist?'

If I had had my own car with me I would have driven away. 'M. Morin,' I said, 'there are different kinds of hunger. You seem only to cater for one kind.' He went ahead of me into a small study—a desk, a table, two comfortable chairs, and some bookshelves oddly bare—I could see no sign of his own books. There was a bottle of brandy on the table, ready perhaps for the stranger and the blizzard that would never again come together in this place.

'Sit down,' he said, 'sit down. You must forgive me if I was discourteous. I am unused to company. I will go and find the wine I spoke of. Make yourself at home.' I had never seen a man less at home himself. It was as if he were camping in a house that belonged to another.

While he was away, I looked more closely at his bookshelves. He had not re-bound any of his paper-backs and his shelves had the appearance of bankrupt stock: small tears and dust and the discoloration of sunlight. There was a great deal of theology, some poetry, very few novels. He came back with the wine and a plate of salami. When he had tasted the wine himself, he poured me a glass. 'It will do,' he said.

'It's excellent. Remarkable.'

'A small vineyard twenty miles away. I will give you the address before you go. For me, on a night like this, I prefer brandy.' So perhaps it was really for himself and not for the stranger, I thought, that the bottle stood ready.

'It's certainly cold.'

'It was not the weather I meant.'

'I have been looking at your library. You read a lot of theology?'

'Not now.'

'I wonder if you would recommend . . .' But I had even less success with him than with the chaplain.

'No. Not if you want to believe. If you are foolish enough to want that you must avoid theology.'

'I don't understand.'

He said, 'A man can accept anything to do with God until scholars begin to go into the details and the implications. A man can accept the Trinity, but the arguments that follow . . .' He gave a gesture of rejection. 'I would never try to determine some point in differential calculus with a two-times-two table. You end by disbelieving the calculus.' He poured out two more glasses and drank his own as though it were vodka. 'I used to believe in revelation, but I never believed in the capacity of the human mind.'

'You used to believe?'

'Yes, Mr Dunlop—was that the name?—*used*. If you are one of those who come seeking belief, go away. You won't find it here.'

'But from your books . . .'

'You will find none of them,' he said, 'on my shelves.'

'I noticed you have some theology.'

'Even disbelief,' he said, with his eye on the brandy bottle, 'needs bolstering.' I noticed that the brandy affected him very quickly, not only his readiness to communicate with me, but even the physical appearance of his eyeballs. It was as if the little blood-cells had been waiting under the white membrane to burst at once like buds with the third glass. He said, 'Can you find anything more inadequate than the scholastic arguments for the existence of God?'

'I'm afraid I don't know them.'

'The arguments from an agent, from a cause?'

'No.'

'They tell you that in all change there are two elements, that which is changed and that which changes it. Each agent of change is itself determined by some higher agent. Can this go on *ad infinitum?* Oh no, they say, that would not give the finality that thought demands. But does thought demand it? Why shouldn't the chain go on for ever? Man has invented the idea of infinity. In any case how trivial any argument based on what human thought demands must be. The thoughts of you and me and Monsieur Dupont. I would prefer the thoughts of an ape. Its instincts are less corrupted. Show me a gorilla praying and I might believe again.'

'But surely there are other arguments?'

'Four. Each more inadequate than the other. It needs a child to say to these theologians, Why? Why not? Why not an infinite series of causes? Why should the existence of a good and a better imply the existence of a best? This is playing with words. We invent the words and make arguments from them. The better is not a fact: it is only a word and a human judgement.'

'You are arguing,' I said, 'against someone who can't answer you back. You see, M. Morin, I don't believe either. I'm curious, that's all.'

'Ah,' he said, 'you've said that before—curious. Curiosity is a great trap. They used to come here in their dozens to see me. I used to get letters saying how I had converted them by this book or that. Long after I ceased to believe myself I was a carrier of belief, like a man can be a carrier of disease without being sick. Women especially.' He added with disgust, 'I had only to sleep with a woman to make a convert.' He turned his red eyes towards me and really seemed to require an answer when he said, 'What sort of Rasputin life was that?' The brandy by now had really taken a hold; I wondered how many years he had been waiting for some stranger without faith to whom he could speak with frankness.

'Did you never tell this to a priest? I always imagined in your faith . . .'

'There were always too many priests,' he said, 'around me. The priests swarmed like flies. Near me and any woman I knew. First I was an exhibit for their faith. I was useful to them, a sign that even an intelligent man could believe. That was the period of the Dominicans, who liked the literary atmosphere and good wine. Then afterwards when the books stopped, and they smelt something—gamey—in my religion, it was the turn of the Jesuits, who never despair of what they call a man's soul.'

'And why did the books stop?'

'Who knows? Did you never write verses for some girl when you were a boy?'

'Of course.'

'But you didn't marry the girl, did you? The unprofessional poet writes of his feelings and when the poem is finished he finds his love dead on the page. Perhaps I wrote away my belief like the young man writes away his love. Only it took longer—twenty years and fifteen books.' He held up the wine. 'Another glass?'

'I would rather have some of your brandy.' Unlike the wine it was a crude and common mark, and I thought again, For a beggar's sake or his own? I said, 'All the same you go to Mass.'

'I go to Midnight Mass on Christmas Eve,' he said. 'The worst of Catholics goes then—even those who do not go at Easter. It is the Mass of our childhood. And of mercy. What would they think if I were not there? I don't want to give scandal. You must realize I wouldn't speak to any one of my neighbours as I have spoken to you. I am their Catholic author, you see. Their Academician. I never wanted to help anyone believe, but God knows I wouldn't take a hand in robbing them . . .'

'I was surprised at one thing when I saw you there, M. Morin.'

'Yes?'

I said rashly, 'You and I were the only ones who didn't take Communion.'

'That is why I don't go to the church in my own village. That too would be noticed and cause scandal.'

'Yes, I can see that.' I stumbled heavily on (perhaps the brandy had affected me too). 'Forgive me, M. Morin, but I wondered at your age what kept you from Communion. Of course now I know the reason.'

'Do you?' Morin said. 'Young man, I doubt it.' He looked at me across his glass with impersonal enmity. He said, 'You don't understand a thing I have been saying to you. What a story you would make of this if you were a journalist and yet there wouldn't be a word of truth . . .'

I said stiffly, 'I thought you made it perfectly clear that you had lost your faith.'

'Do you think that would keep anyone from the Confessional? You are a long way from understanding the Church or the human mind, Mr Dunlop. Why, it is one of the most common confessions of all for a priest to hear—almost as common as adultery. "Father, I have lost my faith." The priest, you may be sure, makes it himself often enough at the altar before he receives the Host.'

I said—I was angry in return now, 'Then what keeps you away? Pride? One of your Rasputin women?'

'As you so rightly thought,' he said, 'women are no longer a problem at my age.' He looked at his watch. 'Two-thirty. Perhaps I ought to drive you back.'

'No,' I said, 'I don't want to part from you like this. It's the drink that makes us irritable. Your books are still important to me. I know I am ignorant. I am not a Catholic and never shall be, but in the old days your books made me understand that at least it might be possible to believe. You never closed the door in my face as you are doing now. Nor did your characters, Durobier, Sagrin.' I indicated the brandy bottle. 'I told you just now—people are not only hungry and thirsty in that way. Because you've lost *your* faith . . .'

He interrupted me ferociously. 'I never told you that.'

'Then what have you been talking about all this time?'

'I told you I had lost my belief. That's quite a different thing. But how are you to understand?'

'You don't give me a chance.'

He was obviously striving to be patient. He said, 'I will put it this way. If a doctor prescribed you a drug and told you to take it every day for the rest of your life and you stopped obeying him and drank no more, and your health decayed, would you not have faith in your doctor all the more?'

'Perhaps. But I still don't understand you.'

'For twenty years,' Morin said, 'I excommunicated myself voluntarily. I never went to Confession. I loved a woman too much to pretend to myself that I would ever leave her. You know the condition of absolution? A firm purpose of amendment. I had no such purpose. Five years ago my mistress died and my sex died with her.'

'Then why couldn't you go back?'

'I was afraid. I am still afraid.'

'Of what the priest would say?'

'What a strange idea you have of the Church. No, not of what the priest would say. He would say nothing. I dare say there is no greater gift you can give a priest in the confessional, Mr Dunlop, than to return to it after many years. He feels of use again. But can't you understand? I can tell myself now that my lack of belief is a final proof that the Church is right and the faith is true. I had cut myself off for twenty years from grace and my belief withered as the priests said it would. I don't believe in God and His Son and His angels and His saints, but I know the reason why I don't believe and the reason is—the Church is true and what she taught me is true. For twenty years I have been without the sacraments and I can see the effect. The wafer must be more than wafer.'

'But if you went back . . .'

'If I went back and belief did not return? That is what I fear, Mr Dunlop. As long as I keep away from the sacraments, my lack of belief is an argument for the Church. But if I returned and they failed me, then I would really be a man without faith, who had better hide himself quickly in the grave so as not to discourage others.' He laughed uneasily. 'Paradoxical, Mr Dunlop?'

'That is what they said of your books.'

'I know.'

'Your characters carried their ideas to extreme lengths. So your critics said.'

'And you think I do too?'

'Yes, M. Morin.'

His eyes wouldn't meet mine. He grimaced beyond me. 'At least I am not a carrier of disease any longer. You have escaped infection.' He added, 'Time for bed, Mr Dunlop. Time for bed. The young need more sleep.'

'I am not as young as that.'

'To me you seem very young.'

He drove me back to my hotel and we hardly spoke. I was thinking of the strange faith which held him even now after he had ceased to believe. I had felt very little curiosity since that moment of the war when I had spoken to the chaplain, but now I began to wonder again. M. Morin considered he had ceased to be a carrier, and I couldn't help hoping that he was right. He had forgotten to give me the address of the vineyard, but I had forgotten to ask him for it when I said good night.

DREAM OF A
STRANGE LAND

I

The house of the Herr Professor was screened on every side by the plantation of fir-trees which grew among great grey rocks. Although it was only twenty minutes' ride from the capital and then a few minutes from the main road to the north, a visitor had the impression that he was in deep country; he felt himself to be hundreds of miles away from the cafés, the kiosks, the opera-houses and the theatres.

The Herr Professor had virtually retired two years ago when he reached the age of sixty-five. His appointment at the hospital had been filled, he had closed his consulting-room in the capital, and if he continued to work it was only for a few favoured patients who were compelled to drive out to see him, or if they were poor (for he had not clung to a few rich patients only) to take a bus which landed them about ten minutes' walk away at the edge of the trees and the rocks.

It was one of these poorer patients who stood now in the doctor's study listening to his doom. The study had folding pitch-pine doors leading to the living-room, which the patient had never seen. A heavy dark bookcase stood against the wall full of heavy dark books, all obviously medical in character (no one had ever seen the Herr Professor with any lighter literature, nor heard him give an opinion of even the most respected classic. Once questioned on Madame Bovary's poisoning, he had professed complete ignorance of the book, and another time he had shown himself to be equally ignorant of Ibsen's treatment of syphilis in *Ghosts*). The desk was as heavy and dark as the bookcase; it was only a desk as heavy which could have borne without cracking the massive bronze paperweight more than a foot high which represented Prometheus chained to his rock with a hovering eagle thrusting its beak into his liver. (Sometimes, when breaking the news to a patient with cirrhosis, the Professor had referred to his paperweight with dry humour.)

The patient wore a shabby-genteel suit of dark cloth; the cuffs had frayed and been repaired. He wore stout boots which had seen just as long a service, and through the open door in the hall behind him hung an overcoat and an umbrella, while a pair of goloshes stood in the steel trough under the umbrella, the snow not yet melted from their uppers. He was a man past fifty who had spent all his adult years behind the counter of a bank and by patient labour and courtesy he had risen to the position of second cashier. He would never be first cashier, for the first cashier was at least five years younger.

The Herr Professor had a short grey beard and he wore old-fashioned glasses, steel-rimmed, for his short sight. His rather hairy hands were scattered with grave-marks. As he seldom smiled one had very little opportunity to see his strong and perfect teeth. He said firmly, caressing Prometheus as he spoke, 'I warned you when you first came that my treatment might have started too late—to arrest the disease. Now the smear-test shows . . .'

'But, Herr Professor, you have been treating me all these months. No one knows about it. I can go on working at the bank. Can't you continue to treat me a little longer?'

'I would be breaking the law,' the Herr Professor explained, making a motion as though his thumb and forefinger clutched a chalk. 'Contagious cases must always go to the hospital.'

'But you yourself, Herr Professor, have said that it is one of the most difficult of all diseases to catch.'

'And yet you caught it.'

'How? How?' the patient asked himself with the weariness of a man who has confronted the same question time without mind.

'Perhaps it was when you were working on the coast. There are many contacts in a port.'

'Contacts?'

'I assume you are a man like other men.'

'But that was seven years ago.'

'One has known the disease to take ten years to develop.'

'It will be the end of my work, Herr Professor. The bank will never take me back. My pension will be very small.'

'You take an exaggerated view. After a certain period . . . Hansen's disease is eventually curable.'

'Why don't you call it by its proper name?'

'The International Congress decided five years ago to change the name.'

'The world hasn't changed the name, Herr Professor. If you send me to that hospital, everyone will know that I am a leper.'

'I have no choice. But I assure you you will find it very comfortable. There is television, I believe, in every room, and a golf-course.'

The Herr Professor showed no impatience at all, unless the fact that he did not ask the patient to sit and stood himself, stiff and straight-backed behind Prometheus and the eagle, was a sign of it.

'Herr Professor, I implore you. I will not breathe a word to a soul. You can treat me just as well as the hospital can. You've said yourself that the risk of contagion is very small, Herr Professor. I have my savings—they are not very great, but I will give them all . . .'

'My dear sir, you must not try to bribe me. It is not only insulting, it is a gross error of taste. I am sorry. I must ask you to go now. My time is very much occupied.'

'Herr Professor, you have no idea what it means to me. I lead a very simple life, but if a man is alone in the world he grows to love his habits. I go to a café by the lake every day at seven o'clock and stay there till eight. They all know me in the café. Sometimes I play a game of checkers. On Sunday I take the lake steamer to—'

'Your habits will have to be interrupted for a year or two,' the Herr Professor said sharply.

'Interrupted? You say interrupted? But I can never go back. Never. Leprosy is a word—it isn't a disease. They'll never believe leprosy can be cured. You can't cure a word.'

'You will be getting a certificate signed by the hospital authorities,' the Herr Professor said.

'A certificate! I might just as well carry a bell.'

He moved to the door, the hall, his umbrella and the goloshes; the Herr Professor, with a sigh of relief which was almost inaudible beyond the room, seated himself at his desk. But again the patient had turned back. 'Is it that you don't trust me to keep quiet, Herr Professor?'

'I have every belief, I can assure you, that you would keep quiet. For your own sake. But you cannot expect a doctor of my standing to break the law. A sensible and necessary law. If it had not been infringed somewhere by someone you would not be standing here today. Good-bye, Herr—', but the patient had already closed the outer door and had begun to walk back amongst the rocks and firs towards the road, the bus-stop and the capital. The Herr Professor went to the window to make sure that he was truly gone and saw him among the snow-flakes which drifted lightly between the trees; he paused once and gesticulated with his hands as though a new argument had occurred to him which he was practising on a rock. Then he padded on and disappeared from sight.

The Herr Professor opened the sliding doors of the dining-room and made his accurate way to the sideboard, which was heavy like his desk. Instead of the Prometheus there stood on it a large silver flagon inscribed with the Herr Professor's name and a date more than forty years past—an award for fencing—and beside it lay a large silver epergne, also inscribed, a present from the staff of the hospital on his retirement. The Herr Professor took a hard green apple and walked back to his study. He sat down at his desk again and his teeth went crunch, crunch, crunch.

2

Later that morning the Herr Professor received another caller, but this one arrived before the house in a Mercedes-Benz car and the Herr Professor went himself to the door to show him in.

'Herr Colonel,' he said as he pulled forward the only chair of any comfort to be found in his study, 'this I hope is only a friendly call and not a professional one.'

'I am never ill,' the Colonel said with a look of irritated amusement at the very idea. 'My blood-pressure is normal, my weight is what it should be, and my heart's sound. I function like a machine. Indeed I find it difficult to believe that this machine need ever wear out. I have no worries, my nervous system is perfectly adjusted . . .'

'Then I'm relieved to know, Herr Colonel, that this is a social call.'

'The army,' the Colonel went on, crossing his long slim legs encased in English tweed, 'is the most healthy profession possible—naturally I mean in a neutral country like ours. The annual manoeuvres do one a world of good, brace the system, clean the blood . . .'

'I wish I could recommend them to my patients.'

'Oh, we can't have sick men in the army.' The Colonel added with a dry laugh, 'We leave that to the warring nations. They can never have our efficiency.'

The Herr Professor offered the Colonel a cigar. The Colonel took a cutter from a little leather case and prepared the cigar. 'You have met the Herr General?' he asked.

'On one or two occasions.'

'He is celebrating his seventieth birthday tonight.'

'Really? A very well preserved man.'

'Naturally. Now his friends—of whom I count myself the chief—have been arranging a very special occasion for him. You know, of course, his favourite hobby?'

'I can't say . . .'

'The tables. For the last fifty years he has spent most of his leaves at Monte Carlo.'

'He too must have a good nervous system.'

'Of course. Now it occurred to his friends, since he cannot spend his birthday at Monte Carlo for reasons of a quite temporary indisposition, to bring, as it were, the tables to him.'

'How can that be possible?'

'Everything was satisfactorily arranged. A croupier from

Cannes and two assistants. All the necessary equipment. One of my friends was to have lent us his house in the country. You understand that everything has to be very discreet because of our absurd laws. You would think the police on such an occasion would turn a blind eye, but among the higher officials there is a great jealousy of the army. I once heard the Commissioner remark—at a party to which I was surprised to see that he had been invited—that the only wars in which our country had ever been engaged were fought by *his* men.'

'I don't follow.'

'Oh, he was referring to crime. An absurd comparison. What has crime to do with war?'

The Herr Professor said, 'You were telling me that everything had been satisfactorily arranged . . . ?'

'With the Herr General Director of the National Bank. But suddenly today he telephoned to say that a child—a girl as one might expect—had developed scarlatina. The household therefore is in quarantine.'

'The Herr General will be disappointed.'

'The Herr General knows nothing of all this. He understands that a party is being given in his honour in the country—that is all.'

'And you come to me,' the Herr Professor said, trying to hide mystification which he regarded as a professional weakness, 'in case I can suggest . . . ?'

'I come to you, Herr Professor, quite simply to borrow your house for this evening. The problem can be reduced to very simple terms. The house has to be in the country—I have explained to you why. It must have a *salon* of a certain size—to receive the tables; we can hardly have less than three, since the guests will number about a hundred. And the owner of the house must naturally be acceptable to the Herr General. There are houses a great deal larger than yours that the General could not be expected to enter as a guest. We can hardly, in this case, requisition.'

'I am honoured, of course, Herr Colonel, but . . .'

'These doors slide back, I suppose, and can form a room sufficiently large . . . ?'

'Yes, but . . .'

'Pardon me. You were saying?'

'I had the impression that the party was for tonight?'

'Yes.'

'I don't see how there could be time . . .'

'A matter of logistics, Herr Professor. Leave logistics to the army.' He took a notebook from his pocket and wrote down 'lights'. He explained to the Herr Professor, 'We shall have to hang chandeliers. A casino is unthinkable without chandeliers. May I see the other room, please?'

He paced it with his long tweed-clad legs. 'It will make a fine *salle privée* with the doors folded back and the chandeliers substituted for these—forgive me for saying so—rather commonplace centre lights. Your furniture we can store upstairs? Of course we will bring our own chairs. This sideboard, however, can serve as a bar. I see you were a fencer in your time, Herr Professor?'

'Yes.'

'The Herr General used to be very keen on fencing. Now tell me, where do you think we could put the orchestra?'

'Orchestra?'

'My regiment will supply the musicians. If the worst came to the worst I suppose they could play on the stairs.' He stood at the window of the *salon,* looking out at the wintry garden bounded by the dark wood of fir-trees. 'Is that a summerhouse?'

'Yes.'

'The oriental touch is very suitable. If they played there, and if we left a window a little open, the music will surely carry faintly . . .'

'The cold . . .'

'You have a fine stove and the curtains are heavy.'

'The summerhouse is altogether unheated.'

'The men can wear their military overcoats. And then for a fiddler, you know, the exercise . . .'

'And all this for tonight?'

'For tonight.'

The Herr Professor said, 'I have never before violated the law,' and then smiled a quick false smile to cover his failure of nerve.

'You could hardly do so in a better cause,' the Herr Colonel replied.

3

Long before dark the furniture-vans began to arrive. The chandeliers came first, with the wine-glasses, and remained crated in the hall until the electricians drove up, and then the waiters arrived simultaneously with the van that contained seventy-four small gilt chairs. The mover's men had beer in the kitchen with the Herr Professor's housekeeper, waiting for a lorry to turn up with the three roulette-tables. The roulette-wheels, the cloths and the boxes of plastic tokens, of varying colours and shapes according to value, were brought later in a smart private car with the three croupiers, serious men in black suits. The Herr Professor had never seen so many cars parked before his house. He felt a stranger, a guest, and lingered at his bedroom-window, afraid to go out on the stairs and meet the workmen. The long passage outside his room became littered with the furniture from below.

As the red winter sun sank in early afternoon below the black firs the cars began to multiply upon the drive. First a fleet of taxis arrived one behind the other, all bright yellow in colour like an amber chain, and out of these scrambled many burly men in military overcoats carrying musical instruments, which too often stuck in the doors and had to be extricated with care and difficulty: it was hard indeed to understand how the 'cello had ever fitted in—the neck came out first like a dressmaker's dummy and then the shoulders proved too wide. The men in overcoats stood around holding violin-bows like rifles at the ready, and a small man with a triangle shouted advice. Presently they had all disappeared from the front of the house and discordant sounds of tuning came across the snow from the summerhouse built in oriental taste. Something broke in the passage outside, and the Herr Professor, looking out, saw that it was one of the central lamps criticized by the Herr Colonel, which had fallen off the occasional table on which it had been propped. The passage was nearly blocked by the heavy desk from the study, the glass-fronted

bookcase and his three filing cabinets. The Herr Professor sal-
vaged Prometheus and carried the bronze into his bedroom for
safety, though it was the least fragile thing in all the house. There
was a sound of hammers below and the Herr Colonel's voice
could be heard giving orders. The Herr Professor went back into
his bedroom. He sat on the bed and read a little Schopenhauer to
soothe himself.

It was some three-quarters of an hour later that the Herr Colonel found him there. He came briskly in, wearing regimental
evening-dress, which made his legs thinner and longer than ever.
'Zero hour approaches,' he said, 'and we are all but ready. You
would not recognize your house, Herr Professor. It is quite transformed. The Herr General will feel himself in a sunnier and more
liberal clime. The musicians will play a pot-pourri of Strauss and
Offenbach with a little of Lehar, which the Herr General finds
more easy to recognize. I've seen to it that suitable paintings hang
on the walls. You will realize when you come down and see the
salle privée that this has been no ordinary military exercise. A care
for detail marks a good soldier. Tonight, Herr Professor, your
house has become a casino, by the Mediterranean. I had thought
of masking the trees in some way, but there was no way of getting
rid of the snow which continues to fall.'

'Astonishing,' the Herr Professor said. 'Quite astonishing.'
From the distant summerhouse he could hear a melody from
La Belle Hélène, and on the drive outside cars continually
braked. He felt far from home as though he were living in a
strange country.

'If you will excuse me,' he said, 'I will leave everything tonight
in your hands. I hardly know the Herr General. I will have a
sandwich quietly in my room.'

'Quite impossible,' the Herr Colonel said. 'You are the host.
By this time the Herr General knows your name, although of
course he hardly expects the sight which will greet . . . Ah, the
guests are now beginning to arrive. I asked them to come early so
that by the time the Herr General puts in his appearance everything will be in full swing, the wheels turning, the stakes laid, the
croupiers calling . . . the field of battle stretched before him,

rouge et noir. Come, Herr Professor, a little flutter at the tables—
it is time for the two of us to open the ball.'

4

The road was treacherous under the thin and new-fallen snow;
the bus from the capital proceeded at a pace no smarter than a
practice-runner who is unwilling to strain a muscle before the
great race. The patient's feet felt chilled even through his goloshes, or perhaps it was the cold of his errand, a fool's errand.
There was a lot of traffic on the road that night: yellow taxis frequently passed the bus, and small sports-cars full of young men
in uniform or evening-dress, laughing or singing, and once at
a particularly imperious siren—which might have been that of
a police-car or an ambulance—the bus slithered awkwardly to a
stop beside the blue heaps of snow on the margin, and a large
Mercedes went by; in it the patient saw an old man sitting stiffly
upright with a long grey moustache which might have dated
from the neutrality of 1914, wearing an old-fashioned uniform
with a fur hat on his head, pulled down over his ears.

The patient alighted at a halt beside the road; the moon was
nearly full, but he still required the pocket-torch which he carried with him to show the way through the woods: no headlights
of cars helped him now on the private drive to the Herr Professor's house. As he walked through the loose snow at the edge of
the road he tried to practise his final appeal. If that failed there
was nothing for him but the hospital, unless he could summon
enough courage to enter the icy water of the lake and never to return. He felt very little hope, and, for some reason that he could
not understand, when he tried to visualize the Herr Professor at
his desk—angry and impatient at this so late and unforeseen a
visit—he could see only the half-spread wings of the bronze eagle and the jutting beak fastened in the intestines of the prisoner.

He pleaded in an undertone beneath the trees, 'There would be
no danger to anyone at all, Herr Professor. I have always been a
lonely man. I have no parents. My only sister died last year. I see

no one, speak to no one except the clients in the bank. An occasional game of checkers in the café perhaps—that is all. I would cut myself off even further, Herr Professor, if you thought it wiser. As for the bank, I have always been in the habit of wearing gloves when I handle the notes—so many are filthy. I will take any precaution you suggest if you will go on treating me in private, Herr Professor. I am a law-abiding man, but surely the spirit is more important than the letter. I will abide by the spirit.'

The eagle gripped Prometheus with its unrelenting beak, and the patient said sadly as though to prevent the repetition of a phrase he could not bear to hear again, 'I don't like television, Herr Professor—it makes my eyes water, and I have never played golf.'

He halted under the trees, and a lump of snow from a burdened branch fell with a plomp upon his umbrella. It seemed very unlikely, but he thought that he heard strains of distant music borne on a gust of wind and borne away again. He even thought he recognized the melody, something from *La Vie Parisienne*, a waltz sounding for a moment from where the darkness and the snow lay all around. He had seen this place before only in daylight; the snow touched his face, and the stars crackled overhead between the firs; he felt as though he must have missed his path and entered a strange estate where perhaps a dance was in progress . . .

But when he reached the circular drive before the house he recognized the portico, the shape of the windows, the steep slope of the roof from which at intervals the snow slid with a crunch like the sound of a man eating apples. It was all that he could recognize, for he had never seen the house like this, ablaze with light and noisy with voices. Perhaps two neighbouring estates had been built by the same architect, and somehow in the wood he had taken the wrong turning. To make sure, he approached the windows, the hard snow breaking like biscuits under his goloshes.

Two young officers, who were obviously the worse for drink, staggered out from the open doorway. 'I have been betrayed by nineteen,' one of them said, 'that confounded nineteen.'

'And I by zero. I have been faithful to zero for an hour but not once . . .'

The first young man took a revolver from the holster at his side and waved it in the moonlight. 'All that is required now,' he said, 'is a suicide. The atmosphere is imperfect without one.'

'Be careful. It might be loaded.'

'It *is* loaded. Who is that man?'

'I don't know. The gardener probably. Don't fool about with that thing.'

'More bubbly is required,' the first man said. He tried to put his revolver back into the holster, but it slid down into the snow and he carefully secured the empty holster. 'More bubbly,' he repeated, 'before the dream fades.' They moved erratically back into the house. The dark object made a pocket in the snow.

The patient went up to the window, which should, if he had taken the right path, have been the window of the Herr Professor's study, but now he realized for certain that in the darkness he had come to the wrong house. Instead of a small square room with heavy desk and heavy bookcase and steel filing-cabinets was a long room brilliantly lit with cut-glass chandeliers, the walls hung with pictures of dubious taste—young women in diaphanous nightgowns leaning over waterfalls or paddling among water-lilies in a stooping position. A crowd of men wearing uniform and evening-dress swarmed around three roulette tables, and the croupiers' cries came thinly out into the night, '*Faites vos jeux, messieurs, faites vos jeux,*' while somewhere in the black garden an orchestra was playing 'The Blue Danube'. The patient stood motionless in the snow, with his face pressed to the glass, and he thought, The wrong house? But this is not the wrong house; it is the wrong country. He felt that he could never find his way home from here—it was too far away.

At one of the tables, on the right of the croupier, sat the old man whom he had seen pass in the Mercedes. One hand was playing with his moustache, the other with a pile of tokens before him, counting and rearranging them while the ball span and jumped and span, and one foot beat in time to the tune from *The Merry Widow*. A champagne cork from the bar shot diagonally up and struck the chandelier while the croupiers cried again, '*Faites vos jeux, messieurs,*' and the stem of a glass went crack in somebody's fingers.

Then the patient saw the Herr Professor standing with his back to the window at the other end of the great room, beyond the second chandelier, and they regarded each other, with the laughter and cries and glitter of light between them.

The Herr Professor could not properly see the patient—only the outline of a face pressed to the exterior of the pane, but the patient could see the Herr Professor very clearly between the tables, in the light of the chandelier. He could even see his expression, the lost look on his face like that of someone who has come to the wrong party. The patient raised his hand, as though to indicate to the other that he was lost too, but of course the Herr Professor could not see the gesture in the dark. The patient realized quite clearly that, though they had once been well known to each other, it was quite impossible for them to meet, in this house to which they had both strayed by some strange accident. There was no consulting-room here, no file on his case, no desk, no Prometheus, no doctor even to whom he could appeal. *'Faites vos jeux, messieurs,'* the croupiers cried, *'faites vos jeux.'*

5

The Herr Colonel said, 'My dear Herr Professor, after all, you are the host. You should at least lay one stake upon the table.' He took the Herr Professor by his sleeve and led him to the board where the Herr General sat, beating tip, tap, tip to the music of Lehar.

'The Herr Professor wishes to follow your fortune, Herr General.'

'I have little luck tonight, but let him . . .' and the General's fingers wove a design over the cloth. 'At the same time guard yourself with the zero.'

The ball span and jumped and span and came to rest. 'Zero,' the croupier announced and began to rake the other stakes in.

'At least you have not lost, Herr Professor,' the Herr General said. Somewhere far away behind the voices there was a faint explosion.

'The corks are popping,' the Herr Colonel said. 'Another glass of champagne, Herr General?'

'I had hoped it was a shot,' the Herr General said with a rather freezing smile. 'Ah, the old days . . . I remember once in Monte Carlo . . .'

The Herr Professor looked at the window, where he had thought a moment ago that someone looked in as lost as himself, but no one was there.

A DISCOVERY IN
THE WOODS

The village lay among the great red rocks about a thousand feet up and five miles from the sea, which was reached by a path that wound along the contours of the hills. No one in Pete's village had ever travelled further, though Pete's father had once, while fishing, encountered men from another small village beyond the headland, which stabbed the sea twenty miles to the east. The children, when they didn't accompany their fathers to the shingled cove in which the boats lay, would climb up higher for their games—of 'Old Noh' and 'Ware that Cloud'—below the red rocks that dominated their home. Low scrub a few hundred feet up gave place to woodland: trees clung to the rock-face like climbers caught in an impossible situation, and among the trees were the bushes of blackberry, the biggest fruits always sheltered from the sun. In the right season the berries formed a tasty sharp dessert to the invariable diet of fish. It was, taking it all in all, a sparse and simple, yet a happy, life.

Pete's mother was a little under five feet tall; she had a squint and she was inclined to stumble when she walked, but her movements to Pete seemed at their most uncertain the height of human grace, and when she told him stories, as she often did on the fifth day of the week, her stammer had for him the magical effect of music. There was one word in particular, 't-t-t-tree', which fascinated him. 'What is it?' he would ask, and she would try to explain. 'You mean an oak?' 'A t-tree is not an oak. But an oak is a t-t-tree, and so is a b-birch.' 'But a birch is quite different from an oak. Anyone can tell they are not the same, even a long way off, like a dog and a cat.' 'A dog and a c-cat are both animals.' She had from some past generation inherited this ability to generalize, of which he and his father were quite incapable.

Not that he was a stupid child unable to learn from experience. He could even with some difficulty look back into the past for four winters, but the furthest time he could remember was very like a sea-fog, which the wind may disperse for a moment from a rock or a group of trees, but it closes down again. His mother claimed that he was seven years old, but his father said that he was nine and that after one more winter he would be old enough to join the crew of the boat which his father shared with a relation (everybody in the village was in some way related). Perhaps his mother had deliberately distorted his age to postpone the time when he would have to go fishing with the men. It was not only the question of danger—though every winter brought a mortal casualty along with it, so that the size of the village hardly increased more than a colony of ants; it was also the fact that he was the only child. (There were two sets of parents in the village, the Torts and the Foxes, who had more than one child, and the Torts had triplets.) When the time came for Pete to join his father, his mother would have to depend on other people's children for blackberries in the autumn, or just go without, and there was nothing she loved better than blackberries with a splash of goat's milk.

So this, he believed, was to be the last autumn on land, and he was not much concerned about it. Perhaps his father was in the right about his age, for he had become aware that his position as leader of a special gang was now too incontestable: his muscles felt the need of strengthening against an opponent greater than himself. His gang consisted this October of four children, to three of whom he had allotted numbers, for this made his commands sound more abrupt and discipline so much the easier. The fourth member was a seven-year-old girl called Liz, unwillingly introduced for reasons of utility.

They met among the ruins at the edge of the village. The ruins had always been there, and at night the children, if not the adults too, believed them to be haunted by giants. Pete's mother, who was far superior in knowledge to all the other women in the village, nobody knew why, said that her grandmother had spoken of a great catastrophe which thousands of years ago had involved a man called Noh—perhaps it was a thunderbolt from the sky, a huge wave (it would have needed a wave at least a thousand feet high to have extinguished this village), or maybe a plague, so some of the legends went, that had killed the inhabitants and left these ruins to the slow destruction of time. Whether the giants were the phantoms of the slayers or of the slain the children were never quite clear.

The blackberries this particular autumn were nearly over and in any case the bushes that grew within a mile of the village—which was called Bottom, perhaps because it lay at the foot of the red rocks—had been stripped bone-bare. When the gang had gathered at the rendezvous Pete made a revolutionary proposal—that they should enter a new territory in search of fruit.

Number One said disapprovingly, 'We've never done that before.' He was in all ways a conservative child. He had small deep-sunk eyes like holes in stone made by the dropping of water, and there was practically no hair on his head and that gave him the air of a shrivelled old man.

'We'll get into trouble,' Liz said, 'if we do.'

'Nobody need know,' Pete said, 'so long as we take the oath.'

The village by long custom claimed that the land belonging to it extended in a semi-circle three miles deep from the last cottage—even though the last cottage was a ruin of which only the foundations remained. Of the sea too they reckoned to own the water for a larger, more ill-defined area that extended some twelve miles out to sea. This claim, on the occasion when they encountered the boats from beyond the headland, nearly caused a conflict. It was Pete's father who made peace by pointing towards the clouds which had begun to mass over the horizon, one cloud in particular of enormous black menace, so that both parties turned in agreement towards the land, and the fishermen from the village beyond the headland never sailed again so far from their home. (Fishing was always done in grey overcast weather or in fine blue clear weather, or even during moonless nights, when the stars were sufficiently obscured; it was only when the shape of the clouds could be discerned that by general consent fishing stopped.)

'But suppose we meet someone?' Number Two asked.

'How could we?' Pete said.

'There must be a reason,' Liz said, 'why they don't want us to go.'

'There's no reason,' Pete said, 'except the law.'

'Oh, if it's only the law,' Number Three said, and he kicked a stone to show how little he thought of the law.

'Who does the land belong to?' Liz asked.

'To nobody,' Pete said.

'All the same nobody has rights,' Number One said sententiously, looking inwards, with his watery sunk eyes.

'You are right there,' Pete said. 'Nobody has.'

'But I didn't mean what you mean,' Number One replied.

'You think there are blackberries there, further up?' Number Two asked. He was a reasonable child who only wanted to be assured that a risk was worth while.

'There are bushes all the way up through the woods,' Pete said.

'How do you know?'

'It stands to reason.'

It seemed odd to him that day how reluctant they were to take his advice. Why should the blackberry-bushes abruptly stop their growth on the border of their own territory? Blackberries were not created for the special use of Bottom. Pete said, 'Don't you want to pick them one time more before the winter comes?' and they hung their heads, as though they were seeking a reply in the red earth where the ants made roads from stone to stone. At last Number One said, 'Nobody's been there before,' as if that was the worst thing he could think of to say.

'All the better blackberries,' Pete replied.

Number Two said after consideration, 'The wood looks deeper up there and blackberries like the shade.'

Number Three yawned. 'Who cares about blackberries anyway? There's other things to do than pick. It's new ground, isn't it? Let's go and see. Who knows . . . ?'

'Who knows?' Liz repeated in a frightened way and looked first at Pete and then at Number Three as though it were possible that perhaps *they* might.

'Hold up your hands and vote,' Pete said. He shot his own arm commandingly up and Number Three was only a second behind. After a little hesitation Number Two followed suit; then, seeing that there was a majority anyway for going further, Liz raised a cautious hand but with a backward glance at Number One. 'So you're for home?' Pete said to Number One with scorn and relief.

'He'll have to take the oath anyway,' Number Three said, 'or else . . .'

'I don't have to take the oath if I'm going home.'

'Of course you have to or else you'll tell.'

'What do I care about your silly oath? It doesn't mean a thing. I can take it and tell just the same.'

There was a silence: the other three looked at Pete. The whole foundation of their mutual trust seemed to be endangered. No one had ever suggested breaking the oath before. At last Number Three said, 'Let's bash him.'

'No,' Pete said. Violence, he knew, was not the answer. Number One would run home just the same and tell everything. The whole blackberry-picking would be spoilt by the thought of the punishment to come.

'Oh hell,' Number Two said. 'Let's forget the blackberries and play Old Noh.'

Liz, like the girl she was, began to weep. 'I want to pick blackberries.'

But Pete had been given time to reach his decision. He said, 'He's going to take the oath and he's going to pick blackberries too. Tie his hands.'

Number One tried to escape, but Number Two tripped him up. Liz bound his wrists with her hair-ribbon, pulling a hard knot which only she knew—it was for such special skills as this that she had gained her entry into the gang. Number One sat on a chunk of ruin and sneered at them. 'How do I pick blackberries with my hands tied?'

'You were greedy and ate them all. You brought none home. They'll find the stains all over your clothes.'

'Oh, he'll get such a beating,' Liz said with admiration. 'I bet they'll beat him bare.'

'Four against one.'

'Now you are going to take the oath,' Pete said. He broke off two twigs and held them in the shape of a cross. Each of the other three members of the gang gathered saliva in the mouth and smeared the four ends of the cross. Then Pete thrust the sticky points of wood between the lips of Number One. Words were unnecessary: the same thought came inevitably to the mind of everyone with the act: 'Strike me dead if I tell.' After they had dealt forcibly with Number One each followed the same ritual. (Not one of them knew the origin of the oath; it had passed down through generations of such gangs. Once Pete—and perhaps all the others at one time or another had done the same in the darkness of bed—tried to explain to himself the ceremony of the oath: in sharing the spittle maybe they were sharing each other's lives, like mixing blood, and the act was solemnized upon a cross because for some reason a cross always signified shameful death.)

'Who's got a bit of string?' Pete said.

They tied the string to Liz's hair-ribbon and jerked Number One to his feet. Number Two pulled the string and Number Three pushed from behind. Pete led the way, upwards and into the wood, while Liz trailed alone behind; she couldn't move quickly because she had very bandy legs. Now that he realized there was nothing to be done about it, Number One made little trouble; he contented himself with an occasional sneer and lagged enough to keep the cord stretched tight, so that their march was delayed, and nearly two hours passed before they came to the edge of the known territory, emerging from the woods of Bottom on to the rim of a shallow ravine. On the other side the rocks rose again in exactly the same way, with the birch-trees lodged in every crevice up to the sky-line, to which no one from the village of Bottom had ever climbed; in all the interstices of roots and rocks the blackberries grew. From where they stood they could imagine they saw a blue haze like autumn smoke from the great luscious untouched fruit dangling in the shade.

2

All the same they hesitated a while before they started going down; it was as though Number One retained a certain malevolent influence and they had bound themselves to it by the cord. He squatted on the ground and sneered up at them. 'You see you don't dare . . .'

'Dare what?' Pete asked, trying to brush his words away before any doubts could settle on Two or Three or Liz and sap the uncertain power he still possessed.

'Those blackberries don't belong to us,' One said.

'Then who do they belong to?' Pete asked him, noting how Number Two looked at Number One as though he expected an answer.

Three said with scorn, 'Finding's keeping,' and kicked a stone down into the ravine.

'They belong to the next village. You know that as well as I do.'

'And where's the next village?' Pete asked.

'Somewhere.'

'For all you know there isn't another village.'

'There must be. It's common sense. We can't be the only ones—we and Two Rivers.' That was what they called the village which lay beyond the headland.

'But how do you *know*?' Pete said. His thoughts took wing. 'Perhaps we *are* the only ones. Perhaps we could climb up there and go on for ever and ever. Perhaps the world's empty.' He could feel that Number Two and Liz were half-way with him— as for Number Three he was a hopeless case; he cared for nothing. But all the same, if he had to choose his successor he would prefer Number Three's care-for-nothing character than the elderly inherited rules of Number One or the unadventurous reliability of Number Two.

Number One said, 'You are just crazy,' and spat down into the ravine. 'We couldn't be the only ones alive. It's common sense.'

'Why not?' Pete said. 'Who knows?'

'Perhaps the blackberries are poisoned,' Liz said. 'Perhaps we'll get the gripes. Perhaps there's savages there. Perhaps there's giants.'

'I'll believe in giants when I see them,' Pete said. He knew how shallow her fear was; she only wanted to be reassured by someone stronger.

'You talk a lot,' Number One said, 'but you can't even organize. Why didn't you tell us to bring baskets if we were going to pick things?'

'We don't need baskets. We've got Liz's skirt.'

'And it's Liz who'll be thrashed when her skirt's all stained.'

'Not if it's full of blackberries she won't. Tie up your skirt, Liz.'

Liz tied it up, making it into a pannier in front, with a knot behind just above the opening of her small plump buttocks. The boys watched her with interest to see how she fixed it. 'They'll all fall out,' Number One said. 'You ought to have taken the whole thing off an' made a sack.'

'How could I climb holding a sack? You don't know a thing, Number One. I can fix this easy.' She squatted on the ground with a bare buttock on each heel and tied and retied the knot till she was quite satisfied that it was firm.

'So now we go down,' Number Three said.

'Not till I give the order. Number One, I'll release you if you promise to give no trouble.'

'I'll give plenty of trouble.'

'Number Two and Three, you take charge of Number One. You're the rear-guard, see. If we have to retreat in a hurry, you just leave the prisoner behind. Liz and I go ahead to reconnoitre.'

'Why Liz?' Number Three said. 'What good's a girl?'

'In case we have to use a spy. Girl spies are always best. Anyway they wouldn't bash a girl.'

'Pa does,' Liz said, twitching her buttocks.

'But I want to be in the van,' Three said.

'We don't know which is the van yet. They may be watching us now while we talk. They may be luring us on, and then they'll attack in the rear.'

'You're afraid,' Number One said. 'Fainty goose! Fainty goose!'

'I'm not afraid, but I'm boss, I'm responsible for the gang. Listen all of you, in case of danger we give one short whistle. Stay where you are. Don't move. Don't breathe. Two short whistles mean abandon the prisoner and retreat double-quick. One long whistle means treasure discovered, all well, come as quick as you can. Everybody got that clear?'

'Yah,' said Number Two. 'But suppose we're just lost?'

'Stay where you are and wait for a whistle.'

'Suppose *he* whistles—to confuse?' Number Two asked, digging at Number One with his toe.

'If he does gag him. Gag him hard, so his teeth squeak.'

Pete went to the edge of the plateau and gazed down, to choose his path through the scrub; the rocks descended some thirty feet. Liz stood close behind him and held the edge of his shirt. 'Who are *They*?' she whispered.

'Strangers.'

'You don't believe in giants?'

'No.'

'When I think of giants, I shiver—here,' and she laid her hand on the little bare mount of Venus below her panniered skirt.

Pete said, 'We'll start down there between those clumps of gorse. Be careful. The stones are loose and we don't want to make any noise at all.' He turned back to the others, who watched him with admiration, envy and hate (that was Number One). 'Wait till you see us start climbing up the other side and then you come on down.' He looked at the sky. 'The invasion began at noon,' he announced with the precision of an historian recording an event in the past which had altered the shape of the world.

3

'We could whistle now,' Liz suggested. They were half-way up the slope of the ravine by this time, out of breath from the scramble. She put a blackberry in her mouth and added, 'They're sweet. Sweeter than ours. Shall I start picking?' Her thighs and bottom were scratched with briars and smeared with blood the colour of blackberry juice.

Pete said, 'Why, I've seen better than these in our territory. Liz, don't you notice, not one of them's been picked. No one's ever come here. These ones are nothing to what we'll find later. They've been growing for years and years and years—why, I wouldn't be surprised if we came on a whole forest of them with bushes as high as trees and berries as big as apples. We'll leave the little ones for the others if they want to pick them. You and I will climb up higher and find real treasure.' As he spoke he could hear the scrape of the others' shoes and the roll of a loose stone, but they could see nothing because the bushes grew so thick around the trees. 'Come on. If we find treasure first, it's ours.'

'I wish it was real treasure, not just blackberries.'

'It might be real treasure. No one's ever explored here before us.'

'Giants?' Liz asked him with a shiver.

'Those are stories they tell children. Like Old Noh and his ship. There never were giants.'

'Not Noh?'

'What a baby you are.'

They climbed up and up among the birches and bushes, and the sound of the others diminished below them. There was a different smell here: hot and moist and metallic, far away from the salt of the sea. Then the trees and bushes thinned and they were at the summit of the hills. When they looked backwards, Bottom was hidden by the ridge between, but through the trees they could see a line of blue as though the sea had been lifted up almost to their level by some gigantic convulsion. They turned nervously away from it and stared into the unknown land ahead.

4

'It's a house,' Liz said. 'It's a huge house.'

'It can't be. You've never seen a house that size—or that shape,' but he knew that Liz was right. This had been made by men and not by nature. It was something in which people had once lived.

'A house for giants,' Liz said fearfully.

Pete lay on his stomach and peered over the edge of the ravine. A hundred feet down among the red rocks lay a long structure glinting here and there among the bushes and moss which over-grew it—it stretched beyond their sight, trees climbed along its sides, trees had seeded on the roof, and up the length of two enormous chimneys ivy twined and flowering plants with trumpet-mouths. There was no smoke, no sign of any occupant; only the birds, perhaps disturbed by their voices, called warnings among the trees, and a colony of starlings rose from one of the chimneys and dispersed.

'Let's go back,' Liz whispered.

'We can't now,' Pete said. 'Don't be afraid. It's only another ruin. What's wrong with ruins? We've always played in them.'

'It's scary. It's not like the ruins at Bottom.'

'Bottom's not the world,' Pete said. It was the expression of a profound belief he shared with no one else.

The huge structure was tilted at an angle, so that they could almost see down one of the enormous chimneys, which gaped like a hole in the world. 'I'm going down to look,' Pete said, 'but I'll spy out the land first.'

'Shall I whistle?'

'Not yet. Stay where you are in case the others come.'

He moved with caution along the ridge. Behind him the strange thing—not built of stone or wood—extended a hundred yards or more, sometimes hidden, sometimes obscured by trees, but in the direction he now took the cliff was bare of vegetation, and he was able to peer down at the great wall of the house, not straight but oddly curved, like the belly of a fish or . . . He stood still for a moment, looking hard at it: the curve was the enormous magnification of something that was familiar to him. He went thoughtfully on, pondering on the old legend which had been the subject of their games. Nearly a hundred yards further he stopped again. It was as though at this point some enormous hand had taken the house and split it in two. He could look down between the two portions and see the house exposed floor by floor—there must be five, six, seven of them, with nothing stirring inside, except where the bushes had found a lodging and a wing flickered. He could imagine the great halls receding into the dark, and he thought how all the inhabitants of Bottom could have lived in a single room on a single floor and still have found space for their animals and their gear. How many thousand people, he wondered, had once lived in this enormous house? He hadn't realized the world contained so many.

When the house was broken—how?—one portion had been flung upwards at an angle, and only fifty yards from where he stood he could see where the end of it penetrated in the ridge, so that if he wished to explore further he had only to drop a few yards to find himself upon the roof. There trees grew again and made an easy descent. He had no excuse to stay, and suddenly aware of loneliness and ignorance and the mystery of the great house he put his fingers to his mouth and gave one long whistle to summon all the others.

5

They were overawed too, and if Number One had not so jeered at them, perhaps they would have decided to go home with the secret of the house locked in their minds with a dream of one day returning. But when Number One said, 'Softies, Fainties . . .' and shot his spittle down towards the house, Number Three broke silence. 'What are we waiting for?' Then Pete had to act, if he was to guard his leadership. Scrambling from branch to branch of a tree that grew from a plateau of rock below the ridge, he got within six feet of the roof and dropped. He landed on his knees upon a surface cold and smooth as an egg-shell. The four children looked down at him and waited.

The slope of the roof was such that he had to slide cautiously downwards on his bottom. At the end of the descent there was another house which had been built upon the roof, and he realized from where he sat that the whole structure was not one house but a succession of houses built one over the other, and above the topmost house loomed the tip of the enormous chimney. Remembering how the whole thing had been torn apart, he was careful not to slide too fast for fear that he should plunge into the gap between. None of the others had followed him; he was alone.

Ahead of him was a great arch of some unknown material,

and below the arch a red rock rose and split it in two. This was like a victory for the mountains; however hard the material men had used in making the house, the mountains remained the stronger. He came to rest with his feet against a rock and looked down into the wide gap where the rock had come up and split the houses; the gap was many yards across; it was bridged by a fallen tree, and although he could see but a little way down, he had the same sense which he had received above that he was looking into something as deep as the sea. Why was it he half expected to see fishes moving there?

With his hand pressed on the needle of red rock he stood upright and, looking up, was startled to see two unwinking eyes regarding him from a few feet away. Then as he moved again he saw that they belonged to a squirrel, the colour of the rock: it turned without hurry or fear, lifted a plumy tail and neatly evacuated before it leapt into the hall ahead of him.

The hall—it was indeed a hall, he realized, making his way towards it astride the fallen tree, and yet the first impression he had was of a forest, with the trees regularly spaced as in a plantation made by men. It was possible to walk there on a level, though the ground was hummocked with red rock which here and there had burst through the hard paving. The trees were not trees at all but pillars of wood, which still showed in patches a smooth surface, but pitted for most of their length with worm-holes and draped with ivy that climbed to the roof fifty feet up to escape through a great tear in the ceiling. There was a smell of vegetation and damp, and all down the hall were dozens of small green tumuli like woodland-graves.

He kicked one of the mounds with a foot and it disintegrated immediately below the thick damp moss that covered it. Gingerly he thrust his hand into the soggy greenery and pulled out a strut of rotting wood. He moved on and tried again a long curved hump of green which stood more than breast-high—not like a common grave—and this time he stubbed his toes and winced with the pain. The greenery had taken no root here, but had spread from tumulus to hump across the floor, and he was able to pluck away without difficulty the leaves and tendrils. Underneath lay a stone slab in many beautiful colours, green and rose-pink and red the colour of blood. He moved around it, cleaning the surface as he went, and here at last he came on real treasure. For a moment he did not realize what purpose those half-translucent objects could have served; they stood in rows behind a smashed panel, most broken into green rubble, but a few intact, except for the discoloration of age. It was from their shape he realized that they must once have been drinkng pots, made of a material quite different from the rough clay to which he was accustomed. Scattered on the floor below were hundreds of hard round objects stamped with the image of a human head like those his grandparents had dug up in the ruins of Bottom—objects useless except that with their help it was possible to draw a perfect circle and they could be used as forfeits, in place of pebbles, in the game of 'Ware that Cloud'. They were more interesting than pebbles. They had dignity and rareness which belonged to all old things made by man—there was so little to be seen in the world older than an old man. He was tempted momentarily to keep the discovery to himself, but what purpose would they serve if they were not employed? A forfeit was of no value kept secret in a hole, so, putting his fingers to his mouth, he blew the long whistle again.

While waiting for the others to join him, he sat on the stone slab deep in thought and pondered all he had seen, especially that great wall like a fish's belly. The whole huge house, it seemed to him, was like a monstrous fish thrown up among the rocks to die, but what a fish and what a wave to carry it so high.

The children came sliding down the roof, Number One still in tow between them; they gave little cries of excitement and delight; they were quite forgetful of their fear, as though it were the season of snow. Then they picked themselves up by the red rock, as he had done, straddled the fallen tree, and hobbled across the vast space of the hall, like insects caught under a cup.

'There's treasure for you,' Pete said with pride and he was glad to see them surprised into silence at the spectacle; even Number One forgot to sneer, and the cord by which they held him trailed neglected on the ground. At last Number Two said, 'Coo! It's better than blackberries.'

'Put the forfeits into Liz's skirt. We'll divide them later.'

'Does Number One get any?' Liz asked.

'There's enough for all,' Pete said. 'Let him go.' It seemed the moment for generosity, and in any case they needed all their hands. While they were gathering up the forfeits he went to one of the great gaps in the wall that must once have been windows, covered perhaps like the windows of Bottom with straw mats at night, and leant far out. The hills rose and fell, a brown and choppy sea; there was no sign of a village anywhere, not even of a ruin. Below him the great black wall curved out of sight; the place where it touched the ground was hidden by the tops of trees that grew in the valley below. He remembered the old legend, and the game they played among the ruins of Bottom. 'Noh built a boat. What kind of a boat? A boat for all the beasts and Brigit too. What kind of beasts? Big beasts like bears and beavers and Brigit too . . .'

Something went twang with a high musical sound and then there was a sigh which faded into silence. He turned and saw that Number Three was busy at yet another mound—the second biggest mound in the hall. He had unearthed a long box full of the oblongs they called dominoes, but every time he touched a piece a sound came, each a little different, and when he touched one a second time it remained silent. Number Two, in the hope of further treasure, groped in the mound and found only rusty wires which scratched his hands. No more sounds were to be coaxed out of the box, and no one ever discovered why at the beginning it seemed to sing to them.

6

Had they ever experienced a longer day even at the height of midsummer? The sun, of course, stayed longer on the high plateau, and they could not tell how far night was already encroaching on the woods and valleys below them. There were two long narrow passages in the house down which they raced, tripping sometimes on the broken floor—Liz kept to the rear, unable to run fast for fear of spilling the forfeits from her skirt. The passages were lined with rooms, each one large enough to contain a family from Bottom, with strange tarnished twisted fixtures of which the purpose remained a mystery. There was another great hall, this one without pillars, which had a great square sunk in the floor lined with coloured stone; it shelved upwards, so that at one end it was ten feet deep and at the other so shallow that they could drop down to the drift of dead leaves and the scraps of twigs blown there by winter winds, and everywhere the droppings of birds like splashes of soiled snow.

At the end of yet a third hall they came, all of them, to a halt, for there in front of them, in bits and pieces, were five children staring back, a half-face, a head cut in two as though by a butcher's hatchet, a knee severed from a foot. They stared at the strangers and one of them defiantly raised a fist—it was Number Three. At once one of the strange flat children lifted his fist in reply. Battle was about to be joined; it was a relief in this empty world to find real enemies to fight, so they advanced slowly like suspicious cats, Liz a little in the rear, and there on the other side was another girl with skirts drawn up in the same fashion as hers to hold the same forfeits, with a similar little crack under the mount below the belly, but her face obscured with a green rash, one eye missing. The strangers moved their legs and arms and yet remained flat against the wall, and suddenly they were touching nose to nose, and there was nothing there at all but the cold smooth wall. They backed away and approached and backed away: this was something not one of them could understand. So without saying anything to each other, in a private awe, they moved away to where steps led down to the floors below; there they hesitated again, listening and peering, their voices twittering against the unbroken silence, but they were afraid of the darkness, where the side of the mountain cut off all light, so they ran away and screamed defiantly down the long passages, where the late sun slanted in, until they came to rest at last in a group on the great stairs which led upwards into brighter daylight where the enormous chimneys stood.

'Let's go home,' Number One said. 'If we don't go, soon it will be dark.'

'Who's a Fainty now?' Number Three said.

'It's only a house. It's a big house, but it's only a house.'

Pete said, 'It's not a house,' and they all turned and looked their questions at him.

'What do you mean, not a house?' Number Two asked.

'It's a boat,' Pete said.

'You are crazy. Whoever saw a boat as big as this?'

'Whoever saw a house as big as this?' Liz asked.

'What's a boat doing on top of a mountain? Why would a boat have chimneys? What would a boat have forfeits for? When did a boat have rooms and passages?' They threw their sharp objections at him, like handfuls of gravel to sting him into sense.

'It's Noh's boat,' Pete said.

'You're nuts,' Number One said. 'Noh's a game. There was never anyone called Noh.'

'How can we tell? Maybe he did live hundreds of years ago. And if he had all the beasts with him, what could he do without lots of cages? Perhaps those aren't rooms along the passage there; perhaps they are cages.'

'And that hole in the floor?' Liz asked. 'What's that for?'

'I've been thinking about it. It might be a tank for water. Don't you see, he'd have to have somewhere to keep the water-rats and the tadpoles.'

'I don't believe it,' Number One said. 'How would a boat get up here?'

'How would a house as big as this get up here? You know the story. It floated here, and then the waters went down again and left it.'

'Then Bottom was at the bottom of the sea once?' Liz asked. Her mouth fell open and she scratched her buttocks stung with briars and scraped with rock and smeared with bird-droppings.

'Bottom didn't exist then. It was all so long ago . . .'

'He might be right,' Number Two said. Number Three made no comment: he began to mount the stairs towards the roof, and Pete followed quickly and overtook him. The sun lay flat across the tops of the hills which looked like waves, and in all the world there seemed to be nobody but themselves. The great chimney high above shot out a shadow like a wide black road. They stood silent, awed by its size and power, where it tilted towards the cliff above them. Then Number Three said, 'Do you really believe it?'

'I think so.'

'What about all our other games? "Ware that Cloud"?'

'It may have been the cloud which frightened Noh.'

'But where did everybody go? There aren't any corpses.'

'There wouldn't be. Remember the game. When the water went down, they all climbed off the boat two by two.'

'Except the water-rats. The water went down too quickly and one of them was stranded. We ought to find *his* corpse.'

'It was hundreds of years ago. The ants would have eaten him.'

'Not the bones, they couldn't eat those.'

'I'll tell you something I saw—in those cages. I didn't say anything to the others because Liz would have been scared.'

'What did you see?'

'I saw snakes.'

'No!'

'Yes, I did. And they're all turned to stone. They curled along the floor, and I kicked one and it was hard like one of those stone fish they found above Bottom.'

'Well,' Number Three said, 'that seems to prove it,' and they were silent again, weighed down by the magnitude of their discovery. Above their heads, between them and the great chimney, rose yet another house in this nest of houses, and a ladder went up to it from a spot close to where they stood. On the front of the house twenty feet up was a meaningless design in tarnished yellow. Pete memorized the shape, to draw it later in the dust for his father who would never, he knew, believe their story, who would think they had dug the forfeits—their only proof—up in the ruins at the edge of Bottom. The design was like this:

'Perhaps that's where Noh lived,' Number Three whispered, gazing at the design as if it contained a clue to the time of legends, and without another word they both began to climb the ladder, just as the other children came on to the roof below them.

'Where are you going?' Liz called, but they didn't bother to answer her. The thick yellow rust came off on their hands as they climbed and climbed.

The other children came chattering up the stairs and then they saw the man too and were silent.

'Noh,' Pete said.

'A giant,' Liz said.

He was a white clean skeleton, and his skull had rolled on to the shoulder-bone and rested there as though it had been laid on a shelf. All round him lay forfeits brighter and thicker than the forfeits in the hall, and the leaves had drifted against the skeleton, so that they had the impression that he was lying stretched in sleep in a green field. A shred of faded blue material, which the birds had somehow neglected to take at nesting-time, still lay, as though for modesty, across the loins, but when Liz took it up in her fingers it crumbled away to a little powder. Number Three paced the length of the skeleton. He said, 'He was nearly six feet tall.'

'So there *were* giants,' Liz said.

'And they played forfeits,' Number Two said, as though that reassured him of their human nature.

'Moon ought to see him,' Number One said; 'that would take him down a peg.' Moon was the tallest man ever known in Bottom, but he was more than a foot shorter than this length of white bone. They stood around the skeleton with eyes lowered as though they were ashamed of something.

At last Number Two said suddenly, 'It's late. I'm going home,' and he made his hop-and-skip way to the ladder, and after a moment's hesitation Number One and Number Three limped after him. A forfeit went crunch under a foot. No one had picked these forfeits up, not any other of the strange objects which lay gleaming among the leaves. Nothing here was treasure-trove; everything belonged to the dead giant.

At the top of the ladder Pete turned to see what Liz was up to. She sat squatting on the thigh-bones of the skeleton, her naked buttocks rocking to and fro as though in the act of possession. When he went back to her he found that she was weeping.

'What is it, Liz?' he asked.

She leaned forward towards the gaping mouth. 'He's beautiful,' she said, 'he's so beautiful. And he's a giant. Why aren't there giants now?' She began to keen over him like a little old woman at a funeral. 'He's six feet tall,' she cried, exaggerating a little, 'and he has beautiful straight legs. No one has straight legs in Bottom. Why aren't there giants now? Look at his lovely mouth with all the teeth. Who has teeth like that in Bottom?'

'*You* are pretty, Liz,' Pete said, shuffling around in front of her, trying in vain to straighten his own spine like the skeleton's, beseeching her to notice him, feeling jealousy for those straight white bones upon the floor and for the first time a sensation of love for the little bandy-legged creature bucketing to and fro.

'Why aren't there any giants now?' she repeated for the third time, with her tears falling among the bird-droppings. He went sadly to the window and looked out. Below him the red rock split the floor, and up the long slope of the roof he could see the three children scrambling towards the cliff; awkward, with short uneven limbs, they moved like little crabs. He looked down at his own stunted and uneven legs and heard her begin to keen again for a whole world lost.

'He's six feet tall and he has beautiful straight legs.'

MAY WE BORROW YOUR HUSBAND?

I never heard her called anything else but Poopy, either by her husband or by the two men who became their friends. Perhaps I was a little in love with her (absurd though that may seem at my age) because I found that I resented the name. It was unsuited to someone so young and so open—too open; she belonged to the age of trust just as I belonged to the age of cynicism. 'Good old Poopy'—I even heard her called that by the elder of the two interior-decorators (who had known her no longer than I had): a sobriquet which might have been good enough for some vague bedraggled woman of middle age who drank a bit too much but who was useful to drag around as a kind of blind—and those two certainly needed a blind. I once asked the girl her real name, but all she said was, 'Everyone calls me Poopy,' as though that finished it, and I was afraid of appearing too square if I pursued the question further—too middle-aged perhaps as well, so though I hate the name whenever I write it down, Poopy she has to remain: I have no other.

I had been at Antibes working on a book of mine, a biography of the seventeenth-century poet, the Earl of Rochester, for more than a month before Poopy and her husband arrived. I had come there as soon as the full season was over, to a small ugly hotel by the sea not far from the ramparts, and I was able to watch the season depart with the leaves in the Boulevard Général Leclerc. At first, even before the trees had begun to drop, the foreign cars were on the move homeward. A few weeks earlier, I had counted fourteen nationalities, including Morocco, Turkey, Sweden and Luxembourg, between the sea and the Place de Gaulle, to which

I walked every day for the English papers. Now all the foreign number-plates had gone, except for the Belgian and the German and an occasional English one, and, of course, the ubiquitous number-plates of the State of Monaco. The cold weather had come early and Antibes catches only the morning sun—good enough for breakfast on the terrace, but it was safer to lunch indoors or the shadow might overtake the coffee. A cold and solitary Algerian was always there, leaning over the ramparts, looking for something, perhaps safety.

It was the time of year I liked best, when Juan les Pins becomes as squalid as a closed fun-fair with Lunar Park boarded up and cards marked *Fermeture Annuelle* outside the Pam-Pam and Maxim's, and the Concours International Amateur de Striptease at the Vieux Colombiers is over for another season. Then Antibes comes into its own as a small country town with the Auberge de Provence full of local people and old men sit indoors drinking beer or pastis at the *glacier* in the Place de Gaulle. The small garden, which forms a roundabout on the ramparts, looks a little sad with the short stout palms bowing their brown fronds; the sun in the morning shines without any glare, and the few white sails move gently on the unblinding sea.

You can always trust the English to stay on longer than others into the autumn. We have a blind faith in the southern sun and we are taken by surprise when the wind blows icily over the Mediterranean. Then a bickering war develops with the hotel-keeper over the heating on the third floor, and the tiles strike cold underfoot. For a man who has reached the age when all he wants is some good wine and some good cheese and a little work, it is the best season of all. I know how I resented the arrival of the interior-decorators just at the moment when I had hoped to be the only foreigner left, and I prayed that they were birds of passage. They arrived before lunch in a scarlet Sprite—a car much too young for them, and they wore elegant sports clothes more suited to spring at the Cap. The elder man was nearing fifty and the grey hair that waved over his ears was too uniform to be true: the younger had passed thirty and his hair was as black as the other's was grey. I knew their names were Stephen and Tony before they even reached the reception desk, for they had clear, penetrating yet superficial voices, like their gaze, which had quickly lighted on me where I sat with a Ricard on the terrace and registered that I had nothing of interest for them, and passed on. They were not arrogant: it was simply that they were more concerned with each other, and yet perhaps, like a married couple of some years' standing, not very profoundly.

I soon knew a great deal about them. They had rooms side by side in my passage, though I doubt if both rooms were often occupied, for I used to hear voices from one room or the other most evenings when I went to bed. Do I seem too curious about other people's affairs? But in my own defence I have to say that the events of this sad little comedy were forced by all the participants on my attention. The balcony where I worked every morning on my life of Rochester overhung the terrace where the interior-decorators took their coffee, and even when they occupied a table out of sight those clear elocutionary voices mounted up to me. I didn't want to hear them; I wanted to work. Rochester's relations with the actress, Mrs Barry, were my concern at the moment, but it is almost impossible in a foreign land not to listen to one's own tongue. French I could have accepted as a kind of background noise, but I could not fail to overhear English.

'My dear, guess who's written to me now?'

'Alec?'

'No, Mrs Clarenty.'

'What does the old hag want?'

'She objects to the mural in her bedroom.'

'But, Stephen, it's divine. Alec's never done anything better. The dead faun . . .'

'I think she wants something more nubile and less necrophilous.'

'The old lecher.'

They were certainly hardy, those two. Every morning around eleven they went bathing off the little rocky peninsula opposite the hotel—they had the autumnal Mediterranean, so far as the eye could see, entirely to themselves. As they walked briskly

back in their elegant bikinis, or sometimes ran a little way for
warmth, I had the impression that they took their bathes less for
pleasure than for exercise—to preserve the slim legs, the flat
stomachs, the narrow hips for more recondite and Etruscan pas-
times.

Idle they were not. They drove the Sprite to Cagnes, Vence, St
Paul, to any village where an antique store was to be rifled, and
they brought back with them objects of olive wood, spurious old
lanterns, painted religious figures which in the shop would have
seemed to me ugly or banal, but which I suspect already fitted in
their imaginations some scheme of decoration the reverse of commonplace. Not that their minds were altogether on their profession. They relaxed.

I encountered them one evening in a little sailors' bar in the
old port of Nice. Curiosity this time had led me in pursuit, for I
had seen the scarlet Sprite standing outside the bar. They were
entertaining a boy of about eighteen who, from his clothes, I
imagine worked as a hand on the boat to Corsica which was at
the moment in harbour. They both looked very sharply at me
when I entered, as though they were thinking, 'Have we mis-
judged him?' I drank a glass of beer and left, and the younger
said 'Good evening' as I passed the table. After that we had to
greet each other every day in the hotel. It was as though I had
been admitted to an intimacy.

Time for a few days was hanging as heavily on my hands as
on Lord Rochester's. He was staying at Mrs Fourcard's baths in
Leather Lane, receiving mercury treatment for the pox, and I was
awaiting a whole section of my notes which I had inadvertently
left in London. I couldn't release him till they came, and my sole
distraction for a few days was those two. As they packed themselves into the Sprite of an afternoon or an evening I liked to
guess from their clothes the nature of their excursion. Always elegant, they were yet successful, by the mere exchange of one *tri-
cot* for another, in indicating their mood: they were just as well
dressed in the sailors' bar, but a shade more simply; when dealing with a Lesbian antique dealer at St Paul, there was a masculine dash about their handkerchiefs. Once they disappeared
altogether for the inside of a week in what I took to be their old-

est clothes, and when they returned the older man had a contusion on his right cheek. They told me they had been over to Corsica. Had they enjoyed it? I asked.

'Quite barbaric,' the young man Tony said, but not, I thought, in praise.

He saw me looking at Stephen's cheek, and he added quickly, 'We had an accident in the mountains.'

It was two days after that, just at sunset, that Poopy arrived with her husband. I was back at work on Rochester, sitting in an overcoat on my balcony, when a taxi drove up—I recognized the driver as someone who plied regularly from Nice airport. What I noticed first, because the passengers were still hidden, was the luggage, which was bright blue and of an astonishing newness. Even the initials—rather absurdly PT—shone like newly-minted coins. There were a large suitcase and a small suitcase and a hatbox, all of the same cerulean hue, and after that a respectable old leather case totally unsuited to air travel, the kind one inherits from a father, with half a label still left from Shepheard's Hotel or the Valley of the Kings. Then the passenger emerged and I saw Poopy for the first time. Down below, the interior-decorators were watching too, and drinking Dubonnet.

She was a very tall girl, perhaps five feet nine, very slim, very young, with hair the colour of conkers, and her costume was as new as the luggage. She said, 'Finalmente,' looking at the undistinguished facade with an air of rapture—or perhaps it was only the shape of her eyes. When I saw the young man I felt certain they were just married; it wouldn't have surprised me if confetti had fallen out from the seams of their clothes. They were like a photograph in the Tatler; they had camera smiles for each other and an underlying nervousness. I was sure they had come straight from the reception, and that it had been a smart one, after a proper church wedding.

They made a very handsome couple as they hesitated a moment before going up the steps to the reception. The long beam of the Phare de la Garoupe brushed the water behind them, and the floodlighting went suddenly on outside the hotel as if the manager had been waiting for their arrival to turn it up. The two decorators sat there without drinking, and I noticed that the elder one had covered the contusion on his cheek with a very clean white handkerchief. They were not, of course, looking at the girl but at the boy. He was over six feet tall and as slim as the girl, with a face that might have been cut on a coin, completely handsome and completely dead—but perhaps that was only an effect of his nerves. His clothes, too, I thought, had been bought for the occasion, the sports-jacket with a double slit and the grey trousers cut a little narrowly to show off the long legs. It seemed to me that they were both too young to marry—I doubt if they had accumulated forty-five years between them—and I had a wild impulse to lean over the balcony and warn them away— 'Not this hotel. Any hotel but this.' Perhaps I could have told them that the heating was insufficient or the hot water erratic or the food terrible, not that the English care much about food, but of course they would have paid me no attention—they were so obviously 'booked', and what an ageing lunatic I should have appeared in their eyes. ('One of those eccentric English types one finds abroad'—I could imagine the letter home.) This was the first time I wanted to interfere, and I didn't know them at all. The second time it was already too late, but I think I shall always regret that I did not give way to that madness . . .

It had been the silence and attentiveness of those two down below which had frightened me, and the patch of white handkerchief hiding the shameful contusion. For the first time I heard the hated name: 'Shall we see the room, Poopy, or have a drink first?'

They decided to see the room, and the two glasses of Dubonnet clicked again into action.

I think she had more idea of how a honeymoon should be conducted than he had, because they were not seen again that night.

2

I was late for breakfast on the terrace, but I noticed that Stephen and Tony were lingering longer than usual. Perhaps they had decided at last that it was too cold for a bathe; I had the impression, however, that they were lying in wait. They had never been so friendly to me before, and I wondered whether perhaps they regarded me as a kind of cover, with my distressingly normal appearance. My table for some reason that day had been shifted and was out of the sun, so Stephen suggested that I should join theirs: they would be off in a moment, after one more cup . . . The contusion was much less noticeable today, but I think he had been applying powder.

'You staying here long?' I asked them, conscious of how clumsily I constructed a conversation compared with their easy prattle.

'We had meant to leave tomorrow,' Stephen said, 'but last night we changed our minds.'

'Last night?'

'It was such a beautiful day, wasn't it? "Oh", I said to Tony, "surely we can leave poor dreary old London a little longer?" It has an awful staying power—like a railway sandwich.'

'Are your clients so patient?'

'My dear, the clients? You never in your life saw such atrocities as we get from Brompton Square. It's always the same. People who pay others to decorate for them have ghastly taste themselves.'

'You do the world a service then. Think what we might suffer without you. In Brompton Square.'

Tony giggled, 'I don't know how we'd stand it if we had not our private jokes. For example, in Mrs Clarenty's case, we've installed what we call the Loo of Lucullus.'

'She was enchanted,' Stephen said.

'The most obscene vegetable forms. It reminded me of a harvest festival.'

They suddenly became very silent and attentive, watching somebody over my shoulder. I looked back. It was Poopy, all by herself. She stood there, waiting for the boy to show her which table she could take, like a new girl at school who doesn't know the rules. She even seemed to be wearing a school uniform: very tight trousers, slit at the ankle—but she hadn't realized that the summer term was over. She had dressed up like that, I felt certain, so as not to be noticed, in order to hide herself, but there were only two other women on the terrace and they were both wearing sensible tweed skirts. She looked at them nostalgically as the waiter led her past our table to one nearer the sea. Her long legs moved awkwardly in the pants as though they felt exposed.

'The young bride,' Tony said.

'Deserted already,' Stephen said with satisfaction.

'Her name is Poopy Travis, you know.'

'It's an extraordinary name to choose. She couldn't have been *christened* that way, unless they found a very liberal vicar.'

'He is called Peter. Of an undefined occupation. Not Army, I think, do you?'

'Oh no, not Army. Something to do with land perhaps—there's an agreeable *herbal* smell about him.'

'You seem to know nearly all there is to know,' I said.

'We looked at their police *carnet* before dinner.'

'I have an idea,' Tony said, 'that PT hardly represents their activities last night.' He looked across the tables at the girl with an expression extraordinarily like hatred.

'We were both taken,' Stephen said, 'by the air of innocence. One felt he was more used to horses.'

'He mistook the yearnings of the rider's crotch for something quite different.'

Perhaps they hoped to shock me, but I don't think it was that. I really believe they were in a state of extreme sexual excitement; they had received a *coup de foudre* last night on the terrace and were quite incapable of disguising their feelings. I was an excuse to talk, to speculate about the desired object. The sailor had been a stop-gap: this was the real thing. I was inclined to be amused, for what could this absurd pair hope to gain from a young man newly married to the girl who now sat there patiently waiting, wearing her beauty like an old sweater she had forgotten to change? But that was a bad simile to use: she would have been afraid to wear an old sweater, except secretly, by herself, in the playroom. She had no idea that she was one of those who can afford to disregard the fashion of their clothes. She caught my eye and, because I was so obviously English, I suppose, gave me half a timid smile. Perhaps I too would have received the *coup de foudre* if I had not been thirty years older and twice married.

Tony detected the smile. 'A regular body-snatcher,' he said.

My breakfast and the young man arrived at the same moment before I had time to reply. As he passed the table I could feel the tension.

'*Cuir de Russie*,' Stephen said, quivering a nostril. 'A mistake of inexperience.'

The youth caught the words as he went past and turned with an astonished look to see who had spoken, and they both smiled insolently back at him as though they really believed they had the power to take him over . . .

For the first time I felt disquiet.

3

Something was not going well; that was sadly obvious. The girl nearly always came down to breakfast ahead of her husband—I have an idea he spent a long time bathing and shaving and applying his *Cuir de Russie*. When he joined her he would give her a courteous brotherly kiss as though they had not spent the night together in the same bed. She began to have those shadows under the eyes which come from lack of sleep—for I couldn't believe that they were 'the lineaments of gratified desire'. Sometimes from my balcony I saw them returning from a walk—nothing, except perhaps a pair of horses, could have been more handsome. His gentleness towards her might have reassured her mother, but it made a man impatient to see him squiring her across the undangerous road, holding open doors, following a pace behind her like the husband of a princess. I longed to see some outbreak of irritation caused by the sense of satiety, but they never seemed to be in conversation when they returned from their walk, and at table I caught only the kind of phrases people use who are dining together for the sake of politeness. And yet I could swear that she loved him, even by the way she avoided watching him. There was nothing avid or starved about her; she stole her quick glances when she was quite certain that his attention was absorbed elsewhere—they were tender, anxious perhaps, quite undemanding. If one inquired after him when he wasn't there, she glowed with the pleasure of using his name.

'Oh, Peter overslept this morning.' 'Peter cut himself. He's staunching the blood now.' 'Peter's mislaid his tie. He thinks the floor-waiter has purloined it.' Certainly she loved him; I was far less certain of what his feelings were.

And you must imagine how all the time those other two were closing in. It was like a medieval siege: they dug their trenches and threw up their earthworks. The difference was that the besieged didn't notice what they were at—at any rate, the girl didn't; I don't know about him. I longed to warn her, but what could I have said that wouldn't have shocked her or angered her? I believe the two would have changed their floor if that would have helped to bring them closer to the fortress; they probably discussed the move together and decided against it as too overt.

Because they knew that I could do nothing against them, they regarded me almost in the role of an ally. After all, I might be useful one day in distracting the girl's attention—and I suppose they were not quite mistaken in that; they could tell from the way I looked at her how interested I was, and they probably calculated that my interests might in the long run coincide with theirs. It didn't occur to them that, perhaps, I was a man with scruples. If one really wanted a thing scruples were obviously, in their eyes, out of place. There was a tortoiseshell star mirror at St Paul they were plotting to obtain for half the price demanded (I think there was an old mother who looked after the shop when her daughter was away at a *boîte* for women of a certain taste); naturally, therefore, when I looked at the girl, as they saw me so often do, they considered I would be ready to join in any 'reasonable' scheme.

'When I looked at the girl'—realize that I have made no real attempt to describe her. In writing a biography one can, of course, just insert a portrait and the affair is done: I have the prints of Lady Rochester and Mrs Barry in front of me now. But speaking as a professional novelist (for biography and reminiscence are both new forms to me), one describes a woman not so much that the reader should see her in all the cramping detail of colour and shape (how often Dickens's elaborate portraits seem like directions to the illlustrator which might well have been left out of the finished book), but to convey an emotion. Let the reader make his own image of a wife, a mistress, some passer-by 'sweet and kind' (the poet required no other descriptive words), if he has a fancy to. If I were to describe the girl (I can't bring myself at this moment to write her hateful name), it would be not to convey the colour of her hair, the shape of her mouth, but to express the pleasure and the pain with which I recall her—I, the writer, the observer, the subsidiary character, what you will. But if I didn't bother to convey them to her, why should I bother to convey them to you, *hypocrite lecteur?*

How quickly those two tunnelled. I don't think it was more than four mornings after the arrival that, when I came down to breakfast, I found they had moved their table next to the girl's and were entertaining her in her husband's absence. They did it very well; it was the first time I had seen her relaxed and happy—and she was happy because she was talking about Peter. Peter was agent for his father, somewhere in Hampshire—there were three thousand acres to manage. Yes, he was fond of riding and so was she. It all tumbled out—the kind of life she dreamed of having when she returned home. Stephen just dropped in a word now and then, of a rather old-fashioned courteous interest, to keep her going. Apparently he had once decorated some hall in their neighbourhood and knew the names of some people Peter knew—Winstanley, I think—and that gave her immense confidence.

'He's one of Peter's best friends,' she said, and the two flickered their eyes at each other like lizards' tongues.

'Come and join us, William,' Stephen said, but only when he had noticed that I was within earshot. 'You know Mrs Travis?'

How could I refuse to sit at their table? And yet in doing so I seemed to become an ally.

'Not *the* William Harris?' the girl asked. It was a phrase which I hated, and yet she transformed even that, with her air of innocence. For she had a capacity to make everything new: Antibes became a discovery and we were the first foreigners to have made it. When she said, 'Of course, I'm afraid I haven't actually *read* any of your books,' I heard the over-familiar remark for the first time; it even seemed to me a proof of her honesty—I nearly wrote her virginal honesty. 'You must know an awful lot about people,' she said, and again I read into the banality of the remark an appeal—for help against whom, those two or the husband who at that moment appeared on the terrace? He had the same nervous air as she, even the same shadows under the lids, so that they might have been taken by a stranger, as I wrote before, for brother and sister. He hesitated a moment when he saw all of us there and she called across to him, 'Come and meet these nice people, darling.' He didn't look any too pleased, but he sat glumly down and asked whether the coffee was still hot.

'I'll order some more, darling. They know the Winstanleys, and this is *the* William Harris.'

He looked at me blankly; I think he was wondering if I had anything to do with tweeds.

'I hear you like horses,' Stephen said, 'and I was wondering whether you and your wife would come to lunch with us at Cagnes on Saturday. That's tomorrow, isn't it? There's a very good racecourse at Cagnes . . .'

'I don't know,' he said dubiously, looking to his wife for a clue.

'But, darling, of course we must go. You'd love it.'

His face cleared instantly. I really believe he had been troubled by a social scruple: the question whether one accepts invitations on a honeymoon. 'It's very good of you,' he said, 'Mr . . .'

'Let's start as we mean to go on. I'm Stephen and this is Tony.'

'I'm Peter.' He added a trifle gloomily, 'And this is Poopy.'

'Tony, you take Poopy in the Sprite, and Peter and I will go by *autobus*.' (I had the impression, and I think Tony had too, that Stephen had gained a point.)

'You'll come too, Mr Harris?' the girl asked, using my surname as though she wished to emphasize the difference between me and them.

'I'm afraid I can't. I'm working against time.'

I watched them that evening from my balcony as they returned from Cagnes and, hearing the way they all laughed together, I thought, 'The enemy are within the citadel: it's only a question of time.' A lot of time, because they proceeded very carefully, those two. There was no question of a quick grab which I suspect had caused the contusion in Corsica.

4

It became a regular habit with the two of them to entertain the girl during her solitary breakfast before her husband arrived. I never sat at their table again, but scraps of the conversation would come over to me, and it seemed to me that she was never quite so cheerful again. Even the sense of novelty had gone. I heard her say once, 'There's so little to do here,' and it struck me as an odd observation for a honeymooner to make.

Then one evening I found her in tears outside the Musée Grimaldi. I had been fetching my papers, and, as my habit was, I made a round by the Place Nationale with the pillar erected in 1819 to celebrate—a remarkable paradox—the loyalty of Antibes to the monarchy and her resistance to *les Troupes Etrangères,* who were seeking to re-establish the monarchy. Then, according to rule, I went on by the market and the old port and Lou-Lou's restaurant up the ramp towards the cathedral and the Musée, and there in the grey evening light, before the street-lamps came on, I found her crying under the cliff of the château.

I noticed too late what she was at or I wouldn't have said, 'Good evening, Mrs Travis.' She jumped a little as she turned and dropped her handkerchief, and when I picked it up I found it soaked with tears—it was like holding a small drowned animal in my hand. I said, 'I'm sorry,' meaning that I was sorry to have startled her, but she took it in quite another sense. She said, 'Oh, I'm being silly, that's all. It's just a mood. Everybody has moods, don't they?'

'Where's Peter?'

'He's in the museum with Stephen and Tony looking at the Picassos. I don't understand them a bit.'

'That's nothing to be ashamed of. Lots of people don't.'

'But Peter doesn't understand them either. I know he doesn't. He's just pretending to be interested.'

'Oh well . . .'

'And it's not that either. I pretended for a time too, to please Stephen. But he's pretending just to get away from me.'

'You are imagining things.'

Punctually at five o'clock the *phare* lit up, but it was still too light to see the beam.

I said, 'The museum will be closing now.'

'Walk back with me to the hotel.'

'Wouldn't you like to wait for Peter?'

'I don't smell, do I?' she asked miserably.

'Well, there's a trace of Arpège. I've always liked Arpège.'

'How terribly experienced you sound.'

'Not really. It's just that my first wife used to buy Arpège.'

We began walking back, and the mistral bit our ears and gave her an excuse when the time came for the reddened eyes.

She said, 'I think Antibes so sad and grey.'

'I thought you enjoyed it here.'

'Oh, for a day or two.'

'Why not go home?'

'It would look odd, wouldn't it, returning early from a honeymoon?'

'Or go on to Rome—or somewhere. You can get a plane to most places from Nice.'

'It wouldn't make any difference,' she said. 'It's not the place that's wrong, it's me.'

'I don't understand.'

'He's not happy with me. It's as simple as that.'

She stopped opposite one of the little rock houses by the ramparts. Washing hung down over the street below and there was a cold-looking canary in a cage.

'You said yourself . . . a mood . . .'

'It's not his fault,' she said. 'It's me. I expect it seems very stupid to you, but I never slept with anyone before I married.' She gulped miserably at the canary.

'And Peter?'

'He's terribly sensitive,' she said, and added quickly, 'That's a good quality. I wouldn't have fallen in love with him if he hadn't been.'

'If I were you, I'd take him home—as quickly as possible.' I couldn't help the words sounding sinister, but she hardly heard them. She was listening to the voices that came nearer down the ramparts—to Stephen's gay laugh. 'They're very sweet,' she said. 'I'm glad he's found friends.'

How could I say that they were seducing Peter before her eyes? And in any case wasn't her mistake already irretrievable? Those were two of the questions which haunted the hours, dreary for a solitary man, of the middle afternoon when work is finished and the exhilaration of the wine at lunch, and the time for the first evening drink has not yet come and the winter heating is at its feeblest. Had she no idea of the nature of the young man she had married? Had he taken her on as a blind or as a last desperate throw for normality? I couldn't bring myself to believe that. There was a sort of innocence about the boy which seemed to justify her love, and I preferred to think that he was not yet fully formed, that he had married honestly and it was only now that he found himself on the brink of a different experience. And yet if that were the case the comedy was all the crueller. Would everything have gone normally well if some conjunction of the planets had not crossed their honeymoon with that hungry pair of hunters?

I longed to speak out, and in the end I did speak, but not, so it happened, to her. I was going to my room and the door of one of theirs was open and I heard again Stephen's laugh—a kind of laugh which is sometimes with unintentional irony called infectious; it maddened me. I knocked and went in. Tony was stretched on a double bed and Stephen was 'doing' his hair, holding a brush in each hand and meticulously arranging the grey waves on either side. The dressing-table had as many pots on it as a woman's.

'You really mean he told you that?' Tony was saying. 'Why, how are you, William? Come in. Our young friend has been confiding in Stephen. Such really fascinating things.'

'Which of your young friends?' I asked.

'Why, Peter, of course. Who else? The secrets of married life.'

'I thought it might have been your sailor.'

'Naughty!' Tony said. 'But touché too, of course.'

'I wish you'd leave Peter alone.'

'I don't think he'd like that,' Stephen said. 'You can see that he hasn't quite the right tastes for this sort of honeymoon.'

'Now you happen to like women, William,' Tony said. 'Why not go after the girl? It's a grand opportunity. She's not getting what I believe is vulgarly called her greens.' Of the two he was easily the more brutal. I wanted to hit him, but this is not the century for that kind of romantic gesture, and anyway he was stretched out flat upon the bed. I said feebly enough—I ought to have known better than to have entered into a debate with those two—'She happens to be in love with him.'

'I think Tony is right and she would find more satisfaction with you, William dear,' Stephen said, giving a last flick to the hair over his right ear—the contusion was quite gone now. 'From what Peter has said to me, I think you'd be doing a favour to both of them.'

'Tell him what Peter said, Stephen.'

'He said that from the very first there was a kind of hungry femininity about her which he found frightening and repulsive. Poor boy—he was really trapped into this business of marriage. His father wanted heirs—he breeds horses too, and then her mother—there's quite a lot of lucre with that lot. I don't think he had any idea of—of the Shape of Things to Come.' Stephen shuddered into the glass and then regarded himself with satisfaction.

Even today I have to believe for my own peace of mind that the young man had not really said those monstrous things. I believe, and hope, that the words were put into his mouth by that cunning dramatizer, but there is little comfort in the thought, for Stephen's inventions were always true to character. He even saw through my apparent indifference to the girl and realized that Tony and he had gone too far; it would suit their purpose, if I were driven to the wrong kind of action, or if, by their crudities, I lost my interest in Poopy.

'Of course,' Stephen said, 'I'm exaggerating. Undoubtedly he felt a bit amorous before it came to the point. His father would describe her, I suppose, as a fine filly.'

'What do you plan to do with him?' I asked. 'Do you toss up, or does one of you take the head and the other the tail?'

Tony laughed. 'Good old William. What a clinical mind you have.'

'And suppose,' I said, 'I went to her and recounted this conversation?'

'My dear, she wouldn't even understand. She's incredibly innocent.'

'Isn't he?'

'I doubt it—knowing our friend Colin Winstanley. But it's still a moot point. He hasn't given himself away yet.'

'We are planning to put it to the test one day soon,' Stephen said.

'A drive in the country,' Tony said. 'The strain's telling on him, you can see that. He's even afraid to take a siesta for fear of unwanted attentions.'

'Haven't you *any* mercy?' It was an absurd old-fashioned word to use to those two sophisticates. I felt more than ever square. 'Doesn't it occur to you that you may ruin her life—for the sake of your little game?'

'We can depend on you, William,' Tony said, 'to give her creature comforts.'

Stephen said, 'It's no game. You should realize we are saving *him*. Think of the life that he would lead—with all those soft contours lapping him around.' He added, 'Women always remind me of a damp salad—you know, those faded bits of greenery positively swimming . . .'

'Every man to his taste,' Tony said. 'But Peter's not cut out for that sort of life. He's very sensitive,' he said, using the girl's own words. There wasn't any more I could think of to say.

5

You will notice that I play a very unheroic part in this comedy. I could have gone direct, I suppose, to the girl and given her a little lecture on the facts of life, beginning gently with the régime of an English public school—he had worn a scarf of old-boy colours, until Tony had said to him one day at breakfast that he thought the puce stripe was an error of judgement. Or perhaps I could have protested to the boy himself, but, if Stephen had spoken the truth and he was under a severe nervous strain, my intervention would hardly have helped to ease it. There was no move I could make. I had just to sit there and watch while they made the moves carefully and adroitly towards the climax.

It came three days later at breakfast when, as usual, she was sitting alone with them, while her husband was upstairs with his lotions. They had never been more charming or more entertaining. As I arrived at my table they were giving her a really funny description of a house in Kensington that they had decorated for a dowager duchess who was passionately interested in the Napoleonic wars. There was an ashtray, I remember, made out of a horse's hoof, guaranteed—so the dealer said—by Apsley House to have belonged to a grey ridden by Wellington at the Battle of Waterloo; there was an umbrella stand made out of a shellcase found on the field of Austerlitz; a fire-escape made of a scaling ladder from Badajoz. She had lost half that sense of strain listening to them. She had forgotten her rolls and coffee; Stephen had her complete attention. I wanted to say to her, 'You little owl.' I wouldn't have been insulting her—she *had* got rather large eyes.

And then Stephen produced the master-plan. I could tell it was coming by the way his hands stiffened on his coffee-cup, by the way Tony lowered his eyes and appeared to be praying over his *croissant*. 'We were wondering, Poopy—may we borrow your husband?' I have never heard words spoken with more elaborate casualness.

She laughed. She hadn't noticed a thing. 'Borrow my husband?'

'There's a little village in the mountains behind Monte Carlo—Peille it's called—and I've heard rumours of a devastatingly lovely old bureau there—not for sale, of course, but Tony and I, we have our winning ways.'

'I've noticed that,' she said, 'myself.'

Stephen for an instant was disconcerted, but she meant nothing by it, except perhaps a compliment.

'We were thinking of having lunch at Peille and passing the whole day on the road so as to take a look at the scenery. The only trouble is there's no room in the Sprite for more than three, but Peter was saying the other day that you wanted some time to have a hair-do, so we thought . . .'

I had the impression that he was talking far too much to be convincing, but there wasn't any need for him to worry: she saw nothing at all. 'I think it's a marvellous idea,' she said. 'You know, he needs a little holiday from me. He's had hardly a moment to himself since I came up the aisle.' She was magnificently sensible, and perhaps even relieved. Poor girl. She needed a little holiday, too.

'It's going to be excruciatingly uncomfortable. He'll have to sit on Tony's knee.'

'I don't suppose he'll mind that.'

'And, of course, we can't guarantee the quality of food en route.'

For the first time I saw Stephen as a stupid man. Was there a shade of hope in that?

In the long run, of the two, notwithstanding his brutality, Tony had the better brain. Before Stephen had time to speak once more, Tony raised his eyes from the *croissant* and said decisively, 'That's fine. All's settled, and we'll deliver him back in one piece by dinner-time.'

He looked challengingly across at me. 'Of course, we hate to leave you alone for lunch, but I am sure William will look after you.'

'William?' she asked, and I hated the way she looked at me as if I didn't exist. 'Oh, you mean Mr Harris?'

I invited her to have lunch with me at Lou-Lou's in the old port—I couldn't very well do anything else—and at that moment the laggard Peter came out on to the terrace. She said quickly, 'I don't want to interrupt your work . . .'

'I don't believe in starvation,' I said. 'Work has to be interrupted for meals.'

Peter had cut himself again shaving and had a large blob of cottonwool stuck on his chin: it reminded me of Stephen's contusion. I had the impression, while he stood there waiting for someone to say something to him, that he knew all about the conversation; it had been carefully rehearsed by all three, the parts allotted, the unconcerned manner practised well before-hand, even the bit about the food . . . Now somebody had missed a cue, so I spoke.

'I've asked your wife to lunch at Lou-Lou's,' I said. 'I hope you don't mind.'

I would have been amused by the expression of quick relief on all three faces if I had found it possible to be amused by anything at all in the situation.

6

'And you didn't marry again after she left?'

'By that time I was getting too old to marry.'

'Picasso does it.'

'Oh, I'm not quite as old as Picasso.'

The silly conversation went on against a background of fishing-nets draped over a wallpaper with a design of wine-bottles—interior decoration again. Sometimes I longed for a room which had simply grown that way like the lines on a human face. The fish soup steamed away between us, smelling of garlic. We were the only guests there. Perhaps it was the solitude, perhaps it was the directness of her question, perhaps it was only the effect of the *rosé*, but quite suddenly I had the comforting sense that we were intimate friends. 'There's always work,' I said, 'and wine and a good cheese.'

'I couldn't be that philosophical if I lost Peter.'

'That's not likely to happen, is it?'

'I think I'd die,' she said, 'like someone in Christina Rossetti.'

'I thought nobody of your generation read her.'

If I had been twenty years older, perhaps, I could have ex-plained that nothing is quite as bad as that, that at the end of what is called 'the sexual life' the only love which has lasted is the love that has accepted everything, every disappointment, every failure and every betrayal, which has accepted even the sad fact that in the end there is no desire so deep as the simple desire for companionship.

She wouldn't have believed me. She said, 'I used to weep like anything at that poem about "Passing Away". Do you write sad things?'

'The biography I am writing now is sad enough. Two people tied together by love and yet one of them incapable of fidelity. The man dead of old age, burnt-out, at less than forty, and a fashionable preacher lurking by the bedside to snatch his soul. No privacy even for a dying man: the bishop wrote a book about it.'

An Englishman who kept a chandlers' shop in the old port was talking at the bar, and two old women who were part of the family knitted at the end of the room. A dog trotted in and looked at us and went away again with its tail curled.

'How long ago did all that happen?'

'Nearly three hundred years.'

'It sounded quite contemporary. Only now it would be the man from the *Mirror* and not a bishop.'

'That's why I wanted to write it. I'm not really interested in the past. I don't like costume-pieces.'

Winning someone's confidence is rather like the way some men set about seducing a woman; they circle a long way from their true purpose, they try to interest and amuse until finally the moment comes to strike. It came, so I wrongly thought, when I was adding up the bill. She said, 'I wonder where Peter is at this moment,' and I was quick to reply, 'What's going wrong between the two of you?'

She said, 'Let's go.'

'I've got to wait for my change.'

It was always easier to get served at Lou-Lou's than to pay the bill. At that moment everyone always had a habit of disappearing: the old woman (her knitting abandoned on the table), the aunt who helped to serve, Lou-Lou herself, her husband in his blue sweater. If the dog hadn't gone already he would have left at that moment.

I said, 'You forget—you told me that he wasn't happy.'

'Please, please find someone and let's go.'

So I disinterred Lou-Lou's aunt from the kitchen and paid. When we left, everyone seemed to be back again, even the dog.

Outside I asked her whether she wanted to return to the hotel.

'Not just yet—but I'm keeping you from your work.'

'I never work after drinking. That's why I like to start early. It brings the first drink nearer.'

She said that she had seen nothing of Antibes but the ramparts and the beach and the lighthouse, so I walked her around the small narrow backstreets where the washing hung out of the windows as in Naples and there were glimpses of small rooms overflowing with children and grandchildren; stone scrolls were carved over the ancient doorways of what had once been noblemen's houses; the pavements were blocked by barrels of wine and the streets by children playing at ball. In a low room on a ground floor a man sat painting the horrible ceramics which would later go to Vallauris to be sold to tourists in Picasso's old stamping-ground—spotted pink frogs and mauve fish and pigs with slits for coins.

She said, 'Let's go back to the sea.' So we returned to a patch of hot sun on the bastion, and again I was tempted to tell her what I feared, but the thought that she might watch me with the blankness of ignorance deterred me. She sat on the wall and her long legs in the tight black trousers dangled down like Christmas stockings. She said, 'I'm not sorry that I married Peter,' and I was reminded of a song Edith Piaf used to sing, *'Je ne regrette rien'*. It is typical of such a phrase that it is always sung or spoken with defiance.

I could only say again, 'You ought to take him home,' but I wondered what would have happened if I had said, 'You are married to a man who only likes men and he's off now picnicking with his boy friends. I'm thirty years older than you, but at least I have always preferred women and I've fallen in love with you and we could still have a few good years together before the time comes when you want to leave me for a younger man.' All I said was, 'He probably misses the country—and the riding.'

'I wish you were right, but it's really worse than that.'

Had she, after all, realized the nature of her problem? I waited for her to explain her meaning. It was a little like a novel which hesitates on the verge between comedy and tragedy. If she recognized the situation it would be a tragedy; if she were ignorant it was a comedy, even a farce—a situation between an immature girl too innocent to understand and a man too old to have the courage to explain. I suppose I have a taste for tragedy. I hoped for that.

She said, 'We didn't really know each other much before we came here. You know, weekend parties and the odd theatre—and riding, of course.'

I wasn't sure where her remarks tended. I said, 'These occasions are nearly always a strain. You are picked out of ordinary life and dumped together after an elaborate ceremony—almost like two animals shut in a cage who haven't seen each other before.'

'And now he sees me he doesn't like me.'

'You are exaggerating.'

'No.' She added, with anxiety, 'I won't shock you, will I, if I tell you things? There's nobody else I can talk to.'

'After fifty years I'm guaranteed shockproof.'

'We haven't made love—properly, once, since we came here.'

'What do you mean—properly?'

'He starts, but he doesn't finish; nothing happens.'

I said uncomfortably, 'Rochester wrote about that. A poem called "The Imperfect Enjoyment".' I don't know why I gave her this shady piece of literary information; perhaps, like a psychoanalyst, I wanted her not to feel alone with her problem. 'It can happen to anybody.'

'But it's not his fault,' she said. 'It's mine. I know it is. He just doesn't like my body.'

'Surely it's a bit late to discover that.'

'He'd never seen me naked till I came here,' she said with the candour of a girl to her doctor—that was all I meant to her, I felt sure.

'There are nearly always first-night nerves. And then if a man worries (you must realize how much it hurts his pride) he can get stuck in the situation for days—weeks even.' I began to tell her about a mistress I once had—we stayed together a very long time and yet for two weeks at the beginning I could do nothing at all. 'I was too anxious to succeed.'

'That's different. You didn't hate the sight of her.'

'You are making such a lot of so little.'

'That's what he tries to do,' she said with sudden schoolgirl coarseness and giggled miserably.

'We went away for a week and changed the scene, and everything after that was all right. For ten days it had been a flop, and for ten years afterwards we were happy. Very happy. But worry can get established in a room, in the colour of the curtains—it can hang itself up on coat-hangers; you find it smoking away in the ashtray marked Pernod, and when you look at the bed it pokes its head out from underneath like the toes of a pair of shoes.' Again I repeated the only charm I could think of. 'Take him home.'

'It wouldn't make any difference. He's disappointed, that's all it is.' She looked down at her long black legs; I followed the course of her eyes because I was finding now that I really wanted her and she said with sincere conviction, 'I'm just not pretty enough when I'm undressed.'

'You are talking real nonsense. You don't know what nonsense you are talking.'

'Oh no, I'm not. You see—it started all right, but then he touched me'—she put her hands on her breasts—'and it all went wrong. I always knew they weren't much good. At school we used to have dormitory inspection—it was awful. Everybody could grow them big except me. I'm no Jayne Mansfield, I can tell you.' She gave again that mirthless giggle. 'I remember one of the girls told me to sleep with a pillow on top—they said they'd struggle for release and what they needed was exercise. But of course it didn't work. I doubt if the idea was very scientific.' She added, 'I remember it was awfully hot at night like that.'

'Peter doesn't strike me,' I said cautiously, 'as a man who would want a Jayne Mansfield.'

'But you understand, don't you, that, if he finds me ugly, it's all so hopeless.'

I wanted to agree with her—perhaps this reason which she had thought up would be less distressing than the truth, and soon enough there would be someone to cure her distrust. I had noticed before that it is often the lovely women who have the least confidence in their looks, but all the same I couldn't pretend to her that I understood it her way. I said, 'You must trust me.

There's nothing at all wrong with you and that's why I'm talking to you the way I am.'

'You are very sweet,' she said, and her eyes passed over me rather as the beam from the lighthouse which at night went past the Musée Grimaldi and after a certain time returned and brushed all our windows indifferently on the hotel front. She continued, 'He said they'd be back by cocktail-time.'

'If you want a rest first'—for a little time we had been close, but now again we were getting further and further away. If I pressed her now she might in the end be happy—does conventional morality demand that a girl remains tied as she was tied? They'd been married in church; she was probably a good Christian, and I knew the ecclesiastical rules: at this moment of her life she could be free of him, the marriage could be annulled, but in a day or two it was only too probable that the same rules would say, 'He's managed well enough, you are married for life.'

And yet I couldn't press her. Wasn't I after all assuming far too much? Perhaps it was only a question of first-night nerves; perhaps in a little while the three of them would be back, silent, embarrassed, and Tony in his turn would have a contusion on his cheek. I would have been very glad to see it there; egotism fades a little with the passions which engender it, and I would have been content, I think, just to see her happy.

So we returned to the hotel, not saying much, and she went to her room and I to mine. It was in the end a comedy and not a tragedy, a farce even, which is why I have given this scrap of reminiscence a farcical title.

7

I was woken from my middle-aged siesta by the telephone. For a moment, surprised by the darkness, I couldn't find the light-switch. Scrambling for it, I knocked over my bedside lamp—the telephone went on ringing, and I tried to pick up the holder and knocked over a tooth-glass in which I had given myself a whisky. The little illuminated dial of my watch gleamed up at me marking

8.30. The telephone continued to ring. I got the receiver off, but this time it was the ashtray which fell over. I couldn't get the cord to extend up to my ear, so I shouted in the direction of the telephone, 'Hullo!'

A tiny sound came up from the floor which I interpreted as 'Is that William?'

I shouted, 'Hold on,' and now that I was properly awake I realized the light-switch was just over my head (in London it was placed over the bedside table). Little petulant noises came up from the floor as I put on the light, like the creaking of crickets.

'Who's that?' I said rather angrily, and then I recognized Tony's voice.

'William, whatever's the matter?'

'Nothing's the matter. Where are you?'

'But there was quite an enormous crash. It hurt my eardrum.'

'An ashtray,' I said.

'Do you usually hurl ashtrays around?'

'I was asleep.'

'At 8.30? William! William!'

I said, 'Where are you?'

'A little bar in what Mrs Clarenty would call Monty.'

'You promised to be back by dinner,' I said.

'That's why I'm telephoning you. I'm being, *responsible*, William. Do you mind telling Poopy that we'll be a little late? Give her dinner. Talk to her as only you know how. We'll be back by ten.'

'Has there been an accident?'

I could hear him chuckling up the phone. 'Oh, I wouldn't call it an accident.'

'Why doesn't Peter call her himself?'

'He says he's not in the mood.'

'But what shall I tell her?' The telephone went dead.

I got out of bed and dressed and then I called her room. She answered very quickly; I think she must have been sitting by the telephone. I relayed the message, asked her to meet me in the bar, and rang off before I had to face answering any questions.

But I found it was not so difficult as I feared to cover up; she was immensely relieved that somebody had telephoned. She had sat there in her room from half-past seven onwards thinking of all the dangerous turns and ravines on the Grande Corniche, and when I rang she was half afraid that it might be the police or a hospital. Only after she had drunk two dry Martinis and laughed quite a lot at her fears did she say, 'I wonder why Tony rang you and not Peter me?'

I said (I had been working the answer out), 'I gather he suddenly had an urgent appointment—in the loo.'

It was as though I had said something enormously witty.

'Do you think they are a bit tight?' she asked.

'I wouldn't wonder.'

'Darling Peter,' she said, 'he deserved the day off,' and I couldn't help wondering in what direction his merit lay.

'Do you want another Martini?'

'I'd better not,' she said, 'you've made me tight too.'

I had become tired of the thin cold *rosé* so we had a bottle of real wine at dinner and she drank her full share and talked about literature. She had, it seemed, a nostalgia for Dornford Yates, had graduated in the sixth form as far as Hugh Walpole, and now she talked respectfully about Sir Charles Snow, who she obviously thought had been knighted, like Sir Hugh, for his services to literature. I must have been very much in love or I would have found her innocence almost unbearable—or perhaps I was a little tight as well. All the same, it was to interrupt her flow of critical judgements that I asked her what her real name was and she replied, 'Everyone calls me Poopy.' I remembered the PT stamped on her bags, but the only real names that I could think of at the moment were Patricia and Prunella. 'Then I shall simply call you You,' I said.

After dinner I had brandy and she had a kümmel. It was past 10.30 and still the three had not returned, but she didn't seem to be worrying any more about them. She sat on the floor of the bar beside me and every now and then the waiter looked in to see if he could turn off the lights. She leant against me with her hand on my knee and she said such things as 'It must be wonderful to be a writer', and in the glow of brandy and tenderness I didn't mind them a bit. I even began to tell her again about the Earl of Rochester. What did I care about Dornford Yates, Hugh Walpole or Sir Charles Snow? I was even in the mood to recite to her, hopelessly inapposite to the situation though the lines were:

> Then talk not of Inconstancy,
> False Hearts, and broken Vows;
> If I, by Miracle, can be
> This live-long Minute true to thee,
> 'Tis all that Heav'n allows

when the noise—what a noise!—of the Sprite approaching brought us both to our feet. It was only too true that all that heaven allowed was the time in the bar at Antibes.

Tony was singing; we heard him all the way up the Boulevard Général Leclerc; Stephen was driving with the greatest caution, most of the time in second gear, and Peter, as we saw when we came out on to the terrace, was sitting on Tony's knee—nestling would be a better description—and joining in the refrain. All I could make out was

> 'Round and white
> On a winter's night,
> The hope of the Queen's Navee.'

If they hadn't seen us on the steps I think they would have driven past the hotel without noticing.

'You *are* tight,' the girl said with pleasure. Tony put his arm round her and ran her up to the top of the steps. 'Be careful,' she said, 'William's made me tight too.'

'Good old William.'

Stephen climbed carefully out of the car and sank down on the nearest chair.

'All well?' I asked, not knowing what I meant.

'The children have been very happy,' he said, 'and very, very relaxed.'

'Got to go to the loo,' Peter said (the cue was in the wrong place), and made for the stairs. The girl gave him a helping hand and I heard him say, 'Wonderful day. Wonderful scenery. Wonderful . . .' She turned at the top of the stairs and swept us with her

smile, gay, reassured, happy. As on the first night, when they had
hesitated about the cocktail, they didn't come down again. There
was a long silence and then Tony chuckled. 'You seem to have had
a wonderful day,' I said.

'Dear William, we've done a very good action. You've never
seen him so *détendu*.'

Stephen sat saying nothing; I had the impression that today
hadn't gone quite so well for him. Can people ever hunt quite
equally in couples or is there always a loser? The too-grey waves
of hair were as immaculate as ever, there was no contusion on
the cheek, but I had the impression that the fear of the future had
cast a long shadow.

'I suppose you mean you got him drunk?'

'Not with alcohol,' Tony said. 'We aren't vulgar seducers, are
we, Stephen?' But Stephen made no reply.

'Then what was your good action?'

'*Le pauvre petit Pierre.* He was in such a state. He had quite
convinced himself—or perhaps she had convinced him—that he
was *impuissant*.'

'You seem to be making a lot of progress in French.'

'It sounds more delicate in French.'

'And with your help he found he wasn't?'

'After a little virginal timidity. Or near virginal. School hadn't
left him quite unmoved. Poor Poopy. She just hadn't known the
right way to go about things. My dear, he has a superb virility.
Where are you going, Stephen?'

'I'm going to bed,' Stephen said flatly, and went up the steps
alone. Tony looked after him, I thought with a kind of tender
regret, a very light and superficial sorrow. 'His rheumatism
came back very badly this afternoon,' he said. 'Poor Stephen.'

I thought it was well then to go to bed before I should become
'Poor William' too. Tony's charity tonight was all-embracing.

8

It was the first morning for a long time that I found myself alone
on the terrace for breakfast. The women in tweed skirts had been

gone for some days, and I had never before known 'the young men' to be absent. It was easy enough, while I waited for my coffee, to speculate about the likely reasons. There was, for example, the rheumatism . . . though I couldn't quite picture Tony in the character of a bedside companion. It was even remotely possible that they felt some shame and were unwilling to be confronted by their victim. As for the victim, I wondered sadly what painful revelation the night would certainly have brought. I blamed myself more than ever for not speaking in time. Surely she would have learned the truth more gently from me than from some tipsy uncontrolled outburst of her husband. All the same—such egoists are we in our passions—I was glad to be there in attendance . . . to staunch the tears . . . to take her tenderly in my arms, comfort her . . . oh, I had quite a romantic day-dream on the terrace before she came down the steps and I saw that she had never had less need of a comforter.

She was just as I had seen her the first night: shy, excited, gay, with a long and happy future established in her eyes. 'William,' she said, 'can I sit at your table? Do you mind?'

'Of course not.'

'You've been so patient with me all the time I was in the doldrums. I've talked an awful lot of nonsense to you. I know you told me it was nonsense, but I didn't believe you and you were right all the time.'

I couldn't have interrupted her even if I had tried. She was a Venus at the prow sailing through sparkling seas. She said, 'Everything's all right. Everything. Last night—he loves me, William. He really does. He's not a bit disappointed with me. He was just tired and strained, that's all. He needed a day off alone—*détendu*.' She was even picking up Tony's French expressions second-hand. 'I'm afraid of nothing now, nothing at all. Isn't it strange how black life seemed only two days ago? I really believe if it hadn't been for you I'd have thrown in my hand. How lucky I was to meet you and the others too. They're such wonderful friends for Peter. We are all going home next week— and we've made a lovely plot together. Tony's going to come down almost immediately we get back and decorate our house. Yesterday, driving in the country, they had a wonderful discussion about it. You won't know our house when you see it—oh, I forgot, you never *have* seen it, have you? You must come down when it's all finished—with Stephen.'

'Isn't Stephen going to help?' I just managed to slip in.

'Oh, he's too busy at the moment, Tony says, with Mrs Clarenty. Do you like riding? Tony does. He adores horses, but he has so little chance in London. It will be wonderful for Peter—to have someone like that because, after all, I can't be riding with Peter all day long, there will be a lot of things to do in the house, especially now, when I'm not accustomed. It's wonderful to think that Peter won't have to be lonely. He says there are going to be Etruscan murals in the bathroom—whatever Etruscan means; the drawing-room *basically* will be eggshell green and the dining-room walls Pompeian red. They really did an awful lot of work yesterday afternoon—I mean in their heads, while we were glooming around. I said to Peter, "As things are going now we'd better be prepared for a nursery," but Peter said Tony was content to leave all that side to me. Then there are the stables: they were an old coach-house once, and Tony feels we could restore a lot of the ancient character and there's a lamp he bought in St Paul which will just fit . . . it's endless the things there are to be done—a good six months' work, so Tony says, but luckily he can leave Mrs Clarenty to Stephen and concentrate on us. Peter asked him about the garden, but he's not a specialist in gardens. He said, "Everyone to his own métier", and he's quite content if I bring in a man who knows all about roses.

'He knows Colin Winstanley too, of course, so there'll be quite a band of us. It's a pity the house won't be all ready for Christmas, but Peter says he's certain to have wonderful ideas for a really original tree. Peter thinks . . .'

She went on and on like that; perhaps I ought to have interrupted her even then; perhaps I should have tried to explain to her why her dream wouldn't last. Instead, I sat there silent, and presently I went to my room and packed—there was still one hotel open in the abandoned fun-fair of Juan between Maxim's and the boarded-up Striptease.

If I had stayed . . . who knows whether he could have kept on pretending for a second night? But I was just as bad for her as he was. If he had the wrong hormones, I had the wrong age. I didn't see any of them again before I left. She and Peter and Tony were out somewhere in the Sprite, and Stephen—so the receptionist told me—was lying late in bed with his rheumatism.

I planned a note for her, explaining rather feebly my departure, but when I came to write it I realized I had still no other name with which to address her than Poopy.

BEAUTY

The woman wore an orange scarf which she had so twisted around her forehead that it looked like a toque of the twenties, and her voice bulldozed through all opposition—the speech of her two companions, the young motor-cyclist revving outside, even the clatter of soup plates in the kitchen of the small Antibes restaurant which was almost empty now that autumn had truly set in. Her face was familiar to me; I had seen it looking down from the balcony of one of the reconditioned houses on the ramparts, while she called endearments to someone or something invisible below. But I hadn't seen her since the summer sun had gone, and I thought she had departed with the other foreigners. She said, 'I'll be in Vienna for Christmas. I just love it there. Those lovely white horses—and the little boys singing Bach.'

Her companions were English; the man was struggling still to maintain the appearance of a summer visitor, but he shivered in secret every now and then in his blue cotton sports-shirt. He asked throatily, 'We won't see you then in London?' and his wife, who was much younger than either of them, said, 'Oh, but you simply must come.'

'There are difficulties,' she said. 'But if you two dear people are going to be in Venice in the spring . . .'

'I don't suppose we'll have enough money, will we, darling, but we'd love to show you London. Wouldn't we, darling?'

'Of course,' he said gloomily.

'I'm afraid that's quite, quite impossible, because of Beauty, you see.'

I hadn't noticed Beauty until then because he was so well-behaved. He lay flat on the window-sill as inert as a cream bun on a counter. I think he was the most perfect Pekinese I have ever seen—although I can't pretend to know the points a judge ought to look for. He would have been as white as milk if a little coffee had not been added, but that was hardly an imperfection—it enhanced his beauty. His eyes from where I sat seemed deep black, like the centre of a flower, and they were completely undisturbed by thought. This was not a dog to respond to the word 'rat' or to show a youthful enthusiasm if someone suggested a walk. Nothing less than his own image in a glass would rouse him, I imagined, to a flicker of interest. He was certainly well-fed enough to ignore the meal that the others had left unfinished, though perhaps he was accustomed to something richer than *langouste*.

'You couldn't leave him with a friend?' the younger woman asked.

'Leave Beauty?' The question didn't rate a reply. She ran her fingers through the long *café-au-lait* hair, but the dog made no motion with his tail as a common dog might have done. He gave a kind of grunt like an old man in a club who has been disturbed by the waiter. 'All these laws of quarantine—why don't your congressmen do something about them?'

'We call them MPs,' the man said with what I thought was hidden dislike.

'I don't care what you call them. They live in the Middle Ages. I can go to Paris, to Vienna, Venice—why, I could go to Moscow if I wanted, but I can't go to London without leaving Beauty in a horrible prison. With all kinds of undesirable dogs.'

'I think he'd have,' he hesitated with what I thought was admirable English courtesy as he weighed in the balance the correct term—cell? kennel?—'a room of his own.'

'Think of the diseases he might pick up.' She lifted him from the window-sill as easily as she might have lifted a stole of fur and pressed him resolutely against her left breast; he didn't even grunt. I had the sense of something completely possessed. A child at least would have rebelled . . . for a time. Poor child. I don't know why I couldn't pity the dog. Perhaps he was too beautiful.

She said, 'Poor Beauty's thirsty.'

'I'll get him some water,' the man said.

'A half-bottle of Evian if you don't mind. I don't trust the tap-water.'

It was then that I left them, because the cinema in the Place de Gaulle opened at nine.

It was after eleven that I emerged again, and, since the night was fine, except for a cold wind off the Alps, I made a circuit from the Place and, as the ramparts would be too exposed, I took the narrow dirty streets off the Place Nationale—the Rue de Sade, the Rue des Bains . . . The dustbins were all out and dogs had made ordure on the pavements and children had urinated in the gutters. A patch of white, which I first took to be a cat, moved stealthily along the house-fronts ahead of me, then paused, and as I approached snaked behind a dustbin. I stood amazed and watched. A pattern of light through the slats of a shutter striped the road in yellow tigerish bars and presently Beauty slid out again and looked at me with his pansy face and black expressionless eyes. I think he expected me to lift him up, and he showed his teeth in warning.

'Why, Beauty,' I exclaimed. He gave his clubman grunt again and waited. Was he cautious because he found that I knew his name or did he recognize in my clothes and my smell that I belonged to the same class as the woman in the toque, that I was one who would disapprove of his nocturnal ramble? Suddenly he cocked an ear in the direction of the house on the ramparts; it was possible that he had heard a woman's voice calling. Certainly he looked dubiously up at me as though he wanted to see whether I had heard it too, and perhaps because I made no move he considered he was safe. He began to undulate down the pavement with a purpose, like the feather boa in the cabaret act which floats around seeking a top-hat. I followed at a discreet distance.

Was it memory or a keen sense of smell which affected him? Of all the dustbins in the mean street there was only one which had lost its cover—indescribable tendrils drooped over the top.

Beauty—he ignored me as completely now as he would have ignored an inferior dog—stood on his hind legs with two delicately feathered paws holding the edge of the bin. He turned his head and looked at me, without expression, two pools of ink in which a soothsayer perhaps could have read an infinite series of predictions. He gave a scramble like an athlete raising himself on a parallel bar, and he was within the dustbin, and the feathered forepaws—I am sure I have read somewhere that the feathering is very important in a contest of Pekinese—were rooting and delving among the old vegetables, the empty cartons, the squashy fragments in the bin. He became excited and his nose went down like a pig after truffles. Then his back paws got into play, discarding the rubbish behind—old fruit-skins fell on the pavement and rotten figs, fish-heads . . . At last he had what he had come for—a long tube of intestine belonging to God knows what animal; he tossed it in the air, so that it curled round the milk-white throat. Then he abandoned the dustbin, and he galumphed down the street like a harlequin, trailing behind him the intestine which might have been a string of sausages.

I must admit I was wholly on his side. Surely anything was better than the embrace of a flat breast.

Round a turning he found a dark corner obviously more suited than all the others to gnawing an intestine because it contained a great splash of ordure. He tested the ordure first, like the clubman he was, with his nostrils, and then he rolled lavishly back on it, paws in the air, rubbing the *café-au-lait* fur in the dark shampoo, the intestines trailing from his mouth, while the satin eyes gazed imperturbably up at the great black Midi sky.

Curiosity took me back home, after all, by way of the ramparts, and there over the balcony the woman leant, trying, I suppose, to detect her dog in the shadows of the street below. 'Beauty!' I heard her call wearily, 'Beauty!' And then with growing impatience, 'Beauty! Come home! You've done your wee-wee, Beauty. Where are you, Beauty, Beauty?' Such small things ruin our sense of compassion, for surely, if it had not been for that hideous orange toque, I would have felt some pity for the old sterile thing, perched up there, calling for lost Beauty.

CHAGRIN IN THREE PARTS

It was February in Antibes. Gusts of rain blew along the ramparts, and the emaciated statues on the terrace of the Château Grimaldi dripped with wet, and there was a sound absent during the flat blue days of summer, the continual rustle below the ramparts of the small surf. All along the Côte the summer restaurants were closed, but lights shone in Félix au Port and one Peugeot of the latest model stood in the parking-rank. The bare masts of the abandoned yachts stuck up like tooth-picks and the last plane in the winter-service dropped, in a flicker of green, red and yellow lights, like Christmas-tree baubles, towards the airport of Nice. This was the Antibes I always enjoyed; and I was disappointed to find I was not alone in the restaurant as I was most nights of the week.

Crossing the road I saw a very powerful lady dressed in black who stared out at me from one of the window-tables, as though she were willing me not to enter, and when I came in and took my place before the other window, she regarded me with too evident distaste. My raincoat was shabby and my shoes were muddy and in any case I was a man. Momentarily, while she took me in, from balding top to shabby toe, she interrupted her conversation with the *patronne* who addressed her as Madame Dejoie.

Madame Dejoie continued her monologue in a tone of firm disapproval: it was unusual for Madame Volet to be late, but she hoped nothing had happened to her on the ramparts. In winter there were always Algerians about, she added with mysterious apprehension, as though she were talking of wolves, but nonetheless Madame Volet had refused Madame Dejoie's offer to

be fetched from her home. 'I did not press her under the circumstances. Poor Madame Volet.' Her hand clutched a huge pepper-
mill like a bludgeon and I pictured Madame Volet as a weak
timid old lady, dressed too in black, afraid even of protection by
so formidable a friend.

How wrong I was. Madame Volet blew suddenly in with a
gust of rain through the side door beside my table, and she was
young and extravagantly pretty, in her tight black pants, and
with a long neck emerging from a wine-red polo-necked sweater.
I was glad when she sat down side by side with Madame Dejoie,
so that I need not lose the sight of her while I ate.

'I am late,' she said, 'I know that I am late. So many little
things have to be done when you are alone, and I am not yet accustomed to being alone,' she added with a pretty little sob
which reminded me of a cut-glass Victorian tear-bottle. She took
off thick winter gloves with a wringing gesture which made me
think of handkerchiefs wet with grief, and her hands looked suddenly small and useless and vulnerable.

'*Pauvre cocotte*,' said Madame Dejoie, 'be quiet here with me
and forget awhile. I have ordered a *bouillabaisse* with *langouste*.'

'But I have no appetite, Emmy.'

'It will come back. You'll see. Now here is your *porto* and I
have ordered a bottle of *blanc de blancs*.'

'You will make me *tout à fait saoule*.'

'We are going to eat and drink and for a little while we are
both going to forget everything. I know exactly how you are feeling, for I too lost a beloved husband.'

'By death,' little Madame Volet said. 'That makes a great difference. Death is quite bearable.'

'It is more irrevocable.'

'Nothing can be more irrevocable than my situation. Emmy,
he loves the little bitch.'

'All I know of her is that she has deplorable taste—or a deplorable hairdresser.'

'But that was exactly what I told him.'

'You were wrong. I should have told him, not you, for he
might have believed me and in any case my criticism would not
have hurt his pride.'

'I love him,' Madame Volet said, 'I cannot be prudent,' and then suddenly became aware of my presence. She whispered something to her companion, and I heard the reassurance, '*Un anglais.*' I watched her as covertly as I could—like most of my fellow writers I have the spirit of a *voyeur*—and I wondered how stupid married men could be. I was temporarily free, and I very much wanted to console her, but I didn't exist in her eyes, now she knew that I was English, nor in the eyes of Madame Dejoie. I was less than human—I was only a reject from the Common Market.

I ordered a small *rouget* and a half bottle of Pouilly and tried to be interested in the Trollope I had brought with me. But my attention strayed.

'I adored my husband,' Madame Dejoie was saying, and her hand again grasped the pepper-mill, but this time it looked less like a bludgeon.

'I still do, Emmy. That is the worst of it. I know that if he came back . . .'

'Mine can never come back,' Madame Dejoie retorted, touching the corner of one eye with her handkerchief and then examining the smear of black left behind.

In a gloomy silence they both drained their *portos*. Then Madame Dejoie said with determination, 'There is no turning back. You should accept that as I do. There remains for us only the problem of adaptation.'

'After such a betrayal I could never look at another man,' Madame Volet replied. At that moment she looked right through me. I felt invisible. I put my hand between the light and the wall to prove that I had a shadow, and the shadow looked like a beast with horns.

'I would never suggest another man,' Madame Dejoie said. 'Never.'

'What then?'

'When my poor husband died from an infection of the bowels I thought myself quite inconsolable, but I said to myself, Courage, courage. You must learn to laugh again.'

'To laugh,' Madame Volet exclaimed. 'To laugh at what?' But before Madame Dejoie could reply, Monsieur Félix had arrived to perform his neat surgical operation upon the fish for the *bouillabaisse*. Madame Dejoie watched with real interest; Madame Volet, I thought, watched for politeness' sake while she finished a glass of *blanc de blancs*.

When the operation was over Madame Dejoie filled the glasses and said, 'I was lucky enough to have *une amie* who taught me not to mourn for the past.' She raised her glass and cocking a finger as I had seen men do, she added, '*Pas de mollesse.*'

'*Pas de mollesse,*' Madame Volet repeated with a wan enchanting smile.

I felt decidedly ashamed of myself—a cold literary observer of human anguish. I was afraid of catching poor Madame Volet's eyes (what kind of a man was capable of betraying her for a woman who took the wrong sort of rinse?) and I tried to occupy myself with sad Mr Crawley's courtship as he stumped up the muddy lane in his big clergyman's boots. In any case the two of them had dropped their voices; a gentle smell of garlic came to me from the *bouillabaisse,* the bottle of *blanc de blancs* was nearly finished, and, in spite of Madame Volet's protestation, Madame Dejoie had called for another. 'There are no half bottles,' she said. 'We can always leave something for the gods.' Again their voices sank to an intimate murmur as Mr Crawley's suit was accepted (though how he was to support an inevitably large family would not appear until the succeeding volume). I was startled out of my forced concentration by a laugh: a musical laugh: it was Madame Volet's.

'*Cochon,*' she exclaimed. Madame Dejoie regarded her over her glass (the new bottle had already been broached) under beetling brows. 'I am telling you the truth,' she said. 'He would crow like a cock.'

'But what a joke to play!'

'It began as a joke, but he was really proud of himself. *Après seulement deux coups . . .*'

'*Jamais trois?*' Madame Volet asked and she giggled and splashed a little of her wine down her polo-necked collar.

'*Jamais.*'

'*Je suis saoule.*'

'*Moi aussi, cocotte.*'

Madame Volet said, 'To crow like a cock—at least it was a *fantaisie*. My husband has no *fantaisies*. He is strictly classical.'

'*Pas de vices?*'

'*Hélas, pas de vices.*'

'And yet you miss him?'

'He worked hard,' Madame Volet said and giggled. 'To think that at the end he must have been working hard for both of us.'

'You found it a little boring?'

'It was a habit—how one misses a habit. I wake now at five in the morning.'

'At five?'

'It was the hour of his greatest activity.'

'My husband was a very small man,' Madame Dejoie said. 'Not in height of course. He was two metres high.'

'Oh, Paul is big enough—but always the same.'

'Why do you continue to love that man?' Madame Dejoie sighed and put her large hand on Madame Volet's knee. She wore a signet-ring which perhaps had belonged to her late husband. Madame Volet sighed too and I thought melancholy was returning to the table, but then she hiccuped and both of them laughed.

'*Tu es vraiment saoule, cocotte.*'

'Do I truly miss Paul, or is it only that I miss his habits?' She suddenly met my eye and blushed right down into the wine-coloured wine-stained polo-necked collar.

Madame Dejoie repeated reassuringly, '*Un anglais—ou un américain.*' She hardly bothered to lower her voice at all. 'Do you know how limited my experience was when my husband died? I loved him when he crowed like a cock. I was glad he was so pleased. I only wanted him to be pleased. I adored him, and yet in those days—*j'ai peutêtre joui trois fois par semaine.* I did not expect more. It seemed to me a natural limit.'

'In my case it was three times a day,' Madame Volet said and giggled again. '*Mais toujours d'une façon classique.*' She put her hands over her face and gave a little sob. Madame Dejoie put an arm round her shoulders. There was a long silence while the remains of the *bouillabaisse* were cleared away.

2

'Men are curious animals,' Madame Dejoie said at last. The coffee had come and they divided one *marc* between them, in turn dipping lumps of sugar which they inserted into one another's mouths. 'Animals too lack imagination. A dog has no *fantaisie*.'

'How bored I have been sometimes,' Madame Volet said. 'He would talk politics continually and turn on the news at eight in the morning. At eight! What do I care for politics? But if I asked his advice about anything important he showed no interest at all. With you I can talk about anything, about the whole world.'

'I adored my husband,' Madame Dejoie said, 'yet it was only after his death I discovered my capacity for love. With Pauline. You never knew Pauline. She died five years ago. I loved her more than I ever loved Jacques, and yet I felt no despair when she died. I knew that it was not the end, for I knew by then my capacity.'

'I have never loved a woman,' Madame Volet said.

'*Chérie*, then you do not know what love can mean. With a woman you do not have to be content with *une façon classique* three times a day.'

'I love Paul, but he is so different from me in every way . . .'

'Unlike Pauline, he is a man.'

'Oh Emmy, you describe him so perfectly. How well you understand. A man!'

'When you really think of it, how comic that little object is. Hardly enough to crow about, one would think.'

Madame Volet giggled and said, '*Cochon*.'

'Perhaps smoked like an eel one might enjoy it.'

'Stop it. Stop it.' They rocked up and down with little gusts of laughter. They were drunk, of course, but in the most charming way.

3

How distant now seemed Trollope's muddy lane, the heavy boots of Mr Crawley, his proud shy courtship. In time we travel a space as vast as any astronaut's. When I looked up Madame Volet's head rested on Madame Dejoie's shoulder. 'I feel so sleepy,' she said.

'Tonight you shall sleep, *chérie*.'

'I am so little good to you. I know nothing.'

'In love one learns quickly.'

'But am I in love?' Madame Volet asked, sitting up very straight and staring into Madame Dejoie's sombre eyes.

'If the answer were no, you wouldn't ask the question.'

'But I thought I could never love again.'

'Not another man,' Madame Dejoie said. '*Chérie,* you are almost asleep. Come.'

'The bill?' Madame Volet asked as though perhaps she were trying to delay the moment of decision.

'I will pay tomorrow. What a pretty coat this is—but not warm enough, *chérie,* in February. You need to be cared for.'

'You have given me back my courage,' Madame Volet said. 'When I came in here I was *si démoralisée . . .*'

'Soon—I promise—you will be able to laugh at the past . . .'

'I have already laughed,' Madame Volet said. 'Did he really crow like a cock?'

'Yes.'

'I shall never be able to forget what you said about smoked eel. Never. If I saw one now . . .' She began to giggle again and Madame Dejoie steadied her a little on the way to the door.

I watched them cross the road to the car-park. Suddenly Madame Volet gave a little hop and skip and flung her arms around Madame Dejoie's neck, and the wind, blowing through the archway of the port, carried the faint sound of her laughter to me where I sat alone *chez* Félix. I was glad she was happy again. I was glad that she was in the kind reliable hands of Madame Dejoie. What a fool Paul had been, I reflected, feeling chagrin myself now for so many wasted opportunities.

THE OVER-NIGHT BAG

The little man who came to the information desk in Nice airport when they demanded 'Henry Cooper, passenger on BEA flight 105 for London' looked like a shadow cast by the brilliant glitter of the sun. He wore a grey town-suit and black shoes: he had a grey skin which carefully matched his suit, and since it was impossible for him to change his skin, it was possible that he had no other suit.

'Are you Mr Cooper?'

'Yes.' He carried a BOAC over-night bag and he laid it tenderly on the ledge of the information desk as though it contained something precious and fragile like an electric razor.

'There is a telegram for you.'

He opened it and read the message twice over. '*Bon voyage. Much missed. You will be welcome home, dear boy. Mother.*' He tore the telegram once across and left it on the desk, from which the girl in the blue uniform, after a discreet interval, picked the pieces and with natural curiosity joined them together. Then she looked for the little grey man among the passengers who were now lining up at the tourist gate to join the Trident. He was among the last, carrying his blue BOAC bag.

Near the front of the plane Henry Cooper found a window-seat and placed the bag on the central seat beside him. A large woman in pale blue trousers too tight for the size of her buttocks took the third seat. She squeezed a very large handbag in beside the other on the central seat, and she laid a large fur coat on top of both. Henry Cooper said, 'May I put it on the rack, please?'

She looked at him with contempt. 'Put what?'

'Your coat.'

'If you want to. Why?'

'It's a very heavy coat. It's squashing my over-night bag.'

He was so small he could stand nearly upright under the rack. When he sat down he fastened the seat-belt over the two bags before he fastened his own. The woman watched him with suspicion. 'I've never seen anyone do that before,' she said.

'I don't want it shaken about,' he said. 'There are storms over London.'

'You haven't got an animal in there, have you?'

'Not exactly.'

'It's cruel to carry an animal shut up like that,' she said, as though she disbelieved him.

As the Trident began its run he laid his hand on the bag as if he were reassuring something within. The woman watched the bag narrowly. If she saw the least movement of life she had made up her mind to call the stewardess. Even if it were only a tortoise . . . A tortoise needed air, or so she supposed, in spite of hibernation. When they were safely airborne he relaxed and began to read a *Nice-Matin*—he spent a good deal of time on each story as though his French were not very good. The woman struggled angrily to get her big cavernous bag from under the seat-belt. She muttered 'Ridiculous' twice for his benefit. Then she made up, put on thick horn-rimmed glasses and began to re-read a letter which began 'My darling Tiny' and ended 'Your own cuddly Bertha'. After a while she grew tired of the weight on her knees and dropped it on to the BOAC over-night bag.

The little man leapt in distress. 'Please,' he said, 'please.' He lifted her bag and pushed it quite rudely into a corner of the seat. 'I don't want it squashed,' he said. 'It's a matter of respect.'

'What have you got in your precious bag?' she asked him angrily.

'A dead baby,' he said. 'I thought I had told you.'

'On the left of the aircraft,' the pilot announced through the loudspeaker, 'you will see Montélimar. We shall be passing Paris in—'

'You are not serious,' she said.

'It's just one of those things,' he replied in a tone that carried conviction.

'But you can't take dead babies—like that—in a bag—in the economy class.'

'In the case of a baby it is so much cheaper than freight. Only a week old. It weighs so little.'

'But it should be in a coffin, not an over-night bag.'

'My wife didn't trust a foreign coffin. She said the materials they use are not durable. She's rather a conventional woman.'

'Then it's *your* baby?' Under the circumstances she seemed almost prepared to sympathize.

'My wife's baby,' he corrected her.

'What's the difference?'

He said sadly, 'There could well be a difference,' and turned the page of *Nice-Matin*.

'Are you suggesting . . . ?' But he was deep in a column dealing with a Lions Club meeting in Antibes and the rather revolutionary suggestion made there by a member from Grasse. She read over again her letter from 'cuddly Bertha', but it failed to hold her attention. She kept on stealing a glance at the over-night bag.

'You don't anticipate trouble with the customs?' she asked him after a while.

'Of course I shall have to declare it,' he said. 'It was acquired abroad.'

When they landed, exactly on time, he said to her with old-fashioned politeness, 'I have enjoyed our flight.' She looked for him with a certain morbid curiosity in the customs—Channel 10—but then she saw him in Channel 12, for passengers carrying hand-baggage only. He was speaking, earnestly, to the officer who was poised, chalk in hand, over the over-night bag. Then she lost sight of him as her own inspector insisted on examining the contents of her cavernous bag, which yielded up a number of undeclared presents for Bertha.

Henry Cooper was the first out of the arrivals door and he took a hired car. The charge for taxis rose every year when he went abroad and it was his one extravagance not to wait for the airport-bus. The sky was overcast and the temperature only a little above freezing,

but the driver was in a mood of euphoria. He had a dashing com-
radely air—he told Henry Cooper that he had won fifty pounds on
the pools. The heater was on full blast, and Henry Cooper opened
the window, but an icy current of air from Scandinavia flowed
round his shoulders. He closed the window again and said, 'Would
you mind turning off the heater?' It was as hot in the car as in a New
York hotel during a blizzard.

'It's cold outside,' the driver said.

'You see,' Henry Cooper said, 'I have a dead baby in my bag.'

'Dead baby?'

'Yes.'

'Ah well,' the driver said, 'he won't feel the heat, will he? It's
a he?'

'Yes. A he. I'm anxious he shouldn't—deteriorate.'

'They keep a long time,' the driver said. 'You'd be surprised.
Longer than old people. What did you have for lunch?'

Henry Cooper was a little surprised. He had to cast his mind
back. He said, '*Carré d'agneau à la provençale.*'

'Curry?'

'No, not curry, lamb chops with garlic and herbs. And then an
apple-tart.'

'And you drank something I wouldn't be surprised?'

'A half bottle of *rosé*. And a brandy.'

'There you are, you see.'

'I don't understand.'

'With all that inside you, *you* wouldn't keep so well.'

Gillette Razors were half hidden in icy mist. The driver had
forgotten or had refused to turn down the heat, but he remained
silent for quite a while, perhaps brooding on the subject of life
and death.

'How did the little perisher die?' he asked at last.

'They die so easily,' Henry Cooper answered.

'Many a true word's spoken in jest,' the driver said, a little absentmindedly because he had swerved to avoid a car which
braked too suddenly, and Henry Cooper instinctively put his
hand on the over-night bag to steady it.

'Sorry,' the driver said. 'Not my fault. Amateur drivers! Anyway, you don't need to worry—they can't bruise after death, or

can they? I read something about it once in *The Cases of Sir Bernard Spilsbury*, but I don't remember now exactly what. That's always the trouble about reading.'

'I'd be much happier,' Henry Cooper said, 'if you would turn off the heat.'

'There's no point in your catching a chill, is there? Or me either. It won't help *him* where he's gone—if anywhere at all. The next thing you know you'll be in the same position yourself. Not in an over-night bag, of course. That goes without saying.'

The Knightsbridge tunnel as usual was closed because of flooding. They turned north through the park. The trees dripped on empty benches. The pigeons blew out their grey feathers the colour of soiled city snow.

'Is he yours?' the driver asked. 'If you don't mind my inquiring.'

'Not exactly.' Henry Cooper added briskly and brightly, 'My wife's, as it happens.'

'It's never the same if it's not your own,' the driver said thoughtfully. 'I had a nephew who died. He had a split palate— that wasn't the reason, of course, but it made it easier to bear for the parents. Are you going to an undertaker's now?'

'I thought I would take it home for the night and see about the arrangements tomorrow.'

'A little perisher like that would fit easily into the frig. No bigger than a chicken. As a precaution only.'

They entered the large whitewashed Bayswater square. The houses resembled the above-ground tombs you find in continental cemeteries, except that, unlike the tombs, they were divided into flatlets and there were rows and rows of bell-pushes to wake the inmates. The driver watched Henry Cooper get out with the over-night bag at a portico entitled Stare House. 'Bloody orful aircraft company,' he said mechanically when he saw the letters BOAC—without ill-will, it was only a Pavlov response.

Henry Cooper went up to the top floor and let himself in. His mother was already in the hall to greet him. 'I saw your car draw up, dear.' He put the over-night bag on a chair so as to embrace her better.

'You've come quickly. You got my telegram at Nice?'

'Yes, Mother. With only an over-night bag I walked straight through the customs.'

'So clever of you to travel light.'

'It's the drip-dry shirt that does it,' Henry Cooper said. He followed his mother into their sitting-room. He noticed she had changed the position of his favourite picture—a reproduction from *Life* magazine of a painting by Hieronymus Bosch. 'Just so that I don't see it from *my* chair, dear,' his mother explained, interpreting his glance. His slippers were laid out by his armchair and he sat down with an air of satisfaction at being home again.

'And now, dear,' his mother said, 'tell me how it was. Tell me everything. Did you make some new friends?'

'Oh yes, Mother, wherever I went I made friends.' Winter had fallen early on the House of Stare. The over-night bag disappeared in the darkness of the hall like a blue fish into blue water.

'And adventures? What adventures?'

Once, while he talked, his mother got up and tiptoed to draw the curtains and to turn on a reading-lamp, and once she gave a little gasp of horror. 'A little toe? In the marmalade?'

'Yes, Mother.'

'It wasn't English marmalade?'

'No, Mother, foreign.'

'I could have understood a finger—an accident slicing the orange—but a toe!'

'As I understood it,' Henry Cooper said, 'in those parts they use a kind of guillotine worked by the bare foot of a peasant.'

'You complained, of course?'

'Not in words, but I put the toe very conspicuously at the edge of the plate.'

After one more story it was time for his mother to go and put the shepherd's pie into the oven and Henry Cooper went into the hall to fetch the over-night bag. 'Time to unpack,' he thought. He had a tidy mind.

MORTMAIN

How wonderfully secure and peaceful a genuine marriage seemed
to Carter, when he attained it at the age of forty-two. He even enjoyed every moment of the church service, except when he saw
Josephine wiping away a tear as he conducted Julia down the
aisle. It was typical of this new frank relationship that Josephine
was there at all. He had no secrets from Julia; they had often
talked together of his ten tormented years with Josephine, of her
extravagant jealousy, of her well-timed hysterics. 'It was her in-
security,' Julia argued with understanding, and she was quite
convinced that in a little while it would be possible to form a
friendship with Josephine.

'I doubt it, darling.'

'Why? I can't help being fond of anyone who loved you.'

'It was a rather cruel love.'

'Perhaps at the end when she knew she was losing you, but,
darling, there *were* happy years.'

'Yes.' But he wanted to forget that he had ever loved anyone
before Julia.

Her generosity sometimes staggered him. On the seventh day
of their honeymoon, when they were drinking retsina in a little
restaurant on the beach by Sunium, he accidentally took a letter
from Josephine out of his pocket. It had arrived the day before
and he had concealed it, for fear of hurting Julia. It was typical of
Josephine that she could not leave him alone for the brief period
of the honeymoon. Even her handwriting was now abhorrent to
him—very neat, very small, in black ink the colour of her hair. Ju-

lia was platinum-fair. How had he ever thought that black hair was beautiful? Or been impatient to read letters in black ink?

'What's the letter, darling? I didn't know there had been a post.'

'It's from Josephine. It came yesterday.'

'But you haven't even opened it!' she exclaimed without a word of reproach.

'I don't want to think about her.'

'But, darling, she may be ill.'

'Not she.'

'Or in distress.'

'She earns more with her fashion-designs than I do with my stories.'

'Darling, let's be kind. We can afford to be. We are so happy.'

So he opened the letter. It was affectionate and uncomplaining and he read it with distaste.

Dear Philip, I didn't want to be a death's head at the reception, so I had no chance to say goodbye and wish you both the greatest possible happiness. I thought Julia looked terribly beautiful and so very, very young. You must look after her carefully. I know how well you can do that, Philip dear. When I saw her, I couldn't help wondering why you took such a long time to make up your mind to leave me. Silly Philip. It's much less painful to act quickly.

I don't suppose you are interested to hear about my activities now, but just in case you are worrying a little about me—you know what an old worrier you are—I want you to know that I'm working *very* hard at a whole series for—guess, the French *Vogue*. They are paying me a fortune in francs, and I simply have no time for unhappy thoughts. I've been back once—I hope you don't mind—to our apartment (slip of the tongue) because I'd lost a key sketch. I found it at the back of our communal drawer—the ideas-bank, do you remember? I thought I'd taken all my stuff away, but there it was between the leaves of the story you started that heavenly summer, and never finished, at Napoule. Now I'm rambling on when all I really wanted to say was: Be happy both of you. Love, Josephine.

Carter handed the letter to Julia and said, 'It could have been worse.'

'But would she like me to read it?'

'Oh, it's meant for both of us.' Again he thought how wonderful it was to have no secrets. There had been so many secrets during the last ten years, even innocent secrets, for fear of misunderstanding, of Josephine's rage or silence. Now he had no fear of anything at all: he could have trusted even a guilty secret to Julia's sympathy and comprehension. He said, 'I was a fool not to show you the letter yesterday. I'll never do anything like that again.' He tried to recall Spenser's line—'. . . port after stormie seas'.

When Julia had finished reading the letter she said, 'I think she's a wonderful woman. How very, very sweet of her to write like that. You know I was—only now and then of course—just a little worried about her. After all I wouldn't like to lose you after ten years.'

When they were in the taxi going back to Athens she said, 'Were you very happy at Napoule?'

'Yes, I suppose so. I don't remember, it wasn't like this.'

With the antennae of a lover he could feel her moving away from him, though their shoulders still touched. The sun was bright on the road from Sunium, the warm sleepy loving siesta lay ahead, and yet . . . 'Is anything the matter, darling?' he asked.

'Not really . . . It's only . . . do you think one day you'll say the same about Athens as about Napoule? "I don't remember, it wasn't like this." '

'What a dear fool you are,' he said and kissed her. After that they played a little in the taxi going back to Athens, and when the streets began to unroll she sat up and combed her hair. 'You aren't really a cold man, are you?' she asked, and he knew that all was right again. It was Josephine's fault that—momentarily—there had been a small division.

When they got out of bed to have dinner, she said, 'We must write to Josephine.'

'Oh no!'

'Darling, I know how you feel, but really it was a wonderful letter.'

'A picture-postcard then.'

So they agreed on that.

Suddenly it was autumn when they arrived back in London—if not winter already, for there was ice in the rain falling on the tarmac, and they had quite forgotten how early the lights came on at home—passing Gillette and Lucozade and Smith's Crisps, and no view of the Parthenon anywhere. The BOAC posters seemed more than usually sad— 'BOAC takes you there and brings you back.'

'We'll put on all the electric fires as soon as we get in,' Carter said, 'and it will be warm in no time at all.' But when they opened the door of the apartment they found the fires were already alight. Little glows greeted them in the twilight from the depths of the living-room and the bedroom.

'Some fairy has done this,' Julia said.

'Not a fairy of any kind,' Carter said. He had already seen the envelope on the mantelpiece addressed in black ink to 'Mrs Carter'.

Dear Julia, you won't mind my calling you Julia, will you? I feel we have so much in common, having loved the same man. Today was so icy that I could not help thinking of how you two were returning from the sun and the warmth to a cold flat. (I know how cold the flat can be. I used to catch a chill every year when we came back from the south of France.) So I've done a very presumptuous thing. I've slipped in and put on the fires, but to show you that I'll never do such a thing again, I've hidden my key under the mat outside the front door. That's just in case your plane is held up in Rome or somewhere. I'll telephone the airport and if by some unlikely chance you haven't arrived, I'll come back and turn out the fires for safety (and economy! the rates are awful). Wishing you a very warm evening in your new home, love from Josephine.

PS. I did notice that the coffee jar was empty, so I've left a packet of Blue Mountain in the kitchen. It's the only coffee Philip really cares for.

'Well,' Julia said laughing, 'she does think of everything.'

'I wish she'd just leave us alone,' Carter said.

'We wouldn't be warm like this, and we wouldn't have any coffee for breakfast.'

'I feel that she's lurking about the place and she'll walk in at any moment. Just when I'm kissing you.' He kissed Julia with one careful eye on the door.

'You *are* a bit unfair, darling. After all, she's left her key under the mat.'

'She might have had a duplicate made.'

She closed his mouth with another kiss.

'Have you noticed how erotic an aeroplane makes you after a few hours?' Carter asked.

'Yes.'

'I suppose it's the vibration.'

'Let's do something about it, darling.'

'I'll just look under the mat first. To make sure she wasn't lying.'

He enjoyed marriage—so much that he blamed himself for not having married before, forgetting that in that case he would have been married to Josephine. He found Julia, who had no work of her own, almost miraculously available. There was no maid to mar their relationship with habits. As they were always together, at cocktail parties, in restaurants, at small dinner parties, they had only to meet each other's eyes . . . Julia soon earned the reputation of being delicate and easily tired, it occurred so often that they left a cocktail party after a quarter of an hour or abandoned a dinner after the coffee—'Oh dear, I'm so sorry, such a vile headache, so stupid of me. Philip, *you* must stay . . .'

'Of course I'm not going to stay.'

Once they had a narrow escape from discovery on the stairs while they were laughing uncontrollably. Their host had followed them out to ask them to post a letter. Julia in the nick of time changed her laughter into what seemed to be a fit of hysterics . . . Several weeks went by. It was a really successful marriage . . . They liked—between whiles—to discuss its success, each attributing the main merit to the other. 'When I think you might have married Josephine,' Julia said. 'Why didn't you marry Josephine?'

'I suppose at the back of our minds we knew it wasn't going to be permanent.'

'Are we going to be permanent?'

'If we aren't, nothing will ever be.'

It was early in November that the time-bombs began to go off. No doubt they had been planned to explode earlier, but Josephine had not taken into account the temporary change in his habits. Some weeks passed before he had occasion to open what they used to call the ideas-bank in the days of their closest companionship—the drawer in which he used to leave notes for stories, scraps of overheard dialogue and the like, and she would leave roughly sketched ideas for fashion advertisements.

Directly he opened the drawer he saw her letter. It was labelled heavily 'Top Secret' in black ink with a whimsically drawn exclamation mark in the form of a girl with big eyes (Josephine suffered in an elegant way from exophthalmic goitre) rising genie-like out of a bottle. He read the letter with extreme distaste:

Dear, you didn't expect to find me here, did you? But after ten years I can't not now and then say, Good-night or good-morning, how are you? Bless you. Lots of love (really and truly), Your Josephine.

The threat of 'now and then' was unmistakable. He slammed the drawer shut and said 'Damn' so loudly that Julia looked in. 'Whatever is it, darling?'

'Josephine again.'

She read the letter and said, 'You know, I can understand the way she feels. Poor Josephine. Are you tearing it up, darling?'

'What else do you expect me to do with it? Keep it for a collected edition of her letters?'

'It just seems a bit unkind.'

'Me unkind to *her*? Julia, you've no idea of the sort of life that we led those last years. I can show you scars: when she was in a rage she would stub her cigarettes *anywhere*.'

'She felt she was losing you, darling, and she got desperate. They are my fault really, those scars, every one of them.' He could see growing in her eyes that soft amused speculative look which always led to the same thing.

Only two days passed before the next time-bomb went off. When they got up Julia said, 'We really ought to change the mattress. We both fall into a kind of hole in the middle.'

'I hadn't noticed.'

'Lots of people change the mattress every week.'

'Yes. Josephine always did.'

They stripped the bed and began to roll the mattress. Lying on the springs was a letter addressed to Julia. Carter saw it first and tried to push it out of sight, but Julia saw him.

'What's that?'

'Josephine, of course. There'll soon be too many letters for one volume. We shall have to get them properly edited at Yale like George Eliot's.'

'Darling, this is addressed to me. What were you planning to do with it?'

'Destroy it in secret.'

'I thought we were going to have no secrets.'

'I had counted without Josephine.'

For the first time she hesitated before opening the letter. 'It's certainly a bit bizarre to put a letter here. Do you think it got there accidentally?'

'Rather difficult, I should think.'

She read the letter and then gave it to him. She said with relief, 'Oh, she explains why. It's quite natural really.' He read:

Dear Julia, how I hope you are basking in a really Greek sun. Don't tell Philip (Oh, but of course you wouldn't have secrets yet) but I never really cared for the south of France. Always that mistral, drying the skin. I'm glad to think you are not suffering there. We always planned to go to Greece when we could afford it, so I know Philip will be happy. I came in today to find a sketch and then remembered that the mattress hadn't been turned for at least a fortnight. We were rather distracted, you know, the last weeks we were together. Anyway I couldn't bear the thought of your coming back from the lotus islands and find-

ing bumps in your bed the first night, so I've turned it for you.
I'd advise you to turn it every week: otherwise a hole always
develops in the middle. By the way I've put up the winter curtains and sent the summer ones to the cleaners at 153 Brompton
Road. Love, Josephine.

'If you remember, she wrote to me that Napoule had been
heavenly,' he said. 'The Yale editor will have to put in a cross-
reference.'

'You *are* a bit cold-blooded,' Julia said. 'Darling, she's only
trying to be helpful. After all I never knew about the curtains or
the mattress.'

'I suppose you are going to write a long cosy letter in reply,
full of household chat.'

'She's been waiting weeks for an answer. This is an *ancient*
letter.'

'And I wonder how many more ancient letters there are waiting to pop out. By God, I'm going to search the flat through and
through. From attic to basement.'

'We don't have either.'

'You know very well what I mean.'

'I only know you are getting fussed in an exaggerated way.
You really behave as though you are frightened of Josephine.'

'Oh hell!'

Julia left the room abruptly and he tried to work. Later that
day a squib went off—nothing serious, but it didn't help his
mood. He wanted to find the dialling number for oversea tele-
grams and he discovered inserted in volume one of the directory
a complete list in alphabetical order, typed on Josephine's machine on which O was always blurred, a complete list of the
numbers he most often required. John Hughes, his oldest friend,
came after Harrod's; and there were the nearest taxi-rank, the
chemist's, the butcher's, the bank, the dry-cleaner's, the green-
grocer's, the fishmonger's, his publisher and agent, Elizabeth Arden's and the local hairdressers—marked in brackets ('For J
please note, quite reliable and very inexpensive')—it was the first
time he noticed they had the same initials.

Julia, who saw him discover the list, said, 'The angel-woman. We'll pin it up over the telephone. It's really terribly complete.'

'After the crack in her last letter I'd have expected her to include Cartier's.'

'Darling, it wasn't a crack. It was a bare statement of fact. If I hadn't had a little money, we would have gone to the south of France too.'

'I suppose you think I married you to get to Greece.'

'Don't be an owl. You don't see Josephine clearly, that's all. You twist every kindness she does.'

'Kindness?'

'I expect it's the sense of guilt.'

After that he really began a search. He looked in cigarette-boxes, drawers, filing-cabinets, he went through all the pockets of the suits he had left behind, he opened the back of the television-cabinet, he lifted the lid of the lavatory-cistern, and even changed the roll of toilet-paper (it was quicker than unwinding the whole thing). Julia came to look at him, as he worked in the lavatory, without her usual sympathy. He tried the pelmets (who knew what they mightn't discover when next the curtains were sent for cleaning?), he took their dirty clothes out of the basket in case something had been overlooked at the bottom. He went on hands-and-knees through the kitchen to look under the gas-stove, and once, when he found a piece of paper wrapped around a pipe, he exclaimed in a kind of triumph, but it was nothing at all—a plumber's relic. The afternoon post rattled through the letter-box and Julia called to him from the hall—'Oh, good, you never told me you took in the French *Vogue*.'

'I don't.'

'Sorry, there's a kind of Christmas card in another envelope. A subscription's been taken out for us by Miss Josephine Heckstall-Jones. I do call that sweet of her.'

'She's sold a series of drawings to them. I won't look at it.'

'Darling, you are being childish. Do you expect her to stop reading your books?'

'I only want to be left alone with you. Just for a few weeks. It's not so much to ask.'

'You're a bit of an egoist, darling.'

He felt quiet and tired that evening, but a little relieved in mind. His search had been very thorough. In the middle of dinner he had remembered the wedding-presents, still crated for lack of room, and insisted on making sure between the courses that they were still nailed down—he knew Josephine would never have used a screwdriver for fear of injuring her fingers, and she was terrified of hammers. The peace of a solitary evening at last descended on them: the delicious calm which they knew either of them could alter at any moment with a touch of the hand. Lovers cannot postpone as married people can. 'I am grown peaceful as old age tonight,' he quoted to her.

'Who wrote that?'

'Browning.'

'I don't know Browning. Read me some.'

He loved to read Browning aloud—he had a good voice for poetry, it was his small harmless Narcissism. 'Would you really like it?'

'Yes.'

'I used to read to Josephine,' he warned her.

'What do I care? We can't help doing *some* of the same things, can we, darling?'

'There is something I never read to Josephine. Even though I was in love with her, it wasn't suitable. We weren't—permanent.' He began:

> How well I know what I mean to do
> When the long dark autumn-evenings come . . .

He was deeply moved by his own reading. He had never loved Julia so much as at this moment. Here was home—nothing else had been other than a caravan.

> . . . I will speak now,
> No longer watch you as you sit
> Reading by firelight, that great brow
> And the spirit-small hand propping it,
> Mutely, my heart knows how.

He rather wished that Julia had really been reading, but then of
course she wouldn't have been listening to him with such
adorable attention.

> . . . If two lives join, there is oft a scar.
> They are one and one, with a shadowy third;
> One near one is too far.

He turned the page and there lay a sheet of paper (he would have
discovered it at once, before reading, if she had put it in an envelope) with the black neat handwriting.

> Dearest Philip, only to say goodnight to you between the pages of
> your favourite book—and mine. We are so lucky to have ended in
> the way we have. With memories in common we shall for ever be
> a little in touch. Love, Josephine.

He flung the book and the paper on the floor. He said, 'The
bitch. The bloody bitch.'

'I won't have you talk of her like that,' Julia said with surprising strength. She picked up the paper and read it.

'What's wrong with that?' she demanded. 'Do you hate memories? What's going to happen to our memories?'

'But don't you see the trick she's playing? Don't you understand? Are you an idiot, Julia?'

That night they lay in bed on opposite sides, not even touching
with their feet. It was the first night since they had come home
that they had not made love. Neither slept much. In the morning
Carter found a letter in the most obvious place of all, which he
had somehow neglected: between the leaves of the unused single-
lined foolscap on which he always wrote his stories. It began,
'Darling, I'm sure you won't mind my using the old term . . .'

CHEAP IN AUGUST

I

It was cheap in August: the essential sun, the coral reefs, the bamboo bar and the calypsos—they were all of them at cut prices, like the slightly soiled slips in a bargain-sale. Groups arrived periodically from Philadelphia in the manner of school-treats and departed with less *bruit*, after an exact exhausting week, when the picnic was over. Perhaps for twenty-four hours the swimming-pool and the bar were almost deserted, and then another school-treat would arrive, this time from St Louis. Everyone knew everyone else; they had bussed together to an airport, they had flown together, together they had faced an alien customs; they would separate during the day and greet each other noisily and happily after dark, exchanging impressions of 'shooting the rapids', the botanic gardens, the Spanish fort. 'We are doing that tomorrow.'

Mary Watson wrote to her husband in Europe, 'I had to get away for a bit and it's so cheap in August.' They had been married ten years and they had only been separated three times. He wrote to her every day and the letters arrived twice a week in little bundles. She arranged them like newspapers by the date and read them in the correct order. They were tender and precise; what with his research, with preparing lectures and writing letters, he had little time to *see* Europe—he insisted on calling it 'your Europe' as though to assure her that he had not forgotten the sacrifice which she must have made by marrying an American professor from New England, but sometimes little criticisms of 'her Europe' escaped him: the food was too rich, cigarettes too expensive, wine too often served and milk very difficult to obtain at lunchtime—which might indicate that, after all, she ought not to exaggerate her sacrifice. Perhaps it would have been a good thing if James Thomson, who was his special study at the moment, had written *The Seasons* in America—an American fall, she had to admit, was more beautiful than an English autumn.

Mary Watson wrote to him every other day, but sometimes a postcard only, and she was apt to forget if she had repeated the postcard. She wrote in the shade of the bamboo bar where she could see everyone who passed on the way to the swimming-pool. She wrote truthfully, 'It's so cheap in August; the hotel is not half full, and the heat and the humidity are very tiring. But, of course, it's a change.' She had no wish to appear extravagant; the salary, which to her European eyes had seemed astronomically large for a professor of literature, had long dwindled to its proper proportions, relative to the price of steaks and salads—she must justify with a little enthusiasm the money she was spending in his absence. So she wrote also about the flowers in the botanic gardens—she had ventured that far on one occasion—and with less truth of the beneficial changes wrought by the sun and the lazy life on her friend Margaret who from 'her England' had written and demanded her company: a Margaret, she admitted frankly to herself, who was not visible to any eye but the eye of faith. But then Charlie had complete faith. Even good qualities become with the erosion of time a reproach. After ten years of being happily married, she thought, one undervalues security and tranquillity.

She read Charlie's letters with great attention. She longed to find in them one ambiguity, one evasion, one time-gap which he had ill-explained. Even an unusually strong expression of love would have pleased her, for its strength might have been there to counterweigh a sense of guilt. But she couldn't deceive herself that there was any sense of guilt in Charlie's facile flowing informative script. She calculated that if he had been one of the poets he was now so closely studying, he would have completed already a standard-sized epic during his first two months in 'her Europe', and the letters, after all, were only a spare-time occupation. They filled up the vacant hours, and certainly they could have left no room for any other occupation. 'It is ten o'clock at night, it is raining outside and the temperature is rather cool for August, not above fifty-six degrees. When I have said good-night to you, my dear one, I shall go happily to bed with the thought of you. I have a long day tomorrow at the museum and dinner in the evening with the Henry Wilkinsons who are passing through on their way from Athens—you remember the Henry Wilkinsons, don't you?' (Didn't she just?) She had wondered whether, when Charlie returned, she might perhaps detect some small unfamiliar note in his love-making which would indicate that a stranger had passed that way. Now she disbelieved in the possibility, and anyway the evidence would arrive too late—it was no good to her now that she might be justified later. She wanted her justification immediately, a justification not alas! for any act that she had committed but only for an intention, for the intention of betraying Charlie, of having, like so many of her friends, a holiday affair (the idea had come to her immediately the dean's wife had said, 'It's so cheap in Jamaica in August').

The trouble was that, after three weeks of calypsos in the humid evenings, the rum punches (for which she could no longer disguise from herself a repugnance), the warm Martinis, the interminable red snappers, and tomatoes with everything, there had been no affair, not even the hint of one. She had discovered with disappointment the essential morality of a holiday resort in the cheap season; there were no opportunities for infidelity, only for writing postcards—with great brilliant blue skies and seas—to Charlie. Once a woman from St Louis had taken too obvious pity on her, when she sat alone in the bar writing postcards, and invited her to join their party which was about to visit the botanic gardens— 'We are an awfully jolly bunch,' she had said with a big turnip smile. Mary exaggerated her English accent to repel her better and said that she didn't much care for flowers. It had shocked the woman as deeply as if she had said she did not care for television. From the motion of the heads at the other end of the bar, the agitated clinking of the Coca-Cola glasses, she could tell that her words were being repeated from one to another. Afterwards, until the jolly bunch had taken the airport limousine on the way back to St Louis, she was aware of averted heads. She was English, she had taken a superior attitude to flowers, and as she preferred even warm Martinis to Coca-Cola, she was probably in their eyes an alcoholic.

It was a feature common to most of these jolly bunches that they contained no male attachment, and perhaps that was why the attempt to look attractive was completely abandoned. Huge buttocks were exposed in their full horror in tight large-patterned Bermuda shorts. Heads were bound in scarves to cover rollers which were not removed even by lunchtime—they stuck out like small mole-hills. Daily she watched the bums lurch by like hippos on the way to the water. Only in the evening would the women change from the monstrous shorts into monstrous cotton frocks, covered with mauve or scarlet flowers, in order to take dinner on the terrace where formality was demanded in the book of rules, and the few men who appeared were forced to wear jackets and ties though the thermometer stood at close on eighty degrees after sunset. The market in femininity being such, how could one hope to see any male foragers? Only old and broken husbands were sometimes to be seen towed towards an Issa store advertising freeport prices.

She had been encouraged during the first week by the sight of three men with crew-cuts who went past the bar towards the swimming-pool wearing male bikinis. They were far too young for her, but in her present mood she would have welcomed altruistically the sight of another's romance. Romance is said to be contagious, and if in the candle-lit evenings the 'informal' coffee-tavern had contained a few young amorous couples, who could say what men of maturer years might not eventually arrive to catch the infection? But her hopes dwindled. The young men came and went without a glance at the Bermuda shorts or the pinned hair. Why should they stay? They were certainly more beautiful than any girl there and they knew it.

By nine o'clock most evenings Mary Watson was on her way to bed. A few evenings of calypsos, of quaint false impromptus and the hideous jangle of rattles, had been enough. Outside the closed windows of the hotel annexe the boxes of the air-conditioners made a continuous rumble in the starred and palmy night like over-fed hotel guests. Her room was full of dried air which bore no more resemblance to fresh air than the dried figs to the newly picked fruit. When she looked in the glass to brush her hair she often regretted her lack of charity to the jolly bunch from St Louis. It was true she did not wear Bermuda shorts nor coil her hair in rollers, but her hair was streaky nonetheless with heat and the mirror reflected more plainly than it seemed to do at home her thirty-nine years. If she had not paid in advance for a four-weeks *pension* on her individual round-trip tour, with tickets exchangeable for a variety of excursions, she would have turned tail and returned to the campus. Next year, she thought, when I am forty, I must feel grateful that I have preserved the love of a good man.

She was a woman given to self-analysis, and perhaps because it is a great deal easier to direct questions to a particular face rather than to a void (one has the right to expect some kind of a response even from eyes one sees many times a day in a compact), she posed the questions to herself with a belligerent direct stare into the looking-glass. She was an honest woman, and for that reason the questions were all the cruder. She would say to herself, I have slept with no one other than Charlie (she wouldn't admit as sexual experiences the small exciting half-way points that she had reached before marriage); why am I now seeking to find a strange body, which will probably give me less pleasure than the body I already know? It had been more than a month before Charlie brought her real pleasure. Pleasure, she learnt, grew with habit, so that if it were not really pleasure that she now looked for, what was it? The answer could only be the unfamiliar. She had friends, even on the respectable campus, who had admitted to her, in the frank admirable American way, their adventures. These had usually been in Europe—a momentary marital absence had given the opportunity for a momentary excitement, and then with what a sigh of relief they had found themselves safely at home. All the same they felt afterwards that they had enlarged their experience; they understood something that their husbands did not really understand—the real character of a Frenchman, an Italian, even—there were such cases—of an Englishman.

Mary Watson was painfully aware, as an Englishwoman, that

her experience was confined to one American. They all, on the campus, believed her to be European, but all she knew was confined to one man and he was a citizen of Boston who had no curiosity for the great Western regions. In a sense she was more American by choice than he was by birth. Perhaps she was less European even than the wife of the Professor of Romance Languages, who had confided to her that once—overwhelmingly—in Antibes . . . it had happened only once because the sabbatical year was over . . . her husband was up in Paris checking manuscripts before they flew home . . .

Had she herself, Mary Watson sometimes wondered, been just such a European adventure which Charlie mistakenly had domesticated? (She couldn't pretend to be a tigress in a cage, but they kept smaller creatures in cages, white mice, love-birds.) And, to be fair, Charlie too was her adventure, her American adventure, the kind of man whom at twenty-seven she had not before encountered in frowsy London. Henry James had described the type, and at that moment in her history she had been reading a great deal of Henry James: 'A man of intellect whose body was not much to him and its senses and appetites not importunate.' All the same for a while she had made the appetites importunate.

That was her private conquest of the American continent, and when the Professor's wife had spoken of the dancer of Antibes (no, that was a Roman inscription—the man had been a *marchand de vin*) she had thought, The lover I know and admire is American and I am proud of it. But afterwards came the thought: American or New England? Yet to know a country must one know every region sexually?

It was absurd at thirty-nine not to be content. She had her man. The book on James Thomson would be published by the University Press, and Charlie had the intention afterwards of making a revolutionary break from the romantic poetry of the eighteenth century into a study of the American image in European literature—it was to be called *The Double Reflection*: the effect of Fenimore Cooper on the European scene: the image of America presented by Mrs Trollope—the details were not yet worked out. The study might possibly end with the first arrival of Dylan Thomas on the shores of America—at the Cunard quay or at

Idlewild? That was a point for later research. She examined herself again closely in the glass—the new decade of the forties stared frankly back at her—an Englander who had become a New Englander. After all she hadn't travelled very far—Kent to Connecticut. This was not just the physical restlessness of middle age, she argued; it was the universal desire to see a little bit further, before one surrendered to old age and the blank certitude of death.

2

Next day she picked up her courage and went as far as the swimming-pool. A strong wind blew and whipped up the waves in the almost land-girt harbour—the hurricane season would soon be here. All the world creaked around her: the wooden struts of the shabby harbour, the jalousies of the small hopeless houses which looked as though they had been knocked together from a make-it-yourself kit, the branches of the palms—a long, weary, worn-out creaking. Even the water of the swimming-pool imitated in miniature the waves of the harbour.

She was glad that she was alone in the swimming-pool, at least for all practical purposes alone, for the old man splashing water over himself, like an elephant, in the shallow end hardly counted. He was a solitary elephant and not one of the hippo band. They would have called her with merry cries to join them—and it's difficult to be stand-offish in a swimming-pool which is common to all as a table is not. They might even in their resentment have ducked her—pretending like schoolchildren that it was all a merry game; there was nothing she put beyond those thick thighs, whether they were encased in bikinis or Bermuda shorts. As she floated in the pool her ears were alert for their approach. At the first sound she would get well away from the water, but today they were probably making an excursion to Tower Isle on the other side of the island, or had they done that yesterday? Only the old man watched her, pouring water over his head to keep away sunstroke. She was safely alone, which was the next best thing to the adventure she had come here to find. All the same, as she sat on the rim of the pool, and let the sun and wind dry her, she realized the extent of her solitude. She had spoken to no one but black waiters and Syrian receptionists for more than two weeks. Soon, she thought, I shall even begin to miss Charlie—it would be an ignoble finish to what she had intended to be an adventure.

A voice from the water said to her, 'My name's Hickslaughter—Henry Hickslaughter.' She couldn't have sworn to the name in court, but that was how it had sounded at the time and he never repeated it. She looked down at a polished mahogany crown surrounded by white hair; perhaps he resembled Neptune more than an elephant. Neptune was always outsize, and as he had pulled himself a little out of the water to speak, she could see the rolls of fat folding over the blue bathing slip, with tough hair lying like weeds along the ditches. She replied with amusement, 'My name is Watson. Mary Watson.'

'You're English?'

'My husband's American,' she said in extenuation.

'I haven't seen him around, have I?'

'He's in England,' she said with a small sigh, for the geographical and national situation seemed too complicated for casual explanation.

'You like it here?' he asked and lifting a hand-cup of water he distributed it over his bald head.

'So so.'

'Got the time on you?'

She looked in her bag and told him, 'Eleven fifteen.'

'I've had my half hour,' he said and trod heavily away towards the ladder at the shallow end.

An hour later, staring at her lukewarm Martini with its great green unappetizing olive, she saw him looming down at her from the other end of the bamboo bar. He wore an ordinary shirt open at the neck and a brown leather belt; his type of shoes in her childhood had been known as co-respondent, but one seldom saw them today. She wondered what Charlie would think of her pick-up; unquestionably she had landed him, rather as an angler struggling with a heavy catch finds that he has hooked nothing better than an old boot. She was no angler; she didn't know whether a boot would put an ordinary hook out of action altogether, but she knew that *her* hook could be irremediably damaged. No one would approach her if she were in his company. She drained the Martini in one gulp and even attacked the olive so as to have no excuse to linger in the bar.

'Would you do me the honour,' Mr Hickslaughter asked, 'of having a drink with me?' His manner was completely changed; on dry land he seemed unsure of himself and spoke with an old-fashioned propriety.

'I'm afraid I've only just finished one. I have to be off.' Inside the gross form she thought she saw a tousled child with disappointed eyes. 'I'm having lunch early today.' She got up and added rather stupidly, for the bar was quite empty, 'You can have my table.'

'I don't need a drink that much,' he said solemnly. 'I was just after company.' She knew that he was watching her as she moved to the adjoining coffee tavern, and she thought with guilt, at least I've got the old boot off the hook. She refused the shrimp cocktail with tomato ketchup and fell back as was usual with her on a grapefruit, with grilled trout to follow. 'Please no tomato with the trout,' she implored, but the black waiter obviously didn't understand her. While she waited she began with amusement to picture a scene between Charlie and Mr Hickslaughter, who happened for the purpose of her story to be crossing the campus. 'This is Henry Hickslaughter, Charlie. We used to go bathing together when I was in Jamaica.' Charlie, who always wore English clothes, was very tall, very thin, very concave. It was a satisfaction to know that he would never lose his figure—his nerves would see to that and his extreme sensibility. He hated anything gross; there was no grossness in *The Seasons,* not even in the lines on spring.

She heard slow footsteps coming up behind her and panicked. 'May I share your table?' Mr Hickslaughter asked. He had recovered his terrestrial politeness, but only so far as speech was concerned, for he sat firmly down without waiting for her reply. The chair was too small for him; his thighs overlapped like a double mattress on a single bed. He began to study the menu.

'They copy American food; it's worse than the reality,' Mary Watson said.

'You don't like American food?'

'Tomatoes even with the trout!'

'Tomatoes? Oh, you mean tomatoes,' he said, correcting her accent. 'I'm very fond of tomatoes myself.'

'And fresh pineapple in the salad.'

'There's a lot of vitamins in fresh pineapple.' Almost as if he wished to emphasize their disagreement, he ordered shrimp cocktail, grilled trout and a sweet salad. Of course, when her trout arrived, the tomatoes were there. 'You can have mine if you want to,' she said and he accepted with pleasure. 'You are very kind. You are really very kind.' He held out his plate like Oliver Twist.

She began to feel oddly at ease with the old man. She would have been less at ease, she was certain, with a possible adventure: she would have been wondering about her effect on him, while now she could be sure that she gave him pleasure—with the tomatoes. He was perhaps less the old anonymous boot than an old shoe comfortable to wear. And curiously enough, in spite of his first approach and in spite of his correcting her over the pronunciation of tomatoes, it was not really an old American shoe of which she was reminded. Charlie wore English clothes over his English figure, he studied English eighteenth-century literature, his book would be published in England by the Cambridge University Press who would buy sheets, but she had the impression that he was far more fashioned as an American shoe than Hickslaughter. Even Charlie, whose manners were perfect, if they had met for the first time today at the swimming-pool, would have interrogated her more closely. Interrogation had always seemed to her a principal part of American social life—an inheritance perhaps from the Indian smoke-fires: 'Where are you from? Do you know the so and so's? Have you been to the botanic gardens?' It came over her that Mr Hickslaughter, if that were really his name, was perhaps an American reject—not necessarily more flawed than the pottery rejects of famous firms you find in bargain-basements.

She found herself questioning *him,* with circumlocutions, while he savoured the tomatoes. 'I was born in London. I couldn't have been born more than six hundred miles from there

without drowning, could I? But you belong to a continent thousands of miles wide and long. Where were you born?' (She remembered a character in a Western movie directed by John Ford
who asked, 'Where do you hail from, stranger?' The question
was more frankly put than hers.)

He said, 'St Louis.'

'Oh, then there are lots of your people here—you are not
alone.' She felt a slight disappointment that he might belong to
the jolly bunch.

'I'm alone,' he said. 'Room 63.' It was in her own corridor
on the third floor of the annexe. He spoke firmly as though he
were imparting information for future use. 'Five doors down
from you.'

'Oh.'

'I saw you come out your first day.'

'I never noticed you.'

'I keep to myself unless I see someone I like.'

'Didn't you see anyone you liked from St Louis?'

'I'm not all that fond of St Louis, and St Louis can do without
me. I'm not a favourite son.'

'Do you come here often?'

'In August. It's cheap in August.' He kept on surprising her.
First there was his lack of local patriotism, and now his frankness
about money or rather about the lack of it, a frankness that could
almost be classed as an un-American activity.

'Yes.'

'I have to go where it's reasonable,' he said, as though he were
exposing his bad hand to a partner at gin.

'You've retired?'

'Well—I've been retired.' He added, 'You ought to take
salad . . . It's good for you.'

'I feel quite well without it.'

'You could do with more weight.' He added appraisingly, 'A
couple of pounds.' She was tempted to tell him that he could do
with less. They had both seen each other exposed.

'Were you in business?' She was being driven to interrogate.
He hadn't asked her a personal question since his first at the
pool.

'In a way,' he said. She had a sense that he was supremely un-interested in his own doings; she was certainly discovering an America which she had not known existed.

She said, 'Well, if you'll excuse me . . .'

'Aren't you taking any dessert?'

'No, I'm a light luncher.'

'It's all included in the price. You ought to eat some fruit.' He was looking at her under his white eyebrows with an air of dis-appointment which touched her.

'I don't care much for fruit and I want a nap. I always have a nap in the afternoon.'

Perhaps, after all, she thought, as she moved away through the formal dining-room, he is disappointed only because I'm not tak-ing full advantage of the cheap rate.

She passed his room going to her own: the door was open and a big white-haired mammy was making the bed. The room was exactly like her own; the same pair of double beds, the same wardrobe, the same dressing-table in the same position, the same heavy breathing of the air-conditioner. In her own room she looked in vain for the thermos of iced water; then she rang the bell and waited for several minutes. You couldn't expect good service in August. She went down the passage; Mr Hickslaugh-ter's door was still open and she went in to find the maid. The door of the bathroom was open too and a wet cloth lay on the tiles.

How bare the bedroom was. At least she had taken the trouble to add a few flowers, a photograph and half a dozen books on a bedside table which gave her room a lived-in air. Beside his bed there was only a literary digest lying open and face down; she turned it over to see what he was reading—as she might have ex-pected it was something to do with calories and proteins. He had begun writing a letter at his dressing-table and with the simple unscrupulousness of an intellectual she began to read it with her ears cocked for any sound in the passage.

'Dear Joe,' she read, 'the draft was two weeks late last month and I was in real difficulties. I had to borrow from a Syrian who runs a tourist junk-shop in Curaçao and pay him interest. You owe me a hundred dollars for the interest. It's your own fault.

Mum never gave us lessons on how to live with an empty stomach. Please add it to the next draft and be sure to do that, you wouldn't want me coming back to collect. I'll be here till the end of August. It's cheap in August, and a man gets tired of nothing but Dutch, Dutch, Dutch. Give my love to Sis.'

The letter broke off unfinished. Anyway she would have had no opportunity to read more because someone was approaching down the passage. She went to the door in time to see Mr Hickslaughter on the threshold. He said, 'You looking for me?'

'I was looking for the maid. She was in here a minute ago.'

'Come in and sit down.'

He looked through the bathroom door and then at the room in general. Perhaps it was only an uneasy conscience which made her think that his eyes strayed a moment to the unfinished letter.

'She's forgotten my iced water.'

'You can have mine if it's filled.' He shook his thermos and handed it to her.

'Thanks a lot.'

'When you've had your sleep . . .' he began and looked away from her. Was he looking at the letter?

'Yes?'

'We might have a drink.'

She was, in a sense, trapped. She said, 'Yes.'

'Give me a ring when you wake up.'

'Yes.' She said nervously, 'Have a good sleep yourself.'

'Oh, I don't sleep.' He didn't wait for her to leave the room before turning away, swinging that great elephantine backside of his towards her. She had walked into a trap baited with a flask of iced water, and in her room she drank the water gingerly as though it might have a flavour different from hers.

3

She found it difficult to sleep: the old fat man had become an individual now that she had read his letter. She couldn't help comparing his style with Charlie's. 'When I have said good-night to you, my dear one, I shall go happily to bed with the thought of you.' In Mr Hickslaughter's there was an ambiguity, a hint of menace. Was it possible that the old man could be dangerous?

At half past five she rang up room 63. It was not the kind of adventure she had planned, but it was an adventure nonetheless. 'I'm awake,' she said.

'You coming for a drink?' he asked.

'I'll meet you in the bar.'

'Not the bar,' he said. 'Not at the prices they charge for bourbon. I've got all we need here.' She felt as though she were being brought back to the scene of a crime, and she needed a little courage to knock on the door.

He had everything prepared: a bottle of Old Walker, a bucket of ice, two bottles of soda. Like books, drinks can make a room inhabited. She saw him as a man fighting in his own fashion against the sense of solitude.

'Siddown,' he said, 'make yourself comfortable,' like a character in a movie. He began to pour out two highballs.

She said, 'I've got an awful sense of guilt. I did come in here for iced water, but I was curious too. I read your letter.'

'I knew someone had touched it,' he said.

'I'm sorry.'

'Who cares? It was only to my brother.'

'I had no business . . .'

'Look,' he said, 'if I came into your room and found a letter open I'd read it, wouldn't I? Only your letter would be more interesting.'

'Why?'

'I don't write love letters. Never did and I'm too old now.' He sat down on a bed—she had the only easy chair. His belly hung in heavy folds under his sports-shirt, and his flies were a little open. Why was it always fat men who left them unbuttoned? He said, 'This is good bourbon,' taking a drain of it. 'What does your husband do?' he asked—it was his first personal question since the pool and it took her by surprise.

'He writes about literature. Eighteenth-century poetry,' she added, rather inanely under the circumstances.

'Oh.'

'What did you do? I mean when you worked.'

'This and that.'

'And now?'

'I watch what goes on. Sometimes I talk to someone like you. Well, no, I don't suppose I've ever talked to anyone like you before.' It might have seemed a compliment if he had not added, 'A professor's wife.'

'And you read the *Digest*?'

'Ye-eh. They make books too long—I haven't the patience. Eighteenth-century poetry. So they wrote poetry back in those days, did they?'

She said, 'Yes,' not sure whether or not he was mocking her.

'There was a poem I liked at school. The only one that ever stuck in my head. By Longfellow, I think. You ever read Longfellow?'

'Not really. They don't read him much in school any longer.'

'Something about "Spanish sailors with bearded lips and the something and mystery of the ships and the something of the sea." It hasn't stuck at all that well, after all, but I suppose I learned it sixty years ago and even more. Those were the days.'

'The 1900s?'

'No, no. I meant pirates, Kidd and Bluebeard and those fellows. This was their stamping ground, wasn't it? The Caribbean. It makes you kind of sick to see those women going around in their shorts here.' His tongue had been tingled into activity by the bourbon.

It occurred to her that she had never really been curious about another human being; she had been in love with Charlie, but he hadn't aroused her curiosity except sexually, and she had satisfied that only too quickly. She asked him, 'Do you love your sister?'

'Yes, of course, why? How do you know I've got a sister?'

'And Joe?'

'You certainly read my letter. Oh, he's OK.'

'OK?'

'Well, you know how it is with brothers. I'm the eldest in my family. There was one that died. My sister's twenty years younger than I am. Joe's got the means. He looks after her.'

'You haven't got the means?'

'I had the means. I wasn't good at managing them though. We aren't here to talk about myself.'

'I'm curious. That's why I read your letter.'

'You? Curious about me?'

'It could be, couldn't it?'

She had confused him, and now that she had the upper hand, she felt that she was out of the trap; she was free, she could come and go as she pleased, and if she chose to stay a little longer, it was her own choice.

'Have another bourbon?' he said. 'But you're English. Maybe you'd prefer Scotch?'

'Better not mix.'

'No.' He poured her another glass. He said, 'I was wondering— sometimes I want to get away from this joint for a little. What about having dinner down the road?'

'It would be stupid,' she said. 'We've both paid our *pension* here, haven't we? And it would be the same dinner in the end. Red snapper. Tomatoes.'

'I don't know what you have against tomatoes.' But he did not deny the good sense of her economic reasoning: he was the first unsuccessful American she had ever had a drink with. One must have seen them in the street . . . But even the young men who came to the house were not yet unsuccessful. The Professor of Romance Languages had perhaps hoped to be head of a university—success is relative, but it remains success.

He poured out another glass. She said, 'I'm drinking all your bourbon.'

'It's in a good cause.'

She was a little drunk by now and things—which only *seemed* relevant—came to her mind. She said, 'That thing of Longfellow's. It went on—something about "the thoughts of youth are long, long thoughts". I must have read it somewhere. That was the refrain, wasn't it?'

'Maybe. I don't remember.'

'Did you want to be a pirate when you were a boy?'

He gave an almost happy grin. He said, 'I succeeded. That's what Joe called me once—"pirate".'

'But you haven't any buried treasure?'

He said, 'He knows me well enough not to send me a hundred dollars. But if he feels scared enough that I'll come back—he might send fifty. And the interest was only twenty-five. He's not mean, but he's stupid.'

'How?'

'He ought to know I wouldn't go back. I wouldn't do one thing to hurt Sis.'

'Would it be any good if I asked you to have dinner with me?'

'No. It wouldn't be right.' In some ways he was obviously very conservative. 'It's as you said—you don't want to go throwing money about.' When the bottle of Old Walker was half empty, he said, 'You'd better have some food even if it is red snapper and tomatoes.'

'Is your name really Hickslaughter?'

'Something like that.'

They went downstairs, following rather carefully in each other's footsteps like ducks. In the formal restaurant open to all the heat of the evening, the men sat and sweated in their jackets and ties. They passed, the two of them, through the bamboo bar into the coffee tavern, which was lit by candles that increased the heat. Two young men with crew-cuts sat at the next table—they weren't the same young men she had seen before, but they came out of the same series. One of them said, 'I'm not denying that he has a certain style, but even if you *adore* Tennessee Williams . . .'

'Why did he call you a pirate?'

'It was just one of those things.'

When it came to the decision there seemed nothing to choose except red snapper and tomatoes, and again she offered him her tomatoes; perhaps he had grown to expect it and already she was chained by custom. He was an old man, he had made no pass which she could reasonably reject—how could a man of his age make a pass to a woman of hers?—and yet all the same she had a sense that she had landed on a conveyor belt . . . The future was not in her hands, and she was a little scared. She would have been more frightened if it had not been for her unusual consumption of bourbon.

'It was good bourbon,' she commented for something to say, and immediately regretted it. It gave him an opening.

'We'll have another glass before bed.'

'I think I've drunk enough.'

'A good bourbon won't hurt you. You'll sleep well.'

'I always sleep well.' It was a lie—the kind of unimportant lie one tells a husband or a lover in order to keep some privacy. The young man who had been talking about Tennessee Williams rose from his table. He was very tall and thin and he wore a skin-tight black sweater; his small elegant buttocks were outlined in skin-tight trousers. It was easy to imagine him a degree more naked. Would he have looked at her, she wondered, with interest if she had not been sitting there in the company of a fat old man so horribly clothed? It was unlikely; his body was not designed for a woman's caress.

'I don't.'

'You don't what?'

'I don't sleep well.' The unexpected self-disclosure after all his reticences came as a shock. It was as though he had put out one of his square brick-like hands and pulled her to him. He had been aloof, he had evaded her personal questions, he had lulled her into a sense of security, but now every time she opened her mouth, she seemed doomed to commit an error, to invite him nearer. Even her harmless remark about the bourbon . . . She said stupidly, 'Perhaps it's the change of climate.'

'What change of climate?'

'Between here and . . . and . . .'

'Curaçao? I guess there's no great difference. I don't sleep there either.'

'I've got some very good pills . . .' she said rashly.

'I thought you said you slept well.'

'Oh, there are always times. It's sometimes just a question of digestion.'

'Yes, digestion. You're right there. A bourbon will be good for that. If you've finished dinner . . .'

She looked across the coffee tavern to the bamboo bar, where the young man stood *déhanche,* holding a glass of crème-de-menthe between his face and his companion's like an exotically coloured monocle.

Mr Hickslaughter said in a shocked voice, 'You don't care for that type, do you?'

'They're often good conversationalists.'

'Oh, conversation . . . If that's what you want.' It was as though she had expressed an un-American liking for snails or frogs' legs.

'Shall we have our bourbon in the bar? It's a little cooler tonight.'

'And pay and listen to their chatter? No, we'll go upstairs.'

He swung back again in the direction of old-fashioned courtesy and came behind her to pull her chair—even Charlie was not so polite, but was it politeness or the determination to block her way of escape to the bar?

They entered the lift together. The black attendant had a radio turned on, and from the small brown box came the voice of a preacher talking about the Blood of the Lamb. Perhaps it was a Sunday, and that would explain the temporary void around them—between one jolly bunch and another. They stepped out into the empty corridor like undesirables marooned. The boy followed them out and sat down upon a chair beside the elevator to wait for another signal, while the voice continued to talk about the Blood of the Lamb. What was she afraid of? Mr Hickslaughter began to unlock his door. He was much older than her father would have been if he had been still alive; he could be her grandfather—the excuse, 'What will the boy think?' was inadmissible—it was even shocking, for his manner had never ceased to be correct. He might be old, but what right had she to think of him as 'dirty'?

'Damn the hotel key . . .' he said. 'It won't open.'

She turned the handle for him. 'The door wasn't locked.'

'I can sure do with a bourbon after those nancies . . .'

But now she had her excuse ready on the lips. 'I've had one too many already, I'm afraid. I've got to sleep it off.' She put her hand on his arm. 'Thank you so much . . . It was a lovely evening.' She was aware how insulting her English accent sounded as she walked quickly down the corridor leaving it behind her like a mocking presence, mocking all the things she liked best in him: his ambiguous character, his memory of Longfellow, his having to make ends meet.

She looked back when she reached her room: he was standing in the passage as though he couldn't make up his mind to go in. She was reminded of an old man whom she had passed one day on the campus leaning on his broom among the unswept autumn leaves.

4

In her room she picked up a book and tried to read. It was Thomson's *Seasons*. She had carried it with her, so that she could understand any reference to his work that Charlie might make in a letter. This was the first time she had opened it, and she was not held:

> And now the mounting Sun dispels the Fog:
> The rigid Hoar-Frost melts! before his Beam;
> And hung on every Spray, on every Blade
> Of Grass, the myriad Dew-Drops twinkle round.

If she could be so cowardly, she thought, with a harmless old man like that, how could she have faced the real decisiveness of an adventure? One was not, at her age, 'swept off the feet'. Charlie had been proved just as sadly right to trust her as she was right to trust Charlie. Now with the difference in time he would be leaving the Museum, or rather, if this were a Sunday as the Blood of the Lamb seemed to indicate, he would probably have just quit writing in his hotel room. After a successful day's work he always resembled an advertisement for a new shaving-cream: a kind of glow . . . She found it irritating, like living with a halo. Even his voice had a different timbre and he would call her 'old girl' and pat her bottom patronizingly. She preferred him when he was touchy with failure: only temporary failure, of course, the failure of an idea which hadn't worked out, the touchiness of a child's disappointment at a party which has not come up to his expectations, not the failure of the old man—the rusted framework of a ship transfixed once and for all upon the rock where it had struck.

She felt ignoble. What earthly risk could the old man represent to justify refusing him half an hour's companionship? He could no more assault her than the boat could detach itself from the rock and steam out to sea for the Fortunate Islands. She pictured him sitting alone with his half-empty bottle of bourbon seeking unconsciousness. Or was he perhaps finishing the crude blackmailing letter to his brother? What a story she would make of it one day, she thought with self-disgust as she took off her dress, her evening with a blackmailer and 'pirate'.

There was one thing she could do for him: she could give him her bottle of pills. She put on her dressing-gown and retrod the corridor, room by room, until she arrived at 63. His voice told her to come in. She opened the door and in the light of the bed-side lamp saw him sitting on the edge of the bed wearing a crumpled pair of cotton pyjamas with broad mauve stripes. She began, 'I've brought you . . .' and then she saw to her amazement that he had been crying. His eyes were red and the evening darkness of his cheeks sparkled with points like dew. She had only once before seen a man cry—Charlie, when the University Press had decided against his first volume of literary essays.

'I thought you were the maid,' he said. 'I rang for her.'

'What did you want?'

'I thought she might take a glass of bourbon,' he said.

'Did you want so much . . . ? I'll take a glass.' The bottle was still on the dressing-table where they had left it and the two glasses—she identified hers by the smear of lipstick. 'Here you are,' she said, 'drink it up. It will make you sleep.'

He said, 'I'm not an alcoholic.'

'Of course you aren't.'

She sat on the bed beside him and took his left hand in hers. It was cracked and dry, and she wanted to clean back the cuticle until she remembered that was something she did for Charlie.

'I wanted company,' he said.

'I'm here.'

'You'd better turn off the bell-light or the maid will come.'

'She'll never know what she missed in the way of Old Walker.'

When she returned from the door he was lying back against the pillows in an odd twisted position, and she thought again of the ship broken-backed upon the rocks. She tried to pick up his feet to lay them on the bed, but they were like heavy stones at the bottom of a quarry.

'Lie down,' she said, 'you'll never be sleepy that way. What do you do for company in Curaçao?'

'I manage,' he said.

'You've finished the bourbon. Let me put out the lights.'

'It's no good pretending to you,' he said.

'Pretending?'

'I'm afraid of the dark.'

She thought, I'll smile later when I think of who it was I feared. She said, 'Do the old pirates you fought come back to haunt you?'

'I've done some bad things,' he said, 'in my time.'

'Haven't we all?'

'Nothing extraditable,' he explained as though that were an extenuation.

'If you take one of my pills . . .'

'You won't go—not yet?'

'No, no. I'll stay till you're sleepy.'

'I've been wanting to talk to you for days.'

'I'm glad you did.'

'Would you believe it—I hadn't got the nerve.' If she had shut her eyes it might have been a very young man speaking. 'I don't know your sort.'

'Don't you have my sort in Curaçao?'

'No.'

'You haven't taken the pill yet.'

'I'm afraid of not waking up.'

'Have you so much to do tomorrow?'

'I mean ever.' He put out his hand and touched her knee, searchingly, without sensuality, as if he needed support from the bone. 'I'll tell you what's wrong. You're a stranger, so I can tell you. I'm afraid of dying, with nobody around, in the dark.'

'Are you ill?'

'I wouldn't know. I don't see doctors. I don't like doctors.'

'But why should you think . . . ?'

'I'm over seventy. The Bible age. It could happen any day now.'

'You'll live to a hundred,' she said with an odd conviction.

'Then I'll have to live with fear the hell of a long time.'

'Was that why you were crying?'

'No. I thought you were going to stay awhile, and then suddenly you went. I guess I was disappointed.'

'Are you never alone in Curaçao?'

'I pay not to be alone.'

'As you'd have paid the maid?'

'Ye-eh. Sort of.'

It was as though she were discovering for the first time the interior of the enormous continent on which she had elected to live. America had been Charlie, it had been New England; through books and movies she had been aware of the wonders of nature like some great cineramic film with Lowell Thomas cheapening the Painted Desert and the Grand Canyon with his clichés. There had been no mystery anywhere from Miami to Niagara Falls, from Cape Cod to the Pacific Palisades; tomatoes were served on every plate and Coca-Cola in every glass. Nobody anywhere admitted failure or fear; they were like sins 'hushed up'—worse perhaps than sins, for sins have glamour—they were bad taste. But here stretched on the bed, dressed in striped pyjamas which Brooks Brothers would have disowned, failure and fear talked to her without shame, and in an American accent. It was as though she were living in the remote future, after God knew what catastrophe.

She said, 'I wasn't for sale? There was only the Old Walker to tempt *me*.'

He raised his antique Neptune head a little way from the pillow and said, 'I'm not afraid of death. Not sudden death. Believe me, I've looked for it here and there. It's the certain-sure business, closing in on you, like tax-inspectors . . .'

She said, 'Sleep now.'

'I can't.'

'Yes, you can.'

'If you'd stay with me awhile . . .'

'I'll stay with you. Relax.' She lay down on the bed beside him on the outside of the sheet. In a few minutes he was deeply asleep and she turned off the light. He grunted several times and spoke only once, when he said, 'You've got me wrong,' and after that he became for a little while like a dead man in his immobility and his silence, so that during that period she fell asleep. When she woke she was aware from his breathing that he was awake too. He was lying away from her so that their bodies wouldn't touch. She put out her hand and felt no repulsion at all at his excitement. It was as though she had spent many nights beside him in the one bed, and when he made love to her, silently and abruptly in the darkness, she gave a sigh of satisfaction. There was no guilt; she would be going back in a few days, resigned and tender, to Charlie and Charlie's loving skill, and she wept a little, but not seriously, at the temporary nature of this meeting.

'What's wrong?' he asked.

'Nothing. Nothing. I wish I could stay.'

'Stay a little longer. Stay till it's light.' That would not be very long. Already they could distinguish the grey masses of the furniture standing around them like Caribbean tombs.

'Oh yes, I'll stay till it's light. That wasn't what I meant.' His body began to slip out of her, and it was as though he were carrying away her unknown child, away in the direction of Curaçao, and she tried to hold him back, the fat old frightened man whom she almost loved.

He said, 'I never had this in mind.'

'I know. Don't say it. I understand.'

'I guess after all we've got a lot in common,' he said, and she agreed in order to quieten him. He was fast asleep by the time the light came back, so she got off the bed without waking him and went to her room. She locked the door and began with resolution to pack her bag: it was time for her to leave, it was time for term to start again. She wondered afterwards, when she thought of him, what it was they could have had in common, except the fact, of course, that for both of them Jamaica was cheap in August.

A SHOCKING ACCIDENT

Jerome was called into his housemaster's room in the break between the second and the third class on a Thursday morning. He had no fear of trouble, for he was a warden—the name that the proprietor and headmaster of a rather expensive preparatory school had chosen to give to approved, reliable boys in the lower forms (from a warden one became a guardian and finally before leaving, it was hoped for Marlborough or Rugby, a crusader). The housemaster, Mr Wordsworth, sat behind his desk with an appearance of perplexity and apprehension. Jerome had the odd impression when he entered that he was a cause of fear.

'Sit down, Jerome,' Mr Wordsworth said. 'All going well with the trigonometry?'

'Yes, sir.'

'I've had a telephone call, Jerome. From your aunt. I'm afraid I have bad news for you.'

'Yes, sir?'

'Your father has had an accident.'

'Oh.'

Mr Wordsworth looked at him with some surprise. 'A serious accident.'

'Yes, sir?'

Jerome worshipped his father: the verb is exact. As man recreates God, so Jerome re-created his father—from a restless widowed author into a mysterious adventurer who travelled in far places—Nice, Beirut, Majorca, even the Canaries. The time had arrived about his eighth birthday when Jerome believed that his father either 'ran guns' or was a member of the British Secret

Service. Now it occurred to him that his father might have been wounded in 'a hail of machine-gun bullets'.

Mr Wordsworth played with the ruler on his desk. He seemed at a loss how to continue. He said, 'You know your father was in Naples?'

'Yes, sir.'

'Your aunt heard from the hospital today.'

'Oh.'

Mr Wordsworth said with desperation, 'It was a street accident.'

'Yes, sir?' It seemed quite likely to Jerome that they would call it a street accident. The police of course had fired first; his father would not take human life except as a last resort.

'I'm afraid your father was very seriously hurt indeed.'

'Oh.'

'In fact, Jerome, he died yesterday. Quite without pain.'

'Did they shoot him through the heart?'

'I beg your pardon. What did you say, Jerome?'

'Did they shoot him through the heart?'

'Nobody shot him, Jerome. A pig fell on him.' An inexplicable convulsion took place in the nerves of Mr Wordsworth's face; it really looked for a moment as though he were going to laugh. He closed his eyes, composed his features and said rapidly as though it were necessary to expel the story as rapidly as possible. 'Your father was walking along a street in Naples when a pig fell on him. A shocking accident. Apparently in the poorer quarters of Naples they keep pigs on their balconies. This one was on the fifth floor. It had grown too fat. The balcony broke. The pig fell on your father.'

Mr Wordsworth left his desk rapidly and went to the window, turning his back on Jerome. He shook a little with emotion.

Jerome said, 'What happened to the pig?'

2

This was not callousness on the part of Jerome, as it was interpreted by Mr Wordsworth to his colleagues (he even discussed with them whether, perhaps, Jerome was yet fitted to be a warden). Jerome was only attempting to visualize the strange scene to get the details right. Nor was Jerome a boy who cried; he was a boy who brooded, and it never occurred to him at his preparatory school that the circumstances of his father's death were comic—they were still part of the mystery of life. It was later, in his first term at his public school, when he told the story to his best friend, that he began to realize how it affected others. Naturally after that disclosure he was known, rather unreasonably, as Pig.

Unfortunately his aunt had no sense of humour. There was an enlarged snapshot of his father on the piano; a large sad man in an unsuitable dark suit posed in Capri with an umbrella (to guard him against sunstroke), the Faraglione rocks forming the background. By the age of sixteen Jerome was well aware that the portrait looked more like the author of *Sunshine and Shade* and *Rambles in the Balearics* than an agent of the Secret Service. All the same he loved the memory of his father: he still possessed an album fitted with picture-postcards (the stamps had been soaked off long ago for his other collection), and it pained him when his aunt embarked with strangers on the story of his father's death.

'A shocking accident,' she would begin, and the stranger would compose his or her features into the correct shape for interest and commiseration. Both reactions, of course, were false, but it was terrible for Jerome to see how suddenly, midway in her rambling discourse, the interest would become genuine. 'I can't think how such things can be allowed in a civilized country,' his aunt would say. 'I suppose one has to regard Italy as civilized. One is prepared for all kinds of things abroad, of course, and my brother was a great traveller. He always carried a water-filter with him. It was far less expensive, you know, than buying all those bottles of mineral water. My brother always said that his filter paid for his dinner wine. You can see from that what a careful man he was, but who could possibly have expected when he was walking along the Via Dottore Manuele Panucci on his way to the Hydrographic Museum that a pig would fall on him?' That was the moment when the interest became genuine.

Jerome's father had not been a very distinguished writer, but the time always seems to come, after an author's death, when somebody thinks it worth his while to write a letter to the *Times Literary Supplement* announcing the preparation of a biography and asking to see any letters or documents or receive any anecdotes from friends of the dead man. Most of the biographies, of course, never appear—one wonders whether the whole thing may not be an obscure form of blackmail and whether many a potential writer of a biography or thesis finds the means in this way to finish his education at Kansas or Nottingham. Jerome, however, as a chartered accountant, lived far from the literary world. He did not realize how small the menace really was, or that the danger period for someone of his father's obscurity had long passed. Sometimes he rehearsed the method of recounting his father's death so as to reduce the comic element to its smallest dimensions—it would be of no use to refuse information, for in that case the biographer would undoubtedly visit his aunt who was living to a great old age with no sign of flagging.

It seemed to Jerome that there were two possible methods—the first led gently up to the accident, so that by the time it was described the listener was so well prepared that the death came really as an anti-climax. The chief danger of laughter in such a story was always surprise. When he rehearsed this method Jerome began boringly enough.

'You know Naples and those high tenement buildings? Somebody once told me that the Neapolitan always feels at home in New York just as the man from Turin feels at home in London because the river runs in much the same way in both cities. Where was I? Oh, yes. Naples, of course. You'd be surprised in the poorer quarters what things they keep on the balconies of those sky-scraping tenements—not washing, you know, or bedding, but things like livestock, chickens or even pigs. Of course the pigs get no exercise whatever and fatten all the quicker.' He could imagine how his hearer's eyes would have glazed by this time. 'I've no idea, have you, how heavy a pig can be, but these old buildings are all badly in need of repair. A balcony on the fifth floor gave way under one of those pigs. It struck the third floor balcony on its way down and sort of ricochetted into the street. My father was on the way to the Hydrographic Museum when the pig hit him. Coming from that height and that angle it broke his neck.' This was really a masterly attempt to make an intrinsically interesting subject boring.

The other method Jerome rehearsed had the virtue of brevity.

'My father was killed by a pig.'

'Really? In India?'

'No, in Italy.'

'How interesting. I never realized there was pig-sticking in Italy. Was your father keen on polo?'

In course of time, neither too early nor too late, rather as though, in his capacity as a chartered accountant, Jerome had studied the statistics and taken the average, he became engaged to be married: to a pleasant fresh-faced girl of twenty-five whose father was a doctor in Pinner. Her name was Sally, her favourite author was still Hugh Walpole, and she had adored babies ever since she had been given a doll at the age of five which moved its eyes and made water. Their relationship was contented rather than exciting, as became the love-affair of a chartered accountant; it would never have done if it had interfered with the figures.

One thought worried Jerome, however. Now that within a year he might himself become a father, his love for the dead man increased; he realized what affection had gone into the picture-postcards. He felt a longing to protect his memory, and uncertain whether this quiet love of his would survive if Sally were so insensitive as to laugh when she heard the story of his father's death. Inevitably she would hear it when Jerome brought her to dinner with his aunt. Several times he tried to tell her himself, as she was naturally anxious to know all she could that concerned him.

'You were very small when your father died?'

'Just nine.'

'Poor little boy,' she said.

'I was at school. They broke the news to me.'

'Did you take it very hard?'

'I can't remember.'

'You never told me how it happened.'

'It was very sudden. A street accident.'

'You'll never drive fast, will you, Jemmy?' (She had begun to call him 'Jemmy'.) It was too late then to try the second method—the one he thought of as the pig-sticking one.

They were going to marry quietly in a registry-office and have their honeymoon at Torquay. He avoided taking her to see his aunt until a week before the wedding, but then the night came, and he could not have told himself whether his apprehension was more for his father's memory or the security of his own love.

The moment came all too soon. 'Is that Jemmy's father?' Sally asked, picking up the portrait of the man with the umbrella.

'Yes, dear. How did you guess?'

'He has Jemmy's eyes and brow, hasn't he?'

'Has Jerome lent you his books?'

'No.'

'I will give you a set for your wedding. He wrote so tenderly about his travels. My own favourite is *Nooks and Crannies*. He would have had a great future. It made that shocking accident all the worse.'

'Yes?'

Jerome longed to leave the room and not see that loved face crinkle with irresistible amusement.

'I had so many letters from his readers after the pig fell on him.' She had never been so abrupt before.

And then the miracle happened. Sally did not laugh. Sally sat with open eyes of horror while his aunt told her the story, and at the end, 'How horrible,' Sally said. 'It makes you think, doesn't it? Happening like that. Out of a clear sky.'

Jerome's heart sang with joy. It was as though she had appeased his fear for ever. In the taxi going home he kissed her with more passion than he had ever shown and she returned it. There were babies in her pale blue pupils, babies that rolled their eyes and made water.

'A week today,' Jerome said, and she squeezed his hand. 'Penny for your thoughts, my darling.'

'I was wondering,' Sally said, 'what happened to the poor pig?'

'They almost certainly had it for dinner,' Jerome said happily and kissed the dear child again.

THE INVISIBLE JAPANESE GENTLEMEN

There were eight Japanese gentlemen having a fish dinner at Bentley's. They spoke to each other rarely in their incomprehensible tongue, but always with a courteous smile and often with a small bow. All but one of them wore glasses. Sometimes the pretty girl who sat in the window beyond gave them a passing glance, but her own problem seemed too serious for her to pay real attention to anyone in the world except herself and her companion.

She had thin blonde hair and her face was pretty and *petite* in a Regency way, oval like a miniature, though she had a harsh way of speaking—perhaps the accent of the school, Roedean or Cheltenham Ladies' College, which she had not long ago left. She wore a man's signet-ring on her engagement finger, and as I sat down at my table, with the Japanese gentlemen between us, she said, 'So you see we could marry next week.'

'Yes?'

Her companion appeared a little distraught. He refilled their glasses with Chablis and said, 'Of course, but Mother . . .' I missed some of the conversation then, because the eldest Japanese gentleman leant across the table, with a smile and a little bow, and uttered a whole paragraph like the mutter from an aviary, while everyone bent towards him and smiled and listened, and I couldn't help attending to him myself.

The girl's fiancé resembled her physically. I could see them as two miniatures hanging side by side on white wood panels. He should have been a young officer in Nelson's navy in the days when a certain weakness and sensitivity were no bar to promotion.

She said, 'They are giving me an advance of five hundred pounds, and they've sold the paperback rights already.' The hard commercial declaration came as a shock to me; it was a shock too that she was one of my own profession. She couldn't have been more than twenty. She deserved better of life.

He said, 'But my uncle . . .'

'You know you don't get on with him. This way we shall be quite independent.'

'*You* will be independent,' he said grudgingly.

'The wine-trade wouldn't really suit you, would it? I spoke to my publisher about you and there's a very good chance . . . if you began with some reading . . .'

'But I don't know a thing about books.'

'I would help you at the start.'

'My mother says that writing is a good crutch . . .'

'Five hundred pounds and half the paperback rights is a pretty solid crutch,' she said.

'This Chablis is good, isn't it?'

'I dare say.'

I began to change my opinion of him—he had not the Nelson touch. He was doomed to defeat. She came alongside and raked him fore and aft. 'Do you know what Mr Dwight said?'

'Who's Dwight?'

'Darling, you don't listen, do you? My publisher. He said he hadn't read a first novel in the last ten years which showed such powers of observation.'

'That's wonderful,' he said sadly, 'wonderful.'

'Only he wants me to change the title.'

'Yes?'

'He doesn't like *The Ever-Rolling Stream*. He wants to call it *The Chelsea Set*.'

'What did you say?'

'I agreed. I do think that with a first novel one should try to keep one's publisher happy. Especially when, really, he's going to pay for our marriage, isn't he?'

'I see what you mean.' Absent-mindedly he stirred his Chablis with a fork—perhaps before the engagement he had always bought champagne. The Japanese gentlemen had finished their fish and with very little English but with elaborate courtesy they were ordering from the middle-aged waitress a fresh fruit salad. The girl looked at them, and then she looked at me, but I think she saw only the future. I wanted very much to warn her against any future based on a first novel called *The Chelsea Set*. I was on the side of his mother. It was a humiliating thought, but I was probably about her mother's age.

I wanted to say to her, Are you certain your publisher is telling you the truth? Publishers are human. They may sometimes exaggerate the virtues of the young and the pretty. Will *The Chelsea Set* be read in five years? Are you prepared for the years of effort, 'the long defeat of doing nothing well'? As the years pass writing will not become any easier, the daily effort will grow harder to endure, those 'powers of observation' will become enfeebled; you will be judged, when you reach your forties, by performance and not by promise.

'My next novel is going to be about St Tropez.'

'I didn't know you'd ever been there.'

'I haven't. A fresh eye's terribly important. I thought we might settle down there for six months.'

'There wouldn't be much left of the advance by that time.'

'The advance is only an advance. I get fifteen per cent after five thousand copies and twenty per cent after ten. And of course another advance will be due, darling, when the next book's finished. A bigger one if *The Chelsea Set* sells well.'

'Suppose it doesn't.'

'Mr Dwight says it will. He ought to know.'

'My uncle would start me at twelve hundred.'

'But, darling, how could you come then to St Tropez?'

'Perhaps we'd do better to marry when you come back.'

She said harshly, 'I mightn't come back if *The Chelsea Set* sells enough.'

'Oh.'

She looked at me and the party of Japanese gentlemen. She finished her wine. She said, 'Is this a quarrel?'

'No.'

'I've got the title for the next book—*The Azure Blue.*'

'I thought azure *was* blue.'

She looked at him with disappointment. 'You don't really want to be married to a novelist, do you?'

'You aren't one yet.'

'I was born one—Mr Dwight says. My powers of observation . . .'

'Yes. You told me that, but, dear, couldn't you observe a bit nearer home? Here in London.'

'I've done that in *The Chelsea Set*. I don't want to repeat myself.'

The bill had been lying beside them for some time now. He took out his wallet to pay, but she snatched the paper out of his reach. She said, 'This is my celebration.'

'What of?'

'*The Chelsea Set*, of course. Darling, you're awfully decorative, but sometimes—well, you simply don't connect.'

'I'd rather . . . if you don't mind . . .'

'No, darling, this is on me. And Mr Dwight, of course.'

He submitted just as two of the Japanese gentlemen gave tongue simultaneously, then stopped abruptly and bowed to each other, as though they were blocked in a doorway.

I had thought the two young people matching miniatures, but what a contrast in fact there was. The same type of prettiness could contain weakness and strength. Her Regency counterpart, I suppose, would have borne a dozen children without the aid of anaesthetics, while he would have fallen an easy victim to the first dark eyes in Naples. Would there one day be a dozen books on her shelf? They have to be born without an anaesthetic too. I found myself hoping that *The Chelsea Set* would prove to be a disaster and that eventually she would take up photographic modelling while he established himself solidly in the wine-trade in St James's. I didn't like to think of her as the Mrs Humphrey Ward of her generation—not that I would live so long. Old age saves us from the realization of a great many fears. I wondered to which publishing firm Dwight belonged. I could imagine the blurb he would have already written about her abrasive powers of observation. There would be a photo, if he was wise, on the back of the jacket, for reviewers, as well as publishers, are human, and she didn't look like Mrs Humphrey Ward.

I could hear them talking while they found their coats at the back of the restaurant. He said, 'I wonder what all those Japanese are doing here?'

'Japanese?' she said. 'What Japanese, darling? Sometimes you are so evasive I think you don't want to marry me at all.'

AWFUL WHEN YOU
THINK OF IT

When the baby looked up at me from its wicker basket and winked—on the opposite seat somewhere between Reading and Slough—I became uneasy. It was as if he had discovered my secret interest.

It is awful how little we change. So often an old acquaintance, whom one has not seen for forty years when he occupied the neighbouring chopped and inky desk, detains one in the street with his unwelcome memory. Even as a baby we carry the future with us. Clothes cannot change us, the clothes are the uniform of our character, and our character changes as little as the shape of the nose and the expression of the eyes.

It has always been my hobby in railway trains to visualize in a baby's face the man he is to become—the bar-lounger, the gadabout, the frequenter of fashionable weddings; you need only supply the cloth cap, the grey topper, the uniform of the sad, smug or hilarious future. But I have always felt a certain contempt for the babies I have studied with such superior wisdom (they little know), and it was a shock last week when one of the brood not only detected me in the act of observation but returned that knowing signal, as if he shared my knowledge of what the years would make of him.

He had been momentarily left alone by his young mother on the seat opposite. She had smiled towards me with a tacit understanding that I would look after her baby for a few moments. What danger after all could happen to *it*? (Perhaps she was less certain of his sex than I was. She knew the shape under the nappies, of course, but shapes can deceive: parts alter, operations are performed.) She could not see what I had seen—the tilted bowler and the umbrella over the arm. (No arm was yet apparent under the coverlet printed with pink rabbits.)

When she was safely out of the carriage I bent towards the basket and asked him a question. I had never before carried my researches quite so far.

'What's yours?' I said.

He blew a thick white bubble, brown at the edges. There could be no doubt at all that he was saying, 'A pint of the best bitter.'

'Haven't seen you lately—you know—in the old place,' I said.

He gave a quick smile, passing it off, then he winked again. You couldn't doubt that he was saying, 'The other half?'

I blew a bubble in my turn—we spoke the same language.

Very slightly he turned his head to one side. He didn't want anybody to hear what he was going to say now.

'You've got a tip?' I asked.

Don't mistake my meaning. It was not racing information I wanted. Of course I could not see his waist under all those pink-rabbit wrappings, but I knew perfectly well that he wore a double-breasted waistcoat and had nothing to do with the tracks. I said very rapidly because his mother might return at any moment, 'My brokers are Druce, Davis and Burrows.'

He looked up at me with bloodshot eyes and a little line of spittle began to form at the corner of his mouth. I said, 'Oh, I know they're not all that good. But at the moment they are recommending Stores.'

He gave a high wail of pain—you could have mistaken the cause for wind, but I knew better. In his club they didn't have to serve dill water. I said, 'I don't agree, mind you,' and he stopped crying and blew a bubble—a little tough white one which lingered on his lip.

I caught his meaning at once. 'My round,' I said. 'Time for a short?'

He nodded.

'Scotch?' I know few people will believe me, but he raised his head an inch or two and gazed unmistakably at my watch.

'A bit early?' I said. 'Pink gin?'

I didn't have to wait for his reply. 'Make them large ones,' I said to the imaginary barman.

He spat at me, so I added, 'Throw away the pink.'

'Well,' I said, 'here's to you. Happy future,' and we smiled at each other, well content.

'I don't know what you would advise,' I said, 'but surely Tobaccos are about as low as they will go. When you think Imps were a cool 80/- in the early Thirties and now you can pick them up for under 60/- . . . This cancer scare can't go on. People have got to have their fun.'

At the word fun he winked again, looked secretively around, and I realized that perhaps I had been on the wrong track. It was not after all the state of the markets he had been so ready to talk about.

'I heard a damn good one yesterday,' I said. 'A man got into a tube train, and there was a pretty girl with one stocking coming down . . .'

He yawned and closed his eyes.

'Sorry,' I said, 'I thought it was new. You tell me one.'

And do you know that damned baby was quite ready to oblige? But he belonged to the school who find their own jokes funny and when he tried to speak, he could only laugh. He couldn't get his story out for laughter. He laughed and winked and laughed again—what a good story it must have been. I could have dined out for weeks on the strength of it. His limbs twitched in the basket; he even tried to get his hands free from the pink rabbits, and then the laughter died. I could almost hear him saying, 'Tell you later, old man.'

His mother opened the door of the compartment. She said, 'You've been amusing baby. How kind of you. Are you fond of babies?' And she gave me such a look—the love-wrinkles forming round the mouth and eyes—that I was tempted to reply with the warmth and hypocrisy required, but then I met the baby's hard relentless gaze.

'Well, as a matter of fact,' I said, 'I'm not. Not really,' I drooled on, losing all my chances before that blue and pebbly stare. 'You know how it is . . . never had one of my own . . . I'm fond of fishes though . . .'

I suppose in a way I got my reward. The baby blew a whole succession of bubbles. He was satisfied; after all a chap shouldn't make passes at another chap's mother, especially if he belongs to the same club—for suddenly I knew inevitably to what club he would belong in twenty-five years' time. 'On me,' he was obviously saying now. 'Doubles all round.' I could only hope that I would not live so long.

DOCTOR CROMBIE

An unfortunate circumstance in my life has just recalled to mind a certain Doctor Crombie and the conversations I used to hold with him when I was young. He was the school doctor until the eccentricity of his ideas became generally known. After he had ceased to attend the school the rest of his practice was soon reduced to a few old people, almost as eccentric as himself—there were, I remember, Colonel Parker, a British Israelite, Miss Warrender who kept twenty-five cats, and a man called Horace Turner who invented a system for turning the National Debt into a National Credit.

Doctor Crombie lived all alone half a mile from the school in a red-brick villa in King's Road. Luckily he possessed a small private income, for at the end his work had come to be entirely paperwork—long articles for the *Lancet* and the *British Medical Journal* which were never published. It was long before the days of television; otherwise a corner might have been found for him in some magazine programme, and his views would have reached a larger public than the random gossips of Bankstead—with who knows what result?—for he spoke with sincerity, and when I was young he certainly to me carried a measure of conviction.

Our school, which had begun as a grammar school during the reign of Henry VIII, had, by the twentieth century, just edged its way into the *Public Schools Year Book*. There were many dayboys, of whom I was one, for Bankstead was only an hour from London by train, and in the days of the old London Midland and Scottish Railways there were frequent and rapid services for commuters. In a boarding-school where the boys are isolated for months at a time like prisoners on Dartmoor, Doctor Crombie's views would have become known more slowly. By the time a boy went home for the holidays he would have forgotten any curious details, and the parents, dotted about England in equal isolation, would have been unable to get together and check up on any unusual stories. It was different at Bankstead, where parents lived a community life and attended sing-songs, but even here Doctor Crombie's views had a long innings.

The headmaster was progressively minded and, when the boys emerged, at the age of thirteen, from the junior school, he arranged, with the consent of the parents, that Doctor Crombie should address them in small groups on the problems of personal hygiene and the dangers which lay ahead. I have only faint memories of the occasion, of the boys who sniggered, of the boys who blushed, of the boys who stared at the ground as though they had dropped something, but I remember vividly the explicit and plain-speaking Doctor Crombie, with his melancholy moustache, which remained blond from nicotine long after his head was grey, and his gold-rimmed spectacles—gold rims, like a pipe, always give me the impression of a rectitude I can never achieve. I understood very little of what he was saying, but I do remember later that I asked my parents what he meant by 'playing with oneself'. Being an only child I was accustomed to play with myself. For example, in the case of my model railway, I was in turn driver, signalman and station-master, and I felt no need of an assistant.

My mother said she had forgotten to speak to the cook and left us alone.

'Doctor Crombie,' I told my father, 'says that it causes cancer.'

'Cancer!' my father exclaimed. 'Are you sure he didn't say insanity?' (It was a great period for insanity: loss of vitality leading to nervous debility and nervous debility becoming melancholia and eventually melancholia becoming madness. For some reasons these effects were said to come before marriage and not after.)

'He said cancer. An incurable disease, he said.'

'Odd!' my father remarked. He reassured me about playing

trains, and Doctor Crombie's theory went out of my head for some years. I don't think my father can have mentioned it to anyone else except possibly my mother and that only as a joke. Cancer was as good a scare during puberty as madness—the standard of dishonesty among parents is a high one. They had themselves long ceased to believe in the threat of madness, but they used it as a convenience, and only after some years did they reach the conclusion that Doctor Crombie was a strictly honest man.

I had just left school by that time and I had not yet gone up to the university; Doctor Crombie's head was quite white by then, though his moustache stayed blond. We had become close friends, for we both liked observing trains, and sometimes on a summer's day we took a picnic-lunch and sat on the green mound of Bankstead Castle from which we could watch the line and see below it the canal with the bright-painted barges drawn by slow horses in the direction of Birmingham. We drank ginger-beer out of stone bottles and ate ham sandwiches while Doctor Crombie studied *Bradshaw*. When I want an image for innocence I think of those afternoons.

But the peace of the afternoon I am remembering now was disturbed. An immense goods-train of coal-waggons went by us—I counted sixty-three, which approached our record, but when I asked for his confirmation, Doctor Crombie had inexplicably forgotten to count.

'Is something the matter?' I asked.

'The school has asked me to resign,' he said, and he took off the gold-rimmed glasses and wiped them.

'Good heavens! Why?'

'The secrets of the consulting-room, my dear boy, are one-sided,' he said. 'The patient, but not the doctor, is at liberty to tell everything.'

A week later I learnt a little of what had happened. The story had spread rapidly from parent to parent, for this was not something which concerned small boys—this concerned all of them. Perhaps there was even an element of fear in the talk—fear that Doctor Crombie might be right. Incredible thought!

A boy whom I knew, a little younger than myself, called Fred Wright, who was still in the sixth form, had visited Doctor

Crombie because of certain pains in the testicles. He had had his first woman in a street off Leicester Square on a half-day excursion—there were half-day excursions in those happy days of rival railway-companies—and he had taken his courage in his hands and visited Doctor Crombie. He was afraid that he had caught what was then known as a social disease. Doctor Crombie had reassured him—he was suffering from acidity, that was all, and he should be careful not to eat tomatoes, but Doctor Crombie went on, rashly and unnecessarily, to warn him, as he had warned all of us at thirteen . . .

Fred Wright had no reason to feel ashamed. Acidity can happen to anyone, and he didn't hesitate to tell his parents of the further advice which Doctor Crombie had given him. When I returned home that afternoon and questioned my parents, I found the story had already reached them as it had reached the school authorities. Parent after parent had checked with one another, and afterwards child after child was interrogated. Cancer as the result of masturbation was one thing—you had to discourage it somehow—but what right had Doctor Crombie to say that cancer was the result of prolonged sexual relations, even in a proper marriage recognized by Church and State? (It was unfortunate that Fred Wright's very virile father, unknown to his son, had already fallen a victim to the dread disease.)

I was even a little shaken myself. I had great affection for Doctor Crombie and great confidence in him. (I had never played trains all by myself after thirteen with the same pleasure as before his hygienic talk.) And the worst of it was that now I had fallen in love, hopelessly in love, with a girl in Castle Street with what we called then bobbed hair; she resembled in an innocent and provincial way two famous society sisters whose photographs appeared nearly every week in the *Daily Mail*. (The years seem to be returning on their tracks, and I see now everywhere the same face, the same hair, as I saw then, but alas, with little or no emotion.)

The next time I went out with Doctor Crombie to watch the trains I tackled him—shyly; there were still words I didn't like to use with my elders. 'Did you really tell Fred Wright that— marriage—is a cause of cancer?'

'Not marriage in itself, my boy. Any form of sexual congress.'

'Congress?' It was the first time I had heard the word used in that way. I thought of the Congress of Vienna.

'Making love,' Doctor Crombie said gruffly. 'I thought I had explained all that to you at the age of thirteen.'

'I just thought you were talking about playing trains alone,' I said.

'What do you mean, playing trains?' he asked with bewilderment as a fast passenger-train went by, in and out of Bankstead station, leaving a great ball of steam at either end of No. 2 platform. 'The 3.45 from Newcastle,' he said. 'I make it a minute and a quarter slow.'

'Three-quarters of a minute,' I said. We had no means of checking our watches. It was before the days of radio.

'I am ahead of the time,' Doctor Crombie said, 'and I expect to suffer inconvenience. The strange thing is that people here have only just noticed. I have been speaking to you boys on the subject of cancer for years.'

'Nobody realized that you meant marriage,' I said.

'One begins with first things first. You were, none of you, in those symposiums which I held, of an age to marry.'

'But maiden ladies,' I objected, 'they die of cancer too.'

'The definition of maiden in common use,' Doctor Crombie replied, looking at his watch as a goods-train went by towards Bletchley, 'is an unbroken hymen. A lady may have had prolonged sexual relations with herself or another without injuring the maidenhead.'

I became curious. A new world was opening to me.

'You mean girls play with themselves too?'

'Of course.'

'But the young don't often die of cancer, do they?'

'They can lay the foundations with their excesses. It was from that I wished to save you all.'

'And the saints,' I said, 'did none of them die of cancer?'

'I know very little about saints. I would hazard a guess that the percentage of such deaths in their case was a small one, but I have never taught that sexual congress is the sole cause of cancer: only that it is the most frequent.'

'But all married people don't die that way?'

'My boy, you would be surprised how seldom many married people make love. A burst of enthusiasm and then a long retreat. The danger is necessarily less in those cases.'

'The more you love the greater the danger?'

'I'm afraid that is a truth which applies to more than the danger of cancer.'

I was too much in love myself to be easily convinced, but his answers came, I had to admit, quickly and readily. When I made some remark about statistics he quickly closed that avenue of hope. 'If they demand statistics,' Doctor Crombie said, 'statistics they shall have. They have suspected many causes in the past and based their suspicion on dubious and debatable statistics. White flour for example. It would not surprise me if one day they did not come to suspect even this little innocent comfort of mine' (he waved his cigarette in the direction of the Grand Junction Canal), 'but can they deny that statistically my solution outweighs all others? Almost one hundred per cent of those who die of cancer have practised sex.'

It was a statement impossible to deny, and for a little it silenced me. 'Aren't you afraid yourself?' I asked him at last.

'You know that I live alone. I am one of the few who have never been greatly tempted in that direction.'

'If all of us followed your advice,' I said gloomily, 'the world would cease to exist.'

'You mean the human race. The inter-pollination of flowers seems to have no ill side-effects.'

'And men were created only to die out?'

'I am no believer in the God of Genesis, young man. I think that the natural processes of evolution see to it that an animal becomes extinct when it makes a wrong accidental deviation. Man will perhaps follow the dinosaurs.' He looked at his watch. 'Now here is something wholly abnormal. The time is close on 4.10 and the four o'clock from Bletchley has not even been signalled. Yes, you may check the time, but this delay cannot be accounted for by a difference in watches.'

I have quite forgotten why the four o'clock was so delayed, and I had even forgotten Doctor Crombie and our conversation until this afternoon. Doctor Crombie survived his ruined practice for a few years and then died quietly one winter night of pneumonia following flu. I married four times, so little had I heeded Doctor Crombie's advice, and I only remembered his theory today when my specialist broke to me with rather exaggerated prudence and gravity the fact that I am suffering from cancer of the lungs. My sexual desires, now that I am past sixty, are beginning to diminish, and I am quite content to follow the dinosaurs into obscurity. Of course the doctors attribute the disease to my heavy indulgence in cigarettes, but it amuses me all the same to believe with Doctor Crombie that it has been caused by excesses of a more agreeable nature.

THE ROOT OF ALL EVIL

This story was told me by my father who heard it directly from his father, the brother of one of the participants; otherwise I doubt whether I would have credited it. But my father was a man of absolute rectitude, and I have no reason to believe that this virtue did not then run in the family.

The events happened in 189–, as they say in old Russian novels, in the small market town of B—. My father was German, and when he settled in England he was the first of the family to go further than a few kilometres from the home commune, province, canton or whatever it was called in those parts. He was a Protestant who believed in his faith, and no one has a greater ability to believe, without doubt or scruple, than a Protestant of that type. He would not even allow my mother to read us fairy-stories, and he walked three miles to church rather than go to one with pews. 'We've nothing to hide,' he said. 'If I sleep I sleep, and let the world know the weakness of my flesh. Why,' he added, and the thought touched my imagination strongly and perhaps had some influence on my future, 'they could play cards in those pews and no one the wiser.'

That phrase is linked in my mind with the fashion in which he would begin this story. 'Original sin gave man a tilt towards secrecy,' he would say. 'An open sin is only half a sin, and a secret innocence is only half innocent. When you have secrets, there, sooner or later, you'll have sin. I wouldn't let a Freemason cross my threshold. Where I come from secret societies were illegal, and the government had reason. Innocent though they might be at the start, like that club of Schmidt's.'

It appears that among the old people of the town where my father lived were a couple whom I shall continue to call Schmidt, being a little uncertain of the nature of the laws of libel and how limitations and the like affect the dead. Herr Schmidt was a big man and a heavy drinker, but most of his drinking he preferred to do at his own board to the discomfort of his wife, who never touched a drop of alcohol herself. Not that she wished to interfere with her husband's potations; she had a proper idea of a wife's duty, but she had reached an age (she was over sixty and he well past seventy) when she had a great yearning to sit quietly with another woman knitting something or other for her grandchildren and talking about their latest maladies. You can't do that at ease with a man continually on the go to the cellar for another litre. There is a man's atmosphere and a woman's atmosphere, and they don't mix except in the proper place, under the sheets. Many a time Frau Schmidt in her gentle way had tried to persuade him to go out of an evening to the inn. 'What and pay more for every glass?' he would say. Then she tried to persuade him that he had need of men's company and men's conversation. 'Not when I'm tasting a good wine,' he said.

So last of all she took her trouble to Frau Muller who suffered in just the same manner as herself. Frau Muller was a stronger type of woman and she set out to build an organization. She found four other women starved of female company and female interests, and they arranged to forgather once a week with their sewing and take their evening coffee together. Between them they could summon up more than two dozen grandchildren, so you can imagine they were never short of subjects to talk about. When one child had finished with the chicken-pox, at least two would have started the measles. There were all the varying treatments to compare, and there was one school of thought which took the motto 'starve a cold' to mean 'if you starve a cold you will feed a fever' and another school which took the more traditional view. But their debates were never heated like those they had with their husbands, and they took it in turn to act hostess and make the cakes.

But what was happening all this time to the husbands? You might think they would be content to go on drinking alone, but

not a bit of it. Drinking's like reading a 'romance' (my father
used the term with contempt, he had never turned the pages of a
novel in his life); you don't need talk, but you need company,
otherwise it begins to feel like work. Frau Muller had thought of
that and she suggested to her husband—very gently, so that he
hardly noticed—that, when the women were meeting elsewhere,
he should ask the other husbands in with their own drinks (no
need to spend extra money at the bar) and they could sit as silent
as they wished with their glasses till bedtime. Not, of course, that
they would be silent all the time. Now and then no doubt one of
them would remark on the wet or the fine day, and another
would mention the prospects for the harvest, and a third would
say that they'd never had so warm a summer as the summer of
188–. Men's talk, which, in the absence of women, would never
become heated.

But there was one snag in this arrangement and it was the
one which caused the disaster. Frau Muller roped in a seventh
woman, who had been widowed by something other than drink,
by her husband's curiosity. Frau Puckler had a husband whom
none of them could abide, and, before they could settle down to
their friendly evenings, they had to decide what to do about him.
He was a little vinegary man with a squint and a completely bald
head who would empty any bar when he came into it. His eyes,
coming together like that, had the effect of a gimlet, and he
would stay in conversation with one man for ten minutes on end
with his eyes fixed on the other's forehead until you expected
sawdust to come out. Unfortunately Frau Puckler was highly respected. It was essential to keep from her any idea that her husband was unwelcome, so for some weeks they had to reject Frau
Muller's proposal. They were quite happy, they said, sitting alone
at home with a glass when what they really meant was that even
loneliness was preferable to the company of Herr Puckler. But
they got so miserable all this time that often, when their wives returned home, they would find their husbands tucked up in bed
and asleep.

It was then Herr Schmidt broke his customary silence. He
called round at Herr Muller's door, one evening when the wives
were away, with a four-litre jug of wine, and he hadn't got

through more than two litres when he broke silence. This lonely drinking, he said, must come to an end—he had had more sleep the last few weeks than he had had in six months and it was sapping his strength. 'The grave yawns for us,' he said, yawning himself from habit.

'But Puckler?' Herr Muller objected. 'He's worse than the grave.'

'We shall have to meet in secret,' Herr Schmidt said. 'Braun has a fine big cellar,' and that was how the secret began; and from secrecy, my father would moralize, you can grow every sin in the calendar. I pictured secrecy like the dark mould in the cellar where we cultivated our mushrooms, but the mushrooms were good to eat, so that their secret growth . . . I always found an ambivalence in my father's moral teaching.

It appears that for a time all went well. The men were happy drinking together—in the absence, of course, of Herr Puckler, and so were the women, even Frau Puckler, for she always found her husband in bed at night ready for domesticities. He was far too proud to tell her of his ramblings in search of company between the strokes of the town-clock. Every night he would try a different house and every night he found only the closed door and the darkened window. Once in Herr Braun's cellar the husbands heard the knocker hammering overhead. At the Gasthof too he would look regularly in—and sometimes irregularly, as though he hoped that he might catch them off their guard. The street-lamp shone on his bald head, and often some late drinker going home would be confronted by those gimlet-eyes which believed nothing you said. 'Have you seen Herr Muller tonight?' or 'Herr Schmidt, is he at home?' he would demand of another reveller. He sought them here, he sought them there—he had been content enough aforetime drinking in his own home and sending his wife down to the cellar for a refill, but he knew only too well, now he was alone, that there was no pleasure possible for a solitary drinker. If Herr Schmidt and Herr Muller were not at home, where were they? And the other four with whom he had never been well acquainted, where were they? Frau Puckler was the very reverse of her husband, she had no curiosity, and Frau

Muller and Frau Schmidt had mouths which clinked shut like the clasp of a well-made handbag.

Inevitably after a certain time Herr Puckler went to the police. He refused to speak to anyone lower than the Superintendent. His gimlet-eyes bored like a migraine into the Superintendent's forehead. While the eyes rested on the one spot, his words wandered ambiguously. There had been an anarchist outrage at Schloss—I can't remember the name; there were rumours of an attempt on a Grand Duke. The Superintendent shifted a little this way and a little that way on his seat, for these were big affairs which did not concern him, while the squinting eyes bored continuously at the sensitive spot above his nose where his migraine always began. Then the Superintendent blew loudly and said, 'The times are evil,' a phrase which he had remembered from the service on Sunday.

'You know the law about secret societies,' Herr Puckler said.

'Naturally.'

'And yet here, under the nose of the police,' and the squint-eyes bored deeper, 'there exists just such a society.'

'If you would be a little more explicit . . .'

So Herr Puckler gave him the whole row of names, beginning with Herr Schmidt. 'They meet in secret,' he said. 'None of them stays at home.'

'They are not the kind of men I would suspect of plotting.'

'All the more dangerous for that.'

'Perhaps they are just friends.'

'Then why don't they meet in public?'

'I'll put a policeman on the case,' the Superintendent said half-heartedly, so now at night there were two men looking around to find where the six had their meeting-place. The policeman was a simple man who began by asking direct questions, but he had been seen several times in the company of Puckler, so the six assumed quickly enough that he was trying to track them down on Puckler's behalf and they became more careful than ever to avoid discovery. They stocked up Herr Braun's cellar with wine, and they took elaborate precautions not to be seen entering—each one sacrificed a night's drinking in order to lead Herr Puckler

and the policeman astray. Nor could they confide in their wives
for fear that it might come to the ears of Frau Puckler, so they
pretended the scheme had not worked and it was every man for
himself again now in drinking. That meant they had to tell a lot
of lies if they failed to be the first home—and so, my father said,
sin began to enter in.

One night too, Herr Schmidt, who happened to be the decoy,
led Herr Puckler on a long walk into the suburbs, and then seeing an open door and a light burning in the window with a comforting red glow and being by that time very dry in the mouth, he
mistook the house in his distress for a quiet inn and walked inside. He was warmly welcomed by a stout lady and shown into a
parlour, where he expected to be served with wine. Three young
ladies sat on a sofa in various stages of undress and greeted Herr
Schmidt with giggles and warm words. Herr Schmidt was afraid
to leave the house at once, in case Puckler was lurking outside,
and while he hesitated the stout lady entered with a bottle of
champagne on ice and a number of glasses. So for the sake of the
drink (though champagne was not his preference—he would
have liked the local wine) he stayed, and thus out of secrecy, my
father said, came the second sin. But it didn't end there with lies
and fornication.

When the time came to go, if he were not to overstay his welcome, Herr Schmidt took a look out of the window, and there, in
place of Puckler, was the policeman walking up and down the
pavement. He must have followed Puckler at a distance, and then
taken on his watch while Puckler went rabbiting after the others.
What to do? It was growing late; soon the wives would be drinking their last cup and closing the file on the last grandchild. Herr
Schmidt appealed to the kind stout lady; he asked her whether
she hadn't a back-door so that he might avoid the man he knew
in the street outside. She had no back-door, but she was a woman
of great resource, and in no time she had decked Herr Schmidt
out in a great cartwheel of a skirt, like peasant-women in those
days wore at market, a pair of white stockings, a blouse ample
enough and a floppy hat. The girls hadn't enjoyed themselves so
much for a long time, and they amused themselves decking his
face with rouge, eye-shadow and lipstick. When he came out of

the door, the policeman was so astonished by the sight that he stood rooted to the spot long enough for Herr Schmidt to billow round the corner, take to his heels down a sidestreet and arrive safely home in time to scour his face before his wife came in.

If it had stopped there all might have been well, but the policeman had not been deceived, and now he reported to the Superintendent that members of the secret society dressed themselves as women and in that guise frequented the gay houses of the town. 'But why dress as women to do that?' the Superintendent asked, and Puckler hinted at orgies which went beyond the natural order of things. 'Anarchy,' he said, 'is out to upset everything, even the proper relationship of man and woman.'

'Can't you be more explicit?' the Superintendent asked him for the second time; it was a phrase of which he was pathetically fond, but Puckler left the details shrouded in mystery.

It was then that Puckler's fanaticism took a morbid turn; he suspected every large woman he saw in the street at night of being a man in disguise. Once he actually pulled off the wig of a certain Frau Hackenfurth (no one till that day, not even her husband, knew that she wore a wig), and presently he sallied out into the streets himself dressed as a woman with the belief that one transvestite would recognize another and that sooner or later he would find himself enlisted in the secret orgies. He was a small man and he played the part better than Herr Schmidt had done— only his gimlet-eyes would have betrayed him to an acquaintance in daylight.

The men had been meeting happily enough now for two weeks in Herr Braun's cellar, the policeman had tired of his search, the Superintendent was in hopes that all had blown over, when a disastrous decision was taken. Frau Schmidt and Frau Muller in the old days had the habit of cooking pasties for their husbands to go with the wine, and the two men began to miss this treat which they described to their fellow drinkers, their mouths wet with the relish of the memory. Herr Braun suggested that they should bring in a woman to cook for them—it would mean only a small contribution from each, for no one would charge very much for a few hours' work at the end of the evening. Her duty would be to bring in fresh warm pasties every half an hour or so as long as their wine-session lasted. He advertised the position openly enough in the local paper, and Puckler, taking a long chance—the advertisement had referred to a men's club—applied, dressed up in his wife's best Sunday blacks. He was accepted by Herr Braun, who was the only one who did not know Herr Puckler except by repute, and so Puckler found himself installed at the very heart of the mystery, with a grand opportunity to hear all their talk. The only trouble was that he had little skill at cooking and often with his ears to the cellar-door he allowed the pasties to burn. On the second evening Herr Braun told him that, unless the pasties improved, he would find another woman.

However Puckler was not worried by that because he had all the information he required for the Superintendent, and it was a real pleasure to make his report in the presence of the policeman, who contributed nothing at all to the inquiry.

Puckler had written down the dialogue as he had heard it, leaving out only the long pauses, the gurgle of the wine-jugs, and the occasional rude tribute that wind makes to the virtue of young wine. His report read as follows:

Inquiry into the Secret Meetings held in the Cellar of Herr Braun's House at 27 —strasse. The following dialogue was overheard by the investigator.

MULLER: If the rain keeps off another month, the wine harvest will be better than last year.

UNIDENTIFIED VOICE: Ugh.

SCHMIDT: They say the postman nearly broke his ankle last week. Slipped on a step.

BRAUN: I remember sixty-one vintages.

DOBEL: Time for a pasty.

UNIDENTIFIED VOICE: Ugh.

MULLER: Call in that cow.

    The investigator was summoned and left a tray of pasties.

BRAUN: Careful. They are hot.

SCHMIDT: This one's burnt to a cinder.

DOBEL: Uneatable.

KASTNER: Better sack her before worse happens.

BRAUN: She's paid till the end of the week. We'll give her till then.

MULLER: It was fourteen degrees at midday.

DOBEL: The town-hall clock's fast.

SCHMIDT: Do you remember that dog the mayor had with black spots?

UNIDENTIFIED VOICE: Ugh.

KASTNER: No, why?

SCHMIDT: I can't remember.

MULLER: When I was a boy we had plum-duff they never make now.

DOBEL: It was the summer of '87.

UNIDENTIFIED VOICE: What was?

MULLER: The year Mayor Kalnitz died.

SCHMIDT: '88.

MULLER: There was a hard frost.

DOBEL: Not as hard as '86.

BRAUN: That was a shocking year for wine.

So it went on for twelve pages. 'What's it all about?' the Superintendent asked.

'If we knew that, we'd know all.'

'It sounds harmless.'

'Then why do they meet in secret?'

The policeman said 'Ugh' like the unidentified voice.

'My feeling is,' Puckler said, 'a pattern will emerge. Look at all those dates. They need to be checked.'

'There was a bomb thrown in '86,' the Superintendent said doubtfully. 'It killed the Grand Duke's best grey.'

'A shocking year for wine,' Puckler said. 'They missed. No wine. No royal blood.'

'The attempt was mistimed,' the Superintendent remembered.

'The town-hall clock's fast,' Puckler quoted.

'I can't believe it all the same.'

'A code. To break a code we have need of more material.'

The Superintendent agreed with some reluctance that the report should continue, but then there was the difficulty of the pasties. 'We need a good assistant-cook for the pasties,' Puckler

said, 'and then I can listen without interruption. They won't object if I tell them that it will cost no more.'

The Superintendent said to the policeman, 'Those were good
pasties I had in your house.'

'I cooked them myself,' the policeman said gloomily.

'Then that's no help.'

'Why no help?' Puckler demanded. 'If I can dress up as a
woman, so can he.'

'His moustache?'

'A good blade and a good lather will see to that.'

'It's an unusual thing to demand of a man.'

'In the service of the law.'

So it was decided, though the policeman was not at all happy
about the affair. Puckler, being a small man, was able to dress in
his wife's clothes, but the policeman had no wife. In the end
Puckler was forced to agree to buy the clothes himself; he did it
late in the evening, when the assistants were in a hurry to leave
and were unlikely to recognize his gimlet-eyes, as they judged the
size of the skirt, blouse, knickers. There had been lies, fornication: I don't know in what further category my father placed the
strange shopping expedition, which didn't, as it happened, go
entirely unnoticed. Scandal—perhaps that was the third offence
which secrecy produced, for a late customer coming into the
shop did in fact recognize Puckler, just as he was holding up the
bloomers to see if the seat seemed large enough. You can imagine
how quickly that story got around, to every woman except Frau
Puckler, and she felt at the next sewing-party an odd—well, it
might have been deference or it might have been compassion.
Everyone stopped to listen when she spoke; no one contradicted
or argued with her, and she was not allowed to carry a tray or
pour a cup. She began to feel so like an invalid that she developed
a headache and decided to go home early. She could see them all
nodding at each other as though they knew what was the matter
better than she did, and Frau Muller volunteered to see her
home.

Of course she hurried straight back to tell them about it.
'When we arrived,' she said, 'Herr Puckler was not at home. Of
course the poor woman pretended not to know where he could

be. She got in quite a state about it. She said he was always there to welcome her when she came in. She had half a mind to go round to the police-station and report him missing, but I dissuaded her. I almost began to believe that she didn't know what he was up to. She muttered about the strange goings-on in town, anarchists and the like, and would you believe it, she said that Herr Puckler told her a policeman had seen Herr Schmidt dressed up in women's clothes.'

'The little swine,' Frau Schmidt said, naturally referring to Puckler, for Herr Schmidt had the figure of one of his own wine-barrels. 'Can you imagine such a thing?'

'Distracting attention,' Frau Muller said, 'from his own vices. For look what happened next. We come to the bedroom, and Frau Puckler finds her wardrobe door wide open, and she looks inside, and what does she find—her black Sunday dress missing. "There's truth in the story after all," she said, "and I'm going to look for Herr Schmidt," but I pointed out to her that it would have to be a very small man indeed to wear her dress.'

'Did she blush?'

'I really believe she knows nothing about it.'

'Poor, poor woman,' Frau Dobel said. 'And what do you think he does when he's all dressed up?' and they began to speculate. So thus it was, my father would say, that foul talk was added to the other sins of lies, fornication, scandal. Yet there still remained the most serious sin of all.

That night Puckler and the policeman turned up at Herr Braun's door, but little did they know that the story of Puckler had already reached the ears of the drinkers, for Frau Muller had reported the strange events to Herr Muller, and at once he remembered the gimlet-eyes of the cook Anna peering at him out of the shadows. When the men met, Herr Braun reported that the cook was to bring an assistant to help her with the pasties and as she had asked for no extra money he had consented. You can imagine the babble of voices that broke out from these silent men when Herr Muller told his story. What was Puckler's motive? It was a bad one or it would not have been Puckler. One theory was that he was planning with the help of an assistant to poison them with the pasties in revenge for being excluded. 'It's not beyond

Puckler,' Herr Dobel said. They had good reason to be suspicious, so my father, who was a just man, did not include unworthy suspicion among the sins of which the secret society was the cause. They began to prepare a reception for Puckler.

Puckler knocked on the door and the policeman stood just behind him, enormous in his great black skirt with his white stockings crinkling over his boots because Puckler had forgotten to buy him suspenders. After the second knock the bombardment began from the upper windows. Puckler and the policeman were drenched with unmentionable liquids, they were struck with logs of wood. Their eyes were endangered from falling forks. The policeman was the first to take to his heels, and it was a strange sight to see so huge a woman go beating down the street. The blouse had come out of the waistband and flapped like a sail as its owner tacked to avoid the flying objects—which now included a toilet-roll, a broken teapot and a portrait of the Grand Duke.

Puckler, who had been hit on the shoulder with a rolling-pin, did not at first run away. He had his moment of courage or bewilderment. But when the frying-pan he had used for pasties struck him, he turned too late to follow the policeman. It was then that he was struck on the head with a chamber-pot and lay in the street with the pot fitting over his head like a vizor. They had to break it with a hammer to get it off, and by that time he was dead, whether from the blow on the head or the fall or from fear or from being stifled by the chamber-pot nobody knew, though suffocation was the general opinion. Of course there was an inquiry which went on for many months into the existence of an anarchist plot, and before the end of it the Superintendent had become secretly affianced to Frau Puckler, for which nobody blamed her, for she was a popular woman—except my father who resented the secrecy of it all. (He suspected that the Superintendent's love for Frau Puckler had extended the inquiry, since he pretended to believe her husband's accusations.)

Technically, of course, it was murder—death arising from an illegal assault—but the courts after about six months absolved the six men. 'But there's a greater court,' my father would always end his story, 'and in that court the sin of murder never goes unrequited. You begin with a secret,' and he would look at me as though he knew my pockets were stuffed with them, as indeed they were, including the note I intended to pass the next day at school to the yellow-haired girl in the second row, 'and you end with every sin in the calendar.' He began to recount them over again for my benefit. 'Lies, drunkenness, fornication, scandal-bearing, murder, the subornation of authority.'

'Subornation of authority?'

'Yes,' he said and fixed me with his glittering eye. I think he had Frau Puckler and the Superintendent in mind. He rose towards his climax. 'Men in women's clothes—the terrible sin of Sodom.'

'And what's that?' I asked with excited expectation.

'At your age,' my father said, 'some things must remain secret.'

TWO GENTLE PEOPLE

They sat on a bench in the Parc Monceau for a long time without speaking to one another. It was a hopeful day of early summer with a spray of white clouds lapping across the sky in front of a small breeze: at any moment the wind might drop and the sky become empty and entirely blue, but it was too late now—the sun would have set first.

In younger people it might have been a day for a chance encounter—secret behind the long barrier of perambulators with only babies and nurses in sight. But they were both of them middle-aged, and neither was inclined to cherish an illusion of possessing a lost youth, though he was better looking than he believed, with his silky old-world moustache like a badge of good behaviour, and she was prettier than the looking-glass ever told her. Modesty and disillusion gave them something in common; though they were separated by five feet of green metal they could have been a married couple who had grown to resemble each other. Pigeons like old grey tennis balls rolled unnoticed around their feet. They each occasionally looked at a watch, though never at one another. For both of them this period of solitude and peace was limited.

The man was tall and thin. He had what are called sensitive features, and the cliché fitted him; his face was comfortably, though handsomely, banal—there would be no ugly surprises when he spoke, for a man may be sensitive without imagination. He had carried with him an umbrella which suggested caution. In her case one noticed first the long and lovely legs as unsensual as those in a society portrait. From her expression she found the summer day sad, yet she was reluctant to obey the command of her watch and go—somewhere—inside.

They would never have spoken to each other if two teenaged louts had not passed by, one with a blaring radio slung over his shoulder, the other kicking out at thé pre-occupied pigeons. One of his kicks found a random mark, and on they went in a din of pop, leaving the pigeon lurching on the path.

The man rose, grasping his umbrella like a riding-whip. 'Infernal young scoundrels,' he exclaimed, and the phrase sounded more Edwardian because of the faint American intonation—Henry James might surely have employed it.

'The poor bird,' the woman said. The bird struggled upon the gravel, scattering little stones. One wing hung slack and a leg must have been broken too, for the pigeon swivelled round in circles unable to rise. The other pigeons moved away, with disinterest, searching the gravel for crumbs.

'If you would look away for just a minute,' the man said. He laid his umbrella down again and walked rapidly to the bird where it thrashed around; then he picked it up, and quickly and expertly he wrung its neck—it was a kind of skill anyone of breeding ought to possess. He looked round for a refuse bin in which he tidily deposited the body.

'There was nothing else to do,' he remarked apologetically when he returned.

'I could not myself have done it,' the woman said, carefully grammatical in a foreign tongue.

'Taking life is *our* privilege,' he replied with irony rather than pride.

When he sat down the distance between them had narrowed; they were able to speak freely about the weather and the first real day of summer. The last week had been unseasonably cold, and even today . . . He admired the way in which she spoke English and apologized for his own lack of French, but she reassured him: it was no ingrained talent. She had been 'finished' at an English school at Margate.

'That's a seaside resort, isn't it?'

'The sea always seemed very grey,' she told him, and for a while they lapsed into separate silences. Then perhaps thinking of the dead pigeon she asked him if he had been in the army. 'No, I was over forty when the war came,' he said. 'I served on a government mission, in India. I became very fond of India.' He began to describe to her Agra, Lucknow, the old city of Delhi, his eyes alight with memories. The new Delhi he did not like, built by a Britisher—Lut-Lut-Lut? No matter. It reminded him of Washington.

'Then you do not like Washington?'

'To tell you the truth,' he said, 'I am not very happy in my own country. You see, I like old things. I found myself more at home—can you believe it?—in India, even with the British. And now in France, I find it's the same. My grandfather was British Consul in Nice.'

'The Promenade des Anglais was very new then,' she said.

'Yes, but it aged. What we Americans build never ages beauti-fully. The Chrysler Building, Hilton hotels . . .'

'Are you married?' she asked. He hesitated a moment before replying, 'Yes,' as though he wished to be quite, quite accurate. He put out his hand and felt for his umbrella—it gave him confi-dence in this surprising situation of talking so openly to a stranger.

'I ought not to have asked you,' she said, still careful with her grammar.

'Why not?' He excused her awkwardly.

'I was interested in what you said.' She gave him a little smile. 'The question came. It was *imprévu*.'

'Are *you* married?' he asked, but only to put her at her ease, for he could see her ring.

'Yes.'

By this time they seemed to know a great deal about each other, and he felt it was churlish not to surrender his identity. He said, 'My name is Greaves, Henry C. Greaves.'

'Mine is Marie-Claire. Marie-Claire Duval.'

'What a lovely afternoon it has been,' the man called Greaves said.

'But it gets a little cold when the sun sinks.' They escaped from each other again with regret.

'A beautiful umbrella you have,' she said, and it was quite

true—the gold band was distinguished, and even from a few feet away one could see there was a monogram engraved there—an H certainly, entwined perhaps with a C or a G.

'A present,' he said without pleasure.

'I admired so much the way you acted with the pigeon. As for me I am *lâche*.'

'That I am quite sure is not true,' he said kindly.

'Oh, it is. It is.'

'Only in the sense that we are all cowards about something.'

'You are not,' she said, remembering the pigeon with gratitude.

'Oh yes, I am,' he replied, 'in one whole area of life.' He seemed on the brink of a personal revelation, and she clung to his coat-tail to pull him back; she literally clung to it, for lifting the edge of his jacket she exclaimed, 'You have been touching some wet paint.' The ruse succeeded; he became solicitous about her dress, but examining the bench they both agreed the source was not there. 'They have been painting on my staircase,' he said.

'You have a house here?'

'No, an apartment on the fourth floor.'

'With an *ascenseur?*'

'Unfortunately not,' he said sadly. 'It's a very old house in the *dix-septième.*'

The door of his unknown life had opened a crack, and she wanted to give something of her own life in return, but not too much. A 'brink' would give her vertigo. She said, 'My apartment is only too depressingly new. In the *huitième*. The door opens electrically without being touched. Like in an airport.'

A strong current of revelation carried them along. He learned how she always bought her cheeses in the Place de la Madeleine— it was quite an expedition from her side of the *huitième*, near the Avenue George V, and once she had been rewarded by finding Tante Yvonne, the General's wife, at her elbow choosing a Brie. He on the other hand bought his cheeses in the Rue de Tocqueville, only round the corner from his apartment.

'You yourself?'

'Yes, I do the marketing,' he said in a voice suddenly abrupt.

She said, 'It is a little cold now. I think we should go.'

'Do you come to the Parc often?'

'It is the first time.'

'What a strange coincidence,' he said. 'It's the first time for me too. Even though I live close by.'

'And I live quite far away.'

They looked at one another with a certain awe, aware of the mysteries of providence. He said, 'I don't suppose you would be free to have a little dinner with me.'

Excitement made her lapse into French. *'Je suis libre, mais vous . . . votre femme . . . ?'*

'She is dining elsewhere,' he said. 'And your husband?'

'He will not be back before eleven.'

He suggested the Brasserie Lorraine, which was only a few minutes' walk away, and she was glad that he had not chosen something more chic or more flamboyant. The heavy bourgeois atmosphere of the *brasserie* gave her confidence, and, though she had small appetite herself, she was glad to watch the comfortable military progress down the ranks of the sauerkraut trolley. The menu too was long enough to give them time to readjust to the startling intimacy of dining together. When the order had been given, they both began to speak at once. 'I never expected . . .'

'It's funny the way things happen,' he added, laying unintentionally a heavy inscribed monument over that conversation.

'Tell me about your grandfather, the consul.'

'I never knew him,' he said. It was much more difficult to talk on a restaurant sofa than on a park bench.

'Why did your father go to America?'

'The spirit of adventure perhaps,' he said. 'And I suppose it was the spirit of adventure which brought me back to live in Europe. America didn't mean Coca-Cola and *Time-Life* when my father was young.'

'And have you found adventure? How stupid of me to ask. Of course you married here?'

'I brought my wife with me,' he said. 'Poor Patience.'

'Poor?'

'She is fond of Coca-Cola.'

'You can get it here,' she said, this time with intentional stupidity.

'Yes.'

The wine-waiter came and he ordered a Sancerre. 'If that will suit you?'

'I know so little about wine,' she said.

'I thought all French people . . .'

'We leave it to our husbands,' she said, and in his turn he felt an obscure hurt. The sofa was shared by a husband now as well as a wife, and for a while the *sole meunière* gave them an excuse not to talk. And yet silence was not a genuine escape. In the silence the two ghosts would have become more firmly planted, if the woman had not found the courage to speak.

'Have you any children?' she asked.

'No. Have you?'

'No.'

'Are you sorry?'

She said, 'I suppose one is always sorry to have missed something.'

'I'm glad at least I did not miss the Parc Monceau today.'

'Yes, I am glad too.'

The silence after that was a comfortable silence: the two ghosts went away and left them alone. Once their fingers touched over the sugar-castor (they had chosen strawberries). Neither of them had any desire for further questions; they seemed to know each other more completely than they knew anyone else. It was like a happy marriage; the stage of discovery was over—they had passed the test of jealousy, and now they were tranquil in their middle age. Time and death remained the only enemies, and coffee was like the warning of old age. After that it was necessary to hold sadness at bay with a brandy, though not successfully. It was as though they had experienced a lifetime, which was measured as with butterflies in hours.

He remarked of the passing head waiter, 'He looks like an undertaker.'

'Yes,' she said. So he paid the bill and they went outside. It was a death-agony they were too gentle to resist for long. He asked, 'Can I see you home?'

'I would rather not. Really not. You live so close.'

'We could have another drink on the *terrasse?*' he suggested with half a sad heart.

'It would do nothing more for us,' she said. 'The evening was perfect. *Tu es vraiment gentil.*' She noticed too late that she had used 'tu' and she hoped his French was bad enough for him not to have noticed. They did not exchange addresses or telephone numbers, for neither of them dared to suggest it: the hour had come too late in both their lives. He found her a taxi and she drove away towards the great illuminated Arc, and he walked home by the Rue Jouffroy, slowly. What is cowardice in the young is wisdom in the old, but all the same one can be ashamed of wisdom.

Marie-Claire walked through the self-opening doors and thought, as she always did, of airports and escapes. On the sixth floor she let herself into the flat. An abstract painting in cruel tones of scarlet and yellow faced the door and treated her like a stranger.

She went straight to her room, as softly as possible, locked the door and sat down on her single bed. Through the wall she could hear her husband's voice and laugh. She wondered who was with him tonight—Toni or François. François had painted the abstract picture, and Toni, who danced in ballet, always claimed, especially before strangers, to have modelled for the little stone phallus with painted eyes that had a place of honour in the living-room. She began to undress. While the voice next door spun its web, images of the bench in the Parc Monceau returned and of the sauerkraut trolley in the Brasserie Lorraine. If he had heard her come in, her husband would soon proceed to action: it excited him to know that she was a witness. The voice said, 'Pierre, Pierre,' reproachfully. Pierre was a new name to her. She spread her fingers on the dressing-table to take off her rings and she thought of the sugar-castor for the strawberries, but at the sound of the little yelps and giggles from next door the sugar-castor turned into the phallus with painted eyes. She lay down and screwed beads of wax into her ears, and she shut her eyes and thought how different things might have been if fifteen years ago she had sat on a bench in the Parc Monceau, watching a man with pity killing a pigeon.

'I can smell a woman on you,' Patience Greaves said with pleasure, sitting up against two pillows. The top pillow was punctured with brown cigarette burns.

'Oh no, you can't. It's your imagination, dear.'

'You said you would be home by ten.'

'It's only twenty past now.'

'You've been up in the Rue de Douai, haven't you, in one of those bars, looking for a *fille*.'

'I sat in the Parc Monceau and then I had dinner at the Brasserie Lorraine. Can I give you your drops?'

'You want me to sleep so that I won't expect anything. That's it, isn't it, you're too old now to do it twice.'

He mixed the drops from the carafe of water on the table between the twin beds. Anything he might say would be wrong when Patience was in a mood like this. Poor Patience, he thought, holding out the drops towards the face crowned with red curls, how she misses America—she will never believe that the Coca-Cola tastes the same here. Luckily this would not be one of their worst nights, for she drank from the glass without further argument, while he sat beside her and remembered the street outside the *brasserie* and how—by accident he was sure—he had been called '*tu*'.

'What are you thinking?' Patience asked. 'Are you still in the Rue de Douai?'

'I was thinking that things might have been different,' he said.

It was the biggest protest he had ever allowed himself to make against the condition of life.

THE LAST WORD AND
OTHER STORIES

THE LAST WORD

The old man was only a little surprised, because he was by now well accustomed to inexplicable events, when he received at the hands of a stranger a passport in a name which was not his own, a visa and an exit permit for a country which he had never expected or even desired to visit. He was indeed very old, and he was accustomed to the narrow life he had led alone without human contacts: he had even found a kind of happiness in deprivation. He had a single room to live and sleep in: a small kitchen and a bathroom. Once a month there came a small but sufficient pension which arrived from Somewhere, but he didn't know where. Perhaps it was connected with the accident years before which had robbed him of his memory. All that had remained in his mind of that occasion was a sharp noise, a flash like lightning and then a long darkness full of confusing dreams from which he finally woke in the same small room that he lived in now.

'You will be fetched at the airport on the 25th,' the stranger told him, 'and be taken to your plane. At the other end you will be met and a room is ready for you. It would be best for you if you spoke to no one on the plane.'

'The 25th? This is December, isn't it?' He found it difficult to keep account of time.

'Of course.'

'Then it will be Christmas Day.'

'Christmas Day was abolished more than twenty years ago. After your accident.'

He was left wondering—how does one abolish a day? When the man left he looked up, half expecting an answer, to a small

wooden crucifix which hung over his bed. One arm of the cross
and with it one arm of the figure had been broken off—he had
found it two years before—or was it three?—in the dustbin
which he shared with his neighbours who never spoke to him. He
said aloud, 'And you? Have they abolished you?' The missing
arm seemed to give him the answer, 'Yes.' There was in a way a
communication between them as though they shared a memory
between them.

With his neighbours there was no communication. Since he
had returned to life in this room he had not spoken to one of
them, for he could feel that they were afraid to speak to him. It
was as if they knew something about him which he didn't know
himself. Perhaps a crime committed before the darkness fell.
There was always a man in the street who could not be regarded
as a neighbour, for he was changed every other day, and he too
spoke to no one at all, not even to the old lady on the top floor
who was inclined to gossip. Once in the street she had used the
name—not the name on the passport—with a sideways look
which took in both of them—the old man and the watcher. It
was a common enough name, John.

Once, perhaps because the day was warm and bright after
weeks of rain, the old man had ventured a remark to the man in
the street as he went to fetch his bread, 'God bless you, my dear
fellow', and the man winced as though struck by a sudden pain
and turned his back. The old man went on to fetch his bread
which was his staple food and he had long been aware that he
was followed to the shop. The whole atmosphere was a bit mysterious, but he was not deeply disturbed. Once he remarked to
his only audience, the damaged wooden figure, 'I think they
want to leave you and me alone.' He was quite content, as
though somewhere in the dark forgotten past he had suffered an
immense burden from which he was now free.

The day which he still thought of as Christmas arrived and so
did the stranger—'To take you to the airport. Have you finished
packing?'

'I haven't much to pack and I have no case.'

'I will fetch one,' and so he did. While he was gone the old man wrapped the wooden figure in his only spare jacket which he put in the case as soon as it was brought and covered it with two shirts and some underclothes.

'Is that all you have?'

'At my age one needs very little.'

'What are you carrying in your pocket?'

'Only a book.'

'Let me see it.'

'Why?'

'I have my orders.'

He snatched it from the old man's hand and looked at the title page.

'You have no right to this. How did it come into your possession?'

'I have had it since childhood.'

'They should have seized it in the hospital. I will have to report this.'

'No one is to blame. I kept it hidden.'

'You were brought in unconscious. You weren't capable of hiding.'

'I expect they were too busy saving my life.'

'I call it criminal carelessness.'

'I think I remember someone did ask me what it was. I told them the truth. A book of ancient history.'

'Forbidden history. This will go to the incinerator.'

'It's not so important,' the old man said. 'Read a little of it first. You will see.'

'I shall do no such thing. I am loyal to the General.'

'Oh, you are right of course. Loyalty is a great virtue. But don't worry. I haven't read much of it for some years. My favourite passages are here in my head, and you can't incinerate my head.'

'Don't be too sure of that,' the man replied. They were his last words before they reached the airport, and there everything strangely changed.

2

An officer in uniform greeted the old man with such great courtesy that he felt as though he were returning to a very distant
past. The officer even gave him a military salute. He said, 'The
General asked me to wish you a comfortable journey.'

'Where are you taking me?'

The officer made no reply to his question, but asked the civil-
ian guard, 'Is this all his luggage?'

'All, but I took away this book.'

'Let me see it.' The officer turned to the title page. 'Of course,'
he said, 'you were doing your duty, but all the same give it him
back. These are special circumstances. He is the guest of the
General, and anyway there's no danger in a book like this now.'

'The law . . .'

'Even laws can become out of date.'

The old man repeated his question in another form. 'What line
am I travelling on?'

'You too, sir, are a little out of date. There is only one line
now—The World United.'

'Oh dear, oh dear, what changes there have been.'

'Don't worry, sir, the time of change is over. The world is settled and at peace. No need for change.'

'Where are you taking me?'

'Only to another province. A mere four hours' flight. In the
General's own plane.'

It was an extraordinary plane. There was what one might call a
sitting-room with ample armchairs, sufficient for only six people,
so that they could be transformed into beds: through an open
door as they passed he could see a bath—he hadn't seen a bath for
years (his small studio had only a shower) and he felt a strong desire to spend the hours which followed stretched out in the warm
water. A bar separated the chairs from the cockpit, and an almost
cringing steward offered him a choice from what appeared to be
the drinks of all nations, if one could speak of all nations in this
United World. Even his poor clothes did not seem to diminish the
steward's respect. Presumably he cringed to any guest of the
General however unsuitable he might think one to be.

The officer took his seat at some distance as though he wished to leave him discreetly at peace with his forbidden book, but what he felt was a deeper desire for the peace and the silence. He was tired out by the mystery of things: the mystery of the small studio which he had left, of the tension coming from God knew where, of this luxury plane and above all of the bath . . . His mind, as it so often did, went in pursuit of his memory, which stopped abruptly at this startling crack of sound and the darkness which followed it . . . how many years ago? It was as if he had been living under a total anaesthetic which was only now beginning to wear thin. Suddenly he was frightened in this great private plane of what memories might await him if he woke. He began to read his book; it opened automatically from long use at a passage he knew by heart: 'He was in the world and the world was made by him and the world knew him not.'

The steward's voice sounded in his ear, 'A little caviare, sir, or a glass of vodka, or would you prefer a glass of dry white wine?'

Without looking up from the familiar page he said, 'No, no thank you. I am not hungry or thirsty.'

The clink of the glass the steward removed brought back a memory. His hand of its own accord tried to lay down something on the table before him, and for a moment in front of him he saw a host of strangers with bowed heads, there was a deep silence and then came that startling crack and the darkness which followed . . .

The steward's voice woke him. 'Your safety belt, sir. We shall be arriving in five minutes.'

3

Another officer awaited him at the bottom of the steps and led him towards a large car. The ceremony, the courtesy, the luxury stirred the hidden memories. He felt no surprise now: it was as though he had experienced all this many years before: he gave mechanically a deprecating movement to the hand and a phrase slipped from his mouth, 'I am a servant of the servants' and remained unfinished as the door slammed.

They drove through streets which were empty except for a few queues outside certain stores. He began to say again, 'I am a servant.' Outside the hotel the manager was awaiting them. He bowed and told the old man, 'I am proud to receive a personal guest of the General. I hope you will have every comfort during your short stay here. You have only to ask . . .'

The old man looked up with astonishment at the fourteen floors. He asked, 'For how long are you keeping me here?'

'You are booked, sir, for one night.'

The officer broke hastily in, 'So that you may see the General tomorrow. He wants you to have a good rest tonight after your journey.'

The old man searched his memory and a name came back. It was as though memory were returning to him in broken pieces. 'General Megrim?'

'No, no. General Megrim died nearly twenty years ago.'

A uniformed doorkeeper saluted him as they entered the hotel. The concierge was ready with the keys. The officer said, 'I will leave you here, sir, and tomorrow morning I will come to fetch you at 11. The General will see you at 11.30.'

The manager accompanied him to the lift.

After they had both gone safely away the concierge turned to the officer. 'Who is this gentleman? The guest of the General? He looks a very poor man from his clothes.'

'He's the Pope.'

'The Pope? What's the Pope?' the concierge asked, but the officer left the hotel without making any reply.

4

When the manager left him the old man was aware of how tired he was, but all the same he examined his surroundings with astonishment. He even felt the deep succulent mattress of the great double bed. He opened the door of the bathroom and saw an array of little bottles. The only thing he bothered to unpack was the wooden statuette he had so carefully hidden. He propped it up against the mirror on the dressing-table. He threw his clothes on a chair and then as though obeying an order lay down on the bed. If he had understood anything of what was happening, perhaps he would have found it impossible to sleep, but understanding nothing he was able to sink down on the deep mattress, where sleep came immediately, and with it a dream, parts of which he remembered on waking.

He had been talking—he saw it all clearly—in some sort of immense barn to an audience of not more than a few dozen people. On one wall hung a mutilated wooden cross and a figure without an arm, like the one hidden in his case. He couldn't remember what he had been saying, for the words were in a language—or several languages—which he didn't know or couldn't remember. The barn slowly decreased in size until it was no larger than the little studio which he had left, and in front of him knelt one old woman with a small girl beside her. *She* did not kneel, but looked at him with a look of contempt which seemed to express a thought as clearly as if she had spoken aloud, 'I don't understand a word you're saying and why can't you speak properly?'

He woke to a terrible sense of failure and lay awake on his bed desperately trying to find a way back into the dream and utter some words which the child might understand. He even tried out a few of them at random. 'Pax,' he said aloud, but that would be as foreign a word to her as it had been to him. He tried another, 'Love'. It came more easily to his lips, but it seemed to him now too commonplace a word with its contradictory meaning. He found that he didn't really know what it meant himself. It was something he was not sure he had ever experienced. Perhaps—before the strange crack in the darkness which followed—he might have had a hint, but surely if love had any real importance a small memory of it would have survived.

His uneasy thoughts were interrupted by the entrance of a waiter who brought him a tray with coffee and a variety of breads and croissants he had never seen at the small bakery which served him with the only meals he took.

'The colonel asked me to remind you, sir, that he will be here

at 11 to take you to the General and that your clothes for the occasion are in the wardrobe. In case you forgot to pack them in
your rather hurried departure you will find razor and brushes
and all that is required in the bathroom.'

'My clothes are on the chair,' he told the waiter and he added
a friendly joke, 'I didn't come here quite naked.'

'I have been told to take them away. All you require is there,'
and he pointed at the wardrobe.

The old man looked at his jacket and trousers, his shirt, socks,
and not for the first time, as the waiter picked them gingerly up,
the thought came to him that they were indeed in need of a wash.
He had seen no reason in all the last years to waste a little of his
small pension at the cleaners when the only people who saw him
regularly were the baker, the men sent to watch him and occasionally a neighbour who would avoid looking in his direction and
even cross the street to avoid him. Clean clothes might be a social
need for others, but he had no social life.

The waiter left him and he stood in his underpants brooding
on the mystery of things. Then there was a knock on the door
and the officer who had brought him entered.

'But you're not dressed yet, and you've eaten nothing. The
General expects us to be on time.'

'The waiter has taken my clothes.'

'Your clothes are in the wardrobe.' He flung the door open and
the old man saw a white surplice and a white cape hanging there.
He said, 'Why? What are you asking? I have no right . . .'

'The General wishes to do you honour. He will be in full dress
uniform himself. There is even a guard of honour waiting for
you. You must wear your uniform too.'

'My uniform?'

'Be quick and shave. There will almost certainly be photographs for the world's press. The United World Press.'

He obeyed and in his confusion cut himself in several places.
Then unwillingly he put on his white robe and the cape. There
was a long mirror on the wardrobe door and he exclaimed with
horror, 'I look like a priest.'

'You were a priest. These robes have been lent by the World
Museum of Myths for the occasion. Hold out your hand.'

He obeyed. Authority had spoken. The officer slipped a ring on one of his fingers. 'The Museum,' he said, 'was reluctant to lend us the ring, but the General insisted. This is an occasion which will never be repeated. Follow me please.' As they were about to leave the wooden object on the dressing-table caught his eye. He said, 'They should never have allowed you to bring that with you.'

The old man had no wish to bring trouble to anyone. 'I hid it carefully,' he said.

'Never mind. I dare say the Museum will be glad to have it.'

'I want to keep it.'

'I don't think you will need it after you have seen the General.'

5

They drove through many strangely empty streets before they reached a great square. In front of what might once have been a palace a line of soldiers was drawn up and there the car stopped. The officer told him, 'We descend here. Don't be alarmed. The General wants to show you proper military honours as a former head of state.'

'Head of state? I don't understand.'

'Please. After you.'

The old man would have tripped on his robe if the officer had not grasped his arm. As he straightened there was a crash of sound and he nearly fell again. It was as though that sharp crack which he had heard once, before the long darkness wrapped him in its folds, was now multiplied a dozen times. The crash seemed to break his head in two and into that gap the memories of a lifetime began to pour in. He repeated, 'I don't understand.'

'In your honour.'

He looked down at his feet and saw the fold of the surplice. He looked at his hand and saw the ring. There was a clash of metal. The soldiers were presenting arms.

6

The General greeted him with courtesy and came directly to the point. He said, 'I want you to understand that I was in no way responsible for the attempt to kill you. It was a grave mistake by one of my predecessors, a General Megrim. Such mistakes are easily made in the later stages of a revolution. It has taken us a hundred years to establish the world state and world peace. In his way he was afraid of you and the few followers you still had.'

'Afraid of me?'

'Yes. You must realize that your Church has been responsible throughout history for many wars. At last we have abolished war.'

'But you are a General. I saw outside a number of soldiers.'

'They remain as the preservers of world peace. Perhaps in another hundred years they will cease to exist just as your Church has ceased to exist.'

'Has it ceased to exist? My memory failed me a long time ago.'

'You are the last living Christian,' the General said. 'You are an historic figure. For that reason I wanted to honour you at the end.'

The General took out a cigarette case and offered it. 'Will you smoke with me, Pope John. I'm sorry I forgot the number. Was it XXIX?'

'Pope? I'm sorry I don't smoke. Why do you call me Pope?'

'The last Pope but still a Pope.' The General lit a cigarette and continued. 'You must understand we have nothing at all against you personally. You occupied a great position. We shared many of the same ambitions. We had a great deal in common. That was one of the reasons why General Megrim considered you a dangerous enemy. You represented, as long as you had followers, an alternative choice. As long as there was an alternative choice there would always be war. I don't agree with the method which he took. To shoot you in such a clandestine way as you were saying—what do you call it?'

'My prayers?'

'No, no. It was a public ceremony already forbidden by law.' The old man felt himself at a loss. 'The Mass?' he asked.

'Yes, yes, I think that was the word. The trouble with what he arranged was that it might have turned you into a martyr and delayed our programme not a little. It's true that there were only a dozen people at that—what do you call it?—Mass. But his method was risky. General Megrim's successor realized that, and I have followed the same quieter line. We have kept you alive. We have never allowed the press to make even an occasional reference to you, or to your quiet life in retirement.'

'I don't altogether understand. You must forgive me. I'm only beginning to remember. When your soldiers fired just now . . .'

'We preserved you because you were the last leader of those who still called themselves Christians. The others gave up without too much difficulty. What a strange pack of names—Jehovah's Witnesses, Lutherans, Calvinists, Anglicans. They all died away one by one with the years. Your lot called themselves Catholic as though they claimed to represent the whole bunch even while they fought them. Historically I suppose you were the first to organize yourselves and claim to follow that mythical Jewish carpenter.'

The old man said, 'I wonder how his arm got broken.'

'His arm?'

'I'm sorry. My mind was wandering.'

'We left what was left of you to the last because you still had a few followers and because we did have certain aims in common. World peace, the destruction of poverty. There was a period when we could use you. Use you to destroy the idea of national countries for the sake of a greater whole. You had ceased to be a real danger, which made General Megrim's action unnecessary—or at any rate premature. Now we are satisfied that all this nonsense is finished, forgotten. You have no followers, Pope John. I have had you watched closely over the last twenty years. Not a single person has tried to contact you. You have no power and the world is one and at peace. You are no longer an enemy to be feared. I am sorry for you, for they must have been very long and tedious years in that lodging of yours. In a way a faith is like old age. It can't go on forever. Communism grew old and died, so did imperialism. Christianity is dead too except for you. I expect you were a good Pope as popes go, and I want to do you the honour of no longer keeping you in these dreary conditions.'

'You are kind. They were not so dreary as you think. I had a friend with me. I could talk to him.'

'What on earth do you mean? You were alone. Even when you went out of your door to buy bread you were alone.'

'He was waiting for me when I came back. I wish his arm had not been broken.'

'Oh, you are talking about that wooden image. The Museum of Myths will be glad to add it to its collection. But the time has come to talk of serious things, not of myths. You see this weapon I am putting on my desk. I don't believe in people being allowed to suffer unnecessarily. I respect you. I am not General Megrim. I want you to die with dignity. The last Christian. This is a moment of history.'

'You intend to kill me?'

'Yes.'

It was relief the old man felt, not fear. He said, 'You will be sending me where I've often wanted to go during the last twenty years.'

'Into darkness?'

'Oh, the darkness I have known was not death. Just an absence of light. You are sending me into the light. I am grateful to you.'

'I had hoped you would take a last meal with me. As a kind of symbol. A symbol of final friendship between two born to be enemies.'

'Forgive me, but I am not hungry. Let the execution go ahead.'

'At least, take a glass of wine with me, Pope John.'

'Thank you. I will take that.'

The General poured out two glasses. His hand shook a little as he drained his glass. The old man raised his as though in salute. He said in a low voice some words which the General could not properly catch, in a language which he did not understand. 'Corpus domini nostri . . .' As his last Christian enemy drank, he fired.

Between the pressure on the trigger and the bullet exploding a strange and frightening doubt crossed his mind: is it possible that what this man believed may be true?

THE NEWS IN ENGLISH

Tonight Lord Haw-Haw of Zeesen was off the air.

All over England the new voice was noticed; precise and rather lifeless, it was the voice of a typical English don.

In his first broadcast he referred to himself as a man young enough to sympathize with what he called 'the resurgence of youth all over the new Germany', and that was the reason—combined with the pedantic tone—he was at once nicknamed Dr Funkhole.

It is the tragedy of such men that they are never alone in the world.

Old Mrs Bishop was knitting by the fire at her house in Crowborough when young Mrs Bishop tuned in to Zeesen. The sock was khaki: it was as if she had picked up at the point where she had dropped a stitch in 1918. The grim comfortable house stood in one of the long avenues, all spruce and laurel and a coating of snow, which are used to nothing but the footsteps of old retired people. Young Mrs Bishop never forgot that moment; the wind beating up across Ashdown Forest against the blacked-out window, and her mother-in-law happily knitting, and the sense of everything waiting for this moment. Then the voice came into the room from Zeesen in the middle of a sentence, and old Mrs Bishop said firmly, 'That's David.'

Young Mary Bishop made a hopeless protest—'It can't be,' but she knew.

'I know my son if you don't know your husband.'

It seemed incredible that the man speaking couldn't hear them, that he should just go on, reiterating for the hundredth time the old lies, as if there were nobody anywhere in the world who knew him—a wife or a mother.

Old Mrs Bishop had stopped knitting. She said, 'Is that the man they've been writing about—Doctor Funkhole?'

'It must be.'

'It's David.'

The voice was extraordinarily convincing: he was going into exact engineering details—David Bishop had been a mathematics don at Oxford. Mary Bishop twisted the wireless off and sat down beside her mother-in-law.

'They'll want to know who it is,' Mrs Bishop said.

'We mustn't tell them,' said Mary.

The old fingers had begun on the khaki sock. She said, 'It's our duty.' Duty, it seemed to Mary Bishop, was a disease you caught with age: you ceased to feel the tug-tug of personal ties; you gave yourself up to the great tides of patriotism and hate. She said, 'They must have made him do it. We don't know what threats—'

'That's neither here nor there.'

She gave weakly in to hopeless wishes. 'If only he'd got away in time. I never wanted him to give that lecture course.'

'He always was stubborn,' said old Mrs Bishop.

'He said there wouldn't be a war.'

'Give me the telephone.'

'But you see what it means,' said Mary Bishop. 'He may be tried for treason if we win.'

'*When* we win,' old Mrs Bishop said.

The nickname was not altered, even after the interviews with the two Mrs Bishops, even after the sub-acid derogatory little article about David Bishop's previous career. It was suggested now that he had known all along that war was coming, that he had gone to Germany to evade military service, leaving his wife and his mother to be bombed. Mary Bishop fought, almost in vain, with the reporters for some recognition that he might have been forced—by threats or even physical violence. The most one paper would admit was that if threats had been used Bishop had taken a very unheroic way out. We praise heroes as though they are rare, and yet we are always ready to blame another man for lack of heroism. The name Dr Funkhole stuck.

But the worst of it to Mary Bishop was old Mrs Bishop's attitude. She turned a knife in the wound every evening at 9.15. The radio set must be tuned in to Zeesen, and there she sat listening to her son's voice and knitting socks for some unknown soldier on the Maginot Line. To young Mrs Bishop none of it made sense—least of all that flat, pedantic voice with its smooth, well-thought-out, elaborate lies. She was afraid to go out now into Crowborough: the whispers in the post office, the old faces watching her covertly in the library. Sometimes she thought almost with hatred, *why has David done this to me? Why?*

Then suddenly she got her answer.

The voice for once broke new ground. It said, 'Somewhere back in England my wife may be listening to me. I am a stranger to the rest of you, but she knows that I am not in the habit of lying.'

A personal appeal was too much. Mary Bishop had faced her mother-in-law and the reporters—she couldn't face her husband. She began to cry, sitting close beside the radio set like a child beside its doll's house when something has been broken in it which nobody can repair. She heard the voice of her husband speaking as if he were at her elbow from a country which was now as distant and as inaccessible as another planet.

'The fact of the matter is—'

The words came slowly out as if he were emphasizing a point in a lecture, and then he went on—to what would concern a wife. The low price of food, the quantity of meat in the shops. He went into great detail, giving figures, picking out odd, irrelevant things—like Mandarin oranges and toy zebras—perhaps to give an effect of richness and variety.

Suddenly Mary Bishop sat up with a jerk as if she had been asleep. She said, 'Oh, God, where's that pencil?' and upset one of the too many ornaments looking for one. Then she began to write, but in no time at all the voice was saying, 'Thank you for having listened to me so attentively,' and Zeesen had died out on the air. She said, 'Too late.'

'What's too late?' said old Mrs Bishop sharply. 'Why did you want a pencil?'

'Just an idea,' Mary Bishop said.

She was led next day up and down the cold, unheated corridors of a War Office in which half the rooms were empty, evacuated. Oddly enough, her relationship to David Bishop was of use to her now, if only because it evoked some curiosity and a little pity. But she no longer wanted the pity, and at last she reached the right man.

He listened to her with great politeness. He was not in uniform. His rather good tweeds made him look as if he had just come up from the country for a day or two, to attend to the war. When she had finished he said, 'It's rather a tall story, you know, Mrs Bishop. Of course it's been a great shock to you—this—well—action of your husband's.'

'I'm proud of it.'

'Just because in the old days you had this—scheme, you really believe—?'

'If he was away from me and he telephoned "The fact of the matter is," it always meant, "This is all lies, but take the initial letters which follow." . . . Oh, Colonel, if you only knew the number of unhappy weekends I've saved him from—because, you see, he could always telephone to me, even in front of his host.' She said with tears in her voice, 'Then I'd send him a telegram . . .'

'Yes. But still—you didn't get anything this time, did you?'

'I was too late. I hadn't a pencil. I only got this—I know it doesn't seem to make sense.' She pushed the paper across. 'SOSPIC. I know it might easily be coincidence—that it does seem to make a kind of word.'

'An odd word.'

'Mightn't it be a man's name?'

The officer in tweeds was looking at it, she suddenly realized, with real interest—as if it was a rare kind of pheasant. He said, 'Excuse me a moment,' and left her. She could hear him telephoning to somebody from another room: the little ting of the bell, silence, and then a low voice she couldn't overhear. Then he returned, and she could tell at once from his face that all was well.

He sat down and fiddled with a fountain-pen—he was obviously embarrassed. He started a sentence and stopped it. Then he brought out in an embarrassed gulp, 'We'll have to apologize to your husband.'

'It meant something?'

He was obviously making his mind up about something difficult and out of the way—he was not in the habit of confiding in members of the public. But she had ceased to be a member of the public.

'My dear Mrs Bishop,' he said, 'I've got to ask a great deal from you.'

'Of course. Anything.'

He seemed to reach a decision and stopped fiddling. 'A neutral ship called the *Pic* was sunk this morning at 4.00 a.m., with a loss of two hundred lives. SOS *Pic*. If we'd had your husband's warning, we could have got destroyers to her in time. I've been speaking to the Admiralty.'

Mary Bishop said in a tone of fury, 'The things they are writing about David. Is there one of them who'd have the courage—?'

'That's the worst part of it, Mrs Bishop. They must go on writing. Nobody must know, except my department and yourself.'

'His mother?'

'You mustn't even tell her.'

'But can't you make them just leave him alone?'

'This afternoon I shall ask them to intensify their campaign—in order to discourage others. An article on the legal aspect of treason.'

'And if I refuse to keep quiet?'

'Your husband's life won't be worth much, will it?'

'So he's just got to go on?'

'Yes. Just go on.'

He went on for four weeks. Every night now she tuned in to Zeesen with a new horror—that he would be off the air. The code was a child's code. How could they fail to detect it? But they did fail. Men with complicated minds can be deceived by simplicity. And every night, too, she had to listen to her mother-in-law's indictment; every episode which she thought discreditable out of a child's past was brought out—the tiniest incident. Women in the last war had found a kind of pride in 'giving' their sons: this, too, was a gift on the altar of a warped patriotism. But now young Mrs Bishop didn't cry: she just held on—it was relief enough to hear his voice.

It wasn't often that he had information to give—the phrase 'the fact of the matter is' was a rare one in his talks. Sometimes there were the numbers of the regiments passing through Berlin, or of men on leave—very small details, which might be of value to military intelligence, but to her seemed hardly worth the risk of a life. If this was all he could do, why, why hadn't he allowed them simply to intern him?

At last she could bear it no longer. She visited the War Office again. The man in tweeds was still there, but this time for some reason he was wearing a black tail coat and a black stock as if he had been to a funeral. He must have been to a funeral, and she thought with more fear than ever of her husband.

'He's a brave man, Mrs Bishop,' he said.

'You needn't tell me that,' she cried bitterly.

'We shall see that he gets the highest possible decoration . . .'

'Decorations!'

'What do you want, Mrs Bishop? He's doing his duty.'

'So are other men. But they come home on leave. Sometime. He can't go on for ever. Soon they are bound to find out.'

'What can we do?'

'You can get him out of there. Hasn't he done enough for you?'

He said gently, 'It's beyond our power. How can we communicate with him?'

'Surely you have agents.'

'Two lives would be lost. Can't you imagine how they watch him?'

Yes. She could imagine all that clearly. She had spent too many holidays in Germany—as the Press had not failed to discover—not to know how men were watched, telephone lines tapped, table companions scrutinized.

He said, 'If there was some way we could get a message to him, it *might* be managed. We do owe him that.'

Young Mrs Bishop said quickly before he could change his mind, 'Well, the code works both ways. The fact of the matter is—! We have news broadcast in German. He might one day listen in.'

'Yes. There's a chance.'

She became privy to the plan because again they needed her help. They wanted to attract his notice first by some phrase peculiar to her. For years they had spoken German together on their annual holiday. That phrase was to be varied in every broadcast, and elaborately they worked out a series of messages which would convey to him the same instructions—to go to a certain station on the Cologne–Wesel line and contact there a railway worker who had already helped five men and two women to escape from Germany.

Mary Bishop felt she knew the place well—the small country station which probably served only a few dozen houses and a big hotel where people went in the old days for cures. The opportunity was offered him, if he could only take it, by an elaborate account of a railway accident at that point—so many people killed—sabotage—arrests. It was plugged in the news as relentlessly as the Germans repeated the news of false sinkings, and they answered indignantly back that there had been no accident.

It seemed more horrible than ever to Mary Bishop—those nightly broadcasts from Zeesen. The voice was in the room with her, and yet he couldn't know whether any message for which he risked his life reached home, and she couldn't know whether their message to him just petered out unheard or unrecognized.

Old Mrs Bishop said, 'Well, we can do without David tonight, I should hope.' It was a new turn in her bitterness—now she would simply wipe him off the air. Mary Bishop protested. She said she must hear—then at least she would know that he was well.

'It serves him right if he's not well.'

'I'm going to listen,' Mary Bishop persisted.

'Then I'll go out of the room. I'm tired of his lies.'

'You're his mother, aren't you?'

'That's not my fault. I didn't choose—like you did. I tell you I won't listen to it.'

Mary Bishop turned the knob. 'Then stop your ears,' she cried in a sudden fury, and heard David's voice coming over.

'The lies,' he was saying, 'put over by the British capitalist Press. There has not even been a railway accident—leave alone any sabotage—at the place so persistently mentioned in the broadcasts from England. Tomorrow I am leaving myself for the so-called scene of the accident, and I propose in my broadcast the day after tomorrow to give you an impartial observer's report, with records of the very railwaymen who are said to have been shot for sabotage. Tomorrow, therefore, I shall not be on the air . . .'

'Oh, thank God, thank God,' Mary Bishop said.

The old woman grumbled by the fire. 'You haven't much to thank Him for.'

All next day she found herself praying, although she didn't much believe in prayer. She visualized that station 'on the Rhine not far from Wesel'—and not far either from the Dutch frontier. There must be some method of getting across—with the help of that unknown worker—possibly in a refrigerating van. No idea was too fantastic to be true. Others had succeeded before him.

All through the day she tried to keep pace with him—he would have to leave early, and she imagined his cup of ersatz coffee and the slow wartime train taking him south and west. She thought of his fear and of his excitement—he was coming home to her. Ah, when he landed safely, what a day that would be! The papers then would have to eat their words—no more Dr Funkhole and no more of this place, side by side with his unloving mother.

At midday, she thought, he has arrived: he has his black discs with him to record the men's voices, he is probably watched, but he will find his chance—and now he is not alone. He has someone with him helping him. In one way or another he will miss his train home. The freight train will draw in—perhaps a signal will stop it outside the station. She saw it all so vividly, as the early winter dark came down and she blacked the windows out, that she found herself thankful he possessed, as she knew, a white mackintosh. He would be less visible waiting there in the snow.

Her imagination took wings, and by dinnertime she felt sure that he was already on the way to the frontier. That night there was no broadcast from Dr Funkhole, and she sang as she bathed and old Mrs Bishop beat furiously on her bedroom floor above.

In bed she could almost feel herself vibrating with the heavy movement of *his* train. She saw the landscape going by outside—there must be a crack in any van in which he lay hid, so that he could mark the distances. It was very much the landscape of Crowborough—spruces powdered with snow, the wide dreary waste they called a forest, dark avenues—she fell asleep.

When she woke she was still happy. Perhaps before night she would receive a cable from Holland, but if it didn't come she would not be anxious because so many things in wartime might delay it. It didn't come.

That night she made no attempt to turn on the radio, so old Mrs Bishop changed her tactics again. 'Well,' she said, 'aren't you going to listen to your husband?'

'He won't be broadcasting.' Very soon now she could turn on his mother in triumph and say, *There, I knew it all the time, my husband's a hero.*

'That was last night.'

'He won't be broadcasting again.'

'What do you mean? Turn it on and let me hear.'

There was no harm in proving that she knew—she turned it on.

A voice was talking in German—something about an accident and English lies, she didn't bother to listen. She felt too happy. 'There,' she said, 'I told you. It's not David.'

And then David spoke.

He said, 'You have been listening to the actual voices of

the men your English broadcasters have told you were shot by
the German police. Perhaps now you will be less inclined to believe the exaggerated stories you hear of life inside Germany today.'

'There,' old Mrs Bishop said, 'I told you.'

And all the world, she thought, *will go on telling me now, for
ever—Dr Funkhole. He never got those messages. He's there for
keeps.* David's voice said with curious haste and harshness, 'The
fact of the matter is—'

He spoke rapidly for about two minutes as if he were afraid
they would fade him at any moment, and yet it sounded harmless
enough—the old stories about plentiful food and how much you
could buy for an English pound—figures. But some of the exam-
ples this time, she thought with dread, are surely so fantastic that
even the German brain will realize something is wrong. How had
he ever dared to show this copy to his chiefs?

She could hardly keep pace with her pencil, so rapidly did he
speak. The words grouped themselves on her pad: *Five U's refu-
elling hodie noon 53.23 by 10.5. News reliable source Wesel so
returned. Talk unauthorized. The end.*

'This order. Many young wives I feel enjoy giving one'—he
hesitated—'one's day's butter in every dozen—' the voice faded,
gave out altogether. She saw on her pad: *To my wife, goodbye d—*

The end, goodbye, the end—the words rang on like funeral
bells. She began to cry, sitting as she had done before, close up
against the radio set. Old Mrs Bishop said with a kind of delight,
'He ought never to have been born. I never wanted him. The
coward,' and now Mary Bishop could stand no more of it.

'Oh,' she cried to her mother-in-law across the little over-
heated over-furnished Crowborough room, 'if only he were a
coward, if only he were. But he's a hero, a damned hero, a hero,
a hero—' she cried hopelessly on, feeling the room reel round
her, and dimly supposing behind all the pain and horror that one
day she would have to feel, like other women, pride.

THE MOMENT OF TRUTH

The near approach of death is like a crime which one is ashamed to confess to friends or fellow workers, and yet there remains a longing to confide in someone—perhaps a stranger in the street. Arthur Burton carried his secret to and fro to the kitchen and back, just as he carried the plates and the orders of the clients, as he had done for years in the Kensington restaurant which was called Chez Auguste. There was nothing French about it except the name and the menu, where the English dishes were given French names, explained at length in English under each title.

Twice in one week an American couple had booked the same table, a small one in a corner under a window, a man of about sixty years and a woman in her late forties—a very happy couple.

There are clients whom one likes at the first encounter and these were among them. They asked Arthur Burton's advice before they ordered and later they expressed their appreciation of his choice. They trusted him even over the wine, and on their second visit, they asked him little questions about himself as though he were a fellow guest whom they were anxious to know better.

'Been here long?' Mr Hogminster asked. (Arthur Burton had learnt his curious name when he telephoned for his reservation.)

'About twenty years,' Burton replied. 'It was a different restaurant when I came called The Queen's.'

'Better in those days?'

Arthur Burton tried to be loyal. 'I wouldn't say better. Simpler. Tastes change.'

'Is he French—your boss?'

'No, sir, but he's been to France a lot, I think.'

'We're happy to have your help. We don't know all these French words in the menu.'

'But it's put in English, sir.'

'I guess we don't understand that sort of English either. Anyway we'll be along again tomorrow. If you let us have the same table—Arthur, isn't it? I think I heard the boss call you Arthur?'

'That's right, sir. I'll see that you have this table.'

'And your help, Arthur,' Mrs Hogminster said.

He was touched by the use of his first name and the smile of real friendship which he received from Mrs Hogminster. In all his years as a waiter, he had known nothing like it before.

Arthur Burton was in the habit of observing the customers superficially, if only to keep an interest in his job which it was too late to change. He was alone in life, so there was no initiative for a change and now he was well aware that it was too late. The crime of death had touched him.

Often when he went home at night—if a bed-sitting-room with a shared shower could be called a home—he would remember certain customers: married customers who seemed to lunch together without interest, watching those who came in with a certain envy if the newcomers had words to say to each other: obvious new lovers who paid attention to no one else: sometimes a married young woman (he always looked at the left hand) with a look of anxiety, accompanied by a much older man. She lowered her voice or even ceased to talk when neighbours took the next table and Arthur Burton wished that he could have left it empty, so that they would be free to solve their problem.

When he got home that night, he thought of Mr and Mrs Hogminster. He wished he had spoken more to them. He felt that he could trust them, like strangers in the street. He might at least have hinted at the crime which separated him from the manager, the cook, the other waiters, the washers-up—only hinted of course, he wouldn't like them to be distressed.

They were half an hour late the next day for their reservation, and the manager wanted him to give up the table to other guests who asked for it. 'They won't be coming,' the manager argued, 'and anyway, there are three other tables to choose from.'

'But they like this table,' Arthur Burton said, 'and I promised they would have it.' He added, 'They are kind good people,' but he probably would have been forced to give way if they had not at that moment arrived.

'Oh, I'm so sorry, Arthur, we are terribly late.' He was touched that she had remembered his name. 'It was the Sales, Arthur. We got involved.'

'*She* got involved,' Mr Hogminster said.

'Oh, it will be your turn tomorrow.'

Arthur told them, 'There are restaurants closer to the men's shops. I can recommend one near Jermyn Street.'

'Oh, but it's Chez Augustine that we love.'

'Chez Auguste,' Mr Hogminster corrected her.

'And Arthur. He chooses so well for us. We don't have to think.'

A man with a secret is a very lonely man, and it was relief to Arthur Burton when he could uncover even a small corner of his secret. He said, 'I'm sorry, ma'am, but tomorrow I won't be here. But I'm sure the manager . . .'

'Not here? *Quelle désastre!* Why?'

'I have to go to hospital.'

'Oh, Arthur, I'm so sorry. What for? Is it serious?'

'A check-up, ma'am.'

'Very wise,' Mr Hogminster said. 'I believe in check-ups.'

'He's had four or is it six.' Mrs Hogminster added, 'I think he enjoys them, but it always worries me. What are they checking you for?'

'They've already done the check-up. Now they have to tell me the result.'

'Oh, I'm sure it will be all right, Arthur.'

'I'm happy you've enjoyed yourselves here, ma'am.'

'We have. All thanks to you.'

Arthur Burton said with truth, 'I'm sorry that we have to say goodbye.'

'Oh no—not yet. We'll be here again on Thursday. Tomorrow, we'll take your advice and eat near the men's shops, but we'll be back the day after to have our last meal at Chez Augustine.'

'Chez Auguste,' Mr Hogminster corrected her again, but she ignored him.

'We are flying to New York on Friday, but we'll certainly see you on Thursday and hear your good news, Arthur. I'm sure it will be good news. I'll be thinking of you and crossing my fingers, but I'm sure, quite sure.'

'I have a check-up every six months,' Mr Hogminster said. 'Always satisfactory.'

'Is there anything special you would like on Thursday, ma'am? I can ask the cook . . .'

'No, no. We'll take what you recommend. Until then—and good luck, Arthur.'

Arthur Burton knew that no good luck awaited him. He had known it even before the check-up by the evasiveness of his doctor. He wondered whether a man in the dock could tell the jury's verdict even before they retired from the court in the days when there was still a death sentence: an emanation of shame at what they were going to pronounce. Yet he had a sense of relief because he had at least confessed half his crime to her and she had not rejected him. If, as he believed, the verdict was death, however they wrapped it up in medical phrases of hope, might she be the stranger in the street to whom he could confess the whole? They would never see each other again. She was leaving for New York on Friday. They had no friends in common to whom she could spread the news of his crime. He felt an odd tenderness for her.

That night Arthur Burton dreamt of her. It was not an erotic dream, nor a love dream, a very commonplace dream in which she played an unimportant part and yet he woke with a sense of relaxation he had not known for many months. It was as though he had spoken to her and somehow she had given him words of sympathy which lent him courage to face his enemies, who were about to disclose the shameful truth.

He had taken a day off his work, though his appointment with the surgeon was not until the evening at five, and then he was kept waiting for nearly an hour. The surgeon asked him to sit down in a tone of such grave sympathy that he was able to guess accurately enough the report which followed. 'An operation urgently required . . . yes, cancer, but you mustn't be frightened by the sound of a word . . . I have known cases as bad as yours . . . taken in time there's always a good hope . . .'

'When do you want to operate?'

'I would like you to come into hospital tomorrow morning, and I'll operate the next day.'

'If I could come in the afternoon. You see—they are expecting me to be back at work tomorrow morning.' It was not of work he was thinking, but of Mrs Hogminster. She would be expecting news from him.

'I would much rather you had a quiet day in bed. However . . . I will be coming to see you with the anaesthetist at six.'

As he lay in bed that night, Arthur Burton thought: doctors and surgeons are not necessarily good psychologists; perhaps, because their interests are so concentrated on the body that they forget the mind, they don't realize how much a tone of voice reveals to the patient. They say 'there's always a good hope', but what the patient hears is 'there is very little hope if any'.

It was not that he was frightened of death. No one could avoid that universal fate, and yet the population of the world was not dominated by fear. All Arthur Burton wanted was to share his knowledge and his secret with a stranger who would not be seriously affected like a wife or a child—he possessed neither—but might with a word of kindly interest share with him this criminal secret—'I am condemned'. Mrs Hogminster was just such a woman. He had read it in her eyes. Somehow the next day he would find a way of conveying to her the truth, when she asked for the result of the check-up, without words which might involve her husband in his crime. She would ask him: 'What did the doctor say, Arthur?' And his answer? No, no words, a small shrug of the shoulders would be enough to convey, 'It's all up. Thank you for thinking of me,' and the glance that she gave him back would just as discreetly tell him she shared his secret.

He would not go alone into the future.

'You needn't keep that table,' the manager said. 'Those Americans were in yesterday and I found them one they liked much better.'

'They were in yesterday?'

'Yes, they do seem to like this place.'

'I thought they were going to the men's Sales.'

'I wouldn't know about that. I think you talk too much to the customers, Arthur. Often they want to feel alone.'

He left hurriedly to meet Mr and Mrs Hogminster at the door. Mrs Hogminster nodded and smiled at Arthur as they went by to a little table isolated in a corner of the restaurant. They had no view now of the street outside, but perhaps, as the manager had suggested, they preferred privacy, and perhaps too they preferred to be served by the manager himself.

It was only at the end of their meal after they had paid their bill that Mrs Hogminster called to him as he passed to the kitchen. 'Arthur, do come and have a word with us.'

He went willingly with a lightening of the heart.

'Arthur, we missed you, but the manager was so kind and we didn't want to hurt his feelings.'

'I hope you enjoyed your lunch, ma'am.'

'Oh, but we always do at Chez Augustine.'

'Chez Auguste,' Mr Hogminster said.

'With the Sales you were so right to send us to Jermyn Street. My husband bought two pairs of pyjamas and can you believe it, three—three—shirts!'

'She chose them of course,' Mr Hogminster said.

Arthur Burton excused himself and went on into the kitchen. The problem which he had so feared had not arisen, but the thought gave him no relief from the depression of his secret. He was going to say nothing to the manager: the next day he would simply not turn up. The hospital could inform them in due course if he were dead or alive.

He spent as little time as he could in the restaurant, though it pained him to see another waiter looking after the Hogminsters and exchanging words with them.

Half an hour later the manager came into the kitchen and spoke to him. He carried a letter in his hand. He said, 'Mrs Hogminster asked me to give you this. They've left for the airport.'

Arthur Burton put the envelope in his pocket. He felt an immense relief. Of course Mrs Hogminster had done the right thing. They couldn't have talked about his secret in the restaurant for others to hear. Now he would be able to carry with him to the hospital her sympathetic question about his secret and read it again next day immediately before the anaesthetist arrived. He felt alone no longer. He would be holding the hand of a stranger in the street. She could never receive the answer to her question, 'What did the doctor tell you?' but she had asked it in her letter and it was that which counted.

Before putting out the light above his hospital bed, he opened the envelope. He was surprised when three one-pound notes came out first.

Mrs Hogminster wrote: 'Dear Arthur, I felt I must write you a word of thanks before we catch our plane. We have so enjoyed our visits to Chez Augustine and shall certainly return one day. And the Sales, we got such wonderful bargains—you were so right about Jermyn Street.'

The letter was signed Dolly Hogminster.

THE MAN WHO STOLE
THE EIFFEL TOWER

It was not so much the theft of the Eiffel Tower which caused me difficulty; it was putting it back before anyone noticed. The whole affair, though I say it myself, was beautifully organized. You can easily imagine what was entailed—a fleet of outsize lorries to carry the Tower out to one of those quiet flat fields you see on the way to Chantilly. There the Tower could lie quite easily on its side. On the way out, on the misty autumn morning, there had been very little traffic, and what traffic there was I can only describe as humble. No one who tried to pass my hundred and two six-wheeled lorries noticed that they were joined like beads by the chain of the Tower. The private cars would pull out for a moment and attempt to pass, but when the drivers of the Fiats and Renaults saw lorry after lorry stretching ahead they simply gave up and followed the procession. On the other hand I provided a wonderfully clear road for cars coming into Paris: for them the long road from Chantilly was as good as a one-way street. They skimmed by and had no time to notice how the Tower lay over the driving coach of every lorry with no interval between: the Tower went out in a kind of sleeping berth, so many hundred metres long.

I have a great affection for the Tower, and it pleased me to see it, after all those years of war and fog and rain and radar, in repose. The first day it was there I walked around it, occasionally touching a strut: the fourth floor looked a little uncomfortable where it bridged a mild and muddy tributary of the Seine, and I had it eased. Then I drove back to the original site—I was still nervous lest anybody should notice. The great concrete blocks stood there with nothing on them. They were so like tombs that somebody had already left a bunch of flowers addressed to the Heroes of the Resistance. Once a taxi drew up containing the last swallow of tourism alighting there before winging westwards across the Atlantic at the approach of winter. He had a girl with him and he staggered a little in his walk. He bent to look at the flowers and straightened himself with a flush on his well-shaven powdered cheeks.

' 'Tsa memorial,' he said.

'*Comment?*' asked the taxi-driver.

The girl said, 'Chester, you said we could lunch here.'

'There ain't no Tower,' the man said.

'*Comment?*'

'What I mean to say is,' he explained, waving his arms for emphasis, 'you brought us to the wrong place.' He made an effort. '*Ici n'est pas la Tour Eiffel.*'

'*Qui. Ici.*'

'*Non. Pas du tout. Ici il n'est pas possible de manger.*'

The driver got out and looked around. I felt a little nervous in case he noticed the absence of the Tower, but he got back into the cab and appealed to me sadly. 'They continually change the names of the streets,' he said.

I spoke to him confidentially. 'It's only lunch they want,' I said. 'Take them to the Tour d'Argent.' Quite happily they drove away and that danger was over.

Of course there was always a risk that the employees might arouse public attention, but I had taken that into account. They were paid by the week, and what man or woman is fool enough to admit that his place of employment has ceased to exist until the week has come round again and the money has been earned? The cafés in the neighbourhood became a great resort for the employees, but no one liked to sit at a table with a fellow-worker in case of awkwardness in conversation. I noticed one uniform cap per *bistro* for an area of a square mile: each man sat contentedly during his hours of duty, drinking a glass of beer or a pastis according to his salary, and rising punctually from his table at the hour for clocking out. I don't think they were even puzzled by the Tower's absence. It could be conveniently forgotten like the income tax. Better not to think about it: if you thought about it somebody might expect you to take action.

The tourists, of course, remained the chief danger. Night fliers assumed a low-lying fog and the Ministry of Air passed to the Foreign Ministry 'for comment' several complaints about radar jamming—a new Russian device in the cold war. But word soon got around among guides and taxi-drivers that when a stranger asked for the Tour Eiffel it was simpler and less complicated to take them to the Tour d'Argent. The management there did not disillusion them, and the view these autumn days was just as good, and they were very happy signing the book at so much a head. I used to drop in and listen to them. 'I got the idea it was more sort of steely,' one of them said. 'I thought you could see through it.' I explained to him how perfectly true that was of the establishment he was in.

A holiday can never go on for ever, and wandering round of a morning putting a little spit and polish on the struts I concluded that the Tower must go back to work before its employees missed their wages. I could only hope that in the course of time it would find another like myself to give it a spell of country air. I assure him there is little risk involved. No one in Paris could admit that the Tower was absent for five days unnoticed—any more than a lover could admit to himself that he had failed to notice the absence of his mistress.

All the same it was a tricky business, the return of the Tower, and entailed a good deal of traffic diversion. To facilitate this I had laid in, from a theatrical costumier's, uniforms of the police, the Gardes Mobiles, the Gardes Républicaines, and the Académie Française. The diversions included a Poujadiste meeting, an Algerian riot and a funeral oration for an obscure dramatic critic by a friend of mine dressed up as the Minister of Education. I say 'dressed up', but of course there was no necessity for him even to change his name, let alone his face, since no one remembered who this Minister was in M. Mollet's Cabinet.

The tourists had the last word, and curiously enough as I stood at the base of my beloved Tower, which seemed to pirouette into the morning mist, it was the same American arriving in a taxi with the same girl. He took a quick look round and said, ' 'Tsnot the Eiffel Tower.'

'*Comment?*'

'Oh, Chester,' the girl said, 'where've they taken us now? They never get it right. I'm so *hungry,* Chester. I've just been dreaming of that *Sole Délice* we had.'

I said to the driver, 'It's the Tour d'Argent they want,' and watched them grind away. The wreath to the Heroes of the Resistance had withered, but I put one dried discoloured flower into my buttonhole and waved my farewell to the Tower. I dared not linger. I might have been tempted to steal it again.

THE LIEUTENANT
DIED LAST

An Unrecorded Victory in 1940

There had been a lot of grumbling in the village of Potter before
the astonishing night when the parachutists descended: grumbling about rations, compulsory service, blackouts, all the usual
things. Then apparent disaster, a touch of heroism, a good many
deaths, put an end to it for a while as it always does, though the
hero, old Bill Purves, the poacher, had more reason to grumble
than any, for he received no decorations—only a grudging commendation from Major Barlow, the local magistrate who let him
off 'this once' with a caution, after he had been caught red-
handed with a rabbit in each deep pocket.

You would hardly expect to find Potter the scene of the first invasion of England since French troops landed near Fishguard in
the Napoleonic War. It is one of those tiny isolated villages you
still find dumped down in deserted corners of what we call in England Metroland—the district where commuters live in tidy villas
within easy distances of the railway, on the edge of scrubby com-
mons full of clay pits and gorse and rather withered trees. Walk
for three miles in any direction from Potter and you will find cement sidewalks, nurses pushing prams, the evening paper boy,
but Potter itself lies off the map—off the motoring map, that is to
say. You have to take a turning marked 'No Through Road' and
bump heavily towards what looks like a farm gate stuck a mile
or more over the shaggy common. Through the gate is nothing
but Potter, and Potter is only one public-house, the Black Boar,
landlord Brewitt, one cash store and post office kept by Mrs
Margesson, a small tin-roofed church where services are held on
the first Sunday in the month, half a dozen cottages, a village

pond, and the gates, grounds and mansion of Lord Drew. But even those gates are not used: Lord Drew has other gates on the London road two miles away and never needs to pass through Potter. One of the cottages is inhabited by old Bill Purves: one wall has been repaired with petrol tins and when the door opens smoke blows out into Potter. He is said to sleep on a bed of rags, but nobody but the local policeman has ever visited him there, and the window is obscured by sacking. Three or four times a year—usually on bank holidays—old Bill Purves visits the Black Boar, buys a bottle of whisky and disappears for twenty-four hours. It was suspected, but never known for certain before the parachutists came, that old Purves slipped on those occasions into Lord Drew's grounds, laid his traps and lay out all day and night with his bottle—he never seemed to know what cold was, any more than an animal, and he was rather like an animal him-self—something grey and fleeting that you see for a moment shambling between hedges. His coat stuck out as if he were a scarecrow on a stick because he carried an old Mauser rifle under his coat, for which he had never paid a licence.

That was the odd scene of the 'invasion', though if you exam-ined Potter carefully you may conclude that it was not an acci-dent that the parachutists landed there. Potter itself could be isolated by a few snips of a wire cutter, and from that little hid-den spot in Metroland half a dozen men acting quickly could do an astonishing amount of damage—a mile and a half across un-frequented common and you had the main line to Scotland and the northern coast, and one supposes that the German air chiefs had planned a number of such attempts which our air defences foiled. Their psychological effect might have been incalculable: they would have destroyed the sense of security Englishmen still feel, the security which allows them to grumble. Look at the ef-fect on Potter.

We are a small island and there isn't a village anywhere which isn't accustomed to the sound of aeroplane engines. The plane they heard in the Black Boar was flying fairly low—perhaps 3,000 feet, but there was nothing out of the ordinary in that.

It was the fag-end of a cloudy spring day. Mrs Margesson in

the cash stores had just closed the post office counter because it was 6.30; the shop remained open for general goods till 8.00, and the lean man who was Lord Drew's undergardener was criticizing the beer in the public bar. 'It's the war they tell you,' he said bitterly. 'Everything's the war.' There wasn't a man left in any of the cottages; they were all in the public bar except old Purves, and the women were washing up the supper things.

Old Purves with his coat sticking queerly out and a bottle of whisky in his deep poacher's pocket was skirmishing along by Lord Drew's wall among the high nettles. The gamekeeper had sworn to get him and he wasn't taking any chances. He was the only one to see the parachutists descend.

He looked up under his old grey brows with a kind of angry astonishment as a number of men suddenly appeared in mid-air under things like enormous parasols. He didn't know what they were; he only had a feeling they were best avoided. 'It didn't seem right,' he said afterwards; he meant that it didn't seem fair, people peeping at you like that out of the sky. That was all he saw for a long time because just at that moment he found the weak point in Lord Drew's wall. The men were in uniform—for their own protection, one supposes; otherwise they would have been liable to the death penalty as non-combatants, but their uniforms caused no immediate astonishment in Potter, because we are so used in these days to uniforms: what with AFS and ARP and all the other initial letters we are prepared for any uniform, even a German uniform. Mrs Brewitt saw them at work on the telegraph and telephone wires and thought they were something to do with the post office. Only her son, who was sixteen and, alas! for him, knowledgeable, said they were Germans. 'Nonsense!' Mrs Brewitt said.

Mrs Margesson in the cash stores hardly looked up when the officer came in. He carried a large-scale map of the district and had a revolver at his belt. His steel helmet made her think, 'manoeuvres'. She said promptly, 'The post office is closed,' because she didn't think he looked like a shop customer. He said, 'Madam', and that struck her as foreign: a Frenchman or a Pole, she thought: he was a young man, very fair, and his uniform was very muddy; he sounded nervous and preoccupied. She smiled. 'Yes. What can I do for you?'

'Please,' he said, 'go at once to the inn.'

'The inn?'

'Yes. You must go at once. Everyone must go.'

'I don't understand.'

He said with embarrassment as though he were making a rather absurd claim, 'I am a German officer and this village is occupied by my men.'

With great presence of mind Mrs Margesson picked up the shop telephone and dialled a police call. The young man made no attempt to stop her. She could at once tell why—the wires had been cut. At that moment through the window she saw Driver, the village constable, being impelled down the road towards the Black Boar by two men in uniform; he had probably been digging in his garden as he was in his shirt sleeves.

More or less the same scene took place all over the village. Everybody who was not already at the Black Boar was rounded up and persuaded, pushed or even carried there. The Germans were determined that nobody should leave the village and carry the alarm, but they missed young Brewitt who had hidden in the outside lavatory and, of course, old Purves.

The German officer addressed them in the public bar. He told them that nobody was in danger from him or his men; all they had to do was keep quiet. The gamekeeper, who had been caught hunting old Purves and had a black eye, said in a loud voice, 'It's a scandal.' The German officer paid him no attention. He went on to warn them that any attempt to escape would be fatal; he said frankly, 'Our chance depends on none of you getting away,' and that reference to a chance—for what chance had a dozen Germans planked down in the middle of England?—suggests that they had a desperate hope they might be picked up again by plane before their presence was discovered. He said, 'You will be closely guarded and any attempt to escape will mean death.' He added with a note of entreaty, 'You've only to remain quiet for a few hours.'

All this time, of course, old Purves had been comfortably

curled up just inside Lord Drew's wall. He knew that the house was shut up and the only possible interference would be the gamekeeper or the policeman. The policeman was digging and would be too tired later to prowl: as for the gamekeeper old Purves despised him. He set a couple of traps, loaded his gun, opened the bottle of whisky and began to drink: he always calculated that a little drink improved his aim, and he had high hopes of a bird or two that evening. He was disturbed by a shot: his first feeling was indignation rather than curiosity. Lord Drew was away: a shot meant a rival poacher. He took another long drink, hid the bottle where he could find it again in a hole in the clay bank, and then peeped over the broken stones of the wall. To his astonishment he saw young Brewitt running and zigzagging down the road that led out of the village to the gate and afterwards to the main road.

What had happened was this. Young Brewitt, who had a romantic mind, remained convinced that what he had seen was actually a party of German soldiers cutting the telephone wires. He even guessed how they had arrived. The romantic mind found no difficulty in the idea. So he hid. He would probably have remained hidden if one of the Germans who had a tidy soul hadn't wanted to visit the lavatory. He pulled open the door and young Brewitt darted out like a rat; the soldier was taken by surprise and let him get a start. He shouted and young Brewitt ran the faster: other soldiers ran out of the inn and one of them fired and missed. It suddenly became very essential to get him. Three men waited with their guns raised until he should reach the gate.

So to his amazement old Purves watched the astonishing behaviour of young Brewitt. The boy leapt and zigzagged down the road; then he came to the gate and scrabbled desperately at the catch; three rifles went off together and young Brewitt fell. 'The bloody Bojers,' Purves said aloud, the old brain creaking rustily back forty years to South Africa and an ambush on the veldt.

Young Brewitt wasn't dead: they had fired, humanely, at his legs; but he was crippled for life. He shared with Purves the heroic events of that evening, but there were always some who said that he had intended to hide all night in the lavatory. About old Purves's movements and intentions there was no doubt at all.

He first of all unearthed the whisky bottle, took a long drink and hid it again; then he had a look at his traps and then he sidled like a ferret out of Lord Drew's grounds into the high nettles. He slid among them crouching, his chin protected by a two weeks' beard: he had got his gun out from under his coat—the old Mauser rifle that went back like his memory forty years to another war; it was as if 1914 to 1918 were an interlude he had hardly noticed at all.

Young Brewitt had been carried back into the Black Boar and two men had been left on guard. The rest with the lieutenant now set off across the common towards the railway line, carrying picks and crowbars, their rifles slung; two carried a box between them. Old Purves working his way, like a 'bloody Bojer' himself, from gorse bush to gorse bush, followed. The sun was setting over by Fenham Heath station three miles away; it shone just over the curve of the horizon on the last prams going home, on the circulating library where the Vicar's wife was changing her detective story, and on the little stream of commuters back from town, carrying attaché cases. That was a quiet, orderly, conventional world to which neither old Purves nor his quarry belonged: they were united out of sight but hardly out of hearing in a common spirit of wildness, vindictiveness, adventure. Old Purves gave an odd little chuckle as he bobbed quickly out of sight behind a gorse bush.

He knew the common, of course, as well as he knew Lord Drew's estate, and at first he thought, because of the tools they carried, which he could now see clearly in the darkening air, that they were bound for the gravel pit, dry and abandoned twenty years ago, a hundred yards from the railway line. A miniature one-track line connected it with a disused siding, and an old steel truck lay on its side, tipped off the rail. But the Bojers passed that by, clambering up the embankment on to the line beyond. Old Purves, worming his way along towards the gravel pit, thought they were a beautiful sight, outlined like that against the sky. They had left their rifles, all but two men, in the bushes below the embankment, so that they could slide quickly and inconspicuously down if a train appeared—on that long stretch of rail you could see an engine's steam two miles away. Now four of them bent and pulled and worked at the rails, two followed the lieutenant further down the line with the box, and two stood rather slackly on guard, watching the empty waste of common and the up and down line.

They never saw old Purves get down into the gravel pit. He scrabbled up to the edge, where a bush hid him, and got a line on one of the armed guards—the unarmed ones could wait. With a man's body clear against the sight, old Purves chuckled. It was like youth again: all sorts of sly memories came back, of nurses at Pretoria and drinking evenings in Jo'burg. He pulled the trigger and before the shattering explosion of the ancient rifle could clear, the man was down, holding his stomach with both hands: his rifle toppled over the embankment and rolled.

It was like one of those trick films that suddenly stop and then go on again, fast. Down the line the officer had swung round with his revolver out: the two men with him had their mouths open. Picks and crowbars suddenly stopped: one of them in mid-air. Then life started again. The guard fired at old Purves's smoke and the bullet kicked gravel up against his cheek: the men working dropped their tools and tumbled down the embankment to where they had left their rifles. Old Purves chose his next victim.

The Germans were shockingly out of luck. The bright sunset was behind the poacher, dazzling their eyes: he had their silhouettes lit up like dummies in a shooting booth. He began to suck excitedly through a gap in his teeth and fired again. A man halfway down the embankment tumbled, but old Purves had given away his position and though he ducked at once, the guard, stretched out now on top of the embankment, nipped a bullet close by his ear. When he took another peep the workmen had got their rifles, though the two men with the box a hundred yards up the line were all unarmed. That meant that four rifles could be brought to bear, not counting the lieutenant who was crawling back. Old Purves chuckled again: it was more fun than rabbit shooting.

But the others too had learnt their lesson: the lieutenant was shouting orders which the poacher couldn't understand. While the guard remained on top of the embankment the others, taking advantage of the bushes, began to circle round to get the sun behind them. Old Purves wasn't disturbed: he knew his battlefield. From one end of the gravel pit ran a trench, but because of the overhanging bushes it couldn't be seen from above: to the watcher on the embankment he was cornered. Old Purves, ducking under the gorse into the little hot tunnel, jolted away, looking more than ever like an earth animal going to ground. The trench sloped gently up and soon he was on all fours, then out he came into the tall bracken. He took a daring look: the guard had his eye fixed on the gravel pit: the two men up the line had left their box and were crawling towards their rifles: the three men and the lieutenant had made a half circle and were now steadily creeping towards the pit—their backs were half turned to him, and again they had the worst of the light.

Old Purves at this point of the game could have retired safely, with all the honours, but he was enjoying himself. He never liked to leave good game alone even if it meant risking capture. He waited until one of the men, in screening himself from the supposed enemy in the gravel pit, had exposed himself to his enemy in the flank—then old Purves let him have it 'proper', or rather he meant to: for the first time he nearly missed altogether: the man dropped his rifle, slumped heavily down nursing his hand. 'Goldarn it,' he said and ducked at once under the bracken.

Not one of the men suspected that the shot had come from the rear. They were almost at the rim of the pit now: the lieutenant gave an order: they leapt to their feet and were over it. But this time old Purves couldn't have made a mistake if he'd tried—firing quickly he got two: only the lieutenant leapt to safety.

By that time the two unarmed men had reached their rifles and the guard had spotted old Purves. Before he could get down a shot from the embankment got his left shoulder. He sat still among the bracken and wished he had some whisky with him. He tried to move, but the swaying bracken gave him away and a bullet missed him by a centimeter. He swore softly: this time the bloody Bojers *had* trapped him and there were still four of them left.

He was saved by a goods engine from Fenham Heath: it was going north with a string of empty trucks. The three men now hugged the ground under the embankment and a whistle warned the lieutenant to keep out of sight. They didn't want a warning carried up the line: they couldn't tell that the nearest troops were twenty miles away at least.

As the engine came into sight old Purves saw his chance. He bolted through the bracken towards the overturned truck which would protect him from all of them but the lieutenant—the lieutenant only had a revolver and the light now was shockingly bad. Nobody fired at him. Then he swung round and sent a shot at the officer who had got out of the gravel pit, but the pain in his shoulder was upsetting his aim and he missed.

All the same, though he didn't know it then, he'd won the game. They were scared and harried and didn't know what to think: all the lieutenant was concerned with now was to get his business finished quickly. He dodged round to his men and they all began a kind of strategic retirement up the line, along the edge of the embankment. Old Purves sent another shot after them, ineffectively. Then he swore gently because he'd only got one shot left.

He watched the four men, a little puzzled. They were climbing up on to the embankment again: he didn't shoot because the light was bad now and his eye was out. One man fired a warning shot at him which nicked a tiny piece off the edge of the truck. The others were opening the box: it seemed to contain string . . . Old Purves was irritated: he didn't like being ignored. He took aim rather wildly and fired.

For a moment it was as if the end of the world had come, blasting up against the truck which sheltered him: there were lamentable cries. When the fury of air and fire had died away, he came out of shelter and picked his way through the bushes—there was nobody left to fire at him. This was massacre.

He didn't like it: it turned his stomach over like dynamiting fish: the strange thing was that the rails were the only things left untorn.

The lieutenant was not dead: he called out in English, 'Kill me. Please kill me.' Old Purves always felt pity for broken animals, but he hadn't a bullet left. Then he saw the officer's revolver three yards away . . . Afterwards he looked through his pockets: there was nothing of value, but a photograph of a naked baby on a hearthrug again made his stomach turn over.

That was really the end of old Purves's battle: the rest was only what they call 'mopping up'. He went back to his traps and drank what was left of his whisky: two rabbits had already been snared. Then with the rabbits in his poacher's pockets and the lieutenant's revolver in his hand he went down cautiously to the Black Boar. There they had listened fearfully to the sound of the shots and the explosion: the guards were nearly as scared as the people of Potter. When old Purves appeared suddenly behind them with the revolver they surrendered at once. They, with two wounded men among the gorse, were the only survivors of the only parachute descent—it had been a discouraging failure for the German High Command because of old Purves's absence from the village, in Lord Drew's grounds. Driver, immediately he was released and saw the rabbits, charged him with poaching and as I have said, a week later he was released with a caution and a rather cold commendation. He was quite gratified: he didn't expect medals and as he said, 'I've got one back on them bloody Bojers.' For a while people visited him and gave him tips in return for history—'They runned just like little rabbits,' he used to say—and for the sight of a few souvenirs, but that source of income soon failed, and he was back in no time on the wrong side of Lord Drew's wall. One souvenir he never showed to anyone—the photograph of the baby on the mat. Sometimes he took it out of a drawer and looked at it himself—uneasily. It made him—for no reason that *he* could understand—feel bad.

A BRANCH OF THE
SERVICE

I

I have been forced reluctantly to retire from a profession which I found of great interest and on a few occasions even dangerous because I have lost my appetite for food. Nowadays I can eat only in order to drink a little—before my meal a glass or two of vodka, and then a half bottle of wine. I find it quite impossible to face a menu, leave alone the heavy three- or even four-course meals in restaurants which my profession demanded.

I owed it to my father that I got the job I am now leaving, though he died before I was, as we call it, recruited. My earliest memories are the smells of a kitchen—they are happy memories even though I now find it a burden to eat. The kitchen was not one in my home: it was, as it were, an abstract kitchen which represented all the kitchens in which my father cooked—kitchens in England, Switzerland, Germany, Italy, and once I believe for a short while in Russia. He was a great chef—but he was never officially recognized. He moved from country to country. He was never out of a job, but he never kept a job long because he always knew better than his employer when it was time for him to leave.

Of my mother I remember nothing—I think she must always have been left behind on our travels. How I enjoyed eating in those days, yet I never learnt how to cook. That was my father's pride and secret. What I learnt were languages—never very well but a smattering of many. I could understand better than I spoke. The man who later recruited me understood that. I remember him saying, 'To understand is the only important thing. We don't want you to talk.'

You may wonder why it was necessary for me to eat large meals in order to keep my job. Even in a good restaurant one does not feel bound to eat more than two courses and one may always linger a long time over the wine. Yes, but I was supposed to be judging the food not the wine, even awarding stars to the food in the fashion of Michelin, but of course stars differently designed. I even had to inspect the lavatories.

In my father's eyes I would never have made a first-class cook, and he didn't wish me to spend my life as a kitchen help. Through an admirer of his English cooking in a little restaurant in St Albans where he worked for a year before quarrelling with his employer, he introduced me to a new organization which called itself International Reliable Restaurants Association, but before I had finished my first six months' training they changed the name. IRRA was a little putting off because of the Irish difficulties, and so they became instead the International Guide to Good Restaurants or the IGGR.

Their advertisements and their reputation rose together; at any rate for English customers, for they soon outbid Michelin. Michelin was too nationalist. Michelin awarded to Paris in those days five stars to eight restaurants, while to London they gave no five stars and only two four stars. The IGGR was far more generous, and that proved an advantage.

I had been an inspector for the IGGR for two years before I was recruited for special duties.

As I learnt during my training in these so-called duties we were not really interested in the number of stars or even in the cleanness of the lavatories. The people with whom we were concerned were unlikely to be found in very expensive restaurants, for costly eating can make the eater conspicuous.

'Rich eaters are not the main interest of this section,' my instructor told me, 'here we look out for an ordinary customer. Especially those who are more than usually ordinary—they are the likely ones.'

I found his lessons at first a little obscure, until he told me a story which explained one of my puzzling memories of Paris. He said, 'Of course in this section we are not concerned with police work, but all the same we have taken a hint from the

French police. Do you remember the lottery sellers who used to come into the bistros and the small restaurants in France?'

'Yes. You never see them now.'

'And yet lottery selling is not illegal. They are gone because they had outlived their usefulness.'

'What was their usefulness?'

'The police showed them the photographs of wanted men—small fry, thieves and the like, and they would go from table to table looking at the faces. This gave us an idea for a rather more important work, a work which involves our ears more than our eyes.'

He made a long pause; he meant I think to arouse our curiosity, and curious we certainly were at having been taken away from tasting food and inspecting lavatories. But we were wrong. There was a gleam of amusement in our speaker's eyes. 'The lavatories are of particular importance,' he said.

'From the point of view of cleanness of course?' a novice (not me) asked.

I still had no idea what our instructor was talking about. 'No, no,' he said. 'Cleanness isn't our concern, but the lavatory is a private place if you want to exchange a word or a packet with a friend. Unless of course your friend is a woman, but we'll come to that possibility later.'

A lot of other possibilities came later.

'There are phrases in conversation that you hear in a restaurant which are worth attention. *Pas de problème* is less interesting in France where it is in such common use, but if one of your neighbours in a small unfashionable restaurant in Manchester (a restaurant which hasn't got even one star) says, "There's no problem" it's worth paying attention.'

I think that he felt among the novices a certain scepticism. He went on, 'A hundred chances to one, of course, nothing of interest—of obvious interest—will follow—but make a note. There remains the one chance. The lavatory too—though perhaps the chances there are a little greater. For example two men peeing beside each other and talking. Our organization fills a gap—an important gap in security. A house is watched—but that again is not our job. The telephone is tapped. Not our job. Even street meetings are in other hands. But restaurants—we are doing a great service to the state.'

A question came to my mind. 'But when once we have given a star to a restaurant we have no excuse to go on eating there?'

'You are wrong. Two stars might be gained for the next edition—or a star could be lost. A certain blackmail is sometimes necessary. You will always be welcome and given the best food.'

The best food—yes, that was my problem. A career of eating. Of course it didn't worry me at the beginning, and what attracted me was not so much being of service to the state as the hint of mystery about the whole affair. The phrase 'no problem' stayed like a tune in my ears.

2

Of course, when first sent on duty one made serious mistakes, but unlike other professions one was excused—even sometimes praised—for a mistake because it might have added a little to one's experience. My first bad mistake—which in any other profession would have ruined my career—happened to be concerned with a lavatory. But I would prefer to speak of my first lucky success which far outweighed my lavatory error, although that success too concerned a lavatory. The occasion took place in a three-starred restaurant, a smart one, but not too smart like the Ritz. In my first three years I was only told to take a watch in the Ritz once, the expense was too great and the chances too small. Waiters there were apt to notice strangers. I had been shown a photograph, but a very bad one, of a suspect who apparently had been seen at this restaurant more than once and was believed to be a foreigner. In his case they had already paid three experienced watchers—one a day—and they were almost ready to give up. His companion at table was always different.

Quite by chance—in our profession nearly everything is a chance—I happened to be sitting at the next table to a solitary man. Some instinct had made me choose the table next to him for I could see little resemblance to photographs I had been shown. However there was a foreign look about him, and perhaps (I might have imagined it) a look of impatience or anxiety, and his table was laid for two. He had ordered a glass of port (not a usual aperitif for an Englishman) and he lingered over it. I lingered too over my very dry Martini, trying to outlinger him.

At last the friend he was awaiting arrived—a woman. I write 'friend', but the greeting which he gave her struck me as very odd—'Pleased to meet you', that very antiquated English phrase, was spoken in a distinctly foreign accent.

For the rest of my meal there could no longer be any malingering. In my training I had been taught that I must always finish my meal and pay my bill while those whom I had chosen to watch were still eating. Of course I could spend quite a lot of time, after paying, with a coffee, but I must be prepared to leave my table a little before those I watched or a very little after. I had to keep in touch, at all costs, but avoid the suspicion of keeping them under observation.

This early experience of mine in the Royalty restaurant was a physically very painful one, for the pair whom I had chosen to watch had a large meal and I have always, as I have said, had a very small appetite. First they chose a mixed salad, then roast beef, then cheese and then to my horror, they ordered a dessert—this too was a foreign touch for in England we finish with cheese. It confirmed for me that the two were of different nationalities, and that 'pleased to meet you' had been an agreed signal. A momentary disagreement over cheese before dessert confirmed me in thinking that the man was French and the woman English.

Their conversation was mainly on the subject of Flaubert about whom the woman was writing a book. Of course it occurred to me that Flaubert might be the pseudonym of a third agent and Madame Bovary of yet another. They made no attempt to lower their voices.

'It's very good of you to see me,' the woman told him. 'I have used your great work on Flaubert a good deal, and it's very kind of you to allow me to quote from it.'

I knew little of Flaubert's life, but I began to learn quite a lot, and there really seemed nothing wrong with the couple.

'I'd have liked to see you once again and show you my text before it goes to the publisher, but I know how busy you are,' the woman said.

'Yes, I would like to see it, but I'm afraid I'm off by an early plane tomorrow. At 9.30.'

I made a mental note to check the time and destination, but I had really lost all suspicion and I would have called it a wasted day if it had not been for the cigarettes. After the meat course, when they were waiting for the cheese trolley, she offered him a cigarette.

He hesitated, and I thought he glanced at me.

'A Benson and Hedges Extra Mild,' she told him.

'Yes, I do like one of those, but do you mind—I only smoke one after I have finished eating. It's a habit.' However she took a cigarette and laid it by his plate.

'You don't mind if I smoke?' she asked.

'Of course not.'

He lit her cigarette and the cheese trolley arrived. She chose a Stilton and he chose a Brie. I chose the smallest bit of Gruyère that I could persuade the waiter to cut and shuddered at the thought of the dessert which was yet to come. I took an ice and after the apple tarts which they picked the woman took a coffee. I did the same. He seemed to have forgotten her cigarette, for he left it still unlit beside his plate. Perhaps a Benson and Hedges, I thought, was too mild for his taste. They continued to talk about Flaubert, but what they said was quite beyond me. At last the man asked for his bill and I quickly did the same, but theirs came first and I had no time to wait for it before I followed them from the restaurant. The man still carried his cigarette. Perhaps he had no intention of smoking it, but didn't wish to offend his companion by throwing it away.

At the door he said goodbye to her. She said, 'We haven't spoken at all of *Education Sentimentale*. If you could manage another meeting . . .'

'I'll certainly do my best,' he said. 'It has been a great pleasure meeting you.' When she had left he turned away towards the lavatory still carrying his cigarette. A tidy man, I thought, he's going to throw it into the toilet, but all the same a reasonless curiosity

had settled in my brain. There was another reason too. I wanted
to practise my new profession. A good cook progresses through
his errors. A short pause and then I followed him walking as quietly as I could.

He was washing his hands when I entered and he had laid the
cigarette to one side out of the way of the water—that eternal un-
smoked cigarette. I snatched it and before he had time to turn I
was out of the lavatory. There was no shout from behind me—
only the sound of pursuing feet. At the hotel entrance I pushed
the porter to one side and ran into the street. Luck was with me.
A taxi had just deposited a customer. As I drove away I saw the
customer rushing after me into the street followed by the waiter
who was waving my unpaid bill. Poor man. I paid it later indi-
rectly with interest by recommending the restaurant for a fourth
star, which it certainly did not deserve.

In the taxi I looked more closely at the cigarette. There was an
odd feeling in the centre—a kind of hardening of the tobacco,
and at one end a kind of roughening in the packing of the cigarette. I was careful not to finger it more. It had already passed
through three hands and was a little damp from its lavatory lodging—there seemed reason enough for all this. All the same I had
learnt in my training to hand over any object however trivial belonging to a suspect, and this I did as soon as I reached the office
of the International Guide to Good Restaurants. Then I sat down
to write my report, and my instinct made me enclose with it the
untidy cigarette.

3

I hadn't given in my report long when the telephone sounded.
'Scramble,' my chief's voice said, and I touched the button which
would make our conversation unintelligible to anyone who
might be tapping our line.

'The woman I feel pretty sure was English and the man
French, I think, but they spoke to each other in English although
they were both experts on Flaubert.'

'I think they wanted you to listen. They were proving, you might say, their innocence.'

'But are they guilty?'

'Guilty as hell. You've done a first-rate job. Come along in an hour and see me.'

When I went to him the cigarette lay torn in half on his desk in a small litter of flakes. 'Benson and Hedges Special Mild,' he said with a smile of satisfaction. 'Low in tar content, but certainly not low in valuable information.' He showed a little bit of wrinkled paper. 'A good way to conceal it,' he said, 'in the middle of a cigarette.'

'What's on it?' I asked.

'We'll soon know. Microdots and a code of course. You've done a good job. It was very acute of you to take the cigarette.'

Such a good job indeed that they forgave me several months later for a very bad mistake which also involved a lavatory.

4

The cigarette had led us to a new suspect for our file, a doctor who had connections with the chemical industry. He was now placed under continuous surveillance; a whole team of us was employed night and day. His open practice was in a small country town not far from the factory which used him as a consultant when one of the employees went sick. He had been very thoroughly vetted by MI5, but our relations were closer to MI6 and there was a good deal of rivalry and even jealousy between the two establishments. The foundation of the international food guide was regarded by MI5 as an intrusion into their territory, and it was true that we had not passed on to them the information contained in the cigarette. Counter-espionage abroad certainly belonged to MI6, but our food guide was international and it would be inefficient to split the English section from the foreign. No watcher was employed more than once in two weeks and always at different mealtimes in order that the suspect would never become aware of a familiar face. Unfortunately for me the doctor was a man of inordinate appetite and after two months my turn came at the hour of dinner—the hour when his appetite was greatest. Unfortunately too I had suffered from a succession of heavy meals earlier. To award a star even to breakfasts had to be considered, and it was extraordinary how many people still preserved a pre-war appetite for what is still called an English breakfast as distinct from a continental one—eggs and bacon, or even worse sausages and bacon, sometimes even preceded by a helping of haddock.

I took over from his watcher outside a quite simple inn which was called the Star and Garter only half a mile from his own house. We were the only diners and I sat down at a table well away from his. I noticed he looked quite often at his watch, but he was obviously not expecting a friend for he had already chosen his meal. To my horror when I looked at the menu I found a set menu at a very reasonable price and he had ordered the first course which was an onion soup and my stomach cannot abide onions. If I left out the soup I would find myself well in advance of him and I would be out of touch with him when I finished the last course. Another watcher was stationed in sight of the door who would take over when he left, but I had to remain till then in sight of the doctor in case he was contacted during his meal. A doctor was always of course liable to a phone call when he was away from home, but the Star and Garter telephone would have been tapped as soon as we knew where he was in the habit of dining.

I allowed myself a glance at him every now and then when he lowered his eyes to the obnoxious soup. To me he looked a thoroughly honest man. Why would an honest man be mixed up with the man of the cigarette? Then I remembered he was a doctor. A doctor doesn't judge his patients. If he had attended the deathbed of a murderer that wouldn't have made him a murderer. If a priest appeared on our microdot file would he be reasonably a guilty man? The doctor finished his soup and ordered roast beef. Reluctantly I did the same. I had to keep in step, though I could already feel the effect of the onion soup. He was a slow eater and read a newspaper between bites. I was glad that he showed no interest in me. It confirmed my impression of his honesty. It was a cold night and I felt sorry for the watcher outside keeping his unnecessary vigil.

To my distress the doctor ordered an apple tart to follow. The only alternative on the little restaurant's menu was an ice-cream, but an ice-cream needs to be eaten with some speed before it melts, so I was forced to order the tart. My trouble was I suffer from acidity, and when the doctor followed the tart with a piece of cheese, I had to leave the table, for I felt the approach of diarrhoea. The lavatory was upstairs and as I left I ordered my bill, so as to be ready to leave on my return if the doctor didn't wait for coffee. If I found him with coffee I could spin out the time with a little difficulty over change and when he left my colleague would take over. 'And see him safely home to bed,' I thought with irritation at this unnecessary routine watch.

I won't go into the unsavoury details of my diarrhoea—it was a severe one and more than five minutes had passed before I went downstairs to the restaurant. I found that the doctor had gone, and I thought with relief, 'My job is over.' I would take something to ease my stomach when I got home.

As I paid my bill I remarked to the waiter, an elderly man, who, I found, was also the landlord, 'Not much custom tonight.'

'At night,' he told me, 'the bar trade's better. And we do more at lunchtime—passing motorists, but the doctor's a good regular and he likes simple food.'

I felt it my duty to inquire a little more about our suspect.

'Doesn't he ever dine at home?'

'No, he's a single man.'

'Not much custom for a doctor in a place this size?'

'There's always the flu. And babies. But of course his main work is up at the chemical factory. Two hundred men. Plenty of patients there. I hope you enjoyed your food, sir, and that we'll see you again. It's a small place but my own, and I keep a sharp eye on the kitchen.'

'I can tell that. Here is my card.'

'International Good Food Guide! My goodness! I never expected to see one of your fellows in my little place. So that's why you went to the lavatory?'

'Yes. We always inspect those. And I looked in on the kitchen on my way,' I lied. 'I could tell at a glance . . .'

'What?'

'Clean. Which I already knew from the food it would be.'

'It's very kind of you, sir. I do hope you'll come again.'

'Not for a year. In the meanwhile we'll give you a mention in the guide.'

'I'm very honoured, sir. Perhaps some of the big shots from the factory will read it.'

'What I advise you in the meantime is to have at least two menus. Perhaps then we could promote you to a star.'

'Never did I dream . . . When I tell the missus . . .'

'By the way what do they do in the factory?'

'All sorts of medicines, sir. Even cures for the hiccups they say. Me, I am content with a bit of Eno's. It serves most purposes.'

I bade him a warm goodbye and gave him a copy of the guide in which his restaurant would appear in the next edition. I was glad to be off because my stomach was still queasy and I had no further duties that day. I would go home and perhaps as the man had reminded me take a glass of Eno's.

I went outside and to my astonishment saw my fellow watcher pretending interest in a shop window across the road. He turned and saw me with equal astonishment.

'What the hell have you come out for?'

'What are you doing here?'

'Waiting for the doctor of course.'

'But the doctor's gone.'

'He hasn't passed that door.'

'Oh the hell. There must be a back door.'

'But why didn't you signal me as soon as you lost touch?'

'I had to go to the loo. I was only gone a few minutes and he wasn't there when I came down. He came in this way and I thought he'd gone out the same way and you'd be following him.'

'He must have had suspicions.'

'I took him for an honest man whatever the damned microdots said.'

'We've certainly messed things up this time.'

5

That was exactly what my boss said when I reported to him. 'You've badly messed things. You should never have left the restaurant before him. Even for a minute.'

'It was the onion soup and the tomatoes.'

'Onion soup and tomatoes! Is that what I have to tell the big chief?'

'I had diarrhoea. I couldn't stay and shit in my trousers.'

'You know I would have sacked you like a shot, if you hadn't made that splendid coup with the cigarette.'

'You needn't sack me. I resign. But I'd swear—microdot or not—that man was honest. He was no traitor.'

'Traitor is a silly word that journalists use. A traitor can be as honest as you or me. That chemical factory has connection with chemical warfare. A man can feel that chemical warfare is a be-trayal of the world we have to live in. He could be fighting for something greater than his country. An honest spy is the most dangerous. He is not spying for money, he's spying for a cause. Look, that cigarette is more important than this mistake. One learns from mistakes, and you are a good learner. You have given me a good idea of how to use your mistake. He may have been suspicious of you. Or it may have been his regular drill. To go in by the front and go out by the back.'

I said, 'I can't go on. I'm sorry. I can't go on.'

'But why? This mistake of yours will be forgiven and for-gotten.'

'But the onion soup. Tomatoes. And all the meat I have to eat. Garlic with the lamb. Cheese as well as dessert. Why do all these suspects have such a good appetite?'

'Perhaps it gives them time to observe the people around them.'

'But *they* never seem to get diarrhoea.'

'About your diarrhoea. I have an idea.' He paused and played with his pencil. 'Suppose we gave you a week's holiday.'

'I don't need a holiday except from onion soup, and toma-toes etc.'

'But I see a way of using them. Suppose you stayed a week at that little hotel and had all your meals there. The doctor would begin to accept you as a regular. You would consult him about your stomach. He might give you a treatment. Of course you would take nothing he gave you, for if he remained suspicious he might try to poison you. Any prescription he gave you would send on to us and we would have it examined. If there was anything dangerous about it our suspicions would be confirmed and we would close in on him.'

'And if they weren't?'

'We'd give him more time. He would need to have *his* suspicions confirmed too if he's a man with scruples. We would think of some way. A warning from somewhere would reach him. Or one of your own reports perhaps. We would watch his reactions very closely. All you would need to do is . . .'

'To eat,' I said. 'No. I've made up my mind. I can't make a career out of eating. No more onion soup, no more tomatoes, no more garlic. I resign.'

So it was that I abandoned the International Guide to Good Restaurants. Sometimes from curiosity I buy a copy of the latest number. At least I have done one good deed in my life. The little country restaurant remains as a 'mention' in the guide, though it has never received a star.

AN OLD MAN'S MEMORY

I am writing in 1995 and old people's memories are short. Small wars come and go, even the deaths in Gaza and Beirut which caused such a stir in the eighties seem to belong to history now, but I doubt whether the year 1994 will ever cease to horrify me. The event of that year has a quality of nightmare about it—deaths in the darkness, in the depths of the sea, deaths by mutilation and drowning. The rotting bodies of the unrecognizable rise occasionally to the surface even today on both sides of the Channel.

Elaborate celebrations were prepared for the opening of the Channel Tunnel and the first two trains were arranged to pass each other in mid-Channel. There had been some dissensions in England, of course, just as there had been in the Paris celebrations of the Revolution in 1989, because of the devastation of the countryside in Kent by the new autoroutes between Dover and London, but the dissidents were few when the first cross-Channel train from Paris arrived in Dover. Mrs Thatcher, who had won her fourth electoral contest, was of course there on the platform to greet the French train as it came up from the sea and halted at Dover to join in the celebration. The French Ambassador was present and for some obscure reason Mrs Thatcher was accompanied by the Minister of Defence. Perhaps it was to reassure a few of the dissidents who remembered the failure of Hitler's plans to invade England after our flight from Dunkirk. If the Tunnel had existed then, would there have been time to destroy it and if it had been destroyed would we have rebuilt it when the war was over?

In 1994 all was well prepared. I wasn't at Dover myself. It was easier to watch the whole affair (or so I believed) on television. As the French train emerged from the Tunnel the 'Marseillaise' was played and afterwards 'Rule, Britannia!', but not 'God save the Queen'. Perhaps the Queen shared some of her people's doubts, but Mrs Thatcher stood up very straight and played the part of Britannia. On the other side of the Channel the President of France waited to greet the British train, but it never arrived. The news reached us just as Mrs Thatcher began her well-prepared speech. Bombs had exploded under the Channel and the British train had been destroyed before it reached Calais with the loss of all lives.

Who were the terrorists?

It was believed that Semtex was the explosive used. In the case of an air disaster in the eighties when a plane had crashed over a village in Scotland it had only needed a radio cassette player to hold three hundred grammes of Semtex. There had been great advances since then, and explosives could be timed now for days not hours in advance. The new explosions went off soon after the British engine passed the half-way line under the Channel. The IRA was of course the prime suspect, because of its activities in Germany and its relations with Gadaffi who was known to have supplied the IRA with Semtex, but the Iranians had never for-given England for its support of Rushdie nor the Americans for having shot down their innocent airliner. As it happened there were even more Americans on board the train than English.

Who had known where to plant the bombs? For four years hundreds of workmen had been employed in constructing the Tunnel. It had been like an open challenge to the terrorists to do their worst. Of all these hundreds it must have been easy enough to find one or two who were ready, in return for large sums of money, to sketch plans of their work in the Tunnel and, the best spots once chosen, to find others to plant cassettes.

Much publicity had been given in the Press to the security measures for which those involved in construction were not ulti-mately responsible. All luggage had been X-rayed, every passen-ger passing through the same sort of arch as we have in our airports had been meticulously checked. But had all appropriate measures been taken in the depths of the Channel itself?

The terrorists were in no hurry. They had plenty of time, four years of time, to plan, to choose, to corrupt.

Two years have passed now and there have been no arrests, but what may surprise even the terrorists is that the Euro-Tunnel Company, encouraged by shareholders and aided by the British and French Governments, has announced that the Tunnel is to be reopened and work has already begun and should be finished by 1997. The costs will be almost as great as building the first Tunnel.

I have spoken of the shortness of an old man's memory, but I wonder if anyone's memory will be short enough in 1997 to persuade a passenger to climb on board the carriage which will take him down into the depths of the Channel, as dimly lit as the great Tunnel under the Alps, but with water and not rock above, and how many corpses still rotting below the rails?

THE LOTTERY TICKET

Mr Thriplow bought his first and last lottery ticket in Vera Cruz. He had had two glasses of tequila to give himself the courage to board the awful little hundred-ton Mexican barge with an auxiliary engine which was the only method of getting to the small tropical state he wanted to visit. He felt himself, as he took the very first sheath of tickets the small girl offered him, driven by fate—perhaps he was. I don't often believe in fate, but when I do I picture it as just such a malicious and humorous personality as would choose, out of all people in the world, Mr Thriplow to fulfil its absurd and august purposes.

Then, as far as concerned an aunt in London and a female cousin in Brisbane, with whom he used to keep up an animated and whimsical correspondence, silence descended on Mr Thriplow. One or two events in that obscure state crept into the News in Brief on the foreign page of *The Times*—an assassination, for instance, which the aunt noted and then told her friends, without conviction, 'Henry must be having quite an exciting time.' He was, but you didn't associate Henry Thriplow with excitement.

About forty-two years old and a very well-to-do bachelor, Thriplow was a timid man, but his timidity took a curious form, for it drove him, whenever he had a holiday abroad, into discomforts you didn't connect with timidity. He couldn't bear social contacts, and so he chose for the scene of his escape those parts of the world where his fellow-tourists didn't congregate. He went, the year I'm writing of, to Mexico, but he didn't go to Mexico City, or Taxco or Cuernavaca or even Oaxaca, although his aunt urged him to look out for a decorated serape and he knew his Australian cousin would value some silver ear-rings. Instead—he gave as his rational excuse that he wanted to investigate the career of Cortes—he chose a grim little tropical state, where there was nothing at all to see but marsh, mosquitoes, banana plantations and a public gaol which probably *did* go back to Cortes.

You came after forty hours by sea, wallowing in almost intolerable discomfort in a boat lit only by oil-lamps in the bow and stern (when the captain wrote his log a sailor stood by with an electric torch), you came in sickness and stench and the weariness induced by the wooden shelf they called a bunk, to the River and the Port. There you lay another day against the bank propped up with the carcasses of old ships, the mosquitoes drilling round like sewing machines. There were a few wooden huts, one little dusty plaza with a statue of Obregon, the buzzards rustled overhead, and out beyond the river the fins of sharks glided by like the periscopes of a fleet of submarines.

Ten hours up the river between the banana plantations lay the capital. Thriplow's ship went ashore twice on the way: the fireflies flickered like a city on either bank, and the oil-lamps gave an effect of curious melodrama to the shapes of the coconut palms and the banana trees. Then round a bend came the real lights of the capital looking sophisticated and important and surprising in that wild obstinate region.

It was false, of course, that effect of sophistication: Thriplow had no need to fear the shrill bargaining tones of American women hunting for serapes: there was nothing in that town to attract anyone—except Thriplow. The barge was tied up to a mud-bank, and Thriplow went ashore over a plank thrust across twelve feet of green sour river: a policeman took his suitcase and shook it, listening for the surge and clank of contraband liquor (spirits were prohibited), and a kindly spectator switched on an electric torch to save him from sliding back into the water.

There was only one possible hotel and after Thriplow had left his suitcase, he walked up into the plaza to see what life there was. All that there was existed there. Some sort of an election was on, he couldn't tell what: red stars and the words Popular Frente decorated all the walls, and round and round the plaza in the deep sour heat the younger people walked—the men one way, the girls another. A blind man in his best white suit and his best straw hat was led by a friend: it was like a religious ceremony, going on and on in all-but-silence, in front of a dentist's (the hideous chair lit up like a wax figure in the window), the Federal Prison with white colonial pillars and an armed soldier and a press of dark faces at the bars, the Treasury, the Presidencia, the Syndicate of Workers and Peasants, and a few private houses where behind the unshuttered windows old ladies swung back and forth and children sat on hard straight bought-by-the-dozen Victorian chairs.

Thriplow could speak very little Spanish: he had a phrase book for his vital needs: and he had little hope that in this blistered and comfortless town there would be anyone at all who spoke English. Sitting nervously up in bed, watching a cockchafer bang against the high ceiling of his great bare room and the ants troop up through the tiles, Thriplow could feel that his object had already been achieved—he could look back on Kensington and his aunt's house and his regular comfortable routine with real nostalgia; he could return—unlike the regular tourist—filled with a passionate sense of the beauty of his own home.

Breakfast next day in the only restaurant; a stroll through the market above which the buzzards hovered with black serrated wings and tiny idiot heads: lunch in the same place: an uneasy sleep upon his bed, a walk up to the plaza, supper, a glass of mineral water to clean his teeth with (Thriplow was careful of his health), and bed again. It wasn't much of a day—there wasn't even a church he could examine (they had been destroyed throughout the state and the priests hunted out), in which he could watch with his faint disapproval the Roman ritual and the native superstition. As for the lottery ticket—he had forgotten that completely.

It came back to his mind at lunch-time on the third day, when a man approached his table with tickets. He asked to see the old list, and there, framed in the centre of the long columns, was his own number, 20375. His first—and last—lottery ticket had won 50,000 pesos—about £2,500 in English money. The flies revolved round the ugly beef on his plate, and a beggar—an Indian with little wisps of hair on the chin and lip—stood just inside the doorway watching the lunchers (he never spoke a word, probably knew no Spanish, he was like the figure in a morality play to remind the well-fed of the hungry).

Mr Thriplow's immediate sensation was shame—he felt like a foreign exploiter, a gringo. He had spent 5 pesos on the ticket: what right had he to all this money? The lottery seller told everybody in the room about it, and they all had to see his ticket and the list and they all told him what he had to do—he understood the word 'banco' all right. As he left the restaurant he tried to salve his conscience a little: he emptied his notecase which held 50 pesos into the Indian's hand. The man showed no pleasure: he moved quickly away, as if he didn't know what God might do next.

The news had reached the bank long before Thriplow arrived there. Smug and sleek and smiling, the half-caste manager came out to greet Thriplow, sweating under the armpits. He had almost as little English as Thriplow had Spanish, but Thriplow could guess from the wide gesture that he was putting the poor resources of the bank at his disposal. It was almost as if the news had reached the vultures too, for they came rustling down across the roofs and settled in the road with their hideous little heads peering this way and that for a death.

Thriplow sat on a hard shiny rocking-chair and listened to the manager. He could only understand a word here and there, as the hot day drooped above them. It sounded as if investments were being discussed: apparently he couldn't take the money out of Mexico. He said, suddenly, petulantly, the heat was getting him down, 'I don't want the money, I don't need the money. This place needs it more than I do,' and was startled to see the immediate comprehension in the manager's brown half-breed eyes.

'You are,' the manager said, 'a benefector,' as if he were making a statement and not asking a question.

'I don't need your money,' Thriplow repeated. He smoothed his pale hair nervously, afraid that he might sound theatrical. 'I should like to do good—for this country.' It was really an enormous sum for a Mexican state so poor as this—he pictured himself with gentle satisfaction as a kind of Carnegie. 'A library perhaps.'

'A benefactor,' the manager said again. All the English words he knew had Latin roots—the result was rather like a tongue-tied Dr Johnson. He picked up a straw hat and said, 'Depart.'

'Where to?'

The man was vague. He said something about the Presidencia. Thriplow let himself drift with fate—and haven't I described fate already as humorous? He drifted—after the absurd straw hat, full of holes like a sieve—up into the plaza, into a waiting-room in the Presidencia. It appeared that his benevolence was to be arranged by the Governor himself—free library, Thriplow wondered, a hospital, a scientific institute, perhaps a debating society? Or alms houses. There were long conversations on the telephone. A man like the traditional bandit in tight trousers with a highly decorated revolver holster watched him—with malevolent good humour over a red scarf.

'The Governor is absent,' the manager said. 'Again we depart,' and he led the way back across the plaza followed by the bandit. He headed for a door marked Dentista and flashed explanatory gold teeth. 'Pain,' he said with satisfaction, 'pain.' They went right in—to the room with the chair and the drill. The sun was reflected from a whitewashed wall back into the room blindingly. The Governor sat in the chair, his mouth plugged open with cotton wool, and a buzzard stalked across the yard like a domestic turkey, looking for offal.

The bank manager explained rapidly in Spanish, and the Governor listened, tipped back in the chair with his mouth open. He was small and fat and middle-aged with a blue chin and a good-humoured boyish expression. The dentist changed a needle and a look of agonized apprehension crossed the Governor's face: he gestured imploringly towards the manager as much as to say, 'Go on talking. Go on. For heaven's sake.'

The manager stopped dramatically with an emphatic sentence: Thriplow had understood nothing. The Governor was almost horizontal: his feet were on a level with the manager's mouth: he tried to heave himself up and nodded violently, dislodging a piece of cotton wool.

Then the dentist swung the drill over and the Governor's face was again convulsed—boyishly. 'Pain,' the manager said. 'Pain. We depart.'

They came out again into the little steamy plaza: a few people sat under the trees drinking gaseous fruit drinks—chemical pinks and yellows. A man came down the steps of the Presidencia, his revolver holster creaking dryly in the stifling day, and a little squad of soldiers went by, small men, Indians, with slovenly olive uniforms and rifles slung anyhow. 'Education,' Thriplow thought, 'that's what these people need,' and his heart swelled happily with a sense of benevolence and power: his old Liberal traditions stirred: one of his ancestors had had a statue erected to him in a foreign land.

The bank manager turned this time away from the bank, away from the Presidencia. He trotted across the square, very hot, very intense, mopping his forehead. The force of his momentum carried Mr Thriplow with him. He was aware of nothing but that little steaming back making for the office of the Workers' and Peasants' Syndicate—nothing but that and a girl who moved away at their approach. It wasn't any beauty which caught Thriplow's attention—there were many girls in this town with better features and Thriplow in any case cared nothing for women—it was a curious lost inimical air she had. She wore her clothes as if they didn't fit. 'Who's that?' he said. She watched him from the centre of the plaza with suspicion.

'Religious,' the manager said, as if that explained anything at all, bobbing through a whitewashed door into a little dry patio. The patio contained a number of packing-cases filled with bottles of mineral water, a dead fountain and some shrivelled flowers, an empty sardine tin.

'Interpretation,' the manager said. He began to talk animatedly in Spanish with someone Thriplow couldn't see through a door. And then the oddest figure of that odd day emerged—a very fat man with curly hair and a jolly face. He was dressed in dirty white drill stretched to bursting round his thighs and he carried a billiard cue: his belt shone with bullets and a heavy holster rattled against his side. He waved the cue cheerfully at Thriplow. He said, 'I speak English—very fine. I am the Chief of

Police in this—' he smiled idiomatically, 'lousy hole.' Somebody struck a billiard ball, and the Chief of Police peered with anxiety into the room.

He said, 'You can't trust them. They are not—sports.' He turned again to Thriplow and went rapidly on: 'This man wants me to tell you the Governor is made very happy by your present.'

'And what,' Thriplow said, 'does he propose to do with it?'

'Progress,' the Chief of Police said. 'We are very backward here.' Again he started at the click of a billiard ball.

'A new school?'

'All in good time,' the Chief said. 'First we must defeat reaction.'

'Reaction?'

'You have heard of the election?'

'I don't want the money used for politics,' Thriplow said.

'Politics, no, no. But this is not politics. Rebellion. They are plotting rebellion. They are getting arms from Germany, Italy, Japan. They are selling Mexico.' He gestured out at the little hot plaza, the fruit drink stalls. 'If they win, it is reaction. The Church comes back, the bishop.' He paused impressively. 'The Inquisition.'

'Oh, surely not,' Mr Thriplow protested.

'Yes, the Inquisition.'

'But I wouldn't like to feel,' Thriplow said, 'that this money . . . well, you know, I am a foreigner . . . I don't want to add to the political bitterness.'

'You will be loved,' the Chief of Police said. 'Your money will be . . . sinking fund . . . for progress. Just give your ticket to this man.' He peered anxiously through the door, and then struck with an idea turned floridly back. 'The gratitude of the State . . . a Statue, or perhaps a drinking fountain, but there is no spring . . . a seat of marble in the plaza with *your* name . . . what is your name, señor?'

'Thriplow.'

'An inscription. From all friends of progress in the State in honour of their foreign benefactor.'

'It's very good of you.'

'Not at all. Where would you like the seat, Señor Tipno? In front of the Syndicate? Or by the Presidencia? Under that tree? We will clear out the fruit-seller.'

'It is really too good of you.'

There was nothing to do at night. The electric dynamo on the ground floor of the hotel buzzed and droned, and in the hotel itself, on the first floor, the lights flickered and the beetles banged on the walls. They came swarming up from the riverside in droves: the floor crept with them. The proprietor and Mr Thriplow sat on wicker chairs swinging back and forth in the thick hot air. After a while the proprietor found a few words of English, a few words of French: a doubtful communication of ideas was set up between him and Thriplow. Somewhere, a long way off, in the direction of the plaza, there was a lot of noise and shouting. 'Election,' the proprietor explained, fanning himself with a Mexico City paper four days old. A boat hooted on the river.

The proprietor began to complain—a dreary lament for the good old days. As far as Thriplow could make out, in the days of Porfirio Diaz they had had a Governor who had died a poor man—it had never happened since. Mr Thriplow tentatively produced the words, 'Reaction . . . Inquisition.'

The proprietor suddenly discovered a phrase: 'Now,' he said, 'we die . . . *comme les chiens*.' Why should a man not have a priest at his deathbed . . . if he wanted it? It might be superstition, but when had a man a better right to superstition than when he was dying? He lapsed gloomily into silence, hitting out at the beetles with his paper.

'But the wealth of the Church,' Thriplow protested. The proprietor didn't get his meaning. '*Iglesia* . . .' Thriplow said. '*L'argent . . . mucho dinero*.' A hollow laugh was his reply. The noise from the plaza went on and on.

Thriplow said, 'After all it is a democracy here . . . You have a vote. If you want reaction, you can vote for it.' He went on a long while explaining democracy to the hotel-keeper: every now and then a word seemed to penetrate—'ballot' for instance. Suddenly the old man gave tongue. It was confusing and a little disturbing. Thriplow felt that he had probably not understood correctly. The word 'lottery ticket' came in, and once Thriplow was convinced that he had been called a fool. The idea that Thriplow got—it was probably an inaccurate one—was this: the Governor's position, in spite of the police and the federal troops and the trade union, was shaky. It was incredible, but it had really seemed that he might lose the election. Because the wages of the police and the soldiers had not been paid for months. The word 'gold teeth' came in, but that could hardly have been the Governor's only extravagance. His opponent had been placarding the town with accusations—and the police had not torn down the notices. But now tonight everybody had been paid—in full—because of the lottery ticket.

Mr Thriplow tried to suggest in English and French that the victory of progress ought not to be endangered by the loss of a few weeks' wages.

The proprietor suddenly and unexpectedly lost his temper—the noise now was so great that he shouted at Mr Thriplow. 'Progress.' The electric light went out completely, and then went on again showing the proprietor's face convulsed. He screamed, '*Pistoleros, Asesinos.*' There was some cheering in the street outside.

Thriplow went out on to the balcony. A platoon of soldiers was going by: they were a little drunk—you could tell it in their broken and stumbling march—but it was not they who were making the noise. Four women, some children and about eight men were screaming themselves hoarse behind the soldiers: with mechanical fervour, 'Viva, Viva, Viva.' People watched them from doorways, taking no part: the soldiers marched unsteadily between the dark river and the silent watchers, little bemused Indian faces, rifles slung, marched close together like untouchables.

'What are they doing?' Thriplow said. The proprietor replied that they were probably going for the other candidate—to arrest him. This time Thriplow felt sure he understood because he had guessed the answer.

'Why?'

The proprietor laughed with despairing amusement and

replied, to make sure, in French and Spanish. '*Trahison, defamacion,*' and in English, 'Who will care?'

'Where does he live?' The soldiers were marching slowly.

The proprietor told Thriplow. Thriplow ran down the stairs, treading on the beetles: as he reached the ground floor, he looked back, and then the light went out again: the old man in the wicker chair at the head of the stairs was whisked into darkness in the middle of a swing—it was like an expression of indifference.

If the soldiers were really on their way to the house and not to their barracks, they were soon outdistanced, and the house was easy to find. Thriplow knocked, and the door came open at once, as if somebody had been waiting, with anxiety, for just such a message. Thriplow passed through into a tiny patio. A woman said, in English, 'What do you want?' It was a very poor place— a lamp on a table exposed one small room like a cell. Thriplow said, 'Where's the candidate?'

'My father has gone,' the woman said.

He looked at her for the first time: it was the girl he had seen in the plaza. She recognized him accusingly. 'You were with the Chief of Police.'

He said, 'They are coming to arrest him.' He began to explain that he abhorred their politics, but he felt a certain responsibility, because of his lottery ticket. He had been hasty.

She said, 'It doesn't matter.' Her calm relieved him: he thought perhaps he had been making a mountain out of a molehill. He saw sewing on the table and remarked, 'I do embroidery too.'

'One has to live.'

'You speak English very well.' It was like a social call.

'Of course,' she said. 'I was educated there.'

'You don't think we need worry your father?'

'He knows,' she said, 'all there is to know.' She watched him with immense reserve.

He had a sense of anticlimax in the little poor patio. He said, 'If I've been the cause of any inconvenience, I must apologize.'

'It was you who gave the money, wasn't it?'

'It was, but you understand . . . no personal feeling. I am a Liberal. I cannot help sympathizing with . . . progress.'

'Oh, yes.'

'I detest Fascism. I cannot understand how a patriot—I am sure your father is a patriot—could take arms from Germany, Italy . . .'

'What a lot you believe,' she said with faint derision. He took another covert look round the patio—the rooms had nothing but the barest needs of life—a table, a chair, a bed hard and unpromising. He felt a kind of fanaticism even in the furniture. He said with distaste, 'You live very frugally.'

'We are very poor,' she said.

A crucifix hung on a wall above an Indian bed, just a raised piece of mud floor covered with a straw mat. He said uneasily, 'They told me you were religious.'

She corrected him, 'A religious. I was in a convent, but they destroyed it. It was where the cement playground is, by the river, and the swings.' She made a mild movement towards the crucifix. 'That is treason. They will probably come and search. They will want all the excuses they can find.'

'But I can't believe . . . now that I see you here . . . that your father is in any real danger.'

'He's in none. They are in danger . . . and you.'

Thriplow was startled. He said: 'You mean the reactionaries? They may start trouble?'

For the second time that night somebody lost temper with Mr Thriplow. She flared suddenly out at him: 'The stupid names you use.' She dropped her voice and said, 'I am sorry. Of course you are English. Poor man, what a fool they've made of you.'

Thriplow was shaken with irritation. He tried to break free of the whole absurd tangle. 'Well, I'm glad your father's safe.'

She said, 'I have not been fair to you. You *should* know. They arrested him half an hour ago. You may have seen the soldiers going back to barracks. They had to fill them with liquor first.'

'Then why did you say . . .' He stopped. He knew why. She was breaking the news to him as if it was *his* father. You owed that to the man responsible. He read the whole story in her dry pitying eyes.

She said, 'You've heard of the law of flight. Of course they never really run away . . .'

Mr Thriplow had no words at all, but somewhere at the back of his mind hate began to stir—hate of the lottery seller, hate of the bank manager, the Governor, the Chief of Police, even of the dead victim of his imprudence, hate of all who had so unexpectedly broken into his life, hate of the new ideas, the new words. Hate increased its boundaries in his heart like an annexing army.

The girl said gently: 'If you liked to give me some money . . . I have none in the house . . . you would feel then perhaps—not so bad about it. You would have done your best for us. You could go home quite happy. You are a good man.' She had the kind of copybook psychological sense you often find in nuns. He took out his pocket-book and gave her everything he had. The action dictated by hate was like an action of love. She said: 'It is more than I need—but perhaps I can bribe someone and get a priest to bury him—from another state. Here, you see, we die like dogs. Thank you.' She was determined to make the affair easy for him. She was abominably aloof on the height of her religious resignation, watching poor devils, like beetles, making their mistakes. She said, 'I can see you are a kind man. Only ignorant . . . of life, I mean,' she added with the devastating pride and simplicity of the convent.

Mr Thriplow went out into the street: he thought of his cousin in Brisbane and his aunt in Kensington: a sour smell poured up from the river, and a beetle struck his cheek and detonated off through the electric night. He heard it strike a wall. Somebody somewhere sang in very simple Spanish—a melancholy song about a rose in a field, and hate spread across Mr Thriplow's Liberal consciousness, ignoring boundaries. He heard the bank manager saying, 'Pain. Pain.' Individuals dropped and shrivelled in the enormous conflagration of his internecine war: he didn't even know the candidate's name. It seemed to Mr Thriplow, treading in his disappointed exile beside the sour river, that it was the whole condition of human life that he had begun to hate. A phrase came back to him out of his childhood about one who had so loved the world, and leaning against a wall Mr Thriplow wept. A passer-by, mistaking him for a fellow-countryman, addressed him in Spanish.

THE NEW HOUSE

Mr Josephs offered Handry a cigar with the air of a curator showing a choice exhibit, but the architect brushed it aside, and tenderly unfolded his plans upon the table. Then he waited in a kind of awe for the first exclamation of pleasure.

Mr Josephs, however, stood by the fender and carefully cut his cigar. He was in no hurry; he had never in his life been in a hurry.

'Nice little patch of ground I've got,' he said airily, and waved his hand to express the sense of size, 'near on a thousand acres.

'I like hills, with a bit of wood on them; park, as you might say. It gives one kind of space. One can build with a—a gesture. That's the word, gesture.' He put his hands behind his back and took a long puff. 'I shall wake up this countryside. It's too sleepy by half. You are a lucky man, Handry, and you've got a big chance. I'll make you rich, Handry, rich enough to clear out of this village and start in London. I like you, old son, I like you.'

Samuel Josephs suddenly noticed the architect's face, the pallor, and the brightness of the eyes. He fetched out a glass and a bottle of port, for no one could deny that the great Josephs was a kindly man. 'Have a drink, Handry. You've been overworking.'

Handry's hand shook as he took the glass and drained it, and a small drop fell upon the blotting paper by his side. It spread like a blotch of blood on a dead man's shirt front.

'I'm grateful, sir,' he said, 'very grateful. I've been in this place close on thirty years. When I started I used to dream of something like this, and I always had that stretch of land in mind. I've measured and worked out every yard of it, and twenty years I've spent on the plan, cutting out and putting in, and altering this and altering that. Every moment of time, between putting up cottages for the folk here, has gone to it. So you see I'm pretty grateful, sir. It means a lot to me.'

'Why, Handry,' said Mr Josephs with that expensive smile, so well known to newspaper readers, 'you're an interesting man; bit of a poet, eh? And this,' he looked anxiously at the lengthening ash, 'is what they call your *magnum opus*. The Bard says something about that, I'm sure, but I can't remember it. Quotations more in your line, I expect.'

'I don't care much for poetry, sir, I'm afraid,' returned the architect. 'It's too immaterial. I prefer land, mortar, bricks; things I can shape and feel.'

'You're wrong, Handry. Take my word for it, you're wrong. I've made my pile and I'm proud of it, but I made it by Vision, Handry, Vision. The motto of all my papers was "Follow the Light". Materialism will never get anywhere; compared with vision it's unsaleable. Ever read Longfellow? No? You should. That's the man for my money. He gets there every time. I took something of his for my Topical News:

> O thou sculptor, painter, poet!
> Take this lesson to thy heart:
> That is best which lyeth nearest;
> Shape from that thy work of art.

Cute, eh? Well, now let's see your work of art, Handry, old man.'

With trembling fingers, Handry held down the covers of his plan, and tried to look on it with the eyes of a stranger. Yes, no one could fail to see its beauty, the delicate, retiring lines, like a shy woman. It would melt into the trees as his own dream into reality. He waited in nervous, blushing expectancy, like a mother showing her first baby to the outer world.

But the praise did not come. There was a long and dreadful silence, and Handry, watching his employer's face, could see his mind searching for some kind remark. Josephs cleared his throat and at last it came. 'Very clever, Handry, I'm sure. Very clever. But not exactly what I want. I want something a bit bigger in conception, something that can be seen for miles around. A land-mark, Handry.'

The architect's deadened silence caught his attention, and he gave him another of his well-known, comforting smiles. 'I don't say, Handry, your drawing hasn't got its points. It has. But you haven't had the practice, old man. Everything you've done has been on too small a scale, and naturally you've been getting into rather a groove. I don't despair of you. With help you are going to knock me up something really good.'

'I suppose,' said Handry wearily, 'you want a Vanbrugh.' He rolled up his plans, and stood up. 'Well, there's no more to be said.' He held out his hand. 'Thanks for giving me a trial, Mr Josephs.'

'Don't be a fool, man,' cried Samuel Josephs sharply. 'I like you, and I'm going to have you. I only want you to work out something a little more noticeable, in white stone with Corinthian pillars. It will take you very little time to make a rough sketch, which we can go over together.'

'It'll take me a very little time, will it?' cried Handry. His face was white again, but his eyes were leaden. 'It's taken me twenty years to finish this plan, and you say it has points. Do you think I'll be the instrument for spoiling this land? You can take the dirty job to your friends in London,' and he turned on his heel.

'Now, Handry, Handry, my dear fellow,' Mr Josephs was quite perturbed, 'don't forget your vision. This is petty, Handry, petty. I offer you five thousand pounds to build me a house. You should remember your client's wishes before your own. To be frank, your plans are quite hopeless, quite hopeless, Handry.'

'Curse you, you fool,' muttered the architect between clenched teeth, holding back a childish outburst of tears.

'Are you going to throw away all that money, my dear fellow, just for stupid pride? Anyway, consult your wife before you come to any rash decision. You can't afford such feelings, Handry. Besides, which of us, I wonder, is the true artist. There is no such thing as idle show, Handry. What says the bard?

> Nothing useless is or low;
> Each thing in its place is best;

> And what seems but idle show,
> Strengthens and supports the rest.

'The light, Handry, don't forget the light.'

But Handry had left the room, had dashed into the road, as though from an evil spell, and yet he knew that all this struggle was vain. He was trapped, held fast by the ropes that bind all, his wife, his family, the world. Soon he would come slinking back, mouthing embarrassed apologies, to perpetrate the betrayal.

The bicyclist smiled bitterly at his companion. 'Isn't it a monstrosity?' he cried. 'This used to be one of the most beautiful views in the country. That fellow Josephs's philanthropy goes too far. His architect was a fellow in the village here, with no more views on art than the average rustic. And the abomination is a waste, for Josephs never lives in it, never comes near it.'

'Good evening,' said the strange little man, who had been standing close by, also regarding the house upon the hill. He was an elderly man, with pathetic, puzzled eyes, and he carried an umbrella. 'You are looking at the house?' he asked. 'It is rather fine, I think, don't you? It is so imposing, and such a landmark. It can be seen for miles, positively, for miles. Once I disliked it, but I had queer ideas in those days. There was a plan . . . Yes, my ideas were queer, very queer. I have a better appreciation now, I think. Do you read Longfellow? You should. He has very inspiriting ideas. I did not always think so, but there, one changes.'

A light gleamed suddenly in his eyes, and he drew himself up proudly. 'I am Handry, you know. The Architect,' he said vaguely, and, umbrella upon arm, sloped away into the shadows.

WORK NOT IN PROGRESS

My Girl in Gaiters

DISCLAIMER: *None of the ecclesiastical dignitaries mentioned is drawn from a real character, and the events of this musical comedy are quite fictitious*

As old age closes down one is frequently asked to tell a story to 'the little ones'—grand-nephews and grand-nieces and the like. 'You write books. You must be able to tell a story.' And yet the ignoble truth is that my ideas for future novels are seldom quite suitable. On these occasions I have to fall back on the musical comedy I have planned for years—a fairy story surely innocent enough for the innocents, but even then I sometimes lose a parent's trust. The name I have given it is *My Girl in Gaiters*.

When the curtain rises twelve bishops of varying ages dressed in gaiters and wearing those curious black hats with little strings attached used by the Anglican church are standing on the stage. They sing the opening chorus. During the first verse a young man comes on to the stage at the side. You can recognize he is a JOURNALIST by his notebook and pencil. He listens to the bishops, who sing a song roughly on these lines

> Thirteen bishops for convocation,
>> Gaitered bishops and true,
> We've come to give you our authorization
>> For the prayers to be offered by you.
> We have given consent to Our Father
>> In spite of its Roman tone;

We have set our seal on a Grace for a meal
    If free from a gluttonous moan.

But we've kept very wary of any Hail Mary
    In spite of the High Church vote,
For we are much too Broad to admit any fraud
    Across the Lambeth moat.

Thirteen bishops for convocation . . .

JOURNALIST [*interrupting*]:
    You counted Bath and Wells as two,
        And if you count again,
    You'll find there are only twelve of you.
        Explain, Your Grace, explain.

The bishops look at each other in consternation and begin to count again.

The explanation of this mysterious occurrence is that one of them has been kidnapped, and soon all will be involved in the same fate. A gang of thugs in London have decided to kidnap the whole of Convocation, in the hope of laying their hands on the chasubles belonging to the Church of England. They are ill-educated men and have mistaken the word chasuble for the word chalice. The twelve thugs are led by a woman who is the brains of the gang (and the only woman in the cast). When I have had an extra glass of champagne I dream that she is played by Vivien Leigh.

The kidnapping of the bishops proves successful and they are locked without their trousers in the cellars of a derelict building belonging to the Ecclesiastical Commission. The thugs then draw lots for who plays who. The ringleader naturally is *ex officio* Archbishop of Canterbury—the first time since Pope Joan that a woman has occupied so high an ecclesiastical post. Unfortunately for the false bishops the Bishop of Melbourne has arrived in London to act as an observer at Convocation. The various stages at which his suspicion is aroused I have yet to work out. They include a country Confirmation where the bishop performing the rite mutters some highly unecclesiastical words when he finds too much hair oil on one boy's head. The Bishop of Melbourne sets himself to track down the offenders.

He penetrates to the heart of the conspiracy at Canterbury where he meets the false Archbishop. There in the rose garden strange feelings of love puzzle and disturb him. The false Archbishop too falls in love with the Bishop of Melbourne and her conscience is stirred. At the end of the second Act she confesses all to the Bishop. In horror he decides to leave England for ever, but his love is too great to turn her over to the police. At the end of the second Act the Bishop of Melbourne is sitting at one side of the stage beside a telephone and the Archbishop of Canterbury, the false Archbishop of Canterbury of course, is sitting at the other side also by a telephone. The Bishop begins with a sad reminiscence of the past.

BISHOP OF MELBOURNE:
>There was a maid at Wallyhoo
>With whom I saw my first sunrise.
>There was a deaconess at Starving Camp
>Who made me blush and close my eyes.
>But my girl in gaiters,
>Oh, my girl in gaiters,
>She has tricks like Walter Pater's
>With her Mona Lisa eyes
>All the secrets of the sea,
>Every kind of ecstasy,
>And when she wants to speak to me
>She lifts the telephone.

FALSE ARCHBISHOP OF CANTERBURY:
>Melbourne, Melbourne,
>Cantuar calling.
>Stop your stalling,
>Drop your moral tone.
>There's a heart beneath a cassock,
>And a knee upon a hassock,
>A motor ride from Dover,

So come right over,
But come alone, damn you, come alone.

BISHOP OF MELBOURNE:
Cantuar, Cantuar,
Melbourne calling,
Can't hear a word you say,
Oh, how faint you are.

[*The two in duet*:]

CANTERBURY:
Melbourne, Melbourne,
Cantuar calling,
Stop your stalling,
Drop your moral tone.

MELBOURNE:
Cantuar, Cantuar,
Melbourne calling.
Can't hear a word you say
Oh, how faint you are.

ARCHBISHOP OF CANTERBURY:
It's your girl in gaiters,
Melbourne, Melbourne,
All the tricks of Walter Pater's
With my Mona Lisa eyes.

BISHOP OF MELBOURNE:
And the damn'dest kind of lies.

[*The* BISHOP *slams down the telephone.*]

CURTAIN of Second Act

(The second act of a musical comedy in my youth always ended in self-sacrifice or misunderstanding.)

Alas! the rest of the musical has not yet been very fully worked out except for the escape of the real bishops from their prison, while the false bishops are on their way to Convocation. The false bishops are hurrying down on to the stage between the stalls. The little ribbons in their hats are now wireless aerials through which they are 'Calling all cars,' 'Calling all cars.' In Convocation the Bishop of Melbourne turns up unexpectedly. The false bishops realize they have been betrayed and round on the Archbishop of Canterbury. She is defended by the Bishop of Melbourne until the arrival of the true bishops in their underclothes routs the impostors.

All is well again between the lovers and they sing a melodious duet. (I am anxious that the charm of the old melodies should be revived in my musical.)

HE:

In my very first parish
A dream I used to cherish
Of a girl in a scarlet gown,
And in the quiet scenery
Of my very Rural Deanery
I decided her name was Brown.

As a very young archdeacon
Very early I'd awaken
And wonder if my dream was Sue.

SHE:

But, oh, what a shock!
Instead of a frock
There's a girl in gaiters for you.

HE:

There's nothing could be lighter
Than my bishop's buckram mitre
When laid in the scales against love.

SHE:

> Add a golden chalice
> And a moated palace?

HE:

> They'd still kick the beam above.
>   Oh, I'd gladly abdicate
>   To a country curate,
> If you'd be the curate's wife.

SHE:

>   What, hurt feelings in the choir
>   And collections for the spire,
> For the rest of a humdrum life?

HE:

> When Matins were over,
> How dotingly I'd hover

SHE:

> Above the 'little stranger' in the pram?

HE:

> When the Guilds got up a dance
> I'd be sitting in a trance

SHE:

> Wending home with me at midnight in a tram?

HE:

>   Oh, I hate the Visitations
>   And the endless Confirmations
> And the lonely nights I spend.

SHE:

> But if I cannot marry
> Because of Dick or Harry—?

HE:

> I'm tired of being celibate,
> I'll gladly be expatriate
> With a loving female friend.

In the last scene the Bishop of Melbourne is returning to Australia up the gangplank of a liner and the former false Archbishop of Canterbury accompanies him. She no longer wears a shovel hat and black gaiters, but a little top hat and scarlet gaiters, and the theme song of the thugs is sung for the last time as the curtain falls. The song was written many years ago by my brother, when Controller of Overseas Services (BBC, not ecclesiastical), and I cannot quite remember the words. It is called 'Top Hats in Hell', and begins:

> In hell they all wear top hats,
> Top hats in hell.

Perhaps that is the one unsuitable song for the young, but then I didn't write it.

MURDER FOR THE
WRONG REASON

I

The low brief cry could have reached but a very little distance
into the night from the open window of the room, and perhaps,
before he died, Mr Hubert Collinson may have realized that it
was hopeless to expect any reply.

A long, tortuous dream is said to last but a few seconds of
time as we record it, and in the short interval that elapsed between the moment when the unexpected knife slipped into his
breast and the moment when his heart ceased to beat,
Mr Collinson may have heard his cry reflected as a faint, tin-
gling echo from the glass of his bookcase and the glass of his
door and the glass of the mirror that had hung on the wall for
so many years, to be used by his female clients.

And yet the sound did find an audience, for half a minute later
a heavy knocking began at the door and a voice called,
'Collinson!' When there was no reply, the man outside put his
shoulder to the locked door and burst it open. He gave a hurried
glance at the body, which was curled in an attitude of obsequious
humility in a swivel chair, and took off his soft hat, not in any
reverence for the dead, but because it was a close night.

His glance at the body seemed perfunctory and without pity, a
professional acceptance of the fact of death. He leant out of the
window and blew a whistle several times, until he received his
answer, shrilled from several quarters of the night at once, as
though a host of invisible playgoers were competing for a taxi.
The sense of this hidden wakefulness in an apparently sleeping

world for a moment disturbed his composure, and it needed the quiet of the dead body behind him to restore it.

He picked up a telephone and, sitting on the edge of Collinson's desk, called a number. While he waited he whistled a soft, dreamy and abstracted tune, a waltz which probably dated back to the man's youth, for he was middle-aged, with tidy, greying hair and small greying moustache, and his mind might have been less concerned with crime than with jostling memories of the old music halls, of how little Nellie Collins had sung that tune at the Old Bedford, directing her gaze at long moustached gentlemen in boxes decorated with large gold Cupids bearing cornucopias. Yet when he received a reply, he became at once sharply attentive and professional.

'Detective-Inspector Mason speaking. This is Hubert Collinson's house. No, I haven't found what we wanted. Collinson's dead. I arrived too late. Oh yes, murder unquestionably. Will you send one of our best men down? Is Collins on night duty? Well then, send Groves.'

He slammed down the receiver and, crossing to the window, called to a constable who had appeared at a heavy, lumbering run at the end of the street. Once again the professional air slipped from him and he sat down on the desk with a melancholy that seemed connected with nothing so tangible as a dead man.

He gave the impression of being a little disgusted with his surroundings, as his eye roved here and roved there, and when his gaze lit for a moment on the bookcase and its rows of yellow-backed novels, his smile was almost a malignant grin. Yet, watching the small wrinkles at the corners of his eyes and the almost surly twist of his upper lip, one would have said that chiefly he was disappointed with himself.

The explanation was to be found, perhaps, in the first words he spoke as the door opened and admitted a heavily-built constable with slightly protuberant eyes. 'I am Detective-Inspector Mason of Scotland Yard,' he said. 'I came just too late,' and he waved his hand perfunctorily at the body in the chair.

'Gaw!' the constable said, dragging the monosyllable out to the length of an alexandrine. He stood in the doorway and stared.

'Come, my man,' Mason said with a kind of irritable amusement, 'have you never seen a body before?'

'Never, sir. This is a respectable neighbourhood.' The man drew a deep breath and became suddenly excited and garrulous. 'This is the first chance I've 'ad, sir, of what you'd call a real crime. They put me in these parts because they said the criminal classes would never stand for my eyes.'

'Try a little iodine every day in a glass of milk.'

'I beg your pardon, sir?'

'Exophthalmic goitre. It doesn't make you very bright, does it? Why haven't you asked me for my papers? I'm not a resident of this respectable suburb.'

'But you said, sir . . .'

'Of course I said. But here I am alone with a dead body. The forms, constable, must be observed. Look through these papers.'

The constable examined them with an air of profound apology, but became suddenly attentive over one of them. 'A search warrant, sir?'

'Yes, he has escaped me, you see.' Mason turned round and, for almost the first time, took a long look at the body. 'Have a good look at this man, constable; look at the way he carries his bald head as a badge of respectability.'

The detective put his finger under the dead man's chin and jerked the face upwards. He bit his lip as he did so, his professional nonchalance punctured by the astonished stare of the eyes that seemed aware of this last breach of respect.

Mason sighed. 'Well, I suppose we must hunt his murderer, but Collinson deserved all that he got. Blackmail,' he added, 'and women.'

'All the same, sir,' the constable said, 'as I see it, bad men aren't always killed for a good reason.'

'Why, constable,' Mason swung round, 'you are a philosopher. And you are right. How right,' he added in a thoughtful murmur.

The constable was encouraged by the praise. 'This is a chance for me, you know, sir,' he said.

'A very small chance, constable. You've been reading fiction,

I'm afraid. One of my brightest young men will soon be on his way here in a car from Scotland Yard. How did the murderer escape?'

'The window, sir.'

'It could hardly have been the chimney, could it?' Mason retorted with nervous irritation. He crossed the room and looked over the window-sill. 'An easy way down a drain-pipe. We'll examine that later for scratches. And how about the door? Was it locked by Collinson or the murderer? Search the man's pockets.'

While the constable obeyed, Mason strolled slowly round the room, examining the pictures on the walls, the books on the shelves, the liver-coloured wallpaper, the highly polished mahogany furniture with the same faint, abstracted interest as a man shows who revisits his old home and sees, less the present flames in the fire than the old dreams beating up the chimney. Yet it must have been the future that veiled Mason's eyes with thought.

'There are no keys here, sir.'

Mason started a little at the voice. 'Then possibly the murderer locked the door and took the key away with him.'

He turned to the dead man's desk and laid his hand on a large wooden box. 'You might begin going through these files, constable. They are probably only bills and receipts.'

'It's locked, sir.'

'Then that's more promising. Break it open. We won't waste time looking for the key. Probably business letters, constable, but there, when your business is blackmail . . . And note this. The murderer hasn't touched it, but of course he may have heard me on the stairs. This is a curious case, constable. I seem to have arrived too soon. If I had arrived later he might have left more clues. No, no, you must put on gloves. There is always the chance of fingerprints.'

Again he began to whistle the same waltz, as though it was connected in his mind in some peculiar way with the idea of death.

'Receipts and bills, sir,' the constable said.

'Shop or private individuals?'

'They all seem shops. I'll just begin at the other end, sir, for luck.'

Mason was at the window. 'That fast car from Scotland Yard, constable. I wonder where it is now. Tearing through this hell of a black night. Saunders will be at the wheel and young Groves beside him. That's a keen young man, constable, and intelligent too. This body will call him as a carrot calls a donkey. There's a big difference between the young and the middle-aged. He's got all his bodies before him, and I've got them all behind. When this business is over, constable, I shall retire from active service.'

The pile of letters in front of the constable grew. 'Take to private inquiries, sir?'

Mason laughed, still with a faint undertone of an elegiac melancholy. 'Oh, I've begun those already, constable.'

'I beg pardon, sir?' The constable raised shocked eyes.

'No, no, I don't mean the same as you. Do you know, I have a feeling about this case. I believe the man is going to prove too clever for us. Motive? I expect there are five hundred men, and as many women, with a motive. The road apparently empty below, you on another part of your beat, I on the stairs, all the respectable inhabitants of this respectable suburb in their respectable beds.

'And then look at the knife he's used. A kind sold by the fifty thousand. A fingerprint, perhaps, though he's clever enough surely to have worn gloves. And in any case, he may not belong to the criminal class. One of these respectable sleepers, perhaps, constable.'

Mason began to whistle gently to himself, bathed in a melancholy peace. Collinson's bald head gleamed softly in the electric light, and if he were to bend towards it, Mason thought that he might very well see his own face reflected in its surface. It made him feel as though the dead man were an old and trusted friend, and trusted surely he must have been throughout his life, trusted to do the wrong, the evil thing.

What must the man have felt and thought when alone? It was difficult for frail human nature to avoid some dangerous lapses into virtue, yet Mason was aware of no such lapse in Collinson.

Yet how could he have regarded his life when he was alone, when his evil was not whipped up by a client's challenge to his cunning? He must, Mason considered, have invented some tale to satisfy himself, some laudatory belief in his own superhuman power. But he lay there in a crouched attitude, humble and astonished. Private inquiries, Mason thought—certainly I have taken them up.

'By Jove, sir, we've got it.' Mason turned and, with fingers trembling a very little with excitement, took the paper that the constable held towards him. When he saw the familiar writing, the room became a little misty and impalpable, swayed round him, so that the mahogany bookcase, the mirrors, the chairs, turned thin and transparent and waved before his eyes like threadbare banners. It was some moments before he could read the writing.

'If you will not see me,' the letter began abruptly, but there could be no doubt that it was addressed to Collinson, 'I will wait on your doorstep and beat you in the street.' It was signed Arthur Callum and bore no date.

'There's nothing else, sir,' the constable said.

'Wait.' Mason removed his eyes with difficulty from the scrap of cheap notepaper that had so evidently been bought in a 2d. packet together with half a dozen envelopes. If he thought hard, he could even make a guess at the small stationers where Arthur Callum would have bought it, one of those stationers whose single window is filled with an untidy medley of objects—bottles of ink, paper clips, address stamps, notebooks, china ornaments, pens, pencils, fancy penwipers. 'So you think this is a clue, constable?'

'Well, sir,' the constable gazed at his superior with amazement, 'the man seems to 'ave 'ad a grudge.'

Mason seemed in no hurry to follow up the trail, and the constable, dreams of promotion flowing through his mind, thought regretfully of the fast car from Scotland Yard tearing nearer through the night.

'Constable,' Mason said slowly, 'didn't you say just now that even bad men were seldom murdered for a good reason? Surely this letter comes from a man with a good reason. You don't beat a man in the street for a disgraceful motive. Look at this letter, too. Why, man, the ink has faded. The letter may have been written years ago.'

'Why did 'e keep it in this box, sir, ready to the 'and? 'E might 'ave been going to show it to someone tonight.'

Mason said slowly, 'I'll tell you why I'm hesitating. I knew Arthur Callum well once. I have not met him, though, for many years,' he added, with an enhancement of that surly twist at the corner of his upper lip. 'My friend—he was my friend—was not capable of this,' but the constable noticed that Mason did not look at the body but at the open window.

A solitary taxi hooted dismally in the street below and a small spatter of rain blew into the room.

'Still, sir, it's the only clue we've got. If we could knock up this man Callum quickly . . . 'E wouldn't expect us on the trail so early. We might find something. You know where 'e lives, sir?' He was pleading with voice and with protuberant eyes, pleading for a chance—the only chance that he might ever be given—of praise and promotion.

He had reached that dead afternoon of life when a man is not young enough to recommend himself by his enthusiasm nor old enough to be resigned by any form of sunset touch. Mason's eyes relented a little; he was moved in spite of himself by the man's pitiable inadequacy.

'You mean,' he said, 'that we should have a look at Callum now before Groves arrives?'

'Do you know where 'e lives, sir?' The constable's voice was trembling a little with excitement and with hope.

'Very close. That again is a curious coincidence, isn't it?' Mason smiled with a kind of grim melancholy. 'It certainly would be amazing, wouldn't it, to solve the whole mystery before Groves arrives.'

He added, with a sudden nervous beating of one hand on the desk, 'I hate these clever young men with their complete lack of understanding. Right, constable, I promise you. We'll surprise him.' Mason raised the letter very close to his face, as though middle age had already gripped his sight and made it fail. 'One last look, constable.'

2

Until he saw again the uncarpeted polished yellow deal, he thought that he had forgotten the appearance of the stairs, but now his mind ran to the opposite extreme and he believed that he could recall every scratch and indentation in the wood, perhaps even its cause. At the top of the stairs he found the door of Arthur Callum's room unlocked.

He pushed it open and was for a moment startled by the familiarity of an engraving over the mantelpiece that represented the raising of Lazarus from the dead. The artist had thrown a melodramatic skill into the bearded face's agony, which might be because of the life to which he returned or because of the death from which he came. The table was as Mason had always known it, littered with books and papers. He smiled a little at what he knew was the symbol rather than the reality of work. Behind the table a curtain shut off the corner of the room that contained Callum's bed.

Mason shut the door softly behind him and turned quickly, with the air of a man facing an enemy whom he mistrusted. And mistrust he did, every feature in the room: the shabby armchair, the leather tobacco pouch on the mantelpiece, the pipe rack, the row of second-hand medical handbooks, the large-eyed stare of the familiar clock. They spoke to him in syllables as measured as the slow beat of time upbraiding him for his intrusion, blaming him for the accumulation of the years between them. 'Callum,' he called in a low voice, 'Callum.'

It may have been because he was staring again at bearded Lazarus that he did not see the curtains part and was faced suddenly with the accomplished fact of Callum standing before him. The years that had altered Mason's face, with a deft line here to mark surliness and there to mark melancholy, had apparently left Arthur Callum young, young but ill, pale and with eyes too dark for health.

Again it needed no voice to emphasize to Mason how unwelcome he was. Each man stood and stared at the other with such an uninterested dissatisfaction as an ugly man might show to his own image in the glass.

'I am sorry,' Mason said at last, 'that I have looked you up so late.' He spoke as though every word had to force its way through a hostile air. 'Too late,' he thought that he heard Callum echo in the same tone. Mason glanced at the clock. 'After all,' he said with a forced and jocular ease, 'it's not long past midnight, and from my knowledge of you, Callum—' and then he stopped, faced with his own blank sense of ignorance. Yes, he had once had knowledge, but there were years between them now.

He said gruffly, 'I've just come from Hubert Collinson's house. You knew him?' Callum nodded; and Mason, in an effort to break through that expressionless face which fronted him like an accusation, said quickly, 'He was murdered tonight.' The satisfaction on Callum's face said as plainly as words that the world was all the better for Collinson's death.

'Oh, I admit it,' Mason said, as though the words had been actually spoken; 'but then a bad man,' he used the constable's phrase, 'is not always killed for a good reason.' He waited for Callum to speak, and while he waited may have thought how strangely unprofessional his conduct was. Somewhere a taxi hooted, but it was the only sound, for Callum did not speak.

'You had a good reason, Callum,' Mason said. His tone was less an accusation than an entreaty, for he was beginning to desire poignantly, bitterly and despairingly that Callum had been the murderer, that Collinson should have been killed for a good reason.

'Listen,' he said, 'this is your letter. At least you cannot deny that,' and he fluttered the letter with its fading ink before Callum's face. 'And the knife—I am the only person in the world who knows the knife is yours.'

He remembered Callum's face at the age of fifteen, pressed against the window of an ironmonger's in Camden Town, while his hand closed on the fifteen shillings which could make the knife his. A mixture of adventure, sentimentality, a curious inverted chivalry had made Callum hide his purchase from all but Mason, and lock it in a drawer where it was presently forgotten, even by its owner; but Mason had not forgotten the emblem roughly engraved by Callum on the handle.

'Oh, yes, the knife is yours,' he said again, and would have drifted back into his memories if he had not suddenly felt that Callum had connected his assertion, had whispered, or perhaps only thought intensely, 'was.' 'Anyway, it's in Collinson's body now,' he said with a brusque brutality. If he had meant to startle Callum, he did not succeed.

Mason began to speak again on the subject of the letter. 'I know,' he said, 'that it was written some years ago. I know the cause of it, too. It occurred before we separated.'

He had known all Callum's acts; even his thoughts were not unknown to him. He, too, has been closely acquainted with Rachel Mann, ambitious Rachel Mann. She had had dark hair that curled closely over the ears, and a peculiar combination of ingenious wide eyes and a cynical, or perhaps only shameless, mouth. His knowledge of her now seemed to him to come less from his own experience than from a reflection of her in Callum's mind, a deep and slightly stained reflection as in an antique mirror.

Callum, he remembered, had declared in his characteristic, challenging fashion, that he was ready to serve seven years for Rachel Mann; but long before those years were over he had lost her and not even gained a Leah. Rachel Mann, already at the age of twenty-five, was a woman who knew exactly what she wanted. She wanted Arthur Callum, but not most. She knew that with her looks and with her brains the stage offered her a fine and pleasantly notorious career. She wanted above all things to be talked about.

Mr Hubert Collinson at that time was largely interested in various theatrical enterprises, and he was also, when she introduced herself to him, interested in Rachel Mann. It was really only Arthur Callum who objected to the form the interest took, and the objections that led him to threaten Hubert Collinson crumbled with many other things when he found that he was too late.

And yet Mason knew very well that the first impetuous anger had something transiently fine in it that had nothing to do with jealousy. Indeed, there was never any reason for jealousy, Rachel Mann considered her relations with Mr Hubert Collinson in a purely business light, while she was genuinely, though intermittently, fond of Arthur Callum.

Mason's face reddened suddenly in a jealous rage against Hubert Collinson. Have I not said that he also had known Rachel Mann? It was unbearable to think that the dead man, with his bald head and his lifeless and imbecile air of surprise, had once discovered all the secrets which an intimacy with Rachel Mann must have held, even a businesslike intimacy.

It was unbearable to know that up till an hour ago Mr Hubert Collinson had been at liberty, whenever he chose, to sit down in his chair and go into his own mind and remember and live over again the scenes—whether passionate or cold could little matter after many years—that he had known with Rachel Mann. And perhaps most unbearable of all was the thought that Hubert Collinson in all probability valued these memories so cheaply he never troubled to recall them. Yet the slightest of them would once have fed Arthur Callum for a lifetime.

Then Mason remembered that this which he was feeling was only jealousy, the rather petty jealousy of a man who had been cheated of something he desired.

Staring at the fading ink, Mason knew that it had not been a jealous man who had written the letter. Indeed, so little jealous had Callum been that he would have given everything to have married Rachel Mann, even after he learned that she was Collinson's mistress; but Rachel Mann would not marry him.

She had no objection, she explained on one terrible evening, to loving him occasionally; but he had neither the money nor the influence to make her a good husband, and apparently not seeing how her words affected him, she offered him her love then and there, not as he had once dreamed and hoped and longed and fought for, for a lifetime, but for three-quarters of an hour before she dined with Collinson.

'And now I suppose, when you think of it,' Mason said slowly and with disgust, as though he assumed that Callum had been able to follow his thoughts, 'you wish that you had accepted that three-quarters of an hour. Then there would have been a memory to share with Collinson. Why,' he went on in a bitter, almost hysterical, outburst, 'instead of killing Collinson, you could have sat together over your wine and swopped your memories.'

Then he remembered how certain he was that Arthur Callum was not the murderer. The certainty pained him. 'Why didn't you kill him,' he implored rather than asked, 'twenty years ago? You had a good reason.'

The phrase sang in Mason's head, along with the constable's utterance. For a long time now he had forgotten that he was Detective Inspector Mason of New Scotland Yard, forgotten the waiting policeman with the hopeful, protuberant eyes, and young, intelligent Groves in his fast car tearing through dark, deserted streets and nameless suburbs.

Callum's impeccability began to seem to Mason a reflection on himself. What right had Callum to claim, even by this silent facing of accusation, an honesty and a chivalry that he, Mason, did hot share? But the anger passed quickly and only the hopeless longing remained, the longing that Callum might have been the murderer, that the reason for Collinson's death might have had something in it fine and unselfish and fearless.

'Suppose,' he caught himself saying, and surely it was an odd way for a detective to address a man whom he had come to arrest, so odd that Mason himself smiled and thought that indeed the time had come for him to retire and to take up private inquiries; 'suppose you had killed him, then, when you wrote this letter? Why, man, you wouldn't have hanged. No jury would have convicted you. You needn't have been afraid.'

But he knew very well that in those days Arthur Callum would not have been affected by fear. 'You fool,' he said, 'you silly, romantic young fool, to let a woman like Rachel Mann break you up. If it was a woman you wanted, couldn't you have gone into Piccadilly and chosen one just as pretty and far less expensive? It all comes down to biology in the end. Now,' he waved his hand in a tired, halting fashion, 'look at the mess you've made. Oh yes, it's you, Callum, and not I, Mason, who have made the mess.'

A sudden burst of wind drove the rain in a loud flurry against the window, and Mason's nerves showed themselves in his start. He turned to face the night and as he did so there sprang into his vision again the clock, the mantelpiece, the risen Lazarus. But there was no need surely for these to affect him. These did not belong to the Callum whom he had once known so intimately; they had only been hung round him by an attentive landlady.

But though they did not belong, like a jewel that has lain long in one place, they had left their mark on the living flesh; their imprint was a part of Callum now, as much a part of him as those things which were wholly Callum's, though he, Mason, had once shared them—a long, dark, overhung lane of dripping trees, and the faint, fresh smell of rain; a river in which the reflection of stars and street lamps were inextricably mingled; a sleeping woman's face; and the sound of a voice singing in the sun behind a hill beside the sea.

Pain spread through Mason's body and brain and heart, until the small room, with its four walls shutting him in, seemed an instrument of lifelong torture, each wall to which he turned reflecting the same memories, despairs, regrets, each wall a mirror that, he protested, distorted, and yet he knew sought out the unexaggerated truth in his heart, and when he shut his eyes, ceiling and floor shut him in the closer with the same message.

Though perhaps, to open the door and go meant the end of this long torture, he hesitated, for at least there was silence in which a man could think, and although thought hurt, any thought was better than the noise and action which waited for him without— the hooting of a car, the spatters of rain, excited voices, whistles blowing in the night, the ring of telephone bells, feet pounding on the stairs. 'Motive? The man was a blackmailer. He had pressed someone too hard. Someone who had a great deal to lose.' The wrong reason.

Callum's silence seemed to be asking him a question. 'Arrest you?' Mason cried. 'I wish I could. Why, I can't even bring you back.' Back now to noise and action and worry and the responsibility of decisions. He flung Callum's door open, passed outside, slammed it behind him, and turned to face a flight of yellow deal stairs, still undisturbed and silent, and standing on the top step, her black dress fading into the dark, her white face only evident, Rachel Mann.

There were many reasons why Mason could not have expected thus to meet her, yet he felt no more surprise than a man feels at the incongruity of some of the images that drift through the unthinking mind. She was there. That was clear in the black sweep of her hair round the ears and the slightly open, slightly pouting lips, their tint a little more vivid than nature had intended.

She, like Arthur Callum, seemed to have remained young during all the years that had jostled Mason this way and that way, pushing him down paths which he had never foreseen and making him a little older, a little more filled with disgust at the ways of himself and the world. It was unfair that during all that time Rachel Mann should have kept her beauty.

'Hubert Collinson is dead,' he said to her in a tone purely conversational, as though he thought the news might interest her, as indeed it should have interested Collinson's former mistress. A long band of yellow light from a street lamp outside fell between them, and the band was constantly speckled and its appearance altered by the invisible gusts of rain which beat irregularly against the glass of the lamp.

It gave the impression of a constant flow and eddy of small objects, and emphasized their own immobility in their patches of shadow. It was as though the tossing years had at last left them still and stranded on separate beaches.

'It should have happened before or never at all,' he added. He was beginning to discover how very frayed his nerves were. He was continually giving way to inexplicable outbursts, less of rage than a kind of nagging elderly rancour. 'Oh, it will surprise you,' he continued, 'to hear that you were not concerned, that you had nothing to do with it, that, Rachel, you were of no importance whatever. Hubert Collinson was murdered for quite another reason.'

His eyes clouded and the storm of his nerves for a moment subsided. 'Yes, you were the right reason, Rachel. Why couldn't you have been what Callum thought you were—worth while? Why didn't you marry him? You don't understand Callum, Rachel. I know him better than does anyone else in the world, so you must let me tell you about him. He's a scientist gone wrong. He wanted to be a doctor because he had a passionate devotion to a sentimental idea of service. But he hasn't a clear enough idea of what he wants to serve. He thought it was you, and now it will narrow down to himself. Rachel, you and I know how deadly dull that last is. You and I. You and I.' The phrase continued to echo on in his mind long after the words had faded out, but still the woman made no movement, whether of pity, horror or surprise.

'But you are responsible, yes, you are responsible,' Mason broke out again. 'It's you who broke Callum. Collinson had to die. We both of us know that. But he needn't have died for a wrong reason.' He was infuriated by her silence and calm. It seemed to him a form of conceit. 'I am Rachel Mann and nothing that anyone may say or do can affect me. Bluster, be bitter, be pitiful, sinful, virtuous. I shall feel not the faintest reflection.'

There had always been something of that attitude in her, the germ, so to speak, of the present great calm, as the youngest and loveliest body bears in it the germ, however small, of death. 'Yes, it's you who have killed Collinson,' he continued in a quieter tone, for loud words seemed less able than silence to cross the gentle eddy and flow in the stream of light between them. 'If it were not for you, Callum would never have met Collinson.'

He thought that he saw her eyes alter very slightly into a polite, mechanical, uninterested question. 'Oh no, I'm not going to arrest him.' He waved his hand. 'He's safe enough back there, but I mustn't forget *myself* just because he doesn't belong, any more than you belong, to this hour and place. Rachel, suppose'—the word rang in his brain like a cracked bell set swinging in a deserted house—'suppose you had married Callum.'

A succession of images swayed through his mind, of days and nights of a great passion, tenderness and continually of peace. He forgot for a short moment how irrevocably the present had arrived, that Collinson was dead and his death must inevitably involve another.

He forgot the days during which he had watched the slow dis-integration of his own character, the growing self-disgust, deceit and corruption, he forgot even that he was Detective-Inspector Mason of New Scotland Yard and remembered only a night when he had faced Rachel Mann as he faced her now and said, with the same trembling passion, clinging to a hope which he knew but would not admit was illusory, 'Rachel, marry me.'

The patch of polished yellow deal lit by the streaming light glimmered more brightly, dissolved, became a glass through which he again could see the surroundings of Callum's room, the table, the scattered books, the tortured face of Lazarus hanging from the wall, and Rachel Mann alone with him in the room. The stillness of her face altered a very little, the eyes glanced over his shoulder at the clock, the lips began to open, trembled on the verge of their infamous proposal.

Mason winced in the expectation of pain, and then the years swept between and brushed away the face and the lips which were about to speak words that seemed no longer infamous, but an amusing and satisfying suggestion, for after all everything came down to biology in the end, he reflected, and began to laugh.

3

He was still laughing as he lowered the letter and faced again the constable's impatient and protuberant eyes. Between them the electric light on Hubert Collinson's desk shed a soft carpet of gold, and behind the policeman's head Hubert Collinson's clock showed that two more minutes, valuable for their loneliness and for the absence of young intelligent Groves, had fled. He was be-ginning to feel an affection for the constable, so closely thrown together were they by their isolation and by the mute witness of their contact.

'Oh no, constable,' he said, the relics of laughter making his voice tremble, 'Callum is not the man we want.'

'No, sir?' The eyes goggled with disappointment but remained filled with a childlike faith in the prescience of Scotland Yard.

'For the last few minutes, constable, I have been holding private inquiries.'

'Yes, sir?' ·

'And I have come to the conclusion, constable, that you are going to have your triumph over Groves. A spectacular triumph. Look, we have eight minutes still, and the air is full of clues.'

'I thought you said, sir, you arrived too soon.'

'I've changed my mind. Listen, constable, luck favours you. I happen to know that this letter was written more than fifteen years ago, and the quarrel concerned a woman. You can take my word for it—I knew both Callum and the woman very well— that the quarrel has been dead for almost as long as the letter has lain in Collinson's files. All this I know. Now you must spin your theories, constable. What is the most likely cause of the murder?'

'Blackmail, sir, I should say.'

'And you would also say that the murderer had a certain position to lose to make him sufficiently desperate for this, or even to make him worth blackmailing. That disposes of Callum, constable, a penniless medical student. I can see that you are a sharp man, and you are saying to yourself that the murderer is probably an elderly man. He would not otherwise, unless born with a silver spoon, be high enough game for Collinson. An aristocrat or an elderly man, then, is not too wild a surmise.' Mason found now that his nerves were quite steady, and he was enjoying the last game of his professional career. 'Now look at the knife, constable. What do you notice?'

'There's a kind of badge engraved on it, sir, amateur work, sir, I should say.'

'That doesn't matter. Look at the angle of the knife.'

'It's very crooked, sir.'

'The man who struck that blow put his body's weight into it.

He couldn't trust the strength of his wrist, you see. Yes, an elderly man, constable, or else a very effete aristocrat.'

He laughed at the admiration in the policeman's eyes. The man evidently believed that he was face to face with the detective of fiction, the detective of lightning deductions. 'Has the origin ever occurred to you, constable,' he said—it amused him to delay his own inquiries, to play cat and mouse with the slipping minutes—'of Sherlock Holmes's cleverness? It's simply that the author knows the answer and works backwards. That's what I'm doing.'

'You know the answer, sir?' The policeman's admiration, far from diminishing, had increased.

'Yes, I know the answer, but you must discover it for yourself. This is your chance. You have still six minutes. Now tell me again how the murderer escaped.'

'Out of the window, sir.'

'Any scratches on the window-sill? No, but then of course he may have worn soft shoes. Come and look out of the window. A convenient drain-pipe and a thirty foot fall. We could have done it easily enough when we were young, but now—this is a moment for elegiacs, constable. We have decided that he was probably an elderly man.'

'If 'e'd 'eard you on the stairs, 'e'd 'ave risked it, sir.'

'True. Remember he was a man with a weak wrist. He should have fallen hard in the flower bed underneath. Run down and see if you can find footprints.'

While the policeman was out of the room, Mason strolled around it, with a sour disgust at his own sentiment, looking for any relics of Rachel Mann. This, he thought, is the damnable result of private inquiries. The sooner he was done with the whole business the better. Well, in five minutes Groves would have arrived and the past could hand over worry, searchings, danger, boredom, and perhaps corruption too, to the future.

Still, as his thoughts wandered, his eyes were awake for any signs of Collinson's former mistress. Admirable men, he said to himself, there are none. Rachel Mann had gone and left Collinson with a smoking-room story. The close black hair and the impetuous mouth had become a tale a little scented with the smell of whisky. What a lot of trouble would have been saved if Rachel Mann had left Callum with no more majestic a memory.

Mason began to feel a little tired, though the calmness which had followed his thoughts of stormy 'might have beens' endured. He welcomed the return of the constable as an indication of the passage of time. The game was losing a little of its savour, though it still amused him to think that his last service in a professional capacity would be to a suburban police constable hungry for promotion.

'There are no marks, sir.' The constable's face was puzzled and anxious.

'No, I thought not. You must alter your theory, constable.'

'This is the top floor. 'E couldn't 'ave gone upstairs, sir.' The man's hand suddenly clenched and he lowered his voice. 'You don't mean 'e's in the room now, sir, hiding?'

'In that big cupboard, for instance? Oh no, I hardly think he's there. What do you think about the key, man?'

'The key?'

'The one that isn't in Collinson's pocket, of course. The one that locked the door.'

'Well, sir, Collinson might have locked it, so's 'e could be alone with the man.'

'But why should the man take it?'

'It might've been 'im as locked the door.'

'Yes, on the inside or the outside.'

'Well, sir, if it was on the outside 'e'd 'ave met you.'

'But, man, if it was on the inside, where is he?'

The constable looked round him helplessly. His shoulders drooped a little as he saw the clock. The fast car from Scotland Yard might arrive at any moment now, and he was no nearer the promotion for which opportunity had so desperately awakened his ambitions. He turned to the window, less with the idea of finding any clue than of listening for the car which would end his hopes, and presented to Mason's gaze a greying patch of hair.

Mason expressed a faint sigh of exasperated pity and put his hand into his hip pocket. The policeman, his eyes blurred with self-commiseration, his ears straining to detect through the constant spatter of the rain what he believed was the distant 'burr' of an engine, heard a sudden metallic clatter on the floor and turned. On the floor between him and Mason lay a key.

The policeman remained silent, staring at it, unable to grasp its significance. Only when Mason said sharply, 'Well?' a look of mingled anxiety and fear came into the policeman's eyes. 'You found it, sir?' he asked in slow, puzzled tones, his head drooping towards the key, as though it possessed magnetic power.

Mason let himself down on Collinson's desk with some difficulty. The moment of retirement had come and he felt his age acutely. It was that, indeed, and the disgust and disappointment with himself induced by memory, that had led him to shrink from all the trouble and anxiety and useless strain of deceit which would have as its only result the preservation of life for a few more insignificant years. He could not, however, try as he would, keep his voice to the casual, uninterested note which he desired. It sounded to himself taut and quivering.

'You see, constable, the murderer escaped by the door and locked it behind him. Then he broke in and found the body. May I lend you my handcuffs, constable?' and Mason held them out on the palm of the hand. When the constable remained speechless and stupidly staring, Mason grew impatient.

'Damn you, man, move to it,' he said. 'I hear a car.' As the policeman, still silent and with fumbling shocked fingers fitted the handcuffs on to his superior's wrists, Mason spoke again.

'The credit really belongs to you constable, because you found Arthur Callum's letter, and I was once Arthur Callum. But this murder had nothing to do with Callum. I only wish it had. You don't see a jealous lover here, constable, only an elderly, corrupt police officer who has killed his blackmailer. As you said, a bad man's not always killed for a good reason. Listen, there's the car.'

He turned his back to the door at the sound of light, running feet up the stairs, and Groves was faced, as he entered, only by the white face and protuberant eyes of the police constable and the bald, tip-tilted head of Hubert Collinson and his stare of astonishment.

'You've come too late, Groves,' Mason said, still with his back turned. 'The mystery has been solved without you,' and turning suddenly, he held out his handcuffed wrists in a theatrical gesture which he could not resist. 'Oh no, it's not a mistake,' he added. 'It would have been the perfect murder, Groves, but for this constable. I commend him to you.'

He walked to Hubert Collinson's desk, fixing his eyes on it as though, like a drunken man, he was anxious to assert the straightness of his gait. Actually it was to banish from any absurd visions there might be of a relenting or a pitying Rachel Mann.

Groves, a young alert man in a light mackintosh and a bowler hat, said slowly, 'I don't understand. Is this some sort of joke?'

'Come now'—Mason still spoke to the two men as though he were their superior officer—'you must take my statement,' and not waiting on their stumbling efforts to find pencil and paper, he began to recite in a slow, controlled voice an exact account of his movements and his motive. Even the motive, and his awareness that it was indeed the wrong reason, seemed not to trouble him now.

It was his listeners who were troubled, his listeners reflected many times in the obtrusive mirrors of Hubert Collinson's flat, and later his more numerous listeners at the Old Bailey, judge, jury, counsel; but Rachel Mann remained untroubled, for she had been dead for ten years, and the voice was nothing if it was not terrestrial.

AN APPOINTMENT WITH
THE GENERAL

She felt the unprofessional shyness that she always experienced, with a sense of inadequacy, before an interview—she lacked, as she well knew, the brazen front of the traditional male reporter, but not, or so at this time she still believed, his cynicism—she could be as cynical as any man and with reason.

She found herself now surrounded in the small courtyard of a white suburban villa with half-Indian faces. The men all carried revolvers on their belts and one had a walkie-talk which he kept pressed closely to his ear as though he were waiting with the intensity of a priest for one of his Indian gods to proclaim something. The men are as strange to me, she thought, as the Indians must have seemed to Columbus five centuries ago. The camouflage of their uniforms was like painted designs on naked skin. She said, 'I don't speak Spanish,' as Columbus might have said, 'I don't speak Indian.' She then tried them with French—that was no good—and after that with English, which had been her mother's tongue, but that was no good either. 'I am Marie-Claire Duval. I have an appointment with the General.'

One of the men—an officer—laughed, and at his laugh she wanted to walk straight out of the courtyard, to make her way back to the pseudo-luxury of her hotel, to the half-finished airport, to take the whole dreary way back to Paris. Fear always made her angry. She said, 'Go and tell the General that I am here,' but, of course, no one would understand what she was saying.

One soldier sat on a bench cleaning his automatic. He was stubby and grey-haired. He wore his uniform with the stripes of a sergeant carelessly as though it was just a raincoat which he had huddled on against the thin vagrant rain which was blowing up now from the Pacific. She watched him closely as he cleaned his gun, but he didn't laugh, while the man with the walkie-talk continued to listen to his god and paid her no attention at all.

'Gringo,' the officer said.

'I am not a gringo. I am French,' but of course she knew by this time that he didn't understand any word she said—except gringo. He accused her again with his mocking smile—or so she believed because she didn't speak Spanish. All women, he seemed to be saying to her, were inferior if they hadn't a protector and she was more inferior than most because she spoke no Spanish.

'The General,' she repeated, 'the General,' knowing that she pronounced the word all wrong for a Spaniard, and she fished out of the poor memory she always had for foreign names that of the General's adviser who had made this appointment for her, 'Señor Martinez,' wondering all the time whether the name was right—perhaps it was Rodriguez or Gonzalez or Fernandez.

The sergeant snapped back the chamber of his automatic and spoke to her in almost perfect English from his bench. 'You're Mademoiselle Duval?' he asked.

'Madame Duval,' she said.

'Oh, you're married then?'

'Yes.'

'Well, it doesn't much matter,' he said, and he set his safety catch.

'It does to me.'

'I wasn't thinking of you,' he said. He got up and spoke to the officer. Although by his stripes he was only a sergeant, he had a kind of unmilitary authority about him. She found his manner a little insolent, but he was equally insolent to the officer. He swung his automatic to indicate the door of the small unimportant suburban house. 'You can go in,' he said. 'The General will see you.'

'Is Señor Martinez here—to translate?'

'No. The General wants me to translate. He wants to see you alone.'

'Then how can you translate?'

His smile, she noticed, after all was quite free from insolence in spite of the words he used. 'Ah, but here we say to a girl, "Come with me to be alone." '

She was stopped short again just inside a little hall which contained a bad picture, an occasional table, a nude statue of the late Victorian kind and a life-size china dog, by a soldier who pointed at the tape recorder which was slung over her shoulder.

'Yes,' the sergeant said, 'it would be better if you left that on the table.'

'It's only a recorder. I never learned shorthand. Does it look like a bomb?'

'No. All the same—it would be better. Please.'

She laid it down. She thought, I'll have to trust to my memory, my damnable memory, the memory I hate.

'After all,' she said, 'if I am an assassin you have your gun.'

'A gun is no defence,' he told her.

2

It was more than a month since the editor had invited her to lunch at Fouquet's. She had never met him, but he sent her a neat and courteous letter stamped out in a type which resembled book printing, praising an interview which she had published in another journal. Perhaps the letter read a little condescendingly, as though he were conscious of controlling a review of a higher intellectual grading than the one in which she wrote. It would certainly pay less, always the sign of quality. She accepted his invitation because the morning it arrived she had had one more 'final' quarrel with her husband—the fourth in four years. The first two had been the least damaging—jealousy after all is a form of love; the third was a furious quarrel with all the pain of broken promises, but the fourth was the worst, without love or anger, with just the irritated tiredness that comes from a repeated grievance, from the conviction that the man one lives with is unchangeable, and the sad knowledge that she didn't care much anyway any more. This one *was* the final quarrel she thought.

All that was left for her now was the packing of suitcases. Thank God there were no children to consider.

She came into Fouquet's ten minutes late. She had been kept waiting in restaurants far too often to be punctual. She asked the waiter for Monsieur Jacques Durand's table and saw a man rise to greet her. He was tall and lean and very good-looking—in that he reminded her of her husband. Good looks could be as nauseating as chocolate truffle. He would have had an air of almost overpowering distinction if his greying hair had been a little less well waved over his ears, though the ears, she admitted, were the right masculine size. (She disliked small ears.) She would have taken him for a diplomat if she had not known him to be the editor of that distinguished left-wing weekly which she had seldom read, not being in sympathy with its tendency towards modish politics. Many men who at first sight seem dead come alive in their eyes: but in his case it was the eyes which were the deadest part of him, in spite of their condescending gallantry: only in the gestures of his elegant carcass as he seated her beside him and handed her the menu did he come to a sort of life—a seductive life but a seduction which expressed itself only with words.

He suggested that it would be best if they took the turbot, and when she agreed he told her again in exactly the same phrases that he had used in the letter, how much pleasure her last interview had given him, so perhaps the words really were his and not his secretary's—he would hardly have learnt her words by heart. He added, 'The turbot here is very good.'

'Thank you. It's very kind of you.'

'I've been noticing your work for a long time now, Madame Duval. You get below the surface. Your interviews are not dictated by your victims.'

'I use a tape recorder,' she said.

'I didn't mean literally.' He crackled his toast melba. 'For a long time now, you know,'—his vocabulary seemed limited, perhaps by the rules of journalistic protocol—'I have thought of you as one of us.' Obviously he meant the statement to be a compliment and he paused, probably waiting for her to repeat 'Thank you'. She wondered how long it would be before he began to talk real business. The suitcases were yawning emptily on her bed. She wanted to fill them before her husband returned—it was unlikely, but not impossible, that he would return before dinner.

'Do you know Spanish?' Monsieur Durand asked.

'French and English are my only languages.'

'Not German? Your interview with Helmut Schmidt was beautiful—and so destructive.'

'He speaks English well.'

'I doubt if the General does.' He fell silent over his turbot. It was very good turbot, one of Fouquet's specialities. She thought, 'If I can get out of the apartment before Jean returns it will save a lot of argument.' Argument could be left later to the two *avocats*. There would have to be, she supposed, a meeting of *conciliation*—the thought bored her profoundly. She wanted as quickly as possible to wipe the whole slate clean.

'The situation in Jamaica is another subject I have in mind. You could pick up Jamaica on your way out. You said you speak English, didn't you? A rather more sympathetic approach perhaps to Manley than you are used to. He's one of us, even though for the moment he's "out". The General, I think could be a subject in your usual style. Suitable for your brand of irony. As you can imagine we don't much care for generals—especially Latin-American generals.'

She asked, 'You mean you want to send me somewhere?'

'Well, yes. You are a very attractive woman. And by all accounts the General likes attractive women.'

'Doesn't Manley?' she asked.

'I wish you spoke a little Spanish. You have such a valuable knack of asking the right personal question. Politics, we believe, should never make dull reading. You are not under contract, are you?'

'No, but what General? You don't want me to go to Chile, do you?'

'We are getting a little tired of Chile. I doubt if even you could be very fresh on the subject of Pinochet—and would he receive you? The advantage of a really small republic is that it can be covered—in depth mind you—in a matter of weeks. We can regard it as a microcosm of Latin America. The conflict with the

United States, of course, is more in the open there—because of the bases.'

She looked at her watch. She was wondering if she could get all she wanted for the moment into two suitcases—to go where? 'What bases?' She would not leave a note because it could be used by lawyers.

'The American, of course.'

'You want me to interview the President? Of what republic?'

'Not the President. The General. The President doesn't really count. The General is chief of the revolution.' He poured her out another half-glass of wine. She had only ordered a small carafe. 'You see we are a little bit suspicious of the General. It's true that he has visited Fidel, and that he met Tito at Colombo. But we wonder whether his socialism is not rather skin-deep. He is no Marxist certainly. Your method with Schmidt would suit him admirably. And perhaps on the way there or back a sympathetic portrait of Manley in Jamaica. We feel quite happy about Manley.'

She was still not sure what country it was he wanted her to visit. Geography was not her strong point. Perhaps he *had* mentioned the name, but if he had it had dropped out of sight into the empty suitcases. Anyway it didn't really matter: anywhere was preferable at the moment to Paris. She said, 'When is it you want me to go?'

'As soon as possible. You see there may be a crisis in the next few months, and if that happens . . . you might find yourself only writing the General's obituary.'

'A dead General, I suppose, would certainly not be a socialist good enough for you.'

His laugh, if it could really be called a laugh, was like the scraping of a dry throat, and his eyes, which were now fixed on the menu, the turbot having been meticulously finished, showed no sign that a joke, like an angel, had passed quietly overhead and vanished. 'Oh, as I said, we are rather doubtful about his kind of socialism. May I suggest a little cheese?'

3

'You might find yourself writing his obituary'—the phrase spoken two weeks ago by a modish left-wing editor over the Fouquet menu—came immediately back to Marie-Claire's mind when she encountered the tired and doom-laden eyes of the General. Death was the accepted premature end, she had always understood, for generals in Latin America; the alternative might of course be Miami, but she couldn't see the man before her in Miami, sharing that city with the ex-President of the Republic and the ex-President's wife and his brother-in-law and cousin. Miami was known here, she had already learnt that, as 'The Valley of the Fallen'. The General was dressed in pyjamas and bedroom slippers and his hair was tousled in a boyish way, but no boy would have had eyes so laden with the future. He spoke to her in Spanish and the sergeant translated with correct though rather stiff English.

'The General says you are very welcome in the Republic. He does not know the paper for which you write, but Señor Martinez has told him that it is very well known in France for its liberal views.'

Marie-Claire believed in provocation; Helmut Schmidt had responded promptly with anger and pride, to her first questions, he had given himself away to the merciless tape, but the tape this time had been left behind in the recorder. She said, 'No, not liberal—left-wing. Would it be true to say that the General is much criticized for moving so very reluctantly towards socialism?'

She watched the sergeant closely as he translated, trying to attach a meaning to the Latin-sounding words, and his eyes twinkled back at her as though he were amused at the question and perhaps approved it.

'My General says he is going where his people tell him to go.'

'Or is it the Americans who tell him?'

'My General says that naturally he has to take the Americans into account, that is politics in a country as small as ours, but he need not accept their views. He suggests that you must be tired of standing; you should make yourself comfortable in the armchair.'

Marie-Claire sat down. She felt the General had scored over Helmut Schmidt—and over herself too. She hadn't yet had time to think of her next question—she had expected the General to leave a door open for her to make a quick impromptu question, but he seemed to have closed all doors firmly in her face. There was a long and awkward pause; she was relieved when the General spoke again.

'My General says that he hopes Señor Martinez is helping you in every way he can.'

'Señor Martinez has very kindly lent me his own car, but the chauffeur speaks only Spanish which makes it difficult for me.'

The two of them began to discuss together what she had said at some length. The General slipped off one shoe and stroked his left sole.

'My General says you may dismiss the car and the chauffeur. He has given me orders to look after you—Sergeant Gurdián is my name. I am to take you wherever you may wish to go.'

'Señor Martinez asked me in his letter to make out a programme for him to approve.' Again there was a consultation.

'My General says it is best for you not to have a programme. A programme kills.'

The tired and brooding eyes watched her with what she took to be amusement like those of a chess player who knows that he has made a surprise move and disconcerted his opponent.

'My General says that even a political programme kills. Your editor ought to know that.'

'Señor Martinez thought that I should visit . . .'

'My General says you should always do the opposite of whatever Señor Martinez advises.'

'But I was told that he was Chief Adviser to the General.'

The sergeant shrugged his shoulders and smiled too. 'My General says that while, of course, it is *his* duty to listen to his advisers, it is not *your* duty.'

The General began to talk in a low voice to the sergeant. Marie-Claire had an impression that the interview was slipping disastrously out of her hands. When she had abandoned the recorder she had abandoned her best weapon.

'My General wants to know if your editor is a Marxist.'

'Oh, he supports the Marxists—in a way, but he would never admit to being one himself. Before the war people used to call his type a fellow-traveller. The Communist Party is legal here, isn't it?'

'Yes, it is quite legal to be a Communist. But we have no parties.'

'Not even one?'

'Not one. A man can think what he likes. Is that true in a party?'

She said—and she meant it to be an insult—for in her experience it was only when a man became angry that he told the truth—even Schmidt had told a few truths—'Is your General a fellow-traveller like my editor?'

The General gave her an encouraging smile, and for a moment he looked a little less tired, a little more interested. 'My General says the Communists are for a while travelling on the same train as he is. So are the socialists. But it is he who is driving the train. It is he who will decide at what station to stop, and not his passengers.'

'Passengers usually have tickets for certain destinations.'

'My General says he will be able to explain more easily to you when you have seen something of his country. My General would like before you return to Europe to see for once his country through your eyes. A stranger's eyes. He says they are very beautiful ones.'

So the editor was right, she thought, he likes women, he finds women easy, power is an obvious aphrodisiac . . . Charm too can be an aphrodisiac, Jean had plenty of charm, he had exuded charm with the skill of a politician, but she was finished with charm and aphrodisiacs. She said, 'Now that the General has power, I suppose he finds women easy to come by.' Sergeant Gurdián smiled. He didn't translate.

'I suppose he enjoys his power,' she said. She nearly added, 'And his women.'

She tried a question which she had sometimes found worked surprisingly well. 'What does he dream of? At night I mean. Does he dream of women?' She continued with mockery, 'Or does he dream of the terms he is going to make with the gringos?' The tired and wounded eyes looked at the wall behind her. She could even understand the single phrase he spoke in reply to her question. '*La muerte.*'

'He dreams of death,' the sergeant translated unnecessarily, and I could build an article on that, she thought with self-hatred.

NEWLY COLLECTED

THE BLESSING

The Archbishop was a quarter of an hour late, and Weld, who was uncomfortably pressed into the crowd on the dock, below a heavy glaring sky, resented the delay. It seemed to him absurd that he was there at all. The ceremony could not possibly rate more than a couple of sticks in tomorrow's paper, insufficient to justify even his train-fare from the capital. He suspected that for some obscure reason Smiley, his chief, had wanted him out of the office for the day. Perhaps someone of importance was arriving from London . . . Smiley had not been too pleased when Weld's story of a small pacifist demonstration had been raised to the head of a column on the principal news-page. He had made a slighting reference to the chief sub-editor of the foreign room— 'He never had a sense of values.'

'You never know,' Smiley had said to him that morning with the sour expression which belied his name, 'some of your beloved pacifists may make a protest.'

'It's very improbable. Even if they do . . . '

'Try to make a story out of the ceremony itself. You have a pretty sense of irony. Or so Crowe thinks.' (Crowe was the chief sub-editor.) 'There are no Catholics on the board—as far as I know.'

But were there? Perhaps that was the point of sending him south. Perhaps Smiley was trying to blacken his reputation in London by encouraging him to take a false step.

When he arrived at the port Weld went straight to the *taverna* in the upper town where he could expect to find his colleagues, if anyone beside himself had troubled to come so far for so little.

But he had been over-pessimistic. At least the agencies were represented by their junior men—Hughes of the AP, Collins of the United Press, Tumbril of Reuter's, and of course all the natives. He saw no sign of the *Telegraph*, the *Express* or the *Mail*.

One of the natives was drinking a horrible aperitif made out of artichokes and he was in the course of being interrogated by Tumbril when Weld arrived. Tumbril was a very serious young man, but under these circumstances he had the support of Hughes, who was obviously just as unhappy at being there as Weld.

'You haven't answered Tumbril's question,' Hughes said.

'Oh, heretics like you cannot be expected to understand.' He uttered the word 'heretics' with a smile as an Englishman might have said 'bastards'.

'You told me yourself,' Tumbril persisted, 'that you thought this was an unjust war.' They spoke in English in a hazy hope that the barman might not understand.

'Well . . . perhaps . . . '

'How can you bless the weapons which are to be used in an unjust war?'

'I do not suppose it will make them more efficacious, if that is what you fear.'

'Are you going to bless the canisters of poison gas?'

'There is a difference. The canisters contain only gas—not human beings.'

'What earthly good . . . ?'

'No earthly good. I assure you, no earthly good.'

'You are escaping with a quibble,' Hughes said.

'What is a quibble?'

Collins said to Weld, 'What's yours?'

'A Negroni.'

'What are you here for?'

'What are *you* here for?'

'Caper thought there might possibly be a demonstration.'

'Against an Archbishop? Here? Not a chance.'

'That's what I said. I was going down to the sea with Martha. You know Martha?'

'Oh, yes. Yes.' Martha was the plump and prehensile wife of a

German correspondent who was suspected of strong Nazi sympathies. She was said to look after men's needs with a simple and indiscriminate fervour, and most men felt a strong moral duty to betray her husband.

'Why didn't you bring her with you?'

'I did. She's waiting for me at'—and he named a resort popular with pederasts, lesbians and English tourists.

'You won't have much time. These ceremonies are always late—and prayers drag on so.'

'I was hoping, old man, that you'd do me a favour. Tumbril won't and Hughes—for reasons of his own which I can only surmise—can't. I thought perhaps you'd telephone to me when it's all over at the Grand Hotel—I mean only if something unexpected occurs. I've seen so many of these affairs. I've got this one all written up—I just need an insurance, that's all.'

'Very well. I'll ring you between five and six. It's going to be bloody hot.'

'They'll have rigged up something over the tribune.'

'I'm not going on any tribune. The only chance of a story will be in the crowd.'

'What an optimist you are, Weld.'

'I said the only chance. What's yours?'

'Campari soda. Cigarette?'

'Thanks.' Weld took the cigarette, the tenth of the day, handling it like an enemy. He knew that later in the afternoon his smoker's cough would inevitably begin, rasping the dry throat, keeping him awake all the short night before the sun struck through the shutters at five. He had promised himself not to smoke till the ceremony was over, but the Negroni had weakened his resistance.

'What about the men they are going to kill? Will the blessing help *them*?' Hughes returned to the attack.

'The "unarmed savages" you are always writing about?'

'Not me, old man. If you work for an agency you can't afford fancy words. What's good for the *Express* is poison for the *Mail*. We give them the so-called facts and leave the irony and the indignation to men like Weld here.'

Two hours later Weld stood on the dock in a crowd that smelt of garlic and sweat-soaked cloth. He was a tall man and he could see easily, in spite of the police who were ranked shoulder to shoulder in front of them. There was no tribune, and, when the moment came, very little ceremony. In the space between the troop ship and the crowd tanks were lined up. Sullied with camouflage they looked second-hand, like old cars on a city parking-lot waiting for a buyer or the scrap-heap. The crews lounged a little apart as though disowning them. A child screamed persistently close to Weld and was finally given the breast. Only the flags on the troop ship, the strident posters on the walls of the customs indicated that at least someone had an enthusiasm for the war which was blundering on beyond the sun-polished horizon. The crowd had none. It seemed to Weld they had come here like himself in case something happened. There was a general tone of black because of the number of women, so that he had the sense of forming part of a nation in mourning rather than a nation under arms.

He was looking the other way at the houses beyond the railway, where the bright bed-covers hung from the windows in place of flags, when someone gave an order, and, as he turned, the crews snapped to attention beside their machines, and a little old man in a black cassock with a crimson silk edging shuffled slowly down their ranks. He wore a stole over his shoulders and violet stockings, and he picked his way in silver buckled shoes. The lace on his cotta looked old like himself. A young priest towered over him from behind carrying a purple biretta. There was a small flurry of priests, and in the dazzling day they seemed to scatter like feathers; Weld had the impression of a pigeon being plucked, a small plump pigeon. The crowd was cheering now—so it wasn't, after all, a funeral. As the Archbishop came to each tank he paused and a priest thrust a great prayer-book in front of him from which he read, bending very close to the page as though his old eyes could see no more than an inch or two ahead. Then another priest put a censer into his hand and he swung it to and fro, and whatever breeze there was from the sea sent the blue smoke back towards the crowd, so that for a moment the sweet smell dispersed the sweat and the garlic.

'Ah mother of God, sweet mother of God,' said the man who

stood by Weld, and Weld saw that he was weeping. It shocked him. He had never been quite so close before to superstition. The man's face was wrinkled like a windfall apple which has lain too long upon the ground. 'The good old man, the good old man,' he kept on repeating. 'Ah, the saint of God.' He spoke in the accent of the country, not of the port. Weld was irritated by the man's piety, by his simplicity, or perhaps by the great heat of the day.

'So this is a holy war,' he said scornfully.

The old man looked at him with surprise. 'It is a cursed war,' he said. 'Two men in my village will never come home. Why should we fight over there? The devil makes wars, not God.'

'Then why not let the devil bless the tanks?'

'The devil does not bless. He does not know how to bless.'

'You are against the war,' Weld said, 'and yet you see nothing wrong in an archbishop blessing tanks?'

'Why should he not bless the tanks?' the old man asked. The Archbishop passed on, and the old man clapped and yelled, 'A saint. A saint,' gleefully now as though he and the Archbishop were sharing a joke together. Some children were flinging crackers over the heads of the police, the ceremony was nearly over, and there had been no demonstration. The holy mutter passed out of hearing, while the smell of incense faded.

Weld said to the old man, speaking very simply because his command of the language was weak, 'I do not understand. You say this is a cursed war. Those tanks are going to kill men with spears and old rifles who are defending their country. How can your holy Archbishop bless these instruments of evil?'

'I don't like them myself,' the old man said, 'ugly dangerous things—but then, if you have the desire to bless, you bless.'

'I do not understand.'

'I do a lot of blessing myself,' the old man said. 'It's when you want to love and you can't manage it. You stretch out your hands and you say God forgive me that I can't love but bless this thing anyway. I had a spade, the handle was always coming loose, and I cut my foot with it, so I blessed it—I had to bless it or break it—and I couldn't afford to break it. A woman comes to me every week complaining of my dog. She wants it gelded, poor woman. I can't do that, it's against nature, she calls me all kinds of names,

I hold out my hand—the next thing you know I'm blessing her, poor thing, because I can't love her.'

Weld could not follow. It was as though he had found himself in a very simple landscape, yet one where every path led into a maze from which there was no visible exit.

'But the Archbishop,' he said, 'dressed up like that, the incense, the prayers . . . ' He said, 'All the world knows you have been using mustard gas . . . ' He broke off: it was an absurd accusation to bring against one peasant. 'And these tanks . . . '

'Ugly dangerous things,' the old man repeated. 'They don't even shine like a new plough does. They look as though they had spotted fever. Perhaps the Archbishop hates them—I wouldn't be surprised. We have to bless what we hate. I remember hating once—it was a great grey rat and it killed my pullets. I had it cornered at last, so I put out my hands, and I blessed it. It died after that, run over by the priest's car. Maybe these tanks will die too and the poor souls in them. I've never known a blessing save a life. But then, if you want to bless, you bless. It would be better to love, but that's not always possible.'

It was after five before Weld got back to the *taverna* in the upper town. He telephoned to Collins at the Grand Hotel. Collins replied petulantly—perhaps the afternoon had not gone as well as he had hoped, perhaps Weld had interrupted something, he thought he heard a woman laugh. Collins said, 'I only asked you to telephone if something interesting happened.'

'Nothing happened.'

'Well, all right, goodbye then,' and he rang off without a word of thanks.

Hughes and Tumbril came into the bar, while Weld was telephoning, and so the ritual of paying for rounds of whisky began. Weld found he had lost his packet of cigarettes. It had probably been stolen from him in the crowd. 'A packet of Players,' he said to the barman. The grime of the long hot afternoon had dried his throat. A cigarette would not help, it would only start his cough again, and he hesitated a moment with his hand raised before he took the packet; perhaps he could wait a little longer—say, until the third round.

'Look at Weld,' Hughes said to Tumbril, 'he's blessing the cigarettes.'

'I bless the whisky,' Tumbril said, passing his hand over his glass. 'Sweet product of the fields. Sweet golden grain. I love you dearly as the Archbishop loves his dear old tanks.'

'You don't bless what you love,' Weld said.

'What about your cigarettes then?'

'They are my enemy. They'll kill me in the end.' He couldn't wait any longer. He lit one and almost immediately he began to cough. 'I've never known a blessing save a life,' he said. The sentence sounded like a familiar quotation.

1966

CHURCH MILITANT

As we drove out of the reservation in Father Donnell's old tinpot of a jeep we passed the Archbishop in his Cadillac. It came to rest a few yards off, between the rows of coffee plants. 'If we hadn't stopped at your friend's after lunch,' Father Donnell complained, putting on his brakes, 'we'd have missed him altogether.' He got unwillingly out and went over to the Archbishop who sat at the wheel. The back of the car was full of women in strange, grey clothes on which were sewn grey linen crosses.

Father Donnell came thoughtfully back. He said, 'We can go on, but he wants us to meet him at the Niguru Mission for a chat at teatime. He's going up to my place now. I hope to God there's someone at home besides Patsy One-Eye.'

'Who were those women?' I asked.

Father Donnell replied gloomily and ambiguously, 'I fear the worst.'

That afternoon we called on some women settlers who were living alone very courageously on the edge of the Kikuyu reserve. The shotguns in the hall, the revolvers on their laps, the big Boxer dogs couched protectively by the wire fences called to my mind what life must have been like in the early days of American colonization. Father Donnell was preoccupied. When one of the women mentioned the attack on his mission a few weeks gone, he hadn't the heart to tell a good story. 'Oh, the poor fellows,' he said, 'they didn't know any better.'

'If you hadn't had twenty yards start to the forest——'

'They've been misled,' he said.

The Niguru Mission was quite a different spot from Father Donnell's tin hut on the top of a hill. Outside the reserve, on land owned by Europeans, it had been built in less troublesome times and built to last. I was reminded a little of a military barracks designed by Lutyens. The very sight of it in the distance aroused Father Donnell; he became as mischievous as a small boy from a poor home taken to see a rich and pompous relative.

'We'll pull Father Schmidt's leg,' he said. 'Poor man, living there with all those holy nuns, year in, year out.'

'Have they had any trouble?' I asked.

'Trouble!' Father Donnell exclaimed in his house-proud accent. 'They've got fifty Home Guards stuck around the place and if a dog so much as barks, away goes a rocket and they have the Devons shooting up the drive. What chance have the Mau Mau, poor devils, with a place like that?'

We parked the car as silently as Father Donnell's gears would permit round a corner of the Italianate chapel and went to look for Father Schmidt. In the great square of the place a nun went bustling by and Father Donnell called out to her, 'Hi, sister!'

'How are you, father?'

'Trying to avoid me, are you? Think I've come begging for eggs, eh?'

'I just didn't see you, father.'

'Well, I've some bad news for all of you, sister.'

'Bad news? Is it General Kimathi?'

'What, that poor ignorant fellow? No, sister. The Archbishop's descending on you all, in next to no time! In his brand new Cadillac.'

'But what's he doing this way?'

'I have my fears,' Father Donnell said, moving on.

We found Father Schmidt in his room. He was fast asleep on a couple of chairs, with the shutters drawn to keep the sun out; a very old man with snow-white hair, very close to the last sleep of all. I wouldn't have woken him, but Father Donnell had no such scruples. 'Father Schmidt, Father Schmidt!' he called.

Father Schmidt raised one thick white eyebrow. 'Oh it's you,' he said, and prepared to sleep again.

'Wake up, father. It's serious trouble we have.'

Father Schmidt reluctantly put his feet on the floor. 'Have they attacked you again? I heard no shots last night.'

'They've done worse, Father Schmidt. They've driven away the cows and killed the chickens and we've come to beg for some of your home-made wine.'

'I suppose I can give you a few bottles, perhaps, but what has wine got to do with your cows?'

'Oh, they poisoned our well too. We've nothing to drink, father. And we'll need six of your labourers to carry the things.'

'What is wrong with your car?'

'They burnt that.'

'Then how did you come here?'

'We walked all the way.'

The old man shambled to his feet and made for the cupboard. The bottom shelf was full of bottles.

'We're starving, father. We'll need all those bottles.'

'They have not been filled yet. We will have to take them to the barrel.'

'And bread, father. We've used up all our bread.'

Grumbling gutturally old Father Schmidt produced two loaves and half a pound of butter. 'It is all I have, Father Donnell.'

'And eggs.'

He took three eggs out of a china dish.

'And a side of beef, father.'

'What reason would I have for keeping a side of beef? You know very well I do not eat meat. For that you must go to the sister-in-charge. I have some biscuits. You had better sit down and eat.'

I wondered how far Father Donnell would let the joke go, for there were only a very few sweet biscuits left in the tin and Father Schmidt turned away his face to hide a grimace when Father Donnell dipped a finger towards the tin.

'Look at his face,' Father Donnell said. 'The sweetest tooth this side of the Indian Ocean. Don't be afraid, father. It was a little jest we were having.'

Father Schmidt looked down at his big black boots and said, 'Will you ever grow up, Father Donnell?'

'Ah, don't be angry, father. I'll be as old as you one day. But I've real news for you. The Archbishop's due here any minute with a cargo of ladies.'

'Ladies?'

'The Little Sisters of Charles de Foucauld.'

'Haven't I got enough women in the place?'

'They don't want to have anything to do with you, father. They want a plot in the reserve.'

'Who's going to pay for them?'

'They want to live like African women, build their own huts . . . till the ground . . . I told them I wanted nurses for a hospital, but they'll have none of that they say, except the emptying of the slops. "Perhaps you'll teach in my school?" I said. Oh, no. They'll sweep the floors, they won't teach. I said, "There's no room for you in my small mission," and they said they'd take a bit of ground outside it. "We only want half an hectare," they said. "It belongs to the Kikuyu," I said, "with all this trouble, how can we ask them for land?" "If the Lord wants us here, the Lord will give us half a hectare," they said. What's a hectare and what can you do with women like that?'

'It's not right,' Father Schmidt said. 'They ought to stay in Europe.'

'There's a lot of them in the north.'

'The north is different. There's plenty of room for madness in the desert.'

'Here's the Archbishop,' Father Donnell said, as the Cadillac bumped softly in.

Father Schmidt went to greet him and Father Donnell whispered to me, 'A saint if ever there was one.'

'The Archbishop?'

'Of course not. Oh, he's a good man in his way, but . . . '

The Archbishop entered. His big cross lay at a slight angle over his stomach.

'How are you? How are you?' he said. 'I'm very glad to meet you. It's a beautiful day for a ride if it wasn't for the state of the roads. I like to get out of the city, and the sisters were a good excuse. No, I won't have a cup of tea, thank you. Just one of those sweet biscuits, thank you, thank you. The sisters are looking after

my ladies and showing them the chapel and then we must be off.
I like to get back before it's very late in these dangerous days. Oh,
thank you, thank you, but I seem to be eating them all up, when I
really just wanted to explain about my ladies. They're French, father, like you.'

'I'm no more French,' Father Schmidt said, 'than you're English.'

'Ah, touché, touché,' the Archbishop said with a genial laugh.
His bonhomie was continuous. I was reminded of a cheer-leader
at a baseball match.

'What do they want here?' Father Schmidt asked.

'Well, you know how it is with the Sisters of Charles de Foucauld. They want a bit of land to work like the natives.'

'These parts are unsuitable for women,' Father Schmidt said.

'That's why they want to be here. It's their vocation.' The
Archbishop brushed some crumbs off his waistcoat and said,
'I've given them one plot in the city at Moragumbi.'

'But that is a terrible place,' Father Schmidt said. 'That was
where they dug up those strangled bodies. Their throats will all
be cut,' he added accusingly.

'It's their vocation, father, it's their vocation. You are too materialist. We all of us have our vocations. You and me and Father
Donnell. One mustn't interfere with a vocation.'

'Fifty-five years ago I remember a novice master who didn't
believe in encouraging a vocation.'

'I'm not dealing with novices, father. It's as I said, you are too
materialist, living here comfortably with all these sisters to look
after you.'

'They will not stay alive a month. Who will look after *them*?'

'They'll look after themselves, father.'

'They are women,' Father Schmidt said sadly and wistfully.

The Archbishop took Father Donnell out into the shadowy
square 'to meet the ladies properly'. He walked jauntily, like a
leader: there was no question about his vocation either.

Father Schmidt sat silent over his empty tin of sweet biscuits.
Once he shook his head at his own thoughts.

I wondered how I could cheer him up. I was an outsider, a visit-
ing journalist. I said, 'These empty bottles in your cupboard . . .'

He raised his old eyes.

I said, 'If we loaded half a dozen in the back of Father Donnell's jeep, then when he drives off where'll be such a clatter . . . I don't know what the Archbishop will think.'

Father Schmidt rose. 'It is a very good idea.' He stumped in his big boots towards the cupboard. The Archbishop was talking earnestly to Father Donnell. Neither of them saw us laden with the bottles. Father Schmidt took up a position between me and them, straddling with his legs, making a curtain of his soutane, while I laid the bottles in the bottom of the jeep. Then we went back to where the Archbishop, surrounded by the noncomprehending French faces of his ladies, was having his last word with Father Donnell.

'At a time like this,' Father Donnell said, 'we can't ask the poor creatures for even half an acre.'

'It's to help a vocation.'

'How can you expect the Kikuyu to understand that? They'll think we are stealing the land. And aren't we stealing it?'

'For God, father.'

'I thought God owned the land already. Without us.' He got angrily into his jeep and I followed him. 'Goodbye, your Grace.'

'Goodbye, father. Just think about it. I'm sure you'll come round to my opinion.'

'Goodbye, Father Schmidt.'

'Goodbye, Father Donnell.'

He drove off and the bottles merrily clinked and clanked, but looking back I could see no sign that the Archbishop had heard, nor had Father Donnell. He bumped onwards into the reserve lost in thought. I had to turn on the lights myself. The noise of our progress made me uneasy in the growing darkness. I said, 'Don't you think . . . these bottles . . . '

'Bottles?'

'They are so noisy. If the Mau Mau—' I tried nervously to suggest.

'Poor fellows,' Father Donnell said. 'How could we ever make them understand . . . ?'

1956

DEAR DR FALKENHEIM

Dear Dr Falkenheim.

You have asked me to draw up a report—perhaps I ought to say a case history—dealing with a certain traumatic experience belonging to my son's childhood in connection with the Father Christmas myth. I will try to be precise, not disguising my own feelings because I do realize that the analysis of a child must be to some extent an analysis of his parents. How much more closely 'one flesh' applies to a man's child than to his wife. I have been spending the whole weekend reading the book you recommended by Dr Doppeldorf and I was fascinated by much of it, to learn for example of the punning instincts in the unconscious and of the importance of the irrelevant, so you must not be surprised at irrelevance in my report. And here I am already running on (perhaps I ought to write running away) instead of making the short report you expect of me, but do you really expect a short report? After reading Dr Doppeldorf I suspect not.

I am aware that I am writing flippantly, and I know you will see through the flippancy. What I see is my child coming home every year from school, every December, with his eye blackened or his mouth bleeding, and still with the terrible courage that a child shows alone in a hostile world because he cannot believe that *we* know what life is like. In his eyes I am only concerned about the new price war between Esso and Shell, and my wife is concerned about the Women's Institute, and both of us have to respect his independence and pay no attention. The wound doesn't exist—the bruise came because he walked into a brick wall absent-mindedly.

My son was six years old when the event I am trying to describe occurred. With my wife and son I had left England for Canada only a few months before and we were none of us yet accustomed to the great steely neon-lit city which lay on the foothills of the Rockies more than three thousand feet up. The sky seemed higher and larger than our English skies, above the level of the clouds we knew, and the air was cold and fresh like lake water. From our bungalow which was called Kosy Nuick on the outskirts of the city we could see across the rolling beige ranchland to the snowy peaks of the Rockies; they changed colour every hour of the day—sometimes they were a hard glittering white, sometimes a pale rose and even at moments a deep blue like storm clouds.

I only mention these effects to show that we did not feel in the least exiled in the far West. If anything there was a sense of exhilaration, of freedom, and of a new life beginning. Certainly there was nothing to prepare us for the kind of wanton shock which drove us all away after we had only stayed a few months. We have never returned, so what my son now remembers of the place must be the real memories of a six-year-old. They are an odd assortment when he speaks of them: men dressed like cowboys buying Weetabix in the self-help stores, the garage right up on top of the Perkins building where sitting in the car he could see the river and the tops of the houses and the mountains, the roar and stamp of a multitude of beasts in the cattle trucks at the station, the arch of cloud above the Rockies which heralded what they call the chinook, when the temperature suddenly rises in a matter of hours from twenty degrees below zero to thirty-five above, and of course, but he doesn't speak of that, there is the terrible memory which is the subject of your investigation.

In Western Canada we had found all our English myths—the Easter eggs were there and not the Easter rabbit, and long before Christmas white-bearded men began to distribute chewing gum and paper hats to the children in the toy basements at both the big stores, Perkins and Browne's. Somehow it seems to be tacitly understood by children that these men are only stand-ins for the genuine character, or is there a confusion with the Christian saints whom Catholics believe can appear in more than one place at the same time? Perhaps the idea of a multiple Father Christmas is no more puzzling than all that business of the Trinity which children are expected to accept quite easily at Sunday school. If they are tiresome with their questions, I suppose they are told, as we adults are to this day, that it is an unfathomable mystery.

My son had drawn up early in November his Christmas list. None of the objects on this list could possibly be found in the old men's sacks at Perkins or Browne's, and I don't think he even expected them to be. We were even uncertain—you know how little parents realize about their children—whether he believed in Father Christmas at all. He had been promoted a class at school his first term, coming as he did from England where the standard is higher, and now he was working among the old sceptics of seven and eight. Looking back to my own childhood I seem to remember a period when I kept up the appearance of belief for the sake of my parents: they so obviously enjoyed the ceremony of the stocking, the clandestine appearance in my bedroom in costume in case I had remained wakeful, and certainly one Christmas I *had* been quite wakeful enough to notice that Father Christmas wore size eleven in brown Delta shoes like my father. It's funny how that word Delta has stuck in my mind. You'll probably have a theory about that too, Doctor. The Delta of the Nile perhaps—Moses and the bulrushes—the seven plagues—what a long journey one can make from a pair of fifty shilling shoes.

I said to my wife, 'Why don't we this year just say nothing about Father Christmas? We've made a break with England; surely we can make a break with Father Christmas too.'

'It's fun for me finding the little objects for his stocking,' she said or words to that effect (I am introducing the dialogue as accurately as I can, but after six years . . .). 'Only too soon we'll be buying him silk ties and the Collected Poems of Ezra Pound.'

'Well, there's no reason why the stocking shouldn't continue for a while. We'll detach it from the idea of Father Christmas, that's all. We could even convert it into a bran tub.'

'Then there'd be no heel for the tangerines.'

That year his Christmas list was a little daunting as though it had been drawn up by NATO. It led off with a space gun and a tactical nuclear weapon which he had seen in the window of

Perkins. Almost the least harmful thing on his list, if one could forget the purposes of uranium, was a Geiger counter.

'You aren't telling me, with a list like that, that he still believes in Father Christmas,' I said.

'I don't see why not. I expect you asked in your time for toy soldiers and an air gun. This is only progress.'

'I wonder no one has yet made a toy Hiroshima,' I said, 'to bombard with the tactical nuclear weapons. I've a good mind to patent the idea ready for next Christmas.'

But by next year Father Christmas was as dead as mutton you might say.

We had still not quite definitely made up our minds whether to liquidate the old man this year or next when my wife came home with some excitement from the big self-service stores that looked after the needs of our outer fringe of the city. (It was really unnecessary for any housewife to drive into the city at all, for at this local store you could buy everything from washing machines to paperbacks—and of course Weetabix, and there was a great parking space sufficient for five hundred cars at least.) She said to me, 'Father Christmas is arriving on Christmas Eve by air.'

'By air? With reindeer?' I asked.

'By helicopter. He's going to touch down in the car park just before sunset.'

'We certainly are in the van of progress here.'

'It's Browne's helicopter. They've stolen a march on Perkins. We are the last store on his route. You must admit that if this is to be Colin's last Father Christmas, we've struck a winner.' (That was our general attitude. Sympathetic to the child, sympathetic to Father Christmas, just trying to choose the tactful way of—well of breaking reality gently to the child. I don't remember my parents taking so much trouble.)

Well, there it was, all provided by a paternal store—Father Christmas arriving by helicopter. No payment. A completely free show. There's a kind of generosity in American advertising. And this arrival, of course, had the blessing of all the business interests in the city and all the denominations too. Elias went off by air in a chariot, and Father Christmas was going to descend, but of course, the story of Elias was supposed to be for grown-up people like myself, while Father Christmas was for the kids. (I really hate that word kids, perhaps because kid was a favourite dish of mine in Greece during the war—it's rather as though one called one's children *escalopes de veau*.)

But I have to get back to Christmas Eve whether I want to or not and the parking place outside the glassy self-service store, with a small area no larger than a house roped off for the helicopter, and the three of us waiting for it to arrive from the city and the high sky and the cold air and my wife saying, 'This couldn't happen at home. I love Christmas here,' and we both talked I'm sure about wide open spaces and little cramped Europe and the soaring imagination of the Admen in this city three thousand feet up in the air. Father O'Connor was waiting there with a bunch of veal cutlets from his congregation, wearing cowboy hats and Davy Crockett caps with fur tails and blue jeans and windbreakers with tartan linings. The sun would be going down soon below the Rockies and we heard the helicopter a long way off in the wide green sky; it rose vertically up from some store in the city, hovered like a vulture, and then came buzzing busily towards us, while the babies screamed and gurgled in the perambulators. When Father Christmas looked down from two hundred feet up, below the knifing rotary blades, he must have seen hundreds of open mouths. The helicopter circled above us, and he untied his sack and the air was full of small bright objects dropping down. They fell into the prams and into the cowboy hats and ricochetted all around beside the high heels and the miniature cowboy boots—just the same things which were distributed every day outside the big stores—chewing gum and paper hats—but of course they had more of a sense of glory about them rained like that out of the sky. Then swaying a little, first this way and then that, the helicopter sank slowly plumb in the centre of the roped-off space with its big rubber buffers, and a loudspeaker warned the parents to keep their children away until the blades stopped turning.

The trouble was, no one bothered to warn Father Christmas. The rotary blades above his head were slowing down and he didn't wait for the steps but jumped to the ground with the big sack slung over his shoulder. The windmill over his head was cutting big swaths in the air and hundreds of children screamed

with delight to see him land. Perhaps there was some extra enthusiasm behind the helicopter or perhaps he had the idea that
the children there couldn't see him properly and he moved round
the plane to show himself off there too. But he had quite forgotten, if he had ever known, that a helicopter has a propeller behind as well as overhead and he stepped right into it. The blades
took his body and flung it in a kind of violent dance back the
way he had come and his head was sliced right off and spun
through the air, white detachable beard and all, and it landed a
dozen paces away with open eyes and a look of amazement before the body had time to topple out of its dance.

So it was that the trauma was born—I owe the word to you
and Dr Doppeldorf. My wife wasted a lot of time between the
tranquillizers explaining to the child that after all it was only an
old man called Jeff Drew who had died and not Father Christmas. The papers did their best to contradict her with all the obvious headlines, 'Death of Father Christmas', and the like, and
the authorities contributed to the confusion by giving the old
man, who would have been on poor relief again in a few weeks'
time, a slap-up city funeral with mounted police and wreaths of
holly and a Christmas tree stuck up above the grave covered with
coloured lights, and there was a procession of school children,
though I would not let my son go. I wanted him to forget the affair as quickly as possible, and that is just what he hasn't done.
So now it is that at the age of twelve he has become the mock of
all his contemporaries; each year when December comes around
he suffers from endless practical jokes, and as a result he gets
into fights, which he can't win, how can he? For he's in a perpetual minority of one, because he believes that Father Christmas really existed. 'Of course he's real,' he says, a bit like an early
Christian, 'I saw him die.' He's dead, and so he's indestructible.
Please do what you can, Doctor . . .

1963

THE OTHER SIDE OF
THE BORDER

NOTE

I suppose most novelists' careers are littered with abandoned novels: some may be abandoned because the novelist has lost interest in the story or his characters: some because a more imperative demand-to-be-written pushes out the earlier mood. The other day, looking through a drawer, I came on the MS. of just such a novel, and as I read it the characters, the scene and the half-unfolded story seemed to me to have more interest than many tales of mine that had appeared fully dressed between covers. Why shouldn't this book too, I felt, have its chance? I could identify the year when I began to write it as probably 1936, after I had returned from a journey in Liberia: at any rate, if it has no other merit, the book seems to me stamped unmistakably with the atmosphere of the middle thirties—Hitler is still quite new, dictatorship is only a tang on the breeze blowing from Europe: in England is depression and a kind of Metroland culture.

An odd thing is that though I remember the characters in the book well—Hands, young Morrow, Billings—I can't remember what was going to happen to them. Why did I abandon the book? I think for two main reasons—because another book, *Brighton Rock,* was more insistent to be written, and because I realized that I had already dealt with the main character in a story called *England Made Me.* Hands, I realized, had the same origin as Anthony Farrent in that novel.

Another point interested me: since those days I have been back to the West African port described in Part Two and I realize now that this picture of the place, its whole atmosphere, couldn't be more 'wrong'. I spent a week there in 1936 before this novel was begun, but now I know the port from a year's residence. It is every bit as seedy, depressed and drab as I have described it, but in a totally different way. Denton of Part One on the other hand, which is the town in the Home Counties where I was born and brought up, seems to me right. Between the two lies the whole difference between the passport photograph and the family snapshot.

PART ONE: THE MAP

The first thing young Morrow noticed in the waiting-room was the Map. There it hung where you would naturally expect it in the new offices of the New Syndicate, representing the coast, the rivers running in parallel black threads from the interior, the mountains feathered on the northern border and the forest a splash of green over everything—representing too to Morrow a whole obscure state of mind, a mystery from which he felt he had at last escaped. He was home now. He could understand what went on. Movies were clear. He had a sudden feeling of sentiment for the word 'home', for words like 'the pictures', 'school', 'bus'. There was no obscurity about this varnished and glittering room, the pile of technical magazines upon the table full of advertisements for drills and ore crushers; he could hear the tugs hooting on the Mersey. His young face wore such expressions as 'Cheerio,' 'Glad to be back'. A woman opened the door and said, 'Mr Danvers can see you now.' She was, Morrow supposed, the General Manager's secretary, but she had much more the manner of a nurse—her voice was gentle, friendly and determined, and she gave him a kind of clinical glare as he passed her. Morrow went in.

Mr Danvers rose behind his desk and held out his hand. He hadn't changed at all in two years—time didn't move at home in the same way: he gripped with the same grip he had given Morrow the day he sailed; the signet ring made the same painful impression. And he was just as forthright as he had always been—there were lines Morrow had learnt at school about 'the good grey head that all men loved', which always came to mind.

Mr Danvers said, 'Well, young Morrow, I'm glad to see you, very glad. Take a chair. Help yourself to a cigarette.' He wore hospitality like a flower in the buttonhole: you felt he was going to ask you to smell it. He said, 'Don't think you've been forgotten these last two years. I've had reports of your work—very favourable reports—from Hands.'

It was as if that particular name had been dropped between them too soon; it fell with an effect of embarrassment, like a cup at a tea-party. They were both silent, and then Mr Danvers edged as it were away from the awkward sound. 'The Board have decided to raise your salary.'

'Didn't you get my letter?' Morrow asked.

'I discounted that,' Mr Danvers said gently.

'But I *have* resigned.'

'Forgive me,' Mr Danvers said, 'if I talk to you a little like a father. After all—I knew him. I sat under him.' He sketched in his tone of voice—full of dim respect and gentle memory and kindly amusement—the parsonage house which lay next door to his own rarely visited acres. He said, 'If you leave us, what can you do?'

'I shall find something,' Morrow said and shivered a little: it had been cold on the tug coming off in the early morning over the grey blowy Irish Sea.

'You've been ill,' Mr Danvers said. 'That's the truth of the matter.' He tried to slip the name through less obtrusively this time. '*He* wrote to us,' and then went quickly on, 'you've only to look in that glass.'

He *could* look in the glass: it hung there behind Mr Danvers' desk and attracted his gaze. He saw his own face—it looked the same to him as it had always done—because he'd lived with it. If it had changed, it had changed so gradually that he had never noticed, shaving in the lid of the biscuit tin when his glass had been broken, deliberately, by Hands. He was unhappy when he thought that he hadn't shed a continent from his face.

'You're quite yellow with fever,' Mr Danvers said. 'A skeleton. That attack of dysentery must have got you badly down. I really think it would be a good thing if you went and saw someone at the Hospital for Tropical Diseases. Have a blood test.

And then,' he sketched vaguely in the air, 'the fleshpots, you know. Fatten up.'

The secretary—she seemed after that advice more than ever like a nurse—put her head in at the door. 'Sir Frederick,' she announced softly.

'Ask him to wait just two minutes.' Mr. Danvers went on, rising from his chair, coming round to the front of his desk, holding out his threatening hand, 'The Board likes to look after its servants.'

'But there are things I've simply got to tell you,' Morrow said. 'The whole business—it's fantastic. The gold—and Hands himself—so many deaths—Colley—and then there's Billings.'

'Billings?'

'He must have written you about Billings. He picked him up on the English side of the border. The most appalling . . .'

'Oh, Billings. Of course I remember Billings. You must understand,' Mr Danvers said in a voice of reproof, 'I trust Hands' judgment—absolutely.'

'That's why I've resigned. You mustn't trust it too far. You've got to know—the Board have got to know—' He was taken with the attack of ague he'd been expecting all the morning. His teeth clicked like billiard balls. The secretary had left the door ajar and the draught had set him going.

'There, you see,' Mr Danvers justified himself. He rang the bell and told the secretary, 'My car will take Mr Morrow to his hotel.' He came and laid his hand on Morrow's shoulder. 'Such dreams,' he said. 'We'll talk about it all when you're better.'

'At least,' Morrow said, 'you'll let me write a report?'

'Of course. If you wish,' Mr Danvers said. 'We are always interested. . . .' The secretary stayed behind a moment, and Morrow in the waiting-room allowed himself to be drawn, with a feeling of obscure distress, towards the map. He had believed that back here everything would be very simple: he had resigned: he had his duty to do, and his young yellowed face was like an old intaglio of duty, cut symbolically for a signet ring. Loyalty and duty—they were the only qualities he had to live by, and now that he had resigned he owed no loyalty to Hands. Hands was there—on the map: they had drawn a little ring round

Hands in red ink: a little to the left of Zigita, up beyond Nica-boozu.

2

Hands wiped the soot and steam from the pane and peered out at Willesden Junction. It was safe, if they punched your ticket at Euston, to travel first, but you could never be quite sure. He had a sense of daring, gazing across at the gritty refreshment room—the sense of too many failures slipped from his shoulders: there were limitless possibilities for a man of his experience—experience in Africa, Central America, on the London Midland & Scottish. He felt for a while, all by himself in the first class, that he hadn't failed, he'd been experimenting, seeing life.

A ticket collector passed and for a moment Hands' face seemed to slide—the mouth weakened, the handsome too boyish face turned sullen, he aged perceptibly in seconds, you could see the lines coming out. Then the train began to move and all was well again. He took out his cigarette-case and lit up, as history slid by along the London Midland & Scottish line—an ancient castlework, a canal bridge built for a Jubilee, a pre-war Municipal building estate.

The whole line down to Denton was familiar to him—it was in a way his life, travelling up to the dentist, the pantomime, the oculist, to school: travelling up to catch this boat and that: travelling down it to home. The lights came out in the workmen's cottages: a man on a bicycle paused to light up: an old horse pushed jingling back into the dark dragging a barge, and the idea came to him. Ideas often came to him like that—out of the sooty air, in his bath, shaving. They were like a saint's voices—only they didn't as a rule lead to action good or bad. He didn't really hope for anything from this one—it was just a way of putting things to his father—'I've been getting into touch with various companies'—a hint of mystery and importance: not in his wildest dreams did it involve anyone like Morrow or Danvers or Billings or the hundred blacks whom Morrow calculated had died between 1936 and 1938.

He came breezily out at Denton with his third-class ticket: a cheery word to everyone, the ticket collector, the two porters, the man in the luggage room: he liked to imagine a kind of feudal atmosphere—'Master Hands comes home': he regretted that his father was not somebody other than a retired bank manager. He called 'Good evening' to the single taxi-driver, and then thought—why not blow a shilling on a cab? It didn't look well to have to walk home every evening.

His father was at dinner in the little dark dining-room—the rissoles which always followed the day after the joint—but he must have heard the taxi draw up, for he looked questioningly up. Hands could read on his face a kind of incredulous hope. He was not a man to take a taxi except on great occasions. He said, 'You've had a good day? You've found something?' The room was all carved mahogany and gilt frames and pale water colours: rhododendrons pressed up towards the window, and you could see over the low garden wall the leaning graves of an old cemetery. Nobody was buried there now: only dim inscriptions spoke of falling asleep and peace and hope of resurrection. A cat sat on a flat stone looking in.

'I've made contacts,' Hands said, sitting down and looking distastefully at the rissoles. 'Some big companies. It's a long story.'

'Are they interested—I mean have they any vacancies?'

'This isn't going to be a job of that kind,' Hands said. 'This is going to be more—' The dream grew as he talked. '—more of an administrative job, men under me. It's what I've always wanted, you know—'

But Mr Hands wasn't listening: he was eating a rissole: his old tired grey face had peculiar nobility. For nearly seventy years he had been believing in human nature, against every evidence—it hadn't been good for his promotion in the bank. He was a Liberal, he thought men could govern themselves if they were left alone to it, that wealth did not corrupt and that statesmen loved their country. All that had marked his face until it was a kind of image of what he believed the world to be. But it was breaking up now, since his wife had died and his son had begun to come—regularly—home with his excuses and breezy anecdotes and unjustified contempt. If he lived long enough his face might become more probable, more like the other people's world. He said wearily, 'You've had a tiring day. Shall I get out a little burgundy?'

'Oh, no,' Hands said. 'I'm in training.'

'Harvest burgundy won't hurt you.'

'No, really. I'm not drinking.' He sighed at the cabbage and a very faint smell of whisky percolated through the room. He smelt it himself: it infuriated him. How could a fellow succeed with such a father? Smelling his breath, grudging the taxi, disbelieving. He said stubbornly, 'You know—what I've always needed is—well, to show I can lead men.'

'Can you?' Mr Hands said.

The clock over a black carved mahogany mantel began to strike. 'You wait and see,' Hands said. He remembered the old childish saying that you keep the face you make when a clock strikes—for ever. He tightened his mouth.

'Well,' Mr Hands said hopelessly, 'leaders seem cheap these days.' He began to finish his cabbage: he hadn't troubled to ask about the idea: 'The *Manchester Guardian* today . . .' possibilities of hate moved behind the nobility as he said, 'the Fascists . . .'

'It's no good being a Liberal in these times,' Hands said. He began to lecture his father. 'You don't realize here in Denton. I've been about the world. . . .'

Mr Hands said nothing. He pushed his plate a little on one side and rang the bell: he didn't look at Hands: at the other end of the room where his gaze could unobtrusively rest hung an enlarged tinted photograph of his wife—a high whalebone collar, grey dress, long hair, cheeks stained a wax-like pink and brown spaniel too-devoted eyes—devoted but not to Mr Hands. Mr Hands knew to whom that devotion went. He said absentmindedly to Hands, 'You think there may be a vacancy?'

Hands got furiously up. He said, 'I'm going out.'

'Aren't you going to wait for the blancmange?'

'No. I want to think. I want some air.' A man needed encouragement: he had never, he told himself, had encouragement since his mother died. 'I'm going to take a walk.'

He walked out past the rhododendrons and the forgotten graves into Metroland. Denton sprawled in red villas up the hillside, but there remained in the long High Street, between the estate agents, the cafés and the two super-cinemas, dwindling signs of the old market town—there was a crusader's helmet in the church. People are made by places and this town had formed Hands: he called it 'home', dim sentiment moved in the summer evening among the red brick villas, but it had no real hold on anyone. You bought a season ticket and stayed away. Smoke moved into the sky behind the photographer's roof and showed the 8:52 was in. He would write those letters . . . you never knew . . . and after all the stuff existed, or so he understood. You couldn't live in a place like this: it was somewhere to which you returned for sleep and rissoles by the 7:50 or the 8:52: people had lived here once and died with their feet crossed to show they had been on a crusade, but now . . . He stared into the photographer's window: yellowing photographs peered out of the diamonded Elizabethan pane—a genuine pane, but you couldn't believe it because of the Tudor Café across the street. He saw a face he knew in a wedding group, but it had been taken five years ago: there was something passé about the waistcoat: with a train every hour to town there was no need to be photographed at home these days—except of course for passports in a hurry. He couldn't count how many passport photographs old Millet had made of him.

He pushed the door open (Millet never locked up) and the bell jingled. There was a smell of chemicals, and in the dim bare light an antique pillar of plaster with a velvet top to rest the elbow on. Something hooded stood in a corner, and a metal clamp to fix the neck in. It wasn't up to date, the studio, but old Millet had had a flair for character in his day. As much as the crusader he was a relic of the time when Denton was a place in which to live. He came out now from an inner room, thin and courtly in pince-nez, wearing a velvet jacket—he used to represent the arts in Denton. His grey hair was very smooth and fine and he walked with a stoop—a scholar of the night-school and the institute.

He said, 'Ah, Mr Hands, another passport photograph?'

'Well not exactly, not yet. I came in for a chat, you know.'

'Sit down,' Millet said, 'sit down.' But there was nothing to sit on but a photographic chair, a stiff carved regal seat. The photographer leant on the pillar and said, 'Are you off again?' The door into the inner room was open. He said, 'Mr Hands is a great wanderer. You ought to write a book about all those places you've been in,' and then explained, 'My niece in there. She can't come out. She's sprained her ankle. Now where is it to be, Mr Hands?' He listened hungry for experience.

'Africa,' Hands said. 'The West Coast.'

'And when are you off?'

'It's not fixed definitely.'

'Those will be wild parts?'

'Oh,' Hands said, 'there's ivory, of course. And diamonds. Gold— You have to have men with you you can trust—in an emergency.' He seemed to brood on actual fact—'Old Colley.' He had an audience at last: in the inner room he could just see the girl's face listening. It wasn't a pretty face, and it wasn't very young. He would have liked something a bit better, but it was an audience. 'There are chances in those parts for a man who knows the niggers.'

'They—take handling, I suppose?' Millet said.

'You've got to let them know who's master. I remember once,' he said, and as he started on the long fake tale he felt happy and ready for anything because no one here knew of the last jobs and the borrowed money and the accumulated failures. The whole world was at his feet while the photographer leant on the plaster pillar and under the reading-lamp in the inner room the woman raised her compliant and patient face, the kind of face you feel has known too much unimportant pain, the sprained ankle, the disappointment at the local hop, the varicose veins, a series of small humiliations uncomplainingly borne. 'It was up in the mountains,' Hands said, 'beyond Tapi,' and like Othello he sat there on the hard nobbly throne speaking of pigmies and poisoned arrows, the wild elephant and the leopard and the hidden treasures in the rocks, to old Millet and to Desdemona. He held them fast, he could feel their attention like praise, while the feet of the season ticket-holders went by on the pavement, and the moon swam up above the flinty church and the Tudor Café.

3

The answers came regularly in by the morning and evening post—or else didn't come in at all. The names on the envelopes created a good impression. With so much correspondence nobody could accuse him of not seeking work. They all contained roughly speaking the same reply: the company thanked Mr Hands for his interest, but was unwilling at the moment to increase its commitments. It did not feel any useful purpose could be served by an interview. Hands had borrowed a typewriter when he sent off his original letter and sometimes, for the sake of appearance, he would put in twenty minutes at the machine rap-tapping imaginary replies. 'Hands,' he would tap, 'Hands. Hands. Hands.' Line after line of it, and sometimes the date. 'March 2. March 2. March two. March Two.' Then he came down to lunch with ruffled hair and accepted a glass of harvest burgundy.

The chief companies never replied to his letter: Hands respected them for it. Later he didn't trouble to open all the envelopes marked this and that company or trust. He tore them into little bits in the quiet of his room and went out for a walk past the municipal housing estate, the Norman castle (a tiny piece of ruined wall scheduled as an ancient monument), the watercress beds. He walked by himself and dreamed enormous dreams. Sometimes Millet's niece figured like Cophetua's beggar maid and received his love humbly, sometimes plunging heroically to his death he came out on the other side where his mother waited for him with approval. They looked down together from the region of glory at old Mr Hands—or the Prime Minister—putting up a monument. He was like an adolescent struck suddenly with the curse of physical age: the ignobility of the years weakened his mouth while he dreamed.

He very nearly tore up the letter from the New Syndicate unread, but his fingers had got accustomed to a certain size, and this letter seemed a larger one than usual. In fact, it wasn't: the paper was thicker that was all; and again he nearly tore it up, seeing the usual three or four lines of type. And then he wished he had, reading, 'We shall be pleased to discuss further the subject of your letter of February 12 ult. if you will call at this office between 2 and 5 on Wednesday, March 5 prox. . . .'

It was like having a bluff called at cards. Somebody had taken his suggestion seriously, somebody would demand details, samples, geological facts. His face flushed with his future humiliation. He was frightened. If Mr Hands had not come into breakfast and seen the letter he might have torn it up. But in any case it would have spoiled the dreams: with that letter ignored he couldn't have gone on telling himself—oh, magnificent things, sitting among the gorse bushes on the heath watching the cars go by like common life on the road at the bottom of the hill. He went to the public library and read up all he could: it wasn't much: 'The Geological Formation of Sierra Leone': a book about the Leopard Society in French Guinea: *A White Woman Among Cannibals* by Maisie Whitfield: nothing at all on that obscure republic of which he claimed expert knowledge. He looked at a map of Africa—it didn't mean a thing: he was up against truth. He felt hatred of Mr Danvers who had signed the letter: he read sarcasm into the reply. 'By God,' he thought without conviction, 'I'll make them pay my fare.'

Liverpool looked grey and middle-aged (it could never look old): the wind blew from the Mersey and you couldn't get away from the hooting of the steamers under the low and stormy sky. Rain blew round shabby street corners and suddenly ceased and a pale heartless sun, like a paper streamer flung by a stranger, shone on a tug and a toss of leaden water. Then the thin rain blew again. Nobody knew where the Syndicate offices were. Everybody said, 'I'm a stranger here myself': it was a city of strangers who caught tugs and trains and got away again as quickly as they could. Streets led nowhere: it was like a small town which just went on and on instead of stopping, growing away from the Mersey like a natural formation, a coral reef. In a small news-agent's yard he caught sight of two apple trees, bare and bleak and sooty and barren.

He ran the Syndicate to earth at last—up a side street near the docks, a red brick building with stained glass windows on the lowest floor, a date in chiselled brick over the door, 1873, and a yellow stone close by: 'This foundation stone was laid by Jonas E. Wallbrook, Lord Mayor of Liverpool on Feb. 14, 1873'. There was an insurance office on the ground floor, and on the second floor a philatelic agency, and between the two the New Syndicate. The lift was very small and was worked by a rope.

Hands wore his best suit and an old Mill Hill tie. A little whisky loosened his tongue. 'Not very good weather,' he said to the liftman. They ground laboriously upward.

'It's Liverpool weather,' the man said.

His stomach failed him on the landing: it began to rumble—he had had no appetite for lunch and the liquor and soda water rolled like a barrel inside him. 'I beg your pardon,' he said to the woman who opened the frosted door.

'Have you an appointment with Mr Danvers?'

'Oh, yes, yes. My name is Hands.' He smiled confidentially, he had a way with women—but again his stomach rumbled and his face sullenly set.

The waiting-room was tiny: a small French-polished table, two hard chairs, a copy *The Ironworker, Punch,* and the *Tatler* for January 1932. He opened it at random and came on a picture of deck-chairs and umbrellas, three men in bathing-slips and a girl. 'Mr "Jimmy" Danvers,' he read, 'the popular managing director of the recently formed New Reef Syndicate disporting himself at Juan les Pins'—a baldish head, a high light on a stomach. . . . It had been treasured a long while—everyone was grinning in the sunlight, four years younger, full of all kinds of hopes. The Syndicate apparently had not progressed. Hands went to the window and looked out: a tram went by, sparking slowly: between two warehouses you could see a few grey inches of water moving from left to right: smoke blew backwards and forwards and the soot fell on the Mersey, on the Royal Adelphi Hotel, on apple trees in a back yard.

'Mr Danvers will see you now.'

Hands exchanged greetings with a four-year-old photograph: Mr Danvers hadn't changed at all. He said, 'It's good of you to come all this way . . .' He took out a box of cigars. 'We were very interested.' Hands watched him, waiting for the awkward question and the afternoon deepened and it never came. The word 'gold' wasn't even mentioned: Mr Danvers called it 'it'.

'I've got just the man to send with you,' he said. 'A very trustworthy boy. I want to do him a good turn. His name's Morrow. You'll need someone else too.' The lights came out all over Liverpool: they said Booth's for the Teeth and Codling's Cough Cure: a gull fell out of the sky past a huge glass of harvest burgundy, rose and turned and made for the Mersey. A siren wailed and wailed and Hands said with a touch of bewilderment, loneliness and horror, 'There's a man called Colley. We know each other . . . I'd like to take him too.' There were things he couldn't understand: everything had gone too easily: he might have been selling a gold brick in the Strand to an Australian. He said with bewilderment, 'I thought you'd need to see . . .'

'We've already had samples of it,' Mr Danvers said, 'from another source. A Dutchman. Poor fellow he died—of yellow fever. That's why your letter seemed so timely. We want—the torch handed on.'

'Yellow fever,' Hands said.

'All the best things in life are dangerous,' Mr Danvers said. He opened the drawer of a desk and took out a cardboard box which had once held Egyptian cigarettes. Out of it he picked a small lump of greyish rock. 'You notice the signs,' he said. 'It's there, all right: no doubt of it. Take it. Look at it. The stratification.'

The small grey lump lay in Hands' palm and he thought—he's got me now: I've got to go on, and with a lightening of the heart— It was damned clever: to deceive a man like Danvers who's in the business: it won't be hard after this to deceive him awhile longer, and when he finds out—well—I'll have had my salary for a few weeks at least.

He fingered the stone—was this gold? He had no idea.

4

Colley, standing in the great steel coach station, felt the familiar sadness and unrest of departure. A modern clock-face without numerals, a chromium milk-bar, a faint smell of petrol: they took him back nevertheless to the stone quays and the slap of water, the oil and the seagulls of his usual loneliness. He was only going a few hundred miles north, but that's how new places, new people, always made him feel. It was no good hanging about for half an hour. The grinding of the gears as the buses drew in and out of their lines got on his nerves. Light glittered back from the steel sides, people sat deep down in seats, like expensive theatre stalls, and peered out at him; sometimes they munched chocolate; they looked warm and sleepy and content as if they were definitely going to some place, into the smoke and dust and night outside Victoria; it seemed just as important as when a liner leaves the dock.

It was too familiar. He wanted a drink. There was no one he had to kiss and grin at through the glass. It had been just the same when he was seventeen and went off to Brazil to take the place of a clerk who had died of yellow fever. All the good-byes were always said in Surrey (they became on each occasion more perfunctory), and even that first time he had found his way to the mail-boat's bar while everyone else was throwing paper ribbons. And it was the same the time he went to Africa, except that then the bar had not been open; he'd lain down on his bunk with a comic paper, without the heart to turn the leaf so that now the one dreadful joke was impressed for ever on his mind: a man hunting thrown in a ditch and a yokel bending over a hedge and a piece of dialogue he couldn't even yet understand. You'd think you'd get used to new jobs and going away from the places you know, but the loneliness repeats itself every time.

He went into a bar in the Wilton Road and had a b. and s. He couldn't stand Scotch any more; it had nearly rotted him in Africa, that and the iced crème de menthe the swells all served after every meal. It was one of those big bogus panelled bars you find near railway stations; there was a different tartan on every panel, and people kept coming in and out in a hurry because they had trains to catch: young City men with rolled umbrellas and double-breasted waistcoats on their way to Oxted or Hayward's Heath. When he had drunk two brandies he felt better; he said 'Good evening' to a pair of them, but they just looked him over and went on talking about an interim dividend Dunlop's had declared.

He had another brandy. It seemed to him that he knew them better than anyone else in the world, that he had lived with them all his life, from seventeen to thirty-three, first fellow-novices in strange employments, then senior clerks and eventually in their steady influential progress, the managers who got rid of him. They were bright and bonhomous with each other, they came from the same school, they'd seen the same show the week before at the Prince of Wales, their wives were on the best of terms, and they would no more have trusted each other in business than they would have trusted him. And to him they wouldn't even speak: that was the difference. He knew what was wrong; you can always disguise a frayed sleeve; no one can see much of your socks and your shirt's well out of sight; it's the shoes which give you away. That's why strange women always look at your shoes.

Well, he thought, I'd better be getting on. The bus left at 8:30 and was due in Liverpool some time in the early morning. He couldn't afford another brandy and he wouldn't sleep if he had one. Three brandies were enough to give him the courage of good-bye. It was not that he had been particularly happy in London, but you couldn't help making certain contacts if it was only with a particular table in an A.B.C.; you couldn't even help, perennially at this time of year, wandering back and forth from the Achilles statue to the Marble Arch, feeling certain hopes; they sprang, like the hardy daffodil, regularly to life, the hope of a human relationship based on something which wasn't lust and wasn't interest.

He hated the world—that was the permanent, the first article of his creed—you couldn't help drinking, you couldn't help moving on, but the emotion which made every departure a sad one suggested that somewhere—something—he had no terms for it—there existed. . . . He pushed his coins across the counter and went out into the cool and grimy winter night. The sky paled, like vapour, above Battersea Power Station. Somebody was selling flowers outside the coach station, and a bus pushed its way out into the night.

Flower scent and petrol and the smoke from Pimlico chimneys, the vague spring air, forcing its way with the defenceless persistence of self-seeded grasses between concrete setts, combined to touch his brain with hope. All the jobs he had held up and down the seedy margins of strange continents had left impressions which came up at this time of year into his sour consciousness with an effect of sadness and for some reason beauty: the face of a stoker on a mail boat in '31 and of a dago child; they had mounted for a breath of air on to the steerage deck; he saw their patient lamp-lit faces as they sat side by side on a coil of rope and panted in the heavy night; a one-armed boy in Sierra Leone kneeling at Benediction in a tin church, who had cut his own arm off with a knife when he had broken it gathering palm nuts; a small African village where everyone had died of yellow fever and lay, horribly disfigured but with an air of extreme fidelity, each with his own family, in his own hut. A man in a bowler hat ran by with a suitcase calling out to someone behind, 'We'll be late. We'll be late.'

He too apparently was going north, an elderly man bound (he wanted to show it in his manner) on important business to do with Diesel engines, but not quite important enough to pay his fare by train. None of them in the coach was of *that* importance; a priest sat in the very front seat where he would see nothing but night pressing up against the windscreen: he was a stout young-old man with a little black bag in the rack and an umbrella: he was prepared to sit quiet all the night long reading in a book of devotion; the important man sat with a thin shabby clerk-like companion and talked in a loud voice about the Diesel engines.

Colley picked his way down the centre of the coach to the only empty pair of seats. An elderly woman with a basket of sandwiches and bananas explained to a younger one, 'You got to be prepared for trouble when Ted knows.' A pack of young men (perhaps they were a football team) had filled the back seats with suitcases and paper bags: they blocked the door bellowing with laughter. They were being seen off by two men with grey moustaches and tweed caps who kept on repeating, 'You boys remember—': and the young men slapped them on the back and tried to punch them in the ribs and said, 'You bet.' They had been drinking a little; when a whistle blew and they turned back into the gangway the coach was scented with their stale beery breath. Nobody else could get at the door: a young man outside pressed a pale miserable face to the glass, scrabbling with his fingernails, trying to convey some sense of tenderness and assurance to a girl in black who had been crying. She couldn't get the window down to speak to him; she looked towards the door, but 'You boys remember—' the men outside said, and something about 'Keep on the ball.' Colley leant across a schoolboy and pulled down her window. She didn't thank him, nor did the young man, the whistle had blown, they had no time, they leant towards each other with urgent messages they hadn't time to speak as the bus ground out between the white lines, swung round past the milk-bar and the fruit machines. 'What ho, she bumps,' the young men shouted, coming up the gangway. You could tell that they too were not important enough for the railway fare. They weren't a League team.

It was just like any other sailing at night: the lamps slipping away from you, the turned faces, swinging round by the high stone palace wall in Grosvenor Gardens like a dockside, out into the churn of small tugs and tramps by Hyde Park Corner. Even the young men at the back were momentarily silent as London dragged slowly backward, a kind of summary of London: the Achilles statue, the queue outside the Regal, a policeman, a coffee stall, a Guardsman, and a man in evening dress making tentative passes at a girl in a taxi and then the long wounded length of the Finchley Road, villas and flats and beyond Hendon a patch of grass and a pile of potato peelings, and more villas and a bigger patch of grass, a hole in a field full of old bicycle wheels and parts of car bodies, the country.

The girl sat with her eyes closed and her mouth tight shut as if she were repeating to herself, 'I am asleep. I am asleep.' The schoolboy ate chocolate. A voice from near the front said sharply, importantly, reprovingly, 'Fifty horse-power.' England was like a magnet which had lost its power. There was nothing any longer to hold you to it. It shook you off. Colley thought: I've stuck it long enough for a good reference, and now I may as well shoot it abroad again. But this time he didn't even know what kind of a job it was: except that old Hands had written, 'It might suit you.'

He had a pair of seats to himself. He was the only one who had. He wondered whether there was something in his appearance which kept people away (his shoes were hidden: and in any case these other people's shoes were not so good themselves), but soon he realized the reason. He was seated over the wheel. He was jarred by every unevenness on the Great North Road. They had all been more knowledgeable than he. Like the first time at anything, the novice was 'done'; the time he went to Brazil, he remembered, he had been left the worst place on the whole deck for his canvas chair. Now he was always first at that: the sunniest or the most sheltered corner was his before people had finished saying good-bye. If you had to compete even for your smallest comfort, compete he would with the quickest of them. 'I said oil-burning,' the elderly man screamed above the din of bottom gear as the coach dragged up a long Chiltern hill. The priest whispered softly his devotions, his plump lips hardly moving, vibrating gently on his seat with the engine. The spring night blossomed under the headlamps, a twig of budding beech scraped the windows from a chalky bank, and Colley thought with misery and a kind of thwarted murderous love in his heart, 'Competition. I'll give them competition. Every man for himself'; as if he hadn't already been beaten at *that* game in Brazil, in Africa.

5

'I could recognize at once,' Mr Danvers told the reporter, 'that Hands was a man of extraordinary character. Take a cigar. That's right. And put one in your pocket. What was I saying? Yes. He's an adventurer of the old school. A bit of Sir Walter Raleigh.'

'But Raleigh didn't find gold,' the reporter said.

'Ah,' Mr Danvers countered him quickly, 'but he didn't have proper support. You can take my word for it, the gold is there—you don't imagine we haven't seen satisfactory specimens.'

'And how did Hands come to approach you?'

'I'm going to be frank,' Mr Danvers said. 'I'm not going to let discretion spoil a romantic story. I said, didn't I, that Hands was an adventurer—in the best sense of the word, of course.'

'Like Raleigh,' the reporter said.

'You should hear the stories he has to tell. A rolling stone, you know, and he hasn't gathered any moss—except, of course, the best kind of all, friendships. Worked for others. Threw up the job when he got the wanderlust, moved on. Seeing the world. Learning to deal with all kinds of men. He quelled a strike once—single-handed. Well, he's been home a month or two—and he got restless. A man who hates inaction. And so he thought he'd capitalize his experience. He brought to mind the time he tumbled on this gold in West Africa—the government wasn't doing anything about it—it's a half-caste government, you know. Medieval conditions. Only a few Dutch prospectors were snooping around. There was a big chance for a concession. And so he wrote to a number of companies offering his services. He knows the country, knows the natives, he used to work just over the border in British territory, he's even had contact with members of the government. God knows what he was doing down there. Above all he can handle niggers. In a country like that, it's all-important. Undeveloped. No roads. Everything has to begin from scratch. It's a case of men, not machinery. When you cross over from British Territory, you go back a hundred years. To the time of Stanley, Livingstone,' Mr Danvers said, in-accurately, squinting at his notes.

'What about the other companies?'

'I'm going to be frank again,' Mr Danvers said. 'They didn't believe in him. But then they didn't even grant him an interview. I was sceptical myself till I talked to him. He told me he had had only two other replies, and they were formal notes saying the companies were not considering extending their activities.'

'Of course—to finance this—'

'A new issue of two hundred thousand Ordinary shares. We've taken a page in your paper tomorrow—as I imagine you know.'

'And Hands is going out himself?'

'Of course. This isn't ordinary mining work, young man. It's pioneering: it's adventure. That's the point I want you to make in the paper. Will you take a whisky and soda?'

'I don't drink,' the reporter said.

'Candidly,' Mr Danvers said, 'I want—a Legend. I've spoken to your advertisement manager and you'll be given space. I want Hands—made a figure. It's not only a question of selling shares—I don't want you to think that—it's a question of politics. These niggers need to be impressed. In a way, you know, the man who leads this expedition is an ambassador—the ambassador of Europe, of civilization.'

'Has he technical knowledge of mining?'

'That won't be his main job. His work is to lead the way, handle the men, cut forests, make roads. What an adventure,' Mr Danvers exclaimed; 'if I was a young man I'd go myself.'

'He'll be accompanied by experts?'

'They'll follow, as it were, on his heels.'

'Could I see a map?'

Mr Danvers spread out across his desk the big white sheet—more blank space than anything else.

'There are no reliable maps,' he said, 'yet. We'll have to make our own.' The map was marked 'United States War Department.' The reporter leant over it, pad in hand making notes—it didn't mean a thing to him: it was a paragraph to fill a column. He saw a white space somewhere to the right marked Cannibals, a few strange names like Mendi and Boozie which would sound well on paper, he saw the bottom of a column and a crosshead.

Mr Danvers leant beside him with a possessive smile and bent a double-jointed thumb on a mountain range. 'Up there,' he said, 'we'll get the gold. The problem,' he smeared his thumb towards the sea, 'is whether to bring it down here or take it across the border into British territory. And up here,' the thumb moved north, 'is French territory.' He fell silent, while the reporter made notes: a map is like a crystal in which men see many different things—success and failure, suicide in a second-rate hotel and a government contract, perverse loves and strange homes, a snake in a lavatory. Mr Danvers saw an office building and Doric columns, inlaid furniture, electric clocks and six floors: he saw two hundred thousand Ordinary shares at a premium: he saw no gold.

6

Mr Hands said, 'A moment while I get the encyclopaedia.'

He opened the map of West Africa with an immense desire to understand. The country was very small: 250 miles perhaps from the French border to the sea, 300 miles of seaboard, and the scale was 200 miles to an inch. There was no separate map. Only six towns were marked. He thought of Latvia, Luxembourg, the League of Nations, a picture postcard of Brussels Town Hall. He had no conception whatever of heat, dryness, desolation.

Hands said, 'Of course they treat their own people like dirt.'

Mr Hands thought of suffering minorities everywhere, and the Treaty of Versailles, and looking down at the map he thought, It's a job, he's got a job again, this time perhaps everything will go well, he'll stay and make money, I shall be proud of him, I shall say, 'My son who is the manager . . . writes . . .' and he felt a little shame at the jubilation which moved in his heart.

Hands himself hardly bothered to look. He knew what he would see—that rough rectangular shape was a bluff which hadn't been called, the jackpot if he had the courage to hold his hand, it was success. The world was going to hear of Hands, he was smart, my God how smart, my God. He was afraid. He said, 'I think I'll go and have a word with old Millet,' and with an uncertain swagger, he moved down the Metroland High Street, past the Moorish super-cinema, the dead Crusader and the Tudor Café towards his only listeners.

PART TWO: THE EXPEDITION

Billings wore black in the blinding West African heat: it wasn't respect for the dead minister; it was—paradoxically—because he didn't want to be noticed. Billings trod through the world like an Indian hunter—but the twigs always broke under his feet. In England this suit was really inconspicuous: he was so used to it that he felt on the ship to Africa people would look at him if he changed and wore white, would observe more closely the pigeon breast, the dry and spotty skin, the bloodshot eyes. And then, when he landed in his dusty black and people looked, passing by in their Palm Beach suits, pride wouldn't allow him to change. 'The damned outsider,' he imagined them saying, 'he didn't know beforehand what a white man wears, but he's copying us now.'

He stood there in the tin-roofed church and looked round—the small bare crossless altar, the yellow pitch-pine benches, the big tin tank for total immersion. It was a kind of home. Here he had had authority, holding out the money bag to the blacks. Midday struck outside from the fake Norman church, and the sun weighed down on the tin roof: somewhere outside a steamer wailed. The hymns were still up for the minister's funeral: he changed the numbers ready for Sunday—it was like a gesture to England—Billings had taken over. He dipped his hand in the tank: it hadn't been emptied since the last baptism because of drought: the water was warm and dusty.

Then he went out into the vertical sun, into the shabby street of tin-roofed stores. Nobody was about: the hammocks droned in inner rooms, and the birds of prey squatted like domestic pigeons on the roofs, turning their little moron heads this way and that, spying for carrion. One rose, flapping the midday air with serrated dusty wings, and made across the roofs for the butcher's yard where a dozen of its fellows rooted like turkeys: the others looked down at Billings—black clothes, black ministerial hat—walking with the obsequious pomp of a priest at a funeral. He looked up and met the appraising gaze: they might have been saying as they leant their heads together for confidences, 'He'll do in a few more years. But too much skin and bone.' He thought of death under the awful sun and Mr Baines who had petered out last week while he prayed impromptu by the bed. It was three days now since he had cabled home. He thought defiantly of the emptiness of that death: the consolation of religion—the harmonium in the sitting-room for socials, himself sticking half-way through a prayer. It was a good death, no mummery about it.

He side-stepped away from the fake Norman cathedral. The cross above the door was like an evil eye to Billings: he hated the too eloquent symbols of religion: they seemed to mock him like a Palm Beach suit with lack of breeding—a 'gentleman's religion'. God was a bare room. God was pitch-pine and an undraped table and a piece of dry bread. Between bread and wafer a great gulf was fixed—the bread stuck in the throat for salvation, the wafer melted easily for damnation. The bishop came out of the cathedral and said 'Good morning' pleasantly to Billings, and Billings grunted back. You wait, he thought, you wait: within another thirty years they would both 'see', and he quivered in the secret pride of his own salvation, while the sweat gathered and dripped under the black cloth.

He went into the post office: the big Negro behind the counter watched him insolently: he too belonged to the gentlemen's religion.

Billings said, 'I'm expecting a cable.'

The black wore a clean white suit: he looked Billings up and down—he always did. 'What name?' he asked though he knew it as well as his own, and leaning arrogantly back in his swivel chair, he handed a penny through a window to a small girl outside. 'Three oranges,' he said. 'You can keep the change.'

'Billings.'

'Nothing,' the black said, but as Billings turned, he called after him, 'Hi, wait a moment. There may be something.'

He knew very well there was—the cable from England. He even knew the contents—there was a sneer and a satisfaction in his manner that broke the news. Billings took the envelope in his hand and went out. He had cabled back to the mission centre announcing the minister's death and suggesting, on account of his knowledge of the congregation, that he himself should take the dead man's place: he had spent a great deal on that cable—there was so much to be conveyed—a proper grief and ambition to serve.

He made his way through the siesta-empty street towards his home, but it was less a home than the chapel—the functional rectangular dwelling of God. The sun beat on the black hat and the expected misery.

His hut was raised a foot from the ground because of rats and ants. Outside hung an old photographic sign, a bathing beauty spotted by heat and damp. He could develop films but few people came to Billings for that purpose. No tourists spent much time in this British colony: only at long intervals a cruising steamer stayed for a few hours and people came on shore with Kodaks and snapped—a vulture, the Governor's residence, a Negro woman rolling home from church in her Manchester cotton. But *their* films they kept for London: they didn't trust Billings, though he advertised 'Films developed in six hours'. Only an occasional prospector brought his pack—and a few prosperous blacks—a wedding in Wellesley Street, the opening of the Kru Town court.

And yet a stale smell of hypo always seeped out from under his door—from the dark room—lavatory—to mix and peter out in the fish smell from the market. If I were minister, Billings thought (so long as he didn't open the cable the news mightn't be so bad after all—the committee at home must need time for a decision), if I were minister . . . It meant nearly a pound a week from the collection, it meant his black suit, as it were, regularized, it meant marriage dues and baptisms and authority. In time he could even move out of the damp heat of the town to the European station.

He pushed the door open, and a mongrel puppy, hairless and pink, squirmed on its belly to his feet. It had misbehaved under the table and craved forgiveness, but he couldn't bother with it now. He stood among the advertisements for Kodak and Agfa and opened the cable. It was very short. 'B. Moss answering call. Arriving 16th. Please make arrangements.' He looked out of the window and saw a taxi bouncing down towards the harbour, the air was spotted with buzzards, they moved imperceptibly across the hot immaculate blue. He began to tear the cable up in very small pieces, his fingers worked faster and faster, the scraps fell round the plump and cringing puppy—an epileptic faintness seized him, he said, 'My God, my God,' and clutched the table-edge. The table shook, shook, shook: the heat flapped down on him. Then he was well again, facing life—the little stand of yellowed home-made picture postcards—a Negro woman in Manchester cotton, the Governor's residence—the smell of puppy and hypo—the sweat pouring down under the black cloth. Life for a moment had been frozen by failure, but now it thawed, it dripped on.

He became conscious that a Negro was watching him from the step. He said furiously, 'What do you want?'

'My pictures,' the man said, the voice hollow and toothless like a child's.

'They aren't ready. Come back tomorrow.'

To work, Billings thought, was to pray. He had to begin praying all over again. He kicked the puppy and went on into the dark room—a wash-basin, a shelf, a lavatory seat, a red glass window. He hung his hat on a peg, unpacked a roll of film and bent over the shallow tray of chemicals. He had no interest in the dark strip of film: he weaved it to and fro through the hypo, until another person's life began to show in fits and starts—the negative life where black is white and right is left, but his own positive life shut him in with its unequivocal injustice. He couldn't be certain that B. Moss would ever require his help with the collection: another man might be asked to take it up.

He lifted the film out of the hypo too soon—the white faces of the blacks glowed faintly like transparent insects—and began to wash the negative. He worked absentmindedly (his pictures yellowed within a year) in the red glare of the window. Somebody knocked on his door, but he paid no attention. There were two places where he could be alone with his pride and his resentment—the chapel and the dark room. In the chapel he talked to God and in the dark room he spoke to his own past—the child flung into the water to sink or swim, the scared boy in the playground; he listened to voices saying, 'Creepy Billings' and a woman's appalling laughter. He did not pity himself: he brought up the images as a Jesuit may bring up the images of his Saviour's suffering—to steel himself. They were a discipline which one day would have its value. He would become impervious to contempt.

Again the knock on the door. He hung the negative up to dry and went out into the shop. 'Why,' he said and hesitated, 'it's Mr—'

'Five years ago,' the stranger said, 'and Anderson's store. Don't you remember, Billings, that night . . .'

'It's Hands,' Billings said without enthusiasm.

'I'm staying at the Grand.'

'The Grand?'

'I'm in the money now,' Hands said. He took off his big military-looking khaki sun-helmet and exposed himself for Billings' inspection—the new drill suit, the club tie. He said, 'What a crowd they are up there. Such starch. It might be Government House. I thought I'd slip away and see old Billings. Old Billings will have a bottle poked away.'

An odd expression twisted Billings' face: a sour taste, a happy memory, an unwelcome secret—you couldn't tell. 'Five years,' he said. 'A lot happens in five years.'

'Another window broken in the public library. Anderson sold out to Bates. They've put a pillar box in Gladstone Street. You can't tell me. I only landed this morning but I've been looking round.'

'Things happen to people,' Billings said.

'And here's the cupboard. Let's see what you've got.' He pulled it open—one empty dusty shelf, on another Agfa and Kodak films, a bottle of fruit, Heinz beans, sardines, a tin of Cambridge sausages. 'You don't say,' Hands said, 'you're out of it.'

'I found Christ,' Billings said. 'Didn't they tell you that at the Grand?'

Hands said uncomfortably, 'I didn't hear a word.'

'Of course,' Billings said, 'you never mentioned you were coming here. The street's empty, isn't it? Siesta time. You slipped along.'

'If you mean I'm ashamed—'

'You always were ashamed,' Billings said.

'I always liked you.'

'In secret.'

'Like you liked Christ,' Hands said. He shut the cupboard door. 'What the hell,' he said, 'don't let's quarrel the first minute. I came along,' he lied, 'to ask you to dinner—to meet Colley— you remember Colley—and Morrow, he's new . . .' He hesitated, 'And my wife.'

'You married?' Billings said.

'It's as you say—things happen to people.'

Again the secret look of misery or delight forked Billings' mouth. He said, 'It wouldn't be any harm to celebrate *that*.'

'You've got a bottle?'

'For medical purposes,' Billings said. He went through to his bedroom and fished under his bed, brought out a bottle of cheap brandy. 'I get the toothache,' Billings said. 'It's neuralgia. There's nothing a dentist can do. Sometimes it nearly makes me mad, grinding away. You'll excuse me if I've only got a cup to offer you, but I don't have many visitors.'

'What's happened to Cudlow?'

'He died of yellow fever back in '35.' Billings squinted up over his cup. 'He found Christ first.'

Hands laughed—uneasily.

'We ought to drink your wife's health, oughtn't we? What's her name?'

'Well, it's Ethel. But I call her Ethie.'

'To Mrs Hands.' They drank and Billings refilled the cups.

'She comes of a cultured family,' Hands said. 'You'll like her. You'll have a lot in common. You see her uncle is a photographer.'

'I know the sort of thing,' Billings said. 'Pictures for the *Tatler*—and *Vogue*. You make them lie on the ground and shoot from above while a gramophone plays. It catches on. Society.'

'Something of that sort,' Hands said. 'Could I have a drop more? Just a finger. Thanks.'

'And where's *your* money come from? From the wife?'

'I'm prospecting,' Hands said, 'for gold.'

'Where?'

'Across the border.'

'There's not enough to fill your teeth,' Billings said.

'I don't agree. Don't you remember that old Dutchman who came here? He said there was plenty in the Pandemai hills.'

'They had to ship him back third-class at the consul's expense.'

'But I've got money behind *me*. A whole expedition. Me and Colley—and a man called Morrow. We want servants—and carriers. That's why I came to you. You know the blacks.'

'You couldn't do better than Vandi for head man, but you'll get the carriers cheaper on the other side.' He poured out more brandy. 'I wish I were you. The bush is better than this place. You work and work—and then B. Moss gets the call.'

'Why don't you come? Colley's all right, of course, but I want someone I can *really* trust.' He said with importance. 'A leader has the hell of a lot of responsibility.'

'What's Morrow like?'

'A prig. You feel he's watching you.' He drank again. 'And Ethie—she's all right, but a man needs a man around. Sometimes I feel all a woman cares for'—he made a little shocked expression—'is—you know—what. A leader's got to keep fit.'

'What I don't understand,' Billings said, 'is why they chose you.'

'Sometimes I wonder that myself.' The brandy surged like inspiration on his tongue. 'For years I used to imagine—you know big things. Perhaps it's fate. A man's sometimes kept—for the biggest things. Like Hitler. What was he?'

'I get that feeling too,' Billings said. 'I think of—all of us. A whole crowd who've never had a proper chance. Sneered at. Sacked. And then suddenly—the day comes, and it's we—'

'Is there a spot more brandy?'

'I've dreamed sometimes—of converting thousands. The father of the Negro. Those missionaries out there in the bush—they pamper the niggers with statues and holy medals. It's easy work changing one idol for another. But I'd like to give them—just God.' The cup clinked on the table. 'God bare.'

'By God,' Hands said, 'when you come to think of it, this is a big thing we're on to.'

'You don't have to take the name of God in vain.'

'I'm sorry. But you make me see things.'

'We'll be on our own. No officials nosing round.'

'It's history.'

They stared at each other with awe. 'I suppose,' Hands said, 'that's what made them choose me. They wanted someone—with imagination.'

'And faith,' Billings said.

Somebody knocked at the door. Billings opened it, and there was the blinding day and the buzzards on the rooftops, the little town and life going on. Colley said, 'I thought I'd find you here.' He came suspiciously in out of the glaring noon: and was like doubt in the heart to both of them. He said, 'Your wife's asleep, Hands. I didn't think she looked too good.'

'It's the heat,' Hands said. 'We all know that it takes getting used to.'

'Have you got some brandy there? I've got a thirst.'

'Sorry, old man, it's finished.'

Colley held the bottle to the sunlight, trusting neither of them. He wore a round white sun-helmet which was getting limp already with perspiration. He said, 'I took her up some orange-juice and left it outside her door. I didn't like to wake her.'

'Fine, old man. Where's Morrow?'

'Writing home.' He said with hatred, 'The Sunday letter. To papa.'

'Papa's dead.'

'Mamma then. Or little sister. If there's one thing I can't stand,' Colley said, 'it's priggishness. Thinking yourself better than the rest. That's why we are friends,' he said, turning the contents of the brandy bottle hopelessly into a mug, 'because we are all alike.' Hands and Billings watched him—with embarrassment as if they had been caught out in a crime or a falsehood. . . .

PERMISSIONS

Twenty-One Stories was published by The Viking Press in 1962 and Penguin Books (U.S.A.) in 1981.
(A somewhat different collection was published earlier as *Nineteen Stories*.) Some of the selections
originally appeared in the following publications: *Commonweal, Esquire, Harper's Magazine,
The New Yorker, Story, Tomorrow,* and *Town & Country.*
A Sense of Reality was published by The Viking Press in 1963. Three stories originally appeared in
Harper's Bazaar, Rogue Magazine, and *The Saturday Evening Post.*
May We Borrow Your Husband? was published by The Viking Press in 1967 and Penguin Books (U.S.A.)
in 1978. Some of the stories first appeared in *Esquire, The London Magazine, New Statesman,
Playboy, Punch, The Saturday Evening Post, Status, Vogue,* and *Weekend Telegraph.*
The Last Word and Other Stories was published by Reinhardt Books in association with
Viking Penguin Inc. in 1991 and Penguin Books (U.S.A.) in 1992. Some of the stories first appeared
in *Collier's, Firebird, Graphic, Independent, Oxford Outlook, Punch,* and *Strand.*

FOR THE BEST IN PAPERBACKS, LOOK FOR THE

In every corner of the world, on every subject under the sun, Penguin represents quality and variety—the very best in publishing today.

For complete information about books available from Penguin—including Penguin Classics, Penguin Compass, and Puffins—and how to order them, write to us at the appropriate address below. Please note that for copyright reasons the selection of books varies from country to country.

In the United States: Please write to *Penguin Group (USA), P.O. Box 12289 Dept. B, Newark, New Jersey 07101-5289* or call 1-800-788-6262.

In the United Kingdom: Please write to *Dept. EP, Penguin Books Ltd, Bath Road, Harmondsworth, West Drayton, Middlesex UB7 0DA.*

In Canada: Please write to *Penguin Books Canada Ltd, 90 Eglinton Avenue East, Suite 700, Toronto, Ontario M4P 2Y3.*

In Australia: Please write to *Penguin Books Australia Ltd, P.O. Box 257, Ringwood, Victoria 3134.*

In New Zealand: Please write to *Penguin Books (NZ) Ltd, Private Bag 102902, North Shore Mail Centre, Auckland 10.*

In India: Please write to *Penguin Books India Pvt Ltd, 11 Panchsheel Shopping Centre, Panchsheel Park, New Delhi 110 017.*

In the Netherlands: Please write to *Penguin Books Netherlands bv, Postbus 3507, NL-1001 AH Amsterdam.*

In Germany: Please write to *Penguin Books Deutschland GmbH, Metzlerstrasse 26, 60594 Frankfurt am Main.*

In Spain: Please write to *Penguin Books S. A., Bravo Murillo 19, 1° B, 28015 Madrid.*

In Italy: Please write to *Penguin Italia s.r.l., Via Benedetto Croce 2, 20094 Corsico, Milano.*

In France: Please write to *Penguin France, Le Carré Wilson, 62 rue Benjamin Baillaud, 31500 Toulouse.*

In Japan: Please write to *Penguin Books Japan Ltd, Kaneko Building, 2-3-25 Koraku, Bunkyo-Ku, Tokyo 112.*

In South Africa: Please write to *Penguin Books South Africa (Pty) Ltd, Private Bag X14, Parkview, 2122 Johannesburg.*